Archie's
FAVORITE
HIGH SCHOOL COMICS

Archie's®

FAVORITE

HIGH SCHOOL COMICS

Published by Archie Comic Publications, Inc.
629 Fifth Avenue, Pelham, New York 10803-1242.
www.ArchieComics.com

Printed in U.S.A. First Printing.

ISBN: 978-1-62738-953-2

PUBLISHER/CO-CEO: Jon Goldwater
CO-CEO: Nancy Silberkleit
PRESIDENT: Mike Pellerito
CO-PRESIDENT/EDITOR-IN-CHIEF: Victor Gorelick
CHIEF CREATIVE OFFICER: Roberto Aguirre-Sacasa
CHIEF OPERATING OFFICER: William Mooar
CHIEF FINANCIAL OFFICER: Robert Wintle
SENIOR VICE PRESIDENT,
PUBLISHING & OPERATIONS: Harold Buchholz
SENIOR VICE PRESIDENT,
PUBLICITY & MARKETING: Alex Segura
DIRECTOR, BOOK SALES & OPERATIONS:
Jonathan Betancourt
PRODUCTION MANAGER:
Stephen Oswald
PROJECT COORDINATOR/
BOOK DESIGN:
Duncan McLachlan
EDITORIAL ASSISTANT/
PROOFREADER:
Jamie Lee Rotante

Stories & Art by:

Frank Doyle, Harry Lucey, Terry Szenics,
Mario Acquaviva, Vincent DeCarlo,
Samm Schwartz, Dan DeCarlo,
Rudy Lapick, Victor Gorelick,
George Gladir, Marty Epp, Fernando Ruiz,
Jon D'Agostino, Adam Walmsley, Jim Ruth,
Bill Yoshida, Dan DeCarlo Jr.,
James DeCarlo, Mike Pellowski,
Rex Lindsey, Rich Koslowski, Sy Reit,
Bob Bolling, Chic Stone, Carlos Antunes,
Hal Smith, Stan Goldberg, Al Nickerson,
Tom DeFalco, Bill Galvan, Jack Morelli,
Digikore Studios, Gus LeMoine,
Bill Golliher, Kathleen Webb,
Henry Scarpelli, Sal Contrera,
Vickie Williams, Hy Eisman,
John Workman, Marty Gardner,
Craig Boldman, Dan Parent

Story Introductions by:

Paul Castiglia & Chris Cummins

Welcome to

ARCHIE'S FAVORITE HIGH SCHOOL COMICS

Seventy-five years is a long time to go to high school! Ever since Archie and friends first hit the scene way back in the 1940s, they've spent much of their time in one amazing, timeless place: Riverdale High School, where the teenagers are forever young and the jokes spring eternal!

Relive the glory days with Archie and the gang in this fun, fantastic celebration of the students, teachers and faculty of Riverdale. The hilarious stories included here were hand-selected from Archie's vast archives and are introduced with individualized expert anecdotes. We hope you enjoy reading it as much as we enjoyed making it!

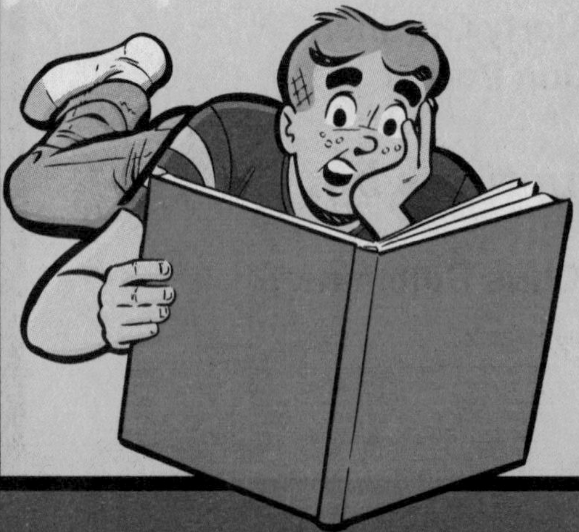

The stories, characters and incidents in this collection are entirely fictional. This book contains some material that was originally created in a less racially and socially sensitive time in our society and reflects attitudes that may be interpreted as offensive today. The stories are reprinted here without alteration for historical reference.

Archie's FAVORITE HIGH SCHOOL COMICS

HIGH SCHOOL HI-JINX

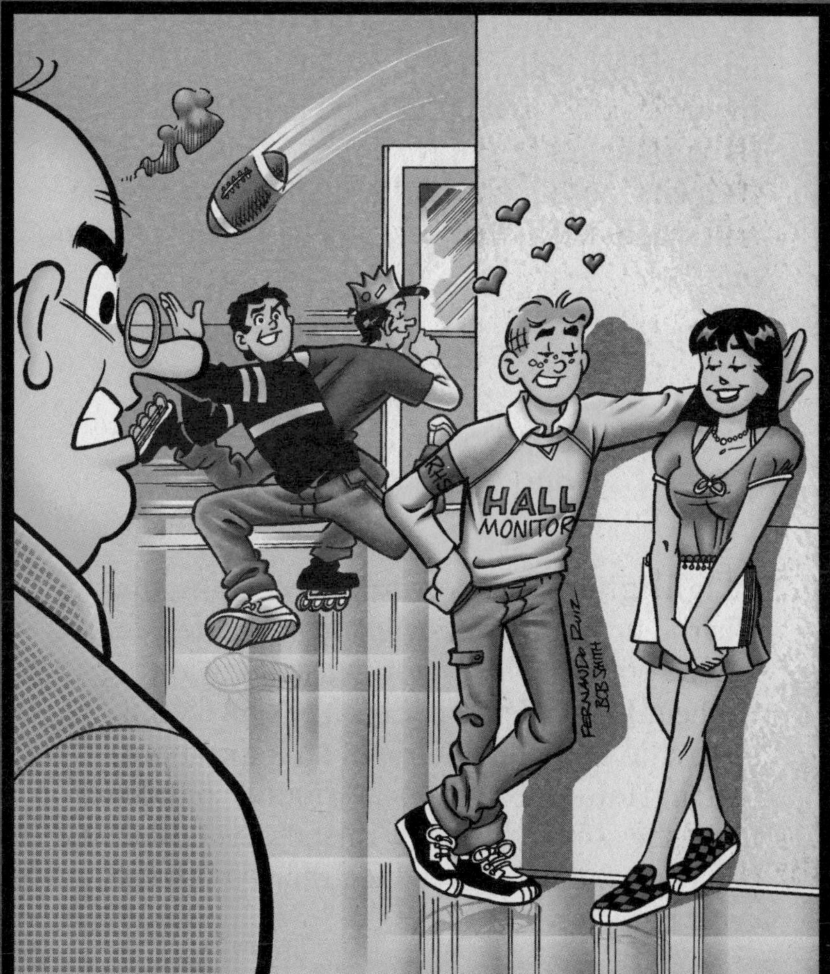
HALL MONITOR
RHS
FERNANDO RUIZ
BOB SMITH

Bowl Game
Archie #119, June 1961
Frank Doyle, Harry Lucey
and Terry Szenics

It's the ultimate recipe for disaster: take one bowling ball, place in accident-prone teen's hand, see that teen off to school and watch the frantic fun begin! No doubt Archie will be throwing nothing but gutter balls as the faculty and students do their best to avoid being *bowled over!*

Bully for You
Archie #156
Frank Doyle, Harry Lucey
and Mario Acquaviva

Highlighted by eye-popping art from Harry Lucey, this side-splitting laugh-fest finds Archie doubting his wrestling skills. Wanting to cheer his student up, Coach Kleats fixes it so Archie beats Big Moose in an impromptu match. However, Archie's newfound confidence unleashes some decidedly unsportsmanlike behavior and he is forced to grapple with the error of his ways.

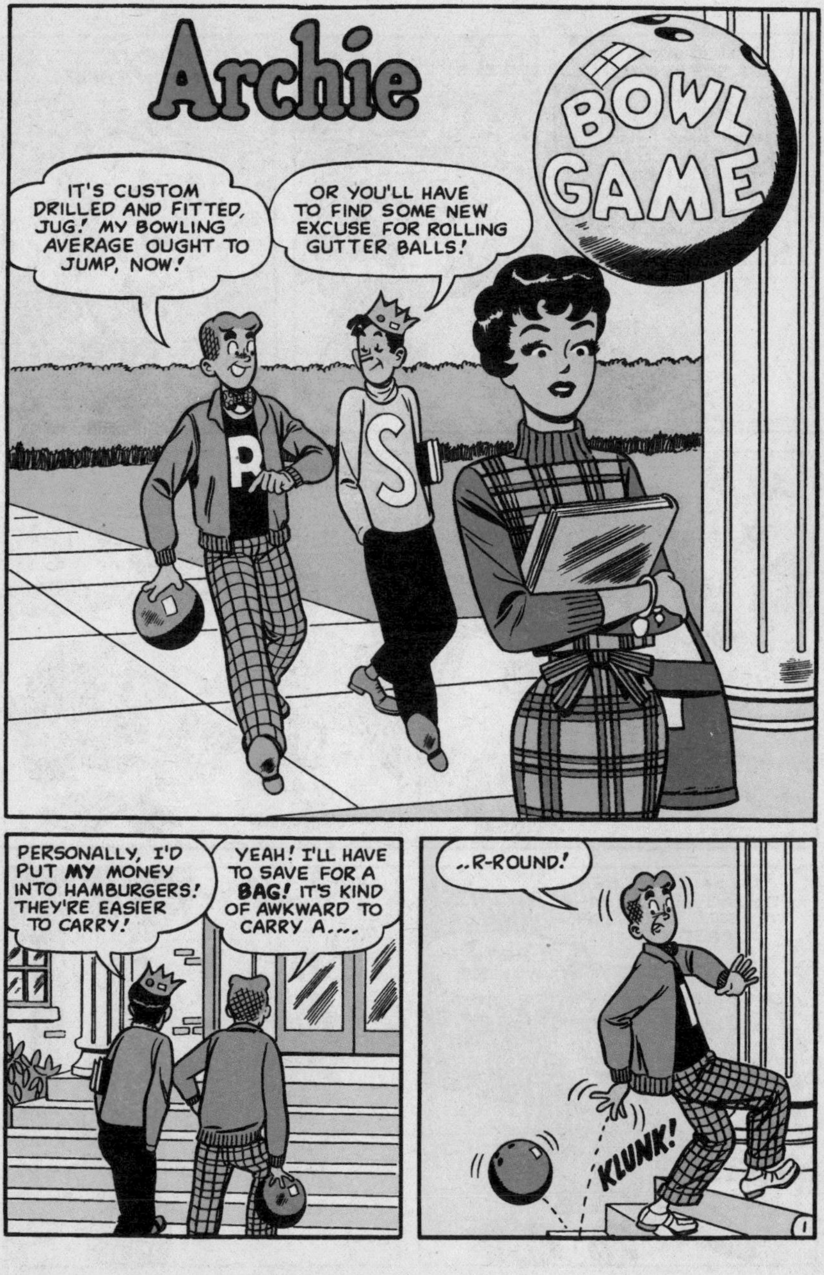
Archie
BOWL GAME
IT'S CUSTOM DRILLED AND FITTED, JUG! MY BOWLING AVERAGE OUGHT TO JUMP, NOW!
OR YOU'LL HAVE TO FIND SOME NEW EXCUSE FOR ROLLING GUTTER BALLS!
PERSONALLY, I'D PUT MY MONEY INTO HAMBURGERS! THEY'RE EASIER TO CARRY!
YEAH! I'LL HAVE TO SAVE FOR A BAG! IT'S KIND OF AWKWARD TO CARRY A....
..R-ROUND!
KLUNK!

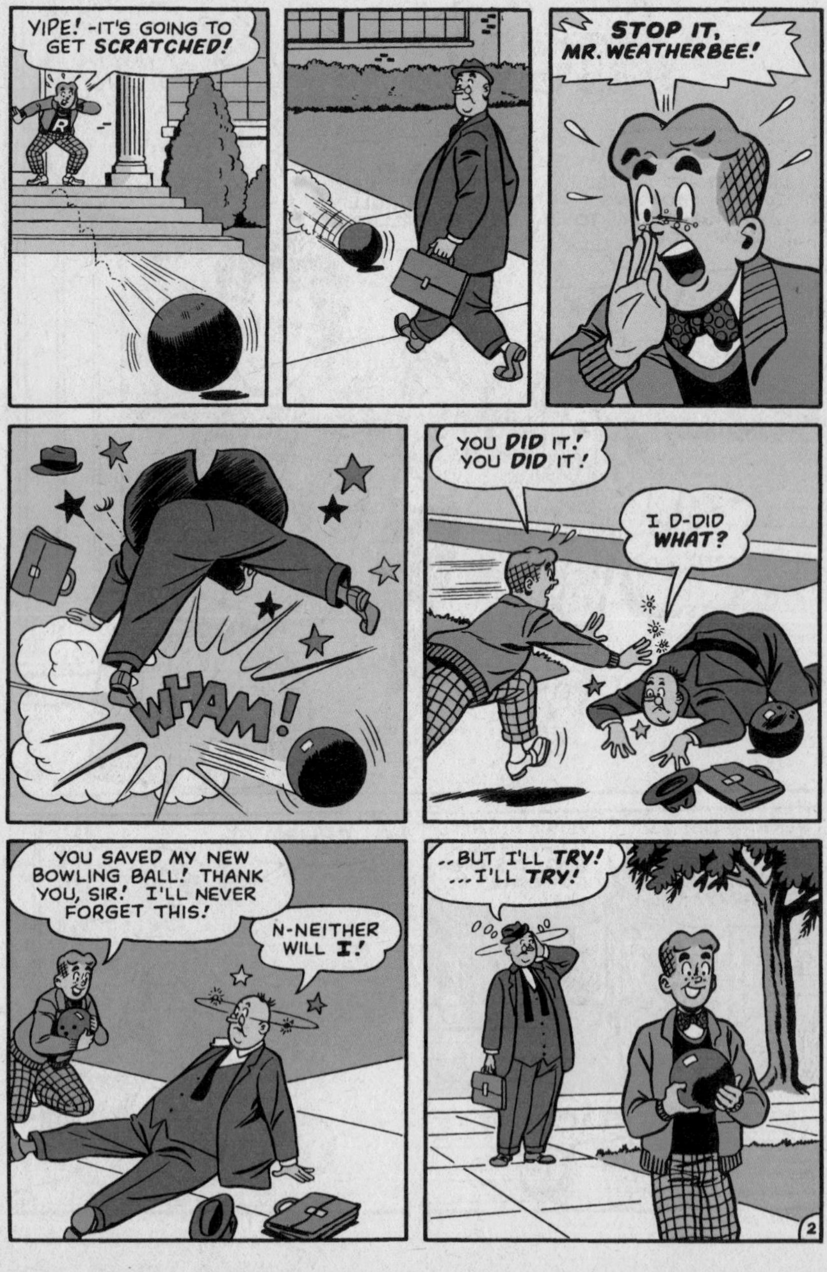
YIPE! -IT'S GOING TO GET SCRATCHED!
STOP IT, MR. WEATHERBEE!
WHAM!
YOU DID IT! YOU DID IT!
I D-DID WHAT?
YOU SAVED MY NEW BOWLING BALL! THANK YOU, SIR! I'LL NEVER FORGET THIS!
N-NEITHER WILL I!
..BUT I'LL TRY! ...I'LL TRY!
2

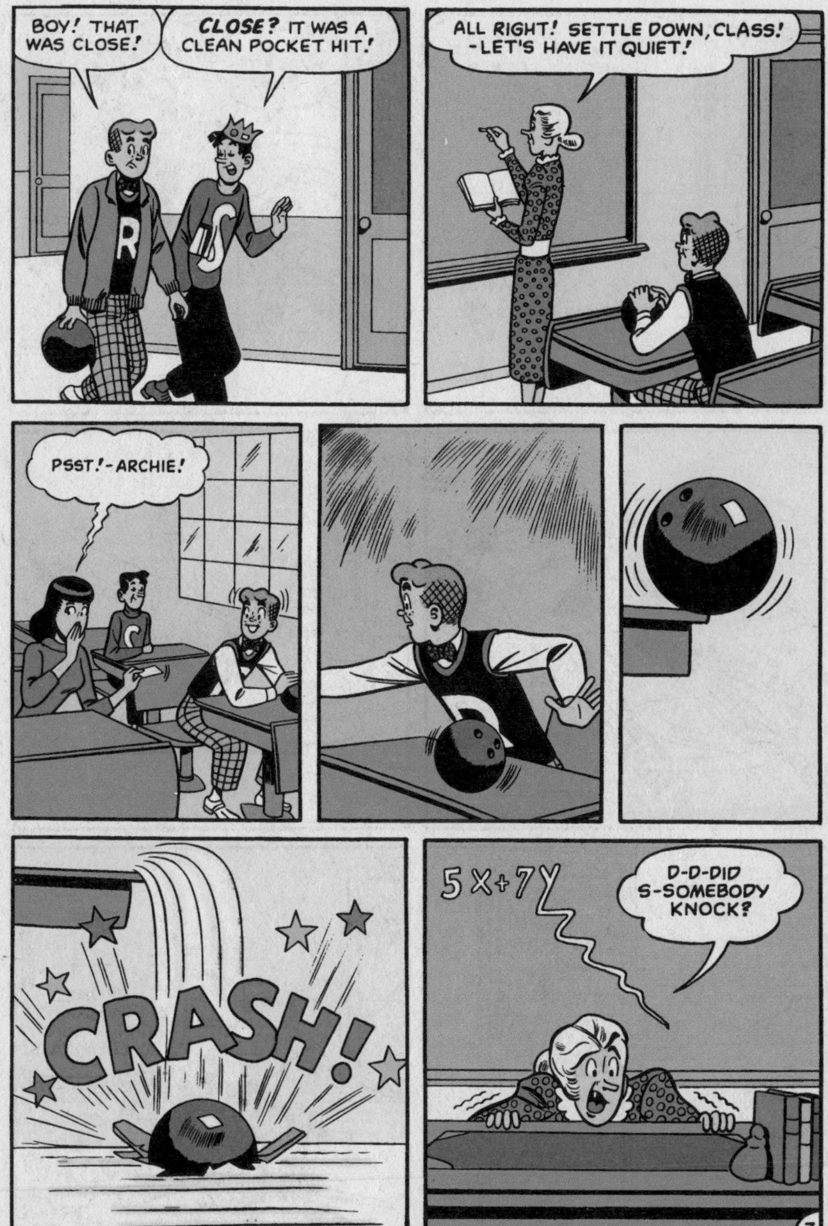
BOY! THAT WAS CLOSE!
CLOSE? IT WAS A CLEAN POCKET HIT!
ALL RIGHT! SETTLE DOWN, CLASS! -LET'S HAVE IT QUIET!
PSST!-ARCHIE!
CRASH!
5X+7Y
D-D-DID S-SOMEBODY KNOCK?
3

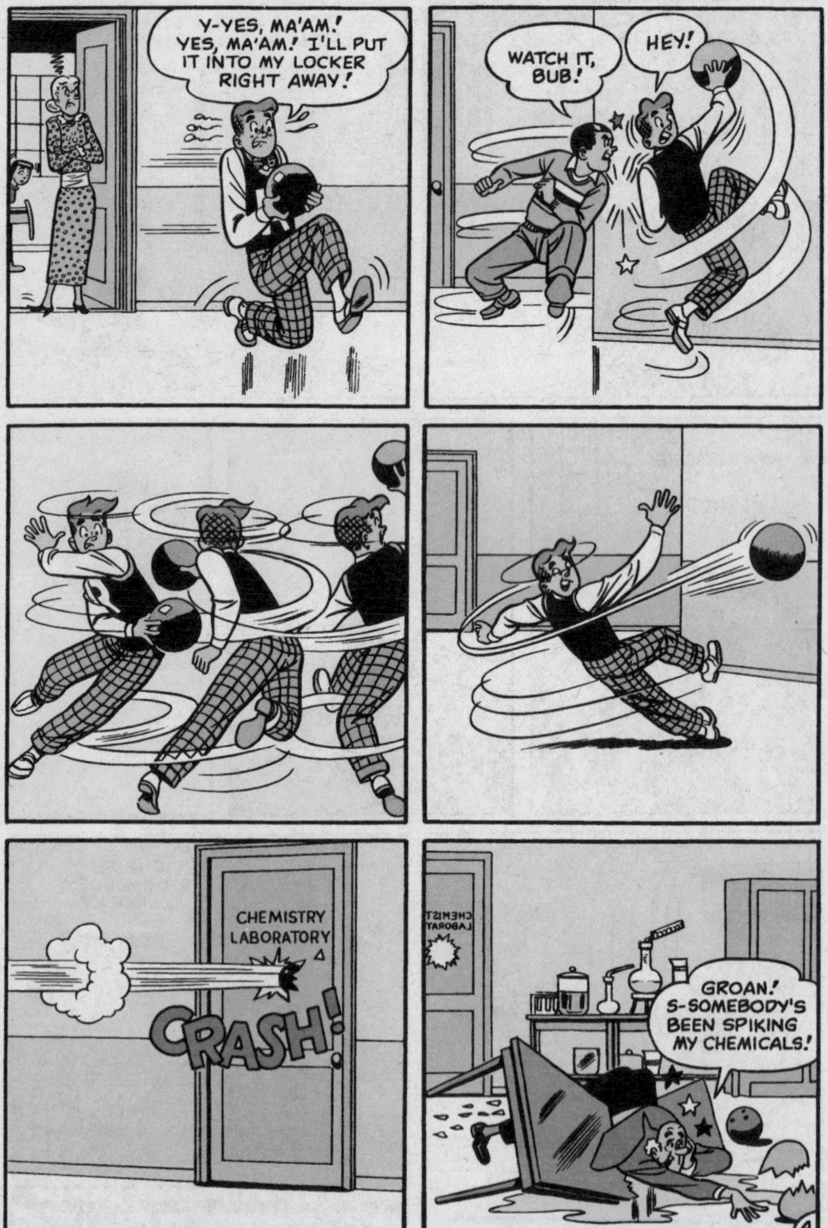
Y-YES, MA'AM! YES, MA'AM! I'LL PUT IT INTO MY LOCKER RIGHT AWAY!
WATCH IT, BUB!
HEY!
CHEMISTRY LABORATORY
CRASH!
GROAN! S-SOMEBODY'S BEEN SPIKING MY CHEMICALS!
4

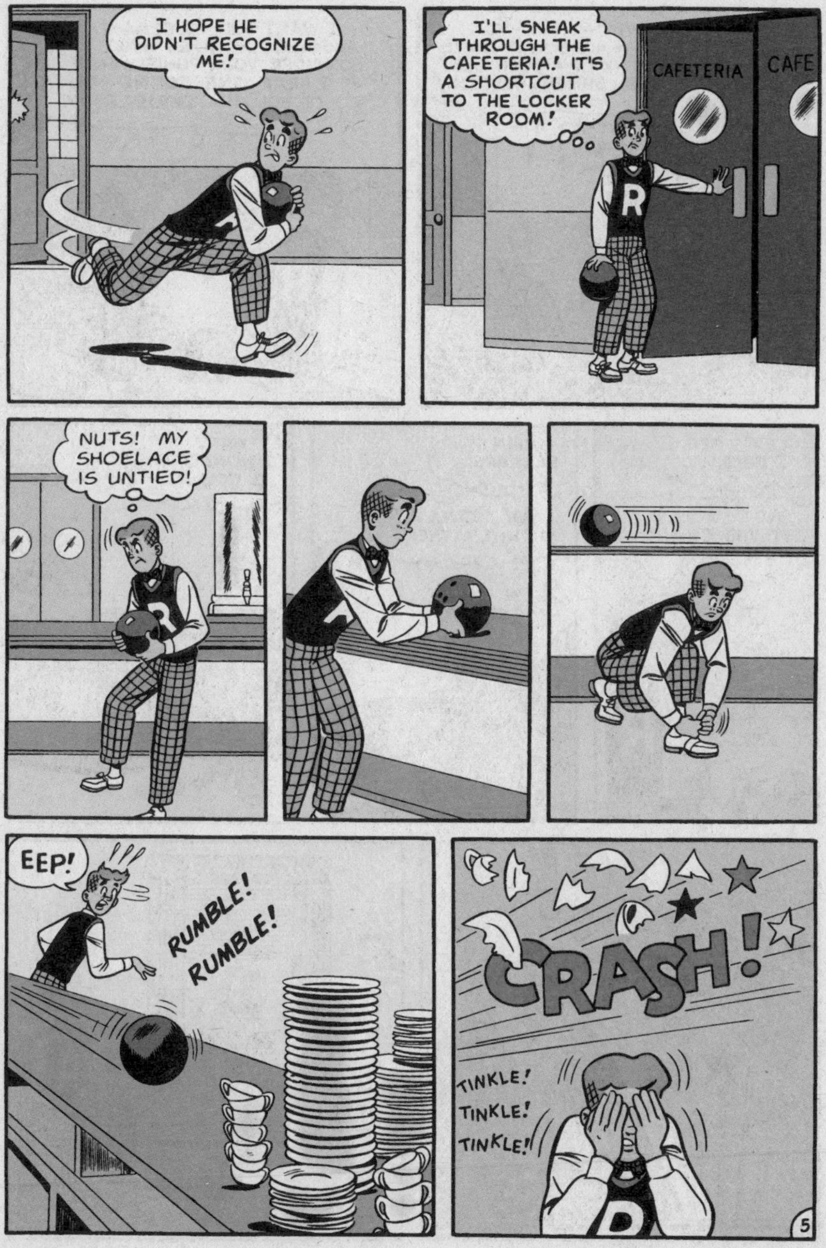
I HOPE HE DIDN'T RECOGNIZE ME!
I'LL SNEAK THROUGH THE CAFETERIA! IT'S A SHORTCUT TO THE LOCKER ROOM!
CAFETERIA
CAFE
NUTS! MY SHOELACE IS UNTIED!
EEP!
RUMBLE! RUMBLE!
CRASH!
TINKLE! TINKLE! TINKLE!
5

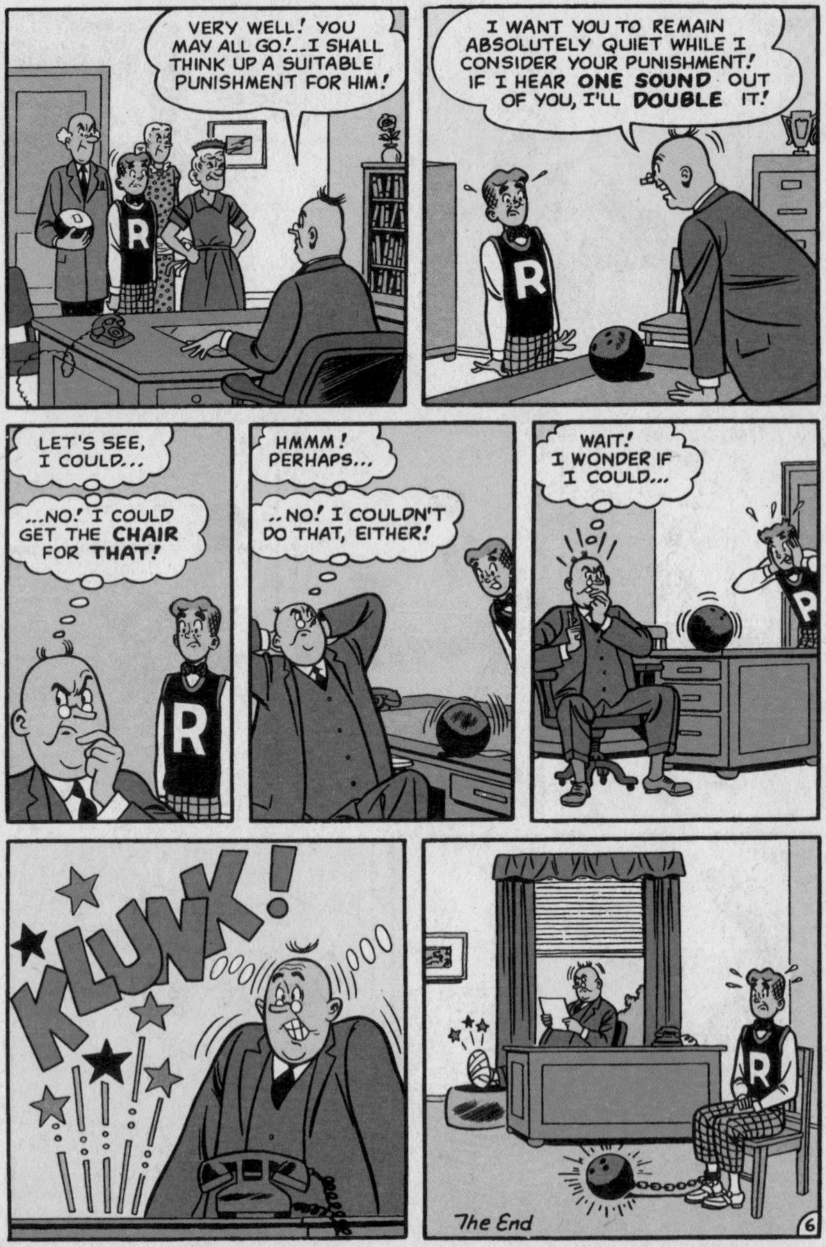
VERY WELL! YOU MAY ALL GO!..I SHALL THINK UP A SUITABLE PUNISHMENT FOR HIM!
I WANT YOU TO REMAIN ABSOLUTELY QUIET WHILE I CONSIDER YOUR PUNISHMENT! IF I HEAR ONE SOUND OUT OF YOU, I'LL DOUBLE IT!
LET'S SEE, I COULD...
...NO! I COULD GET THE CHAIR FOR THAT!
HMMM! PERHAPS...
..NO! I COULDN'T DO THAT, EITHER!
WAIT! I WONDER IF I COULD...
KLUNK!
The End
6

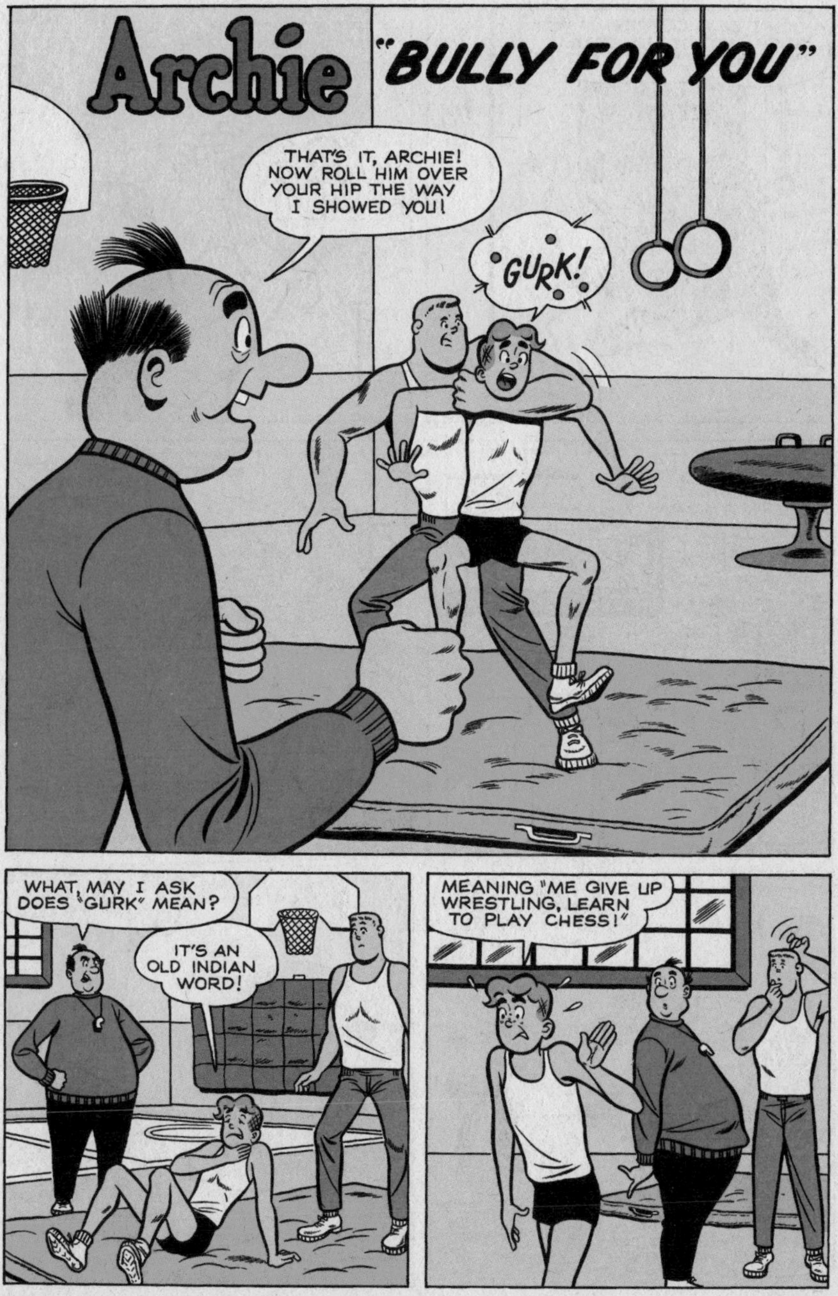
Archie
"BULLY FOR YOU"
THAT'S IT, ARCHIE! NOW ROLL HIM OVER YOUR HIP THE WAY I SHOWED YOU!
GURK!
WHAT, MAY I ASK DOES "GURK" MEAN?
IT'S AN OLD INDIAN WORD!
MEANING "ME GIVE UP WRESTLING, LEARN TO PLAY CHESS!"

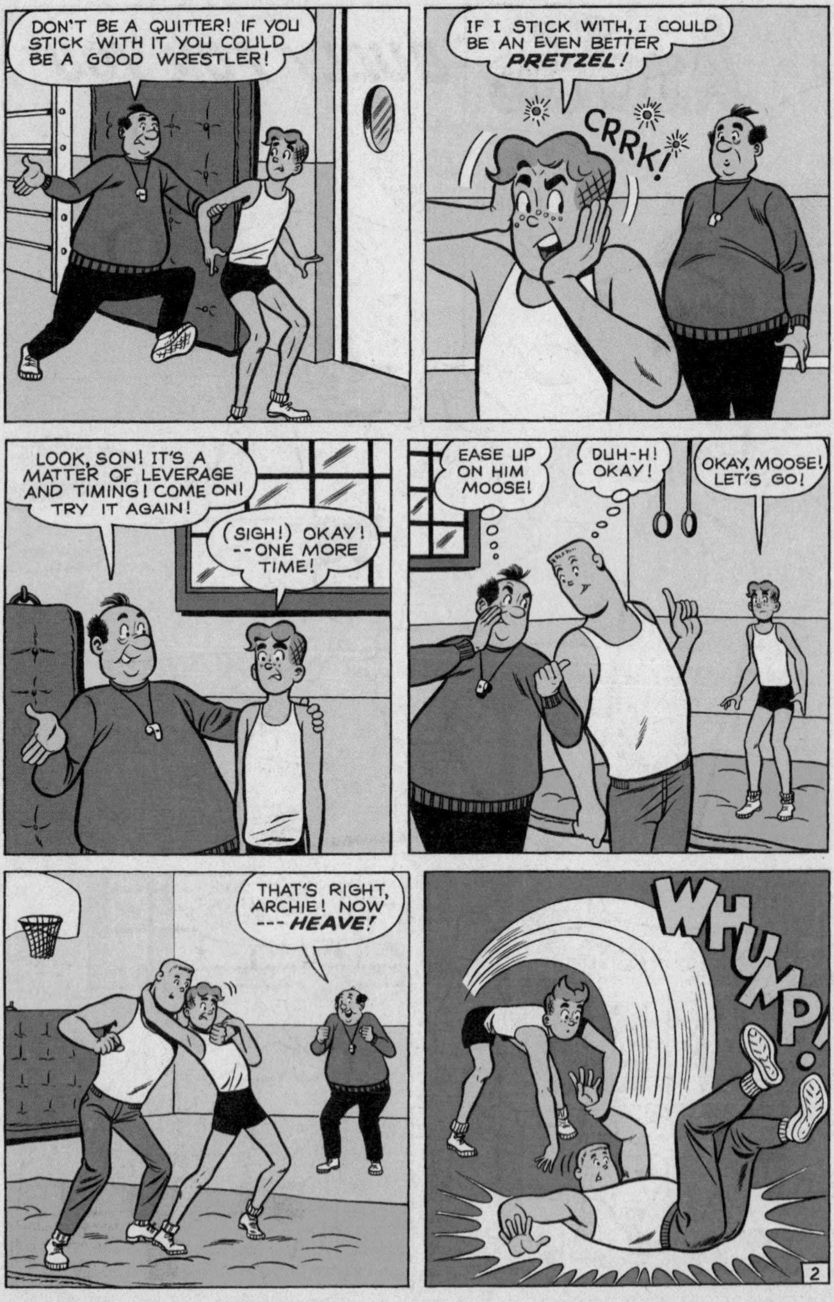
DON'T BE A QUITTER! IF YOU STICK WITH IT YOU COULD BE A GOOD WRESTLER!
IF I STICK WITH, I COULD BE AN EVEN BETTER PRETZEL!
CRRK!
LOOK, SON! IT'S A MATTER OF LEVERAGE AND TIMING! COME ON! TRY IT AGAIN!
(SIGH!) OKAY! --ONE MORE TIME!
EASE UP ON HIM MOOSE!
DUH-H! OKAY!
OKAY, MOOSE! LET'S GO!
THAT'S RIGHT, ARCHIE! NOW --- HEAVE!
WHUMP!
2

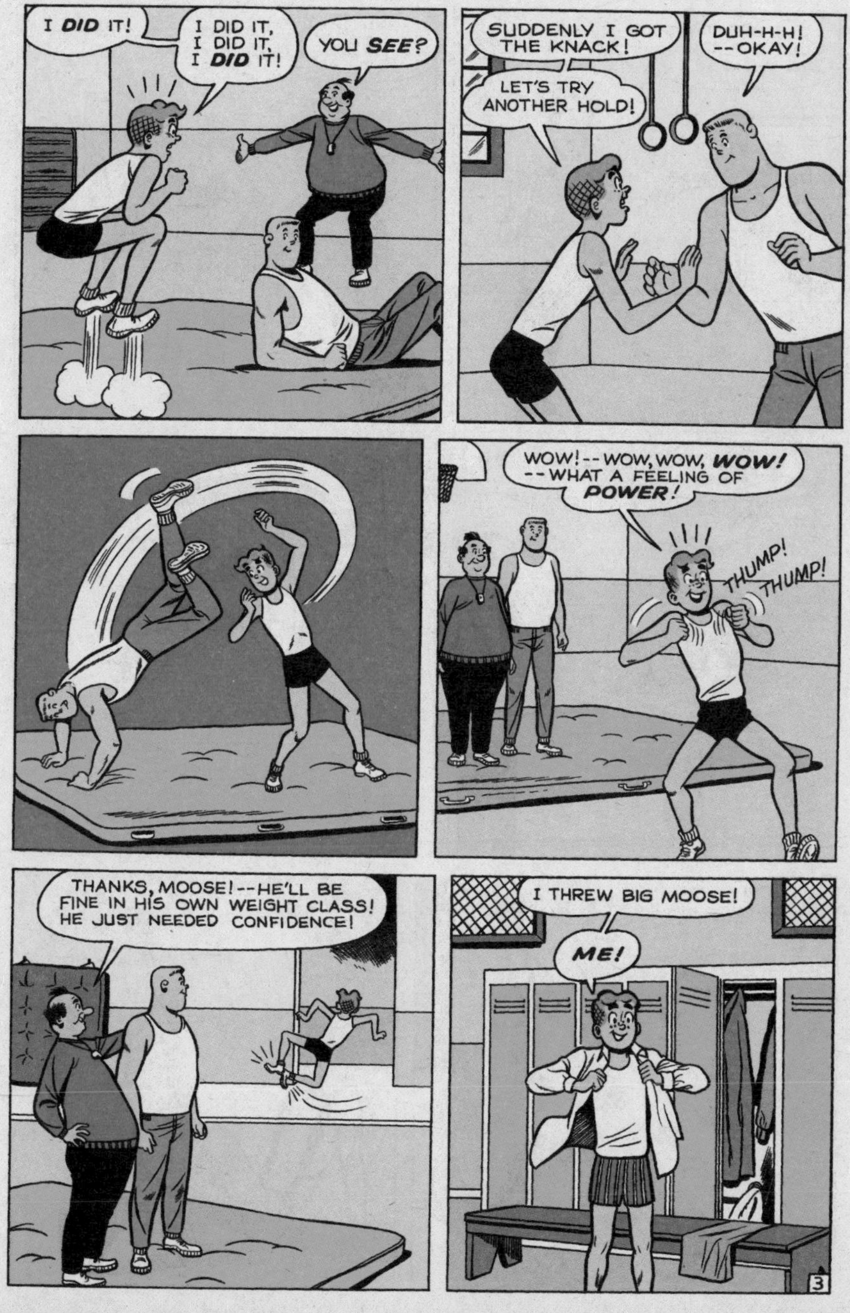
I DID IT!
I DID IT, I DID IT, I DID IT!
YOU SEE?
SUDDENLY I GOT THE KNACK!
LET'S TRY ANOTHER HOLD!
DUH-H-H! --OKAY!
WOW!--WOW, WOW, WOW! --WHAT A FEELING OF POWER!
THUMP!
THUMP!
THANKS, MOOSE!--HE'LL BE FINE IN HIS OWN WEIGHT CLASS! HE JUST NEEDED CONFIDENCE!
I THREW BIG MOOSE!
ME!
3

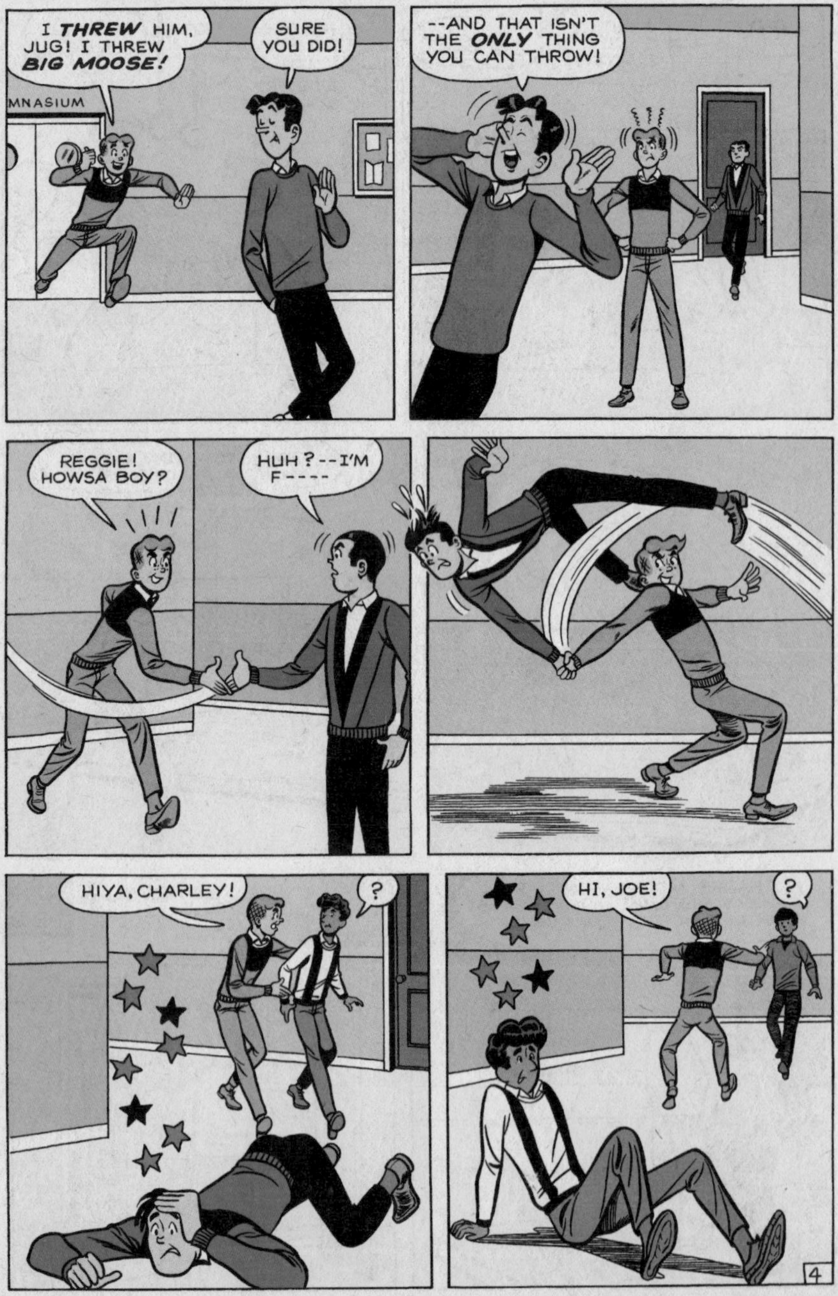
I THREW HIM, JUG! I THREW BIG MOOSE!
SURE YOU DID!
MNASIUM
--AND THAT ISN'T THE ONLY THING YOU CAN THROW!
REGGIE! HOWSA BOY?
HUH? --I'M F----
HIYA, CHARLEY!
?
HI, JOE!
?
4

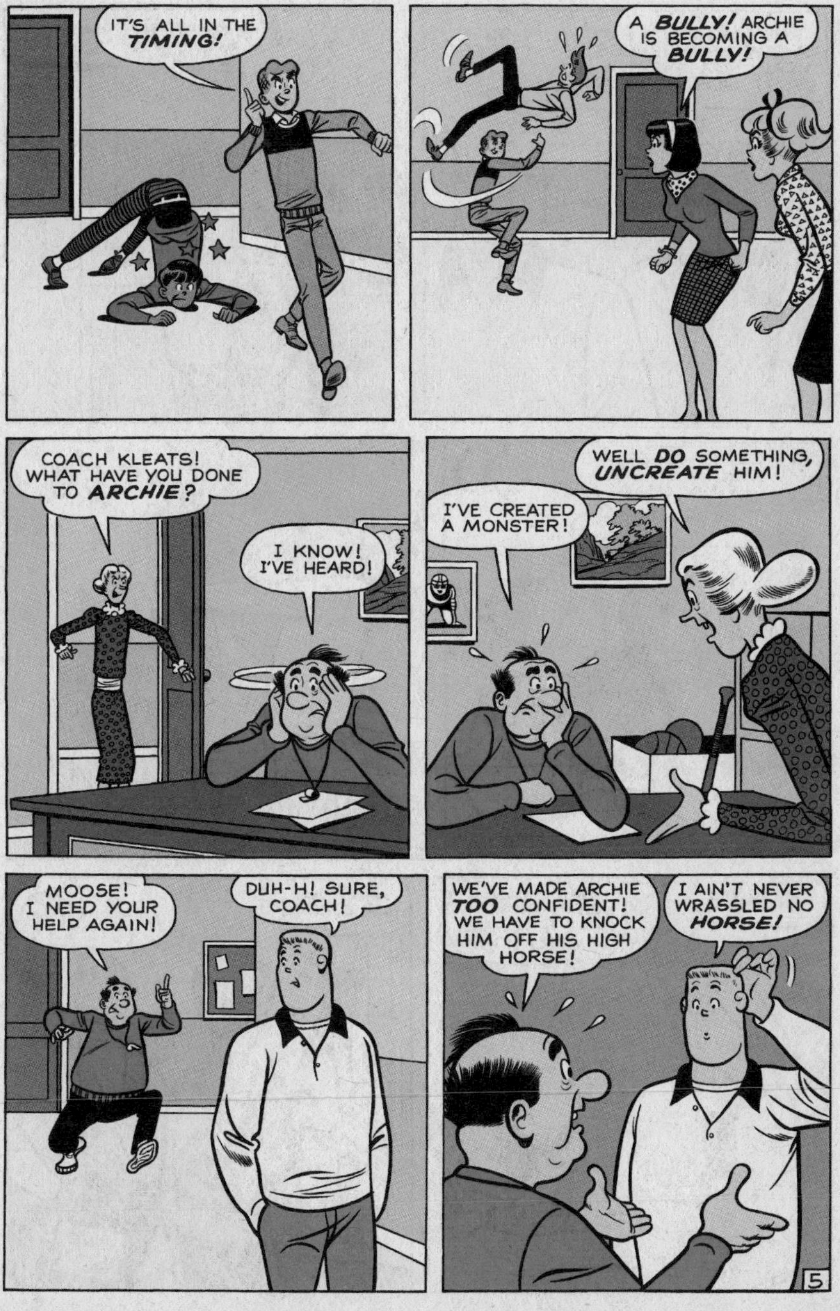
IT'S ALL IN THE TIMING!
A BULLY! ARCHIE IS BECOMING A BULLY!
COACH KLEATS! WHAT HAVE YOU DONE TO ARCHIE?
I KNOW! I'VE HEARD!
I'VE CREATED A MONSTER!
WELL DO SOMETHING, UNCREATE HIM!
MOOSE! I NEED YOUR HELP AGAIN!
DUH-H! SURE, COACH!
WE'VE MADE ARCHIE TOO CONFIDENT! WE HAVE TO KNOCK HIM OFF HIS HIGH HORSE!
I AIN'T NEVER WRASSLED NO HORSE!
5

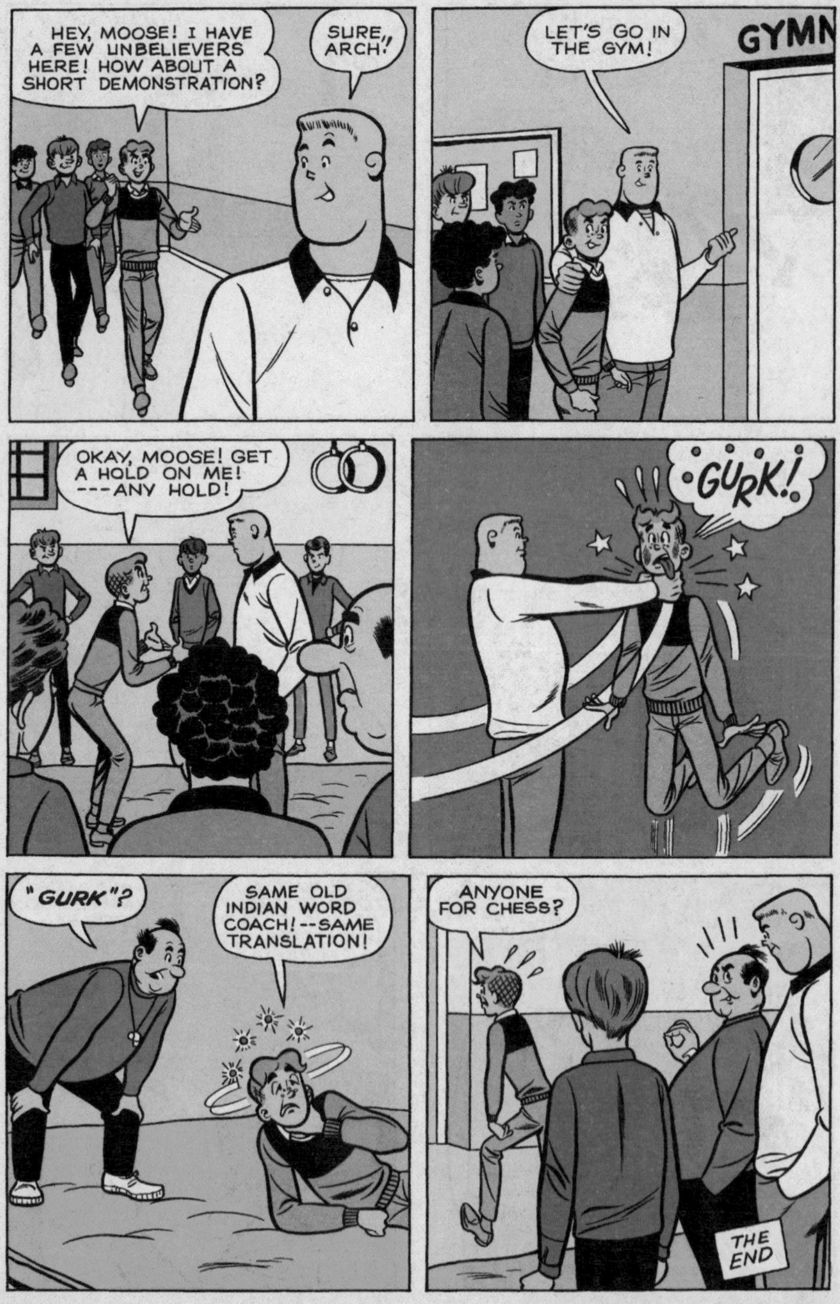
HEY, MOOSE! I HAVE A FEW UNBELIEVERS HERE! HOW ABOUT A SHORT DEMONSTRATION?
SURE, ARCH!
LET'S GO IN THE GYM!
GYMN
OKAY, MOOSE! GET A HOLD ON ME! ---ANY HOLD!
GURK!
"GURK"?
SAME OLD INDIAN WORD COACH! --SAME TRANSLATION!
ANYONE FOR CHESS?
THE END

Fare Enough
Archie #173, June 1967
**Frank Doyle, Harry Lucey
and Vincent DeCarlo**

Archie's determined to stay by Veronica's side... even on the team bus reserved exclusively for football players and cheerleaders! Can Archie outwit Reggie, Coach Kleats and Mr. Weatherbee and hitch a ride, or will he simply be left behind?

Foot Sore
Jughead #105, February 1964
Frank Doyle and Samm Schwartz

Throughout his career with Archie Comics, Samm Schwartz always illustrated unforgettable Jughead stories full of visual charm. This entry is no exception, with a particularly mischievous Jughead inventing yet another comedic solution to a problem brought on by his klutzy behavior. Pancakes, anyone?

Archie in "FARE ENOUGH"

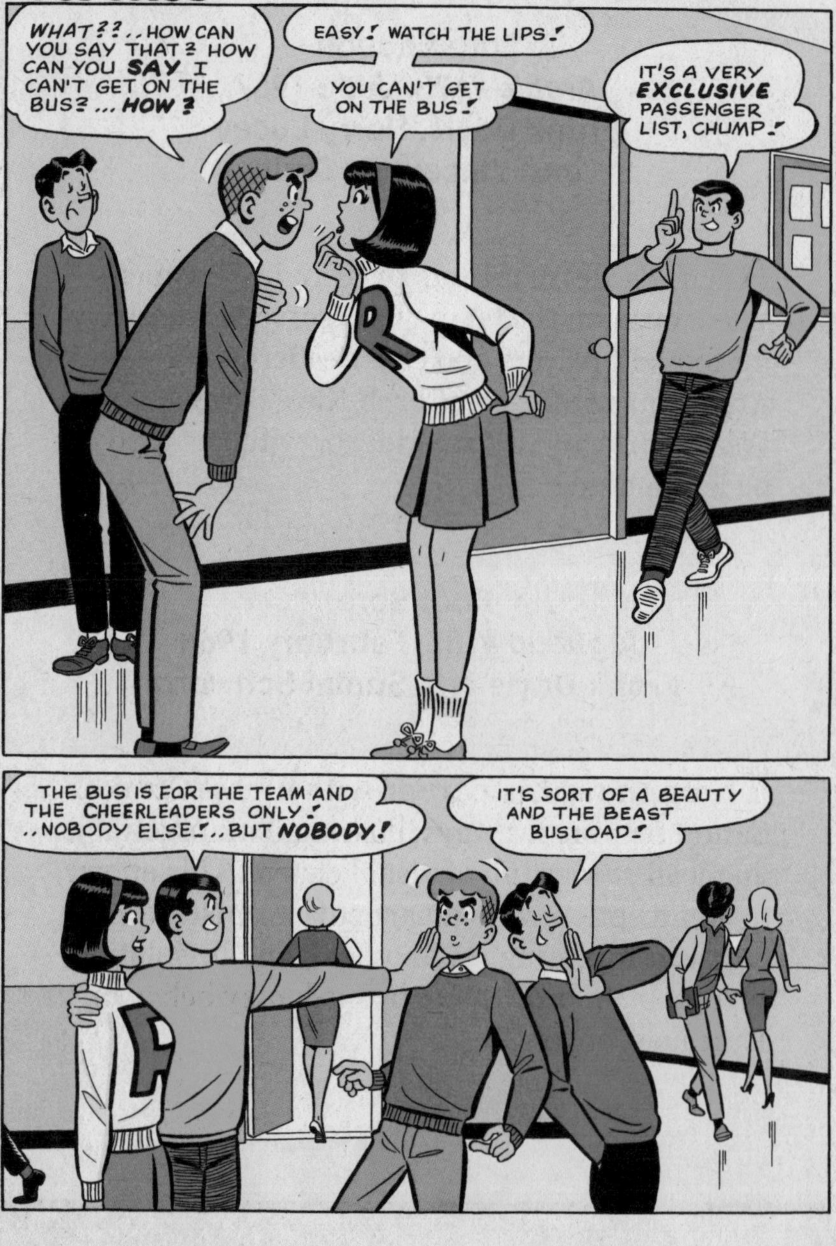
WHAT??..HOW CAN YOU SAY THAT? HOW CAN YOU **SAY** I CAN'T GET ON THE BUS? ... **HOW?**
EASY! WATCH THE LIPS!
YOU CAN'T GET ON THE BUS!
IT'S A VERY **EXCLUSIVE** PASSENGER LIST, CHUMP!
THE BUS IS FOR THE TEAM AND THE CHEERLEADERS ONLY! ..NOBODY ELSE!..BUT **NOBODY!**
IT'S SORT OF A BEAUTY AND THE BEAST BUSLOAD!

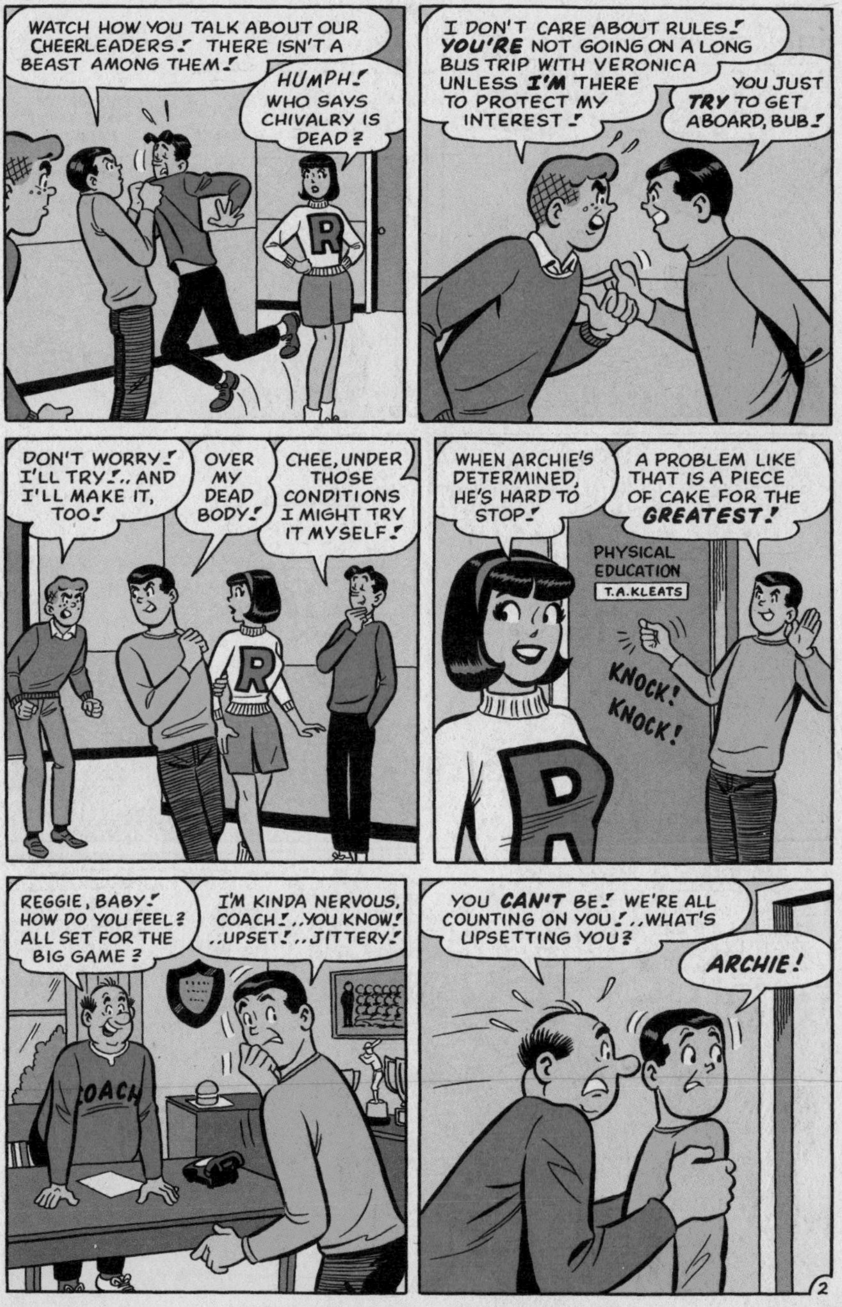
WATCH HOW YOU TALK ABOUT OUR CHEERLEADERS! THERE ISN'T A BEAST AMONG THEM!
HUMPH! WHO SAYS CHIVALRY IS DEAD?
I DON'T CARE ABOUT RULES! YOU'RE NOT GOING ON A LONG BUS TRIP WITH VERONICA UNLESS I'M THERE TO PROTECT MY INTEREST!
YOU JUST TRY TO GET ABOARD, BUB!
DON'T WORRY! I'LL TRY!.. AND I'LL MAKE IT, TOO!
OVER MY DEAD BODY!
CHEE, UNDER THOSE CONDITIONS I MIGHT TRY IT MYSELF!
WHEN ARCHIE'S DETERMINED, HE'S HARD TO STOP!
A PROBLEM LIKE THAT IS A PIECE OF CAKE FOR THE GREATEST!
PHYSICAL EDUCATION
T.A.KLEATS
KNOCK! KNOCK!
REGGIE, BABY! HOW DO YOU FEEL? ALL SET FOR THE BIG GAME?
I'M KINDA NERVOUS, COACH!..YOU KNOW! ..UPSET!..JITTERY!
COACH
YOU CAN'T BE! WE'RE ALL COUNTING ON YOU!..WHAT'S UPSETTING YOU?
ARCHIE!
2

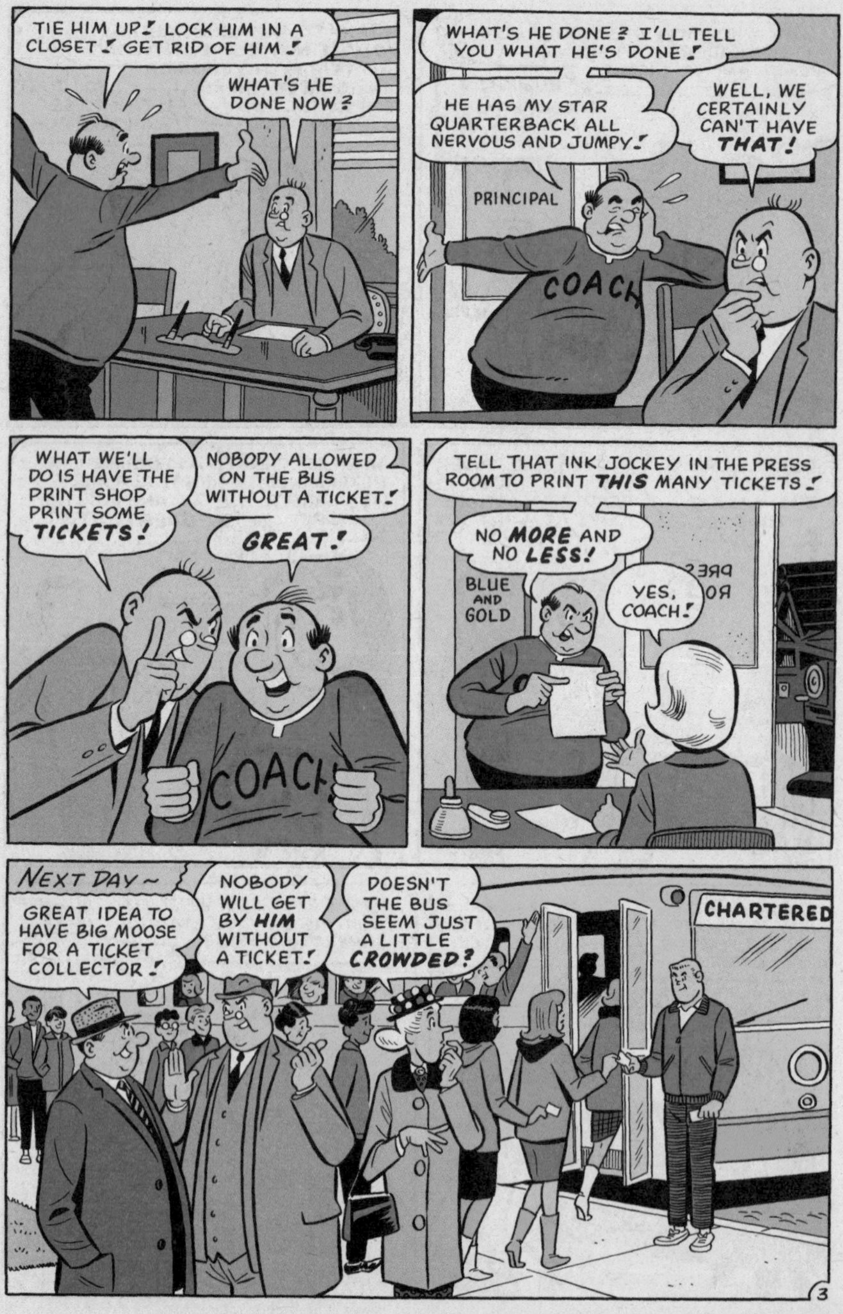
TIE HIM UP! LOCK HIM IN A CLOSET! GET RID OF HIM!
WHAT'S HE DONE NOW?
WHAT'S HE DONE? I'LL TELL YOU WHAT HE'S DONE!
HE HAS MY STAR QUARTERBACK ALL NERVOUS AND JUMPY!
WELL, WE CERTAINLY CAN'T HAVE THAT!
PRINCIPAL
COACH
WHAT WE'LL DO IS HAVE THE PRINT SHOP PRINT SOME TICKETS!
NOBODY ALLOWED ON THE BUS WITHOUT A TICKET!
GREAT!
COACH
TELL THAT INK JOCKEY IN THE PRESS ROOM TO PRINT THIS MANY TICKETS!
NO MORE AND NO LESS!
YES, COACH!
BLUE AND GOLD
NEXT DAY ~
GREAT IDEA TO HAVE BIG MOOSE FOR A TICKET COLLECTOR!
NOBODY WILL GET BY HIM WITHOUT A TICKET!
DOESN'T THE BUS SEEM JUST A LITTLE CROWDED?
CHARTERED
3

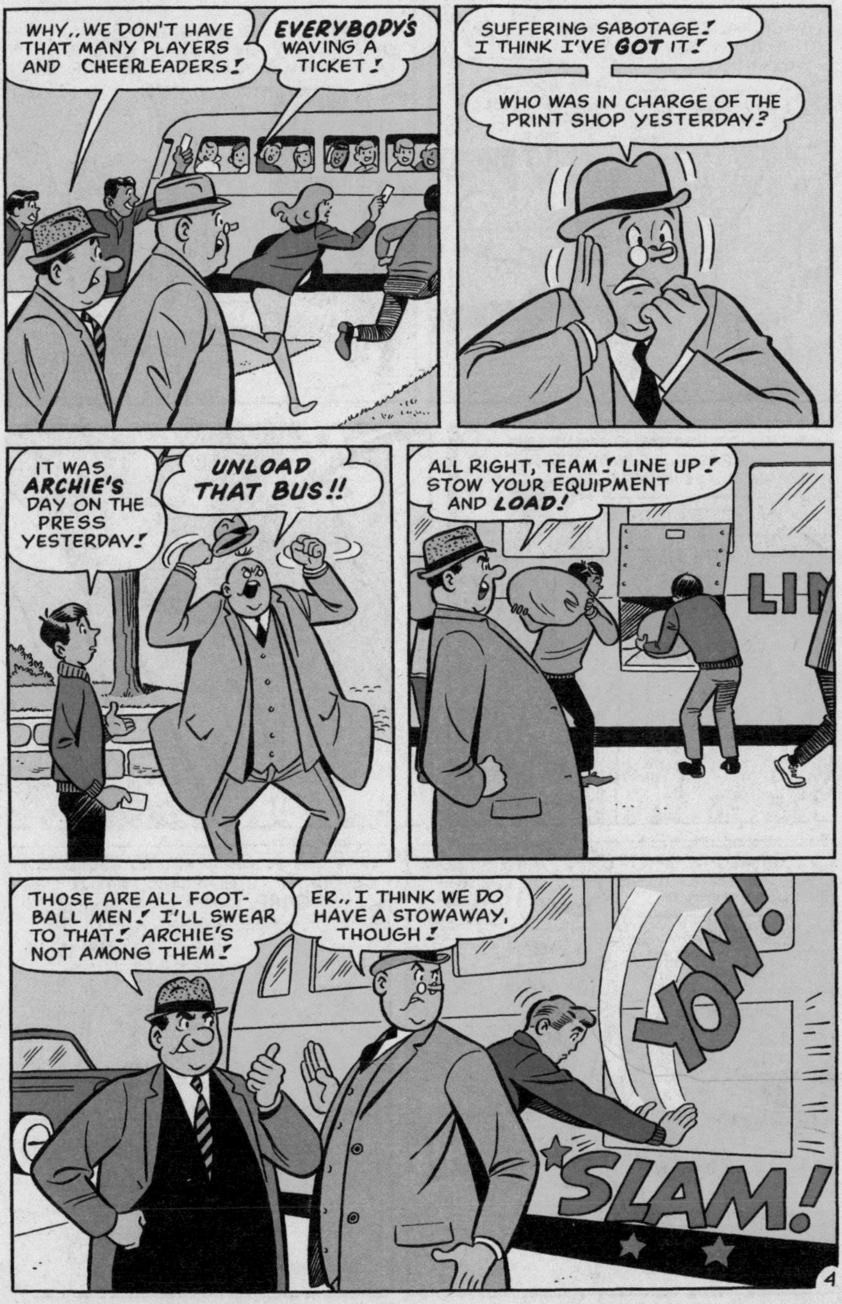
WHY,, WE DON'T HAVE THAT MANY PLAYERS AND CHEERLEADERS!
EVERYBODY'S WAVING A TICKET!
SUFFERING SABOTAGE! I THINK I'VE GOT IT!
WHO WAS IN CHARGE OF THE PRINT SHOP YESTERDAY?
IT WAS ARCHIE'S DAY ON THE PRESS YESTERDAY!
UNLOAD THAT BUS!!
ALL RIGHT, TEAM! LINE UP! STOW YOUR EQUIPMENT AND LOAD!
LI
THOSE ARE ALL FOOT-BALL MEN! I'LL SWEAR TO THAT! ARCHIE'S NOT AMONG THEM!
ER,, I THINK WE DO HAVE A STOWAWAY, THOUGH!
YOW!
SLAM!
4

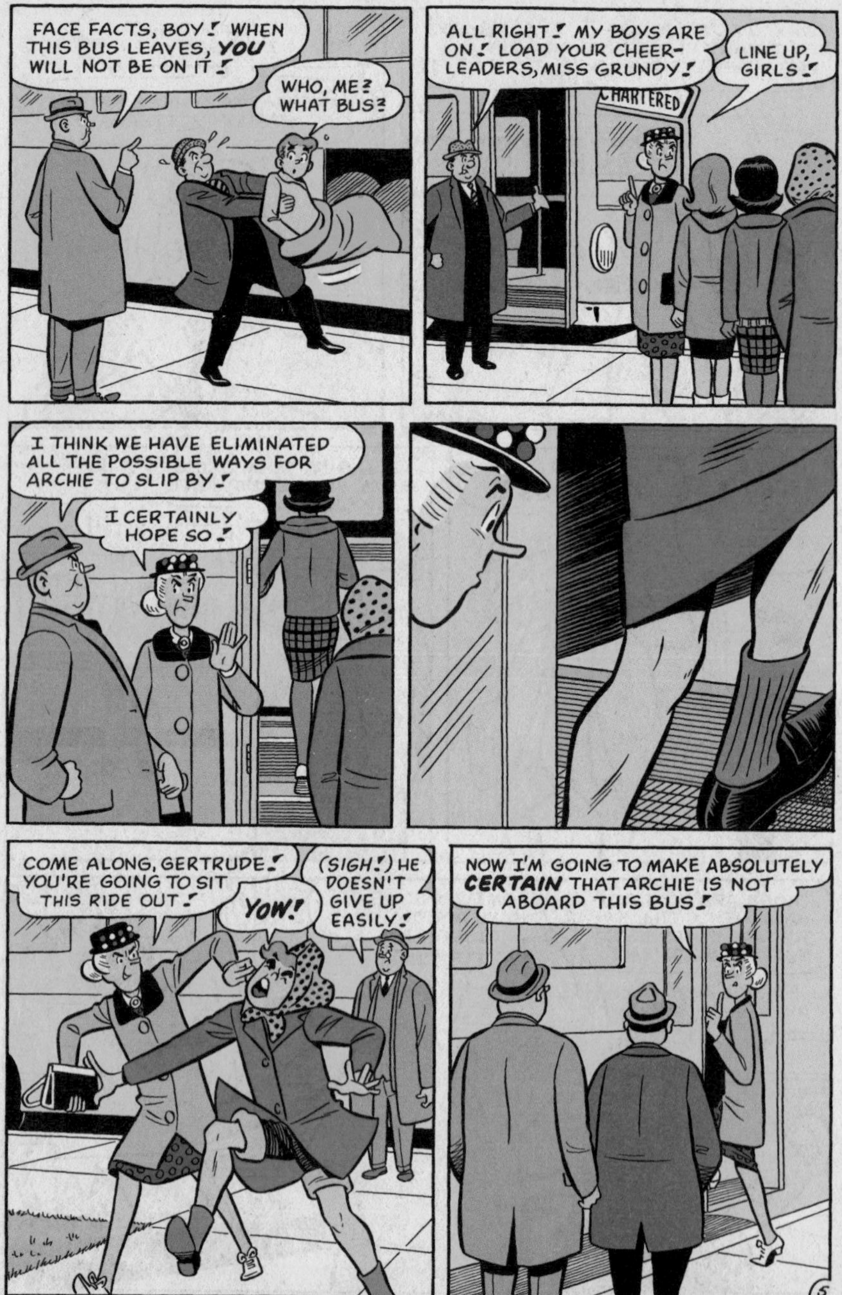

FACE FACTS, BOY! WHEN THIS BUS LEAVES, **YOU** WILL NOT BE ON IT!
WHO, ME? WHAT BUS?
ALL RIGHT! MY BOYS ARE ON! LOAD YOUR CHEER-LEADERS, MISS GRUNDY!
LINE UP, GIRLS!
CHARTERED
I THINK WE HAVE ELIMINATED ALL THE POSSIBLE WAYS FOR ARCHIE TO SLIP BY!
I CERTAINLY HOPE SO!
COME ALONG, GERTRUDE! YOU'RE GOING TO SIT THIS RIDE OUT!
YOW!
(SIGH!) HE DOESN'T GIVE UP EASILY!
NOW I'M GOING TO MAKE ABSOLUTELY **CERTAIN** THAT ARCHIE IS NOT ABOARD THIS BUS!
5

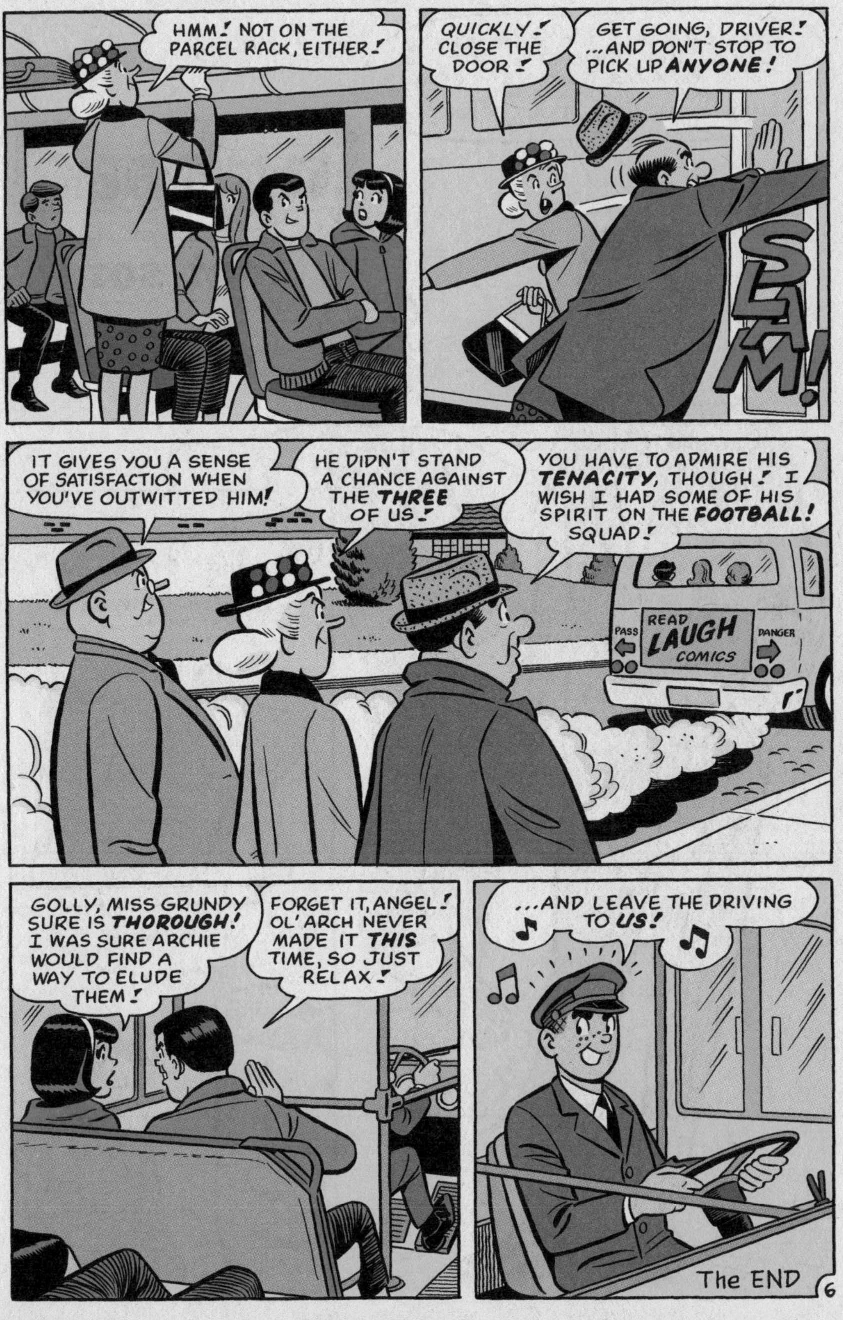
HMM! NOT ON THE PARCEL RACK, EITHER!
QUICKLY! CLOSE THE DOOR!
GET GOING, DRIVER! ...AND DON'T STOP TO PICK UP ANYONE!
SLAM!
IT GIVES YOU A SENSE OF SATISFACTION WHEN YOU'VE OUTWITTED HIM!
HE DIDN'T STAND A CHANCE AGAINST THE THREE OF US!
YOU HAVE TO ADMIRE HIS TENACITY, THOUGH! I WISH I HAD SOME OF HIS SPIRIT ON THE FOOTBALL! SQUAD!
PASS
READ LAUGH COMICS
DANGER
GOLLY, MISS GRUNDY SURE IS THOROUGH! I WAS SURE ARCHIE WOULD FIND A WAY TO ELUDE THEM!
FORGET IT, ANGEL! OL' ARCH NEVER MADE IT THIS TIME, SO JUST RELAX!
...AND LEAVE THE DRIVING TO US!
The END
6

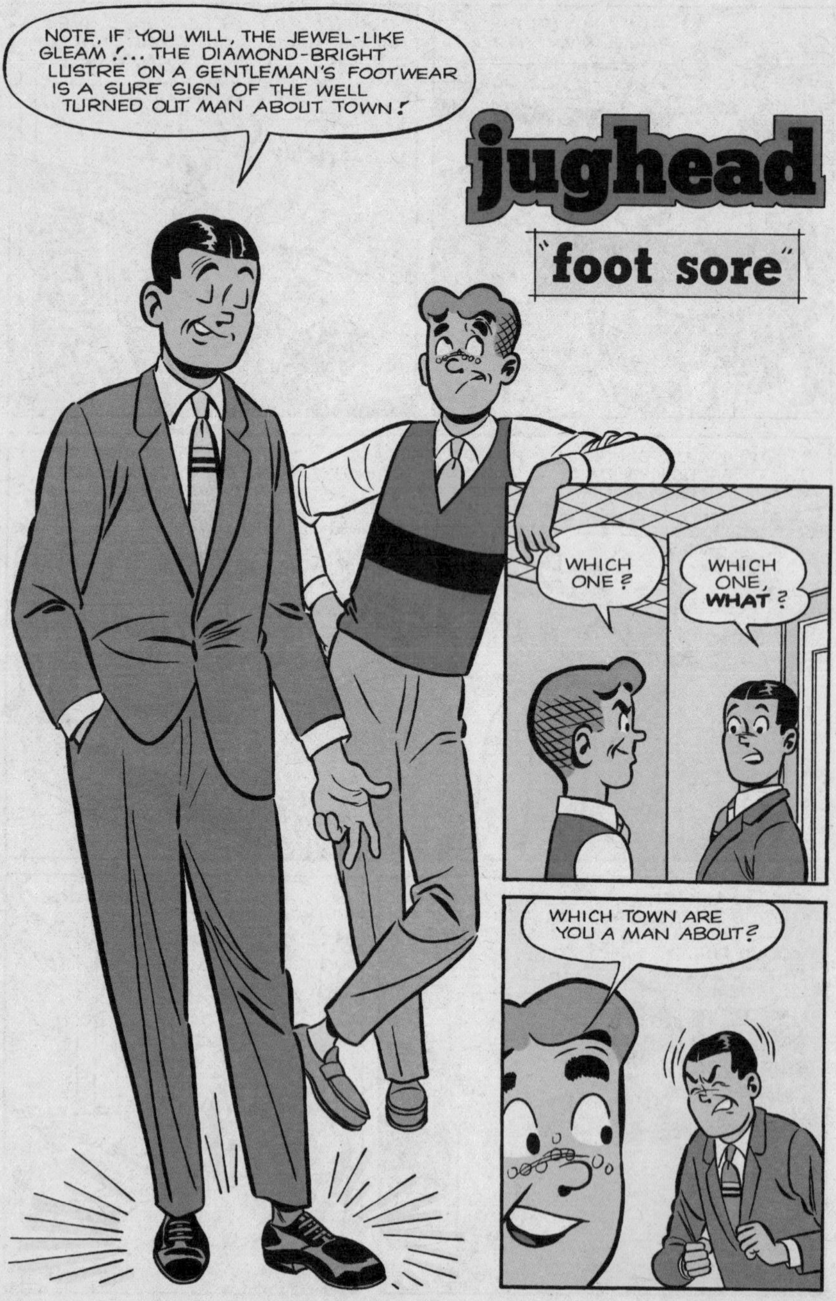
NOTE, IF YOU WILL, THE JEWEL-LIKE GLEAM!... THE DIAMOND-BRIGHT LUSTRE ON A GENTLEMAN'S FOOTWEAR IS A SURE SIGN OF THE WELL TURNED OUT MAN ABOUT TOWN!
jughead
"foot sore"
WHICH ONE?
WHICH ONE, WHAT?
WHICH TOWN ARE YOU A MAN ABOUT?

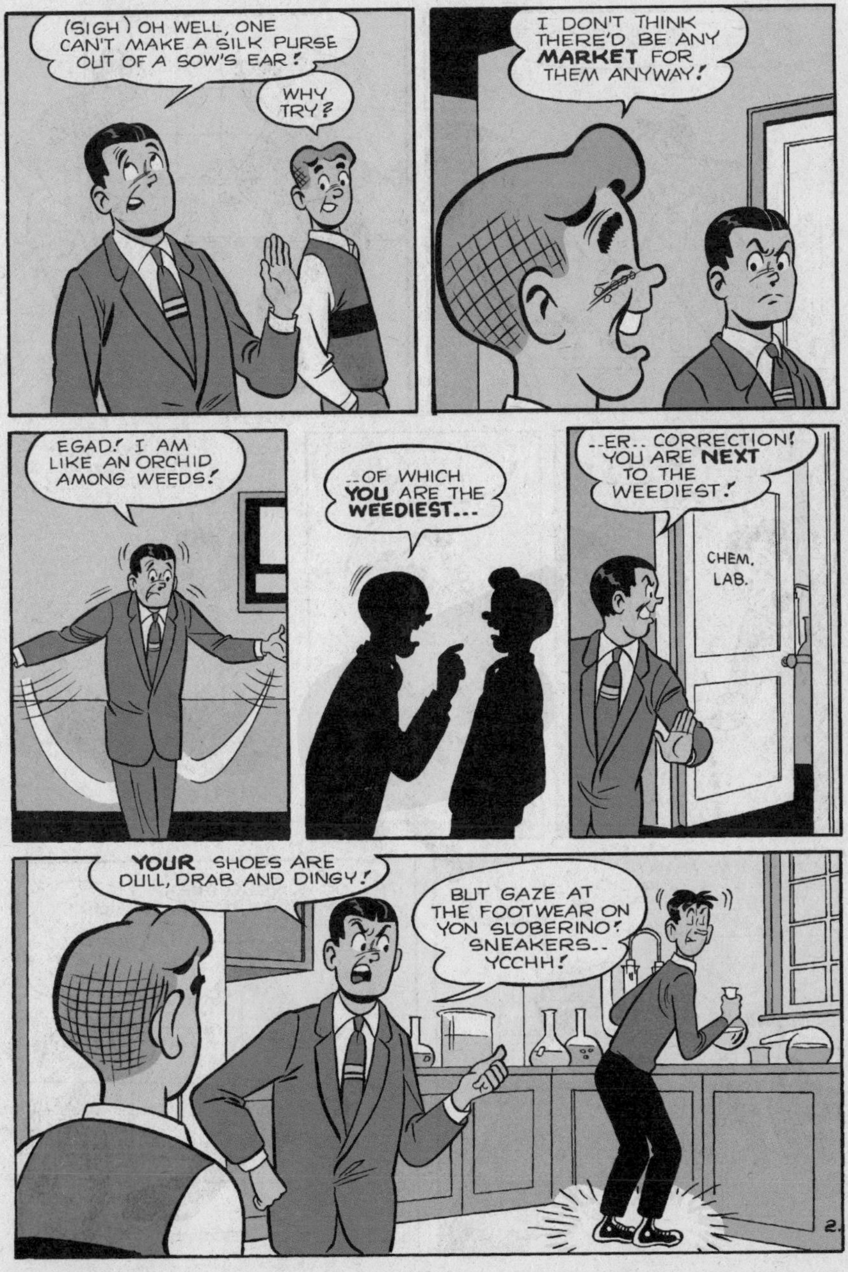
(SIGH) OH WELL, ONE CAN'T MAKE A SILK PURSE OUT OF A SOW'S EAR!
WHY TRY?
I DON'T THINK THERE'D BE ANY **MARKET** FOR THEM ANYWAY!
EGAD! I AM LIKE AN ORCHID AMONG WEEDS!
..OF WHICH **YOU** ARE THE **WEEDIEST...**
--ER.. CORRECTION! YOU ARE **NEXT** TO THE WEEDIEST!
CHEM. LAB.
YOUR SHOES ARE DULL, DRAB AND DINGY!
BUT GAZE AT THE FOOTWEAR ON YON SLOBERINO! SNEAKERS.. YCCHH!
2.

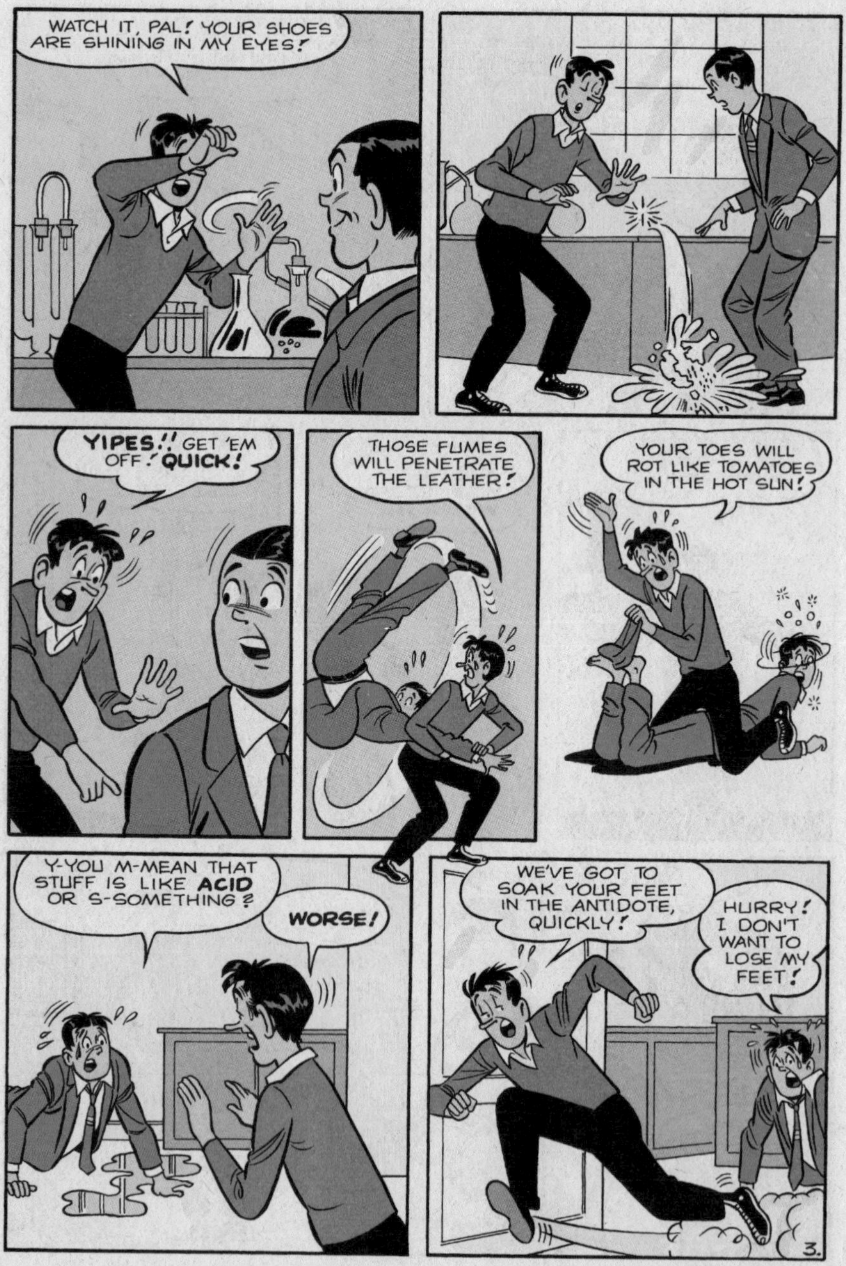
WATCH IT, PAL! YOUR SHOES ARE SHINING IN MY EYES!
YIPES!! GET 'EM OFF! QUICK!
THOSE FUMES WILL PENETRATE THE LEATHER!
YOUR TOES WILL ROT LIKE TOMATOES IN THE HOT SUN!
Y-YOU M-MEAN THAT STUFF IS LIKE ACID OR S-SOMETHING?
WORSE!
WE'VE GOT TO SOAK YOUR FEET IN THE ANTIDOTE, QUICKLY!
HURRY! I DON'T WANT TO LOSE MY FEET!
3.

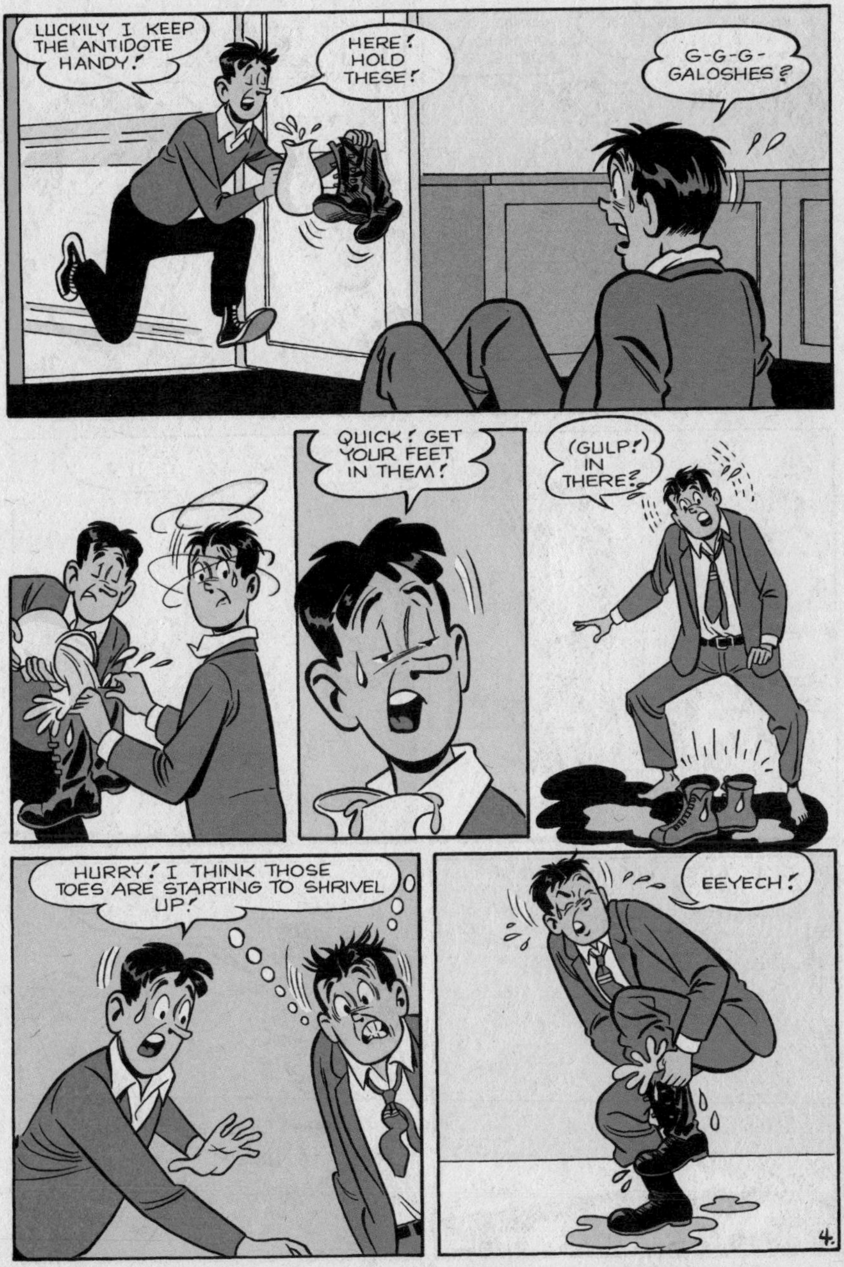
LUCKILY I KEEP THE ANTIDOTE HANDY!
HERE! HOLD THESE!
G-G-G-GALOSHES?
QUICK! GET YOUR FEET IN THEM!
(GULP!) IN THERE?
HURRY! I THINK THOSE TOES ARE STARTING TO SHRIVEL UP!
EEYECH!
4.

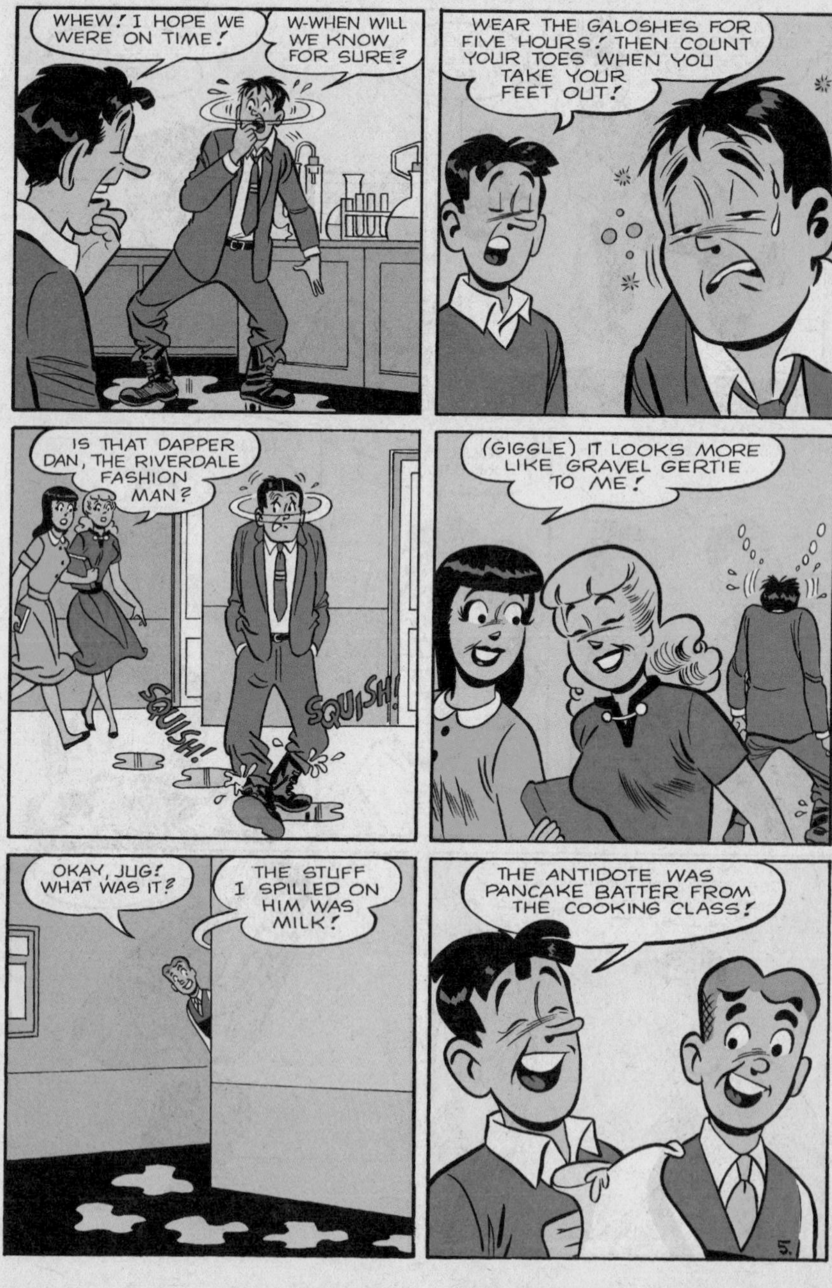
WHEW! I HOPE WE WERE ON TIME!
W-WHEN WILL WE KNOW FOR SURE?
WEAR THE GALOSHES FOR FIVE HOURS! THEN COUNT YOUR TOES WHEN YOU TAKE YOUR FEET OUT!
IS THAT DAPPER DAN, THE RIVERDALE FASHION MAN?
SQUISH!
SQUISH!
(GIGGLE) IT LOOKS MORE LIKE GRAVEL GERTIE TO ME!
OKAY, JUG! WHAT WAS IT?
THE STUFF I SPILLED ON HIM WAS MILK!
THE ANTIDOTE WAS PANCAKE BATTER FROM THE COOKING CLASS!
5.

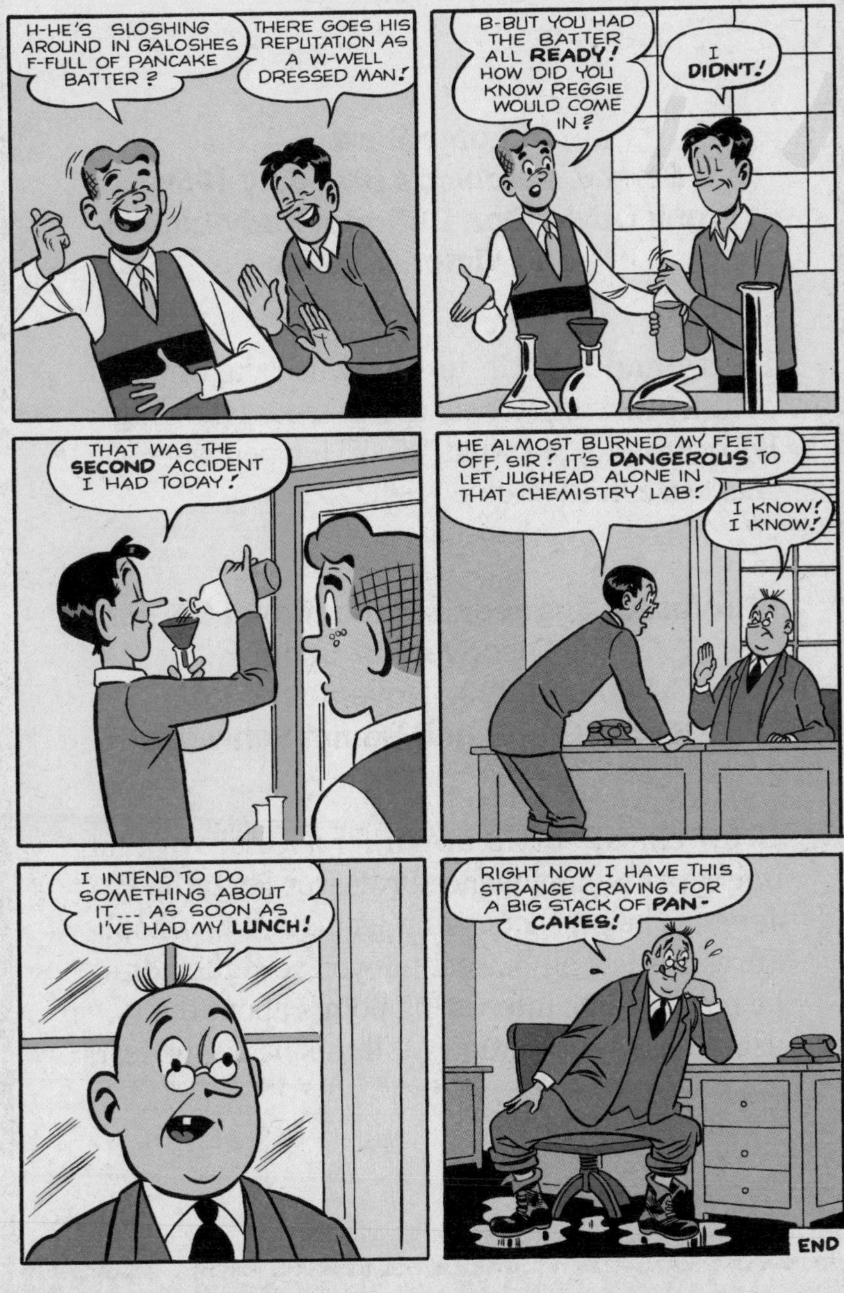
H-HE'S SLOSHING AROUND IN GALOSHES F-FULL OF PANCAKE BATTER?
THERE GOES HIS REPUTATION AS A W-WELL DRESSED MAN!
B-BUT YOU HAD THE BATTER ALL **READY**! HOW DID YOU KNOW REGGIE WOULD COME IN?
I **DIDN'T**!
THAT WAS THE **SECOND** ACCIDENT I HAD TODAY!
HE ALMOST BURNED MY FEET OFF, SIR! IT'S **DANGEROUS** TO LET JUGHEAD ALONE IN THAT CHEMISTRY LAB!
I KNOW! I KNOW!
I INTEND TO DO SOMETHING ABOUT IT... AS SOON AS I'VE HAD MY **LUNCH**!
RIGHT NOW I HAVE THIS STRANGE CRAVING FOR A BIG STACK OF **PAN-CAKES**!
END

Lamb Stew
Betty & Veronica #103, July 1964
Frank Doyle, Dan DeCarlo, Rudy Lapick and Victor Gorelick

Betty had a little lamb—which she won in a raffle! It's sure not *sheepish* about following Betty around, but what "wool" happen when it gets loose in Riverdale High?

Professor Jughead's Educational Corner: The Discovery of School
Jughead #90, November 1962
George Gladir and Samm Schwartz

Now class, settle down for a lecture by that interloper of intelligence Professor Forsythe P. Jones as he presents a unique history of school. Sure, this is a bit biased, but you've got to admit he makes some interesting points about the usefulness of education. Will this be on the test?

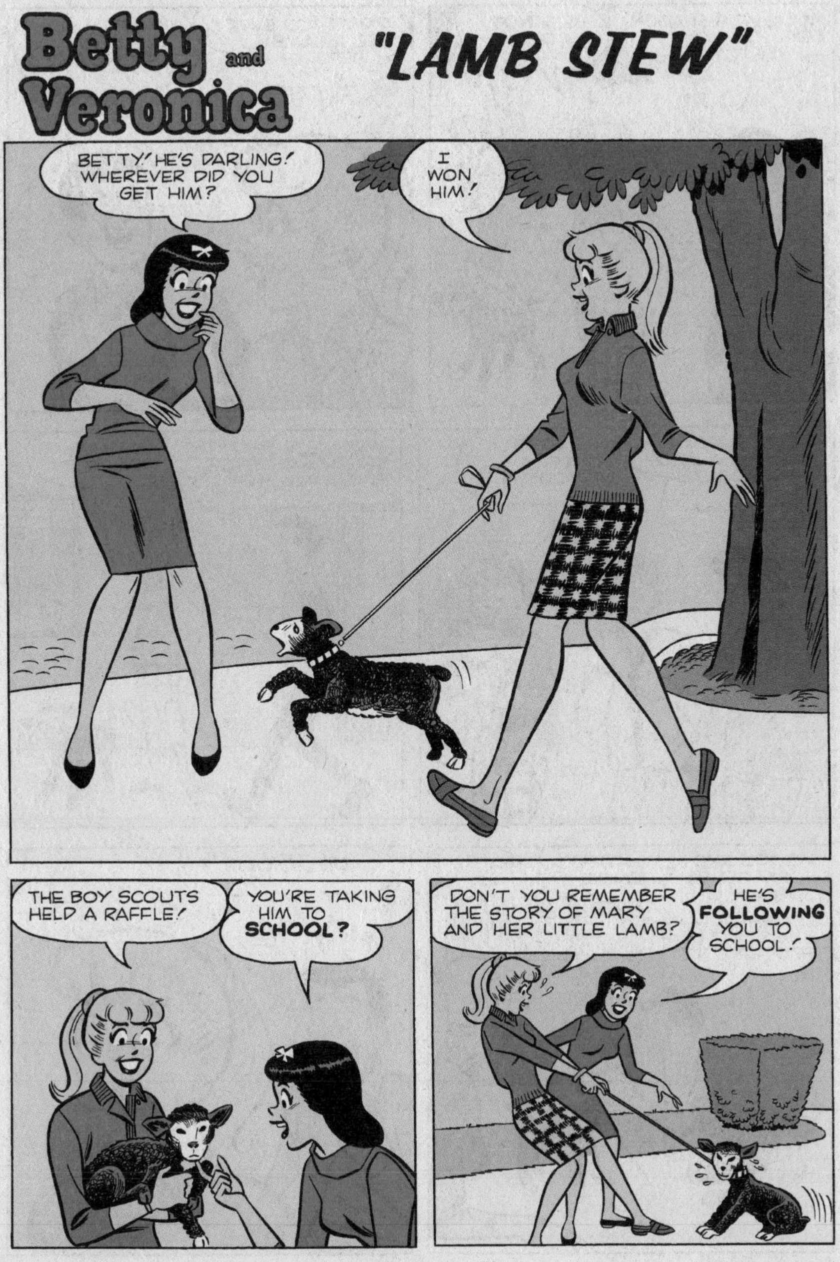
Betty and Veronica
"LAMB STEW"
BETTY! HE'S DARLING! WHEREVER DID YOU GET HIM?
I WON HIM!
THE BOY SCOUTS HELD A RAFFLE!
YOU'RE TAKING HIM TO SCHOOL?
DON'T YOU REMEMBER THE STORY OF MARY AND HER LITTLE LAMB?
HE'S FOLLOWING YOU TO SCHOOL!

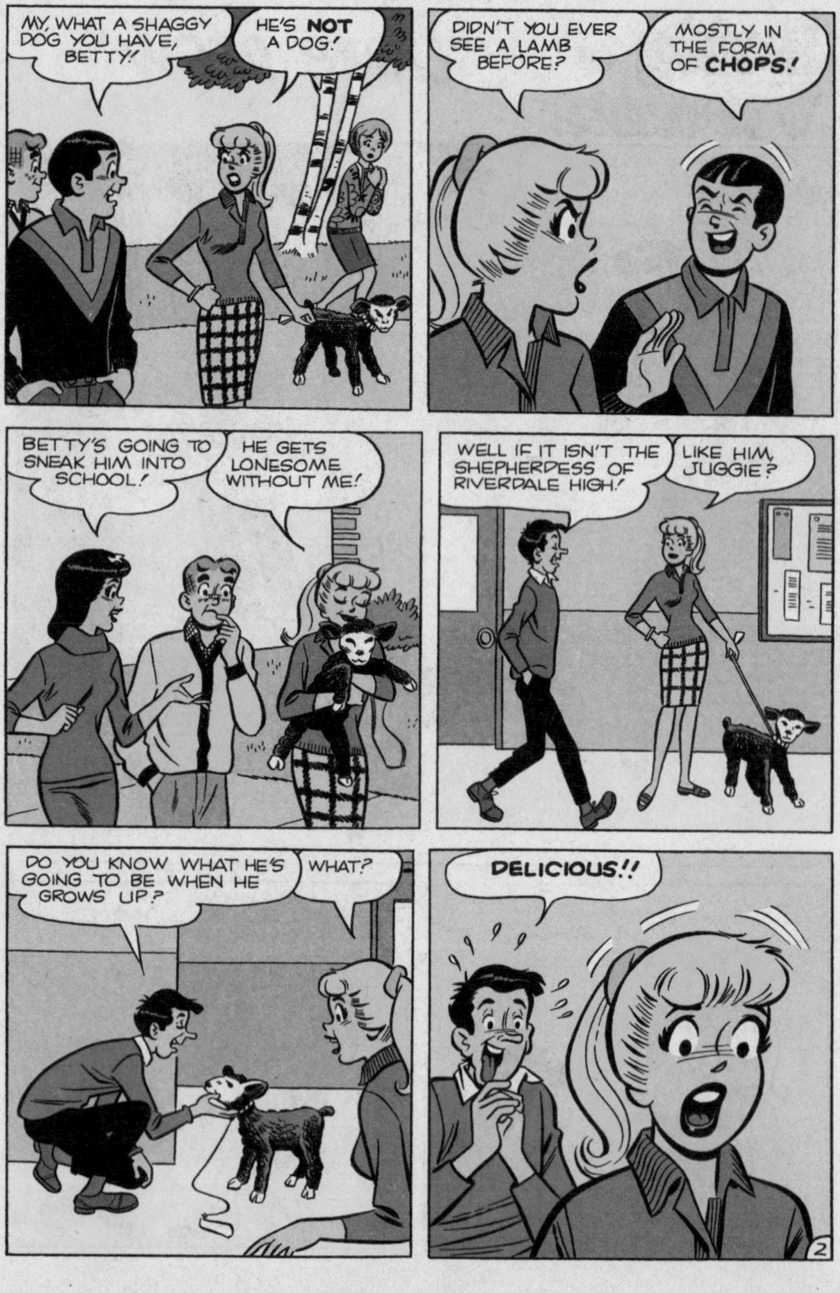
MY, WHAT A SHAGGY DOG YOU HAVE, BETTY!
HE'S **NOT** A DOG!
DIDN'T YOU EVER SEE A LAMB BEFORE?
MOSTLY IN THE FORM OF **CHOPS!**
BETTY'S GOING TO SNEAK HIM INTO SCHOOL!
HE GETS LONESOME WITHOUT ME!
WELL IF IT ISN'T THE SHEPHERDESS OF RIVERDALE HIGH!
LIKE HIM, JUGGIE?
DO YOU KNOW WHAT HE'S GOING TO BE WHEN HE GROWS UP?
WHAT?
DELICIOUS!!
2

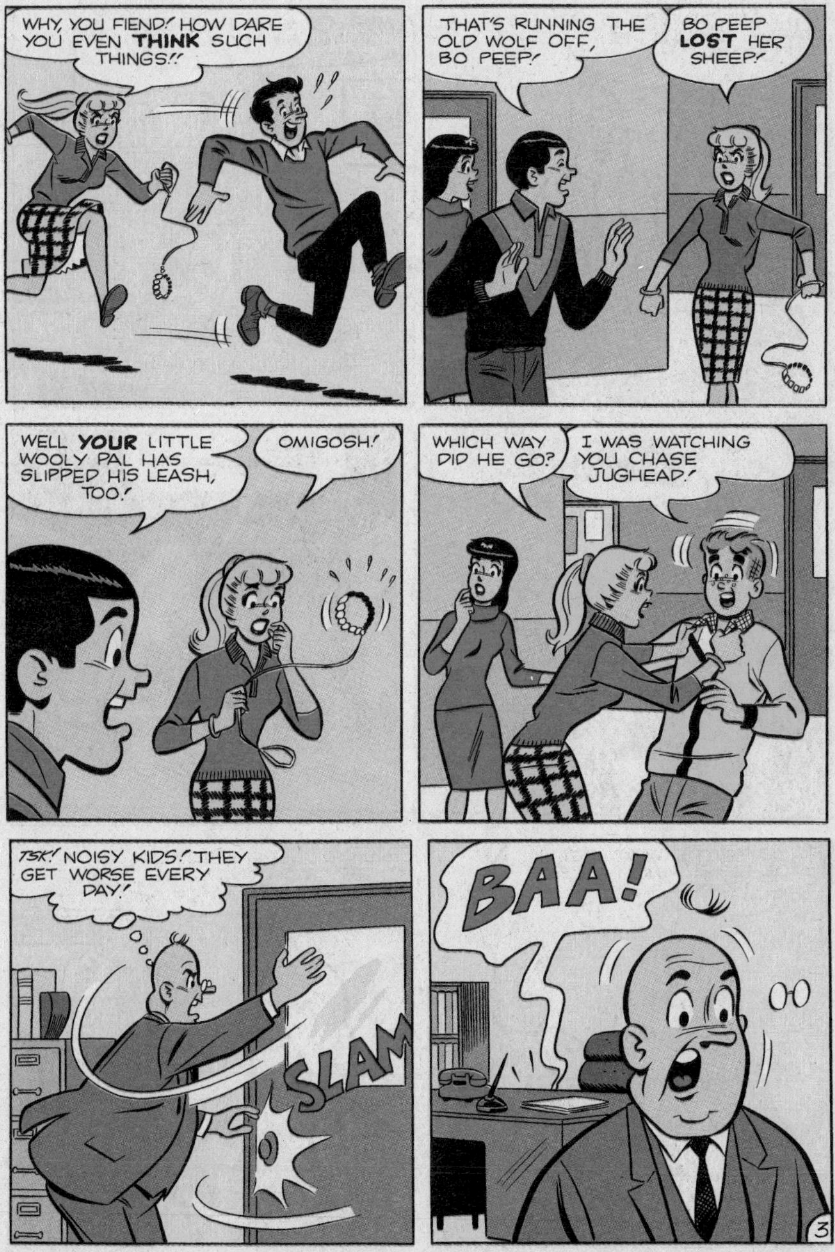
WHY, YOU FIEND! HOW DARE YOU EVEN THINK SUCH THINGS!!
THAT'S RUNNING THE OLD WOLF OFF, BO PEEP!
BO PEEP LOST HER SHEEP!
WELL YOUR LITTLE WOOLY PAL HAS SLIPPED HIS LEASH, TOO!
OMIGOSH!
WHICH WAY DID HE GO?
I WAS WATCHING YOU CHASE JUGHEAD!
TSK! NOISY KIDS! THEY GET WORSE EVERY DAY!
SLAM
BAA!
3

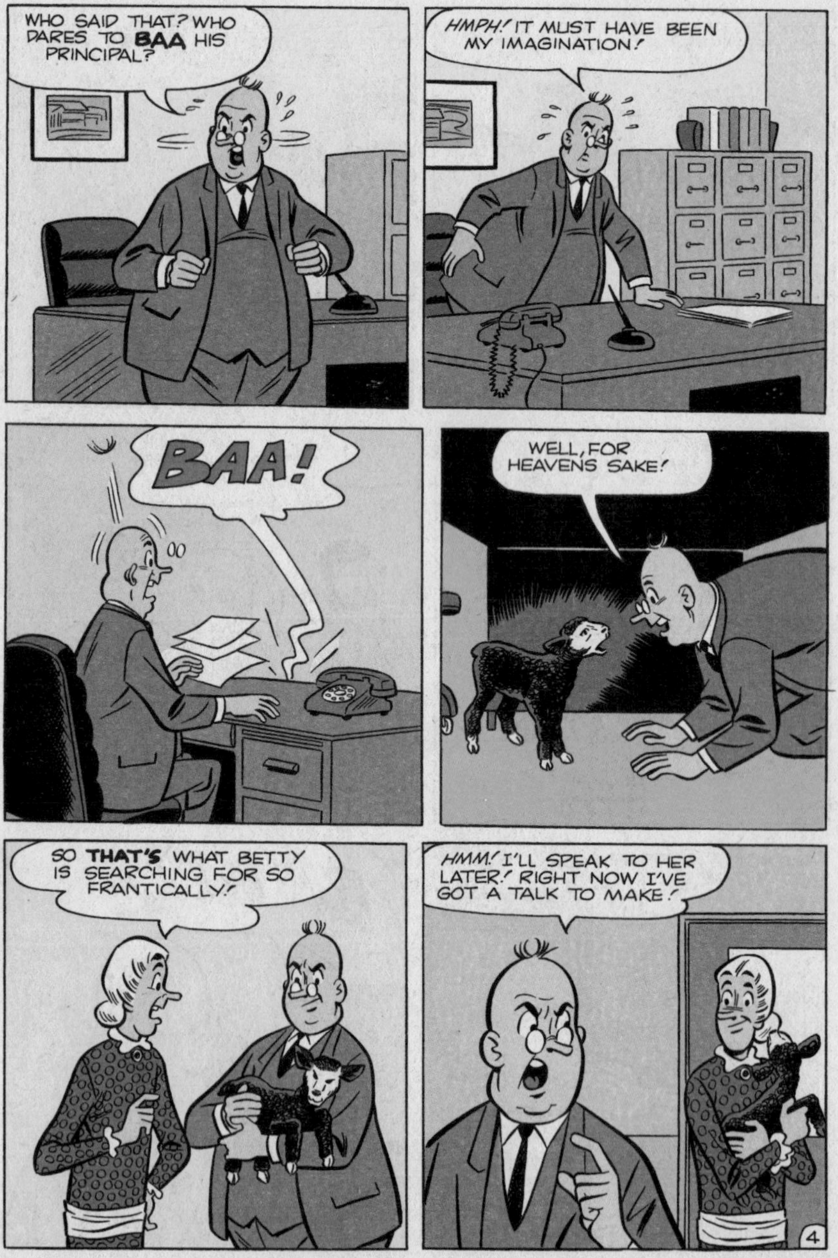
WHO SAID THAT? WHO DARES TO **BAA** HIS PRINCIPAL?
HMPH! IT MUST HAVE BEEN MY IMAGINATION!
BAA!
WELL, FOR HEAVENS SAKE!
SO **THAT'S** WHAT BETTY IS SEARCHING FOR SO FRANTICALLY!
HMM! I'LL SPEAK TO HER LATER! RIGHT NOW I'VE GOT A TALK TO MAKE!
4

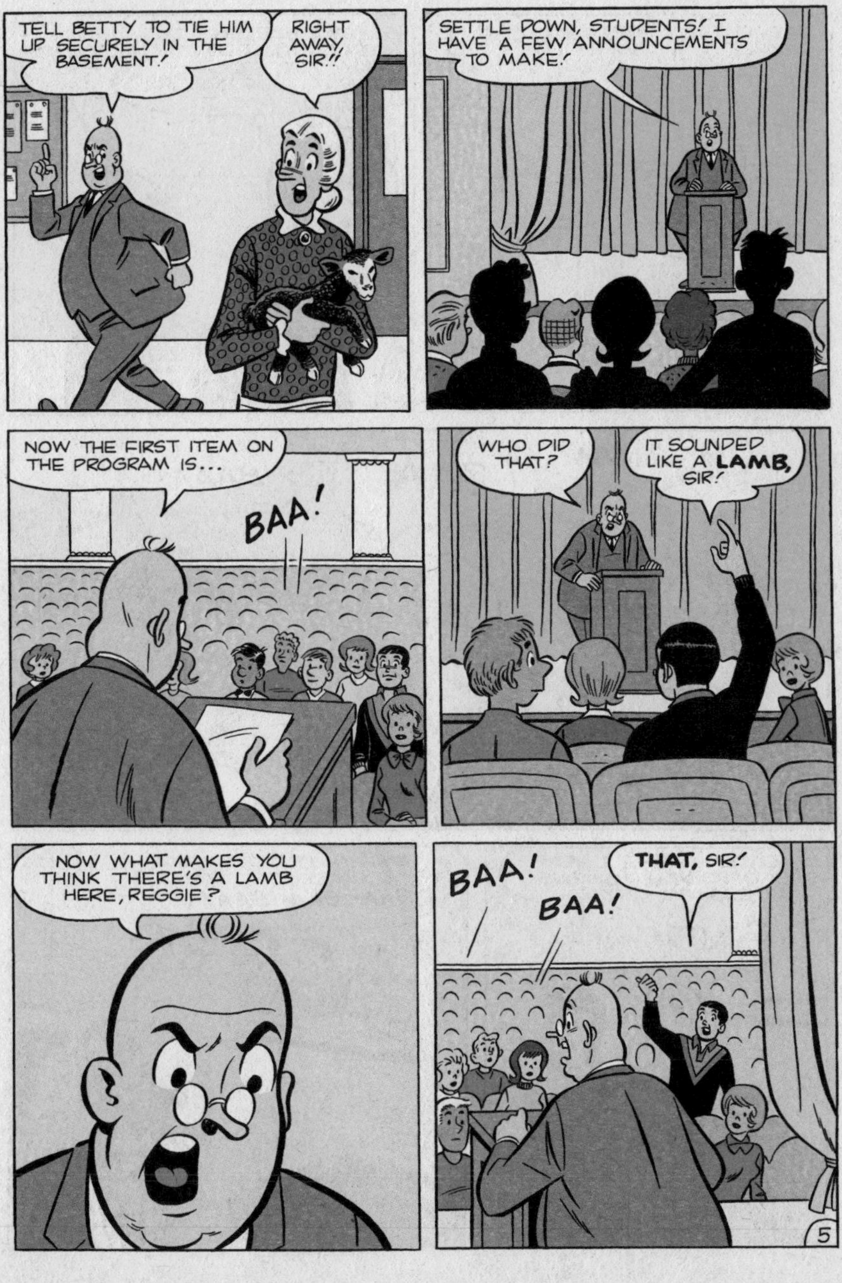
TELL BETTY TO TIE HIM UP SECURELY IN THE BASEMENT!
RIGHT AWAY, SIR!!
SETTLE DOWN, STUDENTS! I HAVE A FEW ANNOUNCEMENTS TO MAKE!
NOW THE FIRST ITEM ON THE PROGRAM IS...
BAA!
WHO DID THAT?
IT SOUNDED LIKE A **LAMB,** SIR!
NOW WHAT MAKES YOU THINK THERE'S A LAMB HERE, REGGIE?
BAA!
BAA!
THAT, SIR!
5

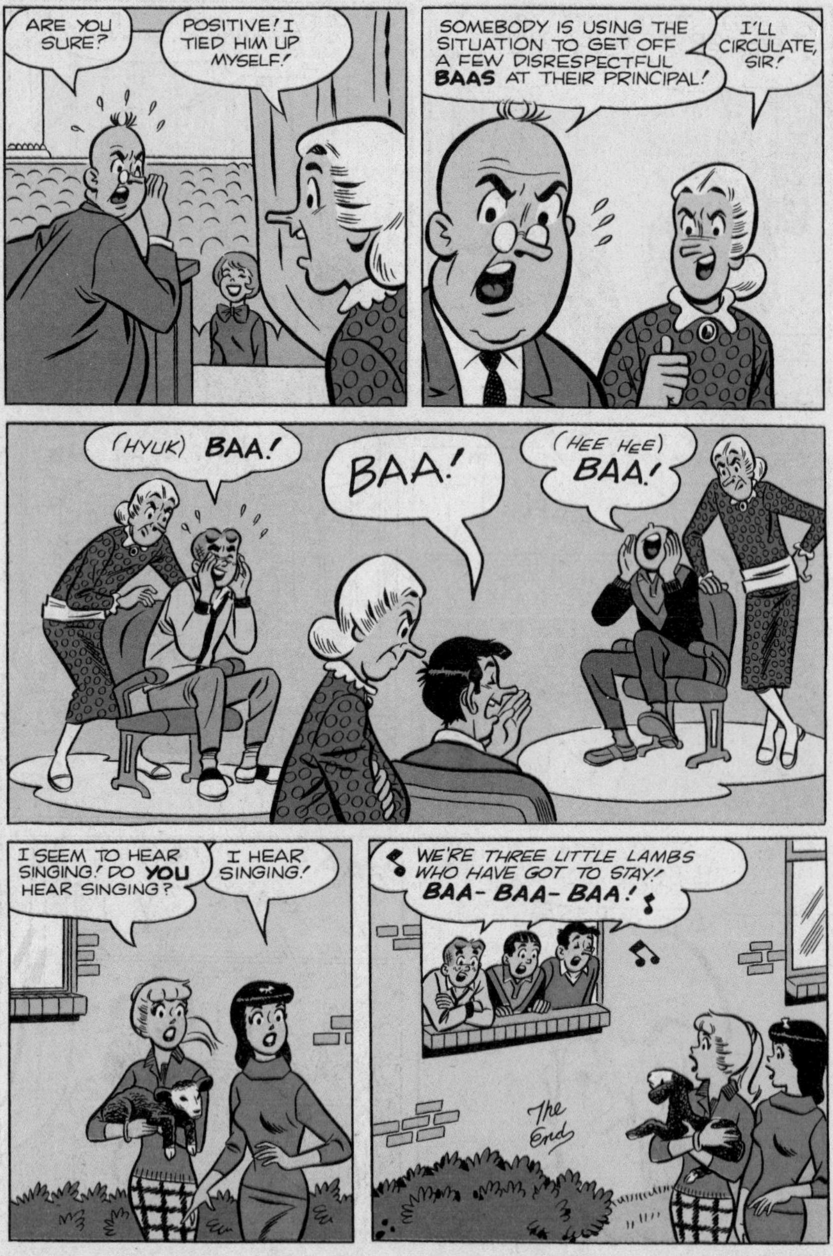
ARE YOU SURE?
POSITIVE! I TIED HIM UP MYSELF!
SOMEBODY IS USING THE SITUATION TO GET OFF A FEW DISRESPECTFUL **BAAS** AT THEIR PRINCIPAL!
I'LL CIRCULATE, SIR!
(HYUK) **BAA!**
BAA!
(HEE HEE) **BAA!**
I SEEM TO HEAR SINGING! DO **YOU** HEAR SINGING?
I HEAR SINGING!
WE'RE THREE LITTLE LAMBS WHO HAVE GOT TO STAY!
BAA- BAA- BAA!
The End

PROFESSOR JUGHEAD'S EDUCATIONAL CORNER

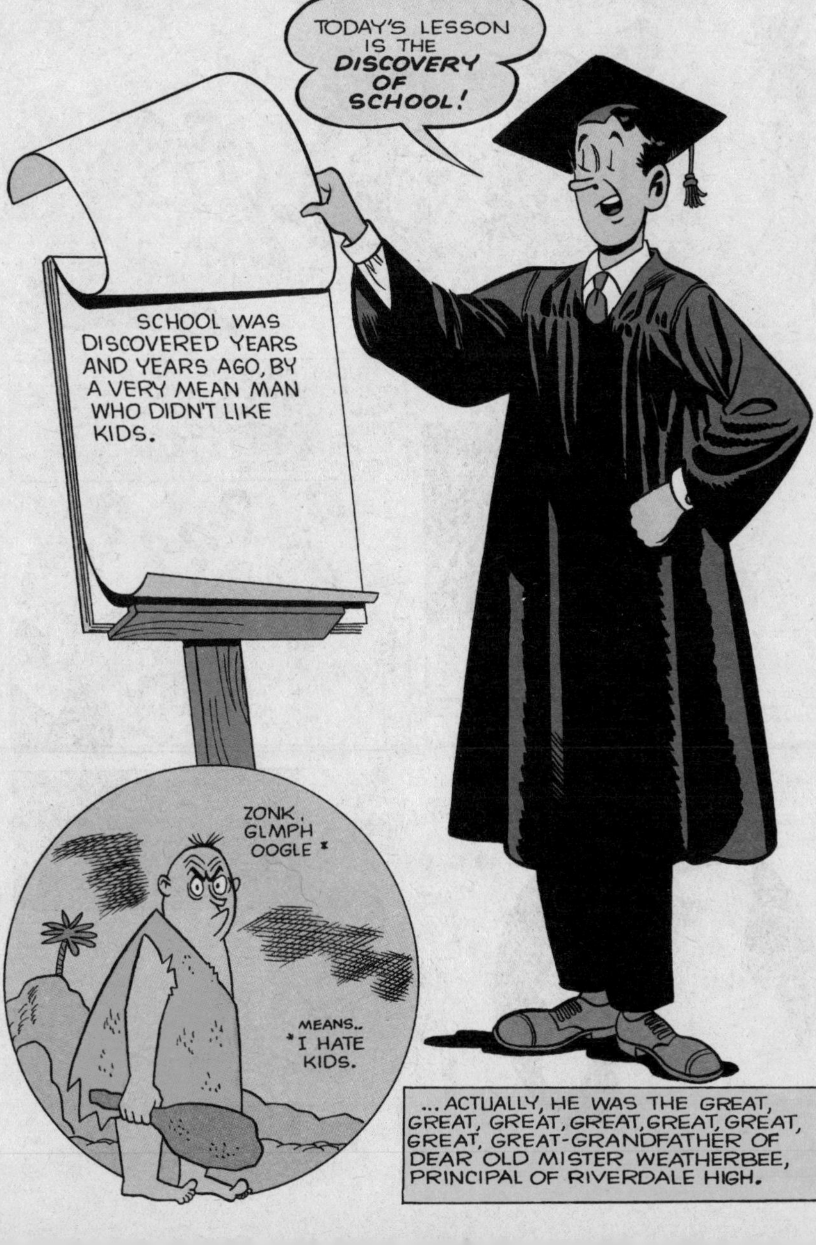
TODAY'S LESSON IS THE DISCOVERY OF SCHOOL!
SCHOOL WAS DISCOVERED YEARS AND YEARS AGO, BY A VERY MEAN MAN WHO DIDN'T LIKE KIDS.
ZONK. GLMPH OOGLE *
MEANS.. * I HATE KIDS.
... ACTUALLY, HE WAS THE GREAT, GREAT, GREAT, GREAT, GREAT, GREAT, GREAT, GREAT-GRANDFATHER OF DEAR OLD MISTER WEATHERBEE, PRINCIPAL OF RIVERDALE HIGH.

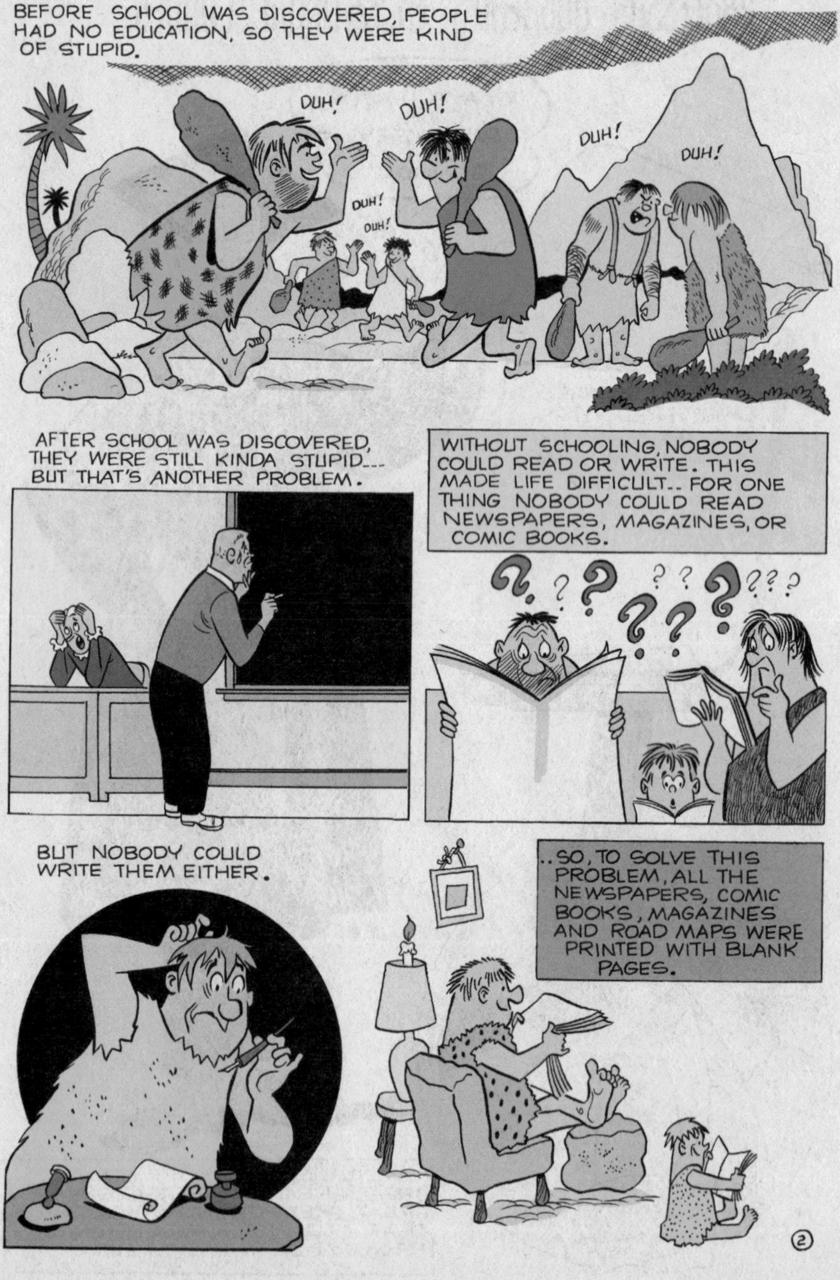
BEFORE SCHOOL WAS DISCOVERED, PEOPLE HAD NO EDUCATION, SO THEY WERE KIND OF STUPID.
DUH!
DUH!
DUH!
DUH!
DUH!
DUH!
AFTER SCHOOL WAS DISCOVERED, THEY WERE STILL KINDA STUPID... BUT THAT'S ANOTHER PROBLEM.
WITHOUT SCHOOLING, NOBODY COULD READ OR WRITE. THIS MADE LIFE DIFFICULT.. FOR ONE THING NOBODY COULD READ NEWSPAPERS, MAGAZINES, OR COMIC BOOKS.
BUT NOBODY COULD WRITE THEM EITHER.
..SO, TO SOLVE THIS PROBLEM, ALL THE NEWSPAPERS, COMIC BOOKS, MAGAZINES AND ROAD MAPS WERE PRINTED WITH BLANK PAGES.
2

SINCE NO ONE KNEW HOW TO READ, IT WAS VERY DIFFICULT TO ORDER A MEAL FROM A RESTAURANT MENU.... ESPECIALLY SINCE THE WAITERS DIDN'T KNOW HOW TO WRITE DOWN THE ORDERS ANYWAY...

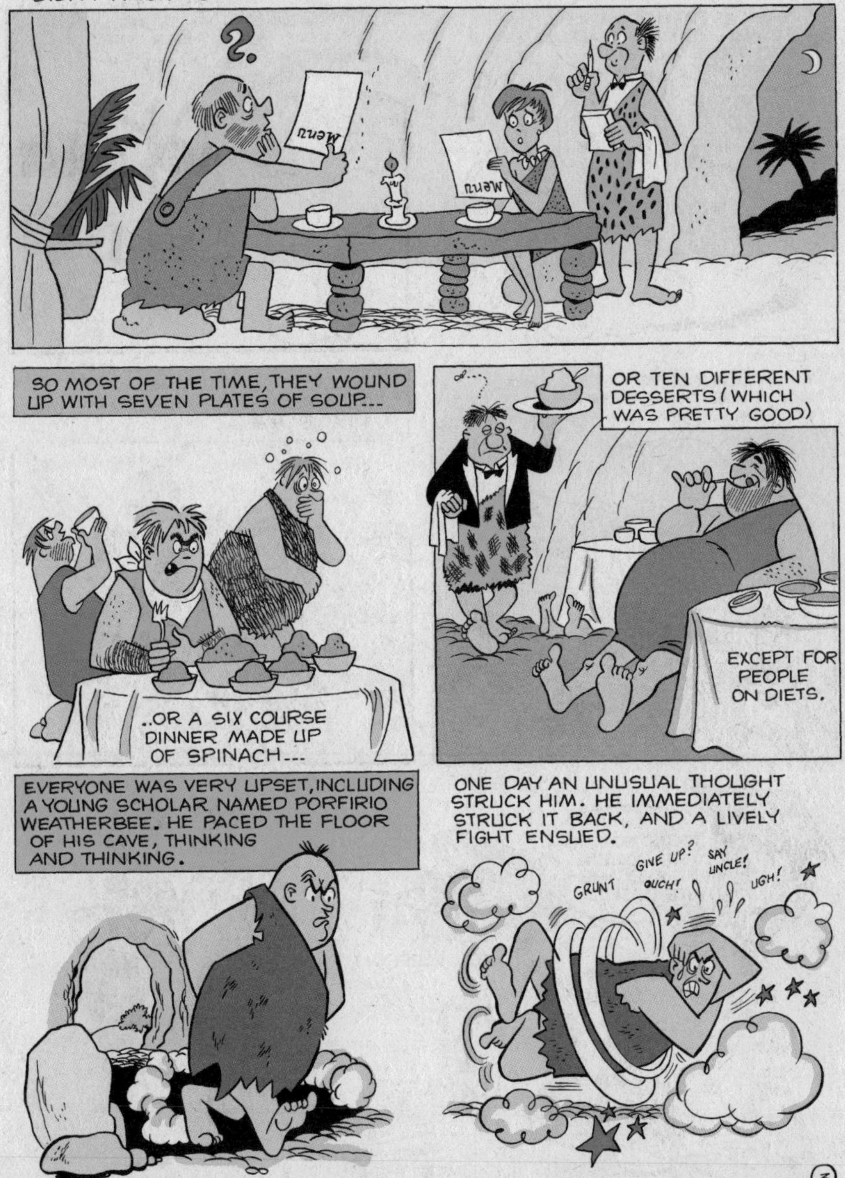
SO MOST OF THE TIME, THEY WOUND UP WITH SEVEN PLATES OF SOUP...
..OR A SIX COURSE DINNER MADE UP OF SPINACH...
OR TEN DIFFERENT DESSERTS (WHICH WAS PRETTY GOOD)
EXCEPT FOR PEOPLE ON DIETS.
EVERYONE WAS VERY UPSET, INCLUDING A YOUNG SCHOLAR NAMED PORFIRIO WEATHERBEE. HE PACED THE FLOOR OF HIS CAVE, THINKING AND THINKING.
ONE DAY AN UNUSUAL THOUGHT STRUCK HIM. HE IMMEDIATELY STRUCK IT BACK, AND A LIVELY FIGHT ENSUED.
GRUNT
GIVE UP?
OUCH!
SAY UNCLE!
UGH!

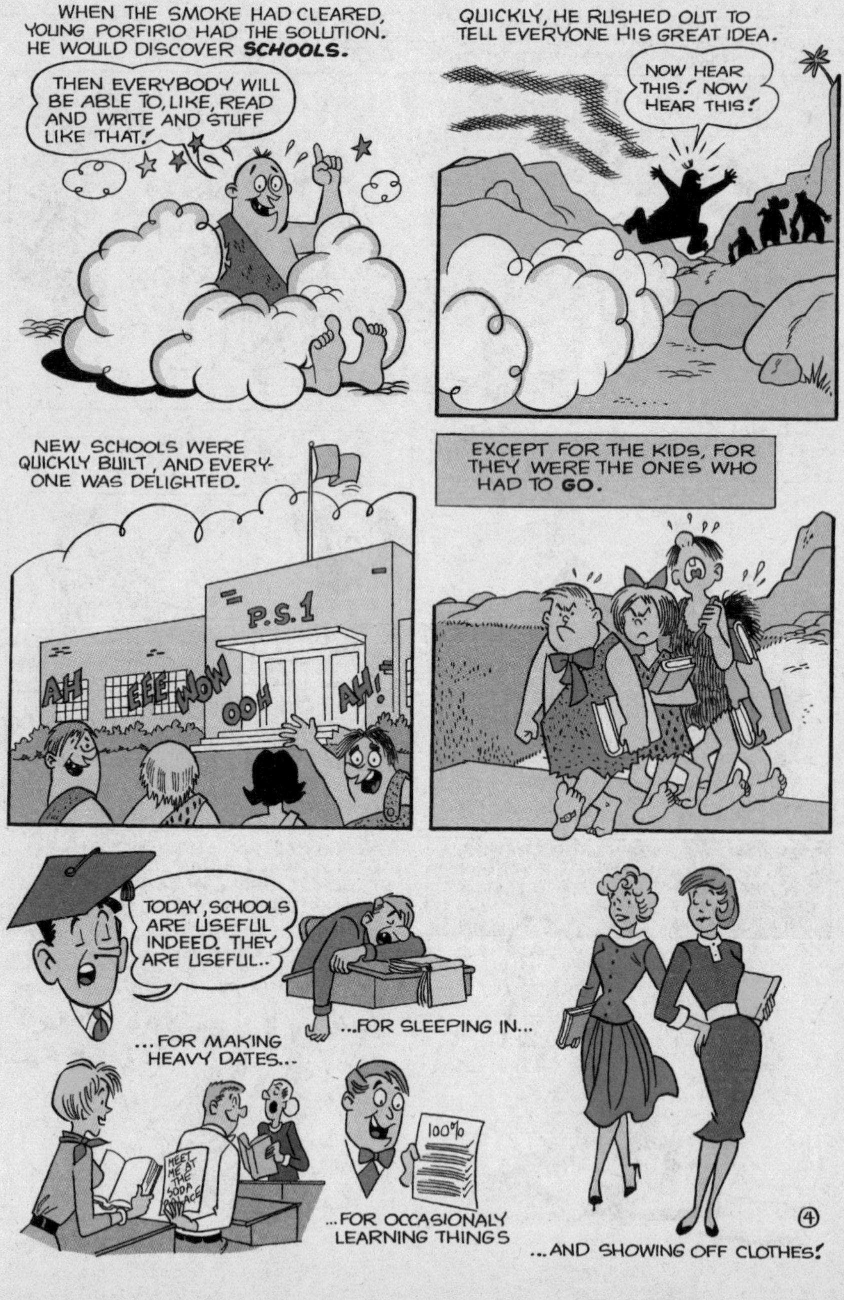
WHEN THE SMOKE HAD CLEARED, YOUNG PORFIRIO HAD THE SOLUTION. HE WOULD DISCOVER SCHOOLS.
THEN EVERYBODY WILL BE ABLE TO, LIKE, READ AND WRITE AND STUFF LIKE THAT!
QUICKLY, HE RUSHED OUT TO TELL EVERYONE HIS GREAT IDEA.
NOW HEAR THIS! NOW HEAR THIS!
NEW SCHOOLS WERE QUICKLY BUILT, AND EVERY-ONE WAS DELIGHTED.
P.S.1
AH
EEE
WOW
OOH
AH!
EXCEPT FOR THE KIDS, FOR THEY WERE THE ONES WHO HAD TO GO.
TODAY, SCHOOLS ARE USEFUL INDEED. THEY ARE USEFUL..
...FOR SLEEPING IN...
...FOR MAKING HEAVY DATES...
MEET ME AT THE SODA PALACE
100%
...FOR OCCASIONALY LEARNING THINGS
...AND SHOWING OFF CLOTHES!
4

Footsore and Weary
Archie #148, August 1964
Frank Doyle, Harry Lucey
and Marty Epp

Archie makes a plaster cast of his foot... not realizing Reggie's replaced the plaster with cement! Will Archie be able to break free or will he be destined to hobble around with a lead foot?

In the Stretch
Archie #146, June 1964
Frank Doyle, Harry Lucey
and Mario Acquaviva

Betty and Veronica cook up some belly-busting laughs when their attempts to make taffy cause sticky trouble throughout Riverdale High. Harry Lucey's art here, er, *stretches* the boundaries of comic book slapstick, resulting in a story that is nothing short of sweet and delicious.

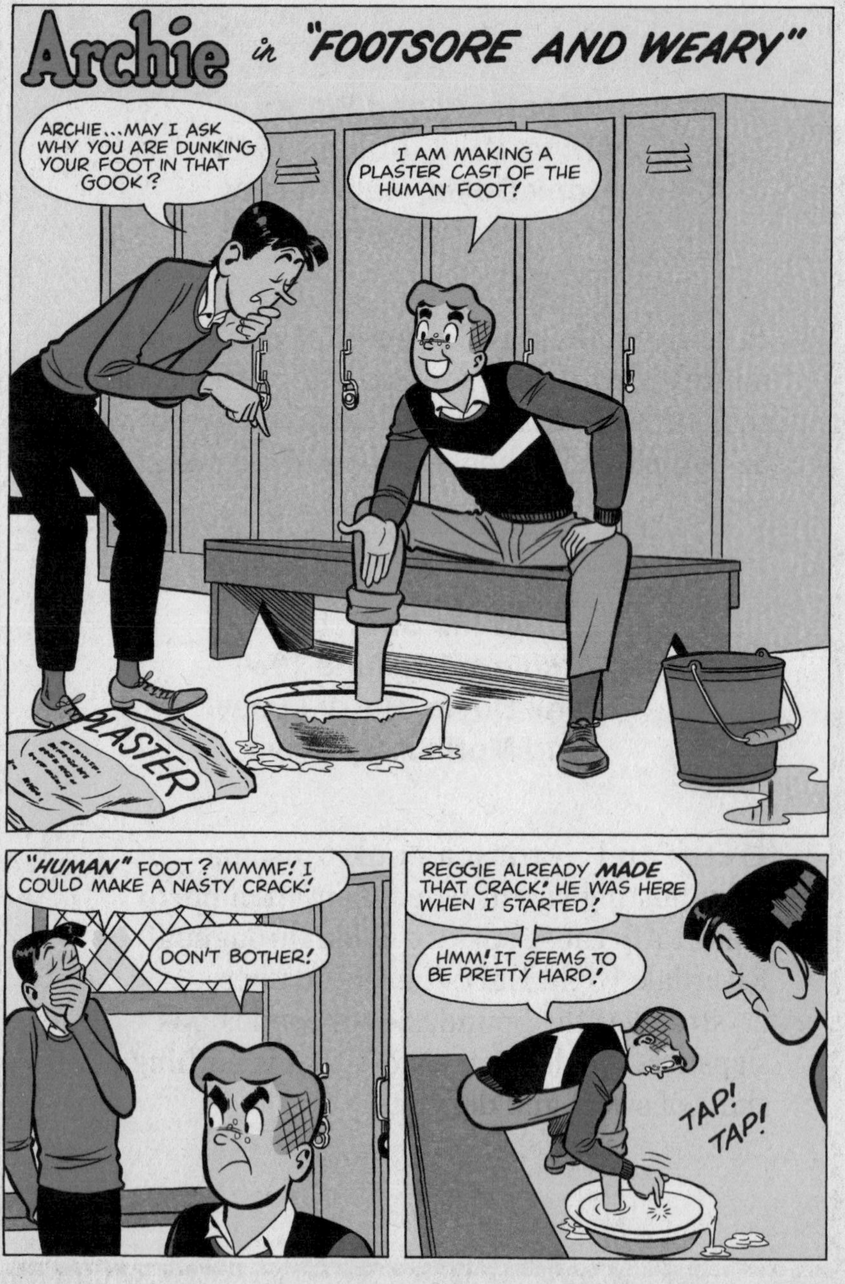
Archie in "FOOTSORE AND WEARY"
ARCHIE...MAY I ASK WHY YOU ARE DUNKING YOUR FOOT IN THAT GOOK?
I AM MAKING A PLASTER CAST OF THE HUMAN FOOT!
PLASTER
"HUMAN" FOOT? MMMF! I COULD MAKE A NASTY CRACK!
DON'T BOTHER!
REGGIE ALREADY MADE THAT CRACK! HE WAS HERE WHEN I STARTED!
HMM! IT SEEMS TO BE PRETTY HARD!
TAP! TAP!

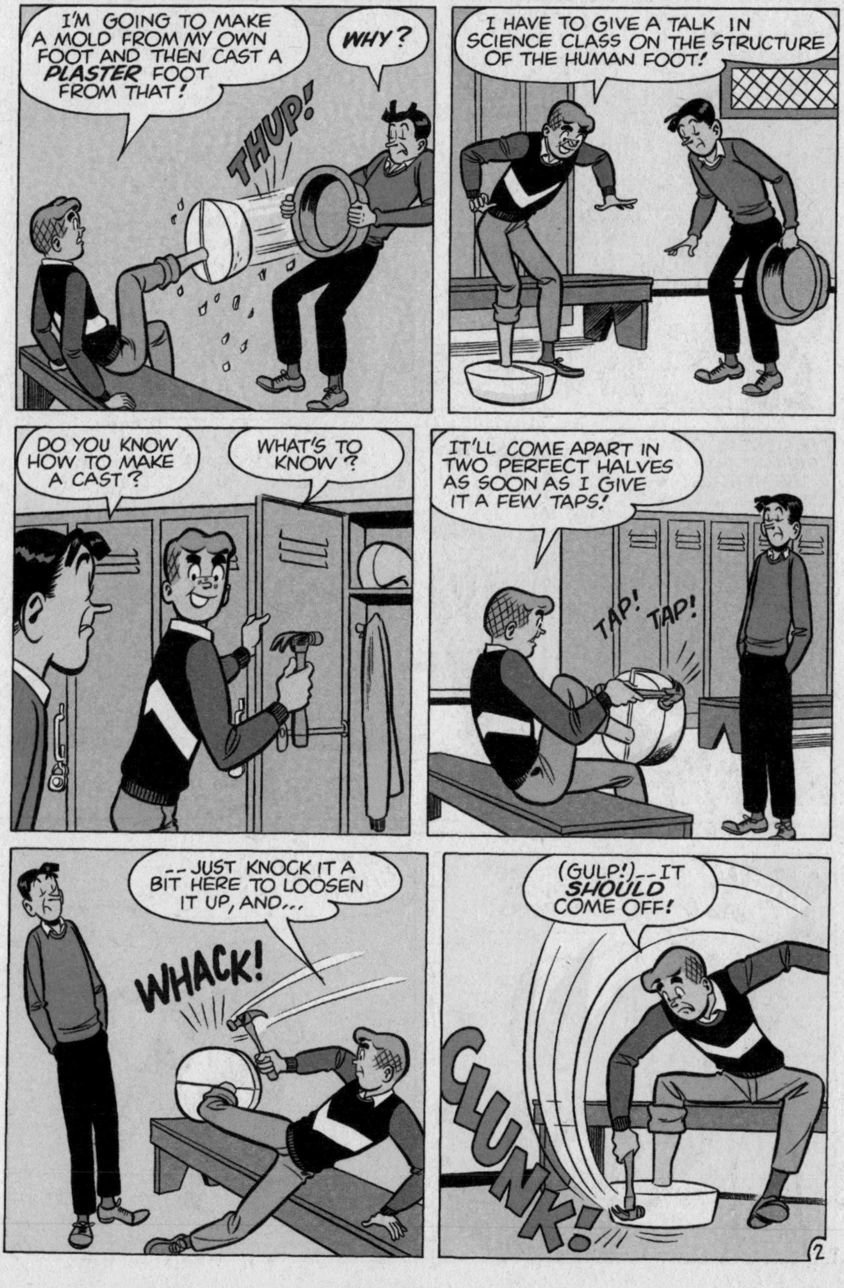

I'M GOING TO MAKE A MOLD FROM MY OWN FOOT AND THEN CAST A PLASTER FOOT FROM THAT!
WHY?
THUP!
I HAVE TO GIVE A TALK IN SCIENCE CLASS ON THE STRUCTURE OF THE HUMAN FOOT!
DO YOU KNOW HOW TO MAKE A CAST?
WHAT'S TO KNOW?
IT'LL COME APART IN TWO PERFECT HALVES AS SOON AS I GIVE IT A FEW TAPS!
TAP! TAP!
--JUST KNOCK IT A BIT HERE TO LOOSEN IT UP, AND...
WHACK!
(GULP!)--IT SHOULD COME OFF!
CLUNK!
2

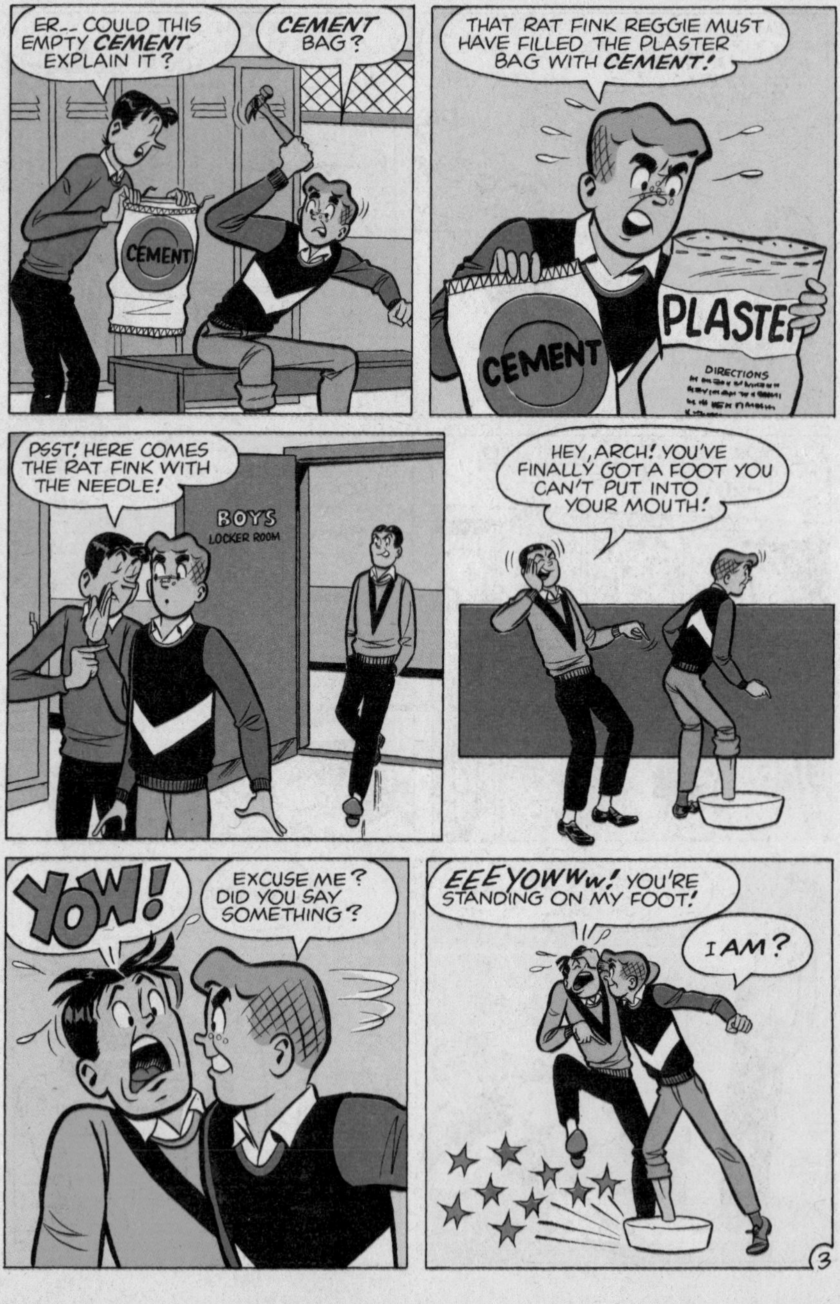
ER-- COULD THIS EMPTY CEMENT EXPLAIN IT?
CEMENT BAG?
CEMENT
THAT RAT FINK REGGIE MUST HAVE FILLED THE PLASTER BAG WITH CEMENT!
CEMENT
PLASTE
DIRECTIONS
PSST! HERE COMES THE RAT FINK WITH THE NEEDLE!
BOYS
LOCKER ROOM
HEY, ARCH! YOU'VE FINALLY GOT A FOOT YOU CAN'T PUT INTO YOUR MOUTH!
YOW!
EXCUSE ME? DID YOU SAY SOMETHING?
EEEYOWWW! YOU'RE STANDING ON MY FOOT!
I AM?
3

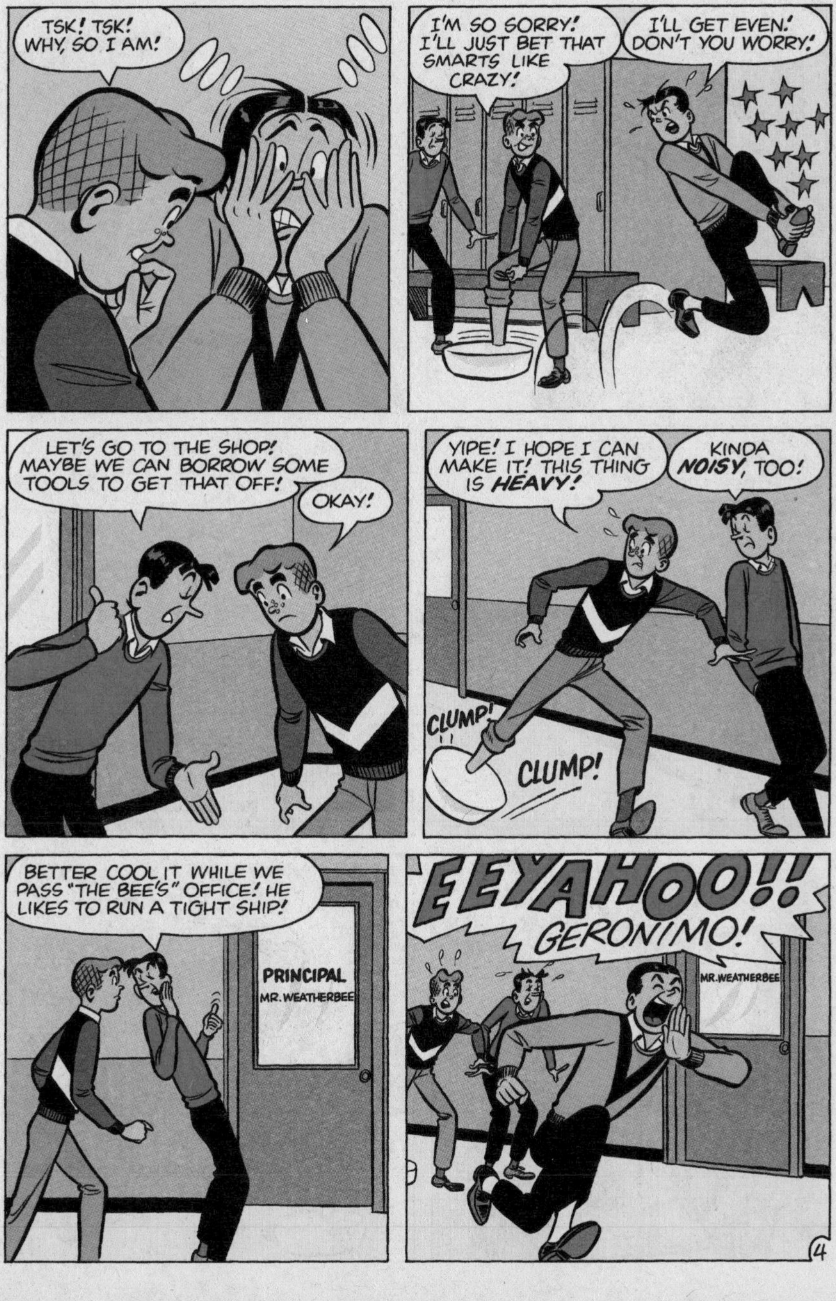
TSK! TSK! WHY, SO I AM!
I'M SO SORRY! I'LL JUST BET THAT SMARTS LIKE CRAZY!
I'LL GET EVEN! DON'T YOU WORRY!
LET'S GO TO THE SHOP! MAYBE WE CAN BORROW SOME TOOLS TO GET THAT OFF!
OKAY!
YIPE! I HOPE I CAN MAKE IT! THIS THING IS HEAVY!
KINDA NOISY, TOO!
CLUMP!
CLUMP!
BETTER COOL IT WHILE WE PASS "THE BEE'S" OFFICE! HE LIKES TO RUN A TIGHT SHIP!
PRINCIPAL
MR. WEATHERBEE
EEYAHOO!! GERONIMO!
MR. WEATHERBEE
4

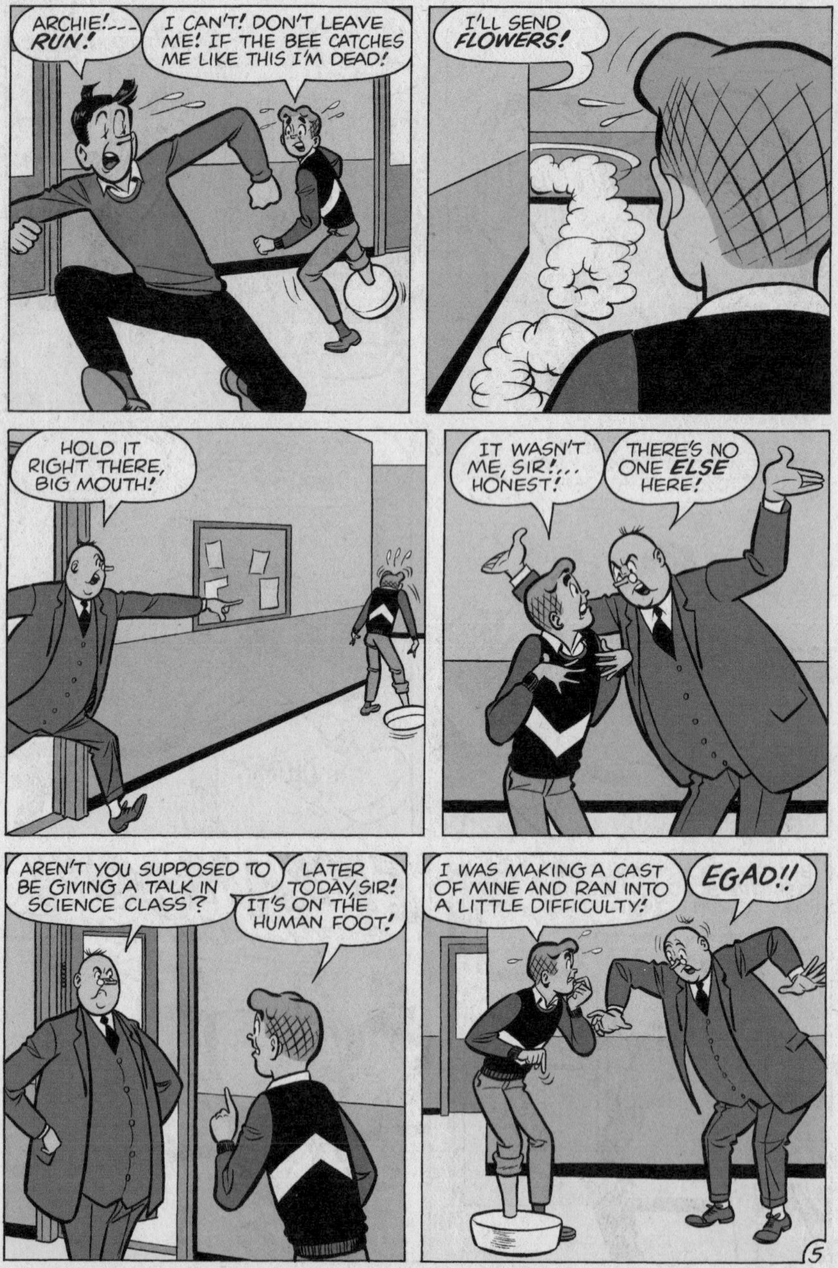
ARCHIE!... RUN!
I CAN'T! DON'T LEAVE ME! IF THE BEE CATCHES ME LIKE THIS I'M DEAD!
I'LL SEND FLOWERS!
HOLD IT RIGHT THERE, BIG MOUTH!
IT WASN'T ME, SIR!... HONEST!
THERE'S NO ONE ELSE HERE!
AREN'T YOU SUPPOSED TO BE GIVING A TALK IN SCIENCE CLASS?
LATER TODAY, SIR! IT'S ON THE HUMAN FOOT!
I WAS MAKING A CAST OF MINE AND RAN INTO A LITTLE DIFFICULTY!
EGAD!!
5

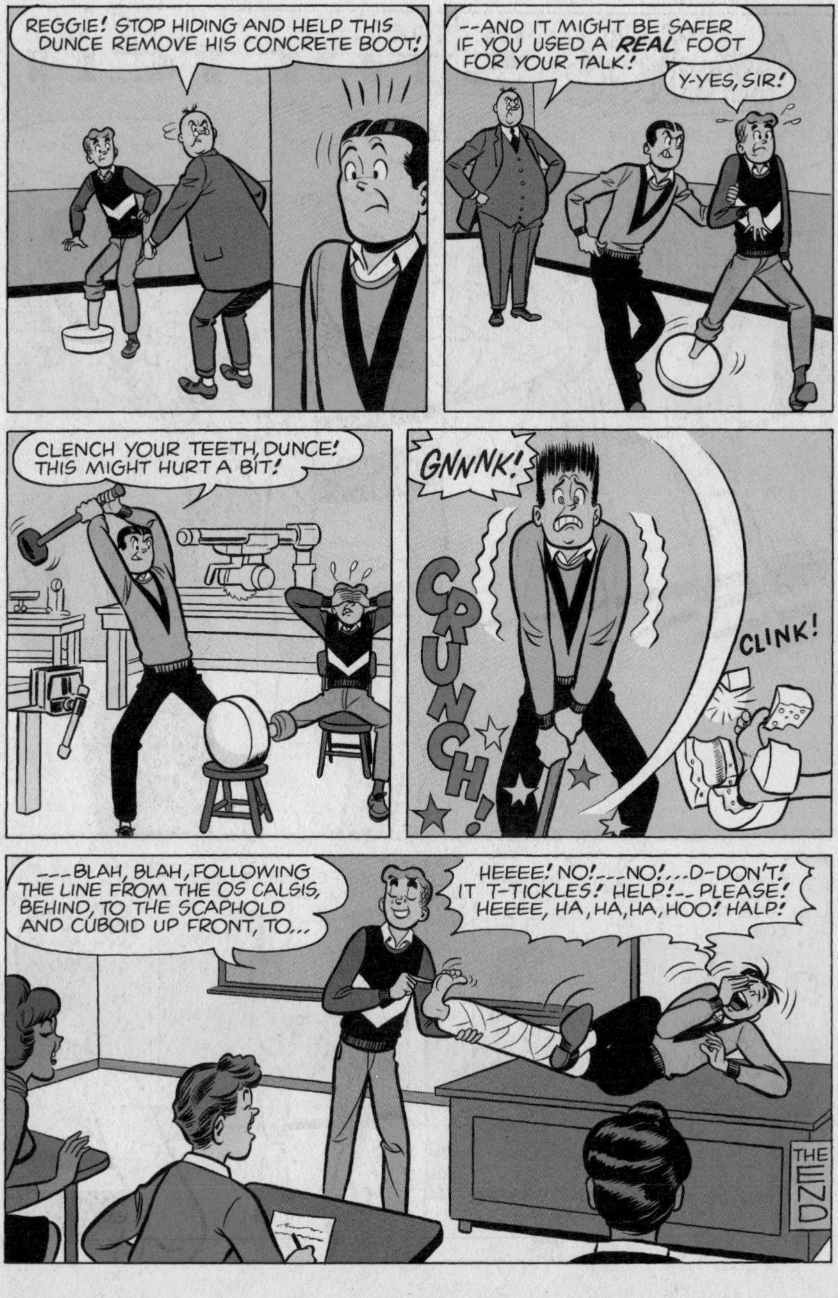
REGGIE! STOP HIDING AND HELP THIS DUNCE REMOVE HIS CONCRETE BOOT!
--AND IT MIGHT BE SAFER IF YOU USED A *REAL* FOOT FOR YOUR TALK!
Y-YES, SIR!
CLENCH YOUR TEETH, DUNCE! THIS MIGHT HURT A BIT!
GNNNK!
CRUNCH!
CLINK!
---BLAH, BLAH, FOLLOWING THE LINE FROM THE OS CALSIS, BEHIND, TO THE SCAPHOLD AND CUBOID UP FRONT, TO...
HEEEE! NO!---NO!...D-DON'T! IT T-TICKLES! HELP!-- PLEASE! HEEEE, HA, HA, HA, HOO! HALP!
THE END

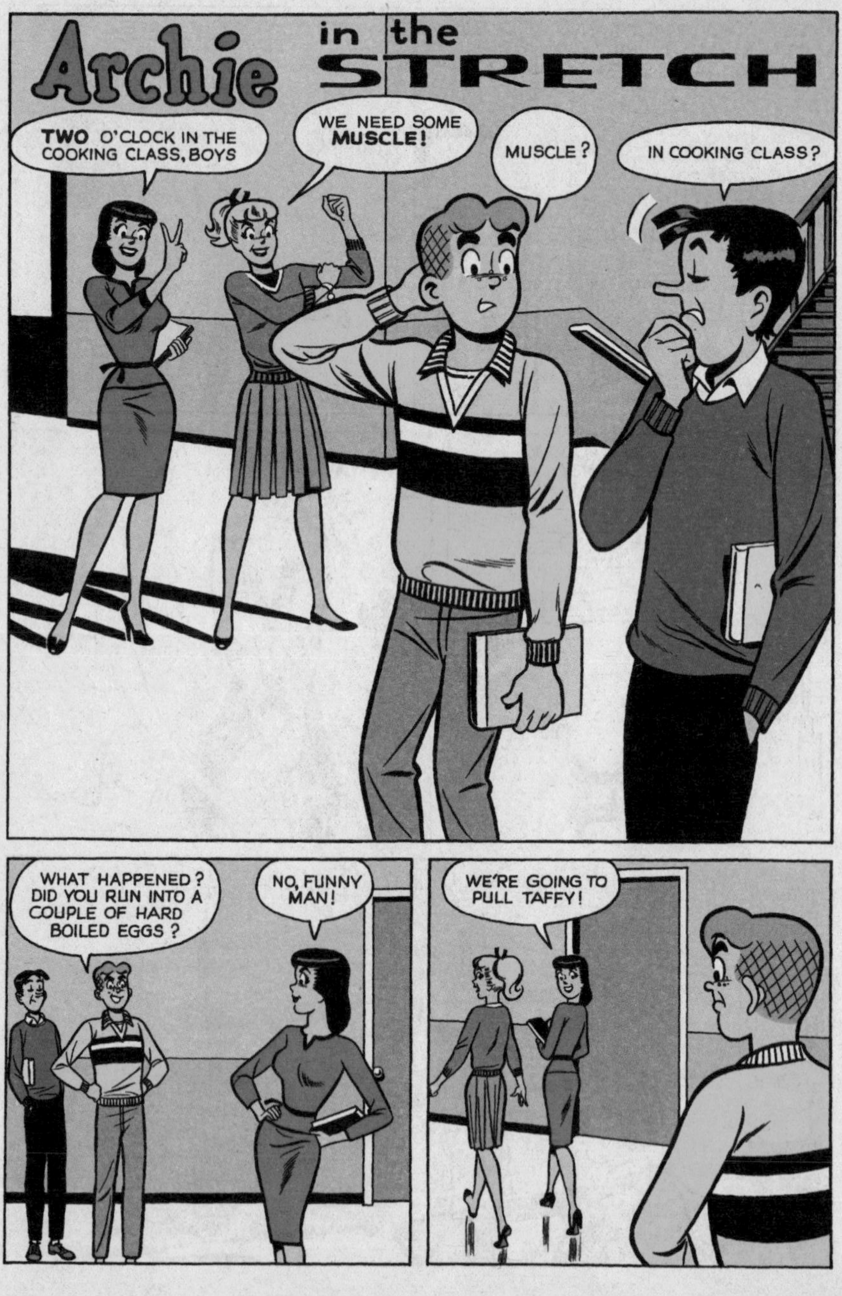
Archie in the STRETCH
TWO O'CLOCK IN THE COOKING CLASS, BOYS
WE NEED SOME MUSCLE!
MUSCLE?
IN COOKING CLASS?
WHAT HAPPENED? DID YOU RUN INTO A COUPLE OF HARD BOILED EGGS?
NO, FUNNY MAN!
WE'RE GOING TO PULL TAFFY!

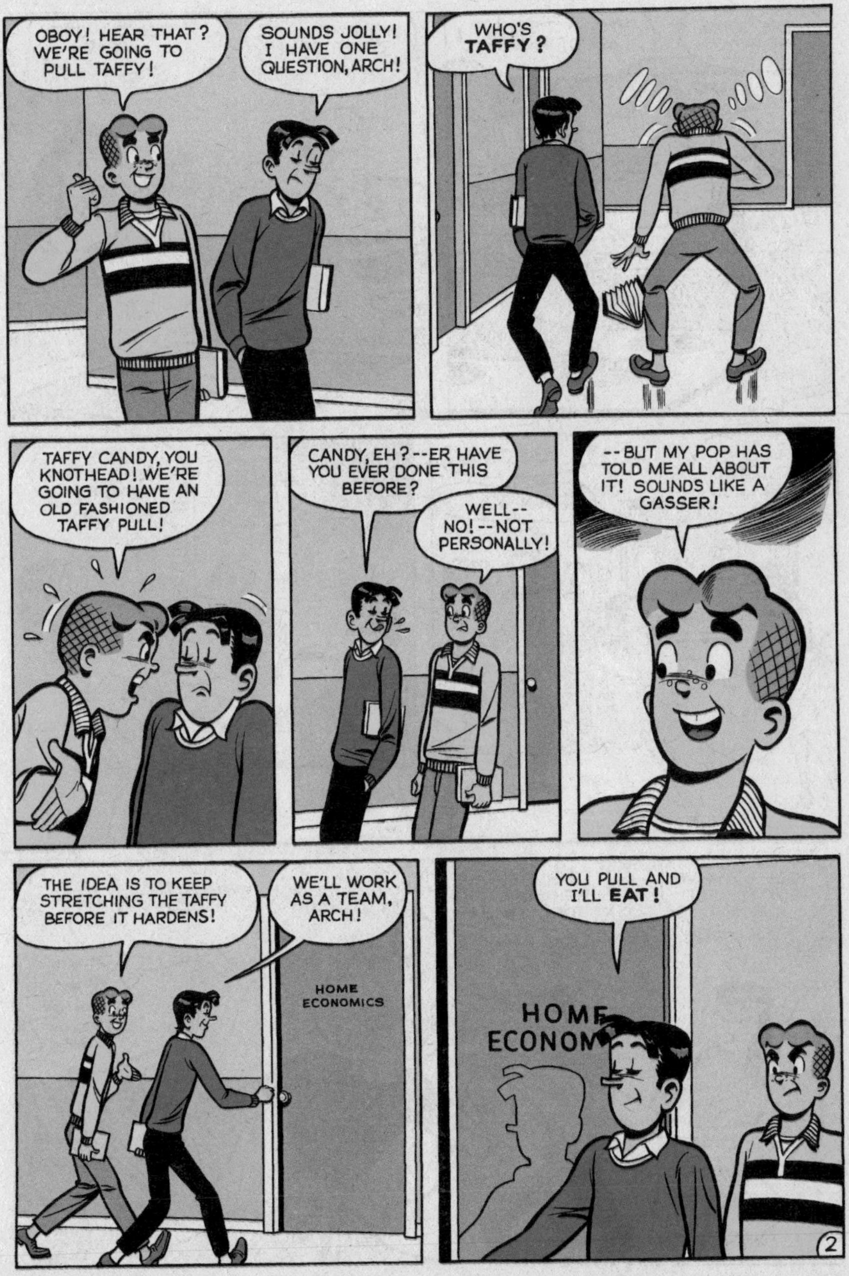
OBOY! HEAR THAT? WE'RE GOING TO PULL TAFFY!
SOUNDS JOLLY! I HAVE ONE QUESTION, ARCH!
WHO'S **TAFFY?**
TAFFY CANDY, YOU KNOTHEAD! WE'RE GOING TO HAVE AN OLD FASHIONED TAFFY PULL!
CANDY, EH?--ER HAVE YOU EVER DONE THIS BEFORE?
WELL-- NO!--NOT PERSONALLY!
--BUT MY POP HAS TOLD ME ALL ABOUT IT! SOUNDS LIKE A GASSER!
THE IDEA IS TO KEEP STRETCHING THE TAFFY BEFORE IT HARDENS!
WE'LL WORK AS A TEAM, ARCH!
HOME ECONOMICS
YOU PULL AND I'LL **EAT!**
2

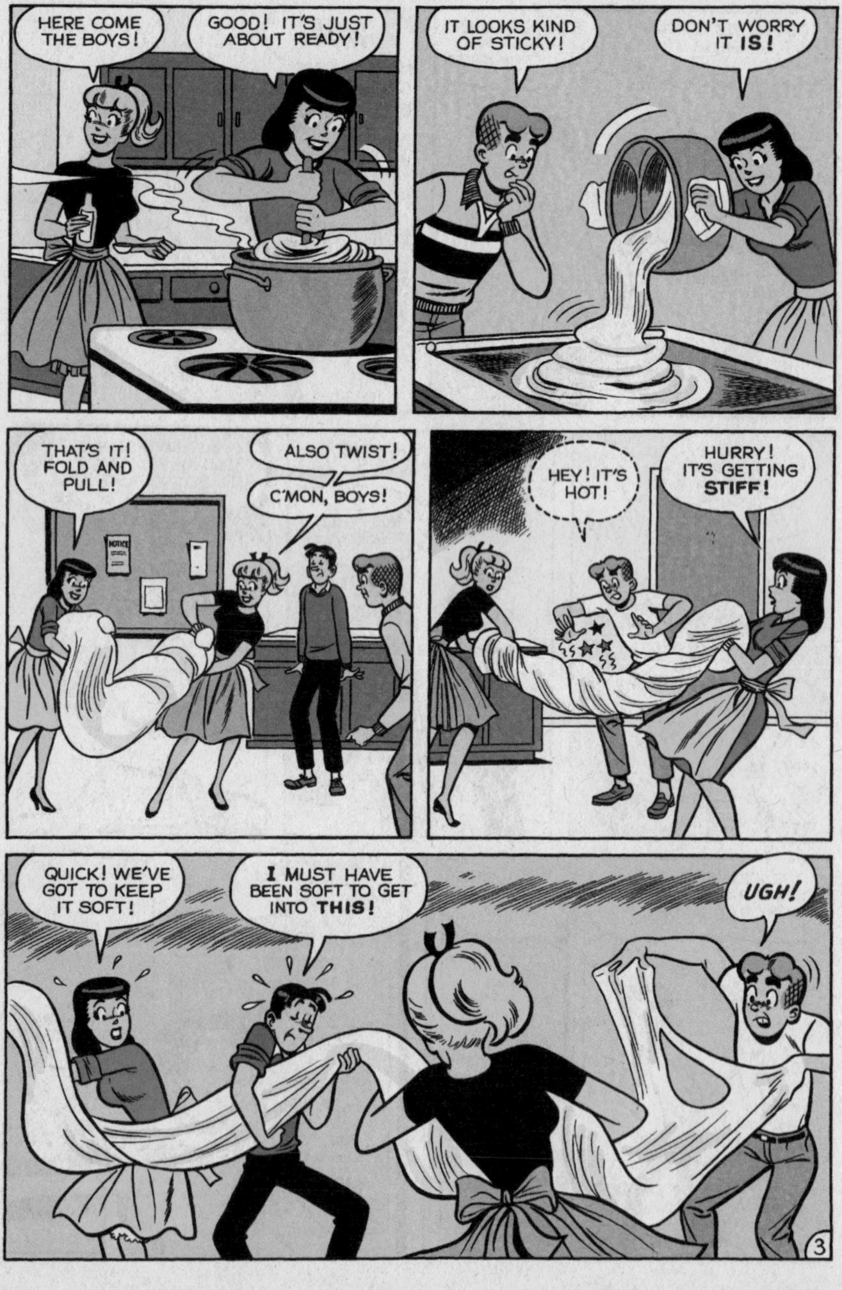
HERE COME THE BOYS!
GOOD! IT'S JUST ABOUT READY!
IT LOOKS KIND OF STICKY!
DON'T WORRY IT IS!
THAT'S IT! FOLD AND PULL!
ALSO TWIST!
C'MON, BOYS!
NOTICE
HEY! IT'S HOT!
HURRY! IT'S GETTING STIFF!
QUICK! WE'VE GOT TO KEEP IT SOFT!
I MUST HAVE BEEN SOFT TO GET INTO THIS!
UGH!
3

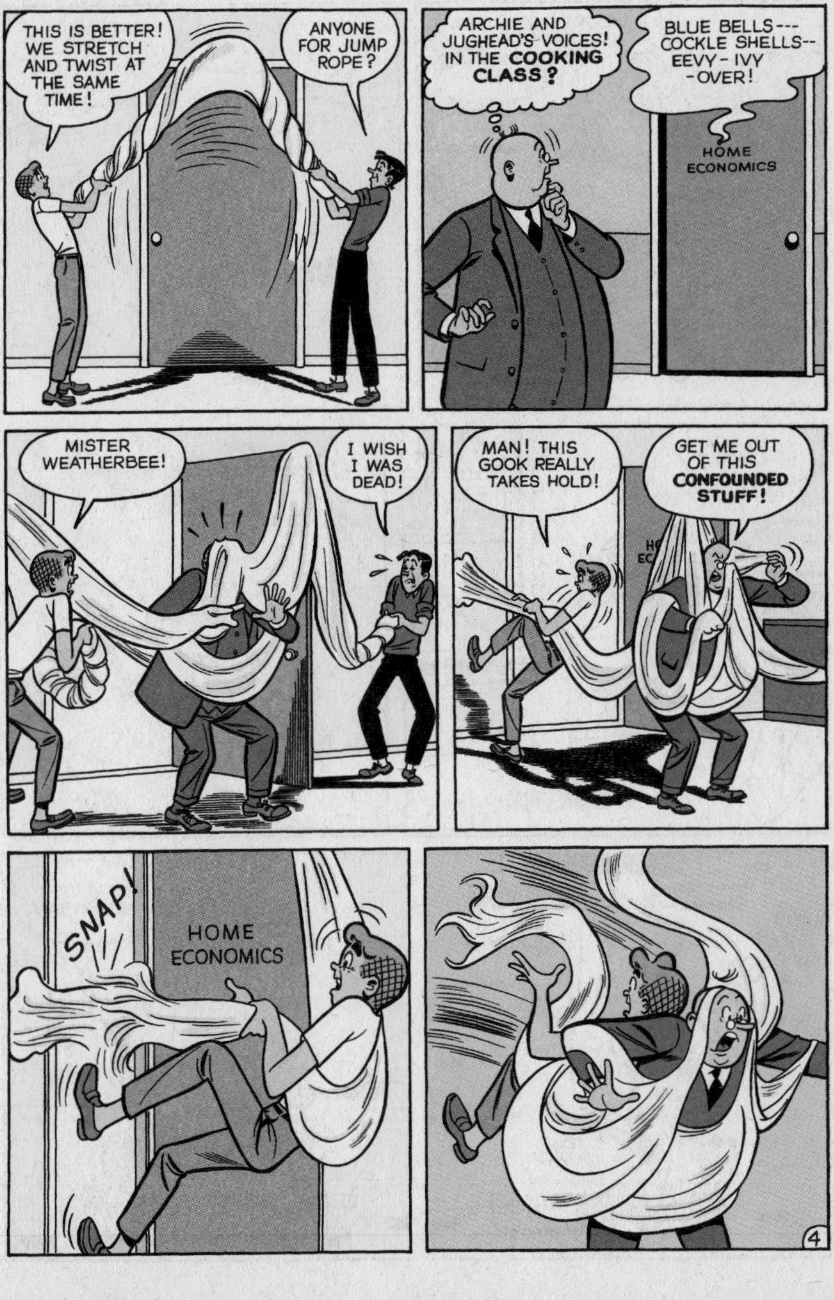
THIS IS BETTER! WE STRETCH AND TWIST AT THE SAME TIME!
ANYONE FOR JUMP ROPE?
ARCHIE AND JUGHEAD'S VOICES! IN THE **COOKING CLASS?**
BLUE BELLS--- COCKLE SHELLS-- EEVY-IVY -OVER!
HOME ECONOMICS
MISTER WEATHERBEE!
I WISH I WAS DEAD!
MAN! THIS GOOK REALLY TAKES HOLD!
GET ME OUT OF THIS **CONFOUNDED STUFF!**
SNAP!
HOME ECONOMICS
4

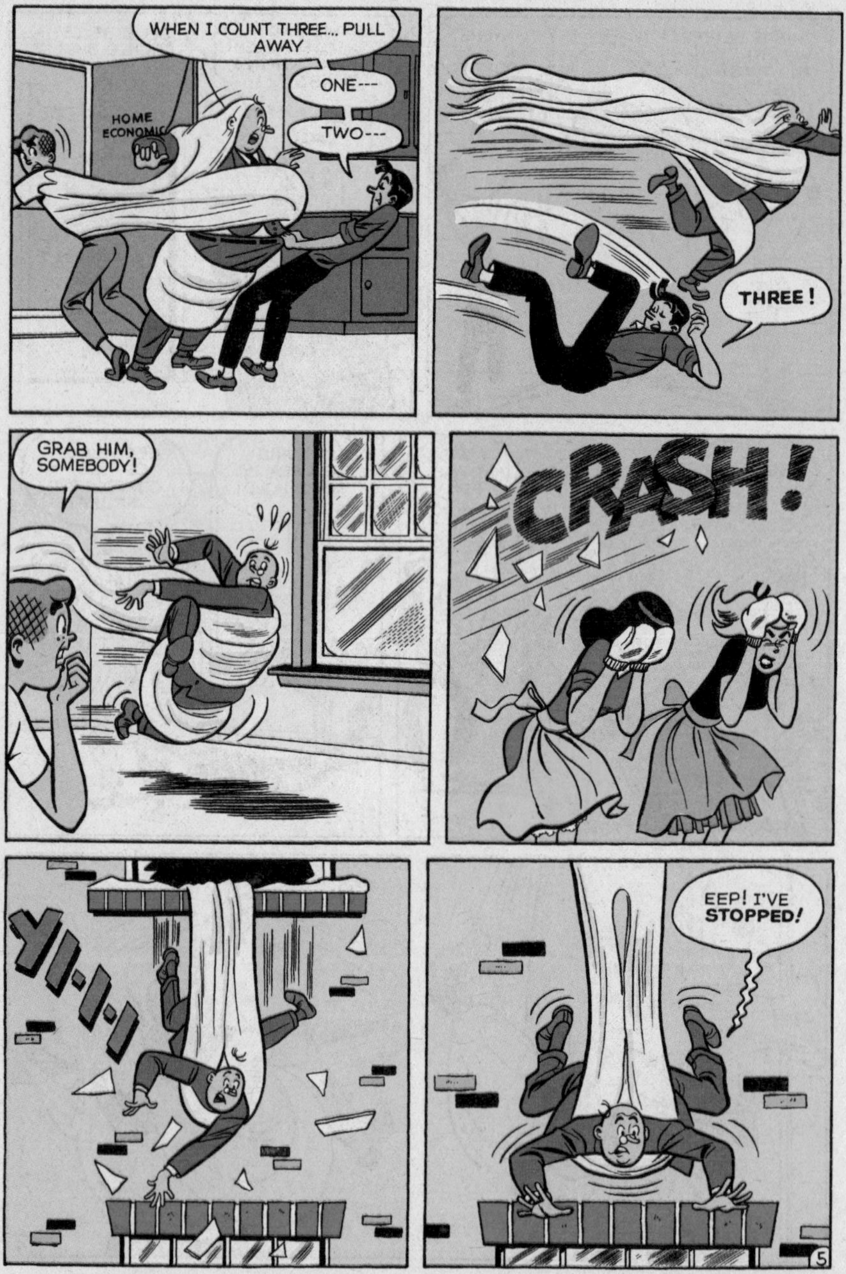
WHEN I COUNT THREE... PULL AWAY
ONE---
TWO---
HOME ECONOMICS
THREE!
GRAB HIM, SOMEBODY!
CRASH!
YI-I-I
EEP! I'VE STOPPED!
5

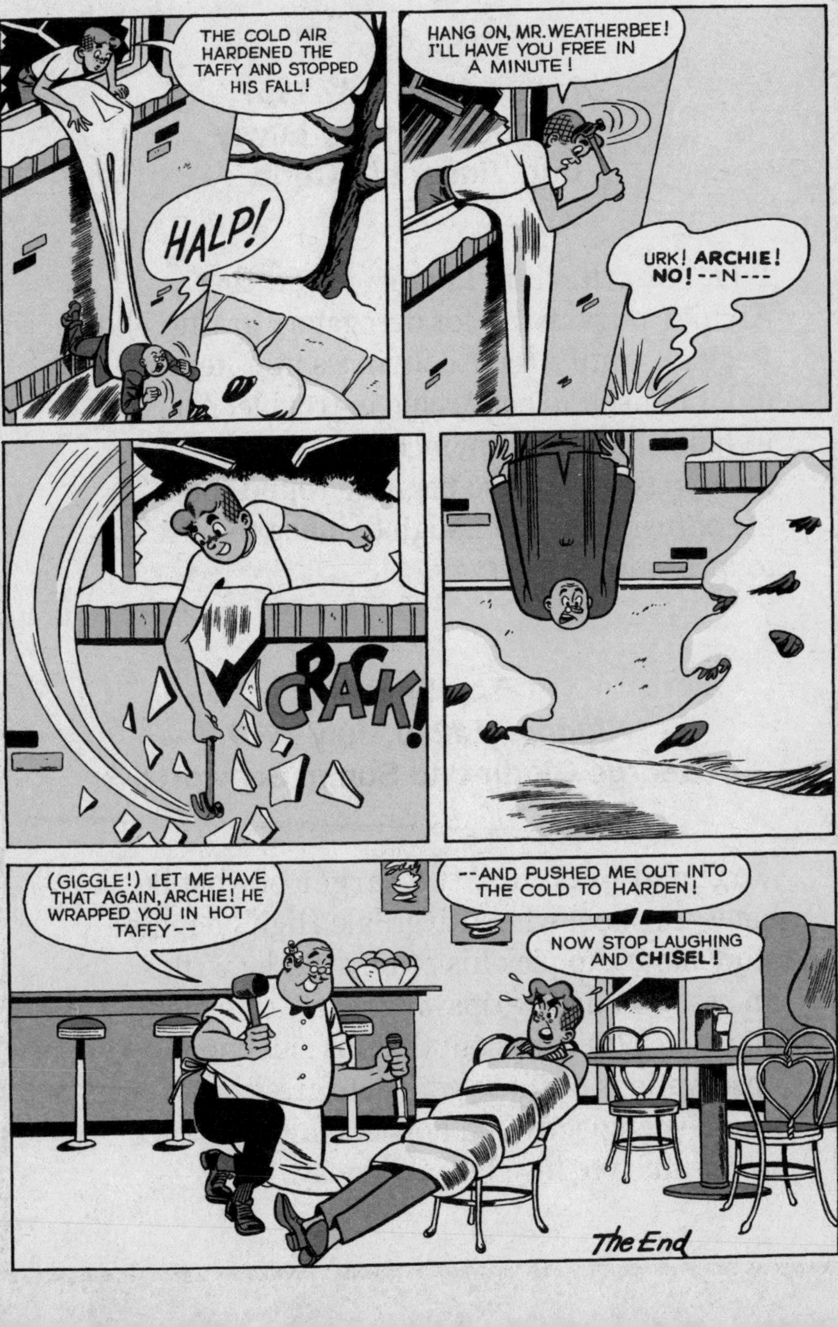
THE COLD AIR HARDENED THE TAFFY AND STOPPED HIS FALL!
HALP!
HANG ON, MR. WEATHERBEE! I'LL HAVE YOU FREE IN A MINUTE!
URK! ARCHIE! NO! --N---
CRACK!
(GIGGLE!) LET ME HAVE THAT AGAIN, ARCHIE! HE WRAPPED YOU IN HOT TAFFY--
--AND PUSHED ME OUT INTO THE COLD TO HARDEN!
NOW STOP LAUGHING AND CHISEL!
The End

The Sign
Archie #174, July 1967
Frank Doyle, Harry Lucey
and Vincent DeCarlo

Mr. Weatherbee is convinced that Archie's responsible for derogatory graffiti about Reggie... until Archie convinces him Reggie did it himself to get Archie in trouble! All is well until Reggie convinces Mr. Weatherbee the opposite... and so begins a round robin of confusion that's enough to make the Bee's toupee spin!

Top Secret
Jughead #290, July 1979
George Gladir and Samm Schwartz

Jughead becomes the target of what he hates the most when Riverdale High's female students try to pick his brain after he writes an essay on dating tips. Jughead? An expert on women? It turns out that his sideline observations of those who date gives him a unique perspective on how to make romance work—much to his eternal dismay.

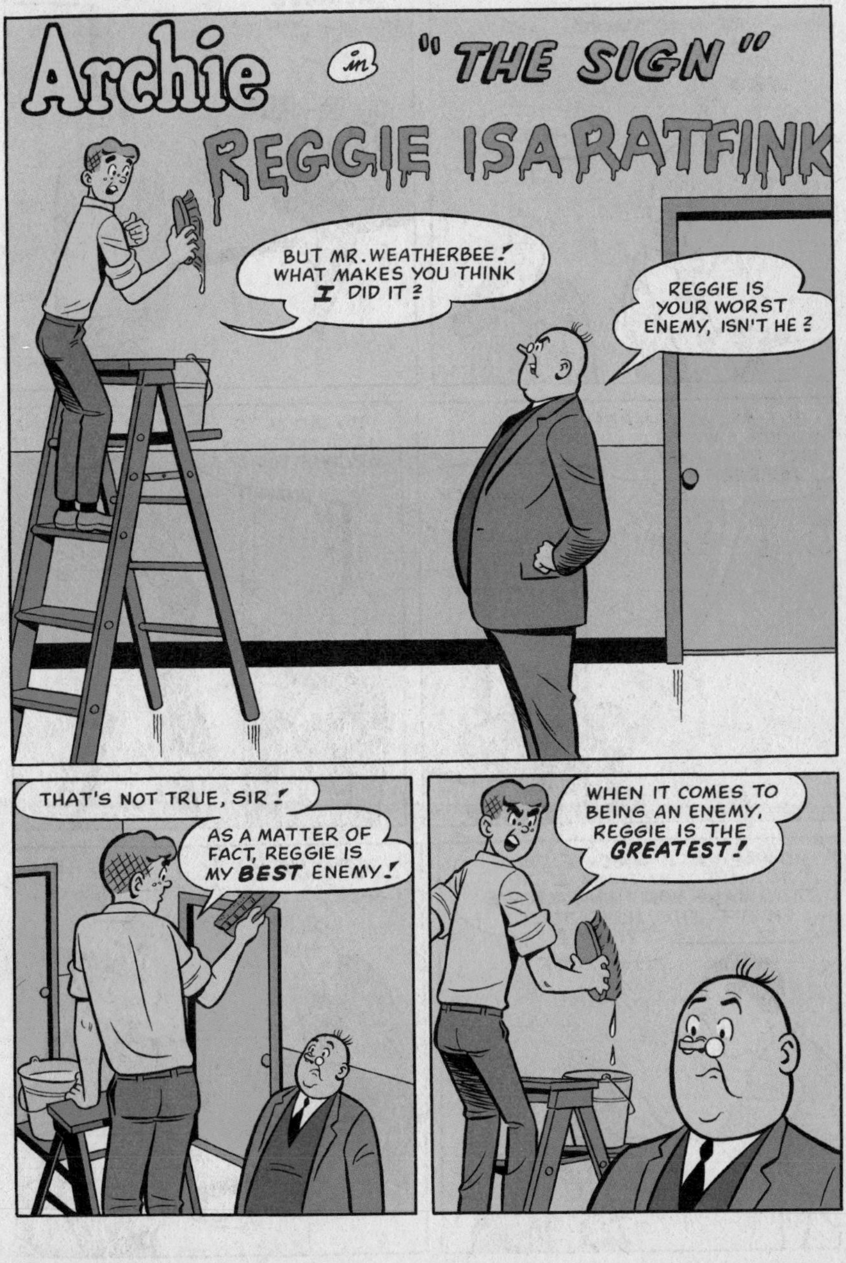
Archie in "THE SIGN"
REGGIE IS A RATFINK
BUT MR. WEATHERBEE! WHAT MAKES YOU THINK I DID IT?
REGGIE IS YOUR WORST ENEMY, ISN'T HE?
THAT'S NOT TRUE, SIR!
AS A MATTER OF FACT, REGGIE IS MY BEST ENEMY!
WHEN IT COMES TO BEING AN ENEMY, REGGIE IS THE GREATEST!

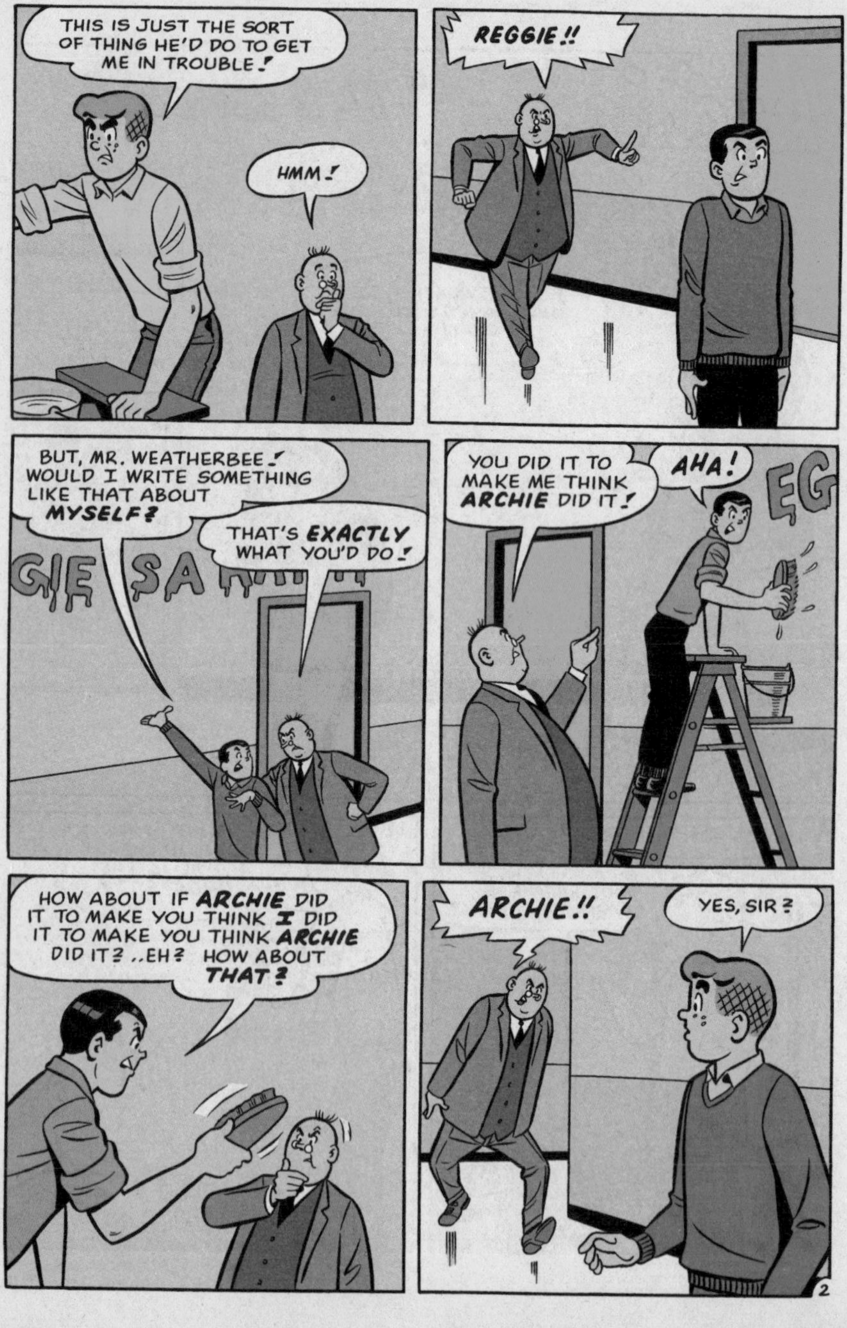
THIS IS JUST THE SORT OF THING HE'D DO TO GET ME IN TROUBLE!
HMM!
REGGIE!!
BUT, MR. WEATHERBEE! WOULD I WRITE SOMETHING LIKE THAT ABOUT MYSELF?
THAT'S EXACTLY WHAT YOU'D DO!
GIE SA
YOU DID IT TO MAKE ME THINK ARCHIE DID IT!
AHA!
EG
HOW ABOUT IF ARCHIE DID IT TO MAKE YOU THINK I DID IT TO MAKE YOU THINK ARCHIE DID IT? ..EH? HOW ABOUT THAT?
ARCHIE!!
YES, SIR?
2

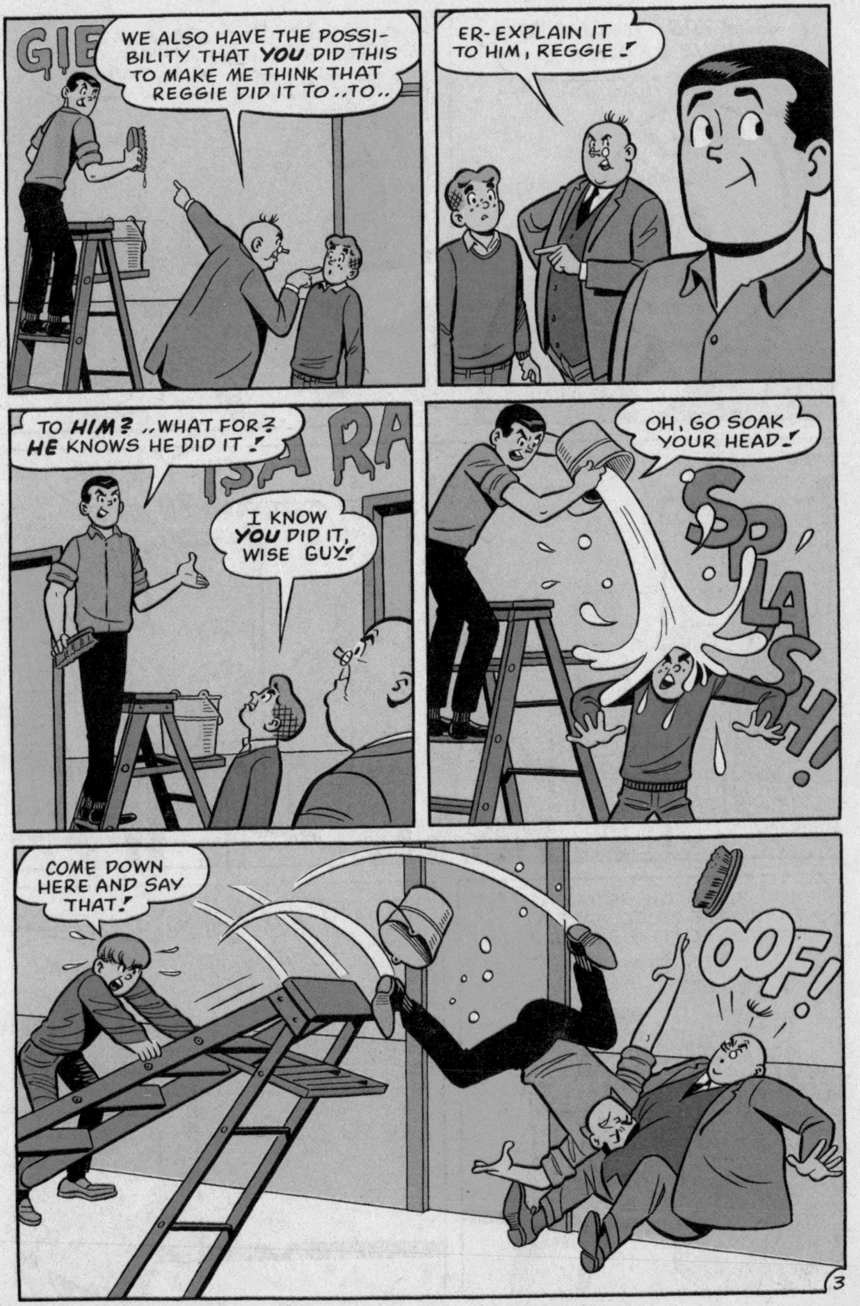
GIE
WE ALSO HAVE THE POSSIBILITY THAT YOU DID THIS TO MAKE ME THINK THAT REGGIE DID IT TO ..TO..
ER- EXPLAIN IT TO HIM, REGGIE!
TO HIM? ..WHAT FOR? HE KNOWS HE DID IT!
'S A RA
I KNOW YOU DID IT, WISE GUY!
OH, GO SOAK YOUR HEAD!
SPLASH!
COME DOWN HERE AND SAY THAT!
OOF!
3

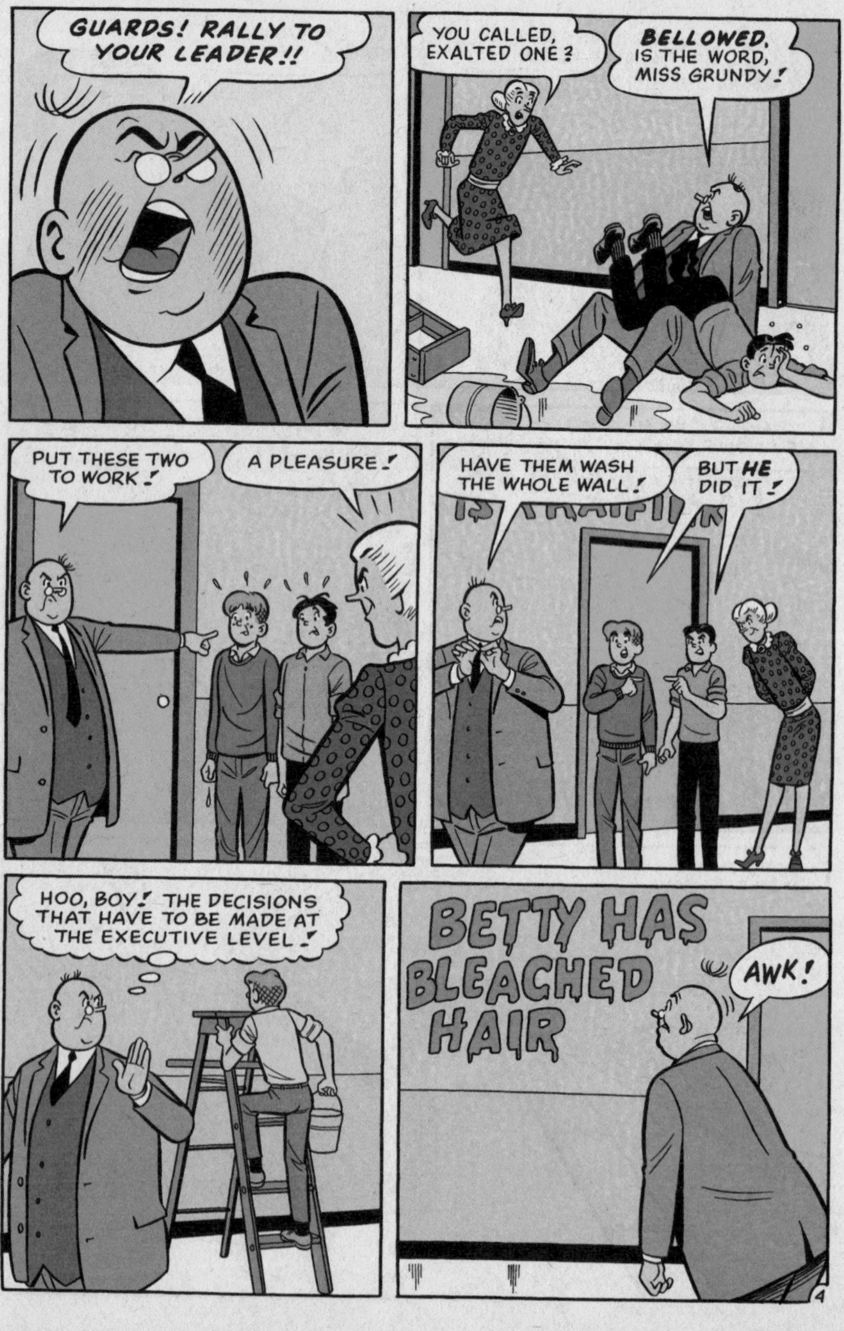
GUARDS! RALLY TO YOUR LEADER!!
YOU CALLED, EXALTED ONE?
BELLOWED, IS THE WORD, MISS GRUNDY!
PUT THESE TWO TO WORK!
A PLEASURE!
HAVE THEM WASH THE WHOLE WALL!
BUT HE DID IT!
HOO, BOY! THE DECISIONS THAT HAVE TO BE MADE AT THE EXECUTIVE LEVEL!
BETTY HAS BLEACHED HAIR
AWK!
4

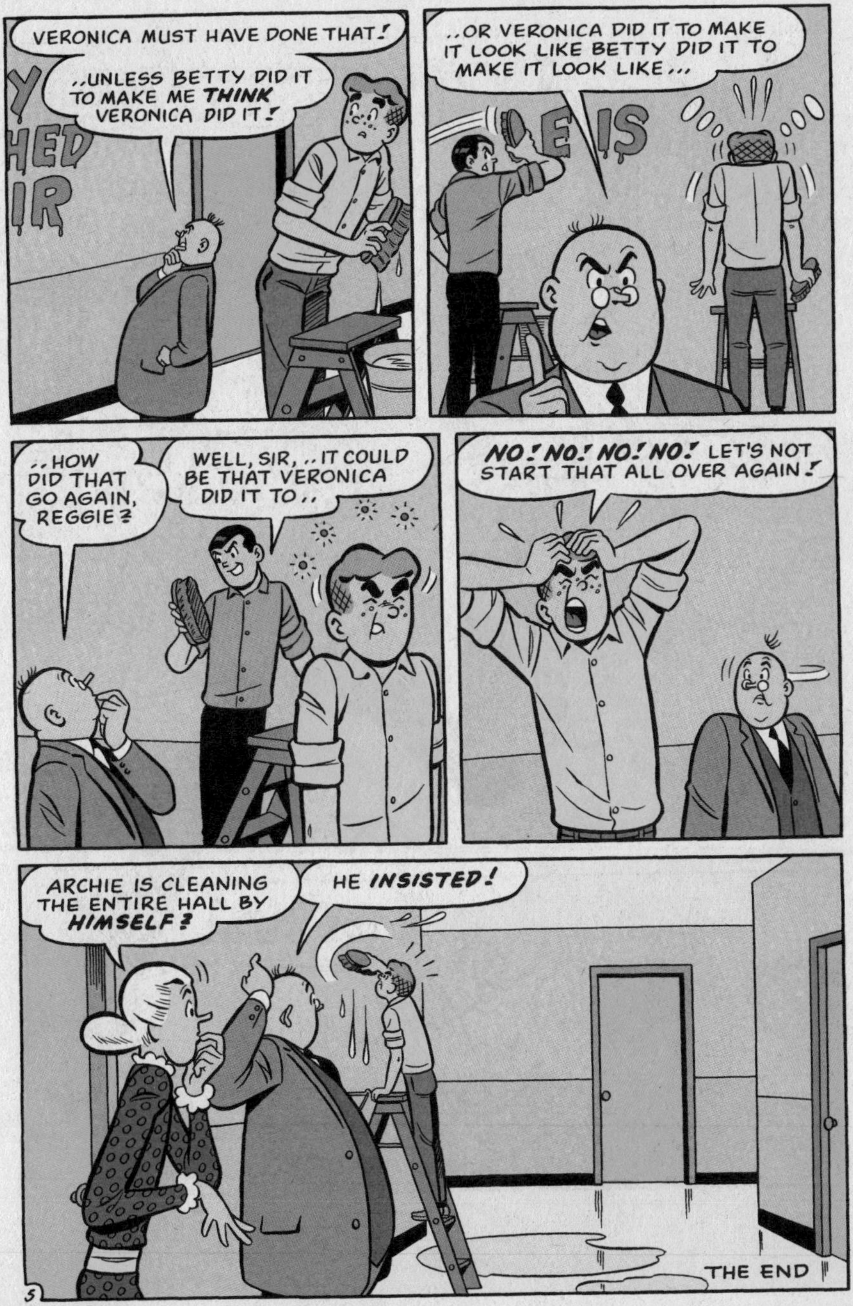

VERONICA MUST HAVE DONE THAT!
..UNLESS BETTY DID IT TO MAKE ME THINK VERONICA DID IT!
..OR VERONICA DID IT TO MAKE IT LOOK LIKE BETTY DID IT TO MAKE IT LOOK LIKE...
..HOW DID THAT GO AGAIN, REGGIE?
WELL, SIR, ..IT COULD BE THAT VERONICA DID IT TO..
NO! NO! NO! NO! LET'S NOT START THAT ALL OVER AGAIN!
ARCHIE IS CLEANING THE ENTIRE HALL BY HIMSELF?
HE INSISTED!
THE END
5

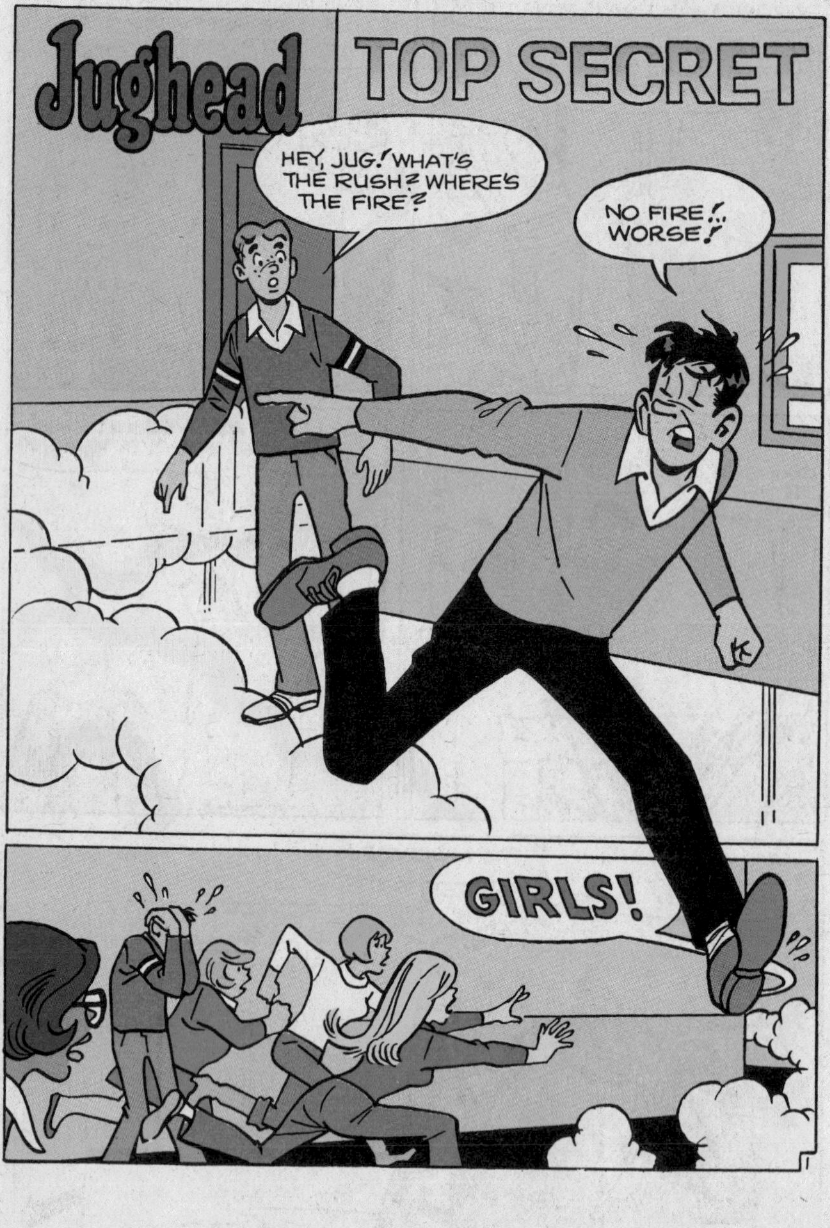
Jughead
TOP SECRET
HEY, JUG! WHAT'S THE RUSH? WHERE'S THE FIRE?
NO FIRE!.. WORSE!
GIRLS!

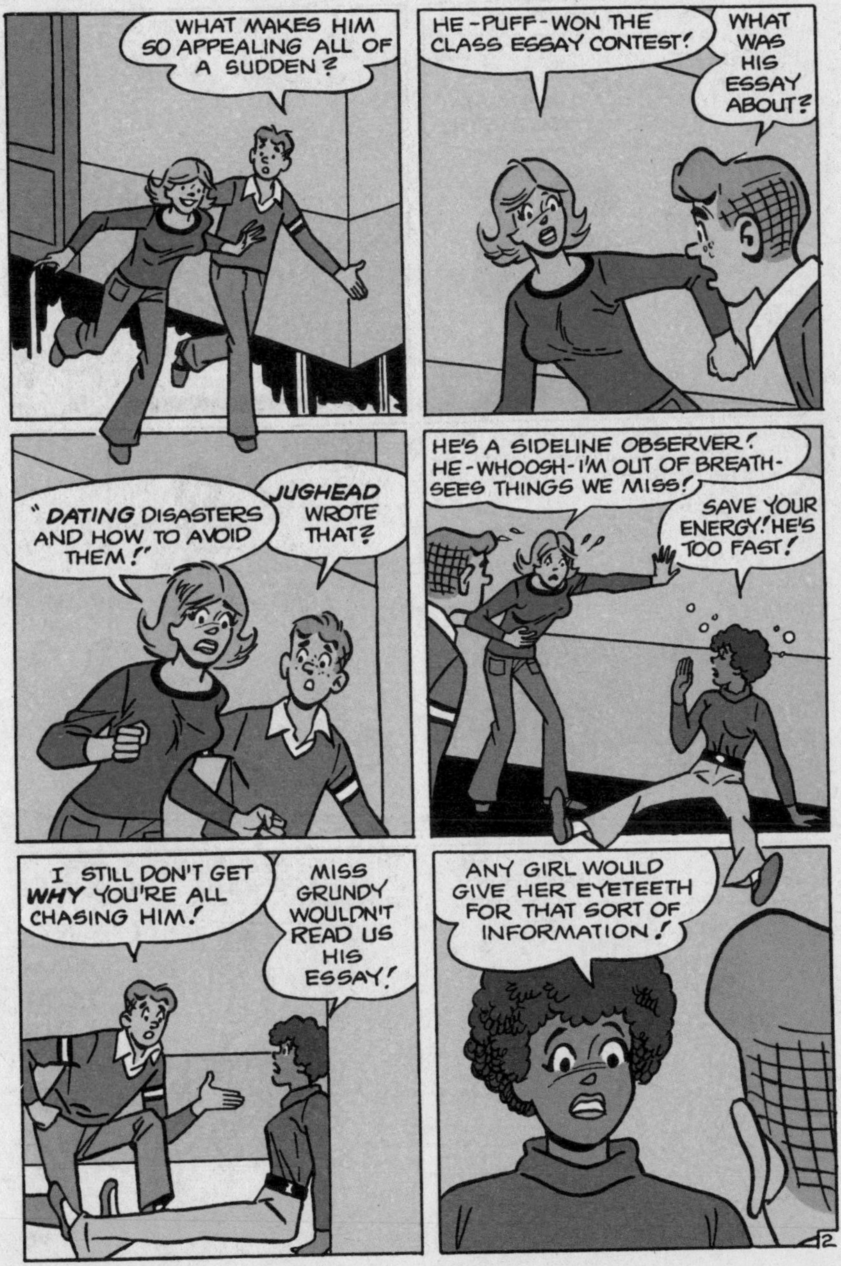
WHAT MAKES HIM SO APPEALING ALL OF A SUDDEN?
HE -PUFF- WON THE CLASS ESSAY CONTEST!
WHAT WAS HIS ESSAY ABOUT?
"DATING DISASTERS AND HOW TO AVOID THEM!"
JUGHEAD WROTE THAT?
HE'S A SIDELINE OBSERVER! HE -WHOOSH- I'M OUT OF BREATH- SEES THINGS WE MISS!
SAVE YOUR ENERGY! HE'S TOO FAST!
I STILL DON'T GET WHY YOU'RE ALL CHASING HIM!
MISS GRUNDY WOULDN'T READ US HIS ESSAY!
ANY GIRL WOULD GIVE HER EYETEETH FOR THAT SORT OF INFORMATION!
2

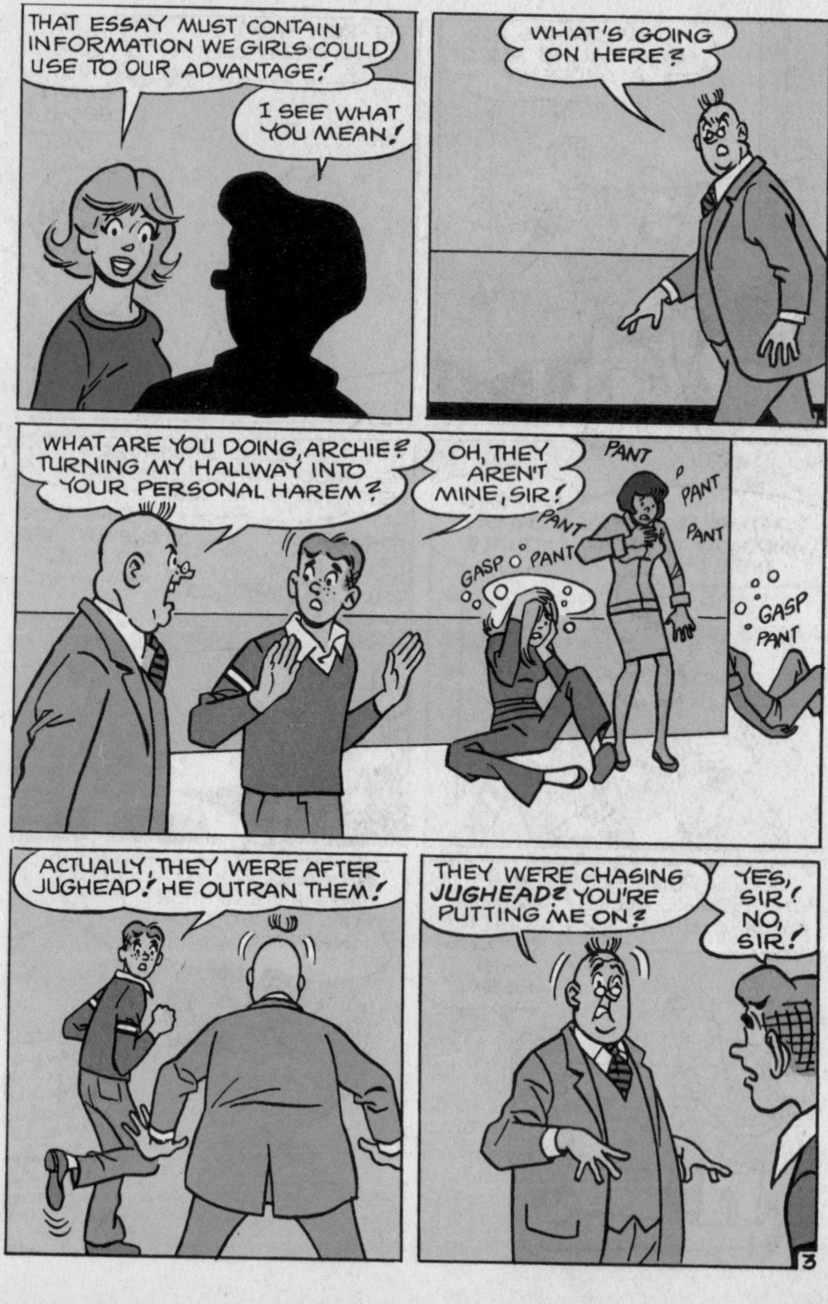
THAT ESSAY MUST CONTAIN INFORMATION WE GIRLS COULD USE TO OUR ADVANTAGE!
I SEE WHAT YOU MEAN!
WHAT'S GOING ON HERE?
WHAT ARE YOU DOING, ARCHIE? TURNING MY HALLWAY INTO YOUR PERSONAL HAREM?
OH, THEY AREN'T MINE, SIR!
PANT
PANT
PANT
PANT
GASP
PANT
GASP
PANT
ACTUALLY, THEY WERE AFTER JUGHEAD! HE OUTRAN THEM!
THEY WERE CHASING JUGHEAD? YOU'RE PUTTING ME ON?
YES, SIR! NO, SIR!
3

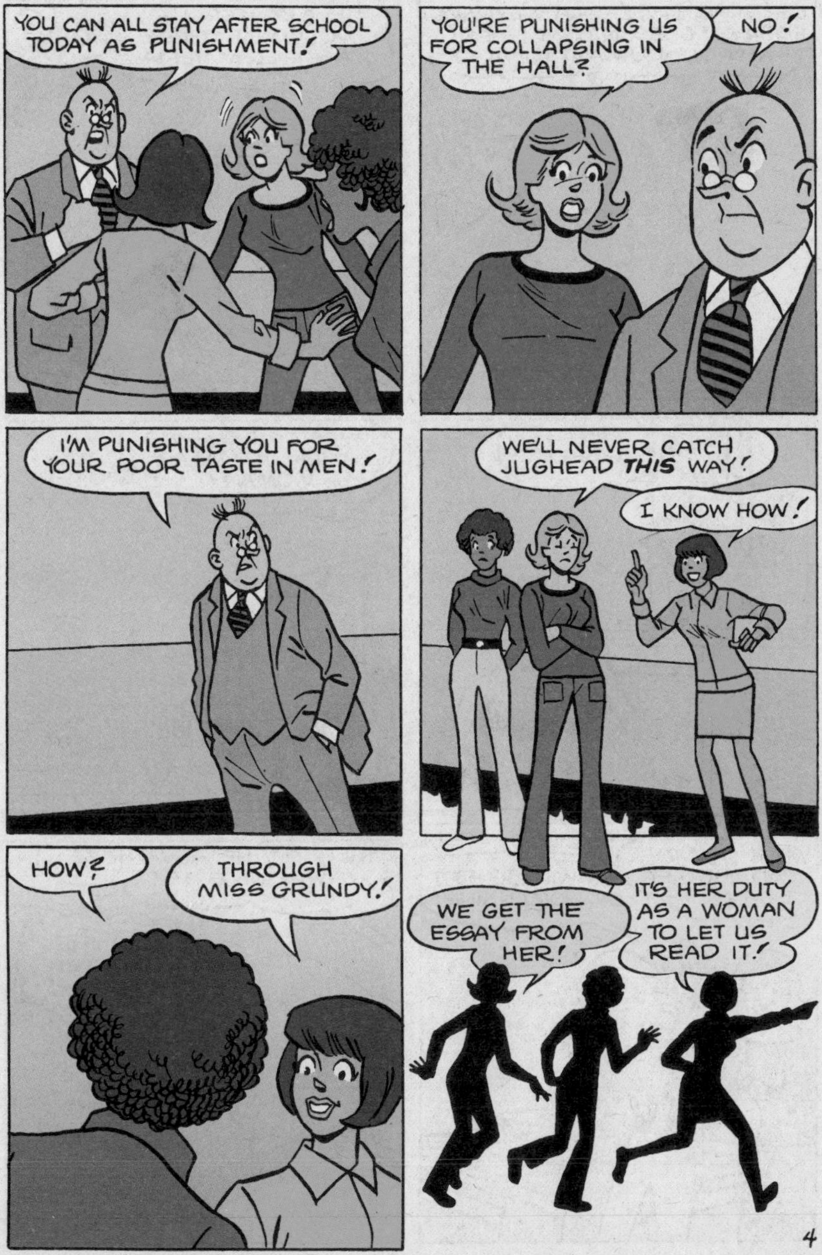
YOU CAN ALL STAY AFTER SCHOOL TODAY AS PUNISHMENT!
YOU'RE PUNISHING US FOR COLLAPSING IN THE HALL?
NO!
I'M PUNISHING YOU FOR YOUR POOR TASTE IN MEN!
WE'LL NEVER CATCH JUGHEAD THIS WAY!
I KNOW HOW!
HOW?
THROUGH MISS GRUNDY!
WE GET THE ESSAY FROM HER!
IT'S HER DUTY AS A WOMAN TO LET US READ IT!

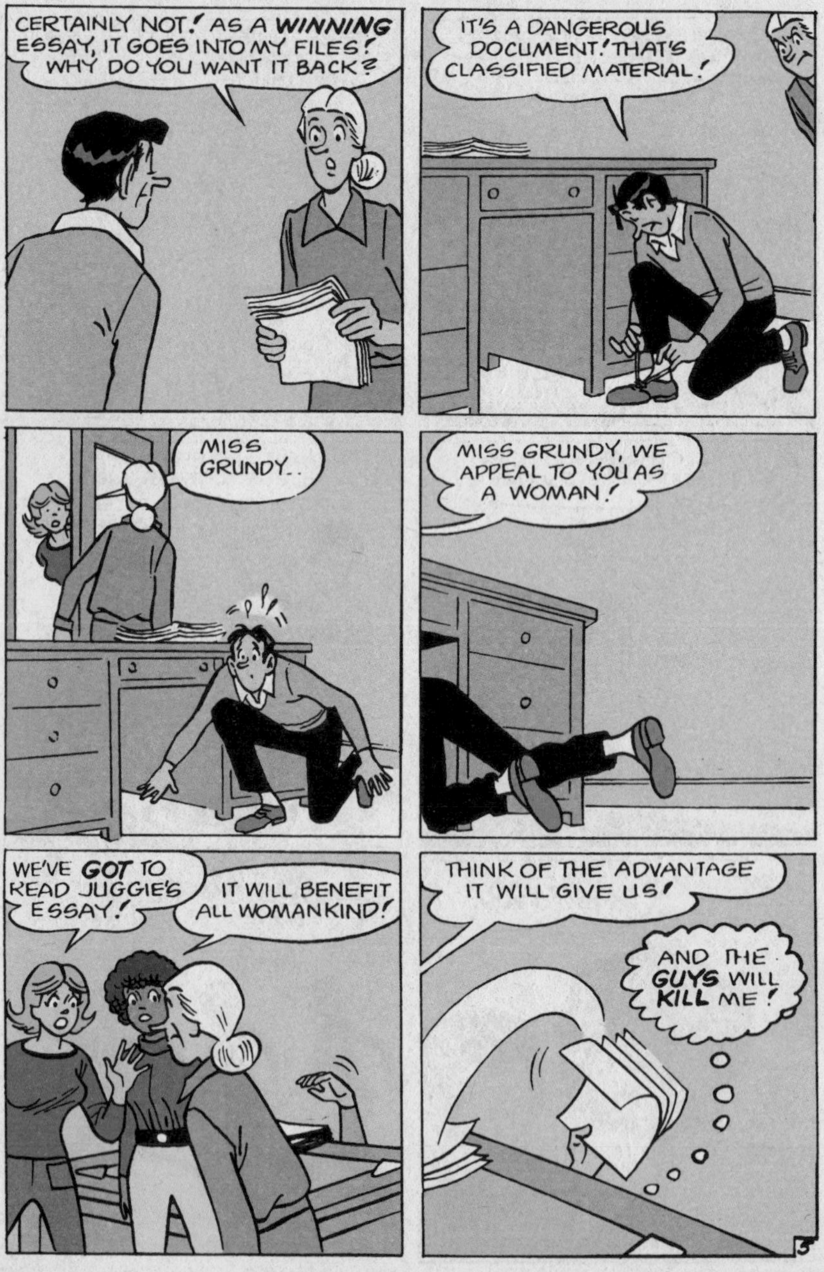
CERTAINLY NOT! AS A WINNING ESSAY, IT GOES INTO MY FILES! WHY DO YOU WANT IT BACK?
IT'S A DANGEROUS DOCUMENT! THAT'S CLASSIFIED MATERIAL!
MISS GRUNDY..
MISS GRUNDY, WE APPEAL TO YOU AS A WOMAN!
WE'VE GOT TO READ JUGGIE'S ESSAY!
IT WILL BENEFIT ALL WOMANKIND!
THINK OF THE ADVANTAGE IT WILL GIVE US!
AND THE GUYS WILL KILL ME!
3

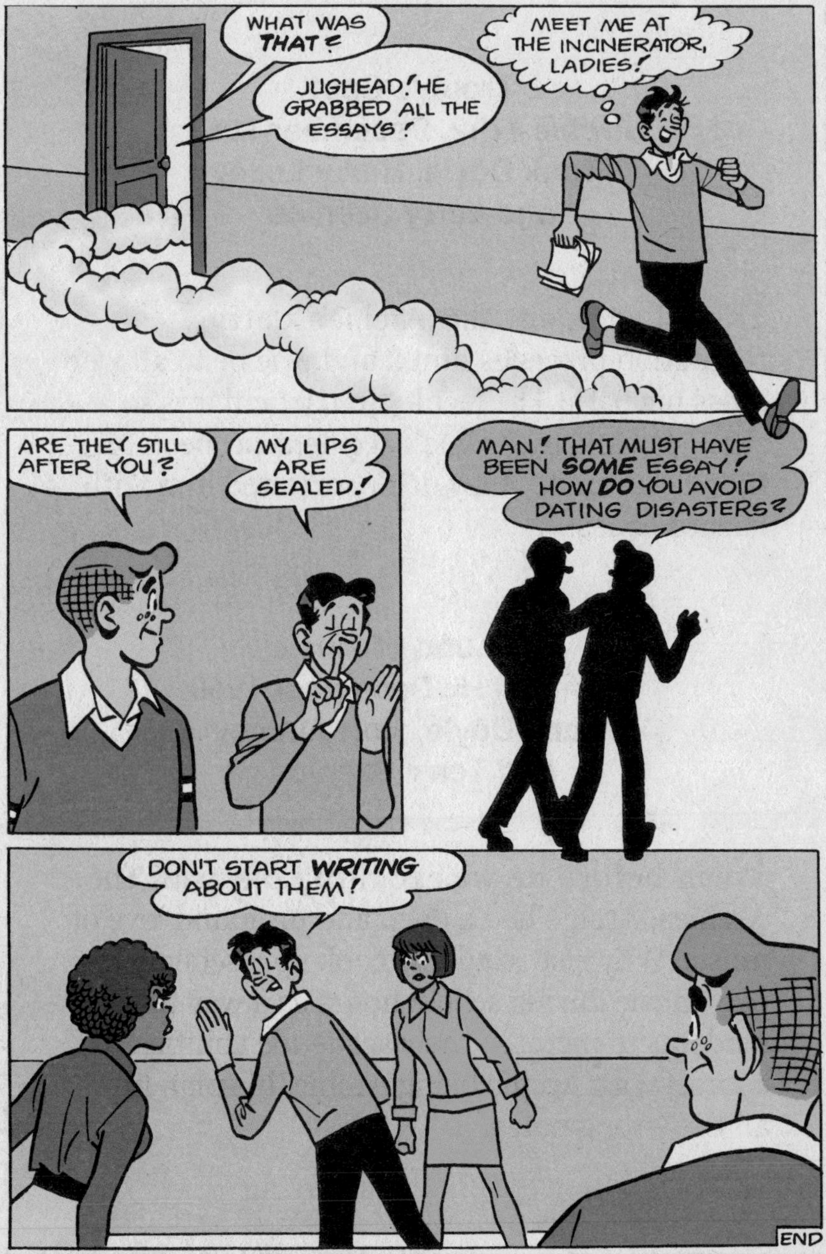
WHAT WAS THAT?
JUGHEAD! HE GRABBED ALL THE ESSAYS!
MEET ME AT THE INCINERATOR, LADIES!
ARE THEY STILL AFTER YOU?
MY LIPS ARE SEALED!
MAN! THAT MUST HAVE BEEN SOME ESSAY! HOW DO YOU AVOID DATING DISASTERS?
DON'T START WRITING ABOUT THEM!
END

Trouble Spot
Archie #142, December 1963
Frank Doyle, Harry Lucey
and Terry Szenics

It's no accident that Archie's klutzy reputation precedes him... and woe be to all who cross his path! The faculty in particular is so shell-shocked by Archie's accident-prone nature that it's a wonder they don't surround him with hazard cones!

Unsound of Music
Archie #115, December 1960
Frank Doyle, Harry Lucey
and Terry Szenics

Even before he was rocking out with The Archies, Archie had a deep and profound love of music. Why else would he cook up a scheme to play music during school hours as a way to get students to increase their academic abilities? Of course, with Archie being Archie, his plan hits all the wrong notes.

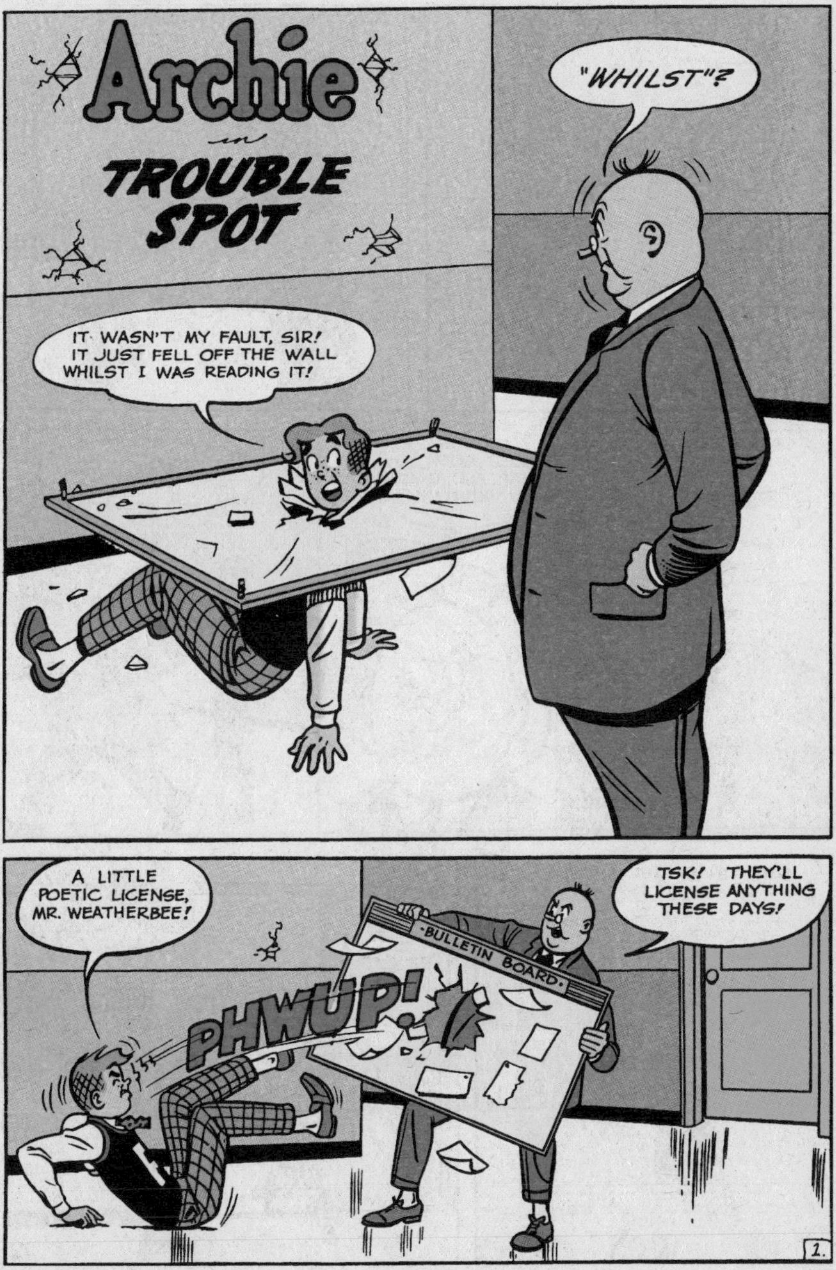
Archie
in
TROUBLE SPOT
IT WASN'T MY FAULT, SIR! IT JUST FELL OFF THE WALL WHILST I WAS READING IT!
"WHILST"?
A LITTLE POETIC LICENSE, MR. WEATHERBEE!
TSK! THEY'LL LICENSE ANYTHING THESE DAYS!
BULLETIN BOARD
PHWUP!
1.

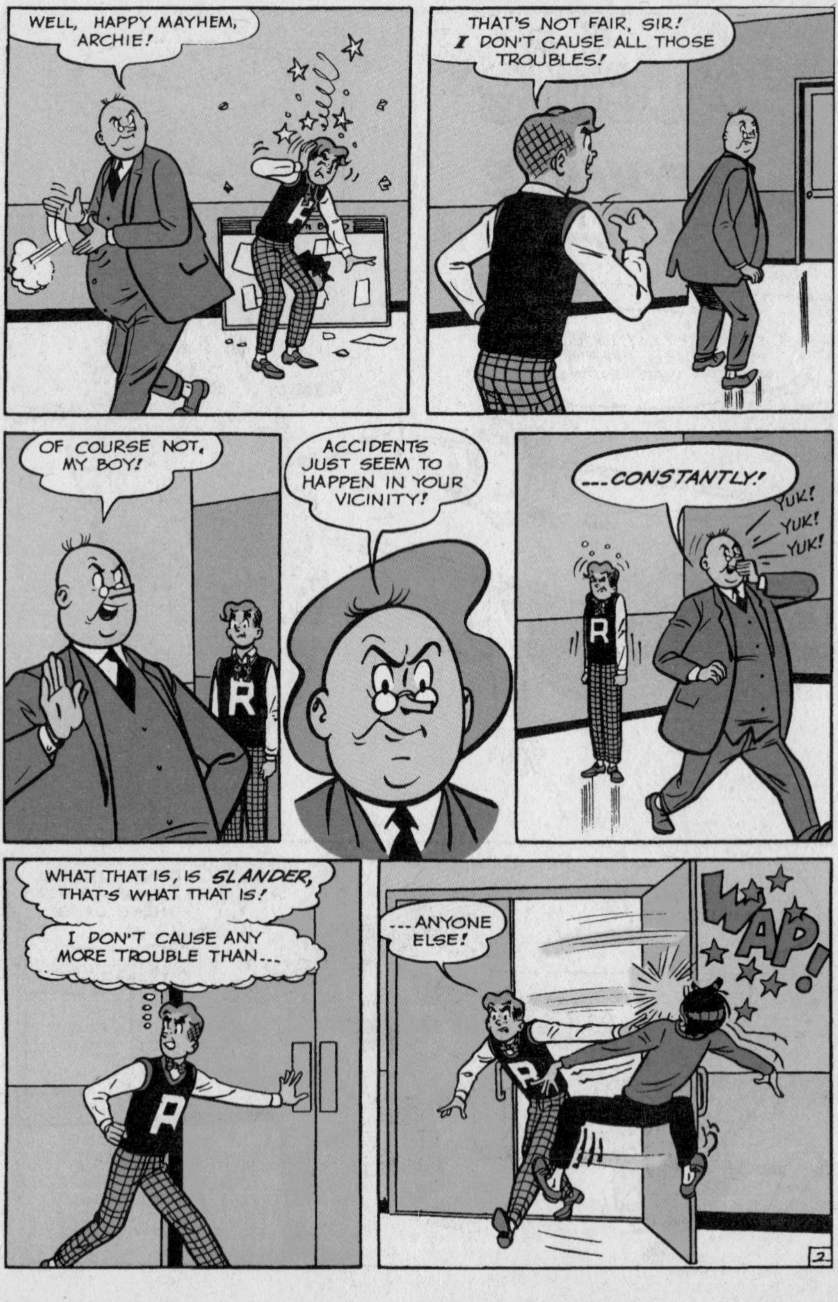
WELL, HAPPY MAYHEM, ARCHIE!
THAT'S NOT FAIR, SIR! I DON'T CAUSE ALL THOSE TROUBLES!
OF COURSE NOT, MY BOY!
ACCIDENTS JUST SEEM TO HAPPEN IN YOUR VICINITY!
---CONSTANTLY!
YUK! YUK! YUK!
WHAT THAT IS, IS SLANDER, THAT'S WHAT THAT IS!
I DON'T CAUSE ANY MORE TROUBLE THAN---
---ANYONE ELSE!
WAP!
2

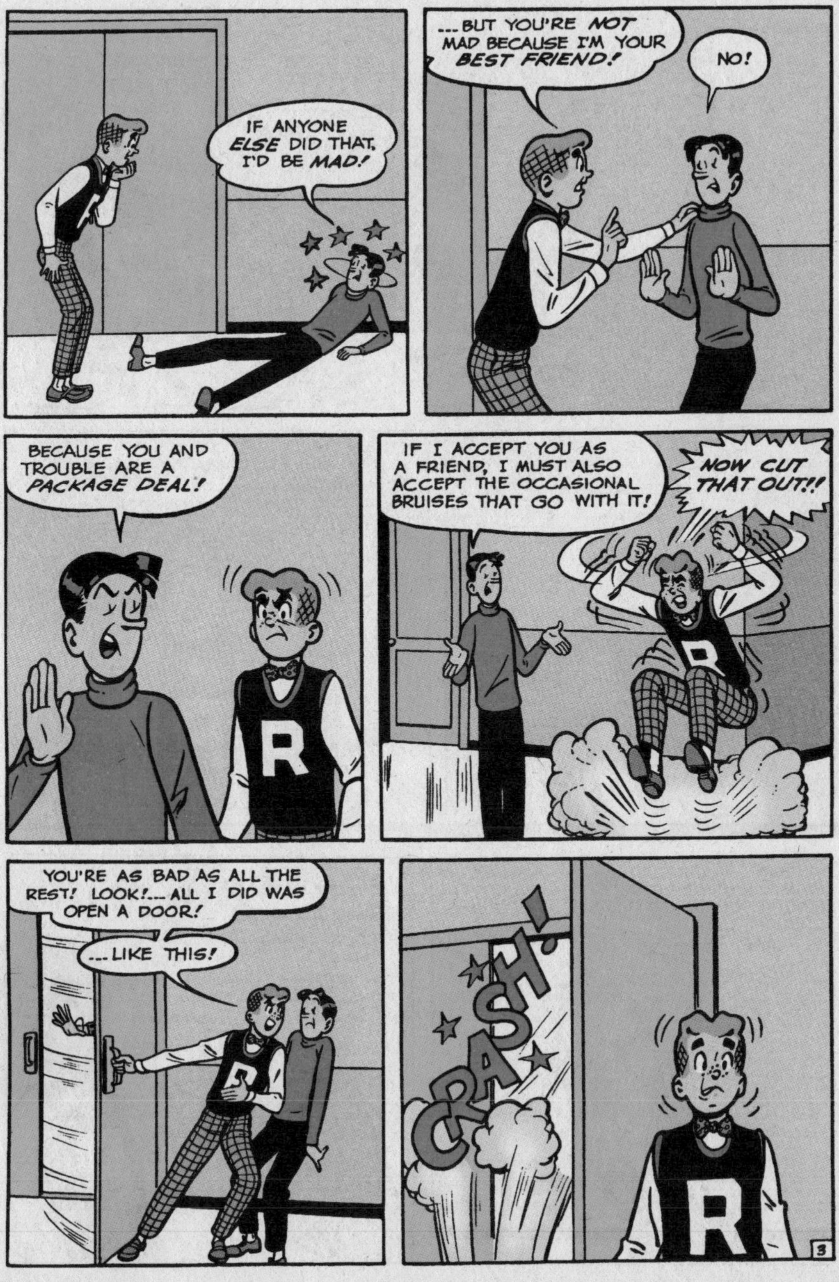
IF ANYONE ELSE DID THAT, I'D BE MAD!
...BUT YOU'RE NOT MAD BECAUSE I'M YOUR BEST FRIEND!
NO!
BECAUSE YOU AND TROUBLE ARE A PACKAGE DEAL!
IF I ACCEPT YOU AS A FRIEND, I MUST ALSO ACCEPT THE OCCASIONAL BRUISES THAT GO WITH IT!
NOW CUT THAT OUT!!
YOU'RE AS BAD AS ALL THE REST! LOOK!... ALL I DID WAS OPEN A DOOR!
...LIKE THIS!
CRASH!
3

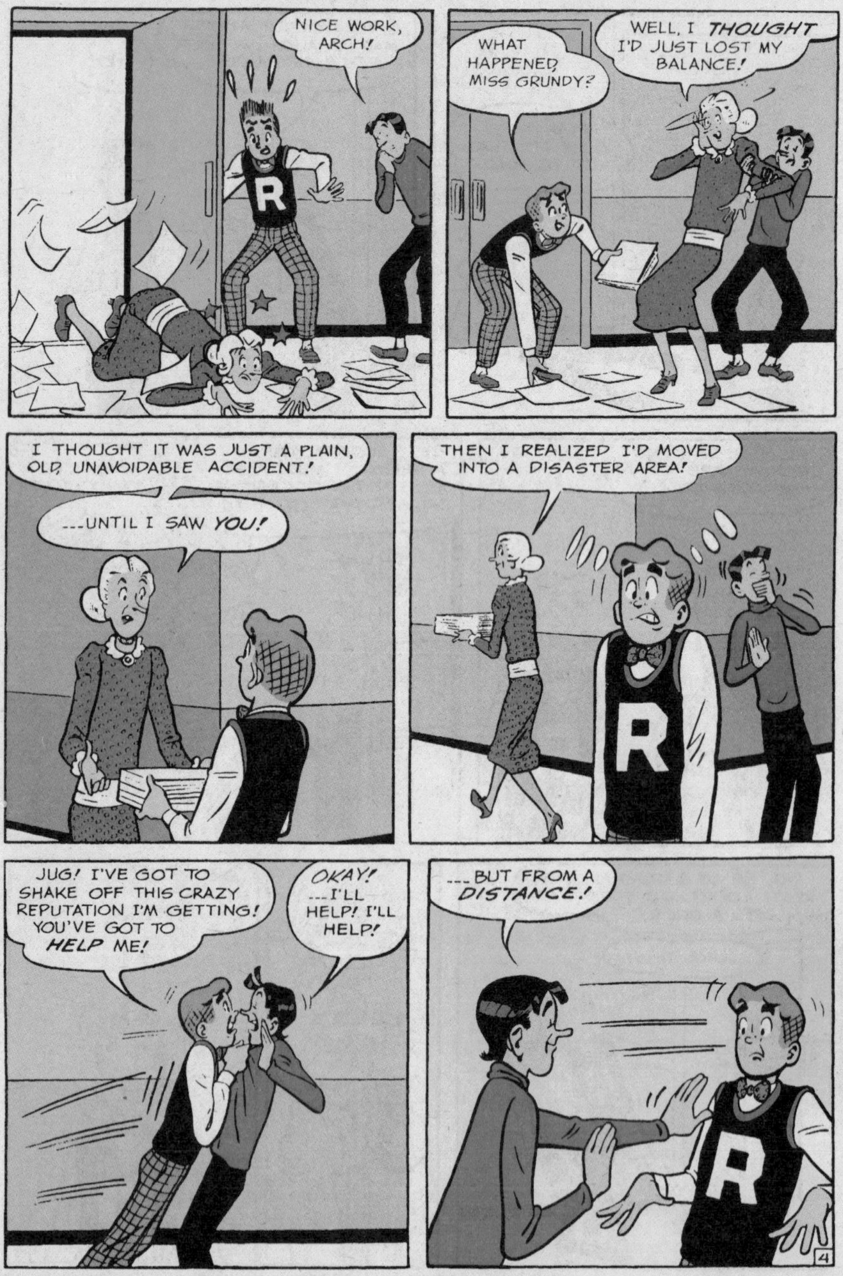
NICE WORK, ARCH!
WHAT HAPPENED, MISS GRUNDY?
WELL, I THOUGHT I'D JUST LOST MY BALANCE!
I THOUGHT IT WAS JUST A PLAIN, OLD, UNAVOIDABLE ACCIDENT!
---UNTIL I SAW YOU!
THEN I REALIZED I'D MOVED INTO A DISASTER AREA!
JUG! I'VE GOT TO SHAKE OFF THIS CRAZY REPUTATION I'M GETTING! YOU'VE GOT TO HELP ME!
OKAY! ---I'LL HELP! I'LL HELP!
---BUT FROM A DISTANCE!
4

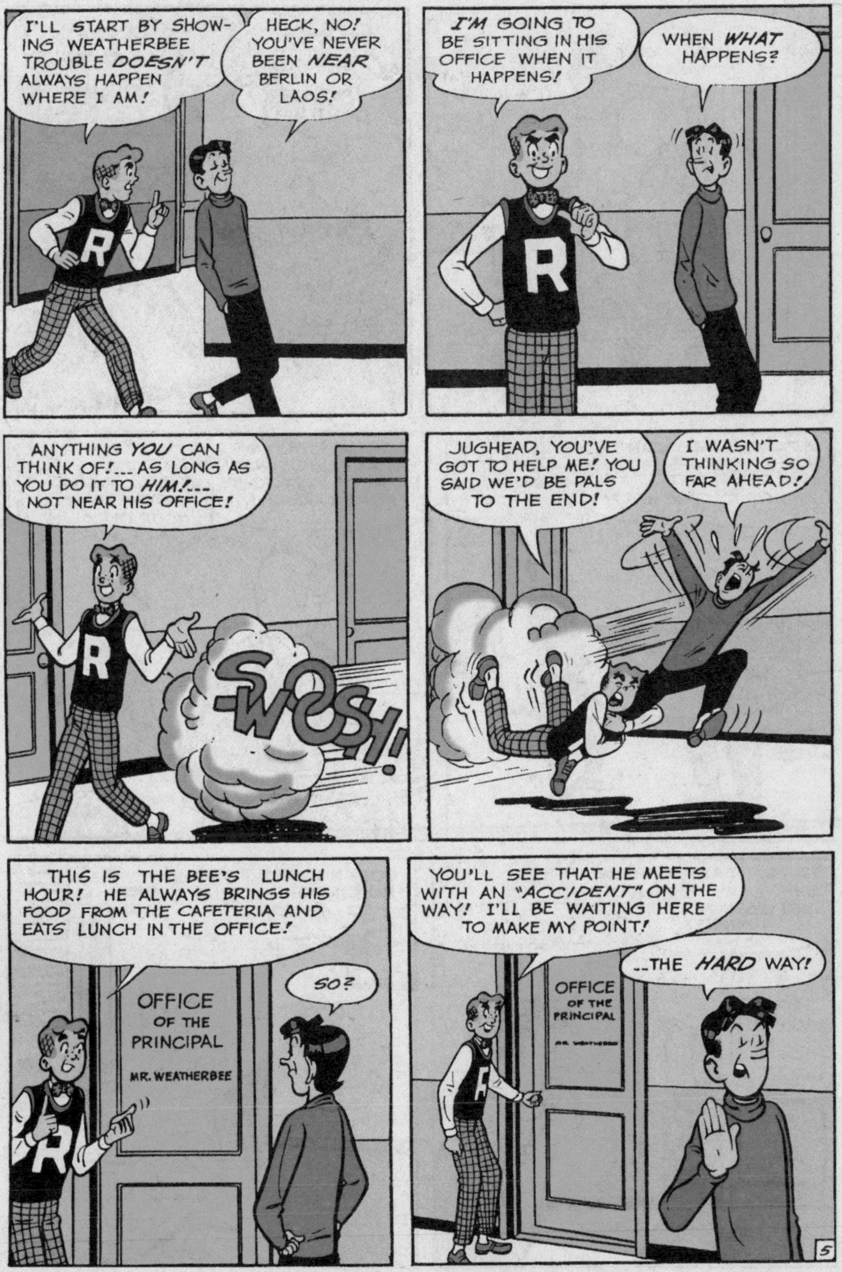
I'LL START BY SHOWING WEATHERBEE TROUBLE DOESN'T ALWAYS HAPPEN WHERE I AM!
HECK, NO! YOU'VE NEVER BEEN NEAR BERLIN OR LAOS!
I'M GOING TO BE SITTING IN HIS OFFICE WHEN IT HAPPENS!
WHEN WHAT HAPPENS?
ANYTHING YOU CAN THINK OF!... AS LONG AS YOU DO IT TO HIM!... NOT NEAR HIS OFFICE!
SWOOSH!
JUGHEAD, YOU'VE GOT TO HELP ME! YOU SAID WE'D BE PALS TO THE END!
I WASN'T THINKING SO FAR AHEAD!
THIS IS THE BEE'S LUNCH HOUR! HE ALWAYS BRINGS HIS FOOD FROM THE CAFETERIA AND EATS LUNCH IN THE OFFICE!
SO?
OFFICE OF THE PRINCIPAL
MR. WEATHERBEE
YOU'LL SEE THAT HE MEETS WITH AN "ACCIDENT" ON THE WAY! I'LL BE WAITING HERE TO MAKE MY POINT!
...THE HARD WAY!
OFFICE OF THE PRINCIPAL
5

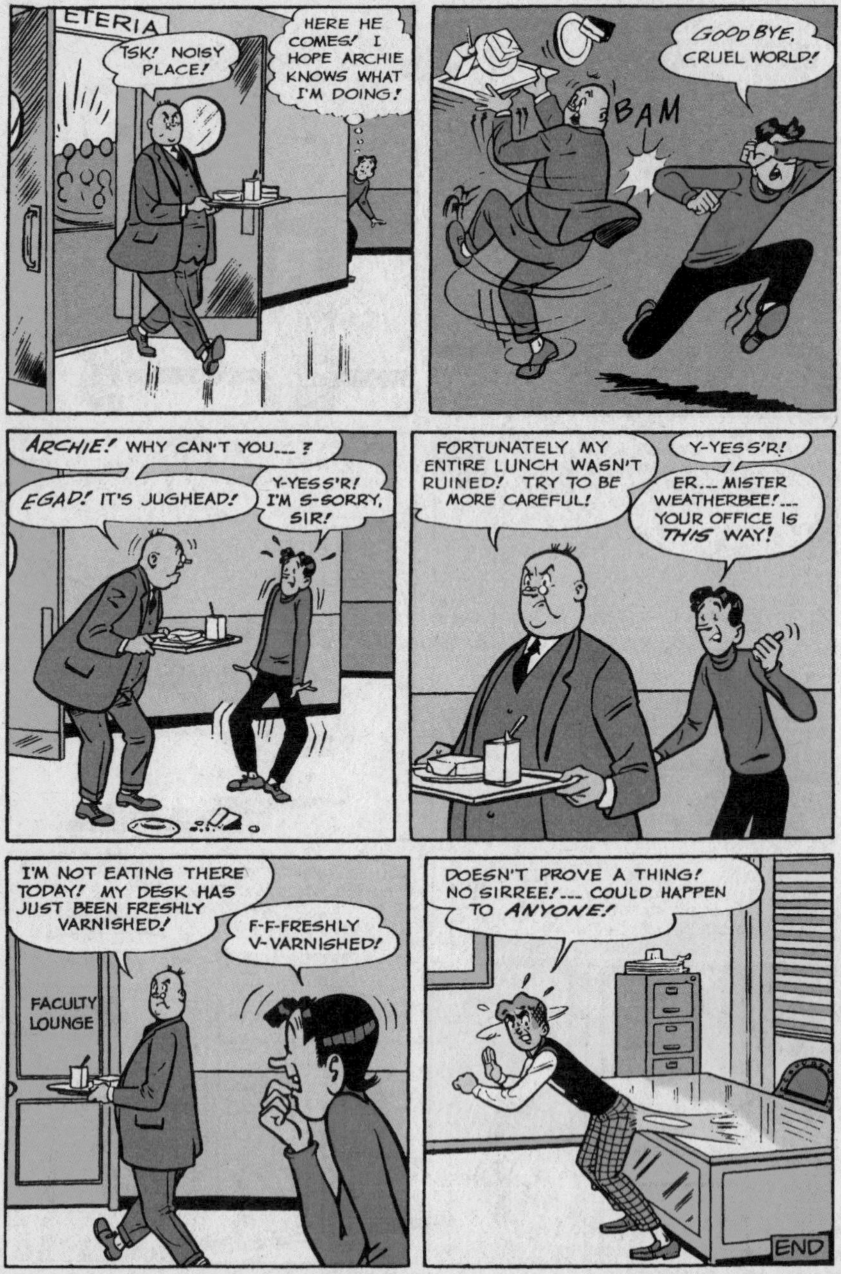
ETERIA
TSK! NOISY PLACE!
HERE HE COMES! I HOPE ARCHIE KNOWS WHAT I'M DOING!
GOOD BYE, CRUEL WORLD!
BAM
ARCHIE! WHY CAN'T YOU...?
EGAD! IT'S JUGHEAD!
Y-YES S'R! I'M S-SORRY, SIR!
FORTUNATELY MY ENTIRE LUNCH WASN'T RUINED! TRY TO BE MORE CAREFUL!
Y-YES S'R!
ER... MISTER WEATHERBEE!... YOUR OFFICE IS THIS WAY!
I'M NOT EATING THERE TODAY! MY DESK HAS JUST BEEN FRESHLY VARNISHED!
F-F-FRESHLY V-VARNISHED!
FACULTY LOUNGE
DOESN'T PROVE A THING! NO SIRREE!... COULD HAPPEN TO ANYONE!
END

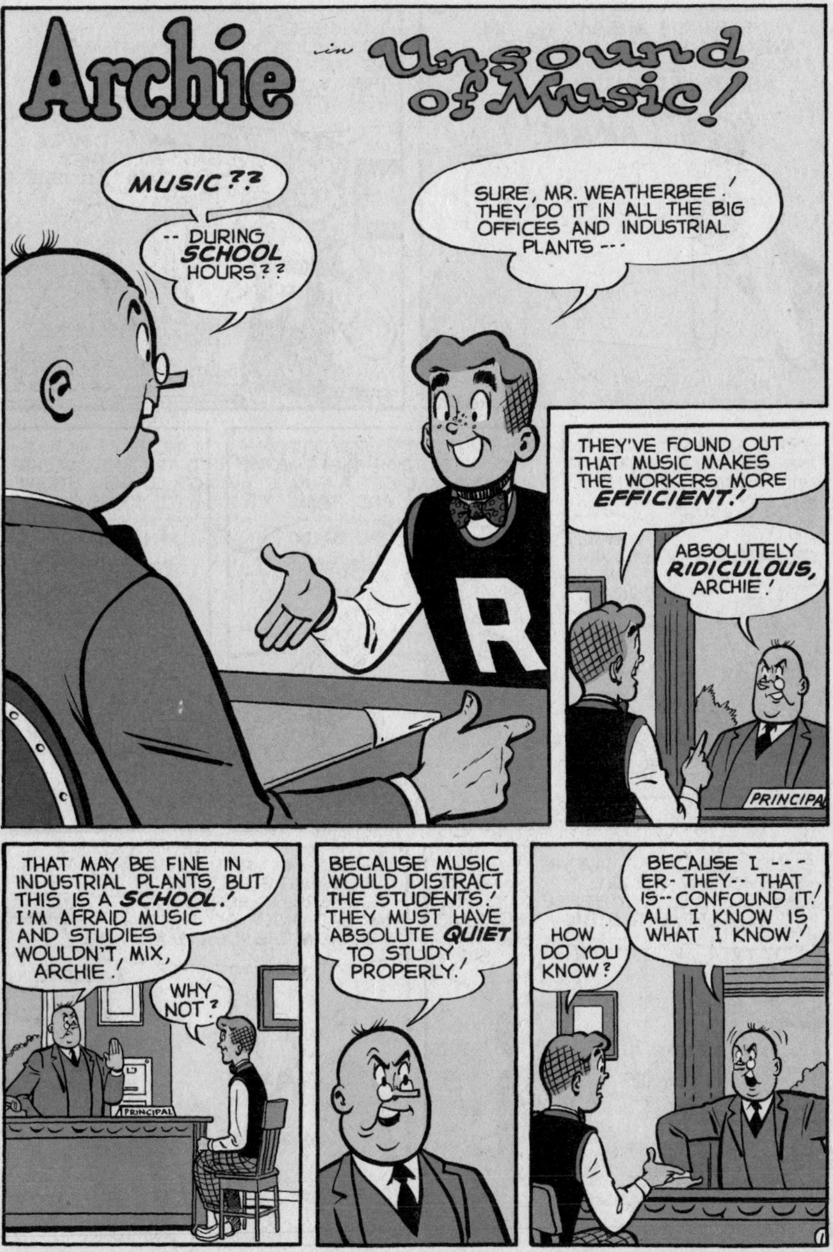
Archie
in
Unsound of Music!
MUSIC??
-- DURING SCHOOL HOURS??
SURE, MR. WEATHERBEE! THEY DO IT IN ALL THE BIG OFFICES AND INDUSTRIAL PLANTS ---
THEY'VE FOUND OUT THAT MUSIC MAKES THE WORKERS MORE EFFICIENT!
ABSOLUTELY RIDICULOUS, ARCHIE!
PRINCIPA
THAT MAY BE FINE IN INDUSTRIAL PLANTS, BUT THIS IS A SCHOOL! I'M AFRAID MUSIC AND STUDIES WOULDN'T, MIX, ARCHIE!
WHY NOT?
PRINCIPAL
BECAUSE MUSIC WOULD DISTRACT THE STUDENTS! THEY MUST HAVE ABSOLUTE QUIET TO STUDY PROPERLY!
HOW DO YOU KNOW?
BECAUSE I --- ER- THEY-- THAT IS-- CONFOUND IT! ALL I KNOW IS WHAT I KNOW!

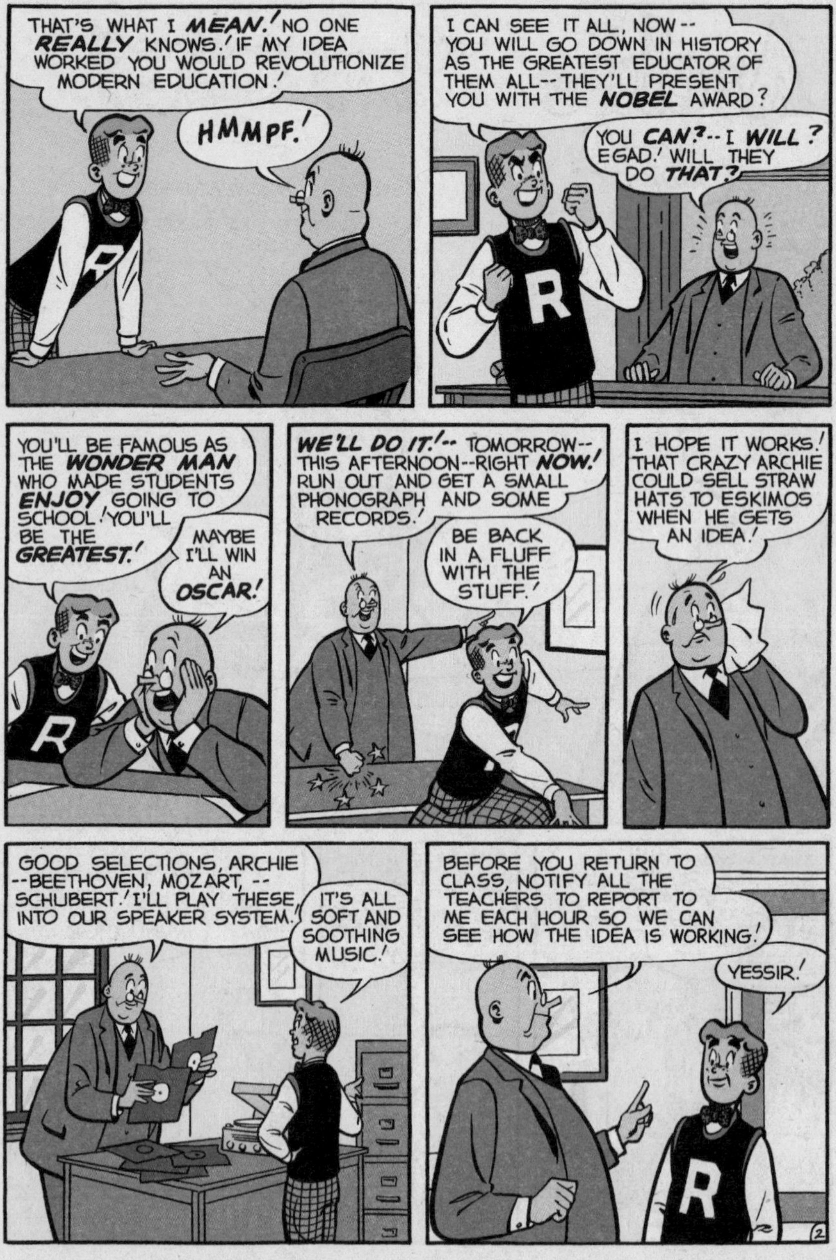
THAT'S WHAT I MEAN! NO ONE REALLY KNOWS! IF MY IDEA WORKED YOU WOULD REVOLUTIONIZE MODERN EDUCATION!
HMMPF!
I CAN SEE IT ALL, NOW -- YOU WILL GO DOWN IN HISTORY AS THE GREATEST EDUCATOR OF THEM ALL -- THEY'LL PRESENT YOU WITH THE NOBEL AWARD?
YOU CAN? -- I WILL? EGAD! WILL THEY DO THAT?
YOU'LL BE FAMOUS AS THE WONDER MAN WHO MADE STUDENTS ENJOY GOING TO SCHOOL! YOU'LL BE THE GREATEST!
MAYBE I'LL WIN AN OSCAR!
WE'LL DO IT! -- TOMORROW -- THIS AFTERNOON -- RIGHT NOW! RUN OUT AND GET A SMALL PHONOGRAPH AND SOME RECORDS!
BE BACK IN A FLUFF WITH THE STUFF!
I HOPE IT WORKS! THAT CRAZY ARCHIE COULD SELL STRAW HATS TO ESKIMOS WHEN HE GETS AN IDEA!
GOOD SELECTIONS, ARCHIE -- BEETHOVEN, MOZART, -- SCHUBERT! I'LL PLAY THESE INTO OUR SPEAKER SYSTEM!
IT'S ALL SOFT AND SOOTHING MUSIC!
BEFORE YOU RETURN TO CLASS, NOTIFY ALL THE TEACHERS TO REPORT TO ME EACH HOUR SO WE CAN SEE HOW THE IDEA IS WORKING!
YESSIR!
2

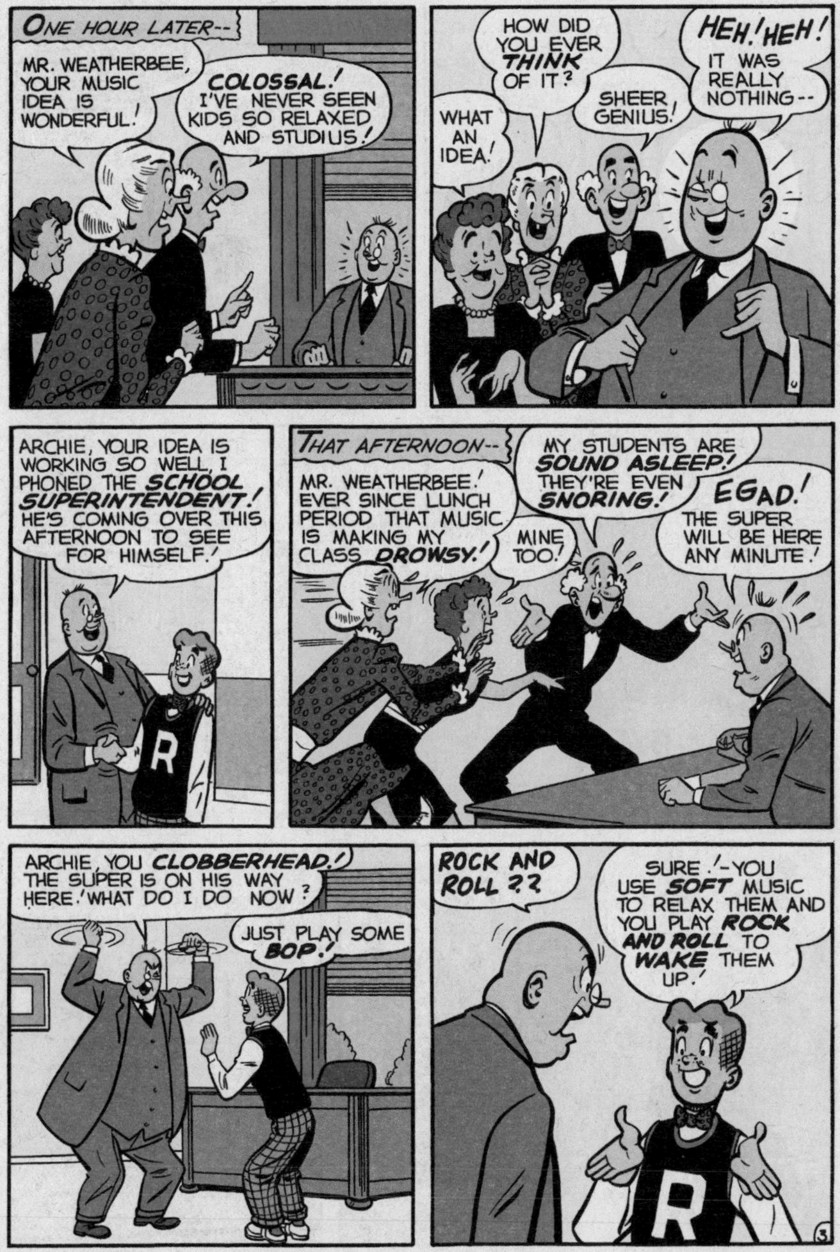
ONE HOUR LATER--
MR. WEATHERBEE, YOUR MUSIC IDEA IS WONDERFUL!
COLOSSAL! I'VE NEVER SEEN KIDS SO RELAXED AND STUDIUS!
WHAT AN IDEA!
HOW DID YOU EVER THINK OF IT?
SHEER GENIUS!
HEH! HEH! IT WAS REALLY NOTHING--
ARCHIE, YOUR IDEA IS WORKING SO WELL, I PHONED THE SCHOOL SUPERINTENDENT! HE'S COMING OVER THIS AFTERNOON TO SEE FOR HIMSELF!
THAT AFTERNOON--
MR. WEATHERBEE! EVER SINCE LUNCH PERIOD THAT MUSIC IS MAKING MY CLASS DROWSY!
MINE TOO!
MY STUDENTS ARE SOUND ASLEEP! THEY'RE EVEN SNORING!
EGAD! THE SUPER WILL BE HERE ANY MINUTE!
ARCHIE, YOU CLOBBERHEAD! THE SUPER IS ON HIS WAY HERE! WHAT DO I DO NOW?
JUST PLAY SOME BOP!
ROCK AND ROLL ??
SURE! -YOU USE SOFT MUSIC TO RELAX THEM AND YOU PLAY ROCK AND ROLL TO WAKE THEM UP!
3

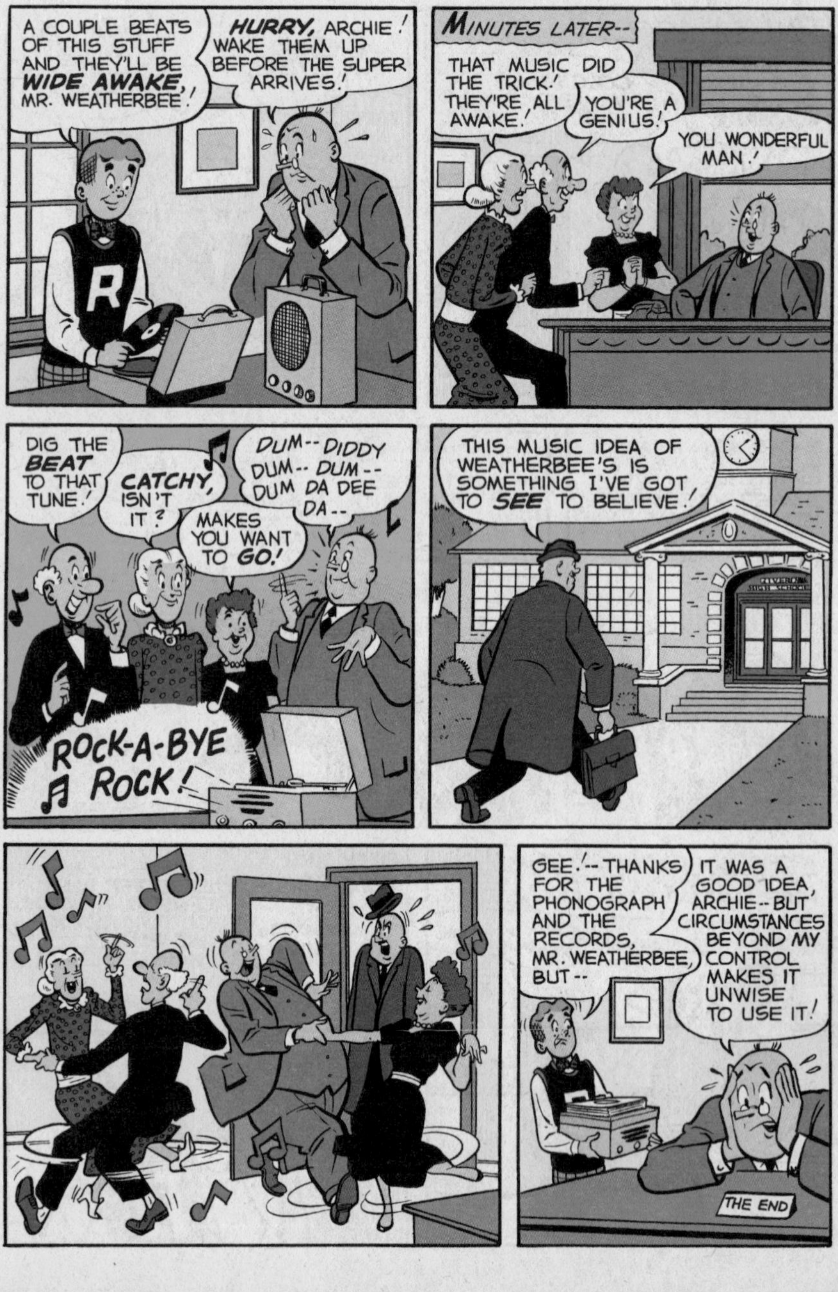
A COUPLE BEATS OF THIS STUFF AND THEY'LL BE WIDE AWAKE, MR. WEATHERBEE!
HURRY, ARCHIE! WAKE THEM UP BEFORE THE SUPER ARRIVES!
MINUTES LATER--
THAT MUSIC DID THE TRICK! THEY'RE ALL AWAKE!
YOU'RE A GENIUS!
YOU WONDERFUL MAN!
DIG THE BEAT TO THAT TUNE!
CATCHY, ISN'T IT?
DUM--DIDDY DUM--DUM--DUM DA DEE DA--
MAKES YOU WANT TO GO!
ROCK-A-BYE ROCK!
THIS MUSIC IDEA OF WEATHERBEE'S IS SOMETHING I'VE GOT TO SEE TO BELIEVE!
GEE!--THANKS FOR THE PHONOGRAPH AND THE RECORDS, MR. WEATHERBEE, BUT--
IT WAS A GOOD IDEA, ARCHIE--BUT CIRCUMSTANCES BEYOND MY CONTROL MAKES IT UNWISE TO USE IT!
THE END

Why Fight It!
Archie Giant Series #21, June 1963
Frank Doyle, Dan DeCarlo, Rudy Lapick
and Vincent DeCarlo

Veronica is determined to shake her boy-crazy reputation... if only she didn't keep running into, falling over, and kissing every boy at school in the process! Can Veronica change her image, or is she forever destined to be the Venus of Riverdale High?

Wittle While You Work
Jughead #115, December 1964
Frank Doyle, Samm Schwartz
and Marty Epp

In this mirthful misadventure, Jughead reveals a hidden talent when he begins carving wood. His abilities soon gain the attention of Mr. Weatherbee, whose desk has fallen victim to Juggie's unique skills. Commissioned to create a Riverdale High totem pole, Jughead, like all great artists, draws inspiration from his own life.

Bonus: Newspaper Strip, January 7, 2001
Craig Boldman and Henry Scarpelli

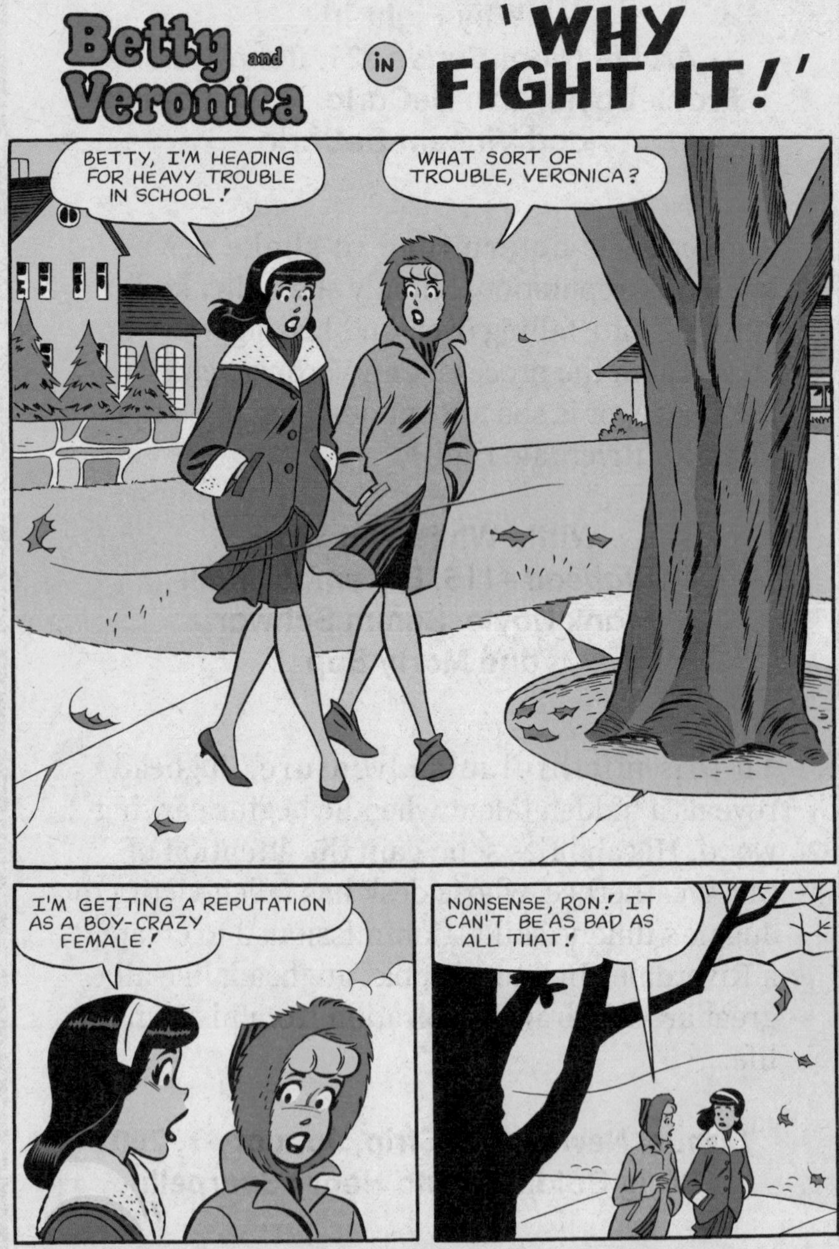
Betty and Veronica
IN
'WHY FIGHT IT!'
BETTY, I'M HEADING FOR HEAVY TROUBLE IN SCHOOL!
WHAT SORT OF TROUBLE, VERONICA?
I'M GETTING A REPUTATION AS A BOY-CRAZY FEMALE!
NONSENSE, RON! IT CAN'T BE AS BAD AS ALL THAT!

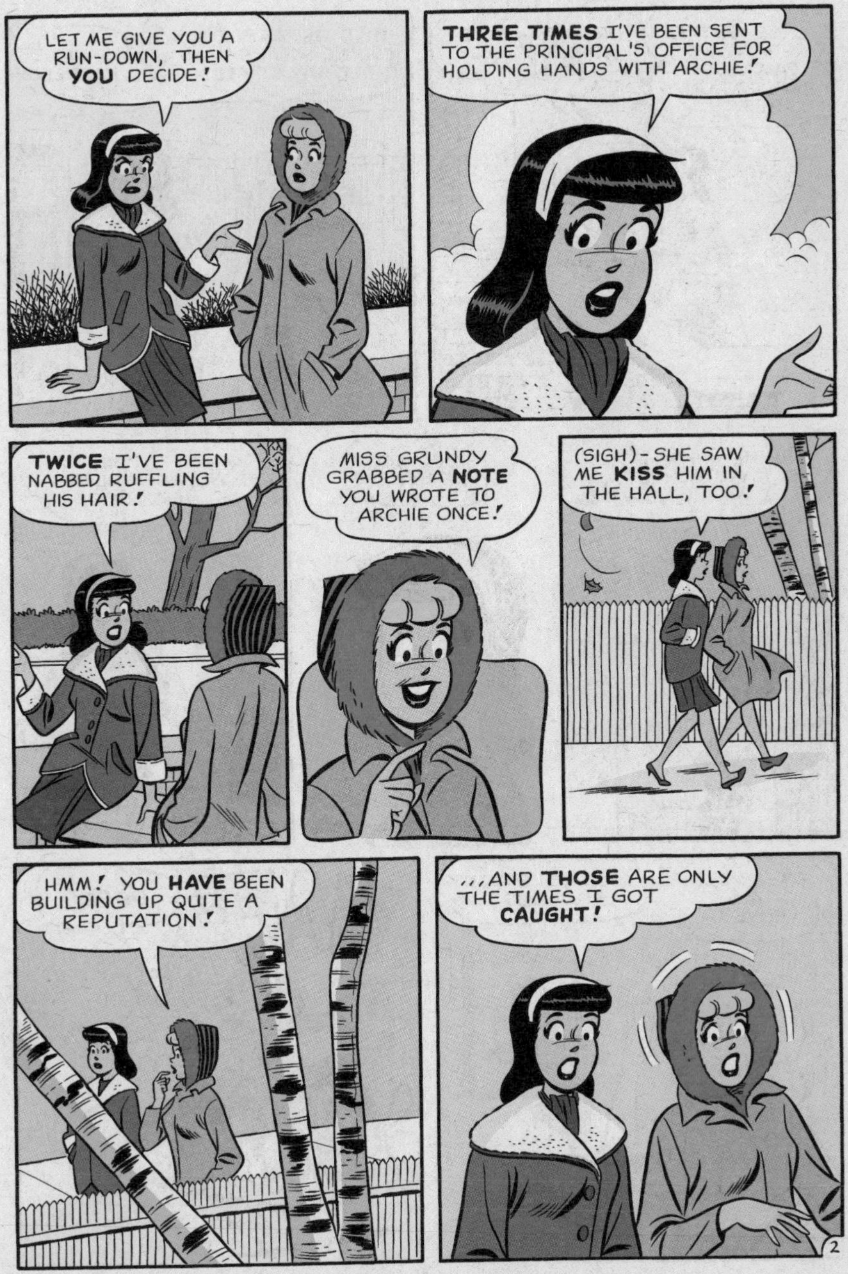
LET ME GIVE YOU A RUN-DOWN, THEN YOU DECIDE!
THREE TIMES I'VE BEEN SENT TO THE PRINCIPAL'S OFFICE FOR HOLDING HANDS WITH ARCHIE!
TWICE I'VE BEEN NABBED RUFFLING HIS HAIR!
MISS GRUNDY GRABBED A NOTE YOU WROTE TO ARCHIE ONCE!
(SIGH)- SHE SAW ME KISS HIM IN THE HALL, TOO!
HMM! YOU HAVE BEEN BUILDING UP QUITE A REPUTATION!
...AND THOSE ARE ONLY THE TIMES I GOT CAUGHT!
2

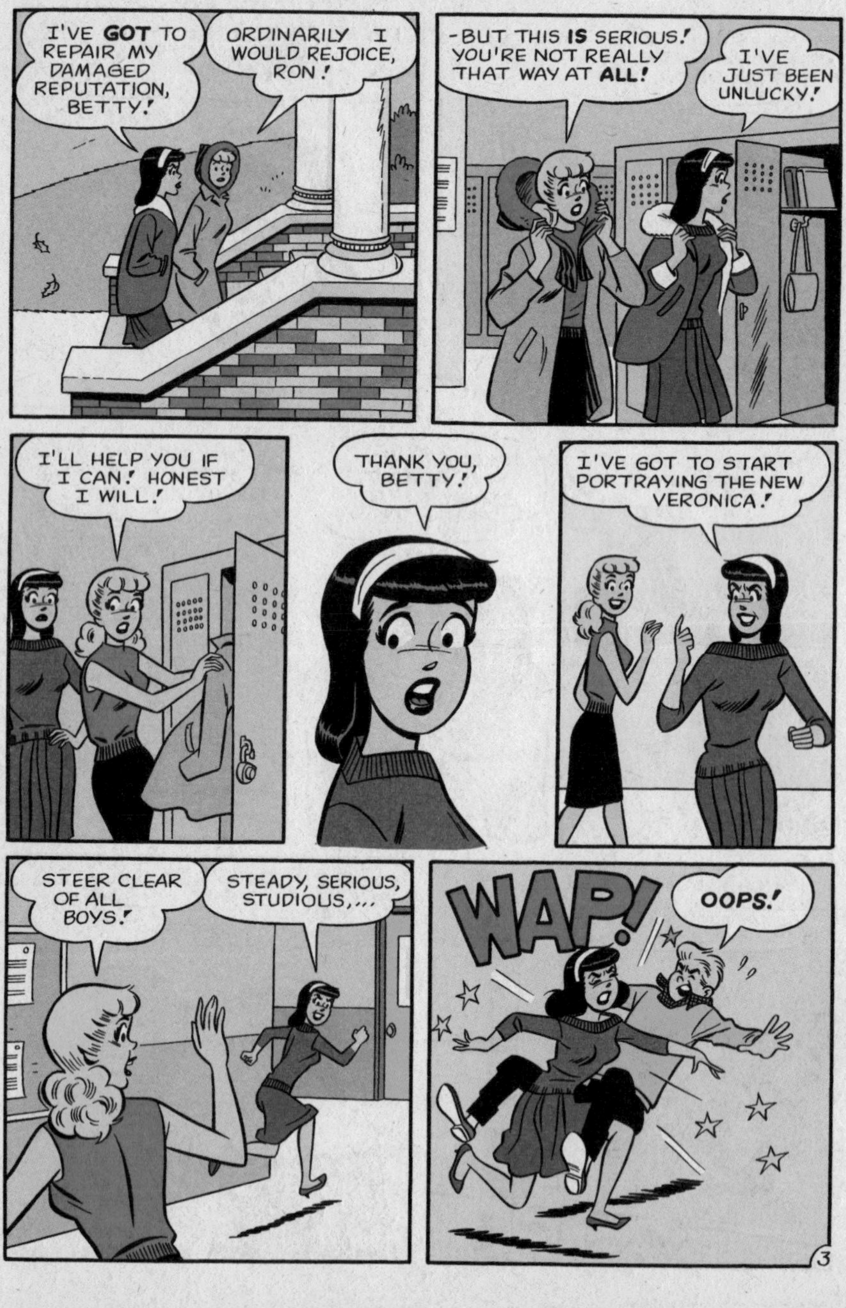
I'VE GOT TO REPAIR MY DAMAGED REPUTATION, BETTY!
ORDINARILY I WOULD REJOICE, RON!
-BUT THIS IS SERIOUS! YOU'RE NOT REALLY THAT WAY AT ALL!
I'VE JUST BEEN UNLUCKY!
I'LL HELP YOU IF I CAN! HONEST I WILL!
THANK YOU, BETTY!
I'VE GOT TO START PORTRAYING THE NEW VERONICA!
STEER CLEAR OF ALL BOYS!
STEADY, SERIOUS, STUDIOUS,...
WAP!
OOPS!
3

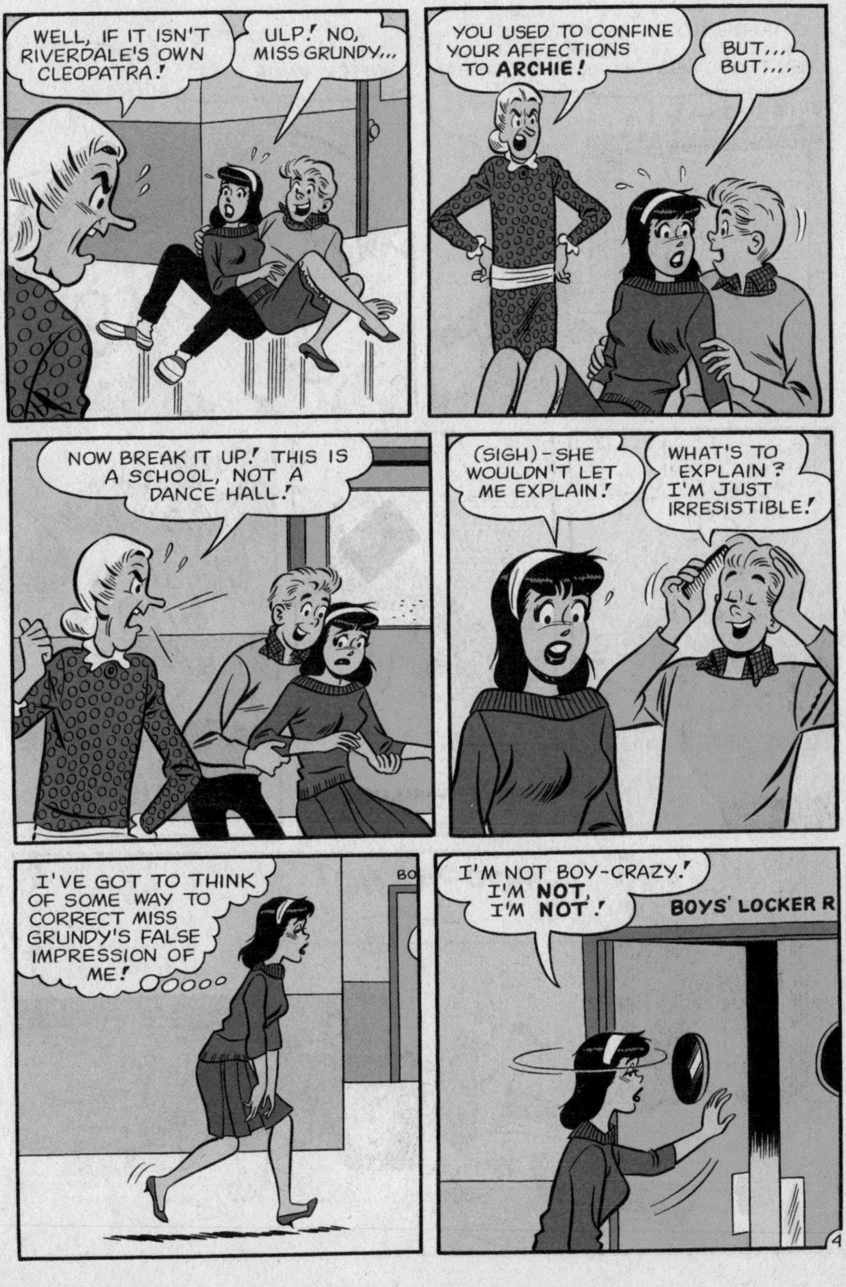
WELL, IF IT ISN'T RIVERDALE'S OWN CLEOPATRA!
ULP! NO, MISS GRUNDY...
YOU USED TO CONFINE YOUR AFFECTIONS TO **ARCHIE**!
BUT... BUT....
NOW BREAK IT UP! THIS IS A SCHOOL, NOT A DANCE HALL!
(SIGH)-SHE WOULDN'T LET ME EXPLAIN!
WHAT'S TO EXPLAIN? I'M JUST IRRESISTIBLE!
I'VE GOT TO THINK OF SOME WAY TO CORRECT MISS GRUNDY'S FALSE IMPRESSION OF ME!
BO
I'M NOT BOY-CRAZY! I'M **NOT**, I'M **NOT**!
BOYS' LOCKER R
4

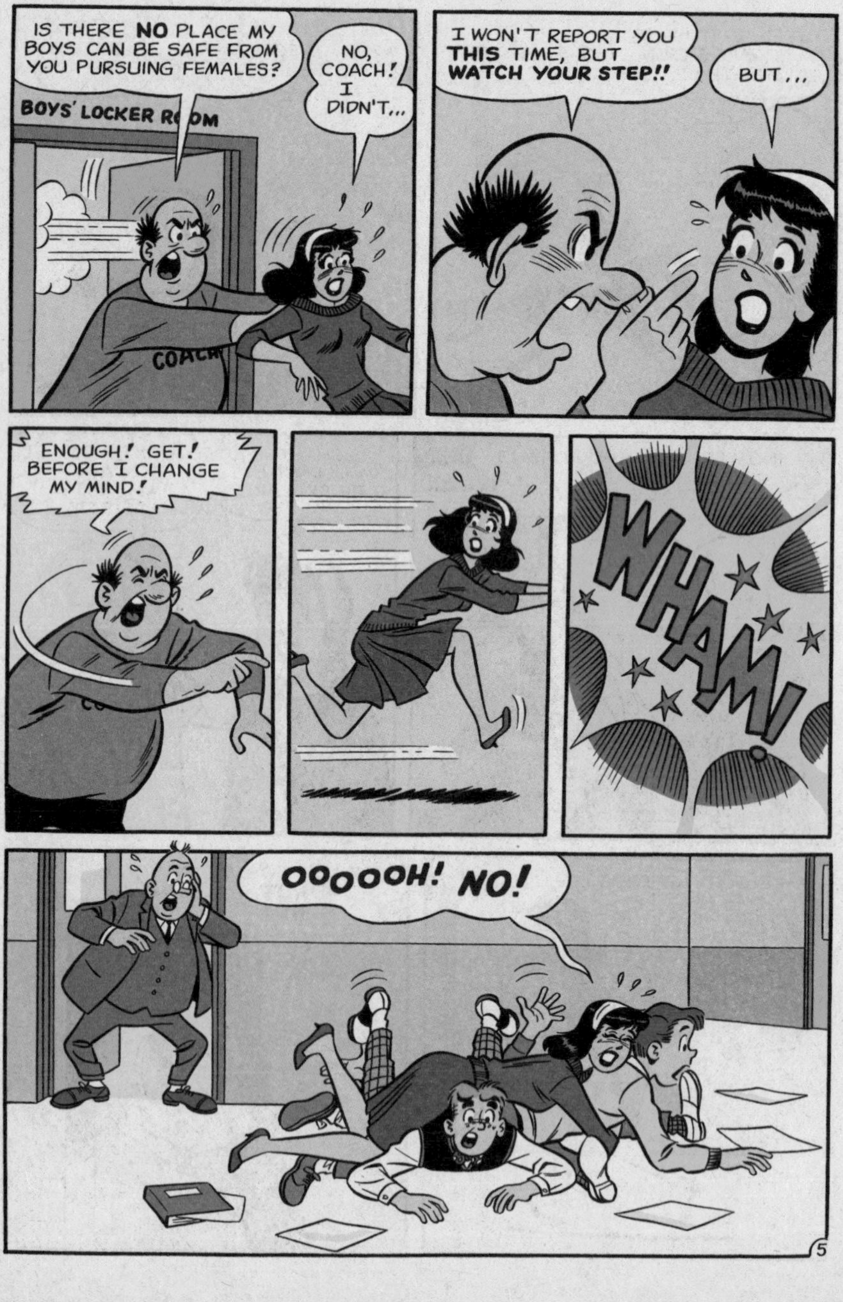
IS THERE NO PLACE MY BOYS CAN BE SAFE FROM YOU PURSUING FEMALES?
BOYS' LOCKER ROOM
NO, COACH! I DIDN'T...
COACH
I WON'T REPORT YOU THIS TIME, BUT WATCH YOUR STEP!!
BUT...
ENOUGH! GET! BEFORE I CHANGE MY MIND!
WHAM!
OOOOOH! NO!
5

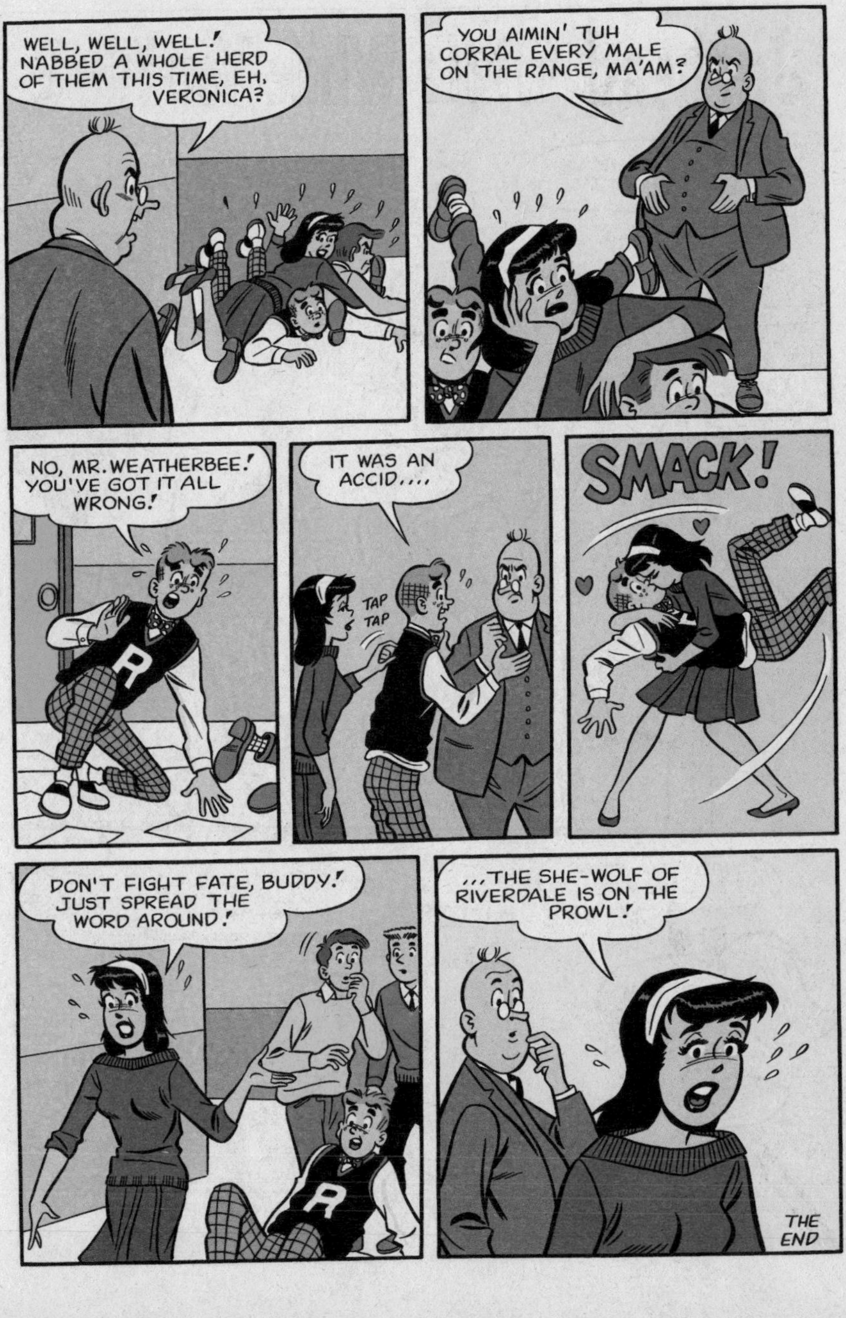
WELL, WELL, WELL! NABBED A WHOLE HERD OF THEM THIS TIME, EH, VERONICA?
YOU AIMIN' TUH CORRAL EVERY MALE ON THE RANGE, MA'AM?
NO, MR. WEATHERBEE! YOU'VE GOT IT ALL WRONG!
IT WAS AN ACCID....
TAP TAP
SMACK!
DON'T FIGHT FATE, BUDDY! JUST SPREAD THE WORD AROUND!
...THE SHE-WOLF OF RIVERDALE IS ON THE PROWL!
THE END

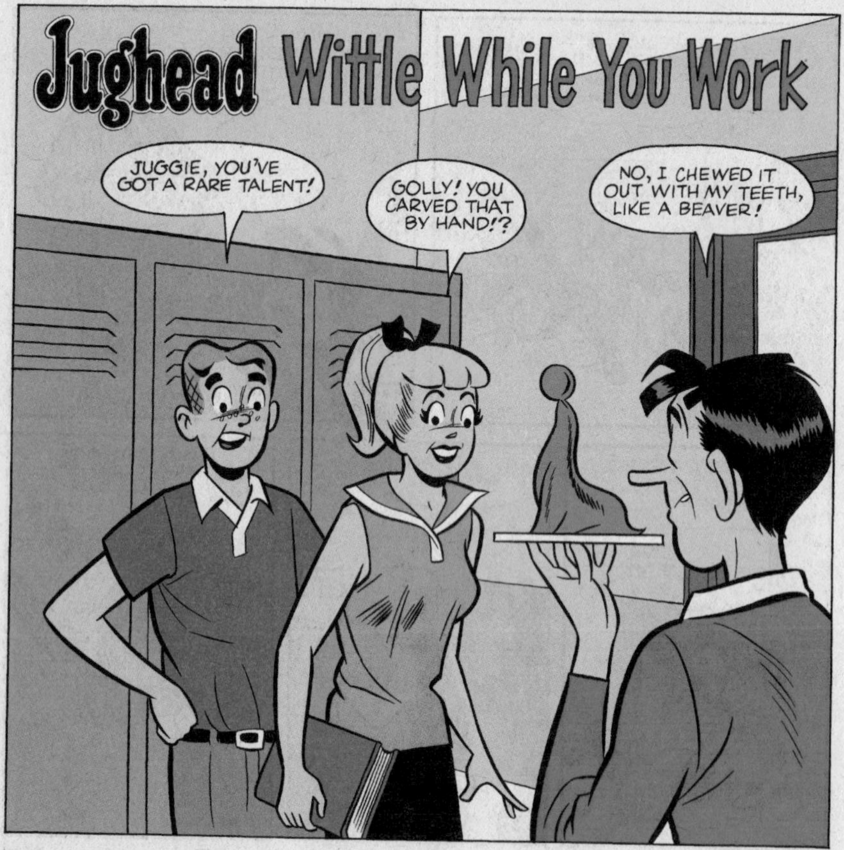
Jughead
Wittle While You Work
JUGGIE, YOU'VE GOT A RARE TALENT!
GOLLY! YOU CARVED THAT BY HAND!?
NO, I CHEWED IT OUT WITH MY TEETH, LIKE A BEAVER!

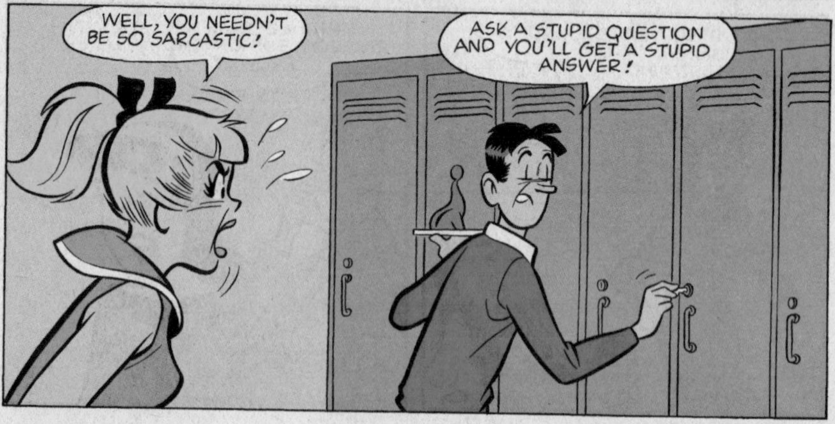
WELL, YOU NEEDN'T BE SO SARCASTIC!
ASK A STUPID QUESTION AND YOU'LL GET A STUPID ANSWER!

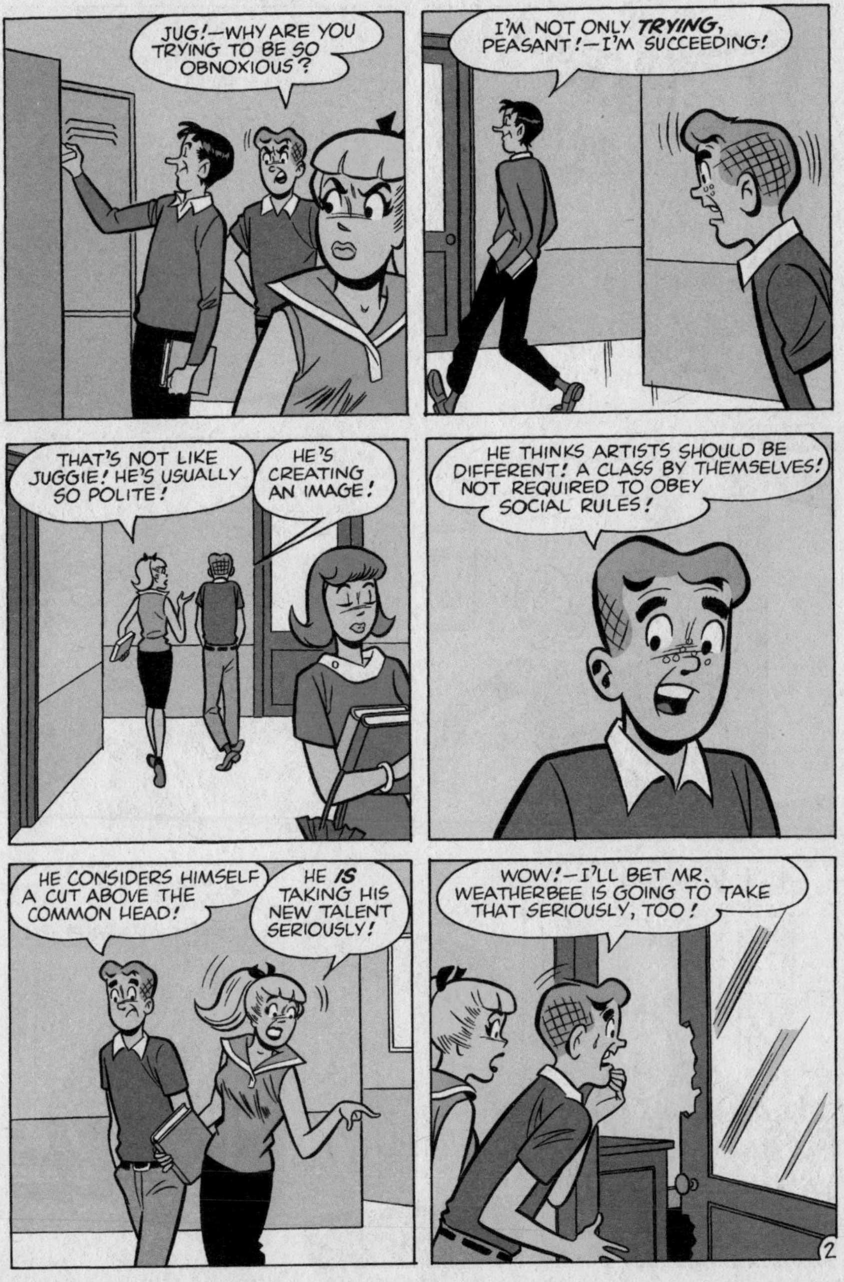
JUG!—WHY ARE YOU TRYING TO BE SO OBNOXIOUS?
I'M NOT ONLY TRYING, PEASANT!—I'M SUCCEEDING!
THAT'S NOT LIKE JUGGIE! HE'S USUALLY SO POLITE!
HE'S CREATING AN IMAGE!
HE THINKS ARTISTS SHOULD BE DIFFERENT! A CLASS BY THEMSELVES! NOT REQUIRED TO OBEY SOCIAL RULES!
HE CONSIDERS HIMSELF A CUT ABOVE THE COMMON HEAD!
HE IS TAKING HIS NEW TALENT SERIOUSLY!
WOW!—I'LL BET MR. WEATHERBEE IS GOING TO TAKE THAT SERIOUSLY, TOO!
2

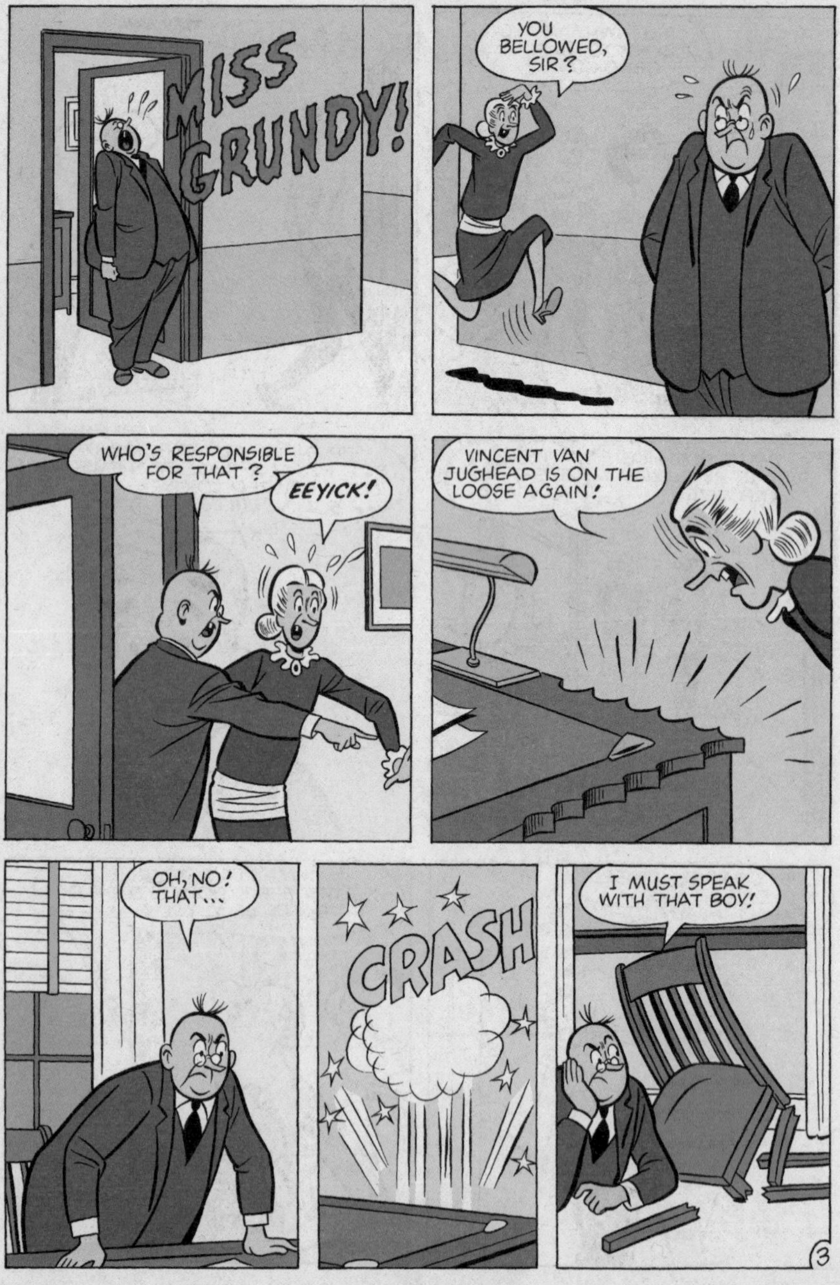
MISS GRUNDY!
YOU BELLOWED, SIR?
WHO'S RESPONSIBLE FOR THAT?
EEYICK!
VINCENT VAN JUGHEAD IS ON THE LOOSE AGAIN!
OH, NO! THAT...
CRASH
I MUST SPEAK WITH THAT BOY!
3

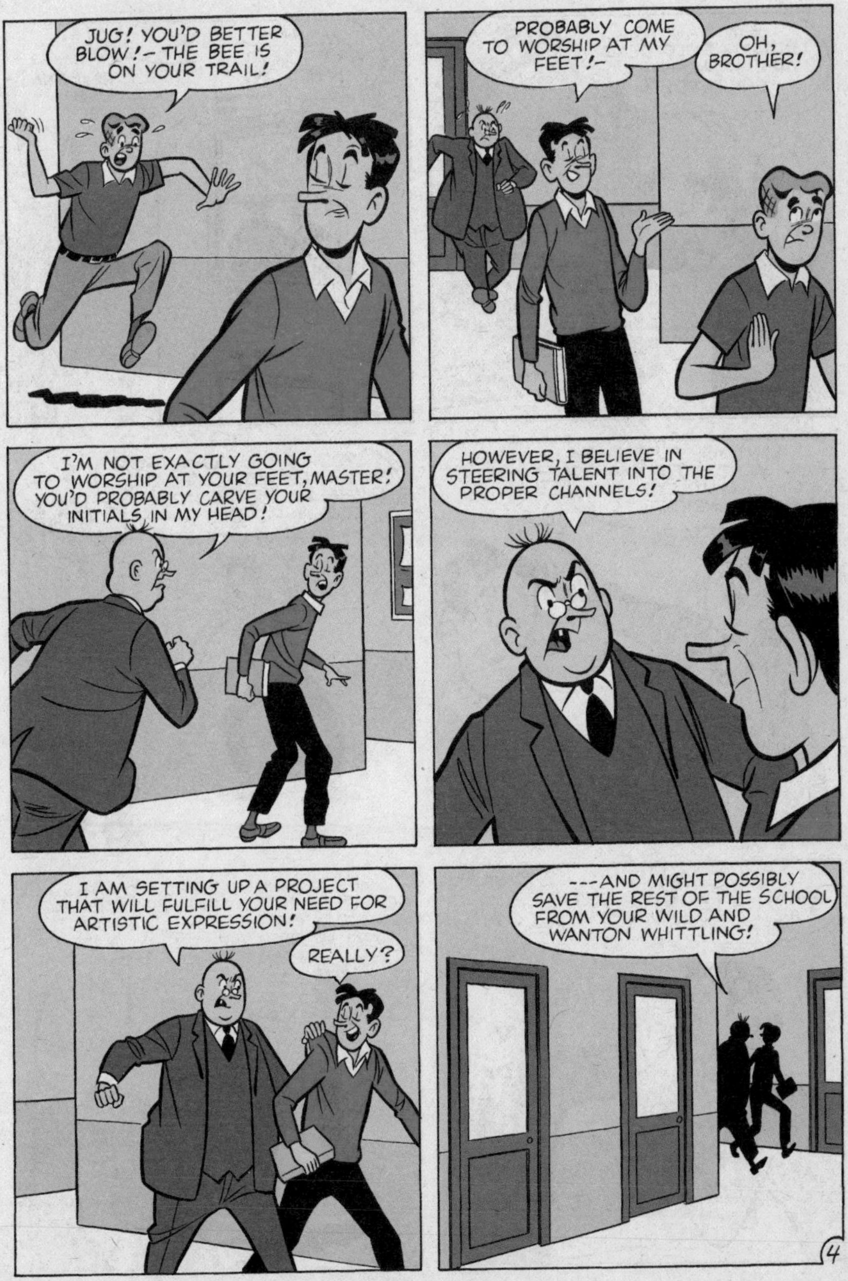
JUG! YOU'D BETTER BLOW!– THE BEE IS ON YOUR TRAIL!
PROBABLY COME TO WORSHIP AT MY FEET!–
OH, BROTHER!
I'M NOT EXACTLY GOING TO WORSHIP AT YOUR FEET, MASTER! YOU'D PROBABLY CARVE YOUR INITIALS IN MY HEAD!
HOWEVER, I BELIEVE IN STEERING TALENT INTO THE PROPER CHANNELS!
I AM SETTING UP A PROJECT THAT WILL FULFILL YOUR NEED FOR ARTISTIC EXPRESSION!
REALLY?
---AND MIGHT POSSIBLY SAVE THE REST OF THE SCHOOL FROM YOUR WILD AND WANTON WHITTLING!
4

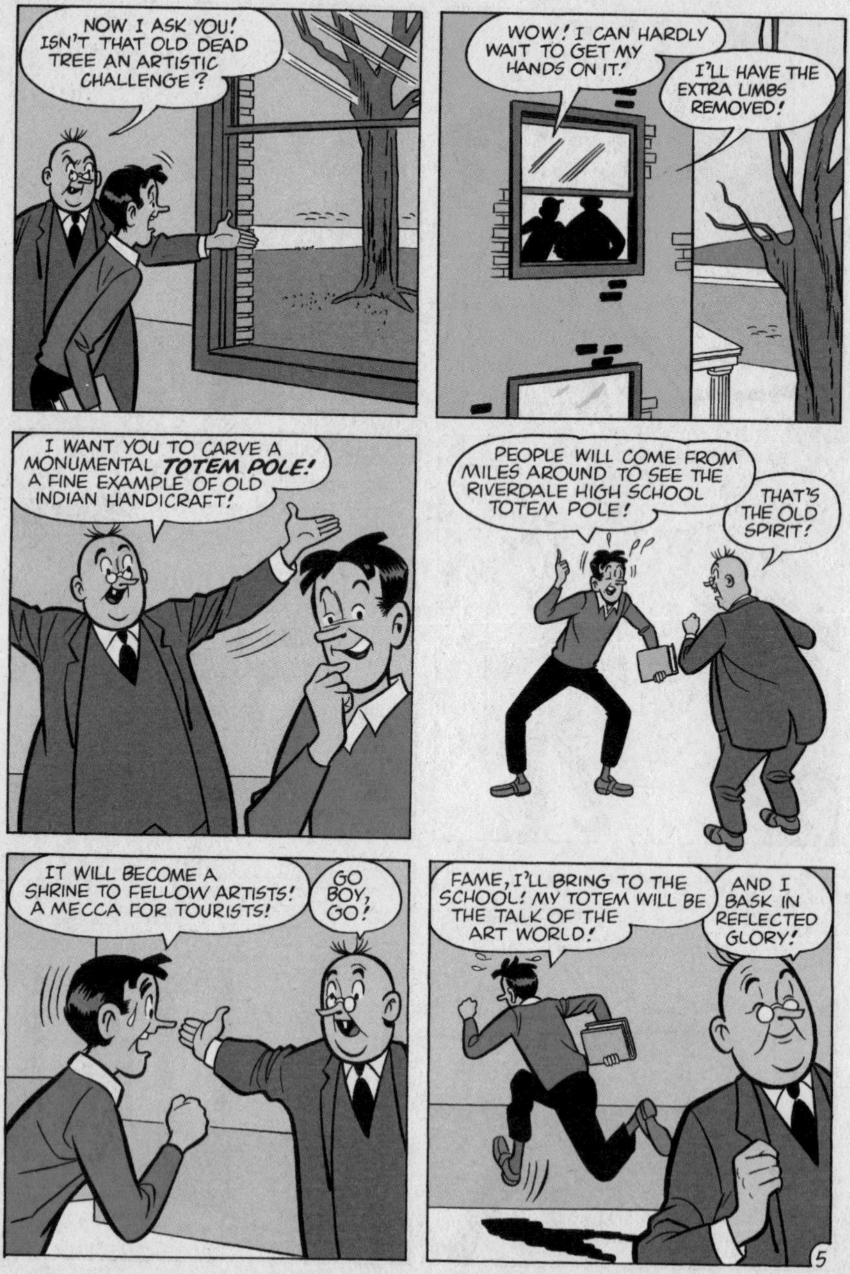
NOW I ASK YOU! ISN'T THAT OLD DEAD TREE AN ARTISTIC CHALLENGE?
WOW! I CAN HARDLY WAIT TO GET MY HANDS ON IT!
I'LL HAVE THE EXTRA LIMBS REMOVED!
I WANT YOU TO CARVE A MONUMENTAL TOTEM POLE! A FINE EXAMPLE OF OLD INDIAN HANDICRAFT!
PEOPLE WILL COME FROM MILES AROUND TO SEE THE RIVERDALE HIGH SCHOOL TOTEM POLE!
THAT'S THE OLD SPIRIT!
IT WILL BECOME A SHRINE TO FELLOW ARTISTS! A MECCA FOR TOURISTS!
GO BOY, GO!
FAME, I'LL BRING TO THE SCHOOL! MY TOTEM WILL BE THE TALK OF THE ART WORLD!
AND I BASK IN REFLECTED GLORY!
5

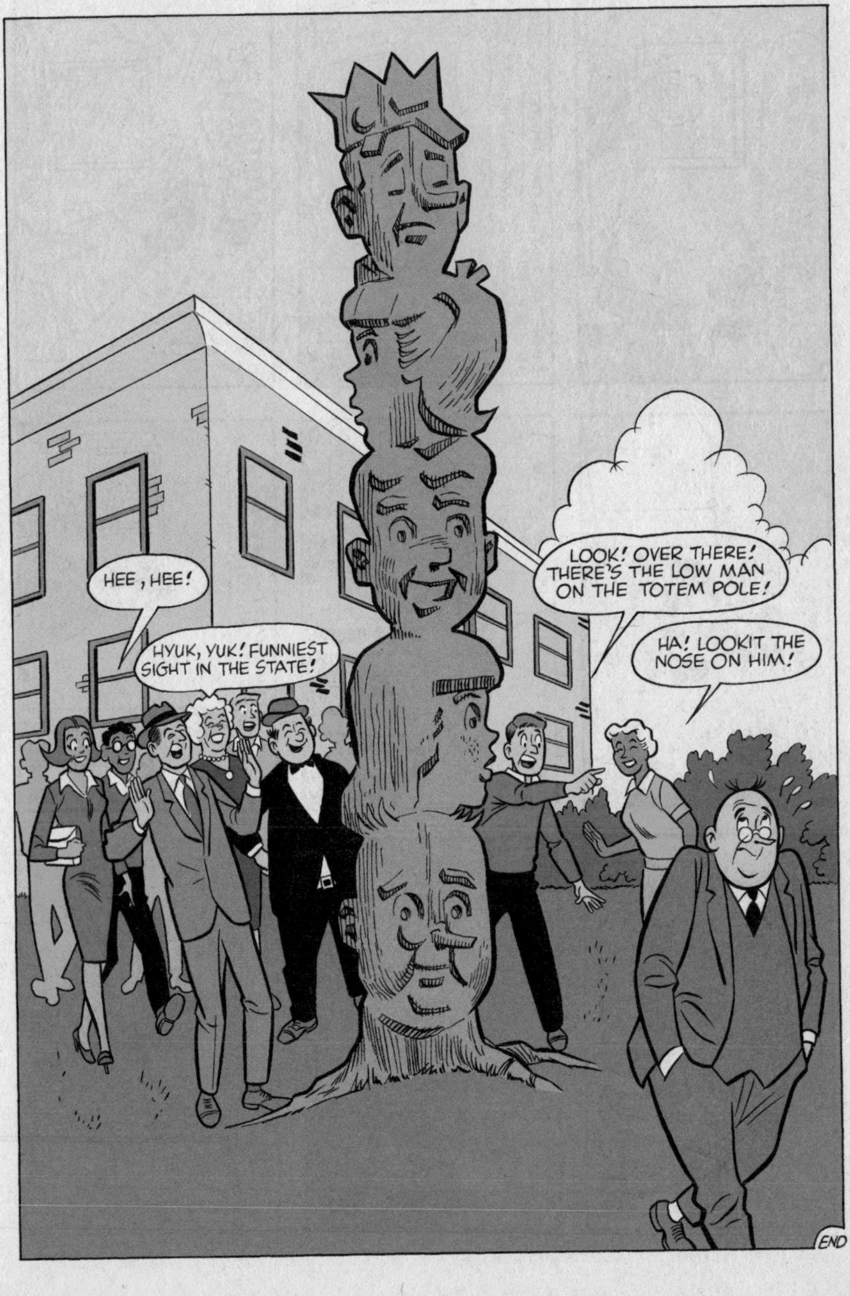
HEE, HEE!
HYUK, YUK! FUNNIEST SIGHT IN THE STATE!
LOOK! OVER THERE! THERE'S THE LOW MAN ON THE TOTEM POLE!
HA! LOOKIT THE NOSE ON HIM!
END

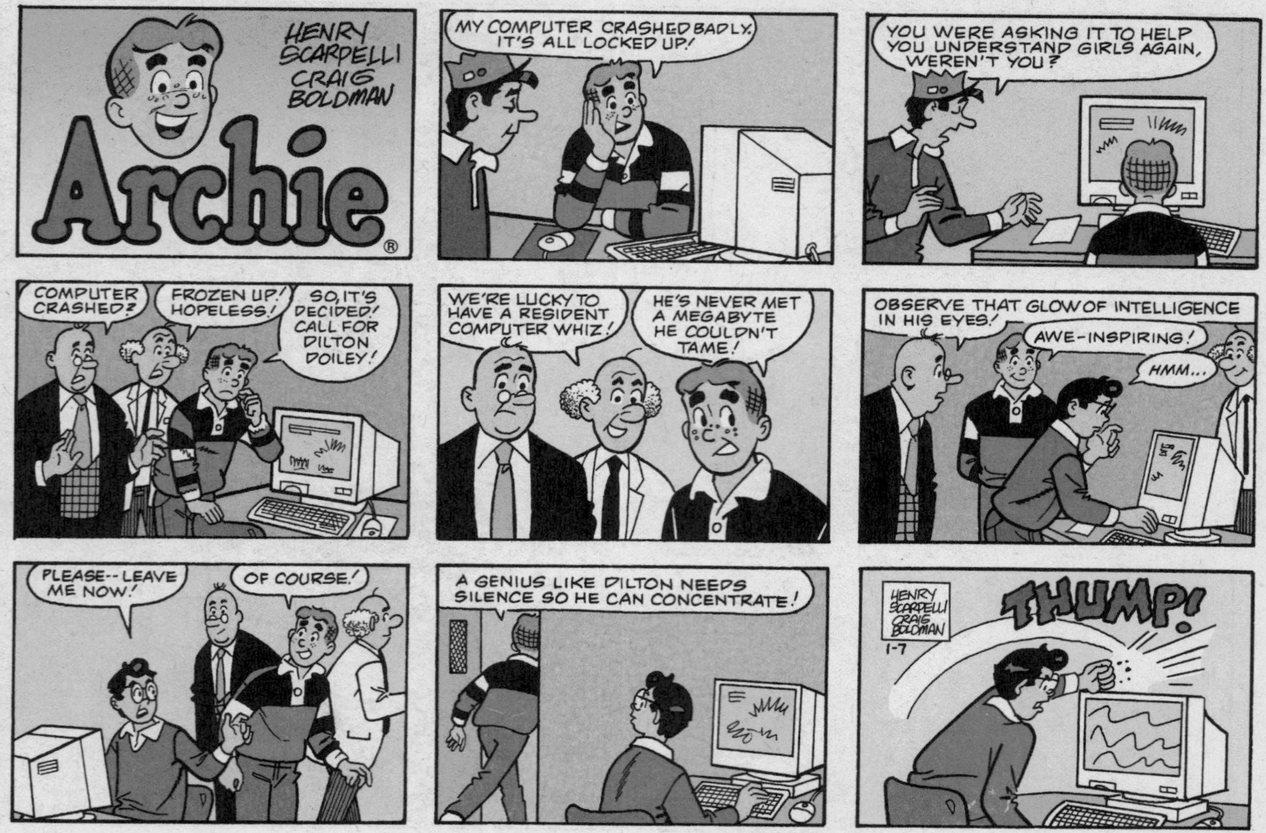
HENRY SCARPELLI CRAIG BOLDMAN
Archie®
MY COMPUTER CRASHED BADLY. IT'S ALL LOCKED UP!
YOU WERE ASKING IT TO HELP YOU UNDERSTAND GIRLS AGAIN, WEREN'T YOU?
COMPUTER CRASHED?
FROZEN UP! HOPELESS!
SO, IT'S DECIDED! CALL FOR DILTON DOILEY!
WE'RE LUCKY TO HAVE A RESIDENT COMPUTER WHIZ!
HE'S NEVER MET A MEGABYTE HE COULDN'T TAME!
OBSERVE THAT GLOW OF INTELLIGENCE IN HIS EYES!
AWE-INSPIRING!
HMM...
PLEASE--LEAVE ME NOW!
OF COURSE!
A GENIUS LIKE DILTON NEEDS SILENCE SO HE CAN CONCENTRATE!
HENRY SCARPELLI CRAIG BOLDMAN
1-7
THUMP!

Archie's FAVORITE HIGH SCHOOL COMICS

HIGH SCHOOL SWEETHEARTS

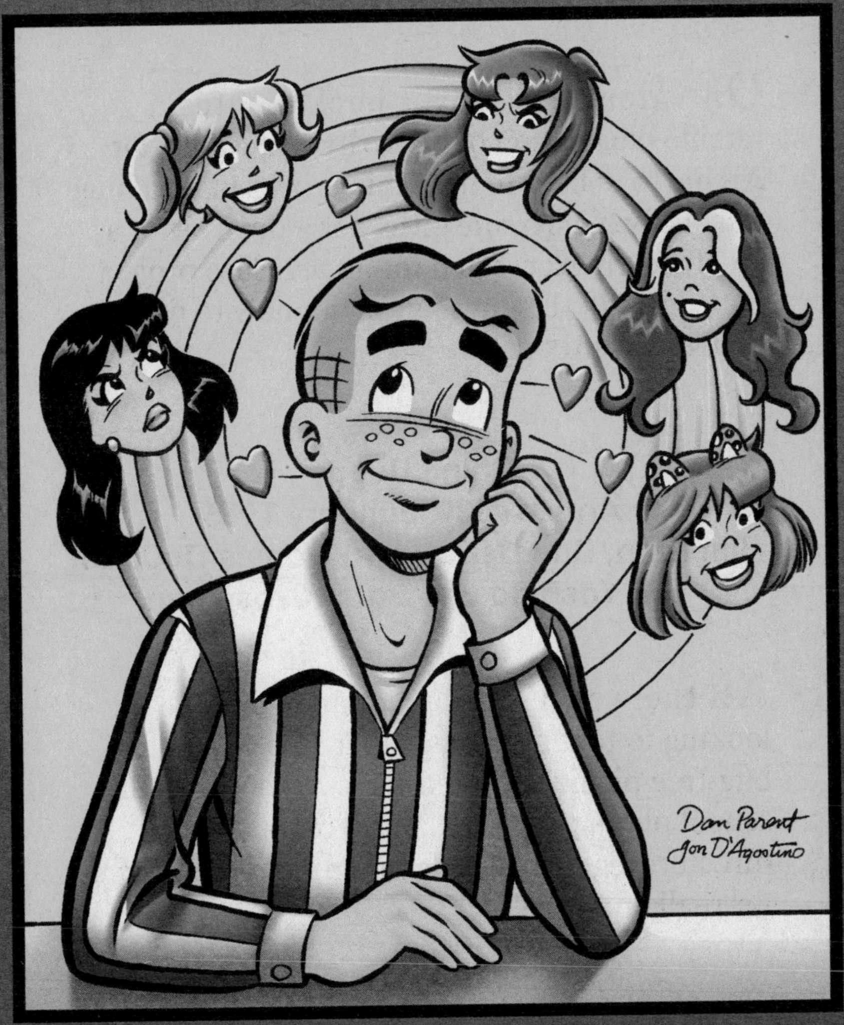
Dan Parent
Jon D'Agostino

Monsterpiece Theater!
Archie & Friends Double Digest #12,
March 2012
Fernando Ruiz, Jon D'Agostino
and Adam Walmsley

On Valentine's Day, Chuck creates a terrific illustration of his girlfriend Nancy for Archie to deliver to her. This proves to be a huge mistake when Archie gives her a drawing of a creature Chuck created for an art class project instead. Will the guys figure out how to fix this monstrous mix-up?

Going Buggy
Archie #339, **January 1986**
Jim Ruth, Dan DeCarlo Jr., James DeCarlo,
Bill Yoshida and Barry Grossman

All the world's a stage... and Archie's looking to take advantage of it. Seeking a bug-free picnic with Veronica, Archie uses the school play's picnic set... little realizing play director Reggie has ordered an influx of insects for realism's sake!

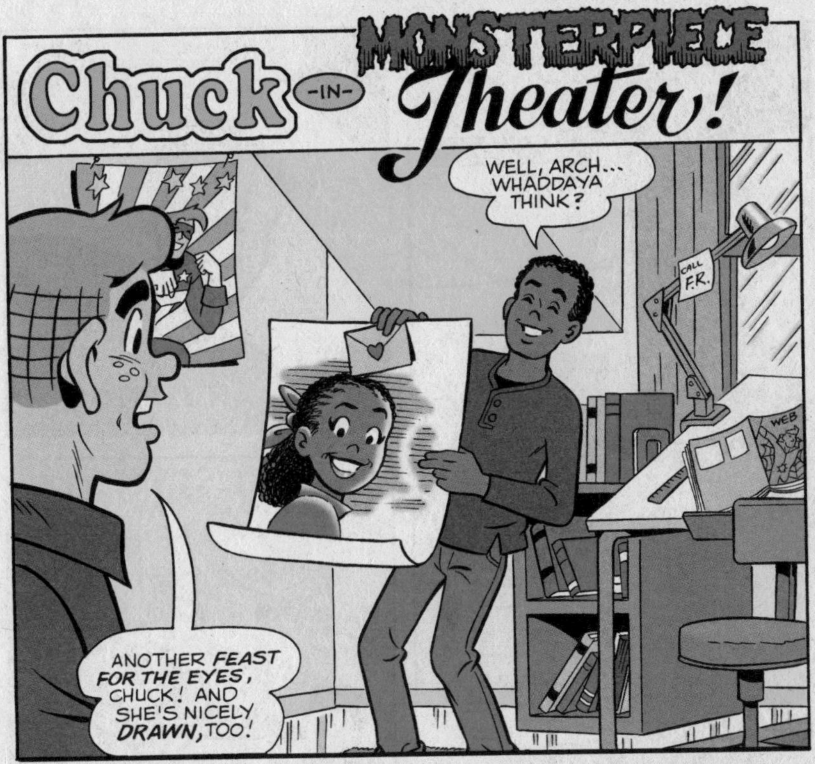
Chuck -IN- MONSTERPIECE Theater!
WELL, ARCH... WHADDAYA THINK?
CALL F.R.
WEB
ANOTHER *FEAST FOR THE EYES*, CHUCK! AND SHE'S NICELY *DRAWN*, TOO!

SCRIPT & PENCILS: FERNANDO RUIZ INKS & LETTERS: JON D'AGOSTINO
COLORS: ADAM WALMSLEY

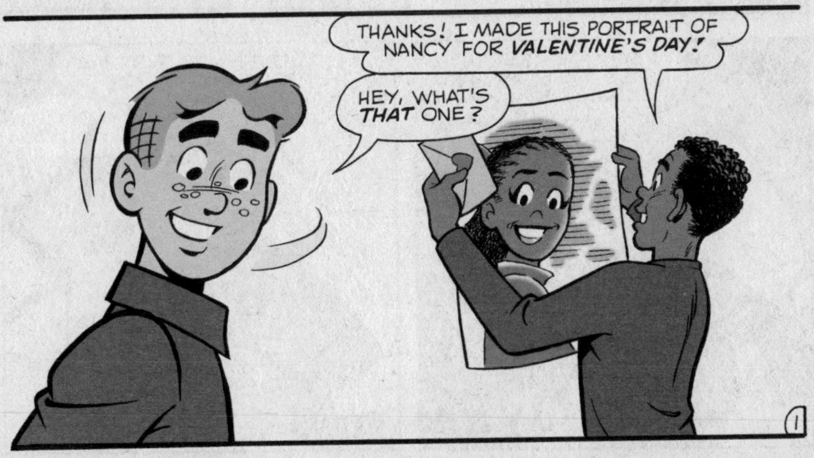
THANKS! I MADE THIS PORTRAIT OF NANCY FOR *VALENTINE'S DAY!*
HEY, WHAT'S *THAT* ONE?
1

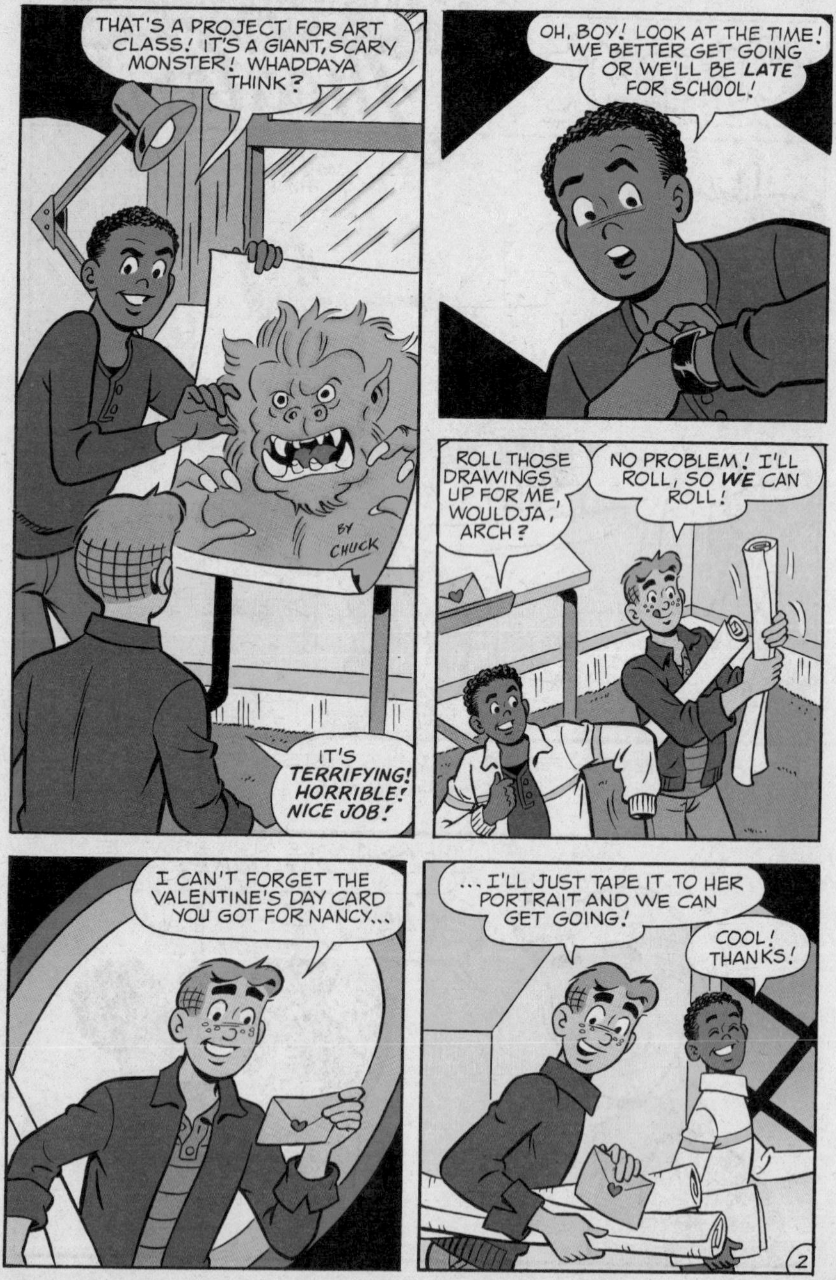
THAT'S A PROJECT FOR ART CLASS! IT'S A GIANT, SCARY MONSTER! WHADDAYA THINK?
BY CHUCK
IT'S TERRIFYING! HORRIBLE! NICE JOB!
OH, BOY! LOOK AT THE TIME! WE BETTER GET GOING OR WE'LL BE LATE FOR SCHOOL!
ROLL THOSE DRAWINGS UP FOR ME, WOULDJA, ARCH?
NO PROBLEM! I'LL ROLL, SO WE CAN ROLL!
I CAN'T FORGET THE VALENTINE'S DAY CARD YOU GOT FOR NANCY...
...I'LL JUST TAPE IT TO HER PORTRAIT AND WE CAN GET GOING!
COOL! THANKS!
2

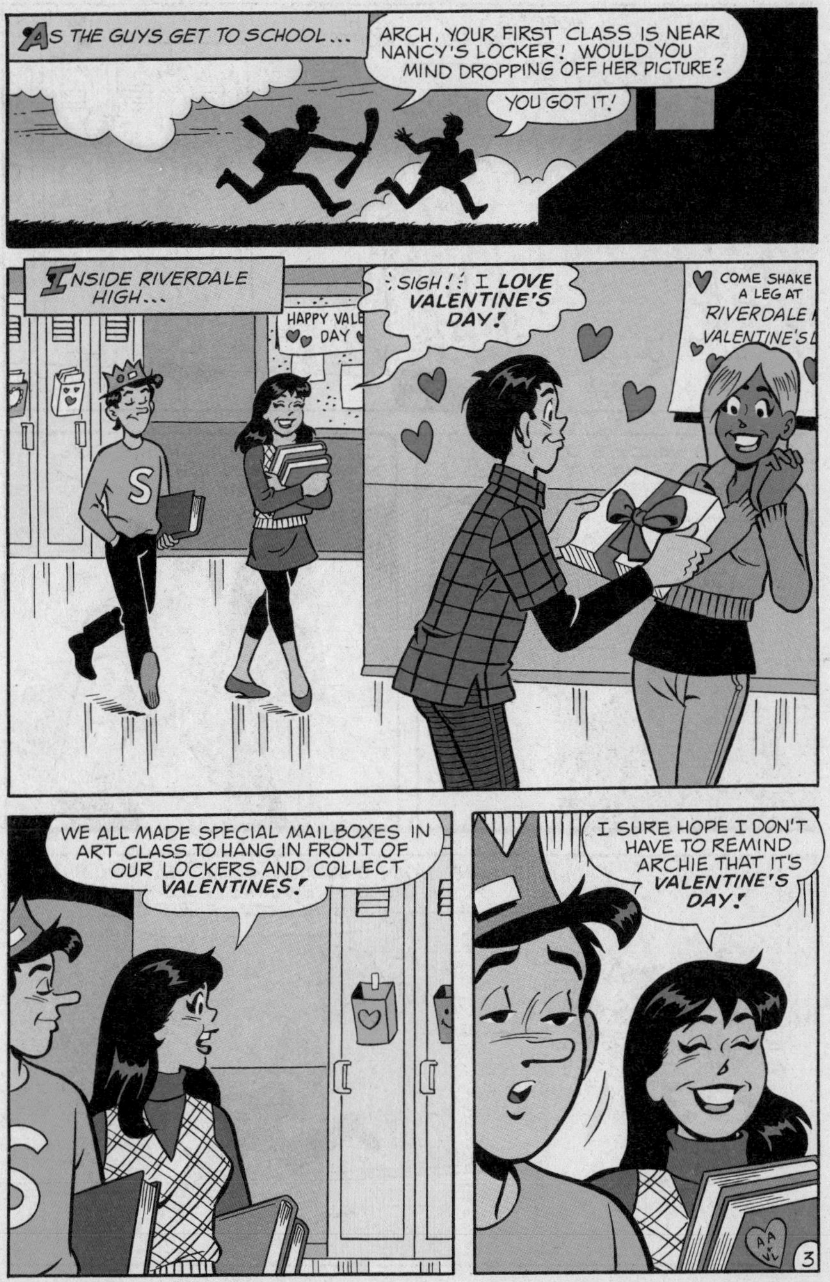
AS THE GUYS GET TO SCHOOL...
ARCH, YOUR FIRST CLASS IS NEAR NANCY'S LOCKER! WOULD YOU MIND DROPPING OFF HER PICTURE?
YOU GOT IT!
INSIDE RIVERDALE HIGH...
HAPPY VALE DAY
SIGH! I LOVE VALENTINE'S DAY!
COME SHAKE A LEG AT RIVERDALE VALENTINE'S
WE ALL MADE SPECIAL MAILBOXES IN ART CLASS TO HANG IN FRONT OF OUR LOCKERS AND COLLECT VALENTINES!
I SURE HOPE I DON'T HAVE TO REMIND ARCHIE THAT IT'S VALENTINE'S DAY!
3

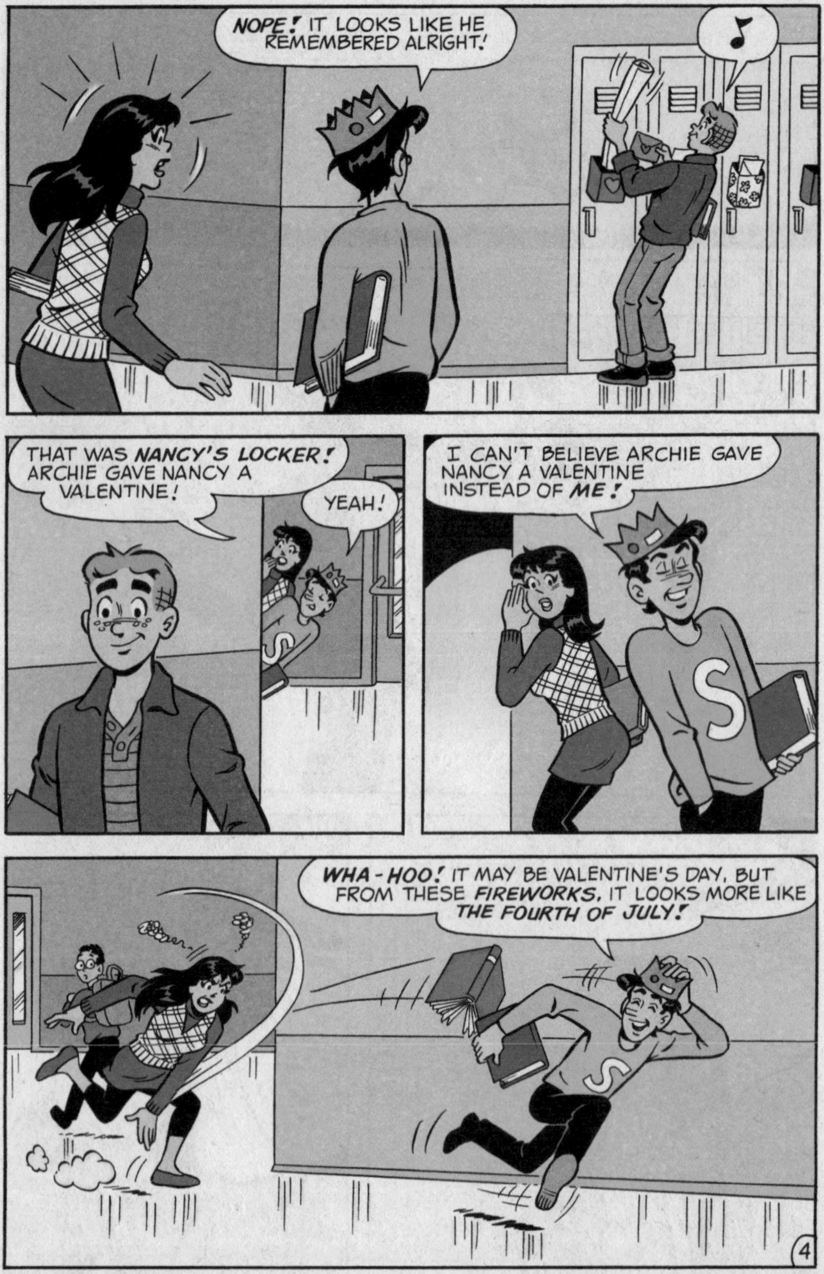
NOPE! IT LOOKS LIKE HE REMEMBERED ALRIGHT!
THAT WAS NANCY'S LOCKER! ARCHIE GAVE NANCY A VALENTINE!
YEAH!
I CAN'T BELIEVE ARCHIE GAVE NANCY A VALENTINE INSTEAD OF ME!
WHA-HOO! IT MAY BE VALENTINE'S DAY, BUT FROM THESE FIREWORKS, IT LOOKS MORE LIKE THE FOURTH OF JULY!
4

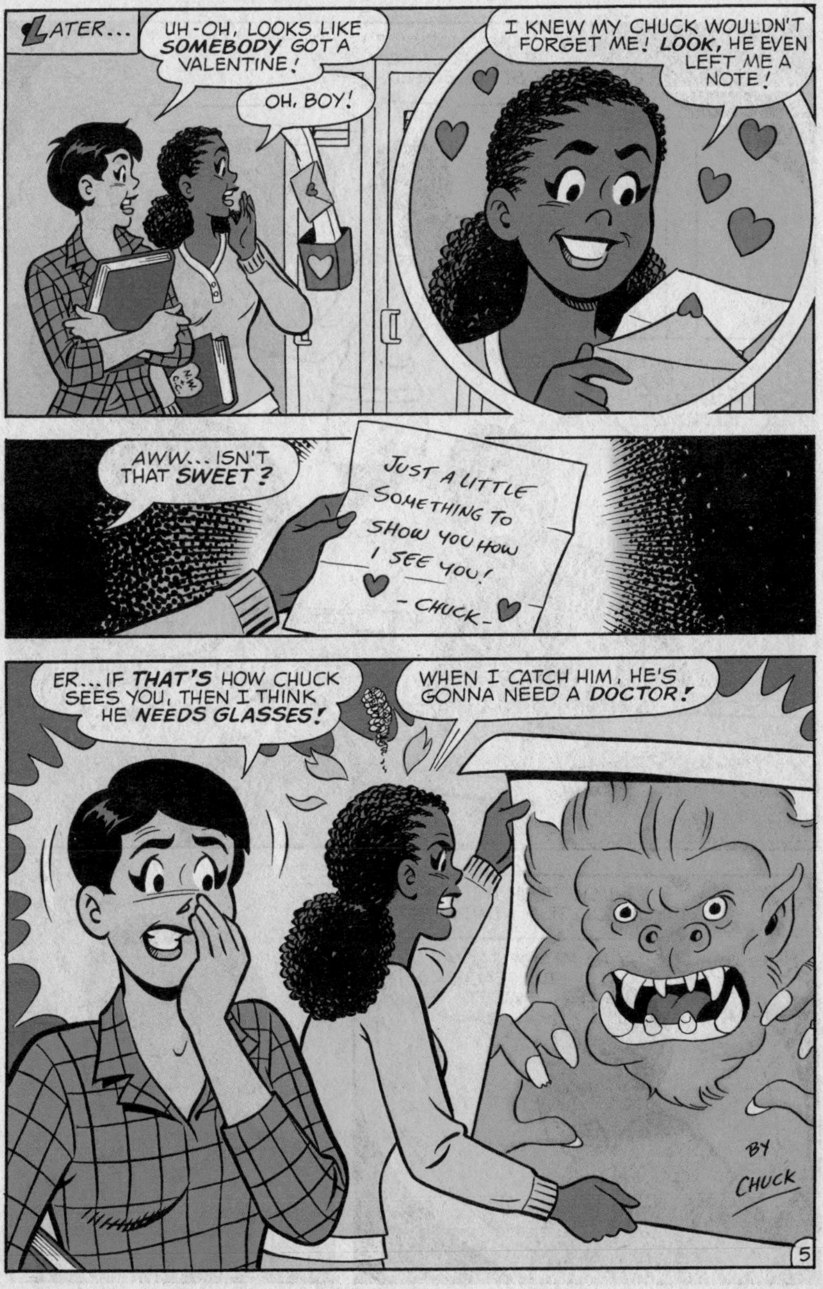
LATER...
UH-OH, LOOKS LIKE SOMEBODY GOT A VALENTINE!
OH, BOY!
I KNEW MY CHUCK WOULDN'T FORGET ME! LOOK, HE EVEN LEFT ME A NOTE!
AWW... ISN'T THAT SWEET?
JUST A LITTLE SOMETHING TO SHOW YOU HOW I SEE YOU! -CHUCK-
ER... IF THAT'S HOW CHUCK SEES YOU, THEN I THINK HE NEEDS GLASSES!
WHEN I CATCH HIM, HE'S GONNA NEED A DOCTOR!
BY CHUCK
5

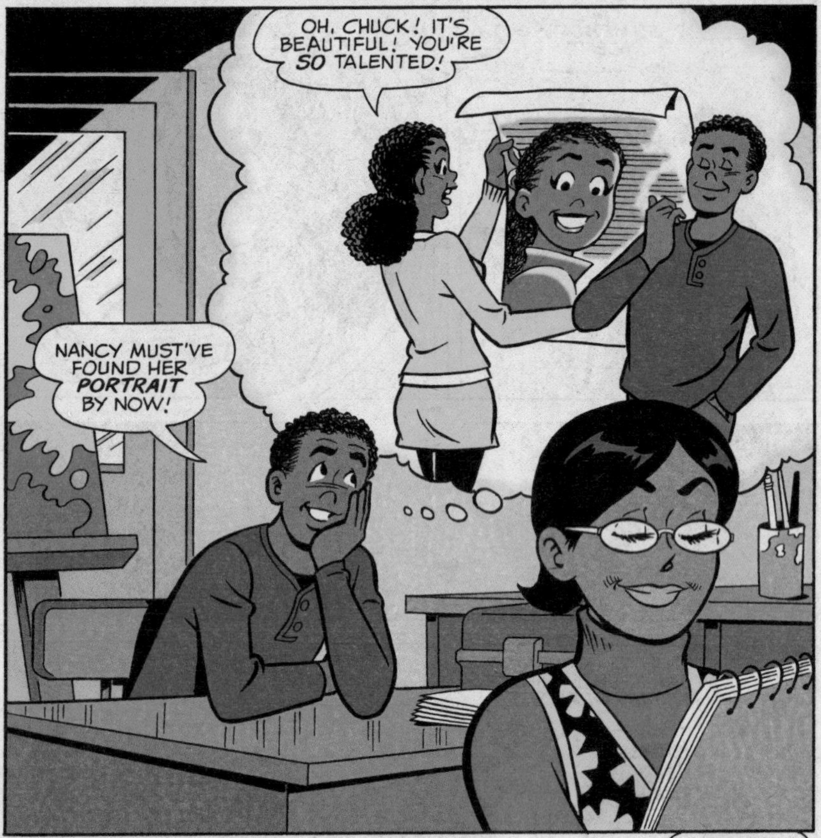
OH, CHUCK! IT'S BEAUTIFUL! YOU'RE SO TALENTED!
NANCY MUST'VE FOUND HER PORTRAIT BY NOW!

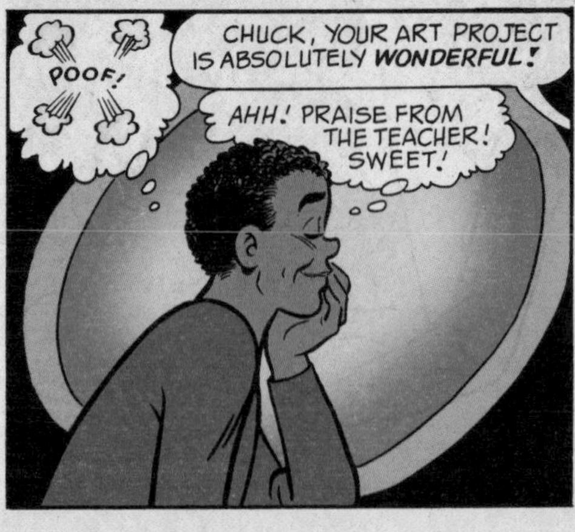
POOF!
CHUCK, YOUR ART PROJECT IS ABSOLUTELY WONDERFUL!
AHH! PRAISE FROM THE TEACHER! SWEET!

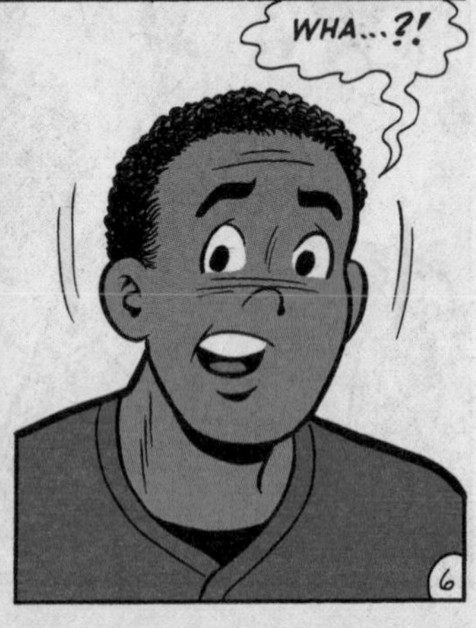
WHA...?!
6

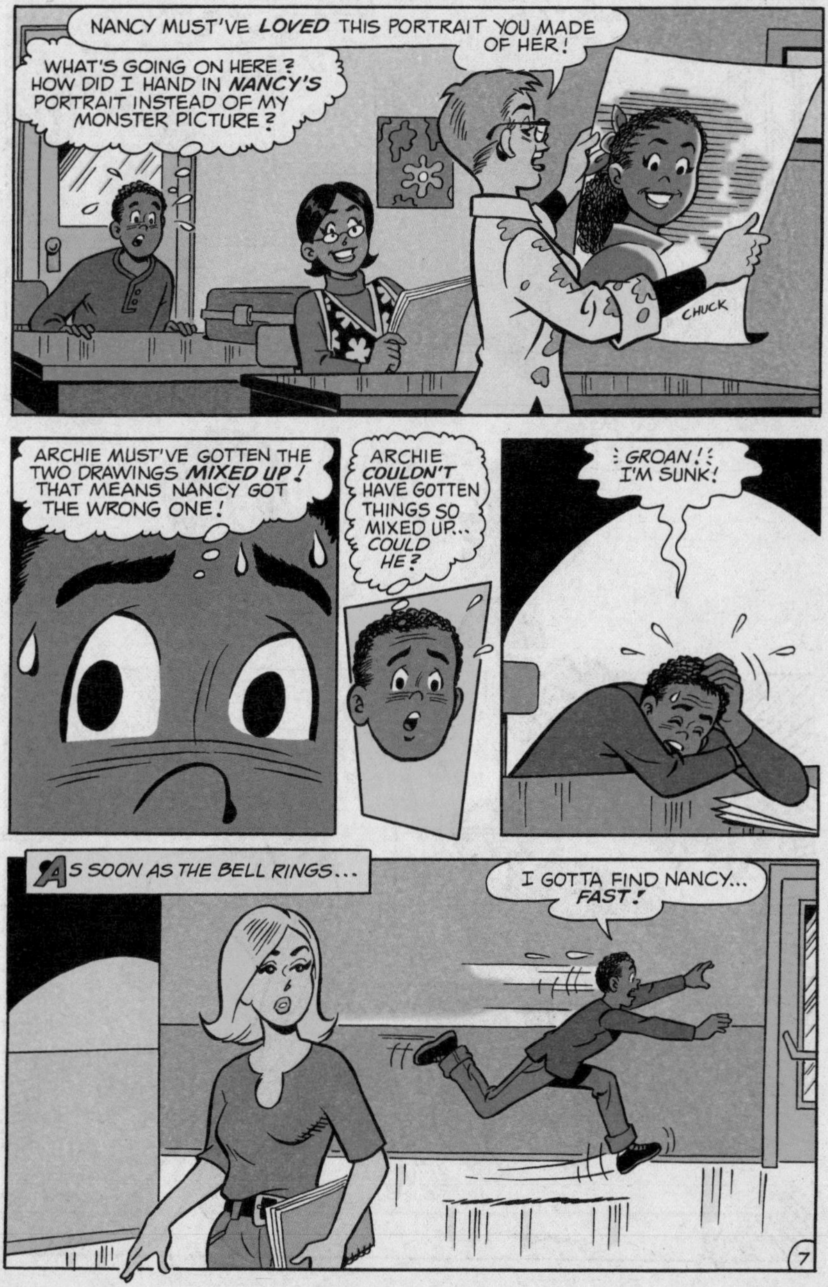
NANCY MUST'VE **LOVED** THIS PORTRAIT YOU MADE OF HER!
WHAT'S GOING ON HERE? HOW DID I HAND IN **NANCY'S** PORTRAIT INSTEAD OF MY MONSTER PICTURE?
CHUCK
ARCHIE MUST'VE GOTTEN THE TWO DRAWINGS **MIXED UP!** THAT MEANS NANCY GOT THE WRONG ONE!
ARCHIE **COULDN'T** HAVE GOTTEN THINGS SO MIXED UP... COULD HE?
GROAN! I'M SUNK!
AS SOON AS THE BELL RINGS...
I GOTTA FIND NANCY... **FAST!**
7

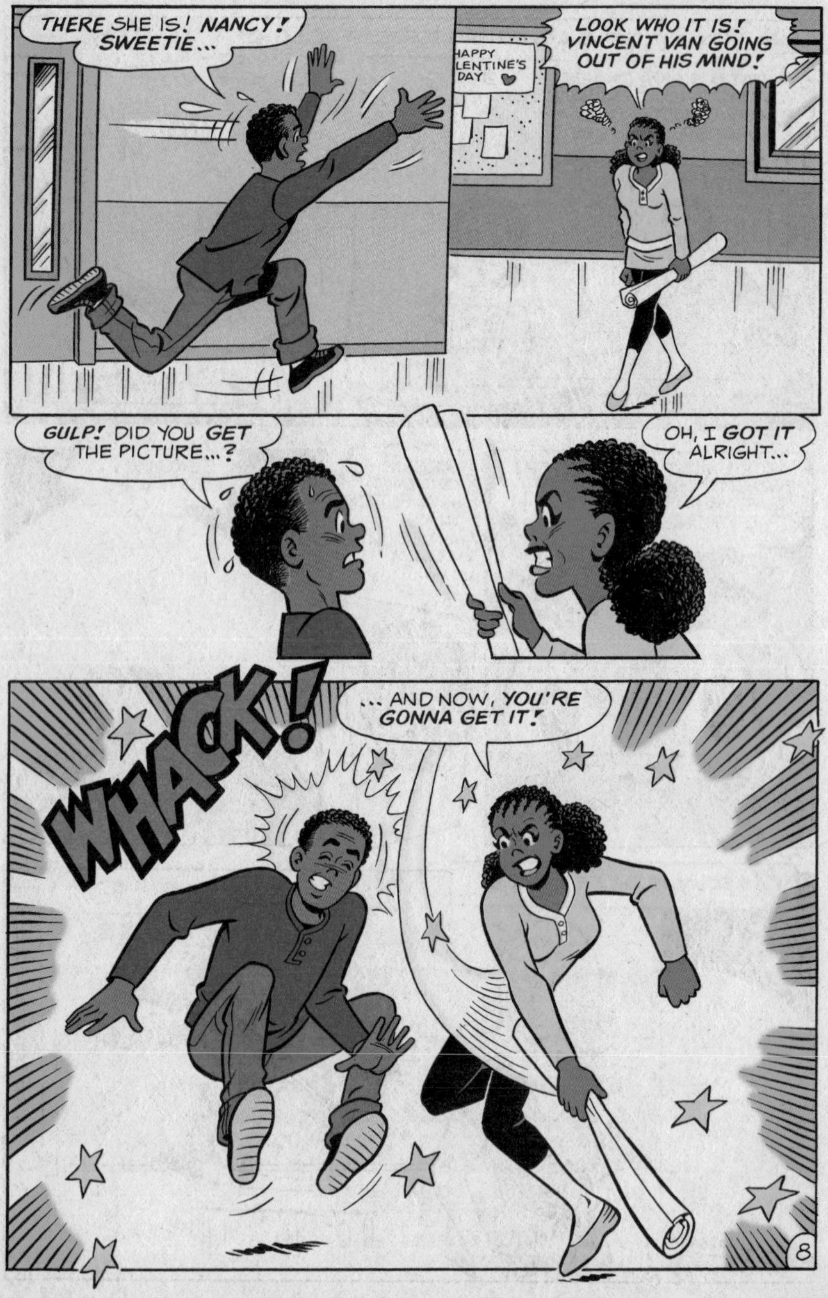
THERE SHE IS! NANCY! SWEETIE...
HAPPY VALENTINE'S DAY
LOOK WHO IT IS! VINCENT VAN GOING OUT OF HIS MIND!
GULP! DID YOU GET THE PICTURE...?
OH, I GOT IT ALRIGHT...
WHACK!
... AND NOW, YOU'RE GONNA GET IT!
8

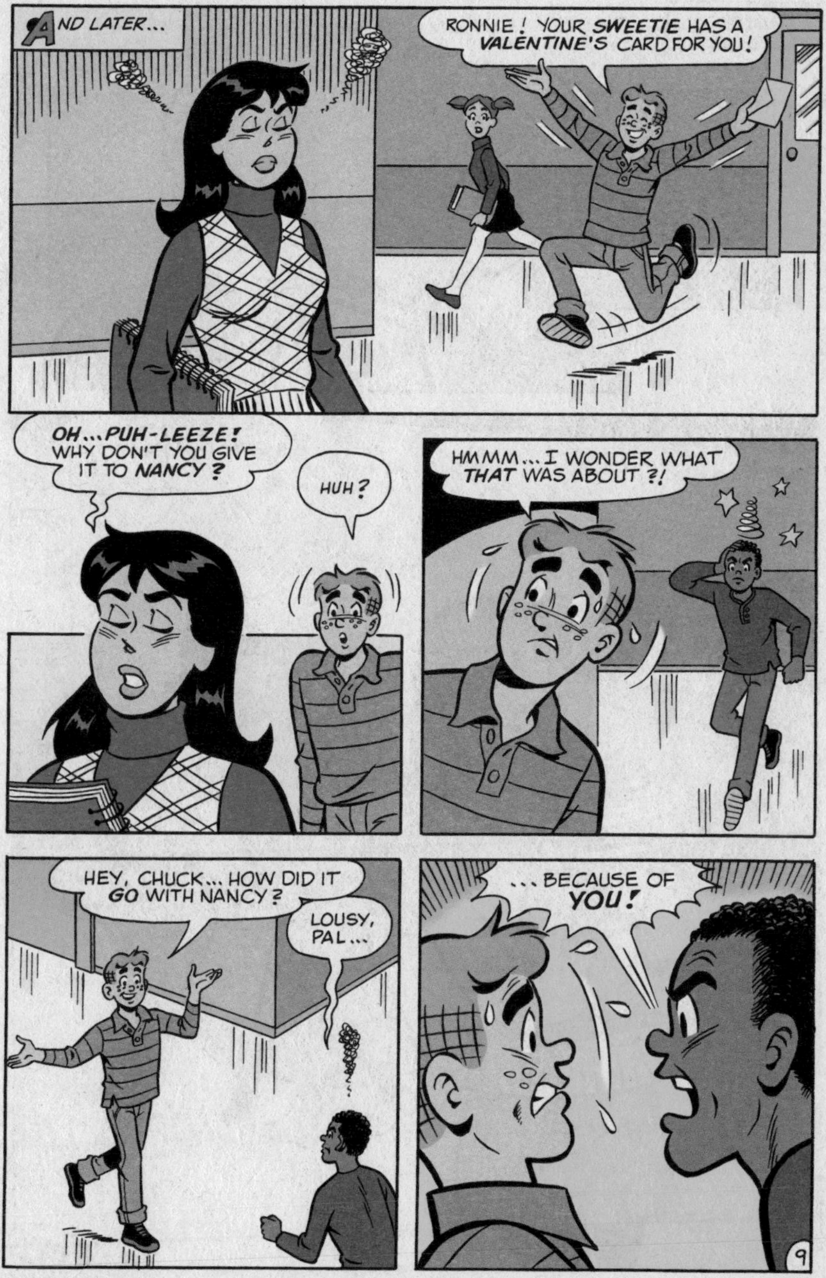
AND LATER...
RONNIE! YOUR SWEETIE HAS A VALENTINE'S CARD FOR YOU!
OH...PUH-LEEZE! WHY DON'T YOU GIVE IT TO NANCY?
HUH?
HMMM...I WONDER WHAT THAT WAS ABOUT?!
HEY, CHUCK... HOW DID IT GO WITH NANCY?
LOUSY, PAL...
...BECAUSE OF YOU!
9

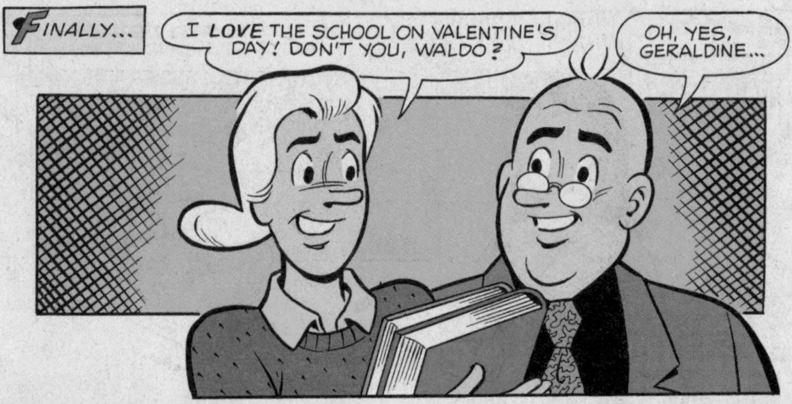
FINALLY...
I LOVE THE SCHOOL ON VALENTINE'S DAY! DON'T YOU, WALDO?
OH, YES, GERALDINE...

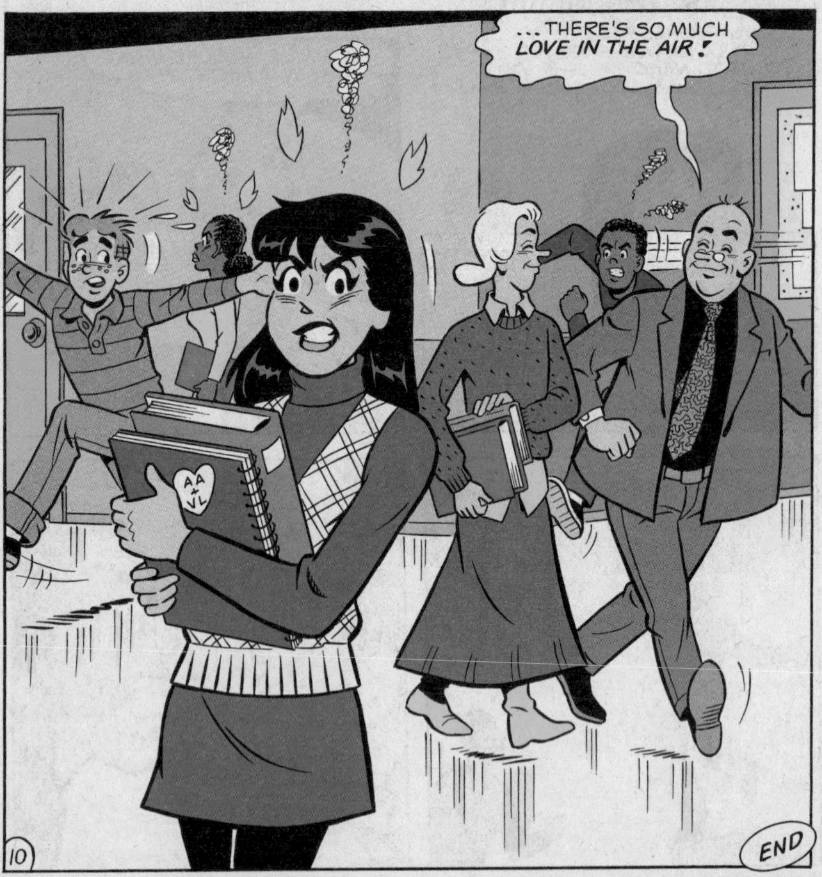
...THERE'S SO MUCH LOVE IN THE AIR!
AA + VL
10
END

Archie in "GOING BUGGY"

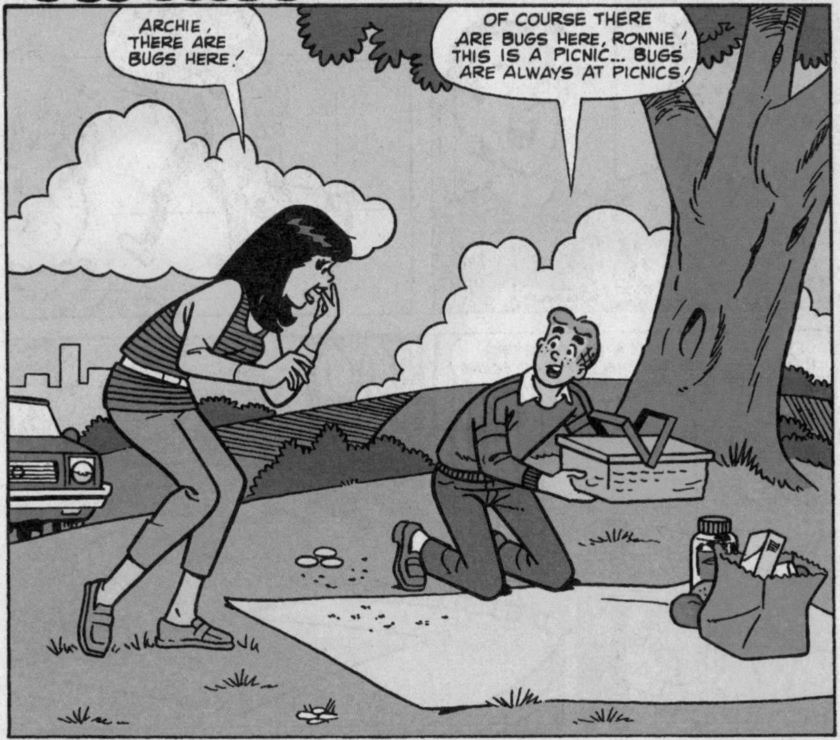
ARCHIE, THERE ARE BUGS HERE!
OF COURSE THERE ARE BUGS HERE, RONNIE! THIS IS A PICNIC... BUGS ARE ALWAYS AT PICNICS!

Script: Jim Ruth / Pencils: Dan DeCarlo Jr. / Inks: Jimmy DeCarlo / Letters: Bill Yoshida / Colors: Barry Grossman

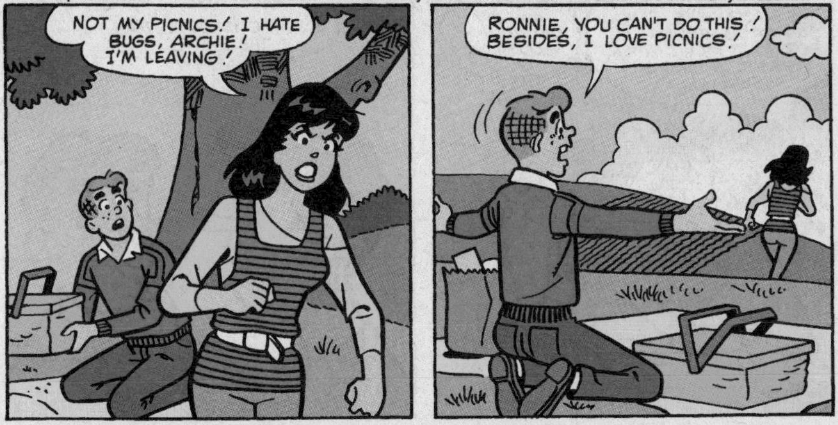
NOT MY PICNICS! I HATE BUGS, ARCHIE! I'M LEAVING!
RONNIE, YOU CAN'T DO THIS! BESIDES, I LOVE PICNICS!

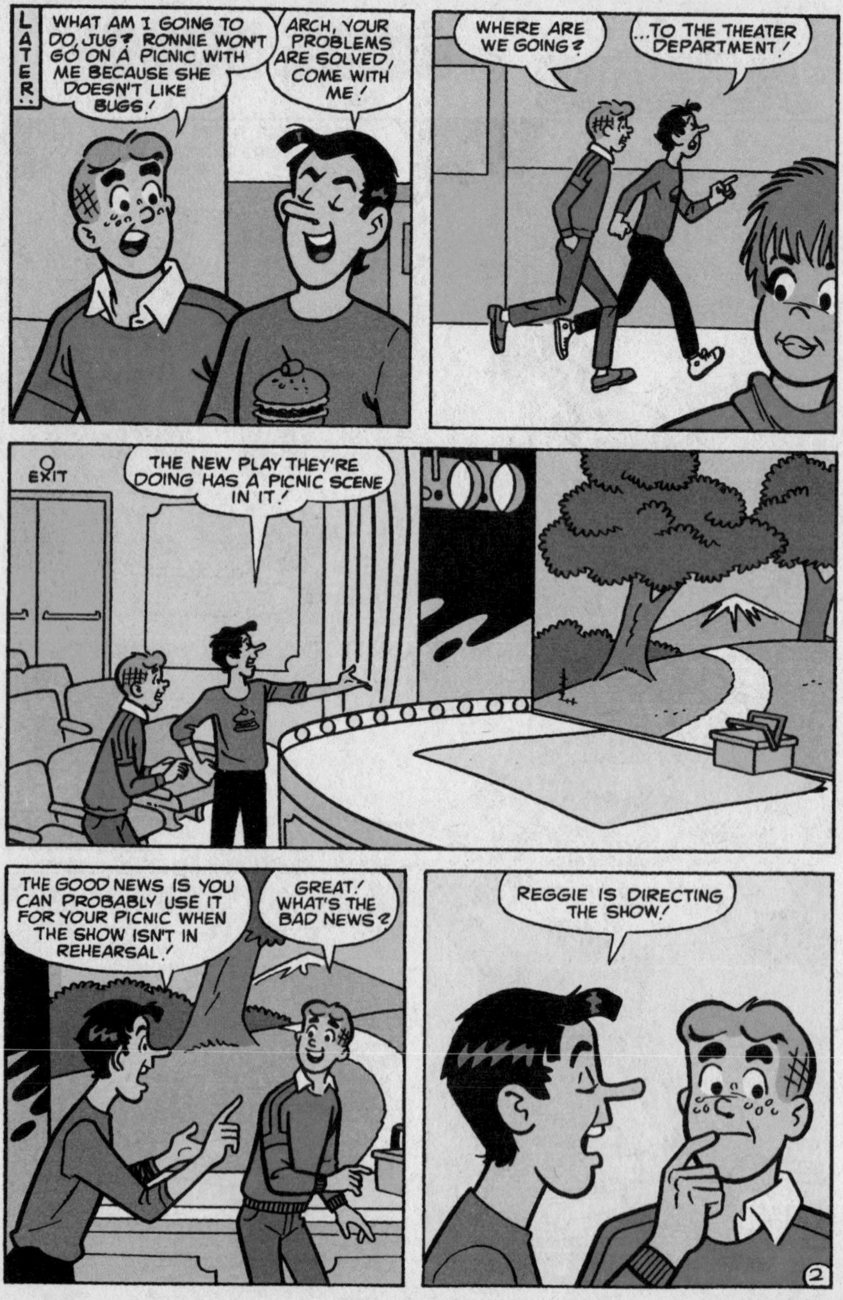
LATER..
WHAT AM I GOING TO DO, JUG? RONNIE WON'T GO ON A PICNIC WITH ME BECAUSE SHE DOESN'T LIKE BUGS!
ARCH, YOUR PROBLEMS ARE SOLVED, COME WITH ME!
WHERE ARE WE GOING?
...TO THE THEATER DEPARTMENT!
EXIT
THE NEW PLAY THEY'RE DOING HAS A PICNIC SCENE IN IT!
THE GOOD NEWS IS YOU CAN PROBABLY USE IT FOR YOUR PICNIC WHEN THE SHOW ISN'T IN REHEARSAL!
GREAT! WHAT'S THE BAD NEWS?
REGGIE IS DIRECTING THE SHOW!
2

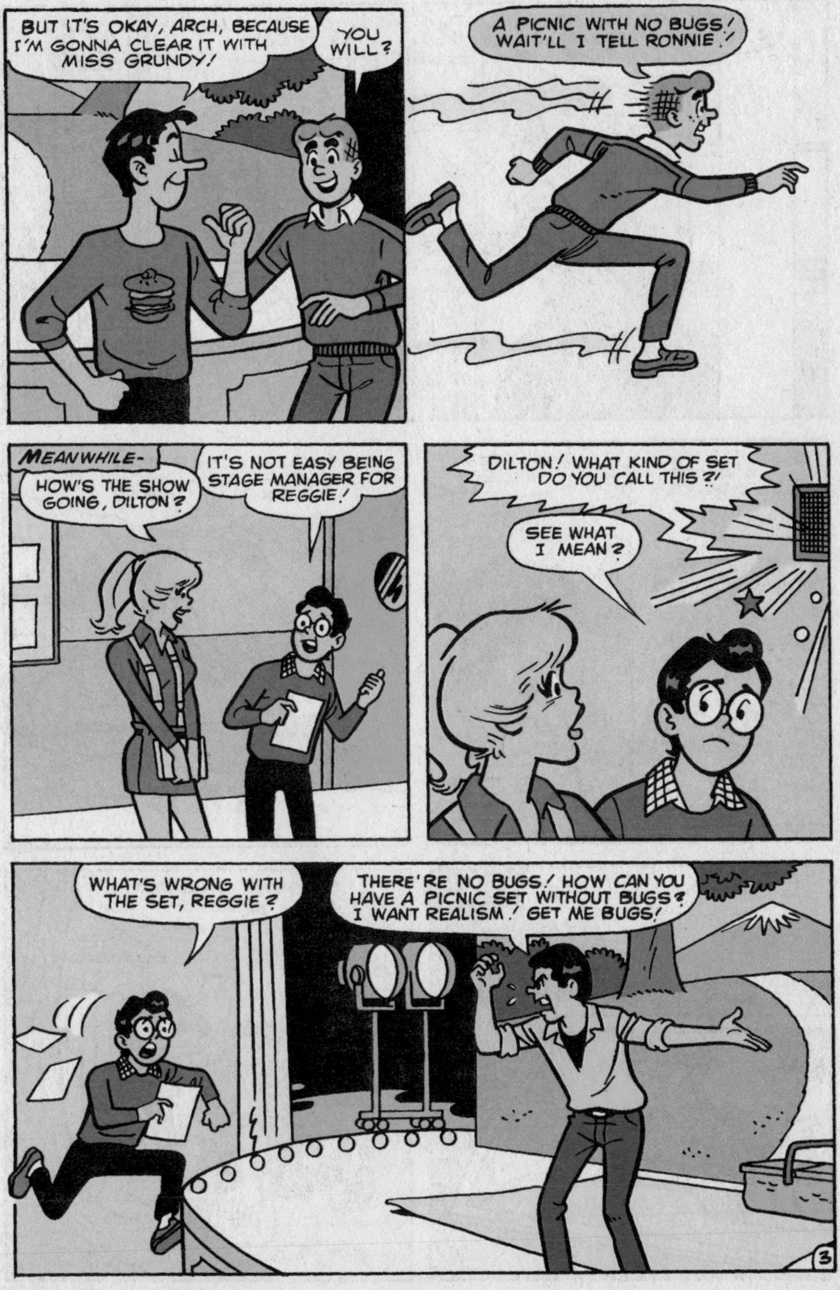
BUT IT'S OKAY, ARCH, BECAUSE I'M GONNA CLEAR IT WITH MISS GRUNDY!
YOU WILL?
A PICNIC WITH NO BUGS! WAIT'LL I TELL RONNIE!
MEANWHILE-
HOW'S THE SHOW GOING, DILTON?
IT'S NOT EASY BEING STAGE MANAGER FOR REGGIE!
DILTON! WHAT KIND OF SET DO YOU CALL THIS?!
SEE WHAT I MEAN?
WHAT'S WRONG WITH THE SET, REGGIE?
THERE'RE NO BUGS! HOW CAN YOU HAVE A PICNIC SET WITHOUT BUGS? I WANT REALISM! GET ME BUGS!
3

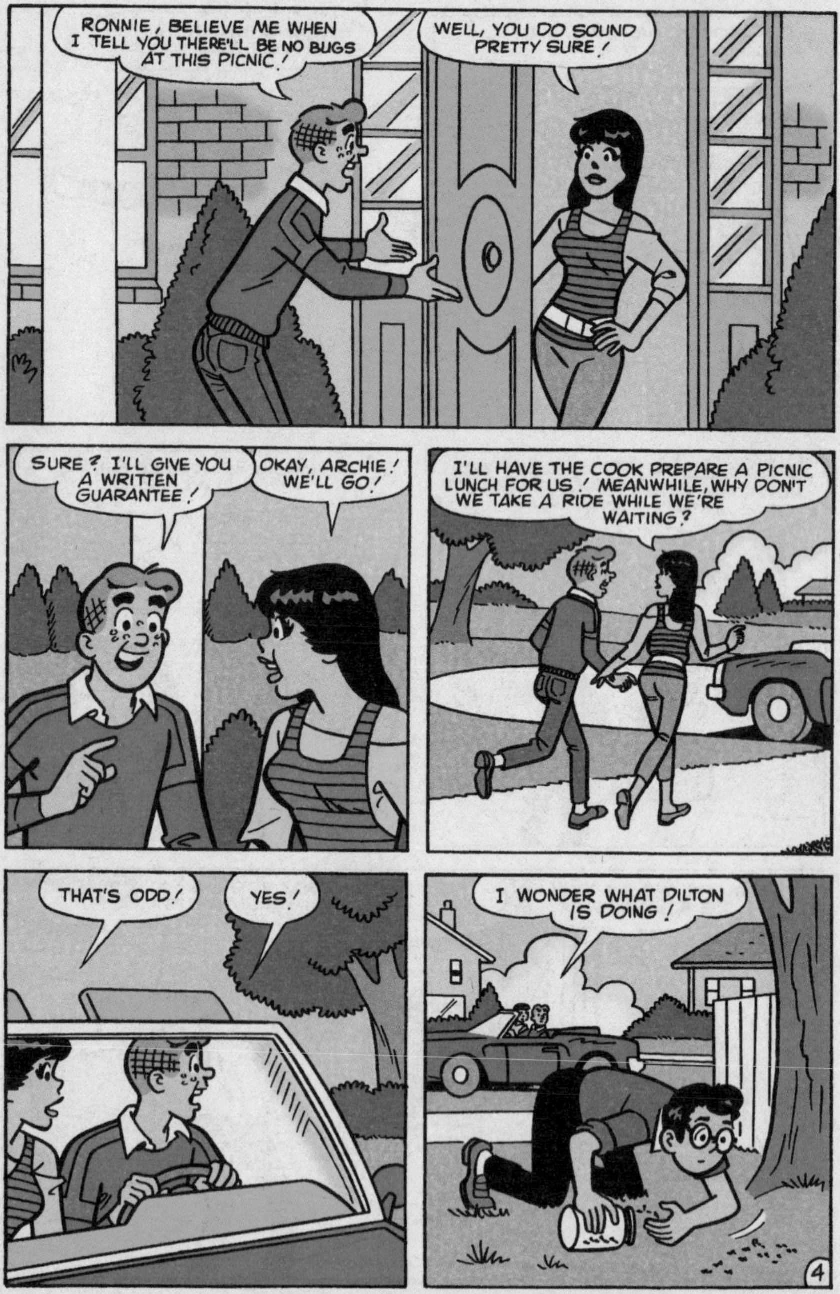
RONNIE, BELIEVE ME WHEN I TELL YOU THERE'LL BE NO BUGS AT THIS PICNIC!
WELL, YOU DO SOUND PRETTY SURE!
SURE? I'LL GIVE YOU A WRITTEN GUARANTEE!
OKAY, ARCHIE! WE'LL GO!
I'LL HAVE THE COOK PREPARE A PICNIC LUNCH FOR US! MEANWHILE, WHY DON'T WE TAKE A RIDE WHILE WE'RE WAITING?
THAT'S ODD!
YES!
I WONDER WHAT DILTON IS DOING!
4

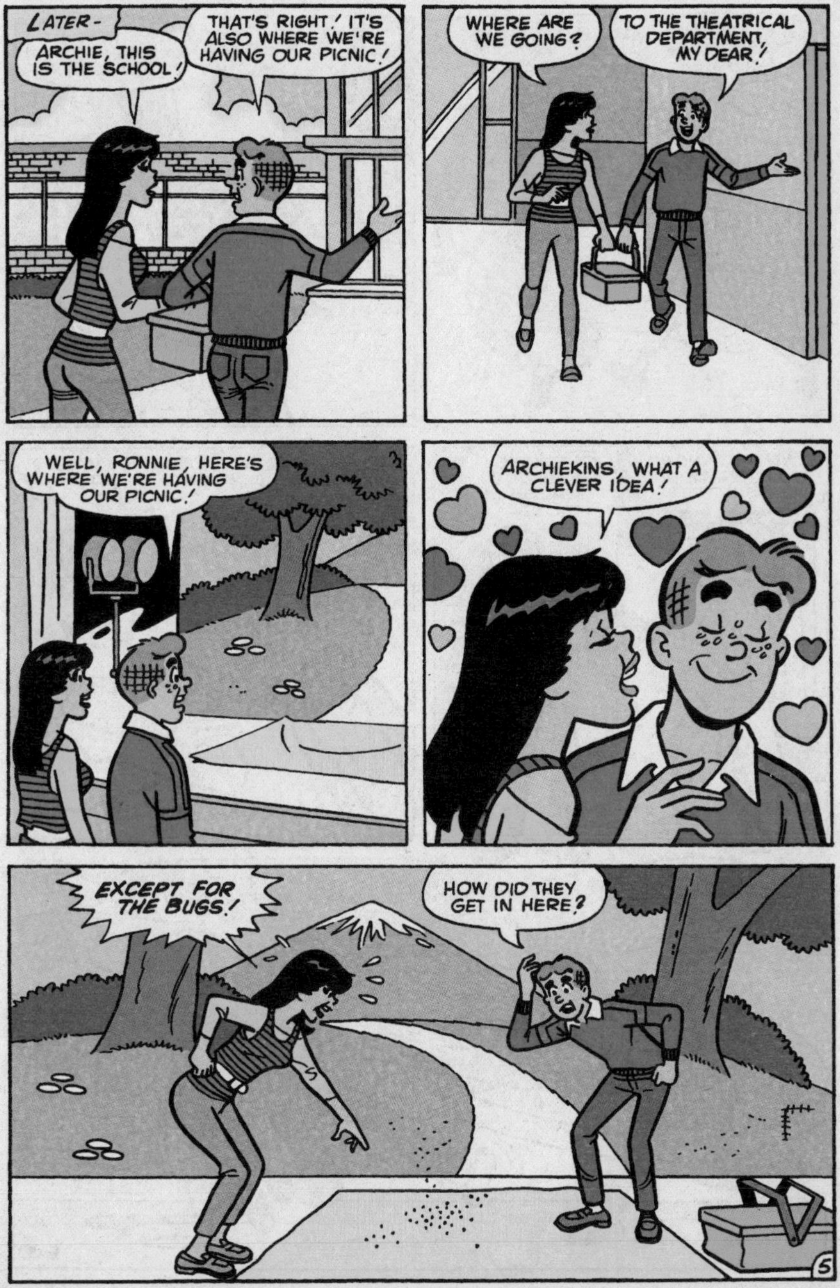
LATER-
ARCHIE, THIS IS THE SCHOOL!
THAT'S RIGHT! IT'S ALSO WHERE WE'RE HAVING OUR PICNIC!
WHERE ARE WE GOING?
TO THE THEATRICAL DEPARTMENT, MY DEAR!
WELL, RONNIE, HERE'S WHERE WE'RE HAVING OUR PICNIC!
ARCHIEKINS, WHAT A CLEVER IDEA!
EXCEPT FOR THE BUGS!
HOW DID THEY GET IN HERE?
5

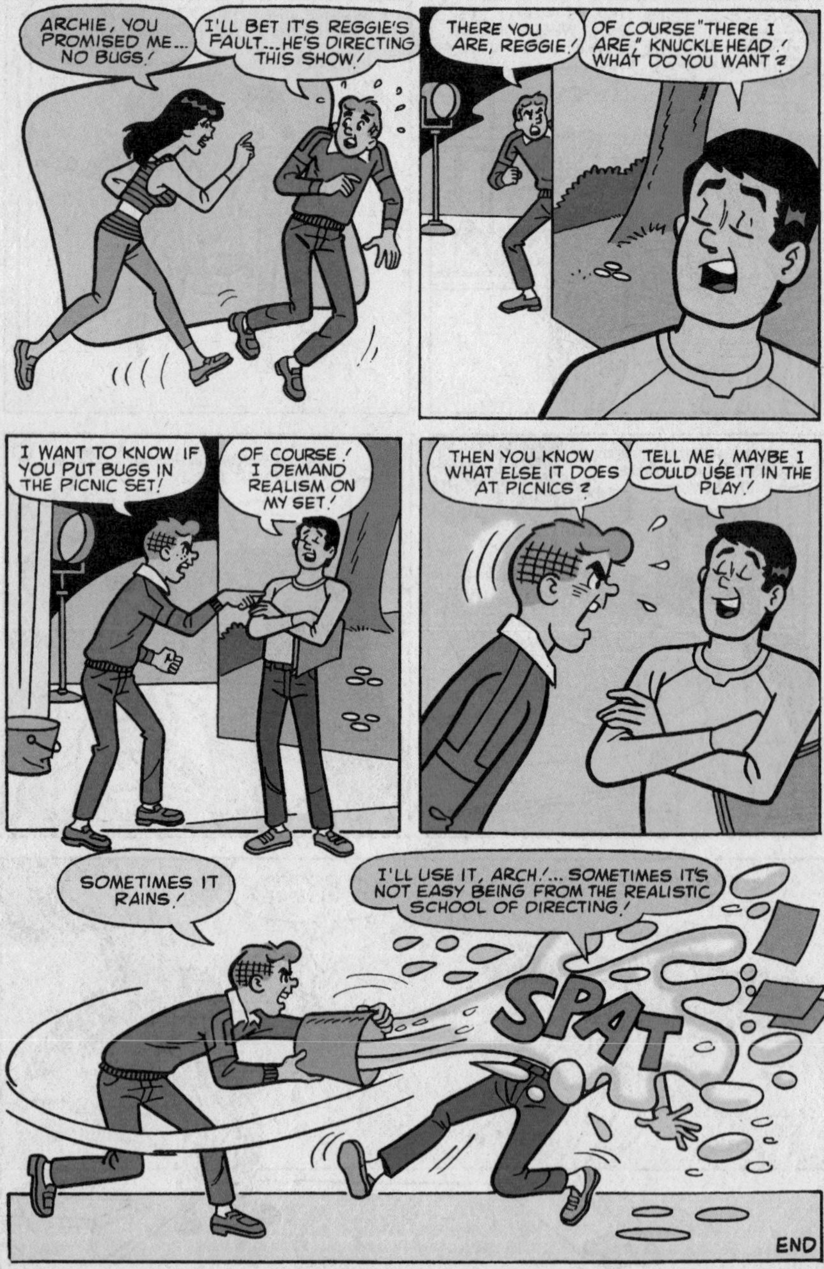
ARCHIE, YOU PROMISED ME... NO BUGS!
I'LL BET IT'S REGGIE'S FAULT... HE'S DIRECTING THIS SHOW!
THERE YOU ARE, REGGIE!
OF COURSE "THERE I ARE," KNUCKLEHEAD! WHAT DO YOU WANT?
I WANT TO KNOW IF YOU PUT BUGS IN THE PICNIC SET!
OF COURSE! I DEMAND REALISM ON MY SET!
THEN YOU KNOW WHAT ELSE IT DOES AT PICNICS?
TELL ME, MAYBE I COULD USE IT IN THE PLAY!
SOMETIMES IT RAINS!
I'LL USE IT, ARCH!... SOMETIMES IT'S NOT EASY BEING FROM THE REALISTIC SCHOOL OF DIRECTING!
SPAT
END

Not So Perfect Date
Archie & Friends #76, December 2003
Mike Pellowski, Rex Lindsey, Rich
Koslowski, Bill Yoshida
and Barry Grossman

It's Moose and Midge's anniversary, and
the big fella has special plans for a romantic date
with his lady to celebrate. The trouble is that his
temper and clumsiness soon get in the way and
the only flirting going on during the couple's
night out is with disaster.

Odd Ball
Archie #130, August 1962
Frank Doyle and Harry Lucey

Ever out to monopolize Veronica for
himself, Reggie tricks Archie into volunteering
as ticket taker at the school dance. But a duped
Archie won't be kept down for long, and he's
determined to share Veronica's "last dance"!

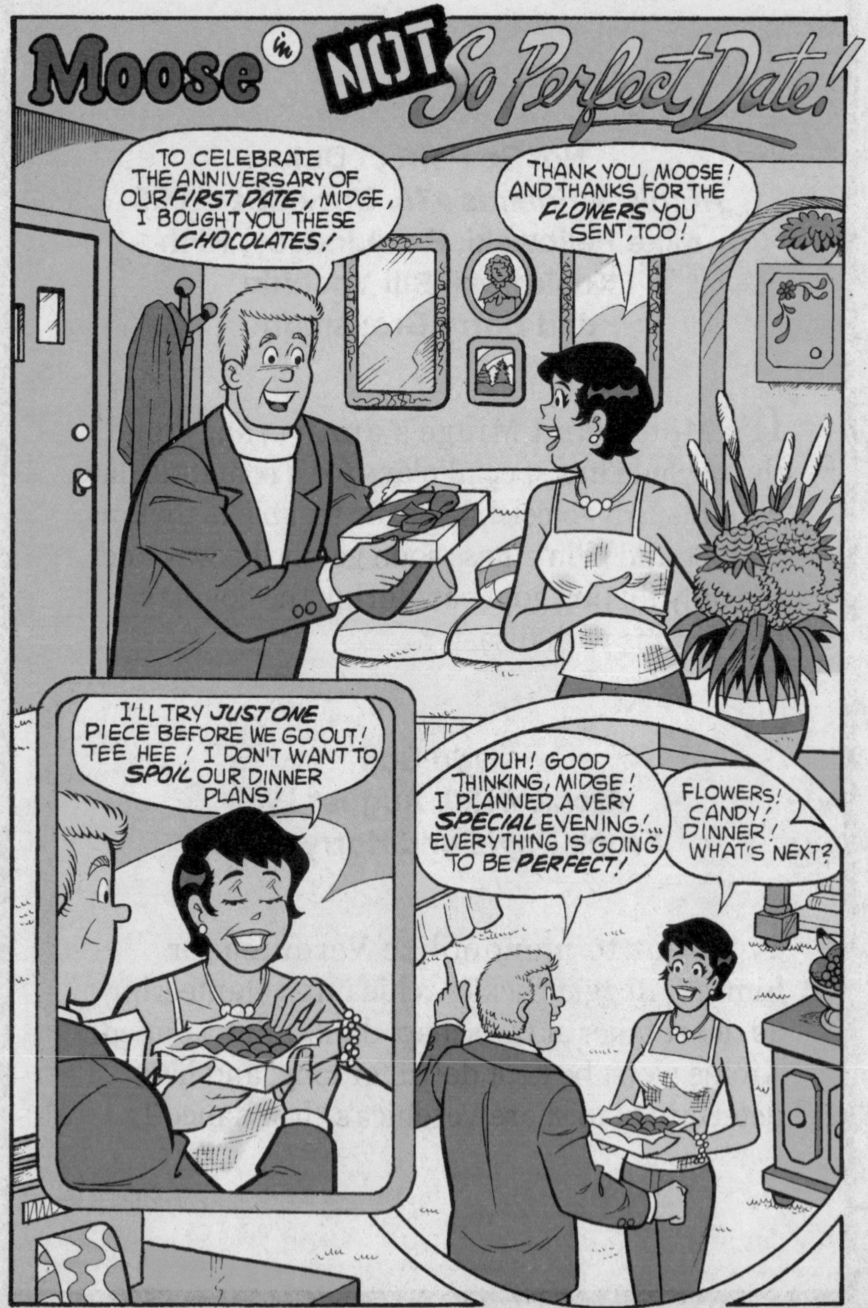
Moose in NOT So Perfect Date!
TO CELEBRATE THE ANNIVERSARY OF OUR FIRST DATE, MIDGE, I BOUGHT YOU THESE CHOCOLATES!
THANK YOU, MOOSE! AND THANKS FOR THE FLOWERS YOU SENT, TOO!
I'LL TRY JUST ONE PIECE BEFORE WE GO OUT! TEE HEE! I DON'T WANT TO SPOIL OUR DINNER PLANS!
DUH! GOOD THINKING, MIDGE! I PLANNED A VERY SPECIAL EVENING!... EVERYTHING IS GOING TO BE PERFECT!
FLOWERS! CANDY! DINNER! WHAT'S NEXT?

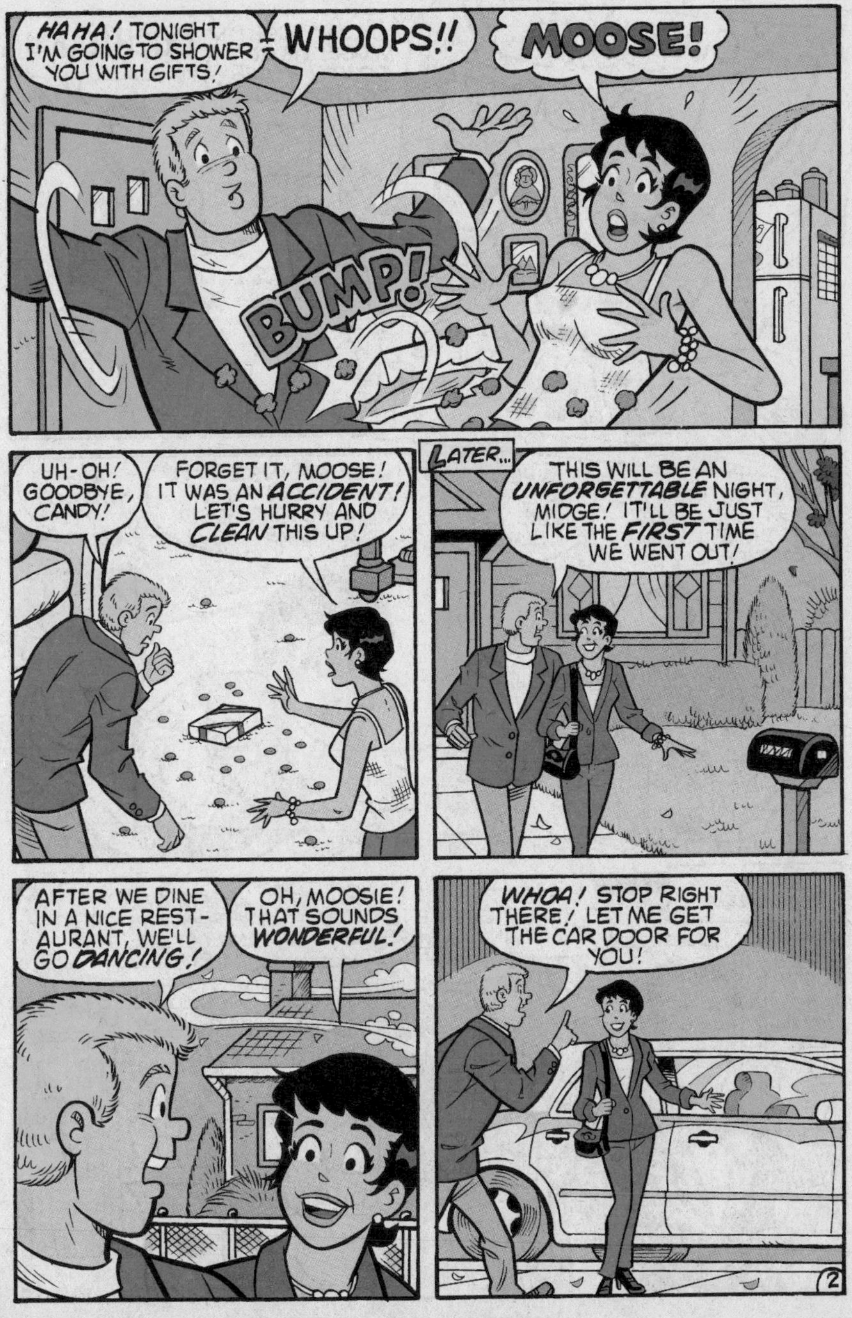
HA HA! TONIGHT I'M GOING TO SHOWER YOU WITH GIFTS!
WHOOPS!!
MOOSE!
BUMP!
UH-OH! GOODBYE, CANDY!
FORGET IT, MOOSE! IT WAS AN ACCIDENT! LET'S HURRY AND CLEAN THIS UP!
LATER...
THIS WILL BE AN UNFORGETTABLE NIGHT, MIDGE! IT'LL BE JUST LIKE THE FIRST TIME WE WENT OUT!
AFTER WE DINE IN A NICE REST-AURANT, WE'LL GO DANCING!
OH, MOOSIE! THAT SOUNDS WONDERFUL!
WHOA! STOP RIGHT THERE! LET ME GET THE CAR DOOR FOR YOU!
2

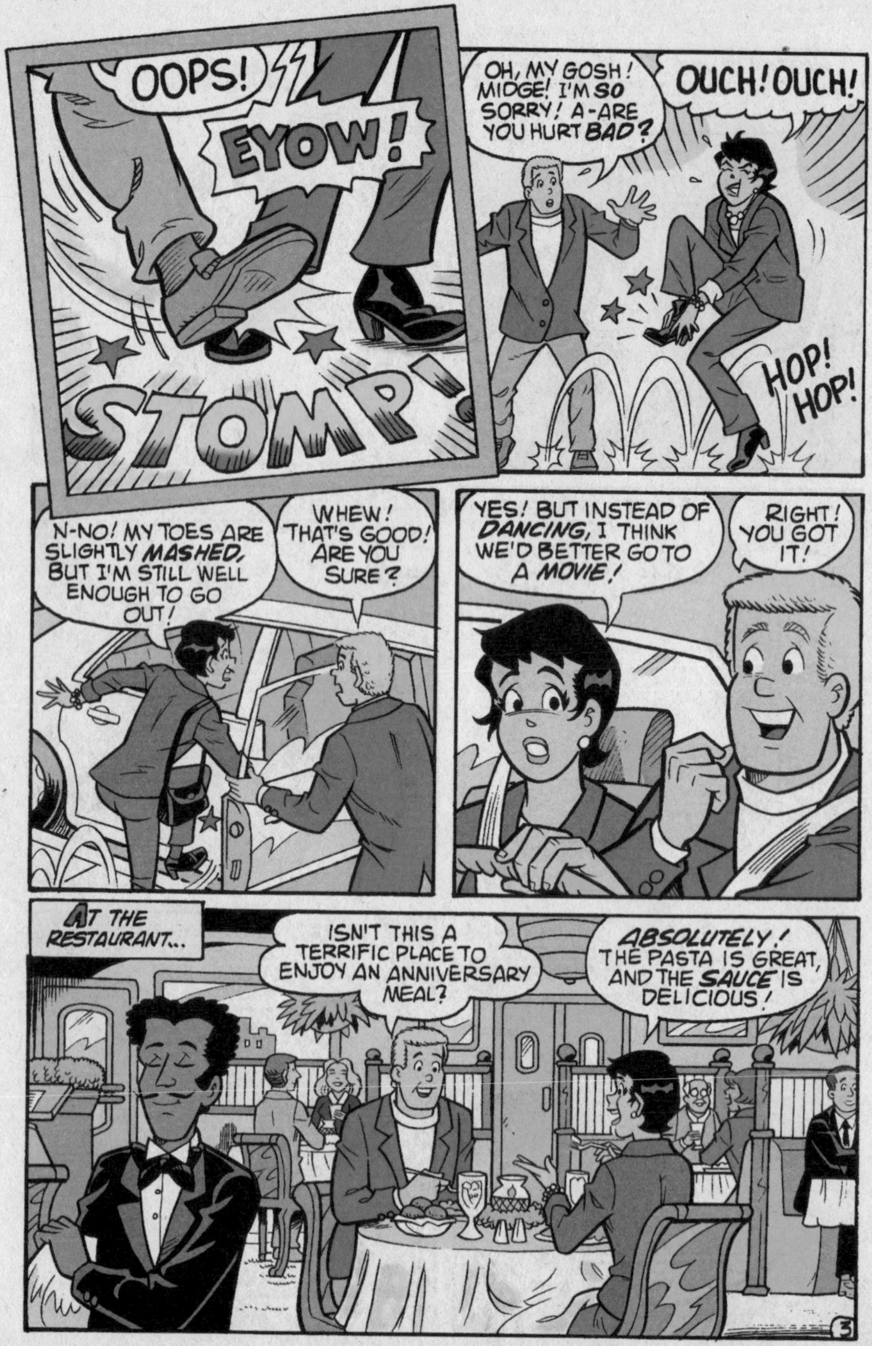
OOPS!
EYOW!
STOMP!
OH, MY GOSH! MIDGE! I'M SO SORRY! A-ARE YOU HURT BAD?
OUCH! OUCH!
HOP! HOP!
N-NO! MY TOES ARE SLIGHTLY MASHED, BUT I'M STILL WELL ENOUGH TO GO OUT!
WHEW! THAT'S GOOD! ARE YOU SURE?
YES! BUT INSTEAD OF DANCING, I THINK WE'D BETTER GO TO A MOVIE!
RIGHT! YOU GOT IT!
AT THE RESTAURANT...
ISN'T THIS A TERRIFIC PLACE TO ENJOY AN ANNIVERSARY MEAL?
ABSOLUTELY! THE PASTA IS GREAT, AND THE SAUCE IS DELICIOUS!
3

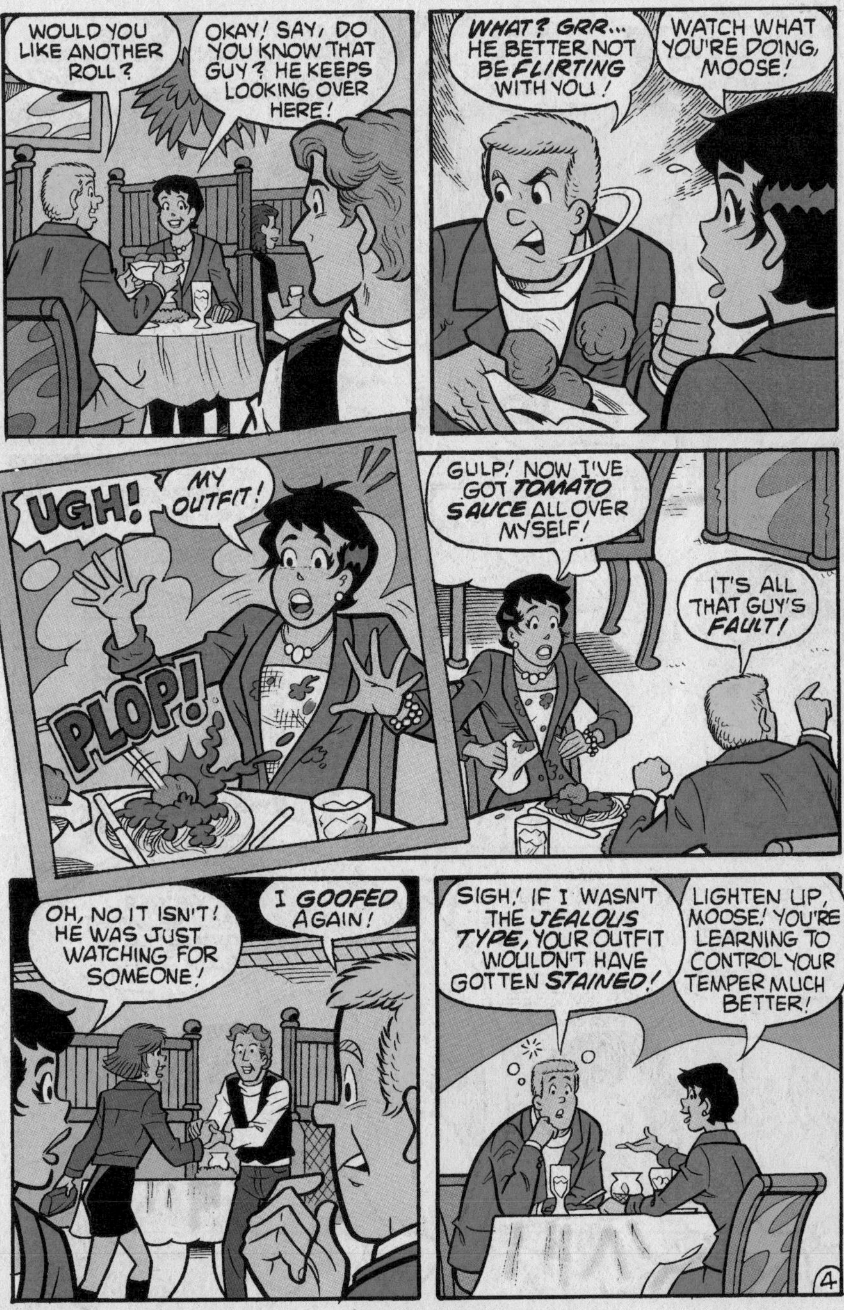
WOULD YOU LIKE ANOTHER ROLL?
OKAY! SAY, DO YOU KNOW THAT GUY? HE KEEPS LOOKING OVER HERE!
WHAT? GRR... HE BETTER NOT BE FLIRTING WITH YOU!
WATCH WHAT YOU'RE DOING, MOOSE!
UGH!
MY OUTFIT!
PLOP!
GULP! NOW I'VE GOT TOMATO SAUCE ALL OVER MYSELF!
IT'S ALL THAT GUY'S FAULT!
OH, NO IT ISN'T! HE WAS JUST WATCHING FOR SOMEONE!
I GOOFED AGAIN!
SIGH! IF I WASN'T THE JEALOUS TYPE, YOUR OUTFIT WOULDN'T HAVE GOTTEN STAINED!
LIGHTEN UP, MOOSE! YOU'RE LEARNING TO CONTROL YOUR TEMPER MUCH BETTER!
4

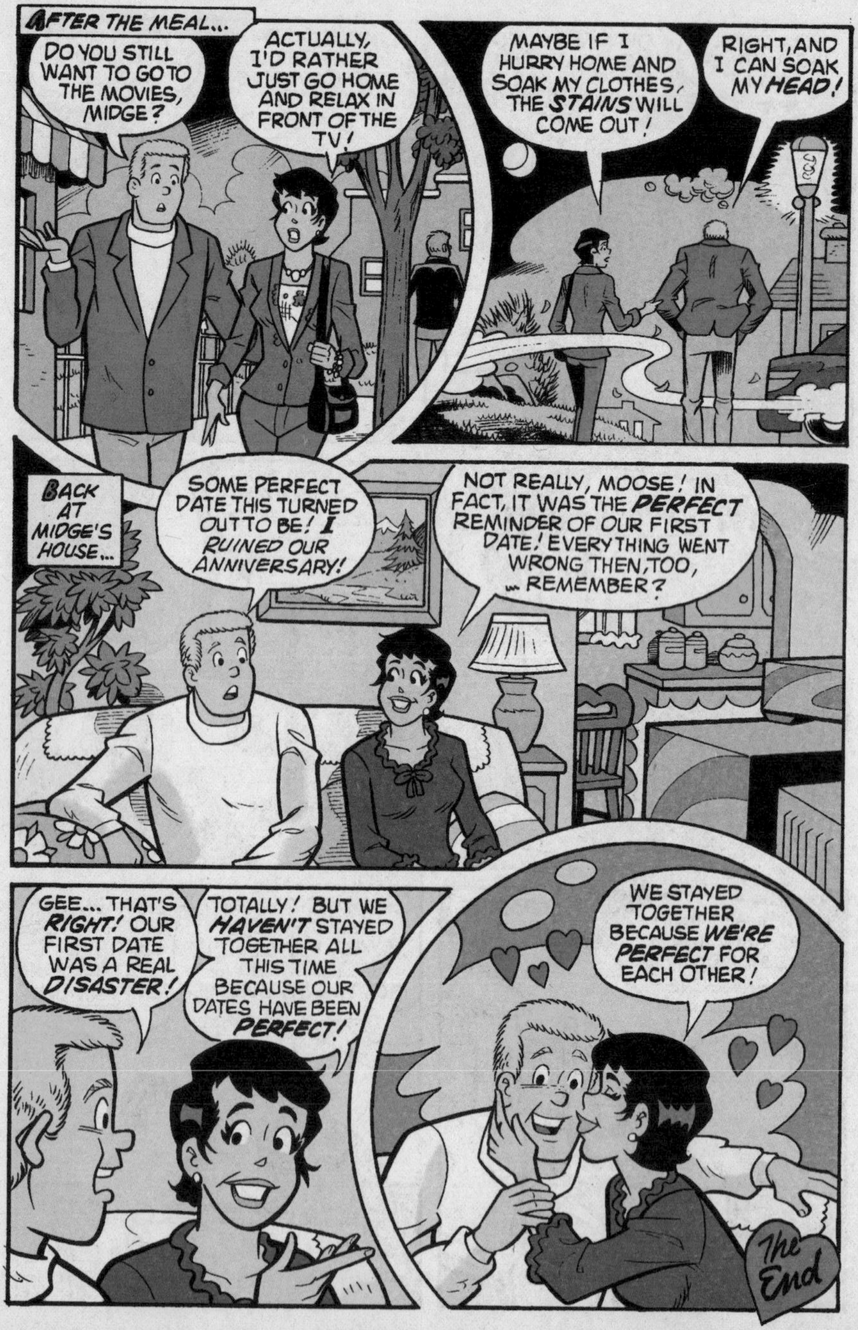
AFTER THE MEAL...
DO YOU STILL WANT TO GO TO THE MOVIES, MIDGE?
ACTUALLY, I'D RATHER JUST GO HOME AND RELAX IN FRONT OF THE TV!
MAYBE IF I HURRY HOME AND SOAK MY CLOTHES, THE STAINS WILL COME OUT!
RIGHT, AND I CAN SOAK MY HEAD!
BACK AT MIDGE'S HOUSE...
SOME PERFECT DATE THIS TURNED OUT TO BE! I RUINED OUR ANNIVERSARY!
NOT REALLY, MOOSE! IN FACT, IT WAS THE PERFECT REMINDER OF OUR FIRST DATE! EVERYTHING WENT WRONG THEN, TOO, ... REMEMBER?
GEE... THAT'S RIGHT! OUR FIRST DATE WAS A REAL DISASTER!
TOTALLY! BUT WE HAVEN'T STAYED TOGETHER ALL THIS TIME BECAUSE OUR DATES HAVE BEEN PERFECT!
WE STAYED TOGETHER BECAUSE WE'RE PERFECT FOR EACH OTHER!
The End

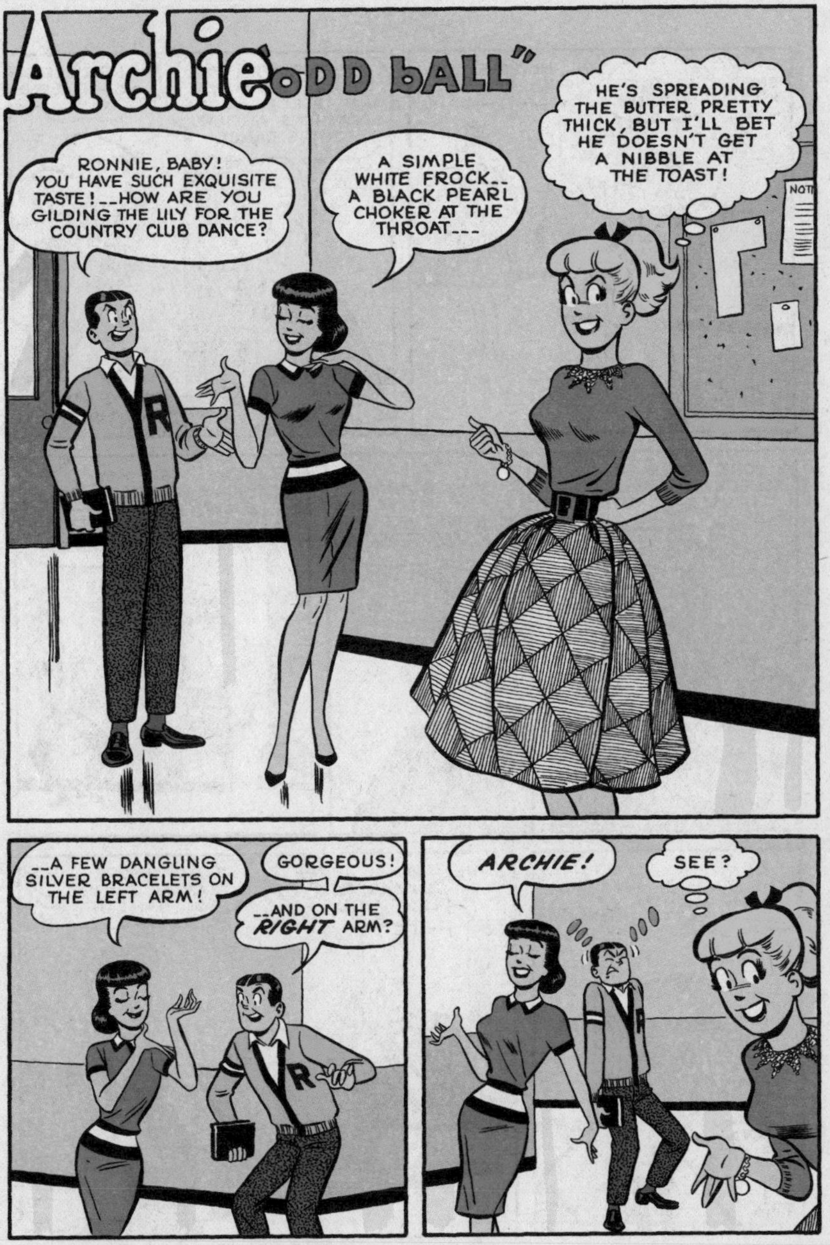
Archie "ODD BALL"
RONNIE, BABY! YOU HAVE SUCH EXQUISITE TASTE!--HOW ARE YOU GILDING THE LILY FOR THE COUNTRY CLUB DANCE?
A SIMPLE WHITE FROCK-- A BLACK PEARL CHOKER AT THE THROAT---
HE'S SPREADING THE BUTTER PRETTY THICK, BUT I'LL BET HE DOESN'T GET A NIBBLE AT THE TOAST!
--A FEW DANGLING SILVER BRACELETS ON THE LEFT ARM!
GORGEOUS!
--AND ON THE *RIGHT* ARM?
ARCHIE!
SEE?

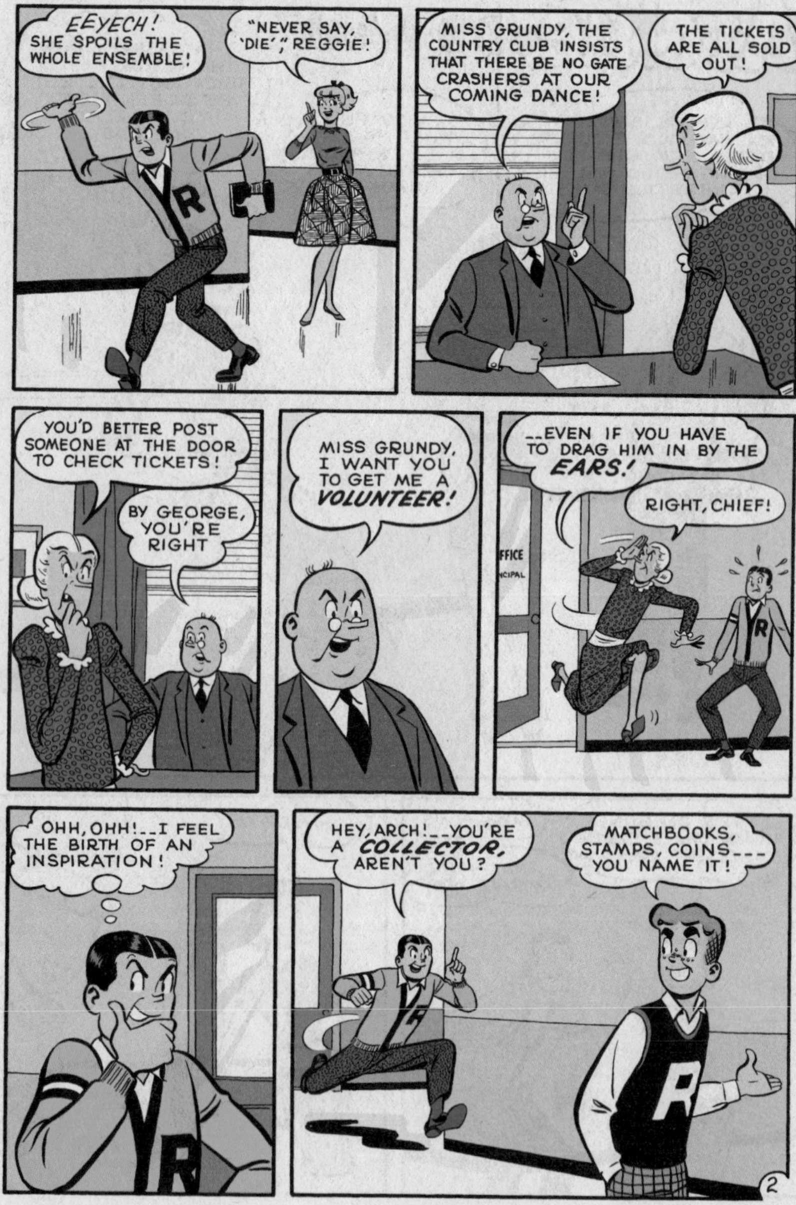
EEYECH! SHE SPOILS THE WHOLE ENSEMBLE!
"NEVER SAY, 'DIE'," REGGIE!
MISS GRUNDY, THE COUNTRY CLUB INSISTS THAT THERE BE NO GATE CRASHERS AT OUR COMING DANCE!
THE TICKETS ARE ALL SOLD OUT!
YOU'D BETTER POST SOMEONE AT THE DOOR TO CHECK TICKETS!
BY GEORGE, YOU'RE RIGHT
MISS GRUNDY, I WANT YOU TO GET ME A VOLUNTEER!
--EVEN IF YOU HAVE TO DRAG HIM IN BY THE EARS!
RIGHT, CHIEF!
OFFICE
NCIPAL
OHH, OHH!--I FEEL THE BIRTH OF AN INSPIRATION!
HEY, ARCH!--YOU'RE A COLLECTOR, AREN'T YOU?
MATCHBOOKS, STAMPS, COINS--- YOU NAME IT!
2

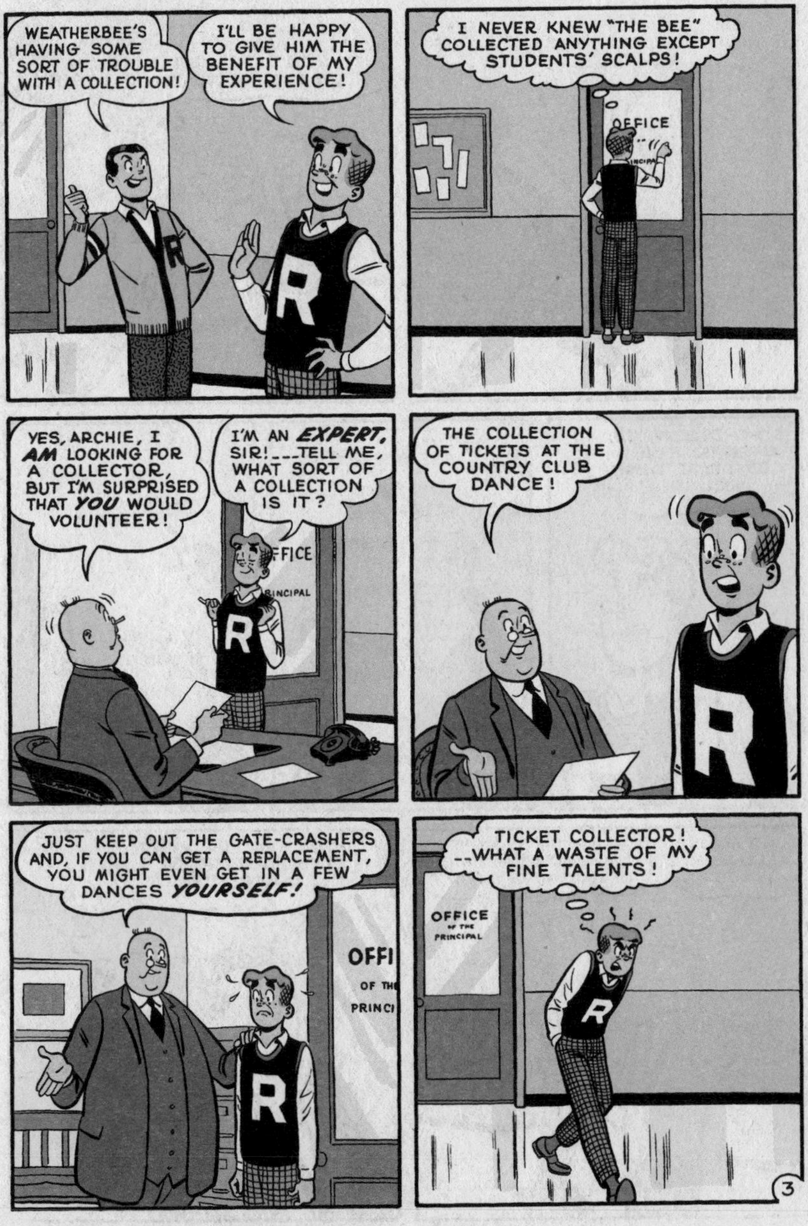
WEATHERBEE'S HAVING SOME SORT OF TROUBLE WITH A COLLECTION!
I'LL BE HAPPY TO GIVE HIM THE BENEFIT OF MY EXPERIENCE!
I NEVER KNEW "THE BEE" COLLECTED ANYTHING EXCEPT STUDENTS' SCALPS!
OFFICE
YES, ARCHIE, I AM LOOKING FOR A COLLECTOR, BUT I'M SURPRISED THAT YOU WOULD VOLUNTEER!
I'M AN EXPERT, SIR!---TELL ME, WHAT SORT OF A COLLECTION IS IT?
FFICE
RINCIPAL
THE COLLECTION OF TICKETS AT THE COUNTRY CLUB DANCE!
JUST KEEP OUT THE GATE-CRASHERS AND, IF YOU CAN GET A REPLACEMENT, YOU MIGHT EVEN GET IN A FEW DANCES YOURSELF!
OFFI
OF THE
PRINCI
TICKET COLLECTOR! --WHAT A WASTE OF MY FINE TALENTS!
OFFICE
OF THE
PRINCIPAL
3

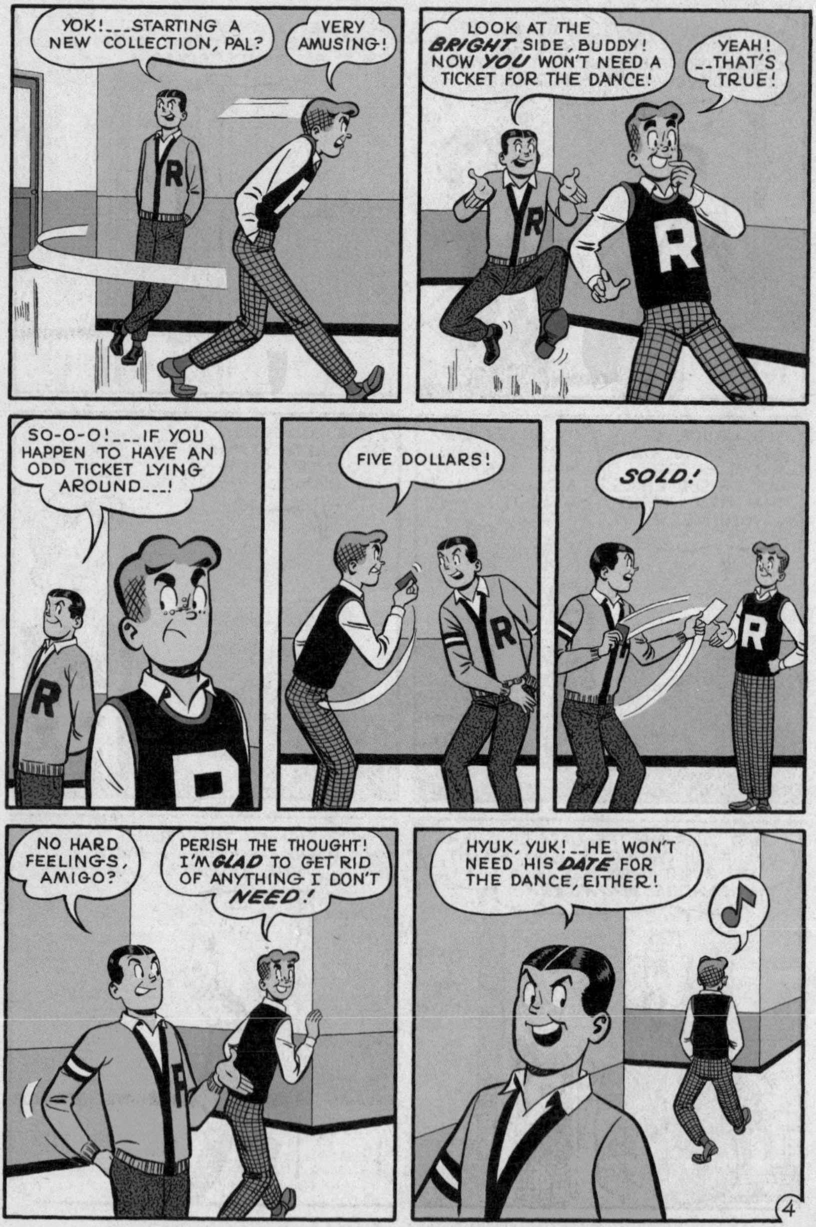
YOK!---STARTING A NEW COLLECTION, PAL?
VERY AMUSING!
LOOK AT THE BRIGHT SIDE, BUDDY! NOW YOU WON'T NEED A TICKET FOR THE DANCE!
YEAH! --THAT'S TRUE!
SO-O-O!---IF YOU HAPPEN TO HAVE AN ODD TICKET LYING AROUND---!
FIVE DOLLARS!
SOLD!
NO HARD FEELINGS, AMIGO?
PERISH THE THOUGHT! I'M GLAD TO GET RID OF ANYTHING I DON'T NEED!
HYUK, YUK!--HE WON'T NEED HIS DATE FOR THE DANCE, EITHER!
4

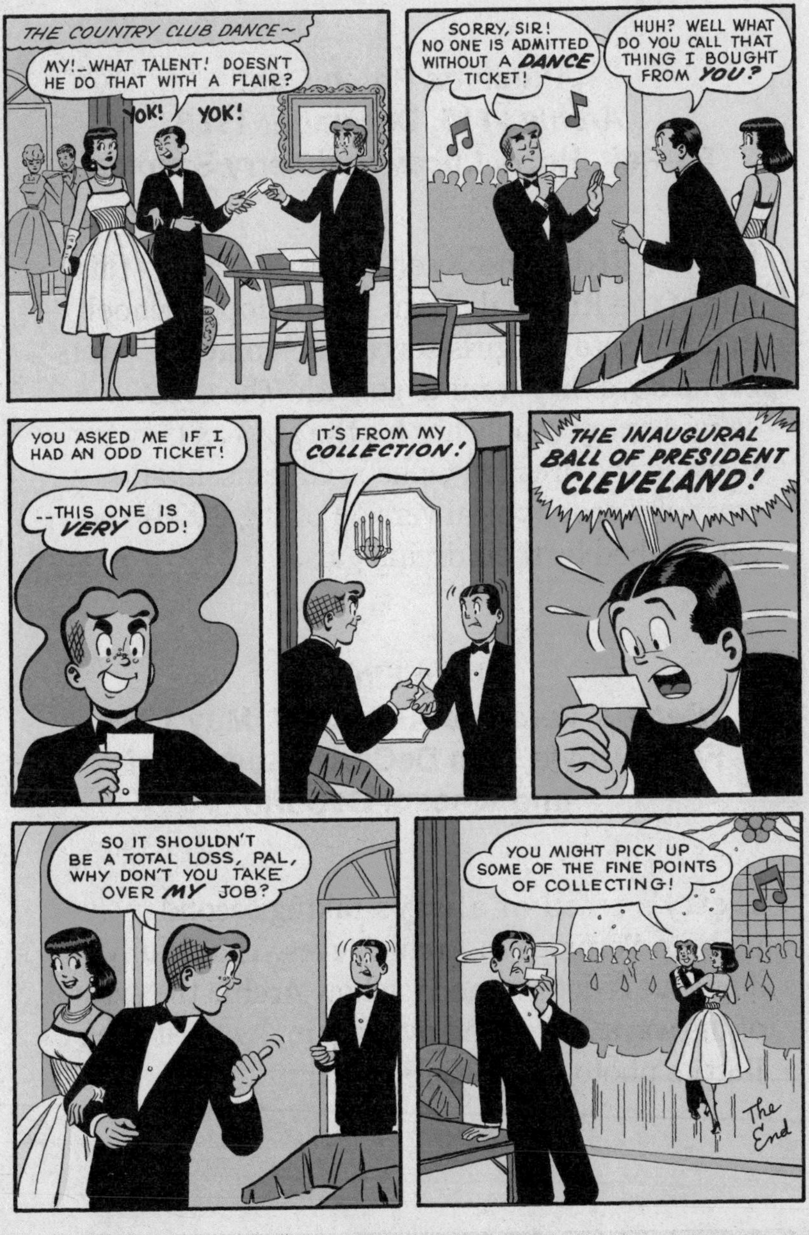
THE COUNTRY CLUB DANCE~
MY!_WHAT TALENT! DOESN'T HE DO THAT WITH A FLAIR?
YOK! YOK!
SORRY, SIR! NO ONE IS ADMITTED WITHOUT A DANCE TICKET!
HUH? WELL WHAT DO YOU CALL THAT THING I BOUGHT FROM YOU?
YOU ASKED ME IF I HAD AN ODD TICKET!
--THIS ONE IS VERY ODD!
IT'S FROM MY COLLECTION!
THE INAUGURAL BALL OF PRESIDENT CLEVELAND!
SO IT SHOULDN'T BE A TOTAL LOSS, PAL, WHY DON'T YOU TAKE OVER MY JOB?
YOU MIGHT PICK UP SOME OF THE FINE POINTS OF COLLECTING!
The End

Patch as Patch Can!
Archie #115, December 1960
Sy Reit, Harry Lucey and Terry Szenics

Ouch! From the Archie vaults comes this tale of the Riverdale High Patch-Hop, a school dance where the girls sew a patch onto the pants of the boys they want to go with. The event causes many headaches for the guys as they try to avoid the dreaded Ophelia Glutenschnable (sort of a prototypical version of Big Ethel) and get patched by their dream gals.

Photo Finish
Betty & Veronica Annual #7, May 1959
Frank Doyle, Dan DeCarlo, Rudy Lapick and Vincent DeCarlo

Betty's tired of always taking second place to Veronica in Archie's eyes. Thankfully, Jughead is determined to show Archie the error of his ways... over and over again, by plastering Betty's photo everywhere!

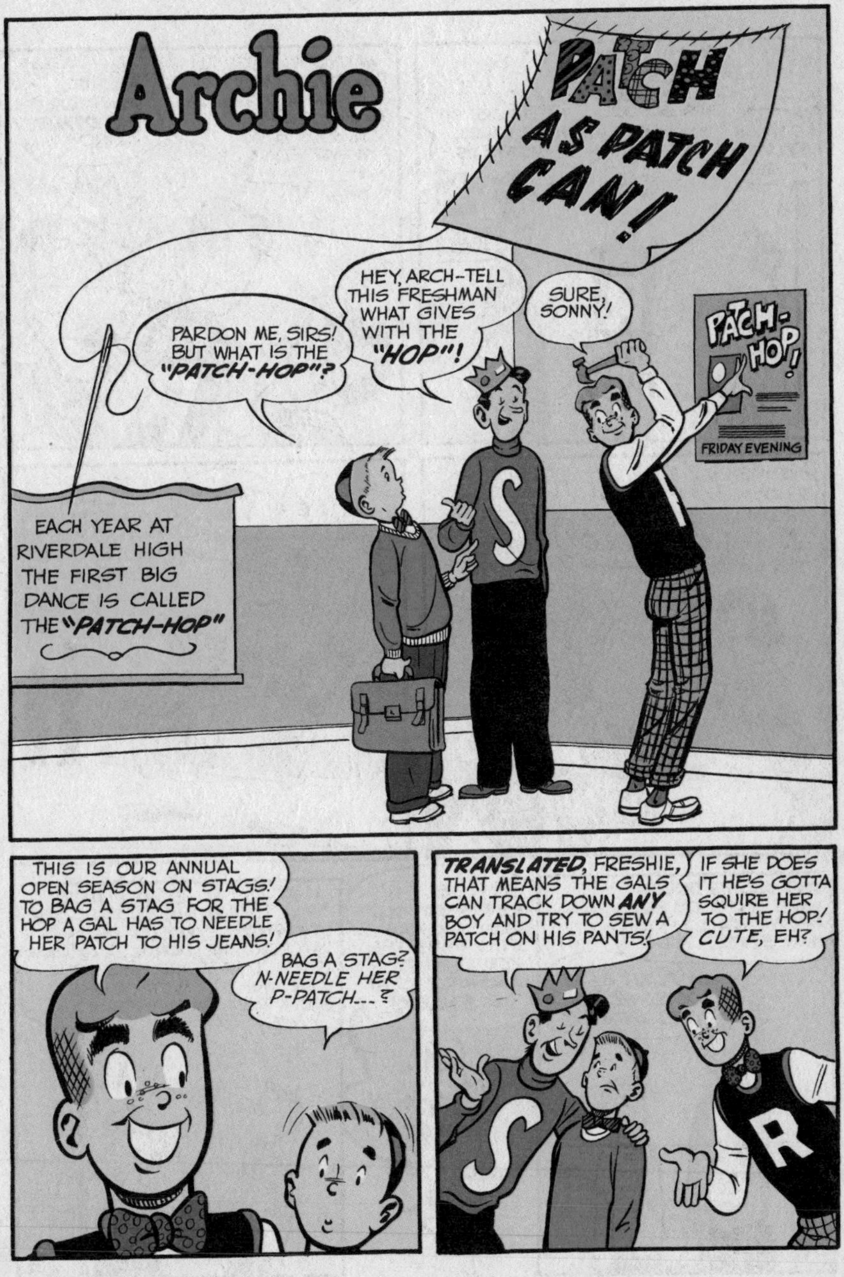
Archie
PATCH AS PATCH CAN!
PATCH-HOP! FRIDAY EVENING
EACH YEAR AT RIVERDALE HIGH THE FIRST BIG DANCE IS CALLED THE "PATCH-HOP"
PARDON ME, SIRS! BUT WHAT IS THE "PATCH-HOP"?
HEY, ARCH--TELL THIS FRESHMAN WHAT GIVES WITH THE "HOP"!
SURE, SONNY!
THIS IS OUR ANNUAL OPEN SEASON ON STAGS! TO BAG A STAG FOR THE HOP A GAL HAS TO NEEDLE HER PATCH TO HIS JEANS!
BAG A STAG? N-NEEDLE HER P-PATCH...?
TRANSLATED, FRESHIE, THAT MEANS THE GALS CAN TRACK DOWN ANY BOY AND TRY TO SEW A PATCH ON HIS PANTS!
IF SHE DOES IT HE'S GOTTA SQUIRE HER TO THE HOP! CUTE, EH?

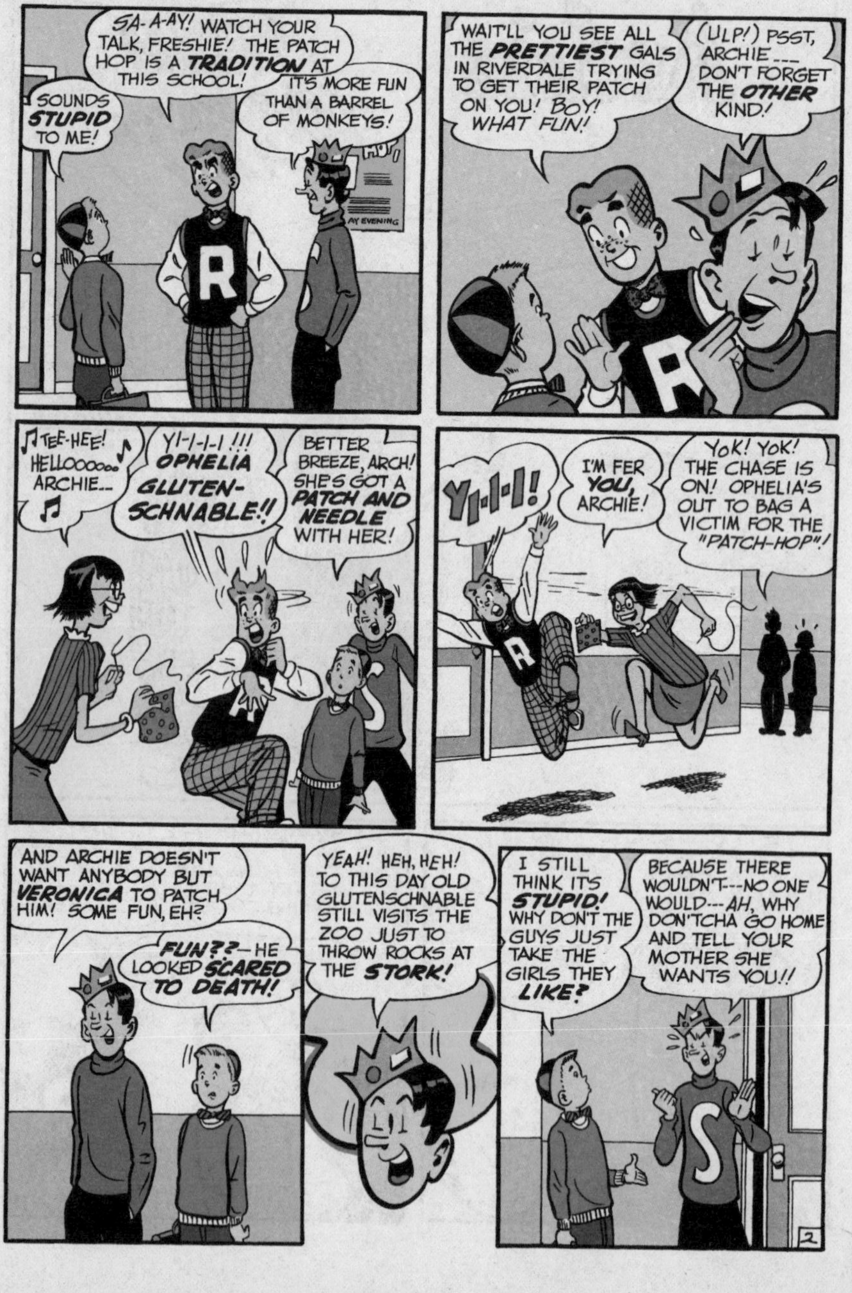
SOUNDS STUPID TO ME!
SA-A-AY! WATCH YOUR TALK, FRESHIE! THE PATCH HOP IS A TRADITION AT THIS SCHOOL!
IT'S MORE FUN THAN A BARREL OF MONKEYS!
AY EVENING
WAIT'LL YOU SEE ALL THE PRETTIEST GALS IN RIVERDALE TRYING TO GET THEIR PATCH ON YOU! BOY! WHAT FUN!
(ULP!) PSST, ARCHIE--- DON'T FORGET THE OTHER KIND!
TEE-HEE! HELLOOOOoo ARCHIE...
YI-I-I-I !!! OPHELIA GLUTEN-SCHNABLE!!
BETTER BREEZE, ARCH! SHE'S GOT A PATCH AND NEEDLE WITH HER!
YI-I-I!
I'M FER YOU, ARCHIE!
YOK! YOK! THE CHASE IS ON! OPHELIA'S OUT TO BAG A VICTIM FOR THE "PATCH-HOP"!
AND ARCHIE DOESN'T WANT ANYBODY BUT VERONICA TO PATCH HIM! SOME FUN, EH?
FUN??—HE LOOKED SCARED TO DEATH!
YEAH! HEH, HEH! TO THIS DAY OLD GLUTENSCHNABLE STILL VISITS THE ZOO JUST TO THROW ROCKS AT THE STORK!
I STILL THINK IT'S STUPID! WHY DON'T THE GUYS JUST TAKE THE GIRLS THEY LIKE?
BECAUSE THERE WOULDN'T---NO ONE WOULD---AH, WHY DON'TCHA GO HOME AND TELL YOUR MOTHER SHE WANTS YOU!!
2

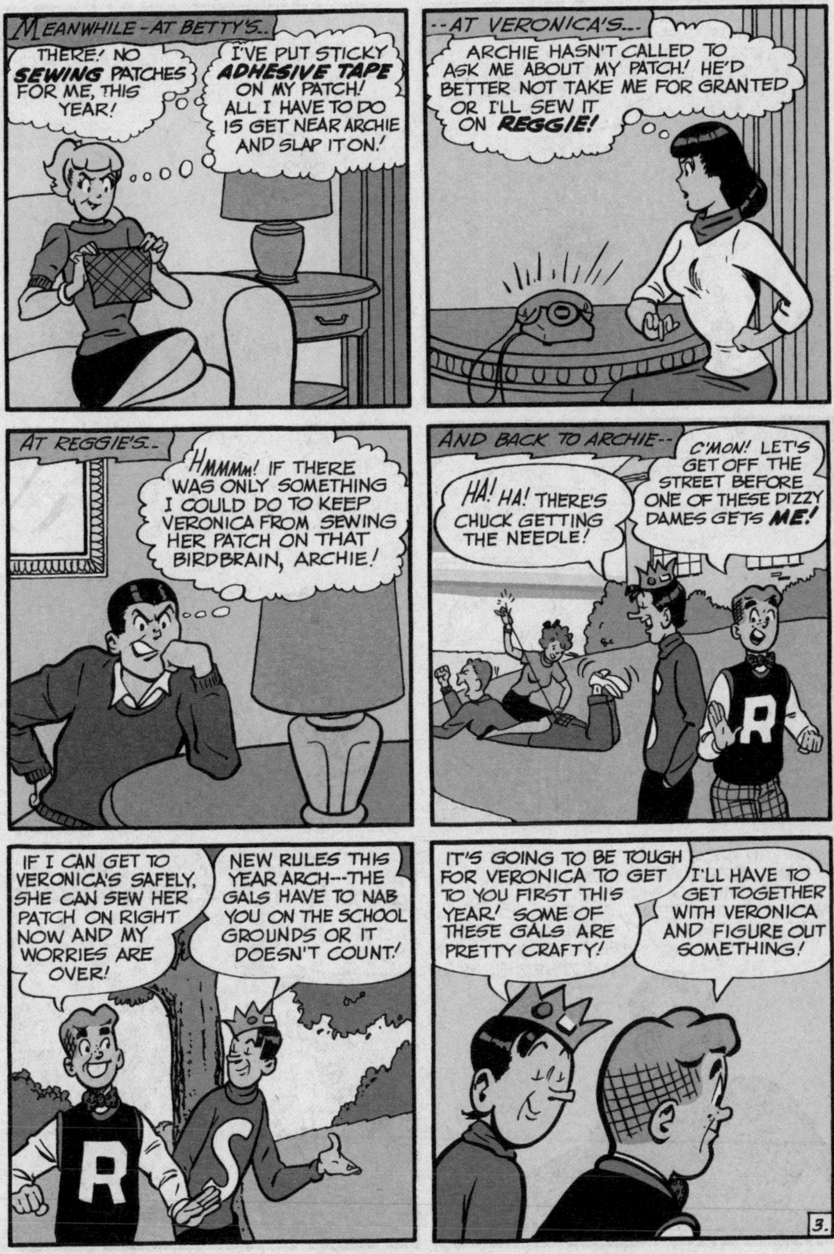
MEANWHILE - AT BETTY'S..
THERE! NO SEWING PATCHES FOR ME, THIS YEAR!
I'VE PUT STICKY ADHESIVE TAPE ON MY PATCH! ALL I HAVE TO DO IS GET NEAR ARCHIE AND SLAP IT ON!
--AT VERONICA'S...
ARCHIE HASN'T CALLED TO ASK ME ABOUT MY PATCH! HE'D BETTER NOT TAKE ME FOR GRANTED OR I'LL SEW IT ON REGGIE!
AT REGGIE'S..
HMMMM! IF THERE WAS ONLY SOMETHING I COULD DO TO KEEP VERONICA FROM SEWING HER PATCH ON THAT BIRDBRAIN, ARCHIE!
AND BACK TO ARCHIE--
HA! HA! THERE'S CHUCK GETTING THE NEEDLE!
C'MON! LET'S GET OFF THE STREET BEFORE ONE OF THESE DIZZY DAMES GETS ME!
IF I CAN GET TO VERONICA'S SAFELY, SHE CAN SEW HER PATCH ON RIGHT NOW AND MY WORRIES ARE OVER!
NEW RULES THIS YEAR ARCH---THE GALS HAVE TO NAB YOU ON THE SCHOOL GROUNDS OR IT DOESN'T COUNT!
IT'S GOING TO BE TOUGH FOR VERONICA TO GET TO YOU FIRST THIS YEAR! SOME OF THESE GALS ARE PRETTY CRAFTY!
I'LL HAVE TO GET TOGETHER WITH VERONICA AND FIGURE OUT SOMETHING!
3.

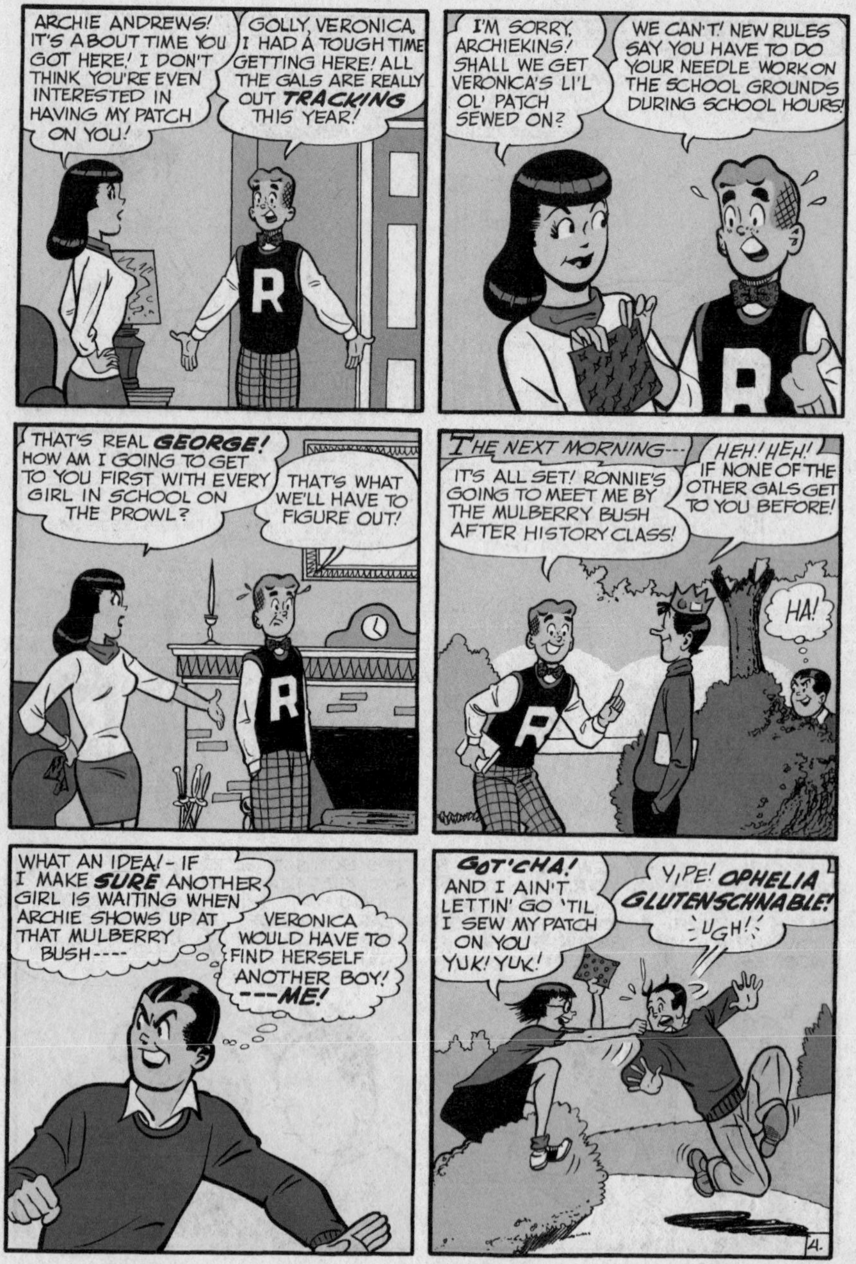

ARCHIE ANDREWS! IT'S ABOUT TIME YOU GOT HERE! I DON'T THINK YOU'RE EVEN INTERESTED IN HAVING MY PATCH ON YOU!
GOLLY, VERONICA, I HAD A TOUGH TIME GETTING HERE! ALL THE GALS ARE REALLY OUT TRACKING THIS YEAR!
I'M SORRY, ARCHIEKINS! SHALL WE GET VERONICA'S LI'L OL' PATCH SEWED ON?
WE CAN'T! NEW RULES SAY YOU HAVE TO DO YOUR NEEDLE WORK ON THE SCHOOL GROUNDS DURING SCHOOL HOURS!
THAT'S REAL GEORGE! HOW AM I GOING TO GET TO YOU FIRST WITH EVERY GIRL IN SCHOOL ON THE PROWL?
THAT'S WHAT WE'LL HAVE TO FIGURE OUT!
THE NEXT MORNING---
IT'S ALL SET! RONNIE'S GOING TO MEET ME BY THE MULBERRY BUSH AFTER HISTORY CLASS!
HEH! HEH! IF NONE OF THE OTHER GALS GET TO YOU BEFORE!
HA!
WHAT AN IDEA! - IF I MAKE SURE ANOTHER GIRL IS WAITING WHEN ARCHIE SHOWS UP AT THAT MULBERRY BUSH----
VERONICA WOULD HAVE TO FIND HERSELF ANOTHER BOY! ---ME!
GOT'CHA! AND I AIN'T LETTIN' GO 'TIL I SEW MY PATCH ON YOU YUK! YUK!
YIPE! OPHELIA GLUTENSCHNABLE!
UGH!
4.

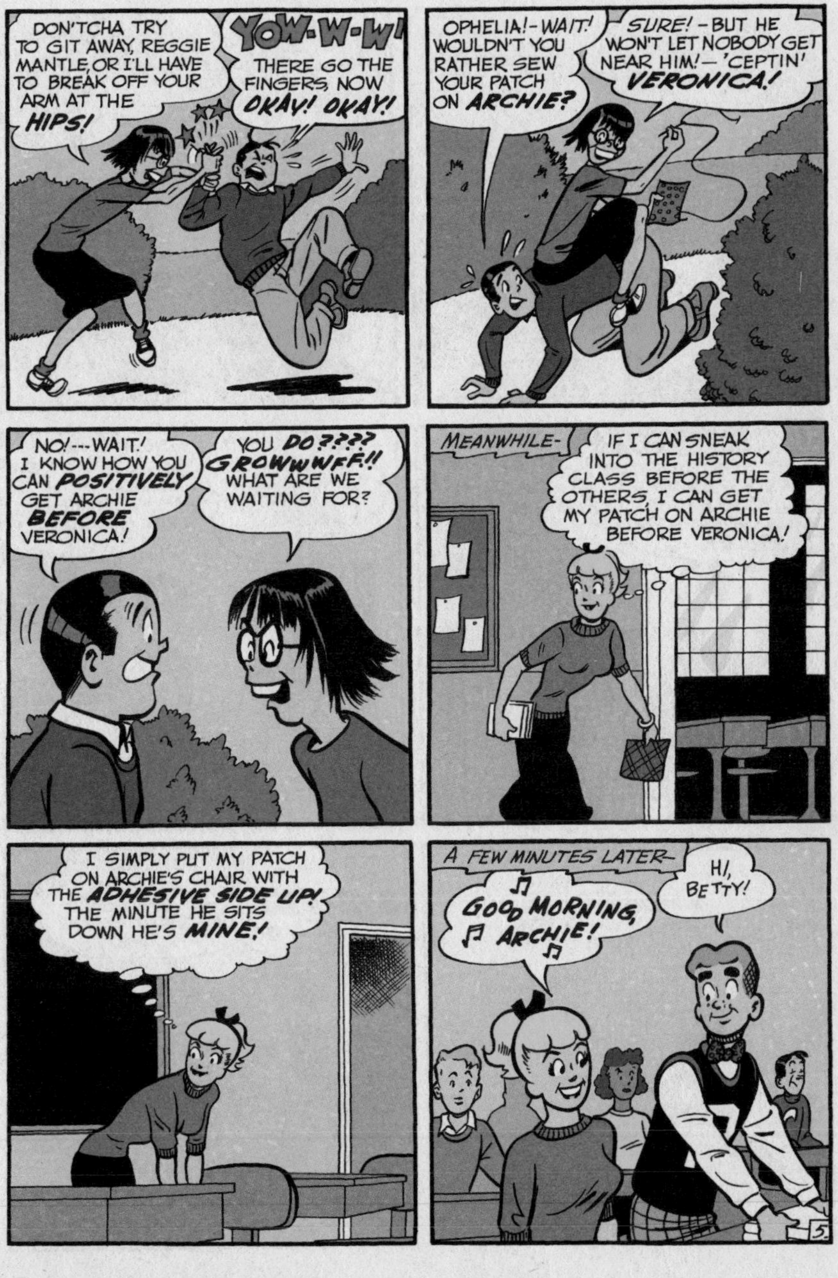
DON'TCHA TRY TO GIT AWAY, REGGIE MANTLE, OR I'LL HAVE TO BREAK OFF YOUR ARM AT THE HIPS!
YOW-W-W!
THERE GO THE FINGERS, NOW OKAY! OKAY!
OPHELIA!-WAIT! WOULDN'T YOU RATHER SEW YOUR PATCH ON ARCHIE?
SURE! -BUT HE WON'T LET NOBODY GET NEAR HIM!- 'CEPTIN' VERONICA!
NO!---WAIT! I KNOW HOW YOU CAN POSITIVELY GET ARCHIE BEFORE VERONICA!
YOU DO???? GROWWWFF!! WHAT ARE WE WAITING FOR?
MEANWHILE-
IF I CAN SNEAK INTO THE HISTORY CLASS BEFORE THE OTHERS, I CAN GET MY PATCH ON ARCHIE BEFORE VERONICA!
I SIMPLY PUT MY PATCH ON ARCHIE'S CHAIR WITH THE ADHESIVE SIDE UP! THE MINUTE HE SITS DOWN HE'S MINE!
A FEW MINUTES LATER-
GOOD MORNING, ARCHIE!
HI, BETTY!
5.

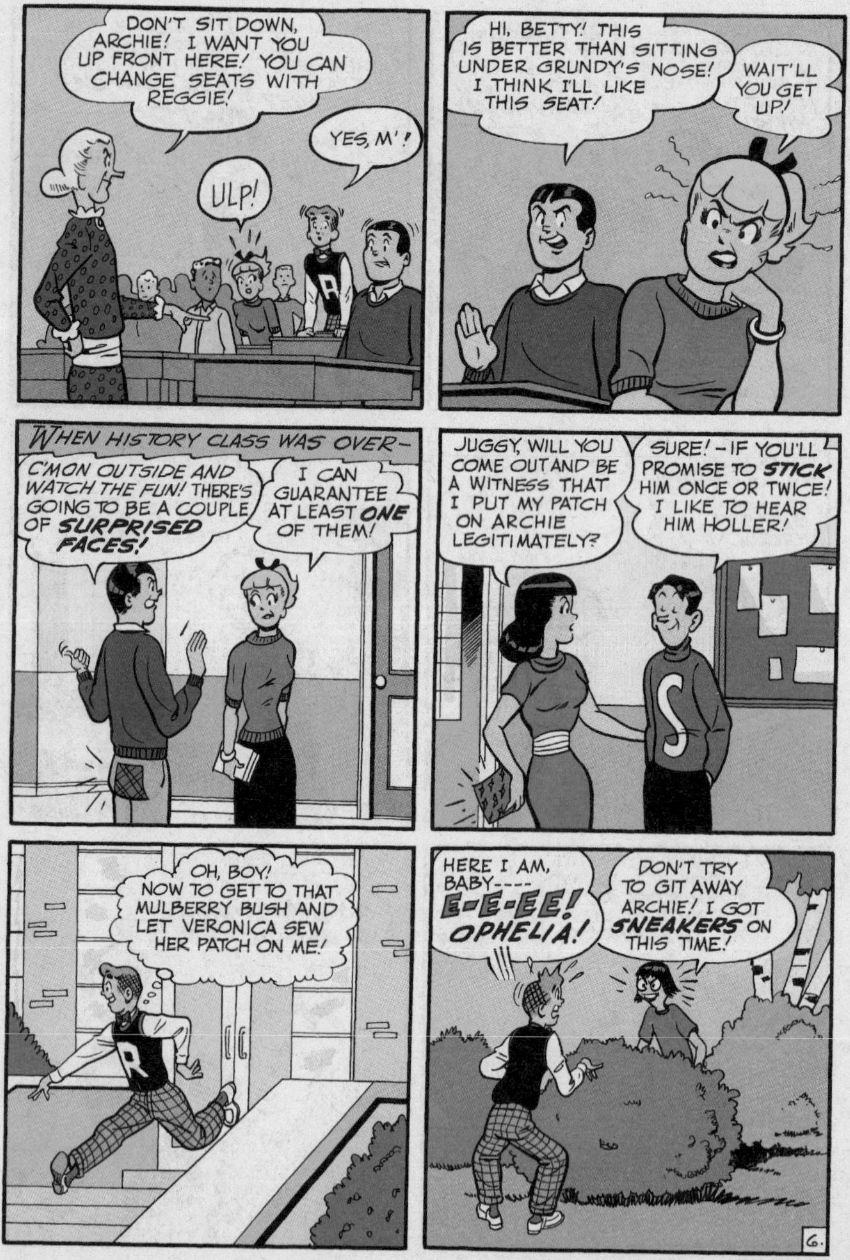
DON'T SIT DOWN, ARCHIE! I WANT YOU UP FRONT HERE! YOU CAN CHANGE SEATS WITH REGGIE!
YES, M'!
ULP!
HI, BETTY! THIS IS BETTER THAN SITTING UNDER GRUNDY'S NOSE! I THINK I'LL LIKE THIS SEAT!
WAIT'LL YOU GET UP!
WHEN HISTORY CLASS WAS OVER–
C'MON OUTSIDE AND WATCH THE FUN! THERE'S GOING TO BE A COUPLE OF SURPRISED FACES!
I CAN GUARANTEE AT LEAST ONE OF THEM!
JUGGY, WILL YOU COME OUT AND BE A WITNESS THAT I PUT MY PATCH ON ARCHIE LEGITIMATELY?
SURE! –IF YOU'LL PROMISE TO STICK HIM ONCE OR TWICE! I LIKE TO HEAR HIM HOLLER!
OH, BOY! NOW TO GET TO THAT MULBERRY BUSH AND LET VERONICA SEW HER PATCH ON ME!
HERE I AM, BABY---- E-E-EE! OPHELIA!
DON'T TRY TO GIT AWAY ARCHIE! I GOT SNEAKERS ON THIS TIME!
6.

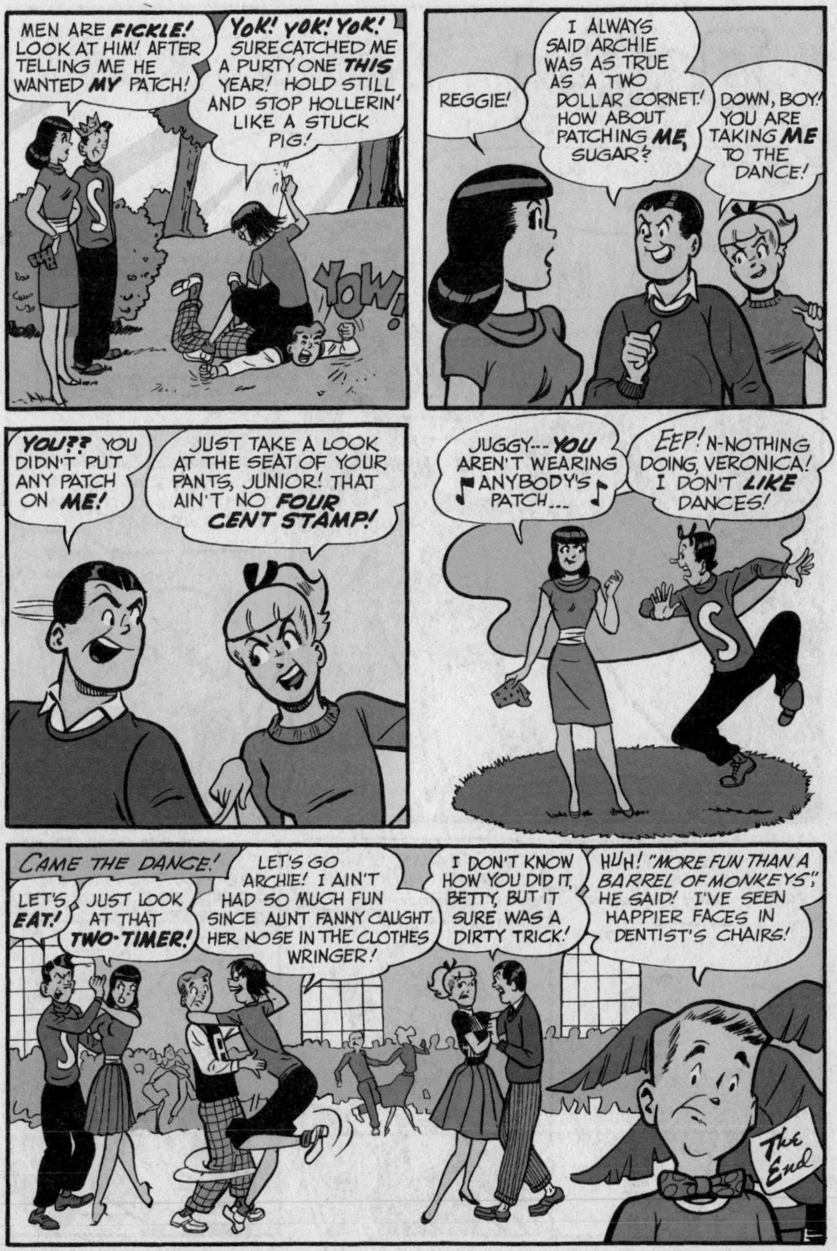
MEN ARE FICKLE! LOOK AT HIM! AFTER TELLING ME HE WANTED MY PATCH!
YOK! YOK! YOK! SURE CATCHED ME A PURTY ONE THIS YEAR! HOLD STILL AND STOP HOLLERIN' LIKE A STUCK PIG!
YOW!
REGGIE!
I ALWAYS SAID ARCHIE WAS AS TRUE AS A TWO DOLLAR CORNET! HOW ABOUT PATCHING ME, SUGAR?
DOWN, BOY! YOU ARE TAKING ME TO THE DANCE!
YOU?? YOU DIDN'T PUT ANY PATCH ON ME!
JUST TAKE A LOOK AT THE SEAT OF YOUR PANTS, JUNIOR! THAT AIN'T NO FOUR CENT STAMP!
JUGGY--- YOU AREN'T WEARING ANYBODY'S PATCH...
EEP! N-NOTHING DOING, VERONICA! I DON'T LIKE DANCES!
CAME THE DANCE!
LET'S EAT!
JUST LOOK AT THAT TWO-TIMER!
LET'S GO ARCHIE! I AIN'T HAD SO MUCH FUN SINCE AUNT FANNY CAUGHT HER NOSE IN THE CLOTHES WRINGER!
I DON'T KNOW HOW YOU DID IT, BETTY, BUT IT SURE WAS A DIRTY TRICK!
HUH! "MORE FUN THAN A BARREL OF MONKEYS", HE SAID! I'VE SEEN HAPPIER FACES IN DENTIST'S CHAIRS!
The End

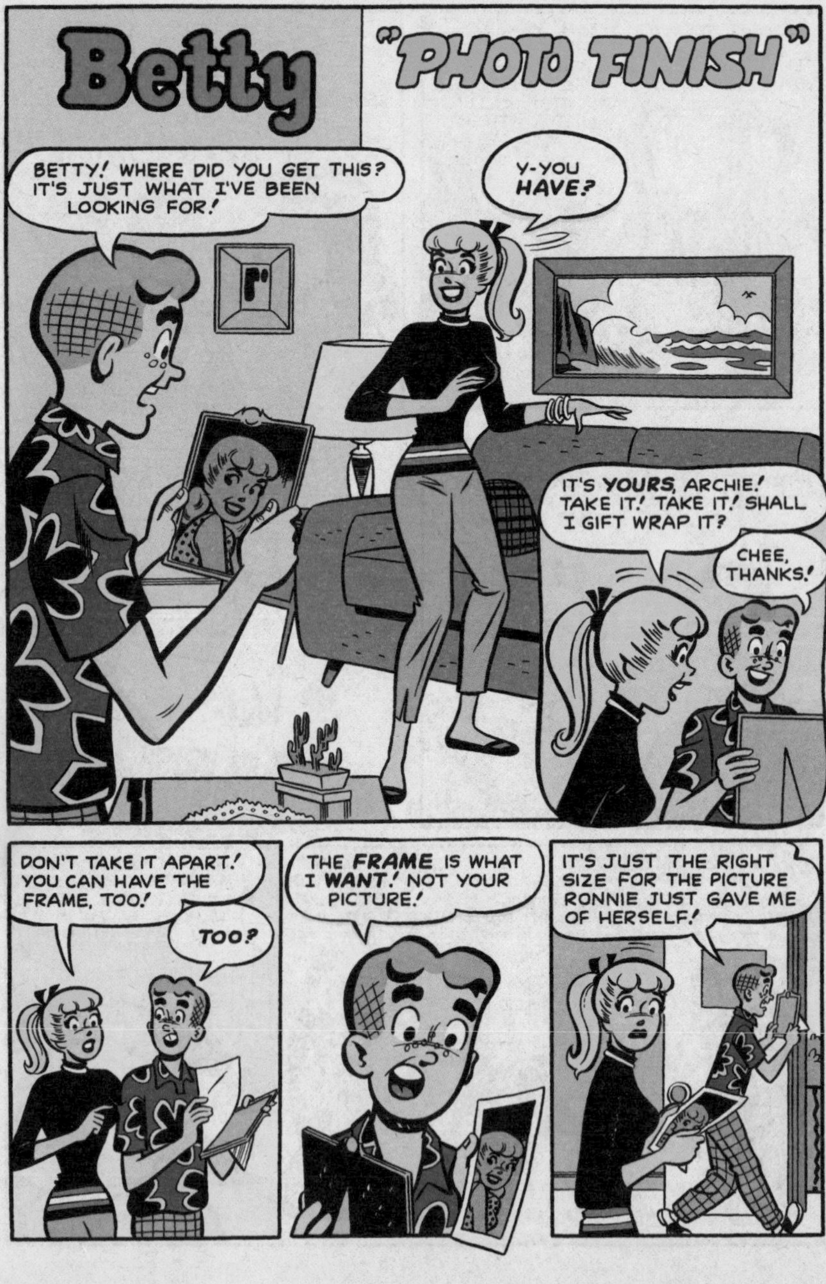
Betty
"PHOTO FINISH"
BETTY! WHERE DID YOU GET THIS? IT'S JUST WHAT I'VE BEEN LOOKING FOR!
Y-YOU HAVE?
IT'S YOURS, ARCHIE! TAKE IT! TAKE IT! SHALL I GIFT WRAP IT?
CHEE, THANKS!
DON'T TAKE IT APART! YOU CAN HAVE THE FRAME, TOO!
TOO?
THE FRAME IS WHAT I WANT! NOT YOUR PICTURE!
IT'S JUST THE RIGHT SIZE FOR THE PICTURE RONNIE JUST GAVE ME OF HERSELF!

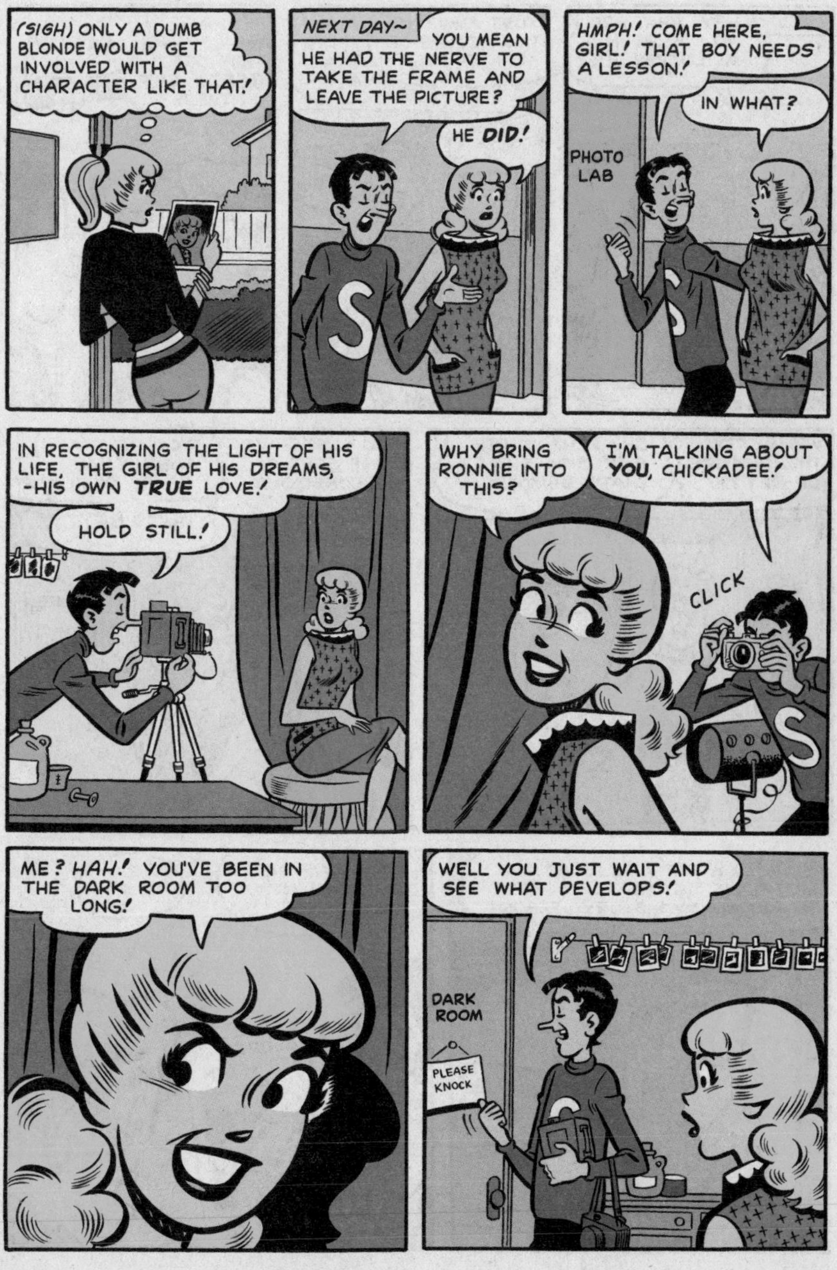
(SIGH) ONLY A DUMB BLONDE WOULD GET INVOLVED WITH A CHARACTER LIKE THAT!
NEXT DAY~
YOU MEAN HE HAD THE NERVE TO TAKE THE FRAME AND LEAVE THE PICTURE?
HE DID!
HMPH! COME HERE, GIRL! THAT BOY NEEDS A LESSON!
IN WHAT?
PHOTO LAB
IN RECOGNIZING THE LIGHT OF HIS LIFE, THE GIRL OF HIS DREAMS, -HIS OWN TRUE LOVE!
HOLD STILL!
WHY BRING RONNIE INTO THIS?
I'M TALKING ABOUT YOU, CHICKADEE!
CLICK
ME? HAH! YOU'VE BEEN IN THE DARK ROOM TOO LONG!
WELL YOU JUST WAIT AND SEE WHAT DEVELOPS!
DARK ROOM
PLEASE KNOCK

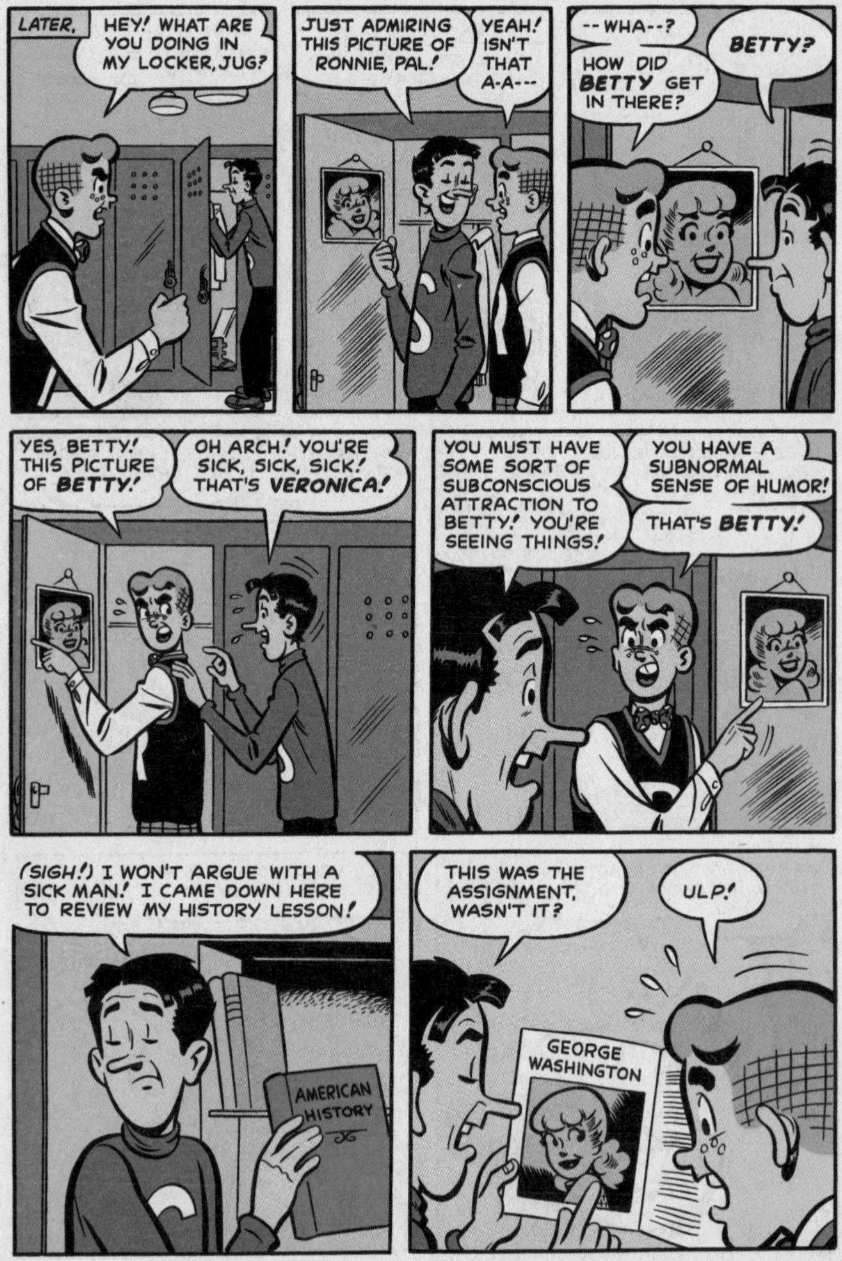
LATER,
HEY! WHAT ARE YOU DOING IN MY LOCKER, JUG?
JUST ADMIRING THIS PICTURE OF RONNIE, PAL!
YEAH! ISN'T THAT A-A---
--WHA--?
HOW DID BETTY GET IN THERE?
BETTY?
YES, BETTY! THIS PICTURE OF BETTY!
OH ARCH! YOU'RE SICK, SICK, SICK! THAT'S VERONICA!
YOU MUST HAVE SOME SORT OF SUBCONSCIOUS ATTRACTION TO BETTY! YOU'RE SEEING THINGS!
YOU HAVE A SUBNORMAL SENSE OF HUMOR!
THAT'S BETTY!
(SIGH!) I WON'T ARGUE WITH A SICK MAN! I CAME DOWN HERE TO REVIEW MY HISTORY LESSON!
AMERICAN HISTORY
THIS WAS THE ASSIGNMENT, WASN'T IT?
ULP!
GEORGE WASHINGTON

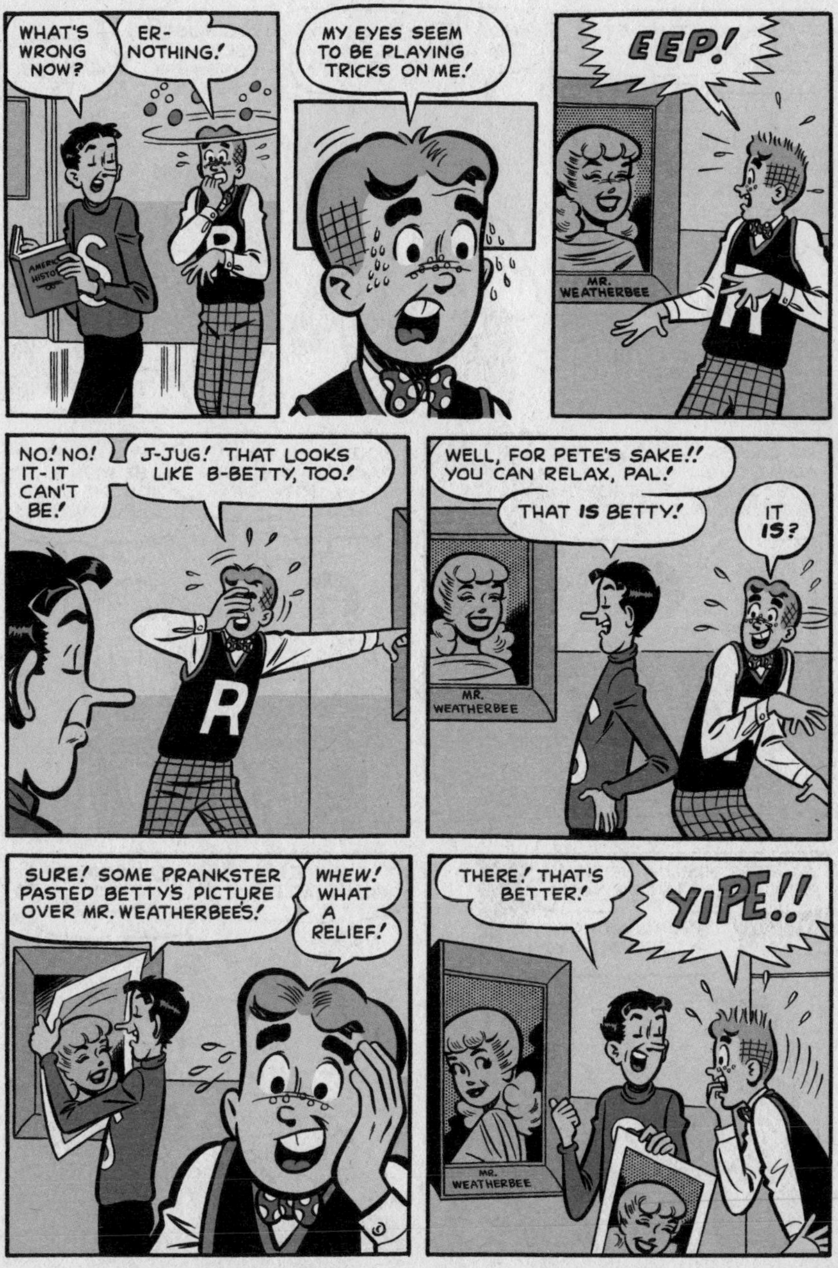
WHAT'S WRONG NOW?
ER- NOTHING.!
MY EYES SEEM TO BE PLAYING TRICKS ON ME.!
EEP!
MR. WEATHERBEE
NO.! NO.! IT-IT CAN'T BE.!
J-JUG.! THAT LOOKS LIKE B-BETTY, TOO.!
WELL, FOR PETE'S SAKE!.! YOU CAN RELAX, PAL.!
THAT IS BETTY.!
IT IS?
MR. WEATHERBEE
SURE.! SOME PRANKSTER PASTED BETTY'S PICTURE OVER MR. WEATHERBEE'S.!
WHEW.! WHAT A RELIEF.!
THERE.! THAT'S BETTER.!
YIPE!!
MR. WEATHERBEE

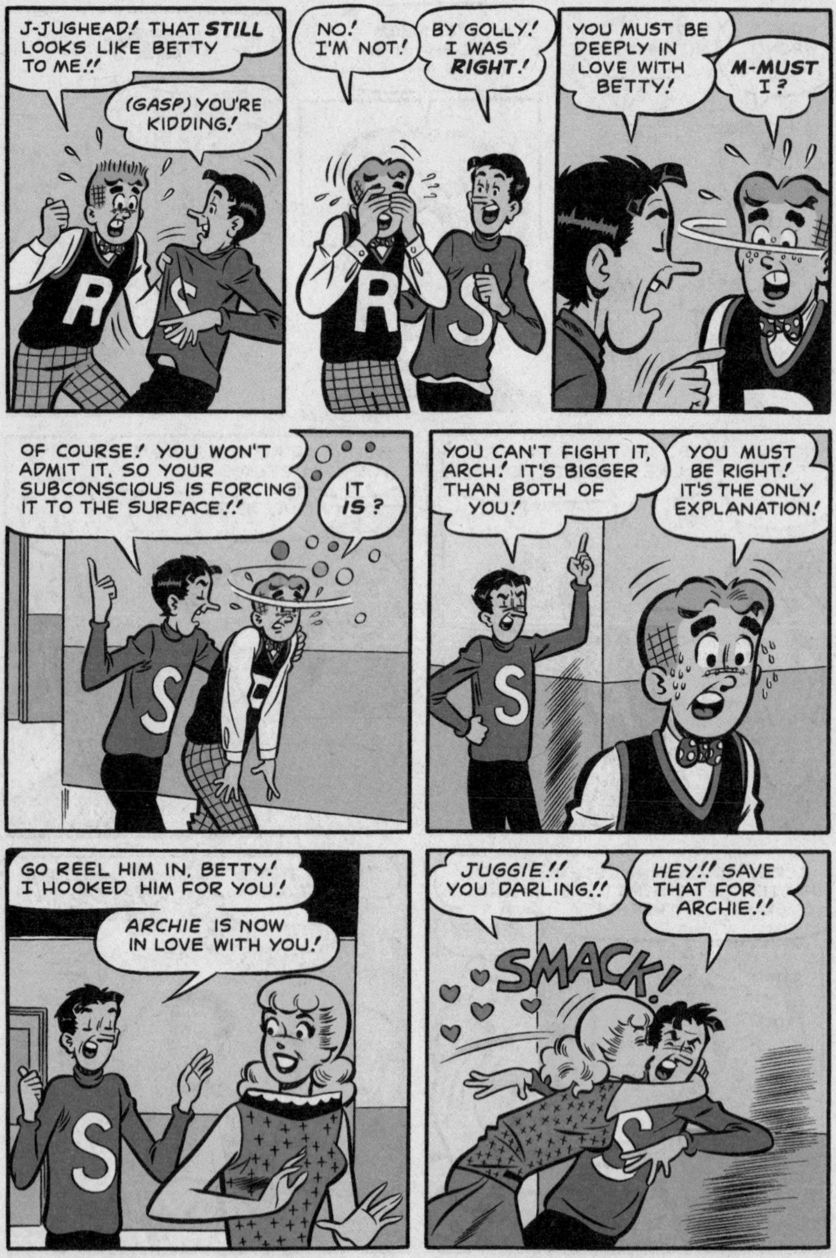
J-JUGHEAD! THAT STILL LOOKS LIKE BETTY TO ME!!
(GASP) YOU'RE KIDDING!
NO! I'M NOT!
BY GOLLY! I WAS RIGHT!
YOU MUST BE DEEPLY IN LOVE WITH BETTY!
M-MUST I?
OF COURSE! YOU WON'T ADMIT IT, SO YOUR SUBCONSCIOUS IS FORCING IT TO THE SURFACE!!
IT IS?
YOU CAN'T FIGHT IT, ARCH! IT'S BIGGER THAN BOTH OF YOU!
YOU MUST BE RIGHT! IT'S THE ONLY EXPLANATION!
GO REEL HIM IN, BETTY! I HOOKED HIM FOR YOU!
ARCHIE IS NOW IN LOVE WITH YOU!
JUGGIE!! YOU DARLING!!
HEY!! SAVE THAT FOR ARCHIE!!
SMACK!

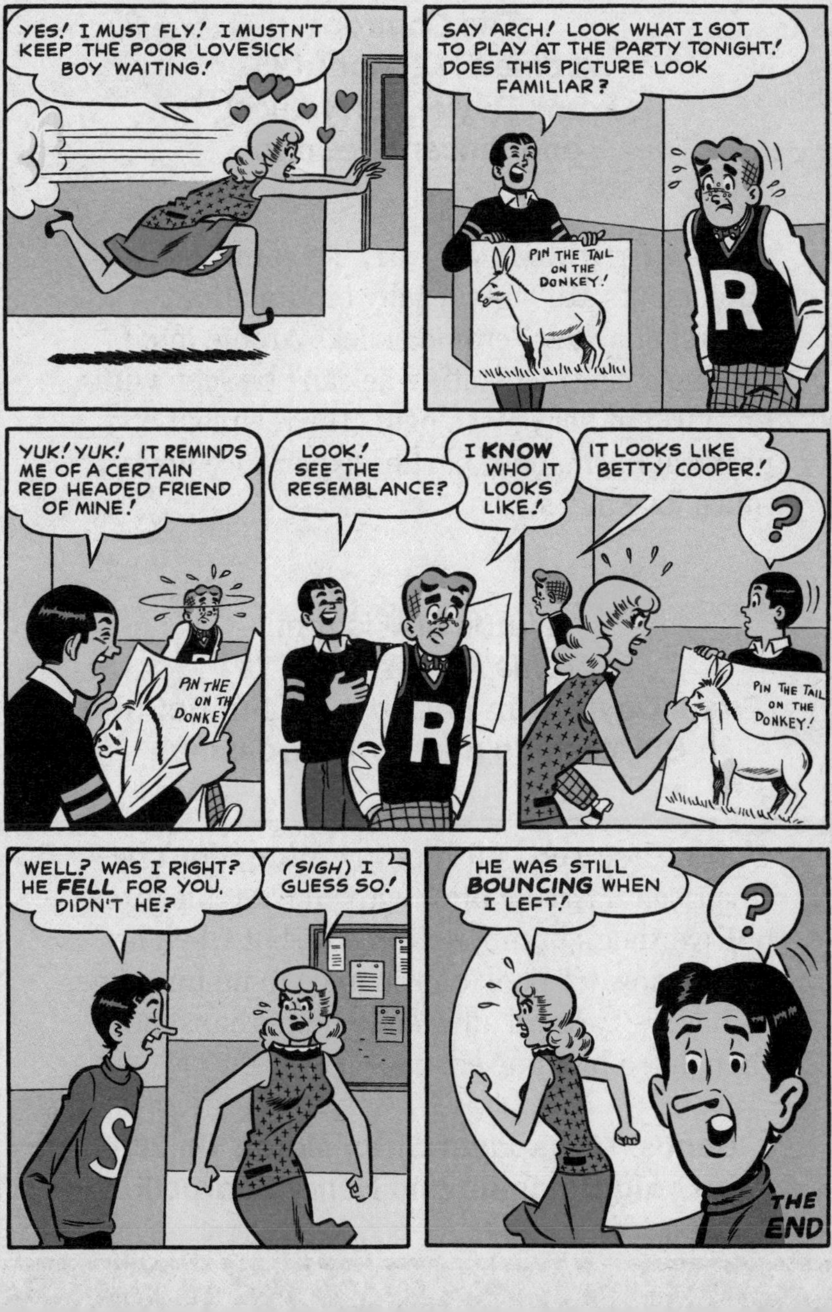
YES! I MUST FLY! I MUSTN'T KEEP THE POOR LOVESICK BOY WAITING!
SAY ARCH! LOOK WHAT I GOT TO PLAY AT THE PARTY TONIGHT! DOES THIS PICTURE LOOK FAMILIAR?
PIN THE TAIL ON THE DONKEY!
YUK! YUK! IT REMINDS ME OF A CERTAIN RED HEADED FRIEND OF MINE!
PIN THE ON TH DONKEY
LOOK! SEE THE RESEMBLANCE?
I KNOW WHO IT LOOKS LIKE!
IT LOOKS LIKE BETTY COOPER!
?
PIN THE TAIL ON THE DONKEY!
WELL? WAS I RIGHT? HE FELL FOR YOU, DIDN'T HE?
(SIGH) I GUESS SO!
HE WAS STILL BOUNCING WHEN I LEFT!
?
THE END

The Contract
Archie #172, April 1967
Frank Doyle, Harry Lucey
and Vincent DeCarlo

All's fair in love in war, but some agreements are more legally binding than others! So when Veronica tricks Archie into signing a contract stating he can't be seen with any girl but her or risk being the recipient of physical harm, both parties experience how much love hurts.

Words of Wisdom
Archie #279, April 1979
Frank Doyle, Dan DeCarlo Jr., Jim DeCarlo,
Bill Yoshida and Barry Grossman

Roses are red, violets are blue, don't be surprised if Archie flirts with you! Archie is one of Riverdale's premiere Romeo's, but when he gets a "how to" book on romance to up his game, he has the girls all aflutter... and perhaps more than just a bit amused!

Bonus: Newspaper Strip, March 14, 2004
Craig Boldman and Henry Scarpelli

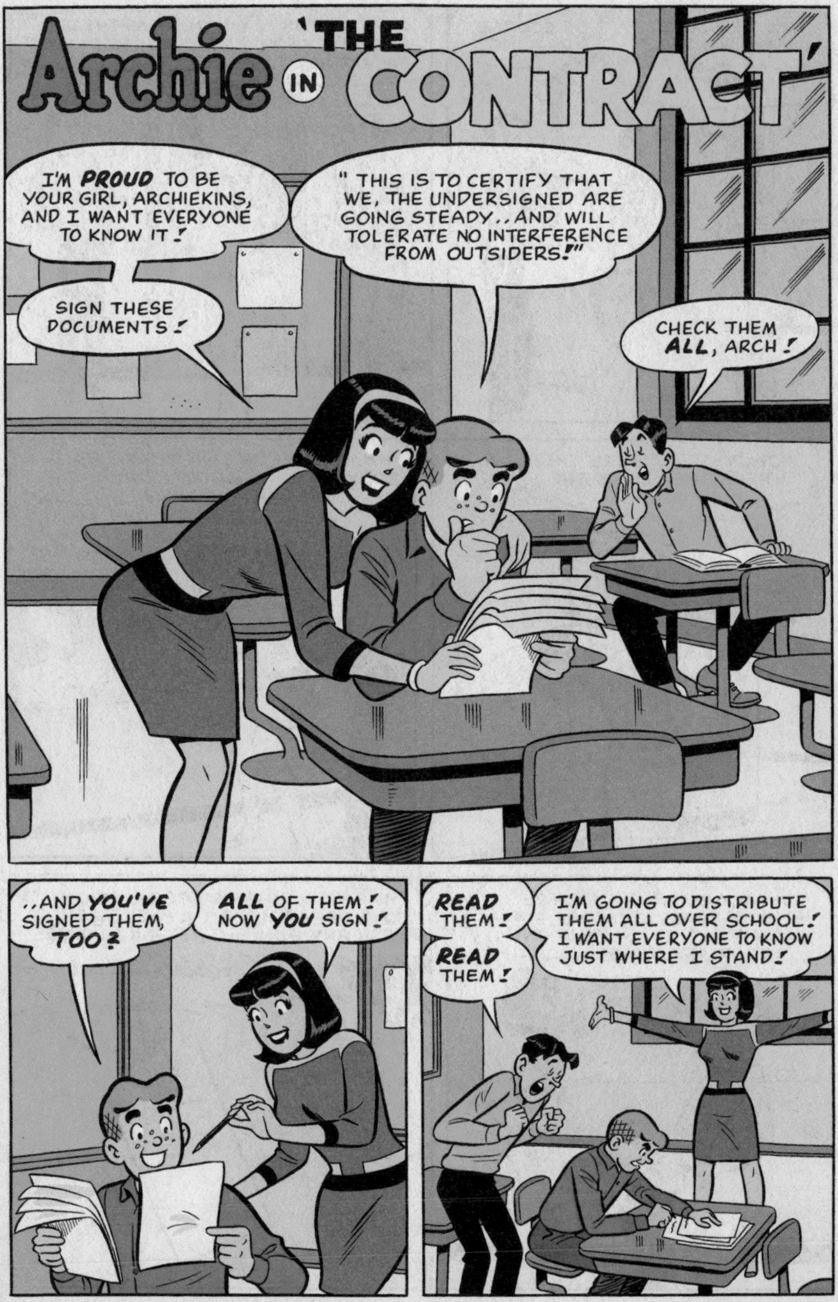
Archie IN 'THE CONTRACT'
I'M PROUD TO BE YOUR GIRL, ARCHIEKINS, AND I WANT EVERYONE TO KNOW IT!
SIGN THESE DOCUMENTS!
" THIS IS TO CERTIFY THAT WE, THE UNDERSIGNED ARE GOING STEADY.. AND WILL TOLERATE NO INTERFERENCE FROM OUTSIDERS!"
CHECK THEM ALL, ARCH!
..AND YOU'VE SIGNED THEM, TOO?
ALL OF THEM! NOW YOU SIGN!
READ THEM!
READ THEM!
I'M GOING TO DISTRIBUTE THEM ALL OVER SCHOOL! I WANT EVERYONE TO KNOW JUST WHERE I STAND!

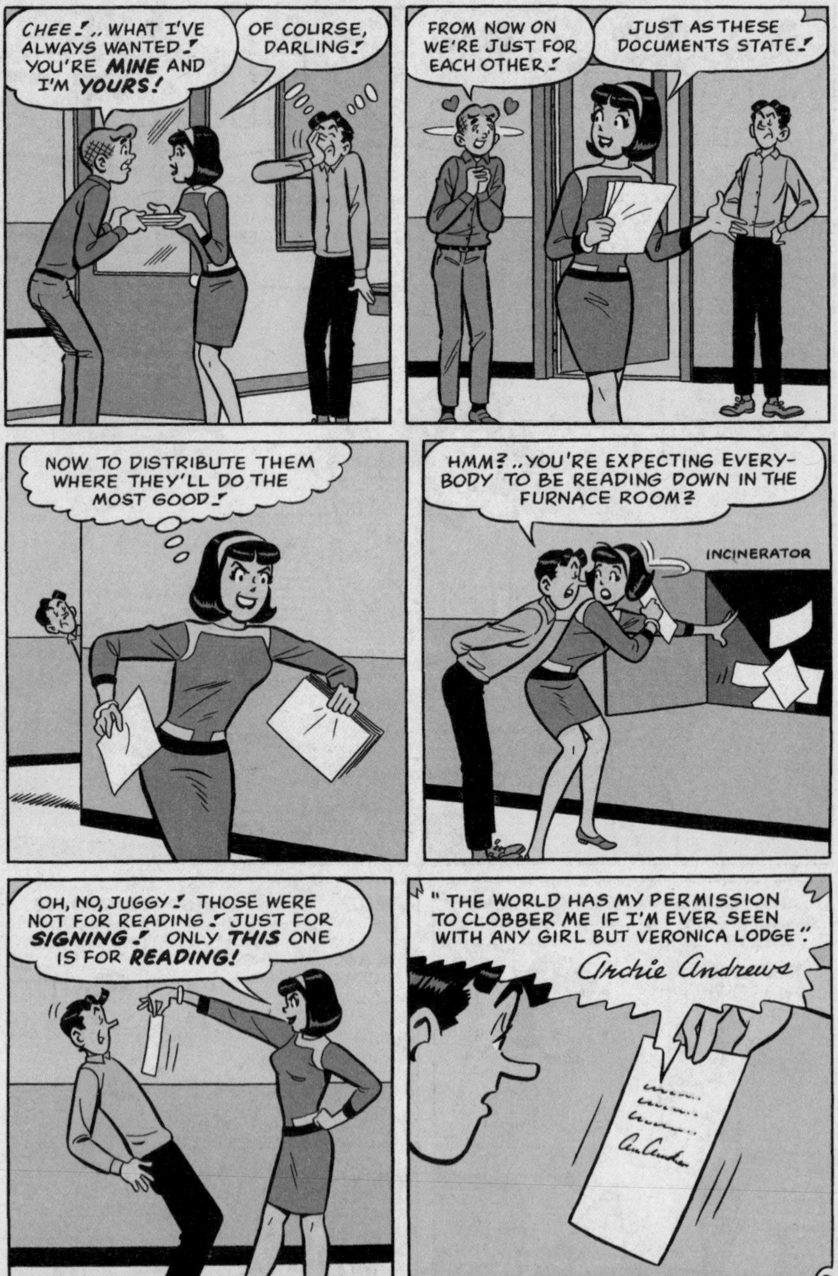
CHEE!.. WHAT I'VE ALWAYS WANTED! YOU'RE MINE AND I'M YOURS!
OF COURSE, DARLING!
FROM NOW ON WE'RE JUST FOR EACH OTHER!
JUST AS THESE DOCUMENTS STATE!
NOW TO DISTRIBUTE THEM WHERE THEY'LL DO THE MOST GOOD!
HMM?..YOU'RE EXPECTING EVERYBODY TO BE READING DOWN IN THE FURNACE ROOM?
INCINERATOR
OH, NO, JUGGY! THOSE WERE NOT FOR READING! JUST FOR SIGNING! ONLY THIS ONE IS FOR READING!
"THE WORLD HAS MY PERMISSION TO CLOBBER ME IF I'M EVER SEEN WITH ANY GIRL BUT VERONICA LODGE."
Archie Andrews
2

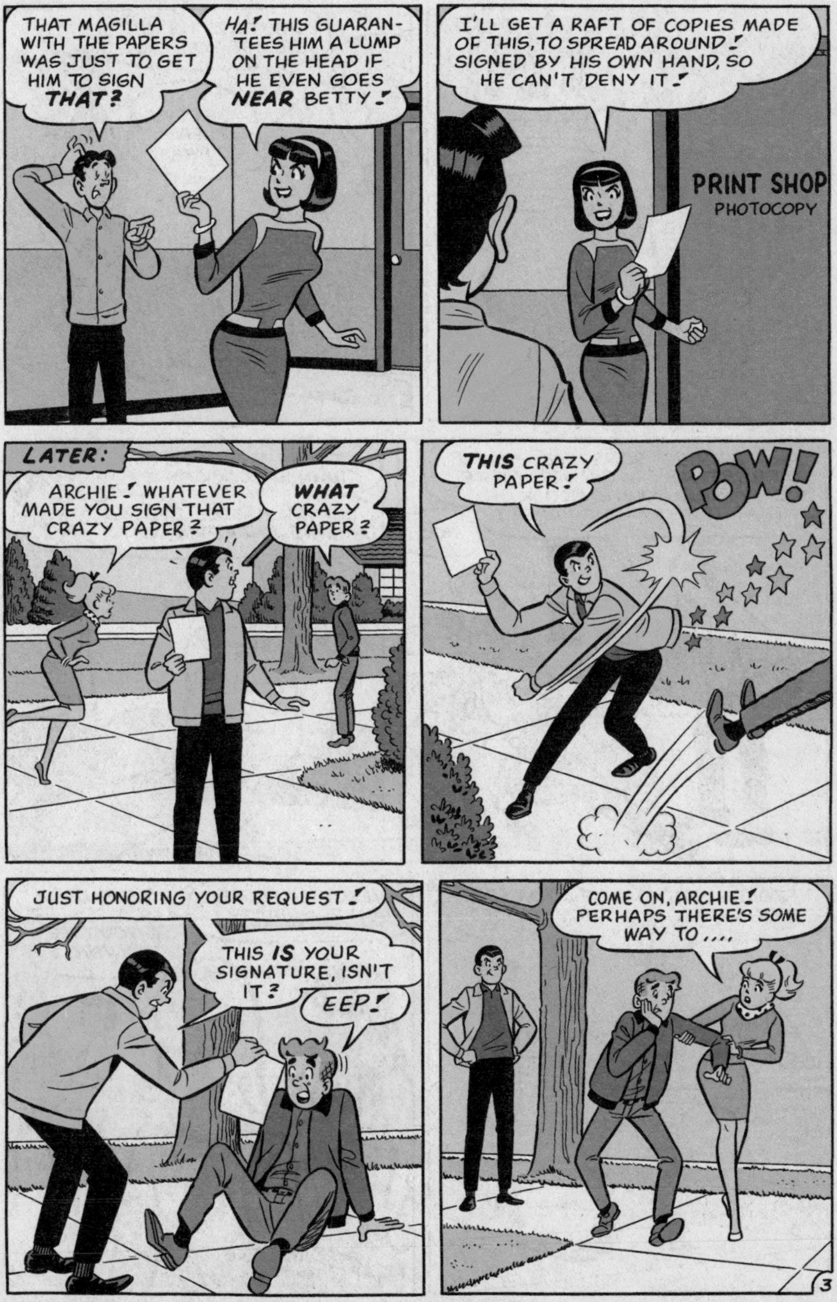
THAT MAGILLA WITH THE PAPERS WAS JUST TO GET HIM TO SIGN THAT?
HA! THIS GUARANTEES HIM A LUMP ON THE HEAD IF HE EVEN GOES NEAR BETTY!
I'LL GET A RAFT OF COPIES MADE OF THIS, TO SPREAD AROUND! SIGNED BY HIS OWN HAND, SO HE CAN'T DENY IT!
PRINT SHOP
PHOTOCOPY
LATER:
ARCHIE! WHATEVER MADE YOU SIGN THAT CRAZY PAPER?
WHAT CRAZY PAPER?
THIS CRAZY PAPER!
POW!
JUST HONORING YOUR REQUEST!
THIS IS YOUR SIGNATURE, ISN'T IT?
EEP!
COME ON, ARCHIE! PERHAPS THERE'S SOME WAY TO....
3

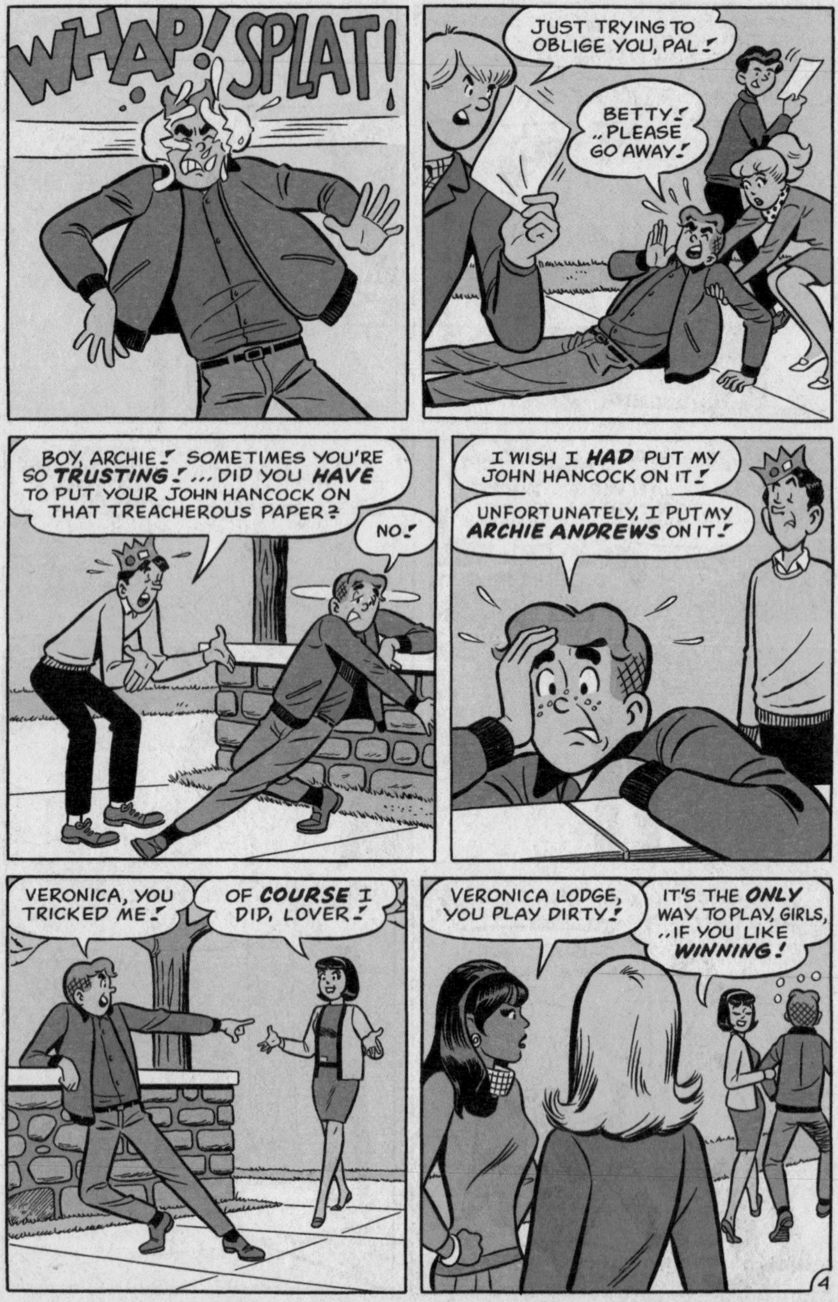
WHAP! SPLAT!
JUST TRYING TO OBLIGE YOU, PAL!
BETTY! ..PLEASE GO AWAY!
BOY, ARCHIE! SOMETIMES YOU'RE SO TRUSTING! ... DID YOU HAVE TO PUT YOUR JOHN HANCOCK ON THAT TREACHEROUS PAPER?
NO!
I WISH I HAD PUT MY JOHN HANCOCK ON IT!
UNFORTUNATELY, I PUT MY ARCHIE ANDREWS ON IT!
VERONICA, YOU TRICKED ME!
OF COURSE I DID, LOVER!
VERONICA LODGE, YOU PLAY DIRTY!
IT'S THE ONLY WAY TO PLAY, GIRLS, ..IF YOU LIKE WINNING!
4

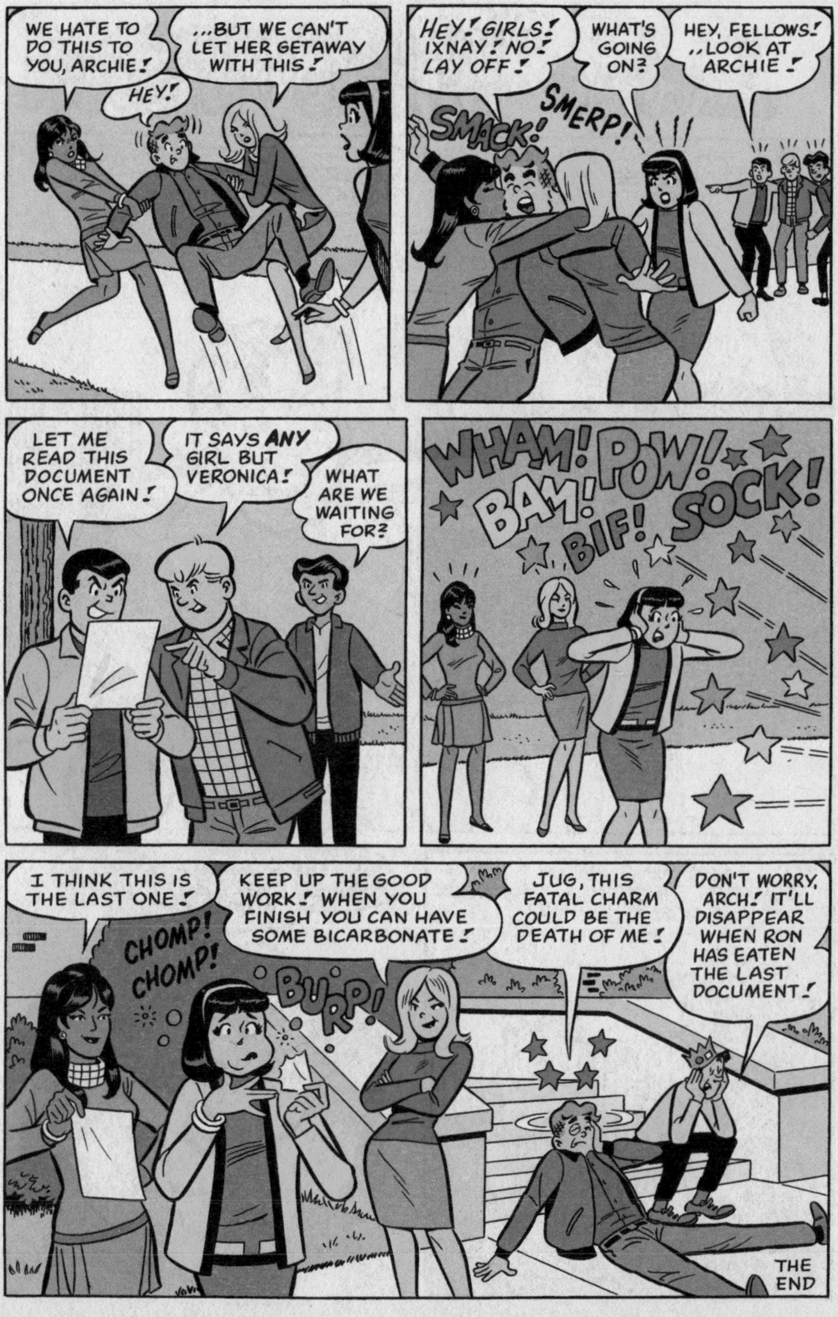
WE HATE TO DO THIS TO YOU, ARCHIE!
...BUT WE CAN'T LET HER GETAWAY WITH THIS!
HEY!
HEY! GIRLS! IXNAY! NO! LAY OFF!
WHAT'S GOING ON?
HEY, FELLOWS! ..LOOK AT ARCHIE!
SMACK!
SMERP!
LET ME READ THIS DOCUMENT ONCE AGAIN!
IT SAYS **ANY** GIRL BUT VERONICA!
WHAT ARE WE WAITING FOR?
WHAM! POW! BAM! BIF! SOCK!
I THINK THIS IS THE LAST ONE!
CHOMP! CHOMP!
KEEP UP THE GOOD WORK! WHEN YOU FINISH YOU CAN HAVE SOME BICARBONATE!
BURP!
JUG, THIS FATAL CHARM COULD BE THE DEATH OF ME!
DON'T WORRY, ARCH! IT'LL DISAPPEAR WHEN RON HAS EATEN THE LAST DOCUMENT!
THE END

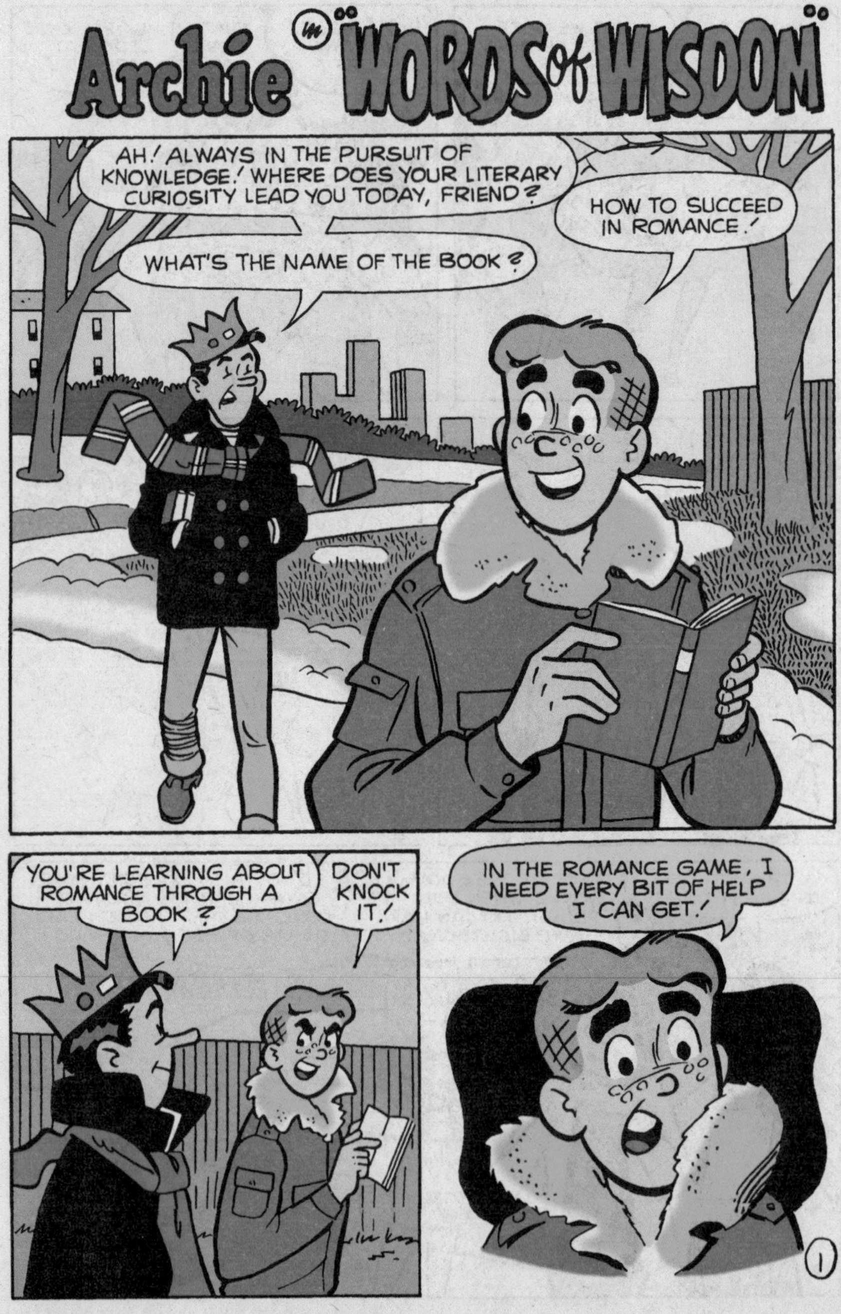
Archie in "WORDS of WISDOM"
AH! ALWAYS IN THE PURSUIT OF KNOWLEDGE! WHERE DOES YOUR LITERARY CURIOSITY LEAD YOU TODAY, FRIEND?
HOW TO SUCCEED IN ROMANCE!
WHAT'S THE NAME OF THE BOOK?
YOU'RE LEARNING ABOUT ROMANCE THROUGH A BOOK?
DON'T KNOCK IT!
IN THE ROMANCE GAME, I NEED EVERY BIT OF HELP I CAN GET!
1

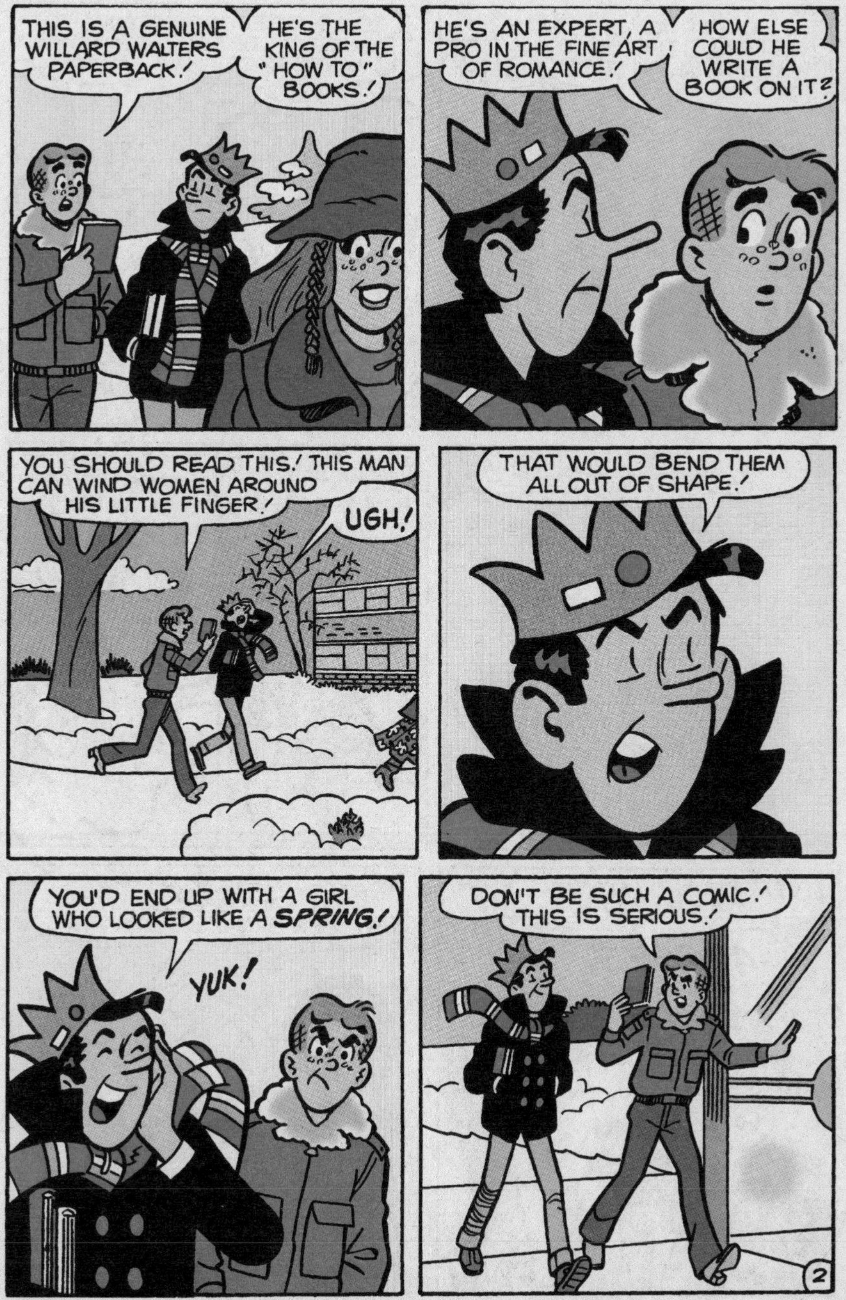
THIS IS A GENUINE WILLARD WALTERS PAPERBACK!
HE'S THE KING OF THE "HOW TO" BOOKS!
HE'S AN EXPERT, A PRO IN THE FINE ART OF ROMANCE!
HOW ELSE COULD HE WRITE A BOOK ON IT?
YOU SHOULD READ THIS! THIS MAN CAN WIND WOMEN AROUND HIS LITTLE FINGER!
UGH!
THAT WOULD BEND THEM ALL OUT OF SHAPE!
YOU'D END UP WITH A GIRL WHO LOOKED LIKE A SPRING!
YUK!
DON'T BE SUCH A COMIC! THIS IS SERIOUS!
2

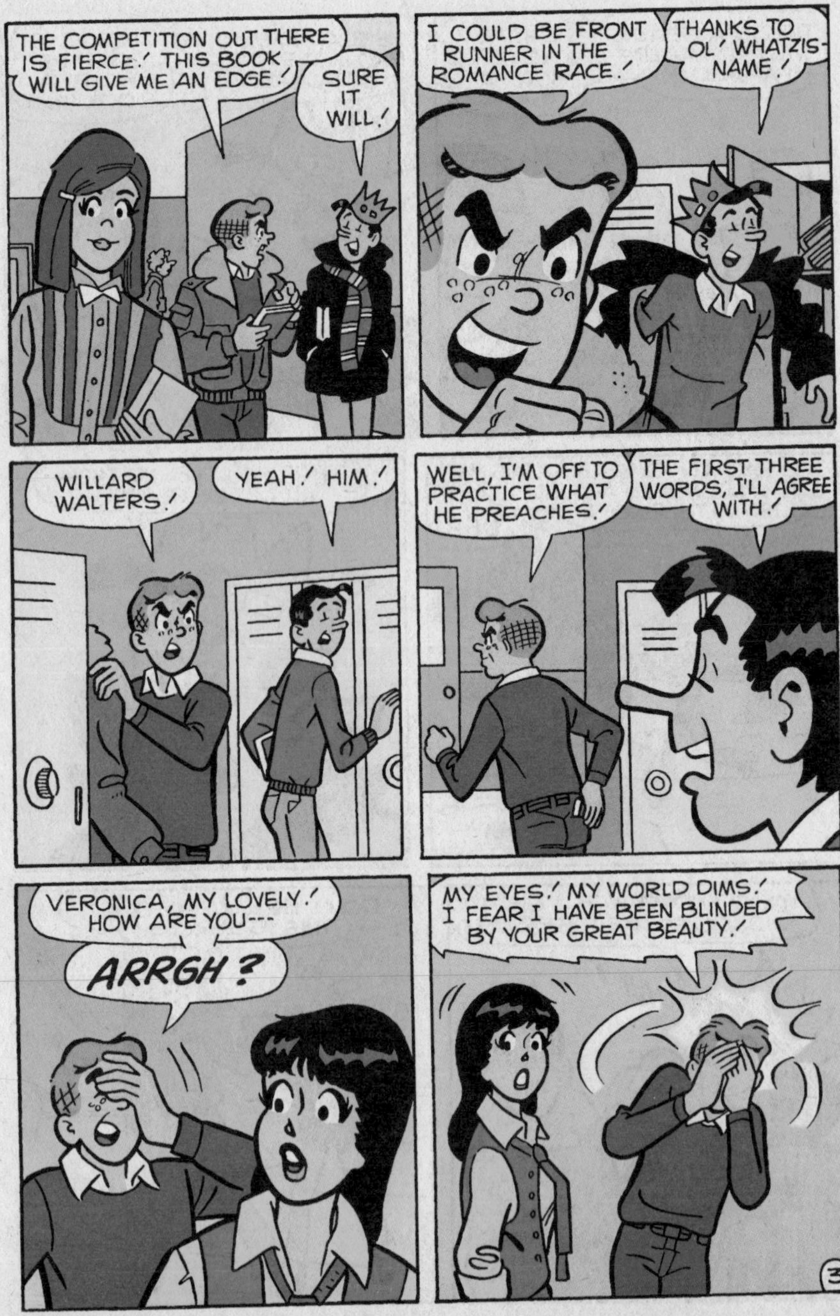
THE COMPETITION OUT THERE IS FIERCE! THIS BOOK WILL GIVE ME AN EDGE!
SURE IT WILL!
I COULD BE FRONT RUNNER IN THE ROMANCE RACE!
THANKS TO OL' WHATZIS-NAME!
WILLARD WALTERS!
YEAH! HIM!
WELL, I'M OFF TO PRACTICE WHAT HE PREACHES!
THE FIRST THREE WORDS, I'LL AGREE WITH!
VERONICA, MY LOVELY! HOW ARE YOU---
ARRGH?
MY EYES! MY WORLD DIMS! I FEAR I HAVE BEEN BLINDED BY YOUR GREAT BEAUTY!
3

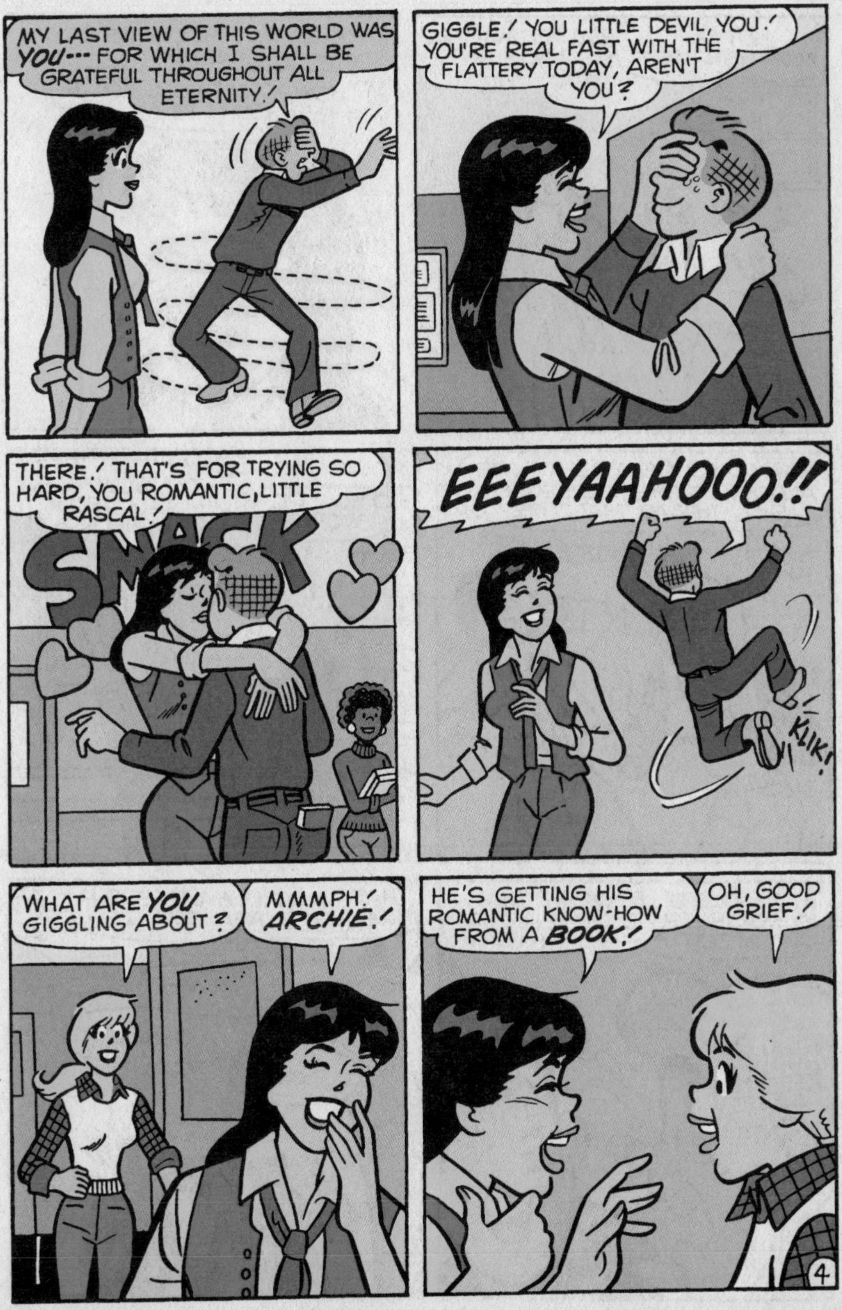
MY LAST VIEW OF THIS WORLD WAS YOU--- FOR WHICH I SHALL BE GRATEFUL THROUGHOUT ALL ETERNITY!
GIGGLE! YOU LITTLE DEVIL, YOU! YOU'RE REAL FAST WITH THE FLATTERY TODAY, AREN'T YOU?
THERE! THAT'S FOR TRYING SO HARD, YOU ROMANTIC, LITTLE RASCAL!
SMACK
EEEYAAHOOO!!
KLIK!
WHAT ARE YOU GIGGLING ABOUT?
MMMPH! ARCHIE!
HE'S GETTING HIS ROMANTIC KNOW-HOW FROM A BOOK!
OH, GOOD GRIEF!
4

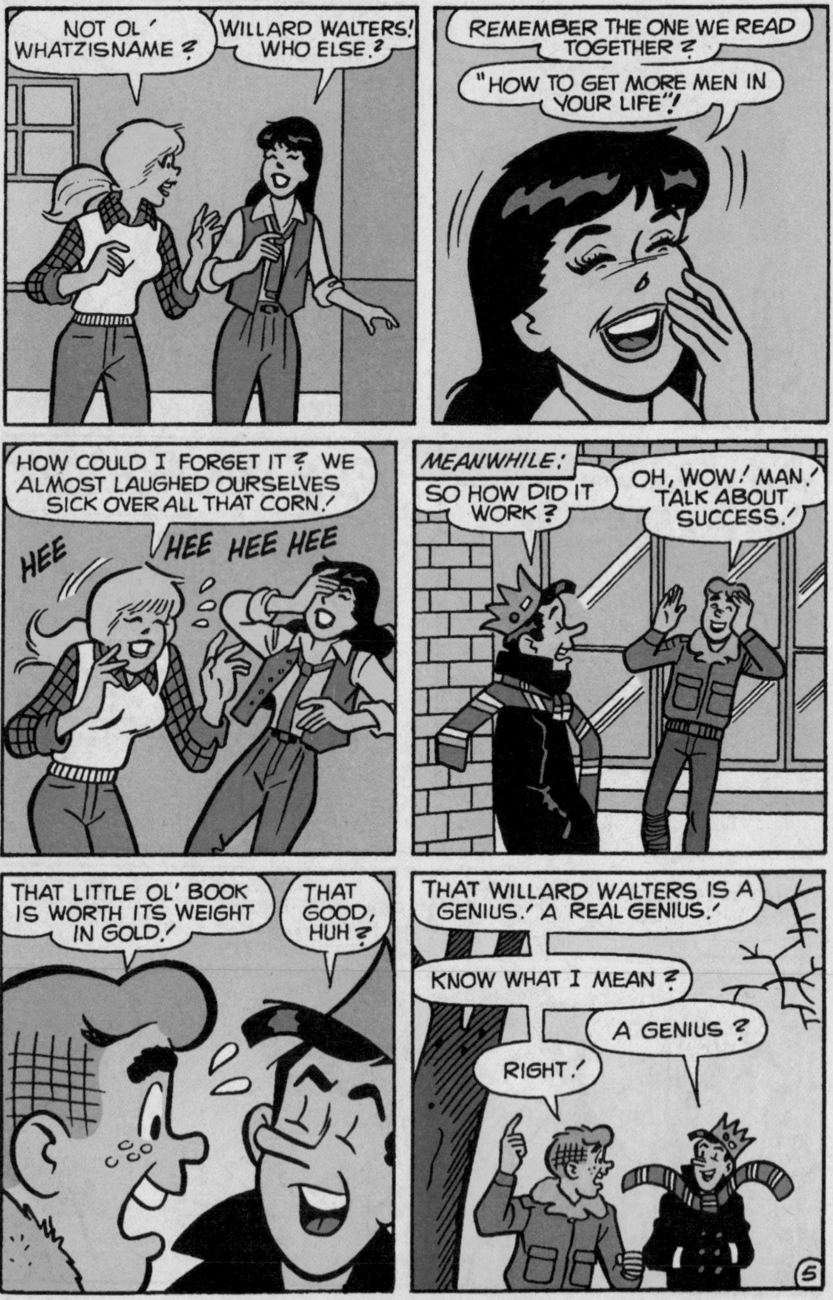
NOT OL' WHATZISNAME ?
WILLARD WALTERS! WHO ELSE ?
REMEMBER THE ONE WE READ TOGETHER ?
"HOW TO GET MORE MEN IN YOUR LIFE"!
HOW COULD I FORGET IT ? WE ALMOST LAUGHED OURSELVES SICK OVER ALL THAT CORN!
HEE
HEE HEE HEE
MEANWHILE:
SO HOW DID IT WORK ?
OH, WOW! MAN! TALK ABOUT SUCCESS!
THAT LITTLE OL' BOOK IS WORTH ITS WEIGHT IN GOLD!
THAT GOOD, HUH ?
THAT WILLARD WALTERS IS A GENIUS! A REAL GENIUS!
KNOW WHAT I MEAN ?
A GENIUS ?
RIGHT!
5

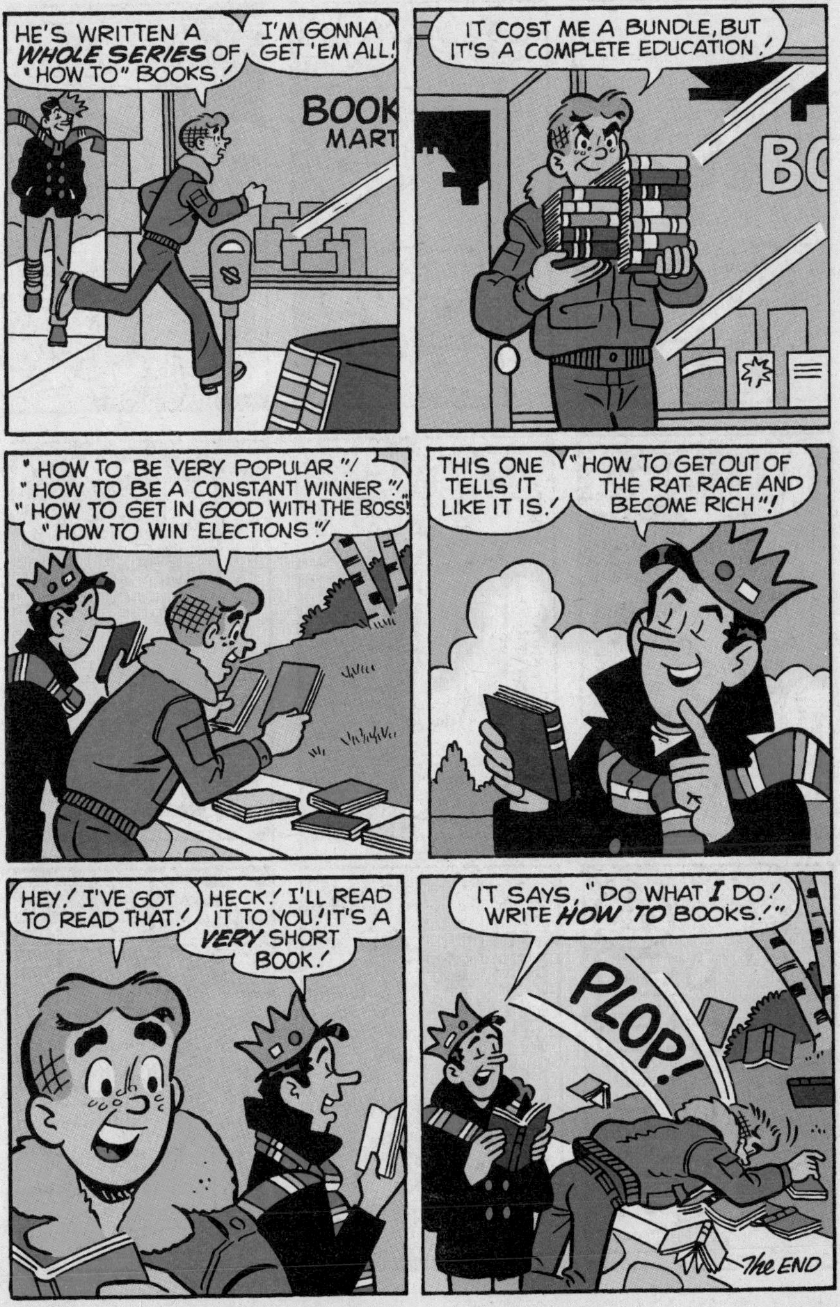
HE'S WRITTEN A WHOLE SERIES OF "HOW TO" BOOKS.!
I'M GONNA GET 'EM ALL!
BOOK MART
IT COST ME A BUNDLE, BUT IT'S A COMPLETE EDUCATION.!
"HOW TO BE VERY POPULAR"! "HOW TO BE A CONSTANT WINNER"! "HOW TO GET IN GOOD WITH THE BOSS"! "HOW TO WIN ELECTIONS"!
THIS ONE TELLS IT LIKE IT IS.!
"HOW TO GET OUT OF THE RAT RACE AND BECOME RICH"!
HEY! I'VE GOT TO READ THAT.!
HECK! I'LL READ IT TO YOU! IT'S A VERY SHORT BOOK.!
IT SAYS, "DO WHAT I DO! WRITE HOW TO BOOKS.!"
PLOP!
The END

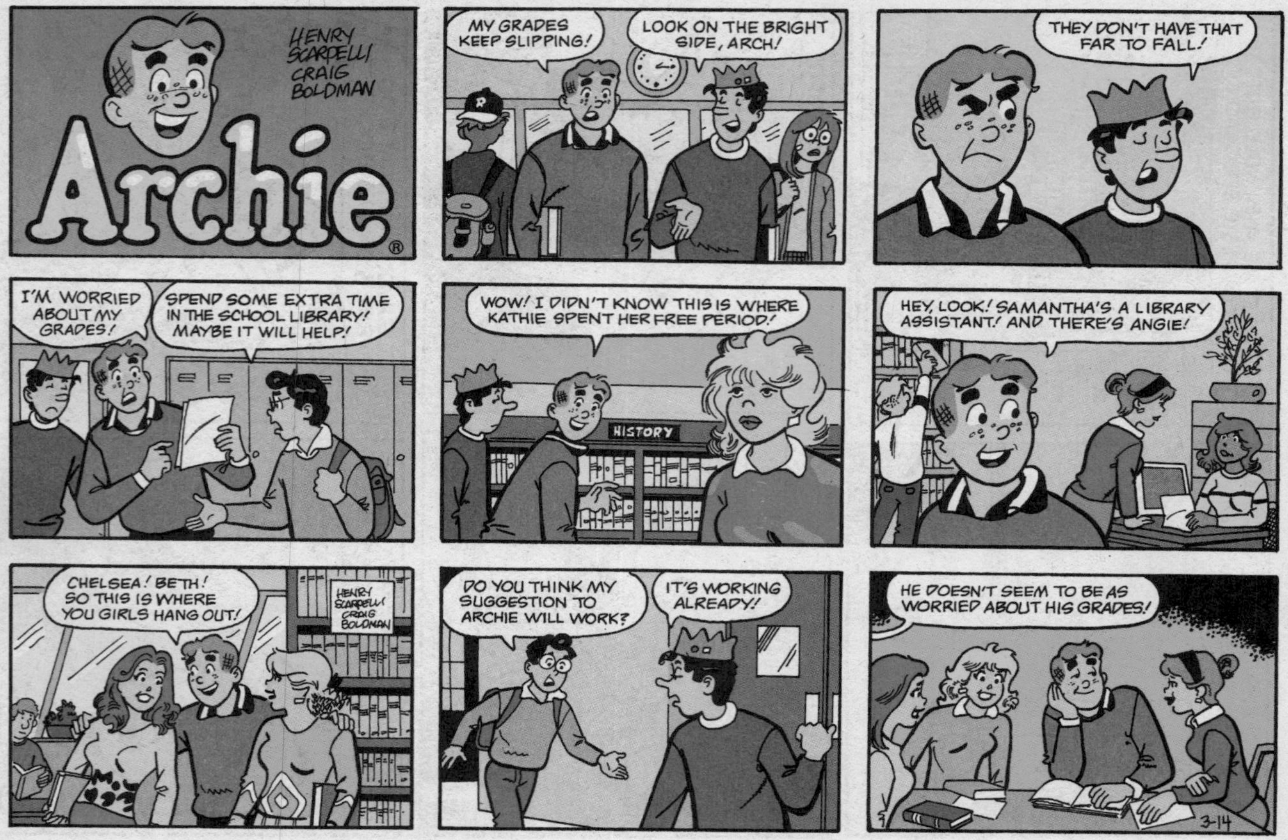
Archie®
HENRY SCARPELLI CRAIG BOLDMAN
MY GRADES KEEP SLIPPING!
LOOK ON THE BRIGHT SIDE, ARCH!
THEY DON'T HAVE THAT FAR TO FALL!
I'M WORRIED ABOUT MY GRADES!
SPEND SOME EXTRA TIME IN THE SCHOOL LIBRARY! MAYBE IT WILL HELP!
WOW! I DIDN'T KNOW THIS IS WHERE KATHIE SPENT HER FREE PERIOD!
HISTORY
HEY, LOOK! SAMANTHA'S A LIBRARY ASSISTANT! AND THERE'S ANGIE!
CHELSEA! BETH! SO THIS IS WHERE YOU GIRLS HANG OUT!
HENRY SCARPELLI CRAIG BOLDMAN
DO YOU THINK MY SUGGESTION TO ARCHIE WILL WORK?
IT'S WORKING ALREADY!
HE DOESN'T SEEM TO BE AS WORRIED ABOUT HIS GRADES!
3-14

Archie's FAVORITE HIGH SCHOOL COMICS

FACULTY FUNNIES

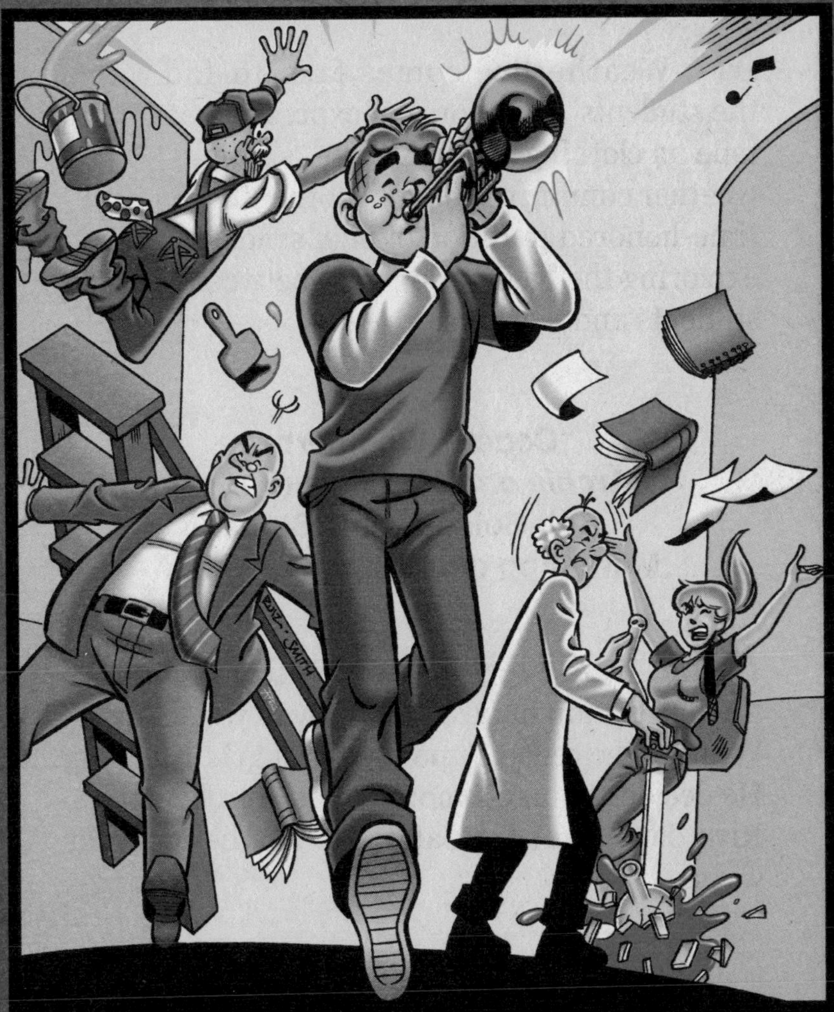

About Face
Pep #156, August 1962
Frank Doyle, Dan DeCarlo, Rudy Lapick and Vincent DeCarlo

Mr. Weatherbee comes face-to-fad with the students' latest form of expression: colored tape on clothing that has them "smiling" whether coming or going! Another in the time-honored tradition of high school tales exploring the "generation gap" between the students and teachers.

"Coach" Weatherbee
Archie and Me #7, April 1966
Bob Bolling, Chic Stone, Marty Epp and Barry Grossman

Little Archie legend Bob Bolling handles the illustration duties for a story in which Mr. Weatherbee reflects upon his past gridiron glory. He decides to take a more hands on role with Riverdale High's football team... for better or for worse.

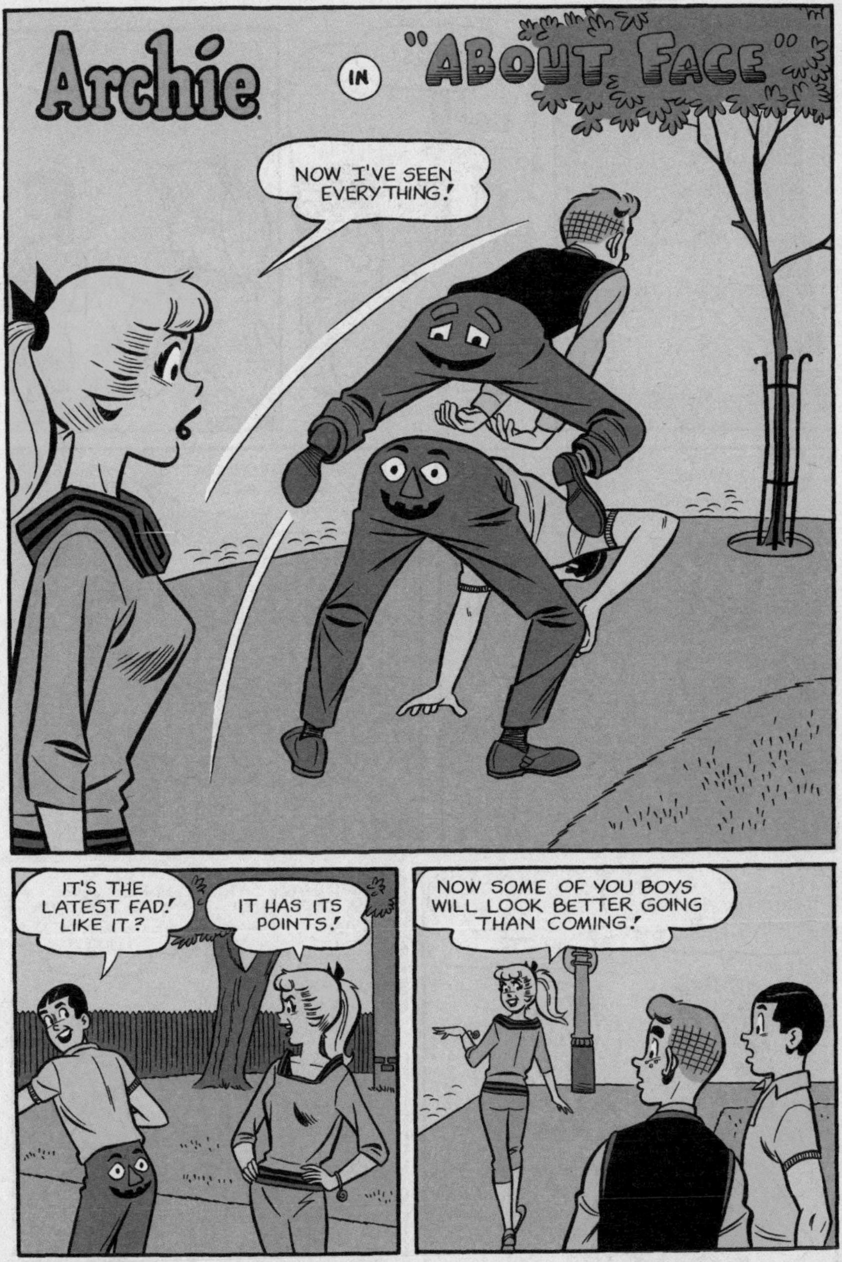
Archie
IN
"ABOUT FACE"
NOW I'VE SEEN EVERYTHING!
IT'S THE LATEST FAD! LIKE IT?
IT HAS ITS POINTS!
NOW SOME OF YOU BOYS WILL LOOK BETTER GOING THAN COMING!

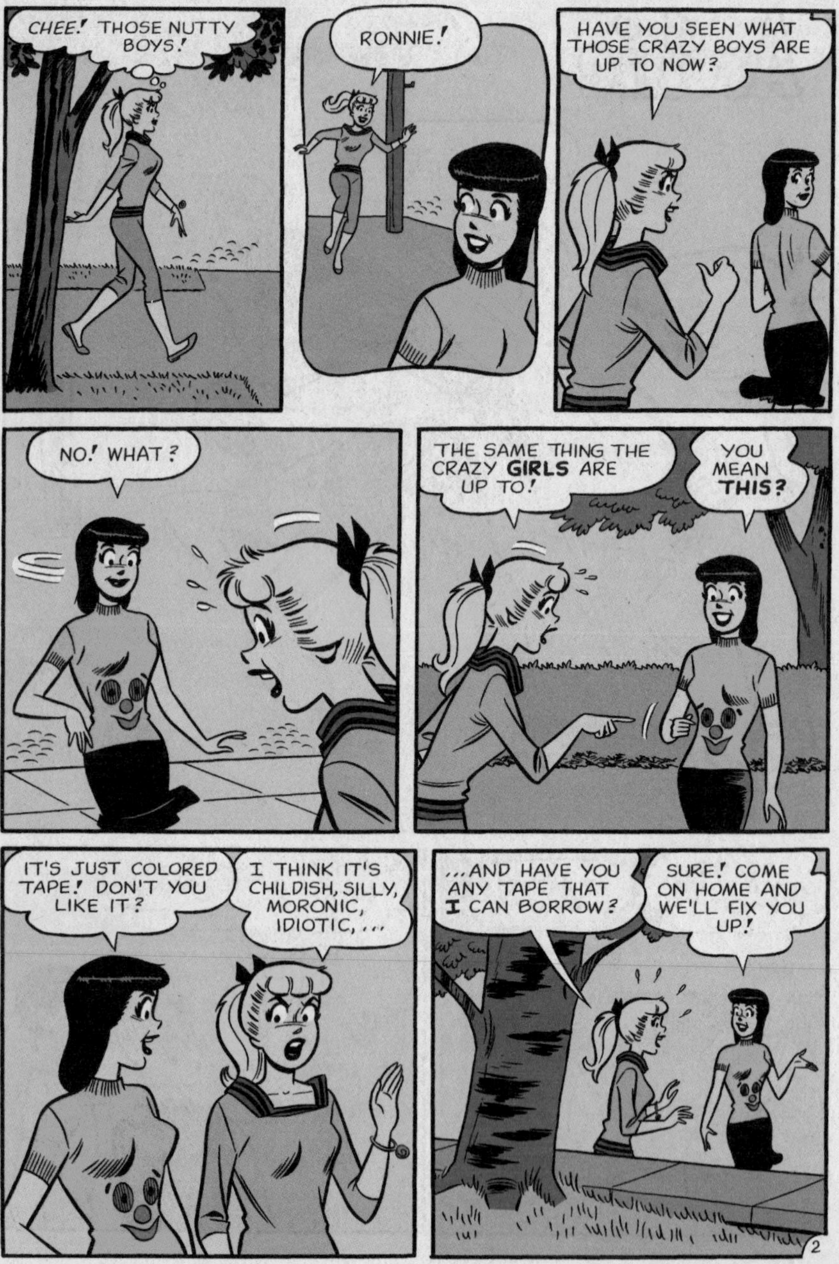
CHEE! THOSE NUTTY BOYS!
RONNIE!
HAVE YOU SEEN WHAT THOSE CRAZY BOYS ARE UP TO NOW?
NO! WHAT?
THE SAME THING THE CRAZY GIRLS ARE UP TO!
YOU MEAN THIS?
IT'S JUST COLORED TAPE! DON'T YOU LIKE IT?
I THINK IT'S CHILDISH, SILLY, MORONIC, IDIOTIC, ...
...AND HAVE YOU ANY TAPE THAT I CAN BORROW?
SURE! COME ON HOME AND WE'LL FIX YOU UP!
2

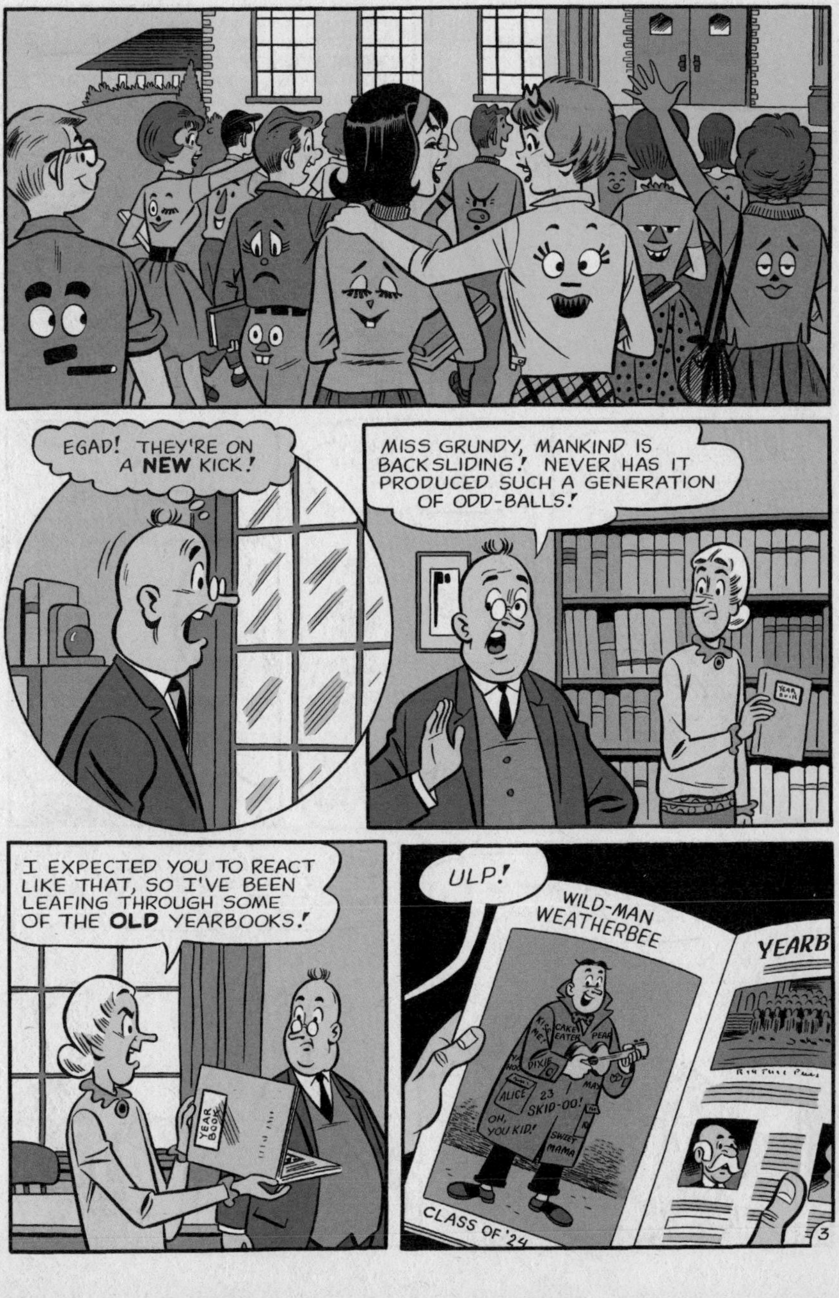
EGAD! THEY'RE ON A **NEW** KICK!
MISS GRUNDY, MANKIND IS BACKSLIDING! NEVER HAS IT PRODUCED SUCH A GENERATION OF ODD-BALLS!
YEAR BOOK
I EXPECTED YOU TO REACT LIKE THAT, SO I'VE BEEN LEAFING THROUGH SOME OF THE **OLD** YEARBOOKS!
YEAR BOOK
ULP!
WILD-MAN WEATHERBEE
CAKE EATER
DIXIE
ALICE
23 SKID-OO!
OH, YOU KID!
SWEET MAMA
CLASS OF '24
YEARB

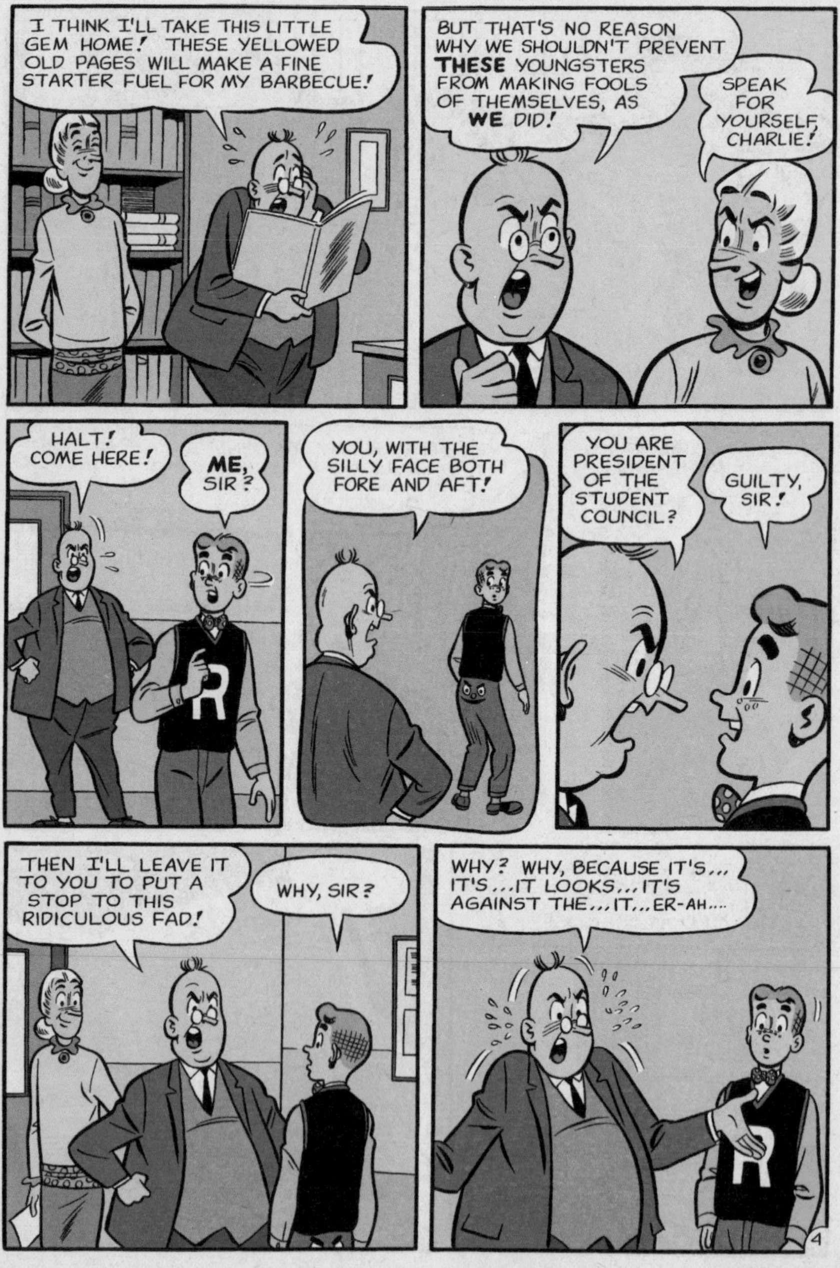
I THINK I'LL TAKE THIS LITTLE GEM HOME! THESE YELLOWED OLD PAGES WILL MAKE A FINE STARTER FUEL FOR MY BARBECUE!
BUT THAT'S NO REASON WHY WE SHOULDN'T PREVENT THESE YOUNGSTERS FROM MAKING FOOLS OF THEMSELVES, AS WE DID!
SPEAK FOR YOURSELF, CHARLIE!
HALT! COME HERE!
ME, SIR?
YOU, WITH THE SILLY FACE BOTH FORE AND AFT!
YOU ARE PRESIDENT OF THE STUDENT COUNCIL?
GUILTY, SIR!
THEN I'LL LEAVE IT TO YOU TO PUT A STOP TO THIS RIDICULOUS FAD!
WHY, SIR?
WHY? WHY, BECAUSE IT'S... IT'S... IT LOOKS... IT'S AGAINST THE... IT... ER-AH....
4

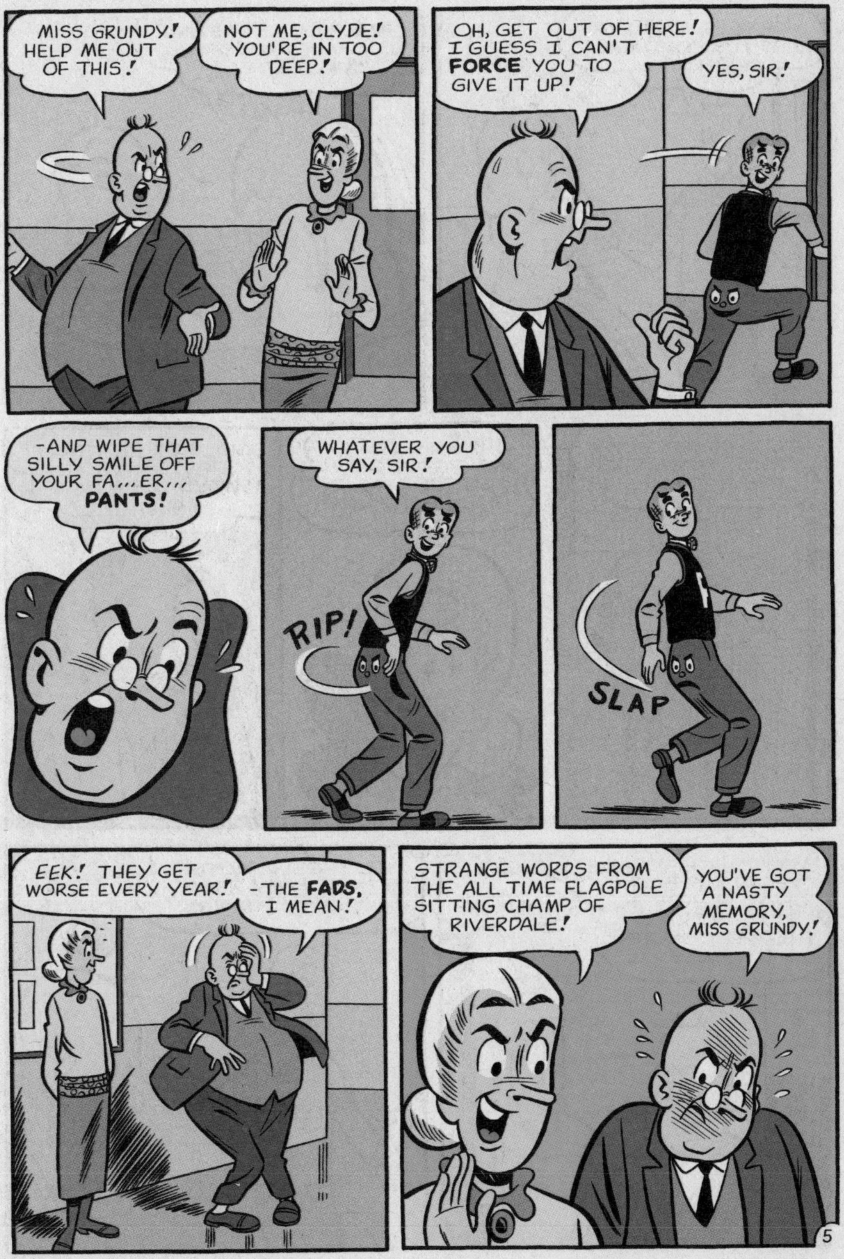
MISS GRUNDY! HELP ME OUT OF THIS!
NOT ME, CLYDE! YOU'RE IN TOO DEEP!
OH, GET OUT OF HERE! I GUESS I CAN'T **FORCE** YOU TO GIVE IT UP!
YES, SIR!
-AND WIPE THAT SILLY SMILE OFF YOUR FA... ER... **PANTS!**
WHATEVER YOU SAY, SIR!
RIP!
SLAP
EEK! THEY GET WORSE EVERY YEAR!
-THE **FADS**, I MEAN!
STRANGE WORDS FROM THE ALL TIME FLAGPOLE SITTING CHAMP OF RIVERDALE!
YOU'VE GOT A NASTY MEMORY, MISS GRUNDY!
5

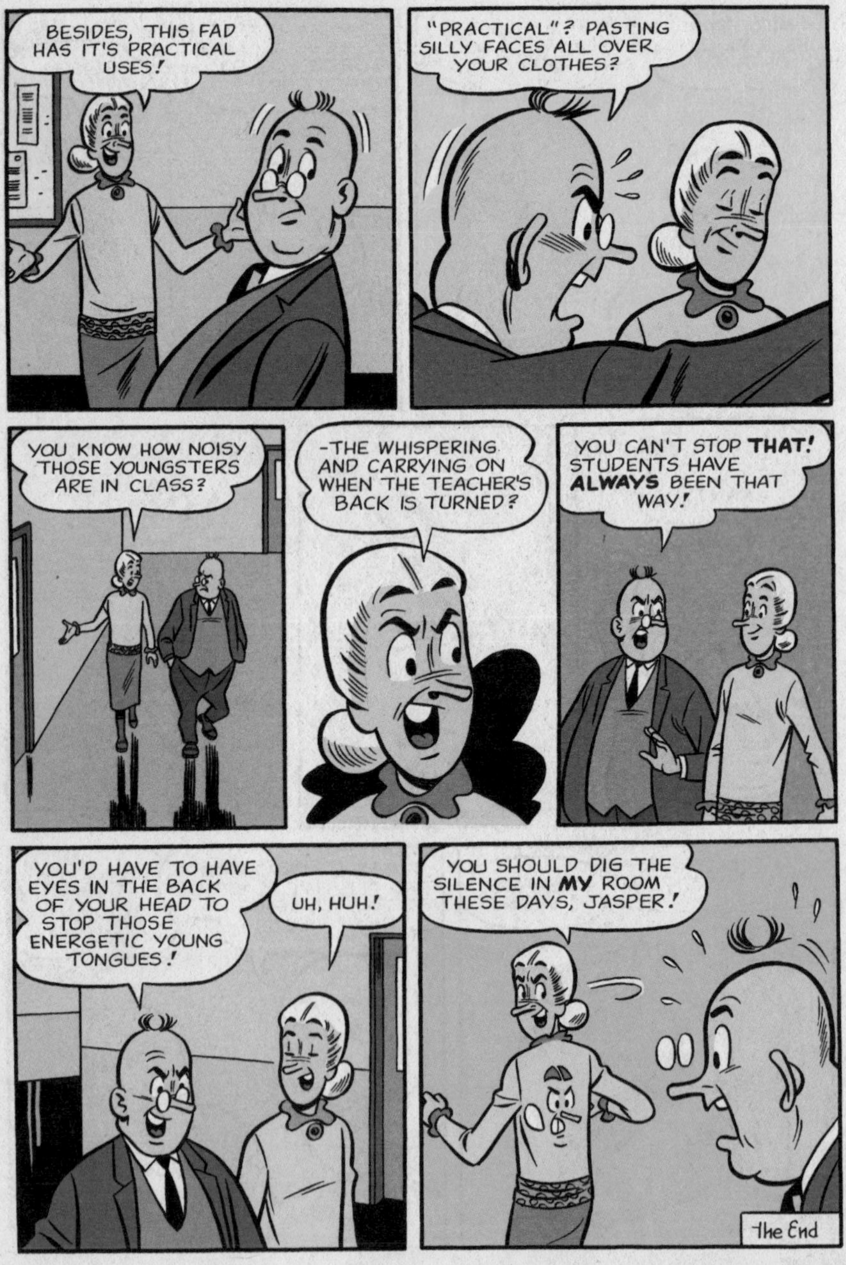
BESIDES, THIS FAD HAS IT'S PRACTICAL USES!
"PRACTICAL"? PASTING SILLY FACES ALL OVER YOUR CLOTHES?
YOU KNOW HOW NOISY THOSE YOUNGSTERS ARE IN CLASS?
-THE WHISPERING AND CARRYING ON WHEN THE TEACHER'S BACK IS TURNED?
YOU CAN'T STOP THAT! STUDENTS HAVE ALWAYS BEEN THAT WAY!
YOU'D HAVE TO HAVE EYES IN THE BACK OF YOUR HEAD TO STOP THOSE ENERGETIC YOUNG TONGUES!
UH, HUH!
YOU SHOULD DIG THE SILENCE IN MY ROOM THESE DAYS, JASPER!
The End

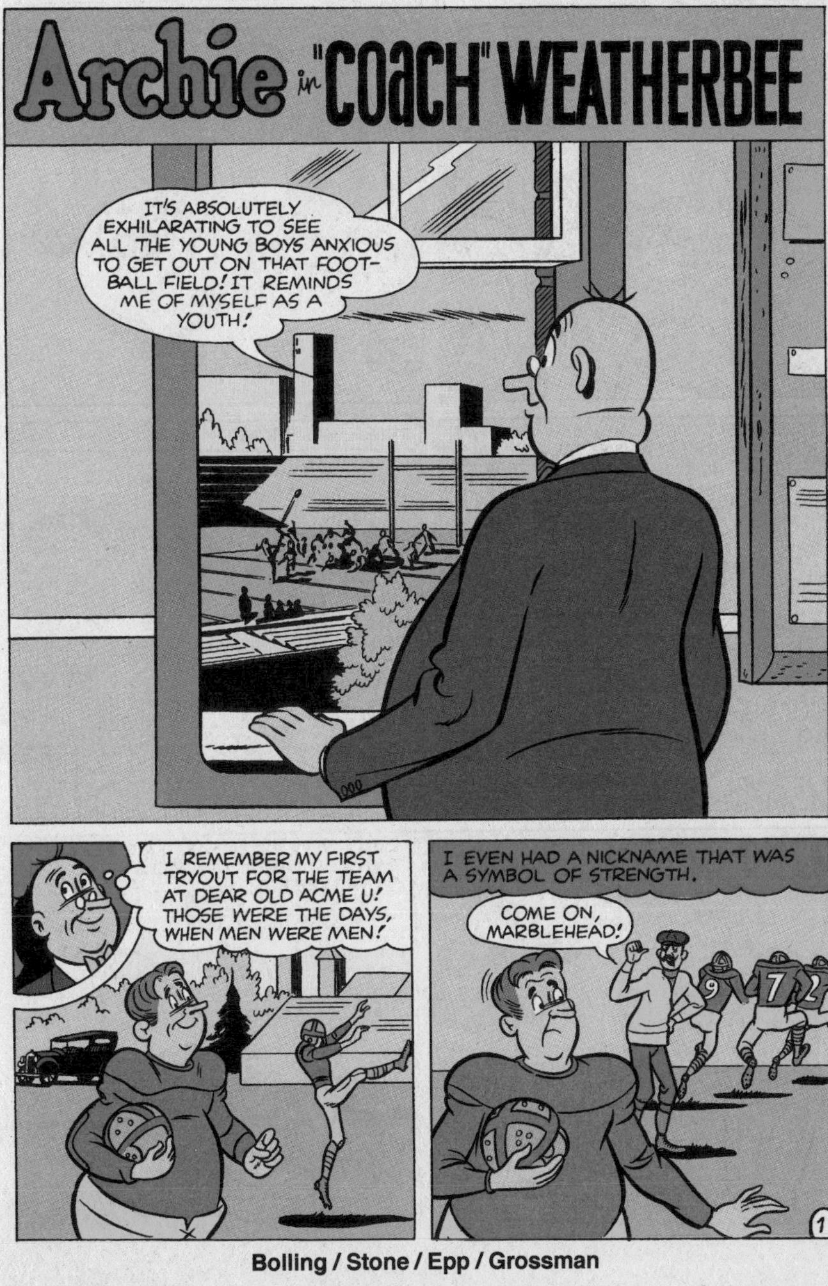
Archie in "COACH" WEATHERBEE
IT'S ABSOLUTELY EXHILARATING TO SEE ALL THE YOUNG BOYS ANXIOUS TO GET OUT ON THAT FOOT-BALL FIELD! IT REMINDS ME OF MYSELF AS A YOUTH!
I REMEMBER MY FIRST TRYOUT FOR THE TEAM AT DEAR OLD ACME U! THOSE WERE THE DAYS, WHEN MEN WERE MEN!
I EVEN HAD A NICKNAME THAT WAS A SYMBOL OF STRENGTH.
COME ON, MARBLEHEAD!
1

Bolling / Stone / Epp / Grossman

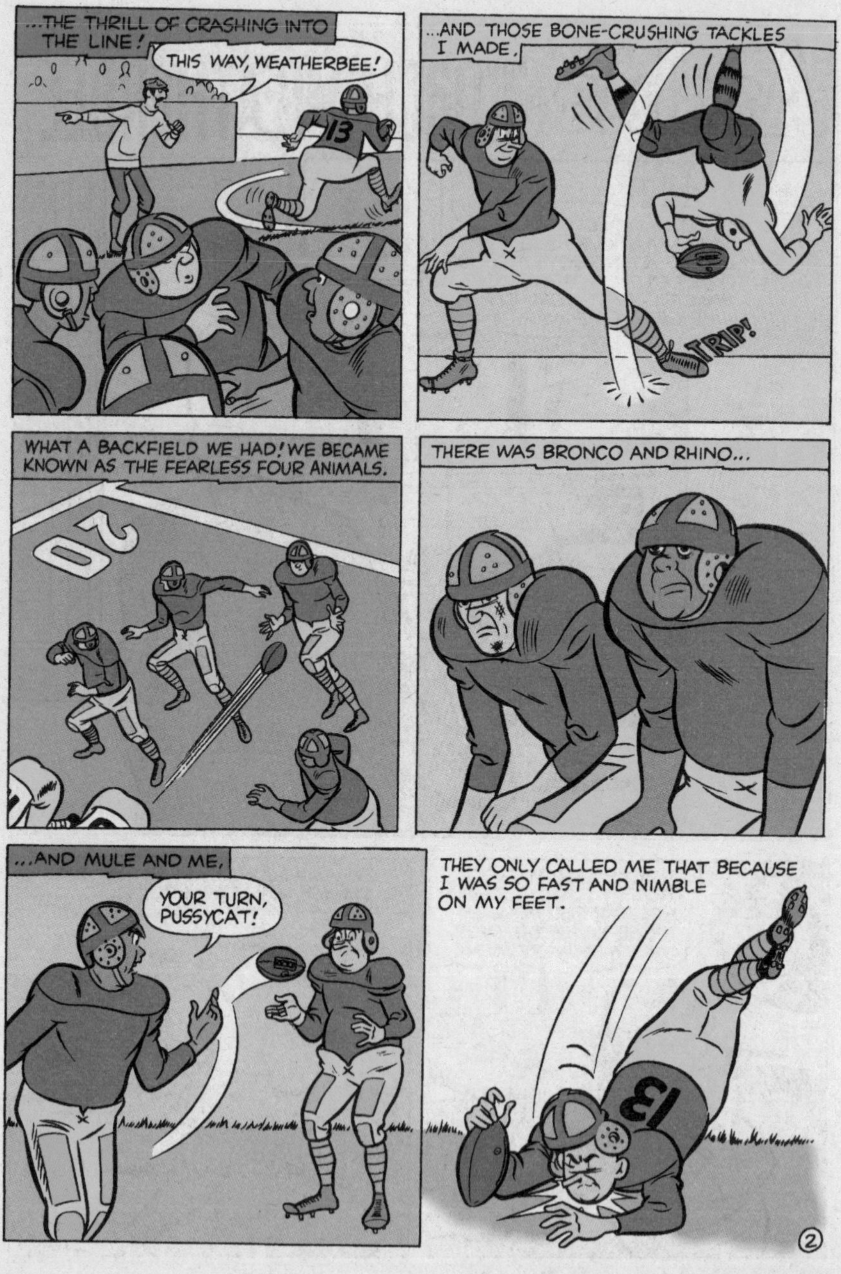
...THE THRILL OF CRASHING INTO THE LINE!
THIS WAY, WEATHERBEE!
...AND THOSE BONE-CRUSHING TACKLES I MADE.
TRIP!
WHAT A BACKFIELD WE HAD! WE BECAME KNOWN AS THE FEARLESS FOUR ANIMALS.
THERE WAS BRONCO AND RHINO...
...AND MULE AND ME.
YOUR TURN, PUSSYCAT!
THEY ONLY CALLED ME THAT BECAUSE I WAS SO FAST AND NIMBLE ON MY FEET.
2

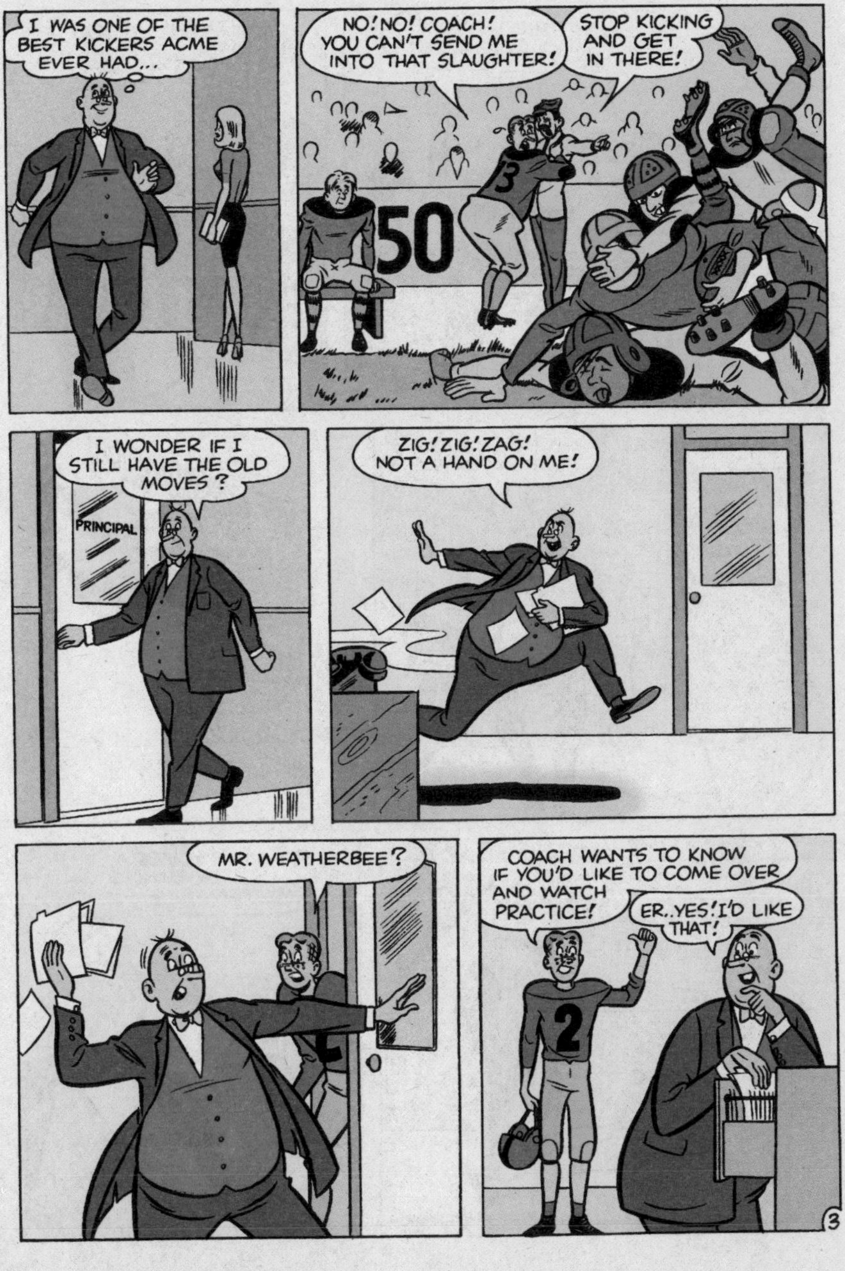
I WAS ONE OF THE BEST KICKERS ACME EVER HAD...
NO! NO! COACH! YOU CAN'T SEND ME INTO THAT SLAUGHTER!
STOP KICKING AND GET IN THERE!
50
I WONDER IF I STILL HAVE THE OLD MOVES?
PRINCIPAL
ZIG! ZIG! ZAG! NOT A HAND ON ME!
MR. WEATHERBEE?
COACH WANTS TO KNOW IF YOU'D LIKE TO COME OVER AND WATCH PRACTICE!
ER..YES! I'D LIKE THAT!
3

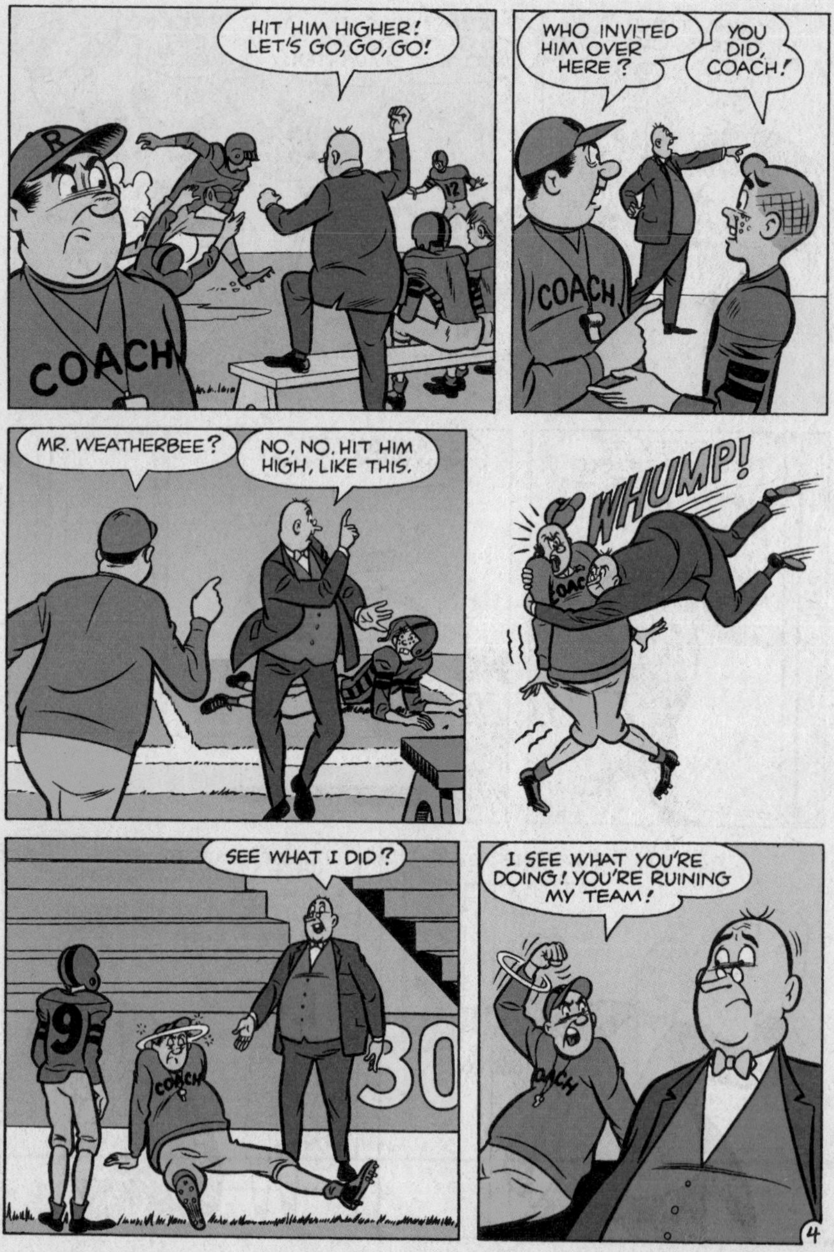
HIT HIM HIGHER! LET'S GO, GO, GO!
COACH
WHO INVITED HIM OVER HERE?
YOU DID, COACH!
COACH
MR. WEATHERBEE?
NO, NO. HIT HIM HIGH, LIKE THIS.
WHUMP!
SEE WHAT I DID?
I SEE WHAT YOU'RE DOING! YOU'RE RUINING MY TEAM!
4

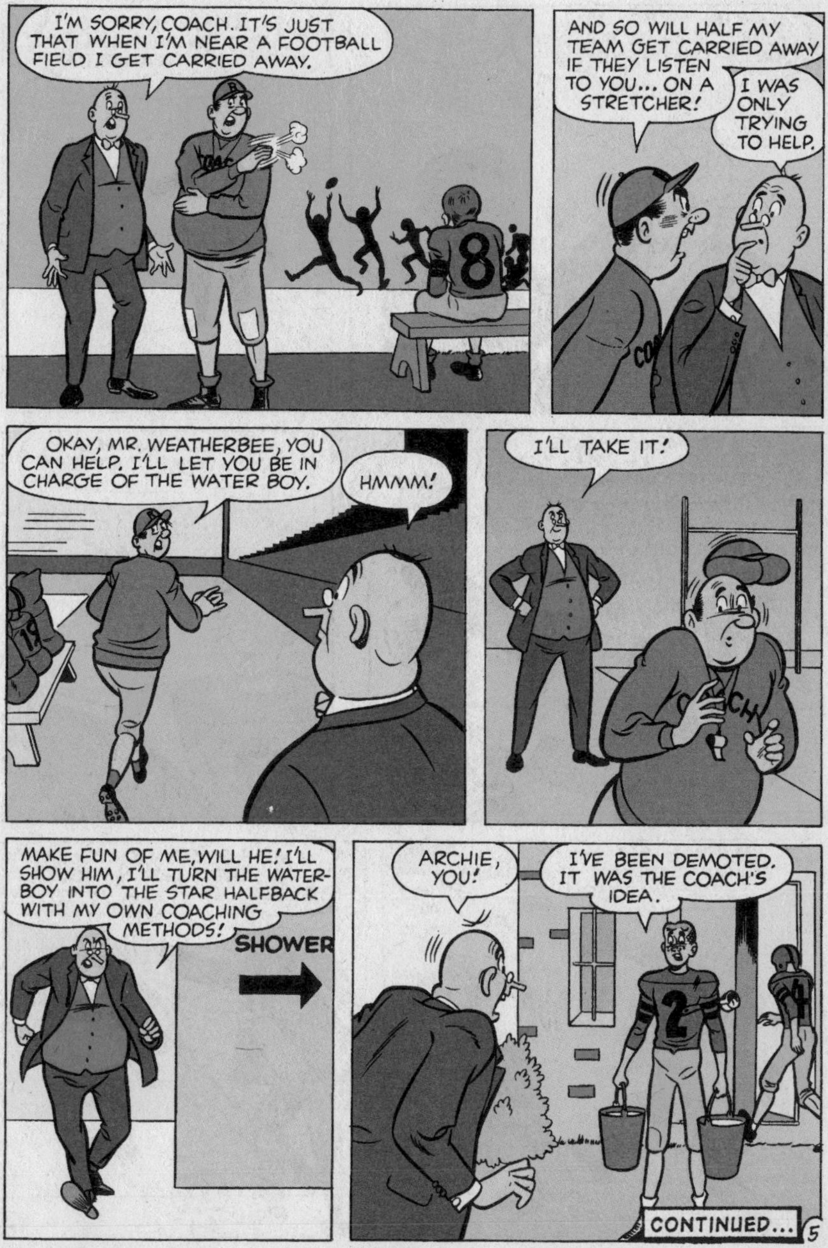
I'M SORRY, COACH. IT'S JUST THAT WHEN I'M NEAR A FOOTBALL FIELD I GET CARRIED AWAY.
AND SO WILL HALF MY TEAM GET CARRIED AWAY IF THEY LISTEN TO YOU... ON A STRETCHER!
I WAS ONLY TRYING TO HELP.
OKAY, MR. WEATHERBEE, YOU CAN HELP. I'LL LET YOU BE IN CHARGE OF THE WATER BOY.
HMMM!
I'LL TAKE IT!
MAKE FUN OF ME, WILL HE! I'LL SHOW HIM, I'LL TURN THE WATER-BOY INTO THE STAR HALFBACK WITH MY OWN COACHING METHODS!
SHOWER
ARCHIE, YOU!
I'VE BEEN DEMOTED. IT WAS THE COACH'S IDEA.
CONTINUED...
5

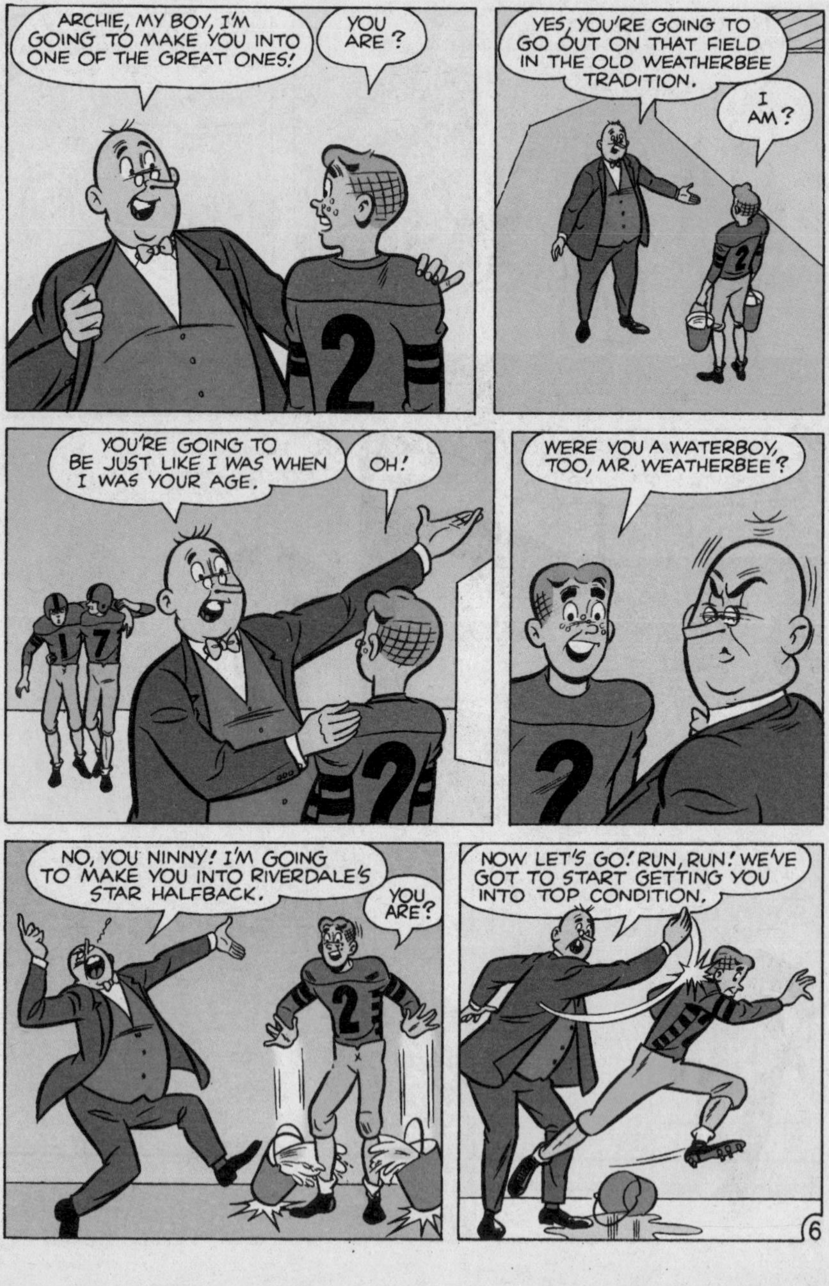
ARCHIE, MY BOY, I'M GOING TO MAKE YOU INTO ONE OF THE GREAT ONES!
YOU ARE?
YES, YOU'RE GOING TO GO OUT ON THAT FIELD IN THE OLD WEATHERBEE TRADITION.
I AM?
YOU'RE GOING TO BE JUST LIKE I WAS WHEN I WAS YOUR AGE.
OH!
WERE YOU A WATERBOY, TOO, MR. WEATHERBEE?
NO, YOU NINNY! I'M GOING TO MAKE YOU INTO RIVERDALE'S STAR HALFBACK.
YOU ARE?
NOW LET'S GO! RUN, RUN! WE'VE GOT TO START GETTING YOU INTO TOP CONDITION.
6

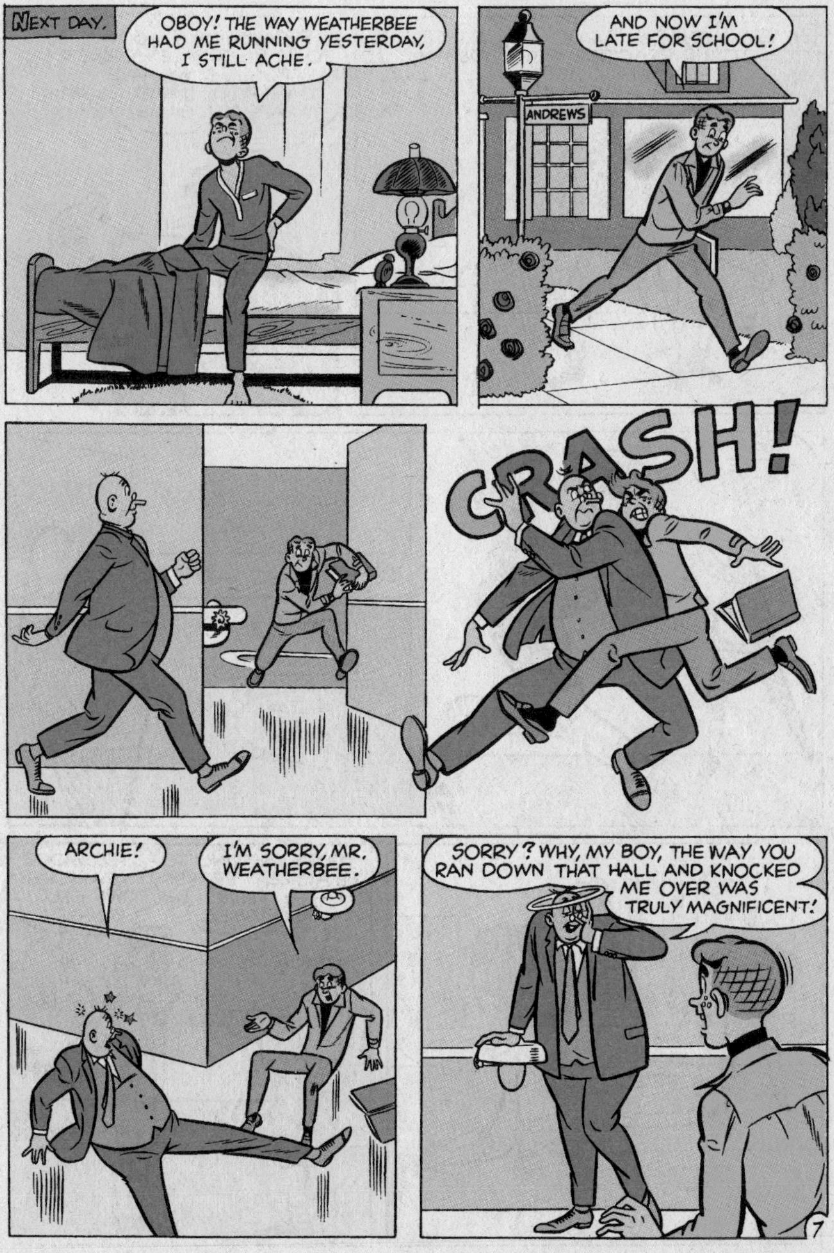
NEXT DAY.
OBOY! THE WAY WEATHERBEE HAD ME RUNNING YESTERDAY, I STILL ACHE.
AND NOW I'M LATE FOR SCHOOL!
ANDREWS
CRASH!
ARCHIE!
I'M SORRY, MR. WEATHERBEE.
SORRY? WHY, MY BOY, THE WAY YOU RAN DOWN THAT HALL AND KNOCKED ME OVER WAS TRULY MAGNIFICENT!
7

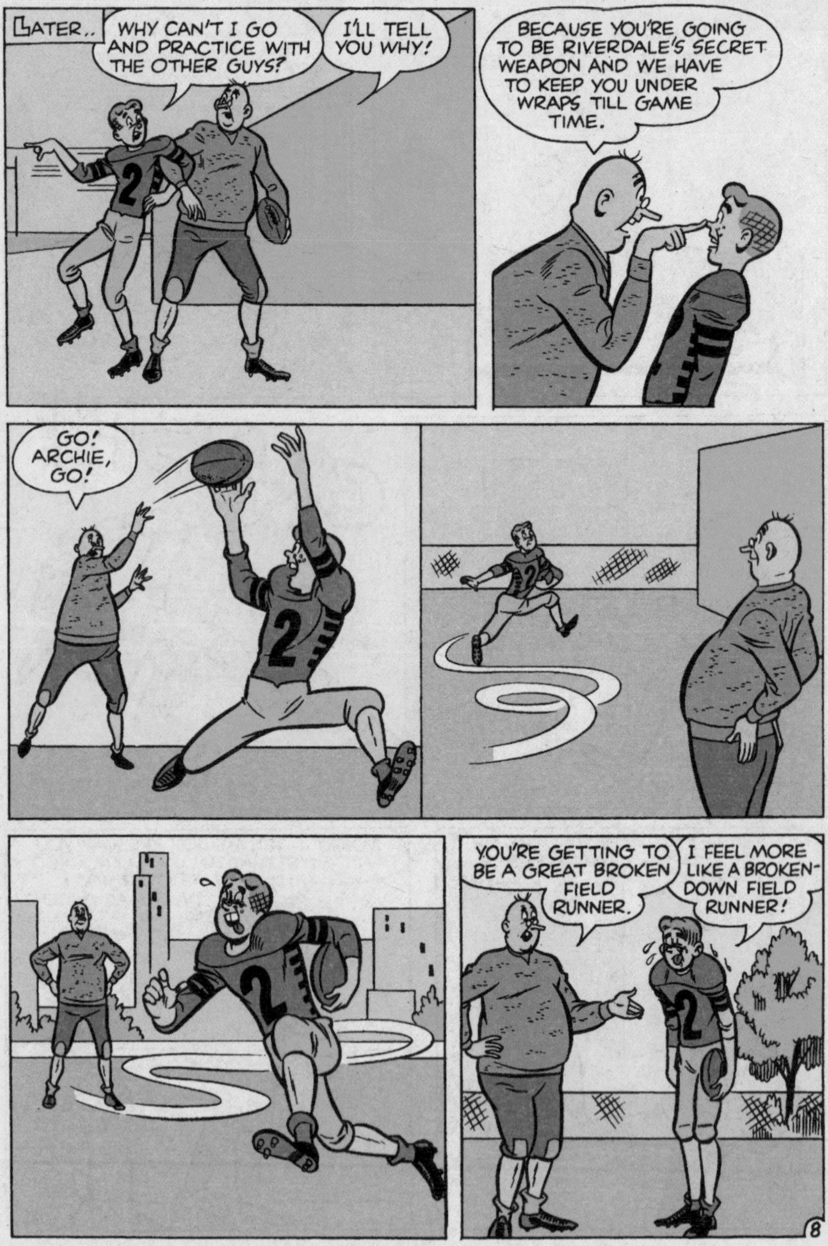
LATER..
WHY CAN'T I GO AND PRACTICE WITH THE OTHER GUYS?
I'LL TELL YOU WHY!
BECAUSE YOU'RE GOING TO BE RIVERDALE'S SECRET WEAPON AND WE HAVE TO KEEP YOU UNDER WRAPS TILL GAME TIME.
GO! ARCHIE, GO!
YOU'RE GETTING TO BE A GREAT BROKEN FIELD RUNNER.
I FEEL MORE LIKE A BROKEN-DOWN FIELD RUNNER!
8

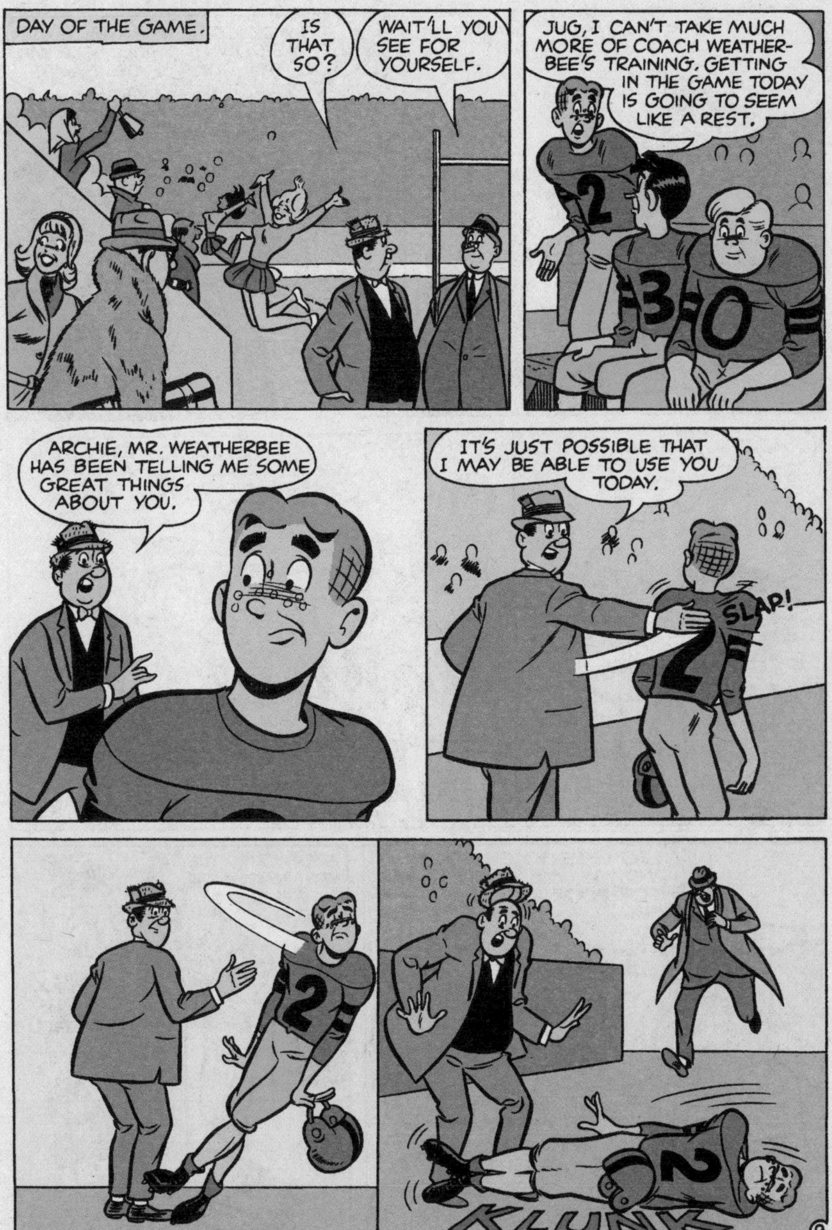
DAY OF THE GAME.
IS THAT SO?
WAIT'LL YOU SEE FOR YOURSELF.
JUG, I CAN'T TAKE MUCH MORE OF COACH WEATHER-BEE'S TRAINING. GETTING IN THE GAME TODAY IS GOING TO SEEM LIKE A REST.
ARCHIE, MR. WEATHERBEE HAS BEEN TELLING ME SOME GREAT THINGS ABOUT YOU.
IT'S JUST POSSIBLE THAT I MAY BE ABLE TO USE YOU TODAY.
SLAP!
KLUNK
9

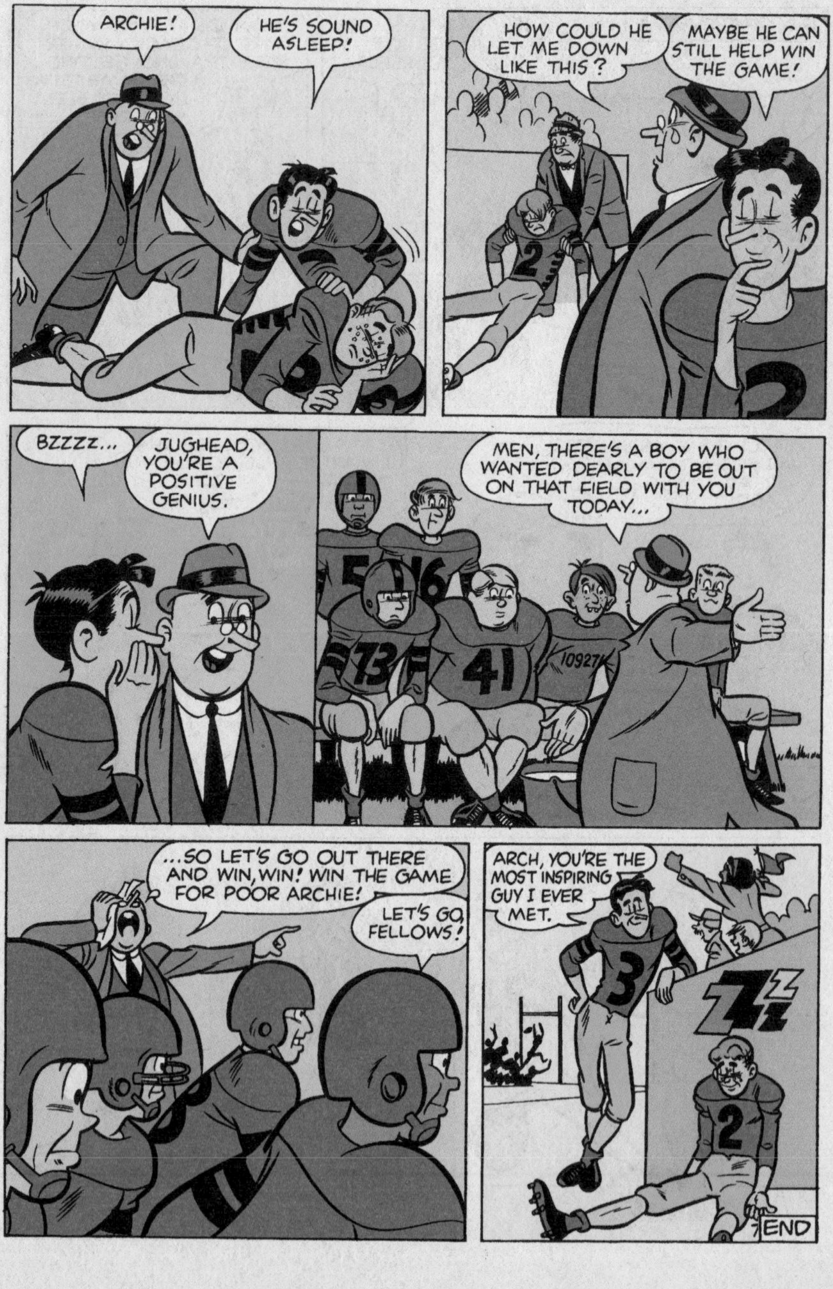
ARCHIE!
HE'S SOUND ASLEEP!
HOW COULD HE LET ME DOWN LIKE THIS?
MAYBE HE CAN STILL HELP WIN THE GAME!
BZZZZ...
JUGHEAD, YOU'RE A POSITIVE GENIUS.
MEN, THERE'S A BOY WHO WANTED DEARLY TO BE OUT ON THAT FIELD WITH YOU TODAY...
...SO LET'S GO OUT THERE AND WIN, WIN! WIN THE GAME FOR POOR ARCHIE!
LET'S GO, FELLOWS!
ARCH, YOU'RE THE MOST INSPIRING GUY I EVER MET.
Z Z Z
END

Bizarre Star
Archie's TV Laugh Out #40, June 1976
**George Gladir, Samm Schwartz
and Barry Grossman**

The annual student/alumni basketball game is on... and this year Mr. Weatherbee has a secret weapon: an alumni-turned pro! But it just might not be the pro the Bee is thinking of. Will the Bee's plan score his team a slam-dunk victory or just get them slammed?!

Boots
Jughead #115, December 1964
**Jim Ruth, Samm Schwartz
and Vincent DeCarlo**

Perhaps Mr. Weatherbee needs to listen to some Nancy Sinatra, because Jughead's boots are clearly made for walking. But Jughead's fancy footwear make a terrible racket, so the principal instructs him to take them off—not realizing the crazy trouble he is about to unleash by doing so.

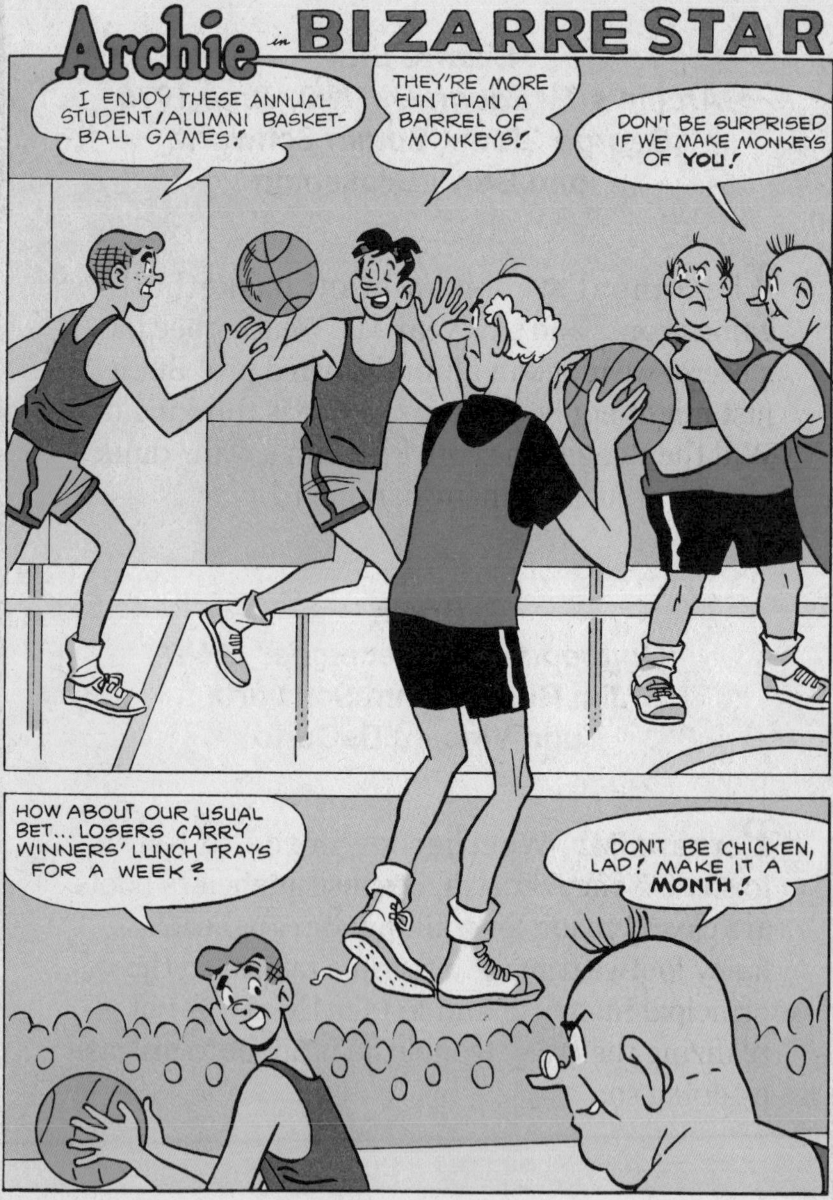
Archie in BIZARRE STAR
I ENJOY THESE ANNUAL STUDENT/ALUMNI BASKET-BALL GAMES!
THEY'RE MORE FUN THAN A BARREL OF MONKEYS!
DON'T BE SURPRISED IF WE MAKE MONKEYS OF YOU!
HOW ABOUT OUR USUAL BET... LOSERS CARRY WINNERS' LUNCH TRAYS FOR A WEEK?
DON'T BE CHICKEN, LAD! MAKE IT A MONTH!

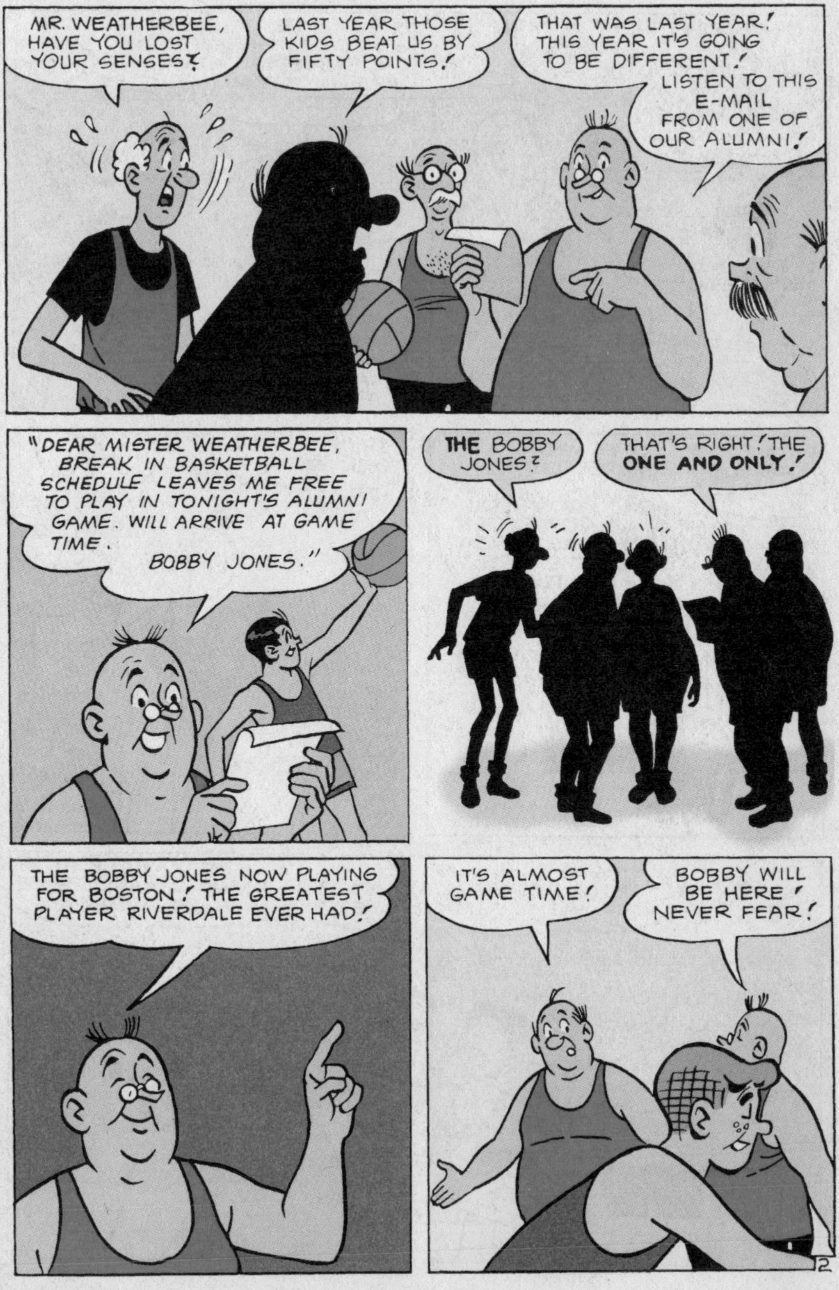
MR. WEATHERBEE, HAVE YOU LOST YOUR SENSES?
LAST YEAR THOSE KIDS BEAT US BY FIFTY POINTS!
THAT WAS LAST YEAR! THIS YEAR IT'S GOING TO BE DIFFERENT!
LISTEN TO THIS E-MAIL FROM ONE OF OUR ALUMNI!
"DEAR MISTER WEATHERBEE, BREAK IN BASKETBALL SCHEDULE LEAVES ME FREE TO PLAY IN TONIGHT'S ALUMNI GAME. WILL ARRIVE AT GAME TIME. BOBBY JONES."
THE BOBBY JONES?
THAT'S RIGHT! THE ONE AND ONLY!
THE BOBBY JONES NOW PLAYING FOR BOSTON! THE GREATEST PLAYER RIVERDALE EVER HAD!
IT'S ALMOST GAME TIME!
BOBBY WILL BE HERE! NEVER FEAR!
2

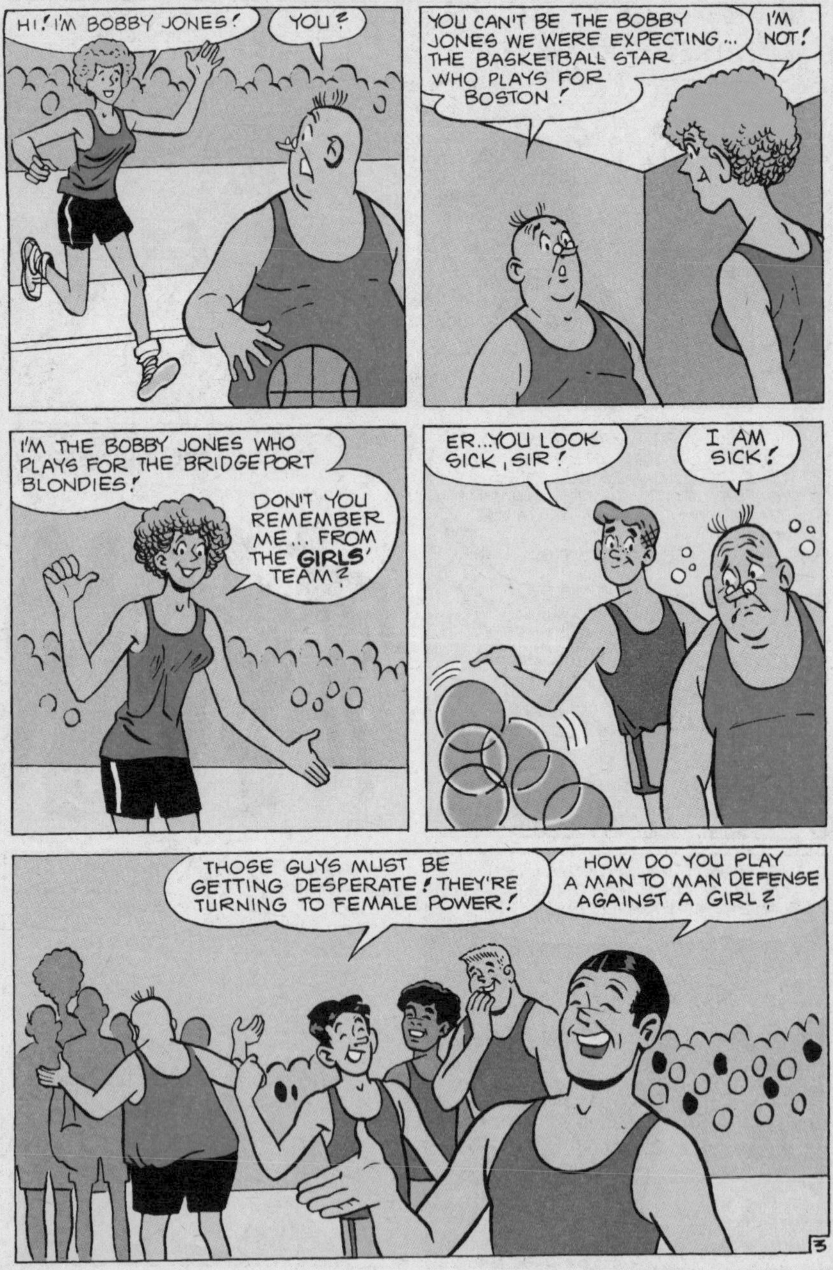
HI! I'M BOBBY JONES!
YOU?
YOU CAN'T BE THE BOBBY JONES WE WERE EXPECTING... THE BASKETBALL STAR WHO PLAYS FOR BOSTON!
I'M NOT!
I'M THE BOBBY JONES WHO PLAYS FOR THE BRIDGEPORT BLONDIES!
DON'T YOU REMEMBER ME... FROM THE **GIRLS'** TEAM?
ER...YOU LOOK SICK, SIR!
I AM SICK!
THOSE GUYS MUST BE GETTING DESPERATE! THEY'RE TURNING TO FEMALE POWER!
HOW DO YOU PLAY A MAN TO MAN DEFENSE AGAINST A GIRL?
3

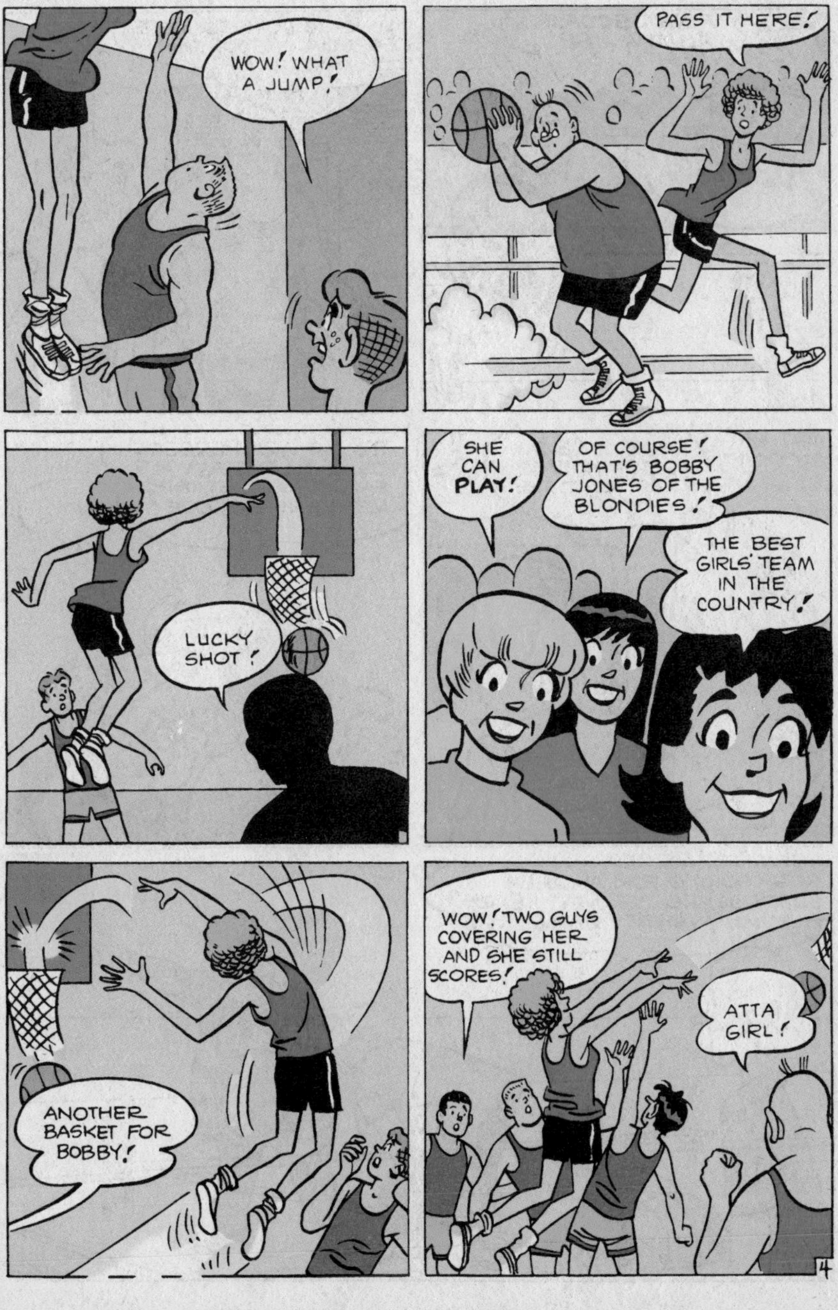
WOW! WHAT A JUMP!
PASS IT HERE!
LUCKY SHOT!
SHE CAN PLAY!
OF COURSE! THAT'S BOBBY JONES OF THE BLONDIES!
THE BEST GIRLS' TEAM IN THE COUNTRY!
ANOTHER BASKET FOR BOBBY!
WOW! TWO GUYS COVERING HER AND SHE STILL SCORES!
ATTA GIRL!
4

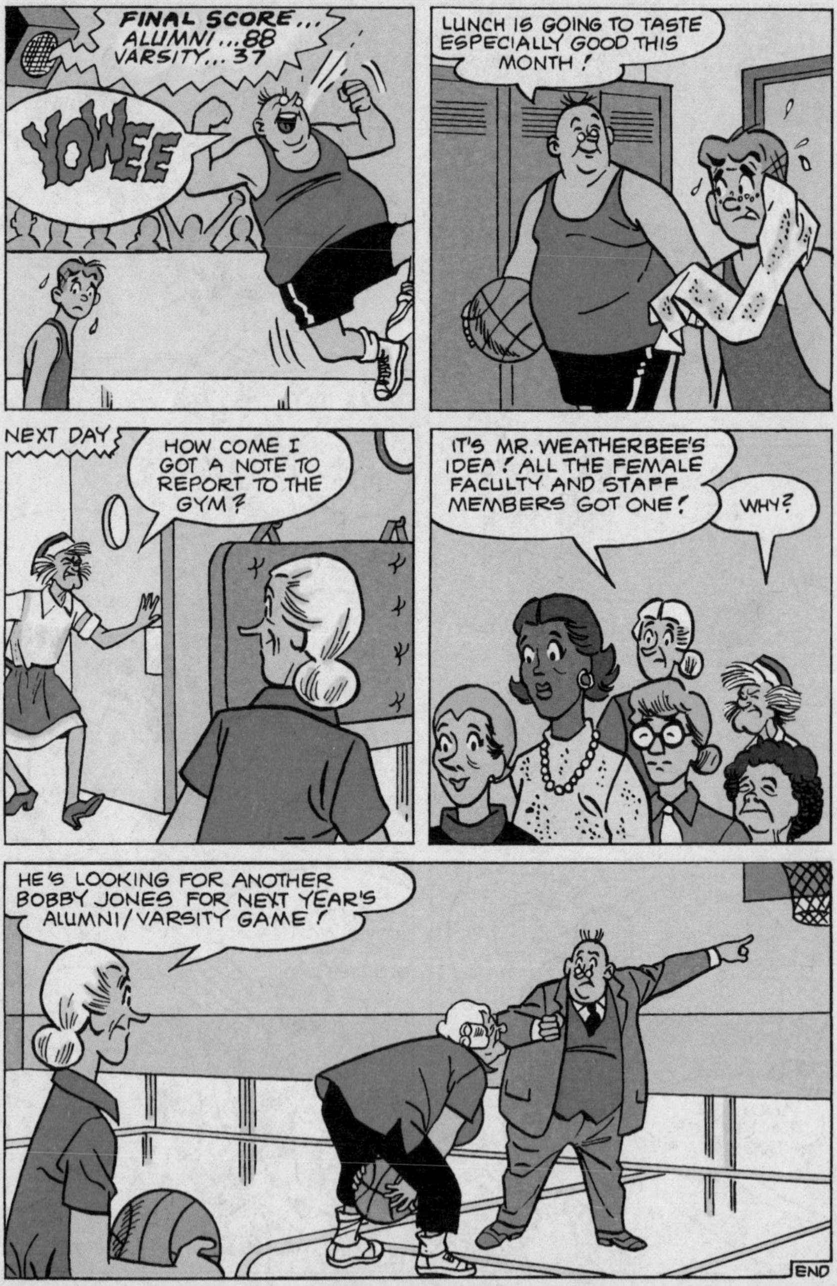
FINAL SCORE... ALUMNI...88 VARSITY...37
YOWEE
LUNCH IS GOING TO TASTE ESPECIALLY GOOD THIS MONTH!
NEXT DAY
HOW COME I GOT A NOTE TO REPORT TO THE GYM?
IT'S MR. WEATHERBEE'S IDEA! ALL THE FEMALE FACULTY AND STAFF MEMBERS GOT ONE!
WHY?
HE'S LOOKING FOR ANOTHER BOBBY JONES FOR NEXT YEAR'S ALUMNI/VARSITY GAME!
END

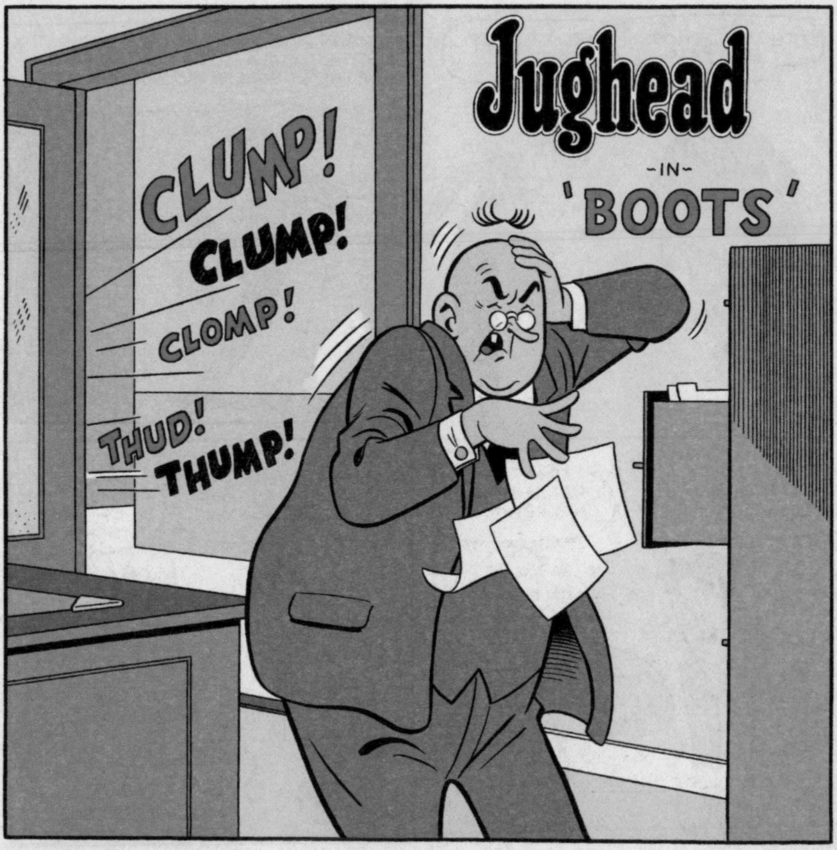
Jughead
-IN-
'BOOTS'
CLUMP!
CLUMP!
CLOMP!
THUD!
THUMP!

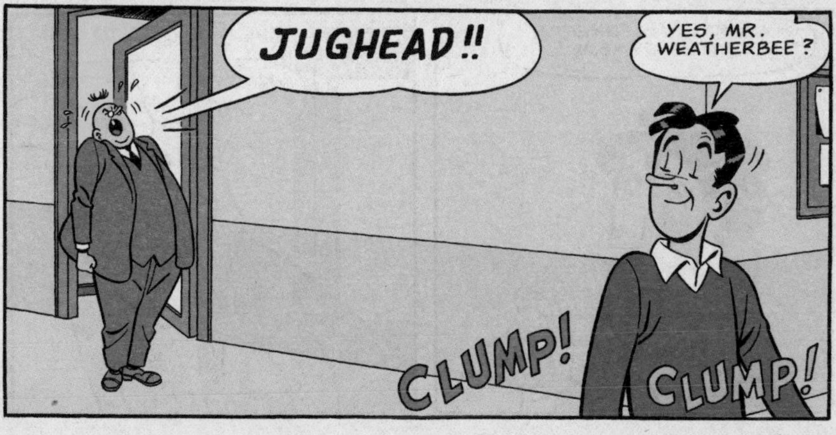
JUGHEAD!!
YES, MR. WEATHERBEE?
CLUMP!
CLUMP!

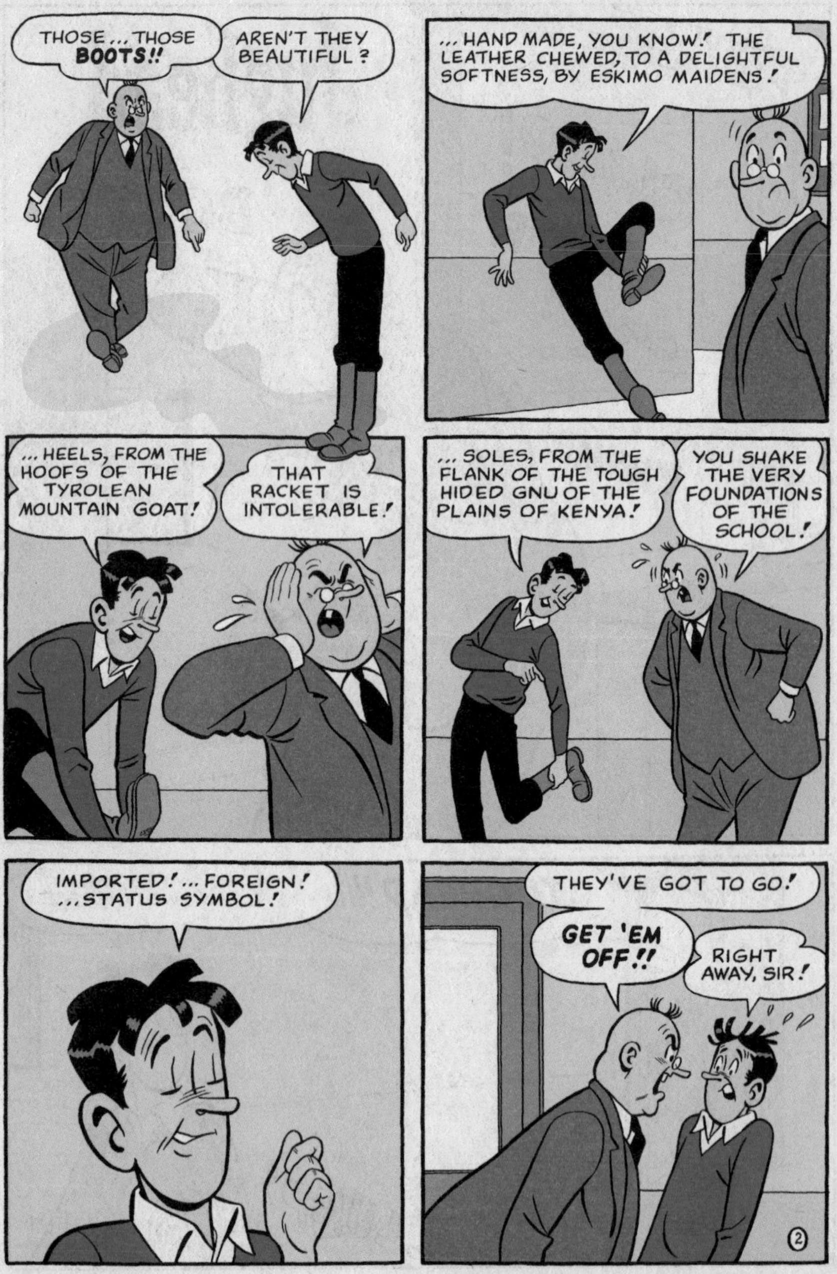
THOSE ... THOSE BOOTS!!
AREN'T THEY BEAUTIFUL ?
... HAND MADE, YOU KNOW! THE LEATHER CHEWED, TO A DELIGHTFUL SOFTNESS, BY ESKIMO MAIDENS!
... HEELS, FROM THE HOOFS OF THE TYROLEAN MOUNTAIN GOAT!
THAT RACKET IS INTOLERABLE!
... SOLES, FROM THE FLANK OF THE TOUGH HIDED GNU OF THE PLAINS OF KENYA!
YOU SHAKE THE VERY FOUNDATIONS OF THE SCHOOL!
IMPORTED! ... FOREIGN! ... STATUS SYMBOL!
THEY'VE GOT TO GO!
GET 'EM OFF!!
RIGHT AWAY, SIR!
2

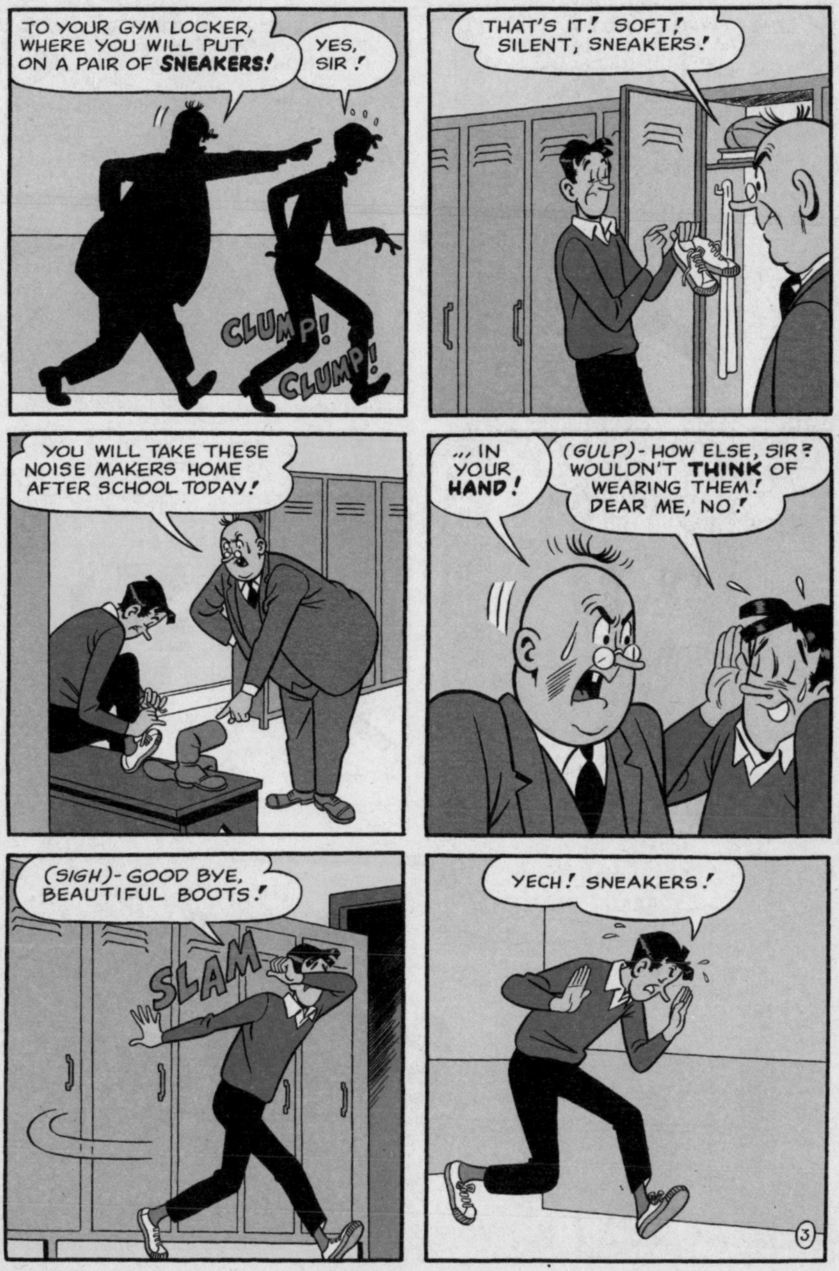
TO YOUR GYM LOCKER, WHERE YOU WILL PUT ON A PAIR OF SNEAKERS!
YES, SIR!
CLUMP!
CLUMP!
THAT'S IT! SOFT! SILENT, SNEAKERS!
YOU WILL TAKE THESE NOISE MAKERS HOME AFTER SCHOOL TODAY!
..., IN YOUR HAND!
(GULP)- HOW ELSE, SIR? WOULDN'T THINK OF WEARING THEM! DEAR ME, NO!
(SIGH)- GOOD BYE, BEAUTIFUL BOOTS!
SLAM
YECH! SNEAKERS!
3

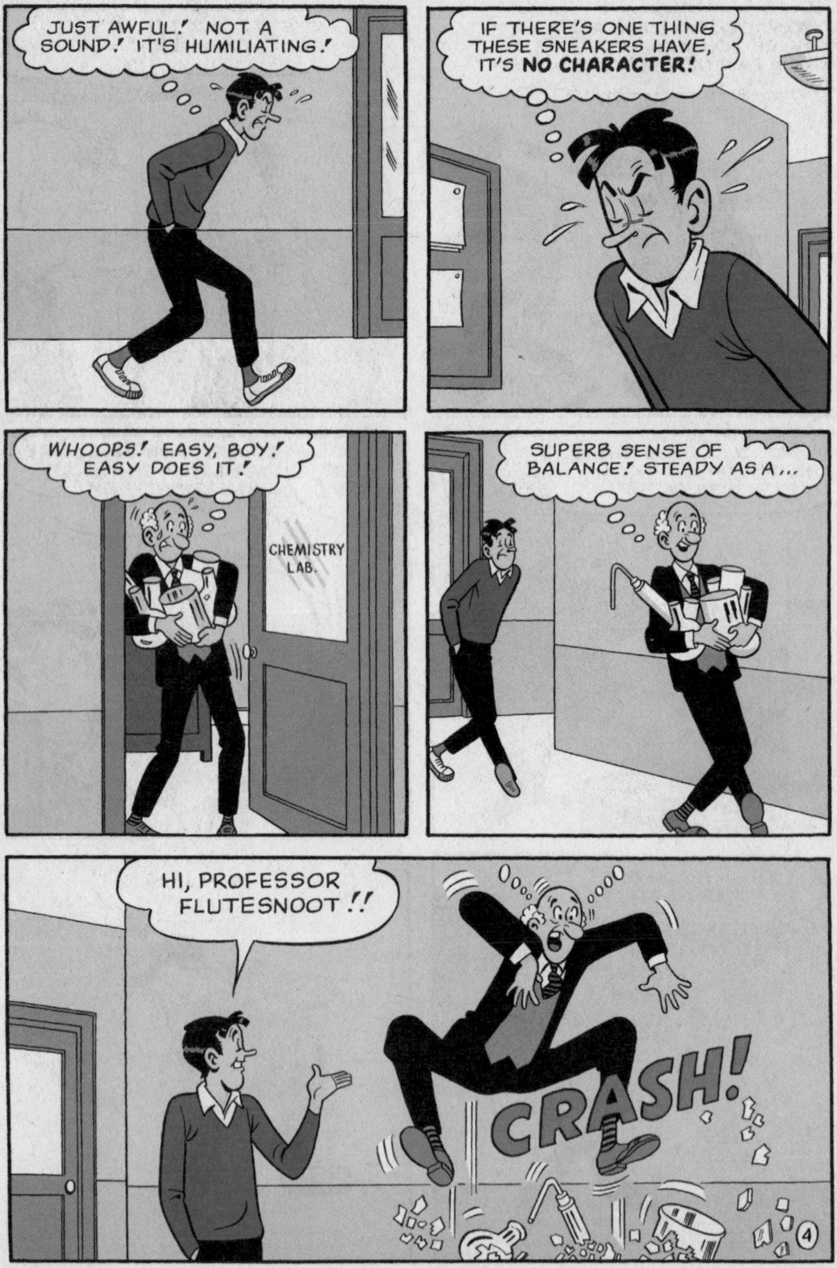
JUST AWFUL! NOT A SOUND! IT'S HUMILIATING!
IF THERE'S ONE THING THESE SNEAKERS HAVE, IT'S NO CHARACTER!
WHOOPS! EASY, BOY! EASY DOES IT!
CHEMISTRY LAB.
SUPERB SENSE OF BALANCE! STEADY AS A...
HI, PROFESSOR FLUTESNOOT!!
CRASH!
4

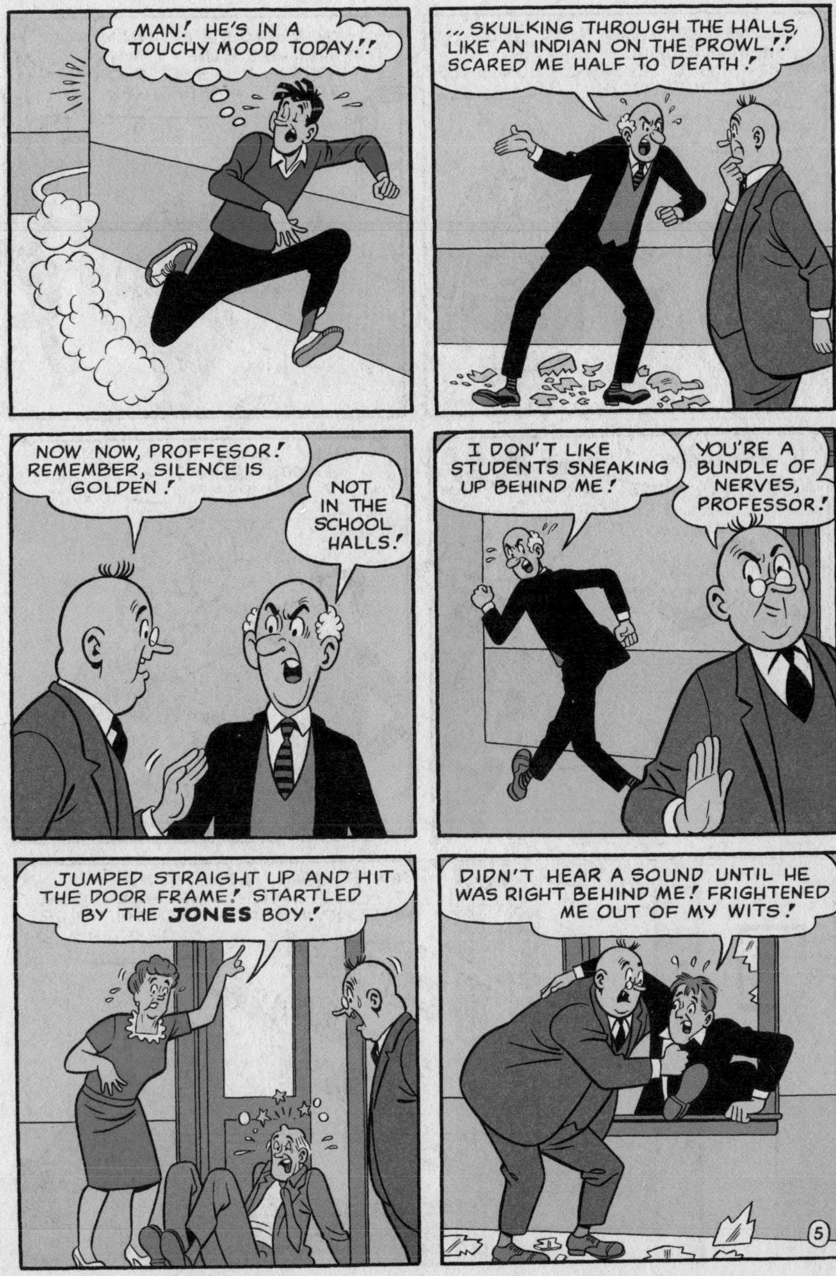
MAN! HE'S IN A TOUCHY MOOD TODAY!!
..., SKULKING THROUGH THE HALLS, LIKE AN INDIAN ON THE PROWL!! SCARED ME HALF TO DEATH!
NOW NOW, PROFFESOR! REMEMBER, SILENCE IS GOLDEN!
NOT IN THE SCHOOL HALLS!
I DON'T LIKE STUDENTS SNEAKING UP BEHIND ME!
YOU'RE A BUNDLE OF NERVES, PROFESSOR!
JUMPED STRAIGHT UP AND HIT THE DOOR FRAME! STARTLED BY THE **JONES** BOY!
DIDN'T HEAR A SOUND UNTIL HE WAS RIGHT BEHIND ME! FRIGHTENED ME OUT OF MY WITS!
5

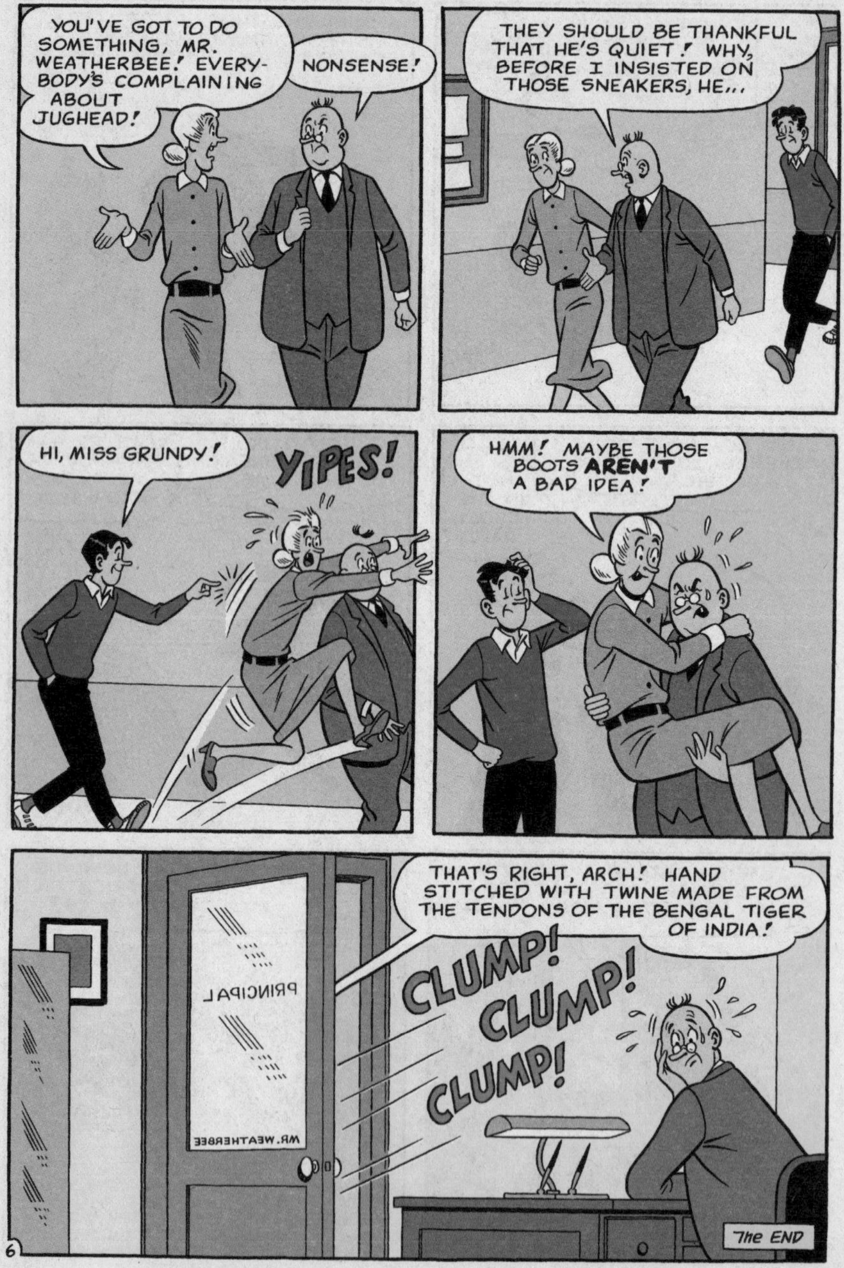
YOU'VE GOT TO DO SOMETHING, MR. WEATHERBEE! EVERYBODY'S COMPLAINING ABOUT JUGHEAD!
NONSENSE!
THEY SHOULD BE THANKFUL THAT HE'S QUIET! WHY, BEFORE I INSISTED ON THOSE SNEAKERS, HE...
HI, MISS GRUNDY!
YIPES!
HMM! MAYBE THOSE BOOTS AREN'T A BAD IDEA!
PRINCIPAL
MR. WEATHERBEE
THAT'S RIGHT, ARCH! HAND STITCHED WITH TWINE MADE FROM THE TENDONS OF THE BENGAL TIGER OF INDIA!
CLUMP! CLUMP! CLUMP!
The END
6

Class of 2027
Tales From Riverdale Digest #18,
April 2007
**Fernando Ruiz, Jon D'Agostino
and Carlos Antunes**

A sideshow seer gives Mr. Weatherbee
a peek into the future... where Riverdale High
is thriving under the leadership of Principal
Archie! Was Mr. Weatherbee's influence greater
than he thought? And will Archie's future
success soften the Bee's wrath when it comes to
Archie's present failures?

The Specialist
Original printing unknown
**George Gladir, Dan DeCarlo Jr.,
Jim DeCarlo, Bill Yoshida
and Barry Grossman**

Because Coach Kleats doesn't possess the
physique of your typical athlete, Archie, Jughead
and Reggie start having some fun at his expense.
They quickly get a refresher course in the errors
of having preconceived notions about people
when the Coach shows off his jaw-dropping
sports abilities. You show 'em, Coach!

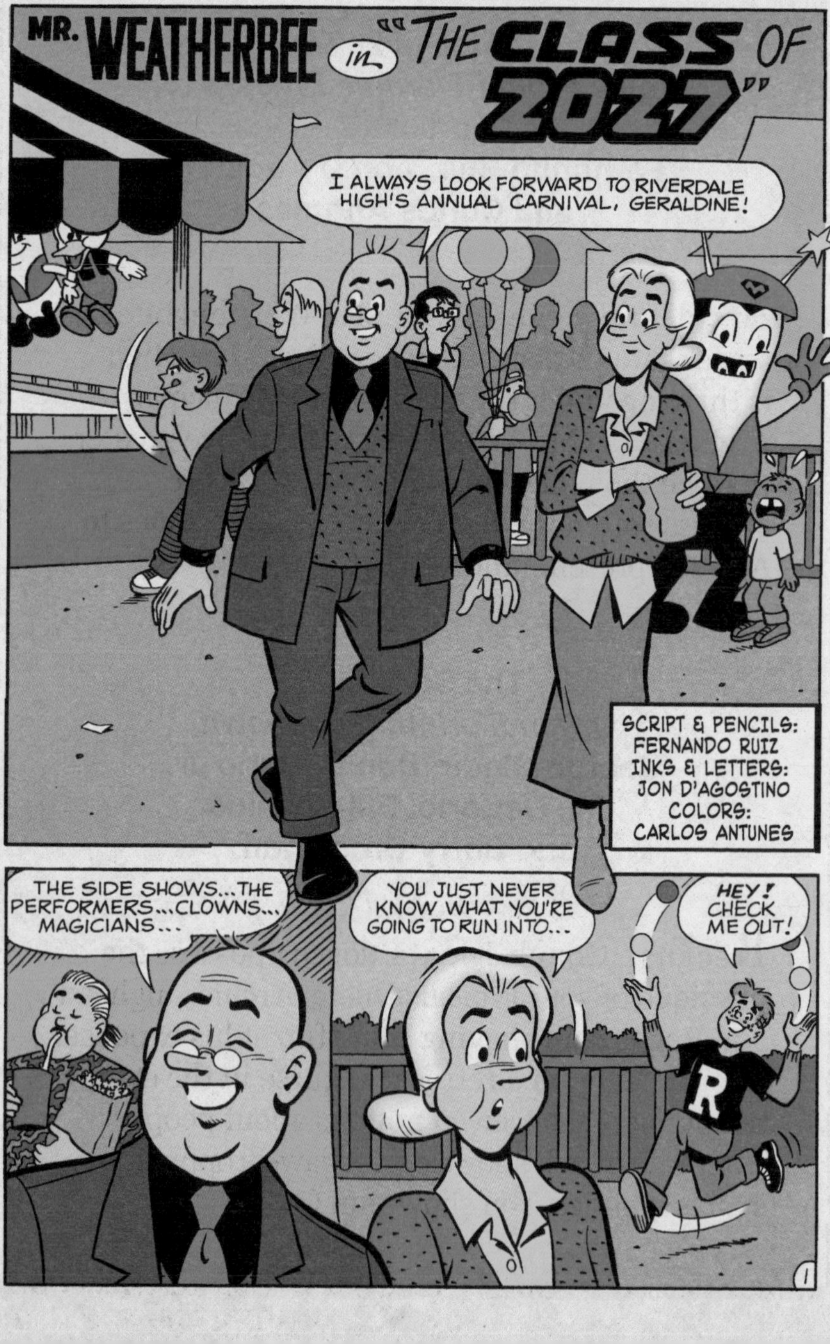
MR. WEATHERBEE in "THE CLASS OF 2027"
I ALWAYS LOOK FORWARD TO RIVERDALE HIGH'S ANNUAL CARNIVAL, GERALDINE!
SCRIPT & PENCILS: FERNANDO RUIZ
INKS & LETTERS: JON D'AGOSTINO
COLORS: CARLOS ANTUNES
THE SIDE SHOWS...THE PERFORMERS...CLOWNS... MAGICIANS...
YOU JUST NEVER KNOW WHAT YOU'RE GOING TO RUN INTO...
HEY! CHECK ME OUT!
1

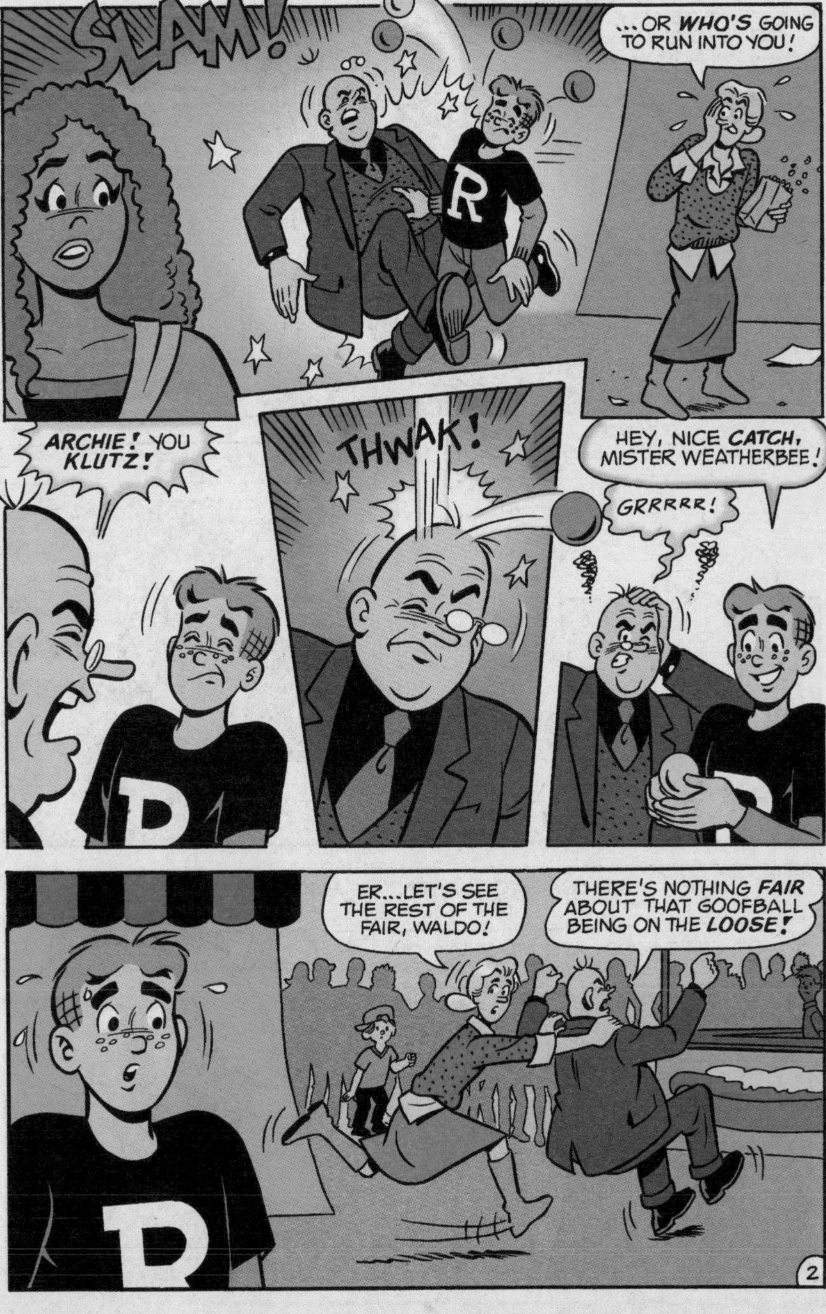
SLAM!
...OR WHO'S GOING TO RUN INTO YOU!
ARCHIE! YOU KLUTZ!
THWAK!
HEY, NICE CATCH, MISTER WEATHERBEE!
GRRRRR!
ER...LET'S SEE THE REST OF THE FAIR, WALDO!
THERE'S NOTHING FAIR ABOUT THAT GOOFBALL BEING ON THE LOOSE!
2

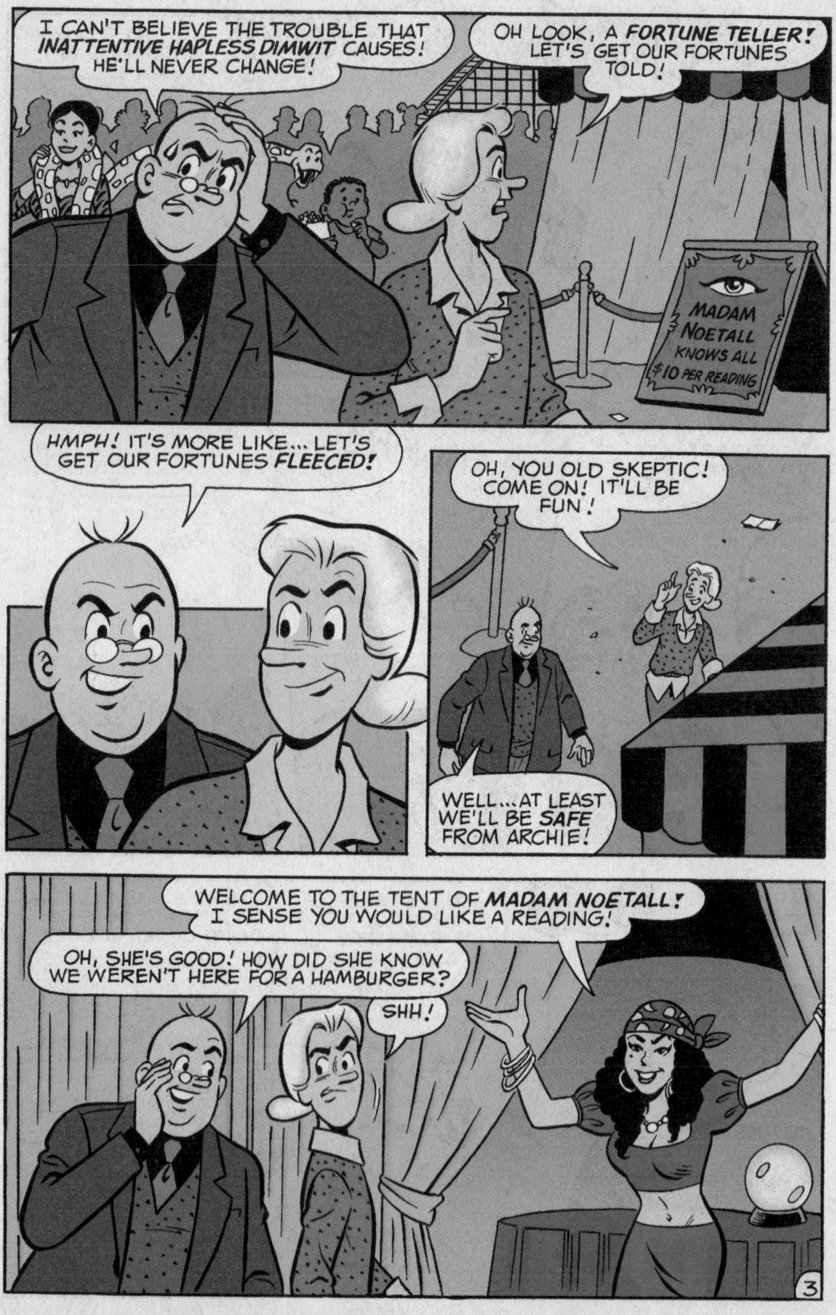
I CAN'T BELIEVE THE TROUBLE THAT INATTENTIVE HAPLESS DIMWIT CAUSES! HE'LL NEVER CHANGE!
OH LOOK, A FORTUNE TELLER! LET'S GET OUR FORTUNES TOLD!
MADAM NOETALL KNOWS ALL $10 PER READING
HMPH! IT'S MORE LIKE... LET'S GET OUR FORTUNES FLEECED!
OH, YOU OLD SKEPTIC! COME ON! IT'LL BE FUN!
WELL... AT LEAST WE'LL BE SAFE FROM ARCHIE!
WELCOME TO THE TENT OF MADAM NOETALL! I SENSE YOU WOULD LIKE A READING!
OH, SHE'S GOOD! HOW DID SHE KNOW WE WEREN'T HERE FOR A HAMBURGER?
SHH!
3

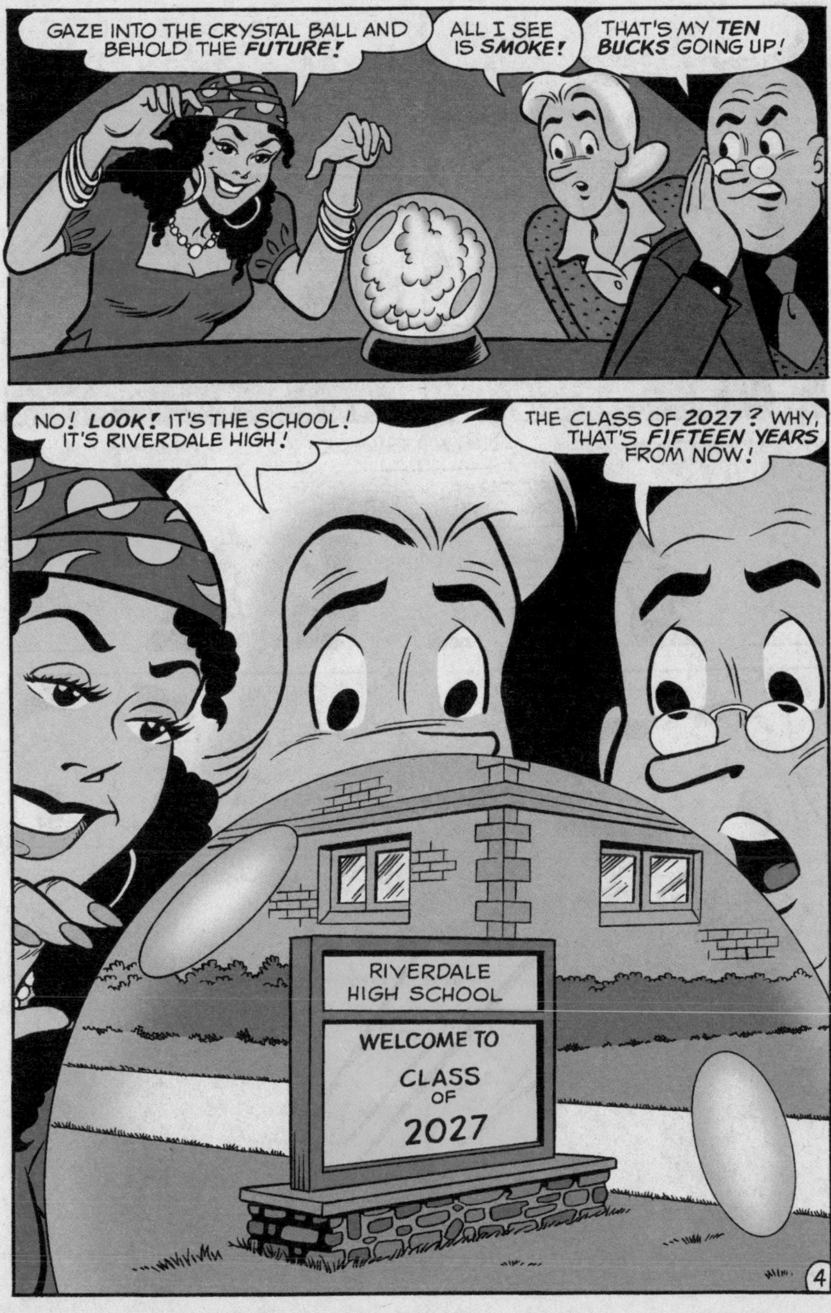
GAZE INTO THE CRYSTAL BALL AND BEHOLD THE *FUTURE!*
ALL I SEE IS *SMOKE!*
THAT'S MY *TEN BUCKS* GOING UP!
NO! *LOOK!* IT'S THE SCHOOL! IT'S RIVERDALE HIGH!
THE CLASS OF *2027?* WHY, THAT'S *FIFTEEN YEARS* FROM NOW!
RIVERDALE HIGH SCHOOL
WELCOME TO CLASS OF 2027
4

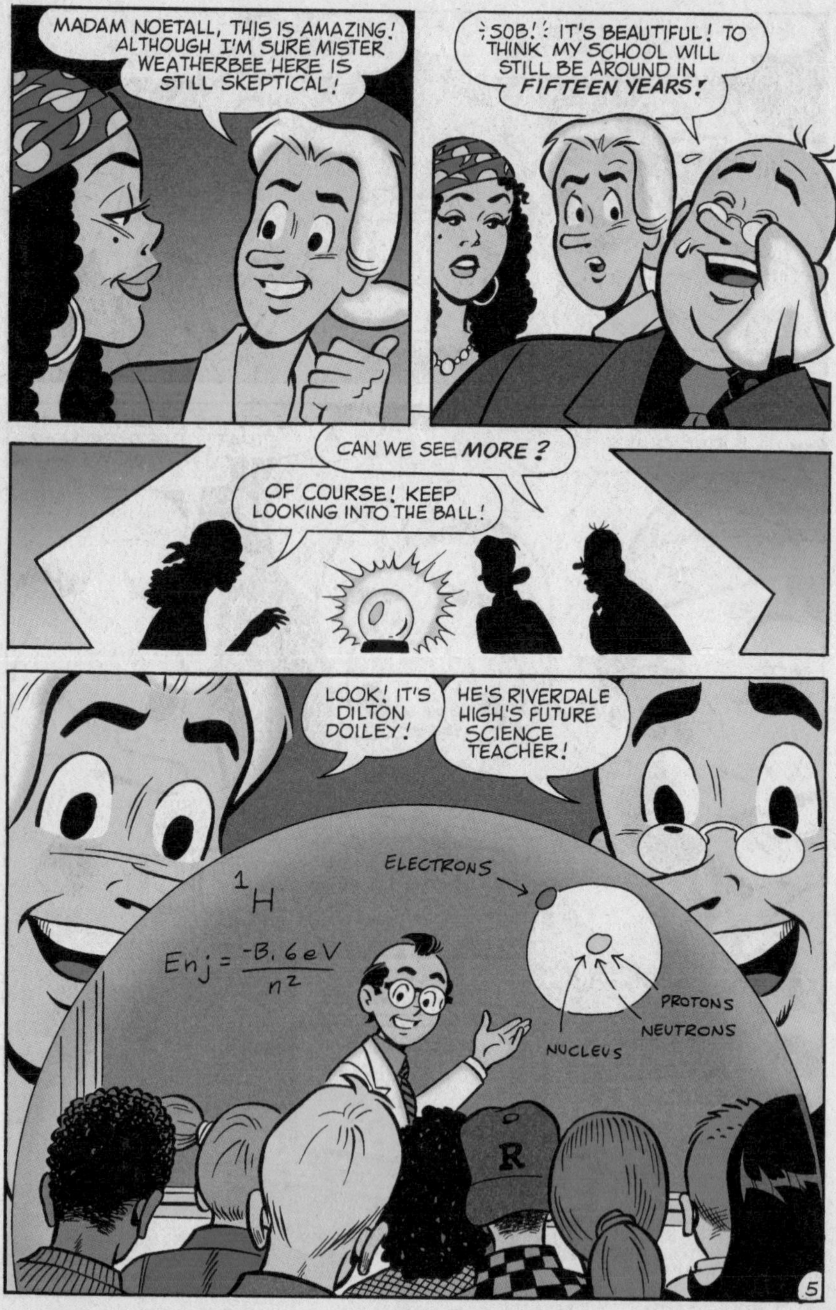
MADAM NOETALL, THIS IS AMAZING! ALTHOUGH I'M SURE MISTER WEATHERBEE HERE IS STILL SKEPTICAL!
SOB! IT'S BEAUTIFUL! TO THINK MY SCHOOL WILL STILL BE AROUND IN *FIFTEEN YEARS!*
CAN WE SEE *MORE?*
OF COURSE! KEEP LOOKING INTO THE BALL!
LOOK! IT'S DILTON DOILEY!
HE'S RIVERDALE HIGH'S FUTURE SCIENCE TEACHER!
^1H
$Enj = \frac{-13.6 eV}{n^2}$
ELECTRONS
PROTONS
NEUTRONS
NUCLEUS
R
5

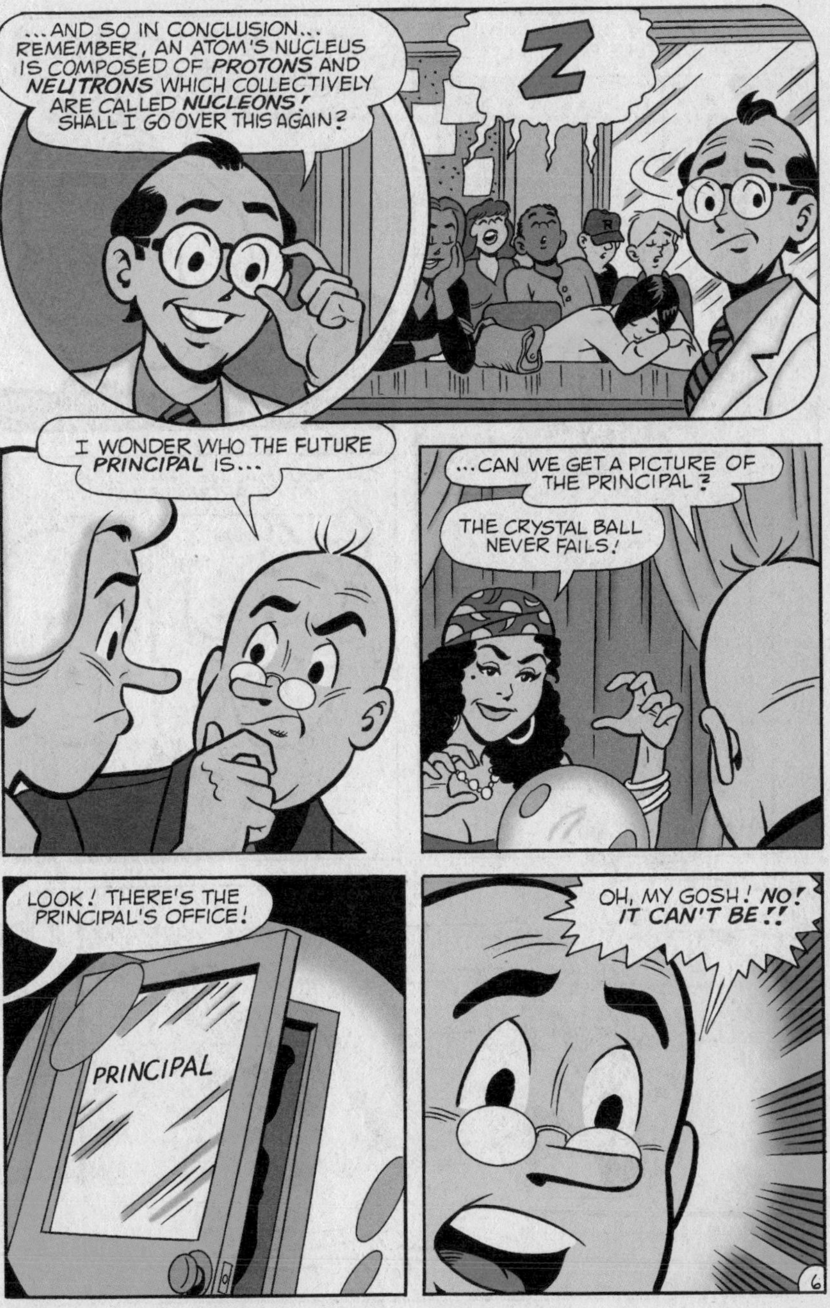
...AND SO IN CONCLUSION... REMEMBER, AN ATOM'S NUCLEUS IS COMPOSED OF PROTONS AND NEUTRONS WHICH COLLECTIVELY ARE CALLED NUCLEONS! SHALL I GO OVER THIS AGAIN?
Z
I WONDER WHO THE FUTURE PRINCIPAL IS...
...CAN WE GET A PICTURE OF THE PRINCIPAL?
THE CRYSTAL BALL NEVER FAILS!
LOOK! THERE'S THE PRINCIPAL'S OFFICE!
PRINCIPAL
OH, MY GOSH! NO! IT CAN'T BE!!
6

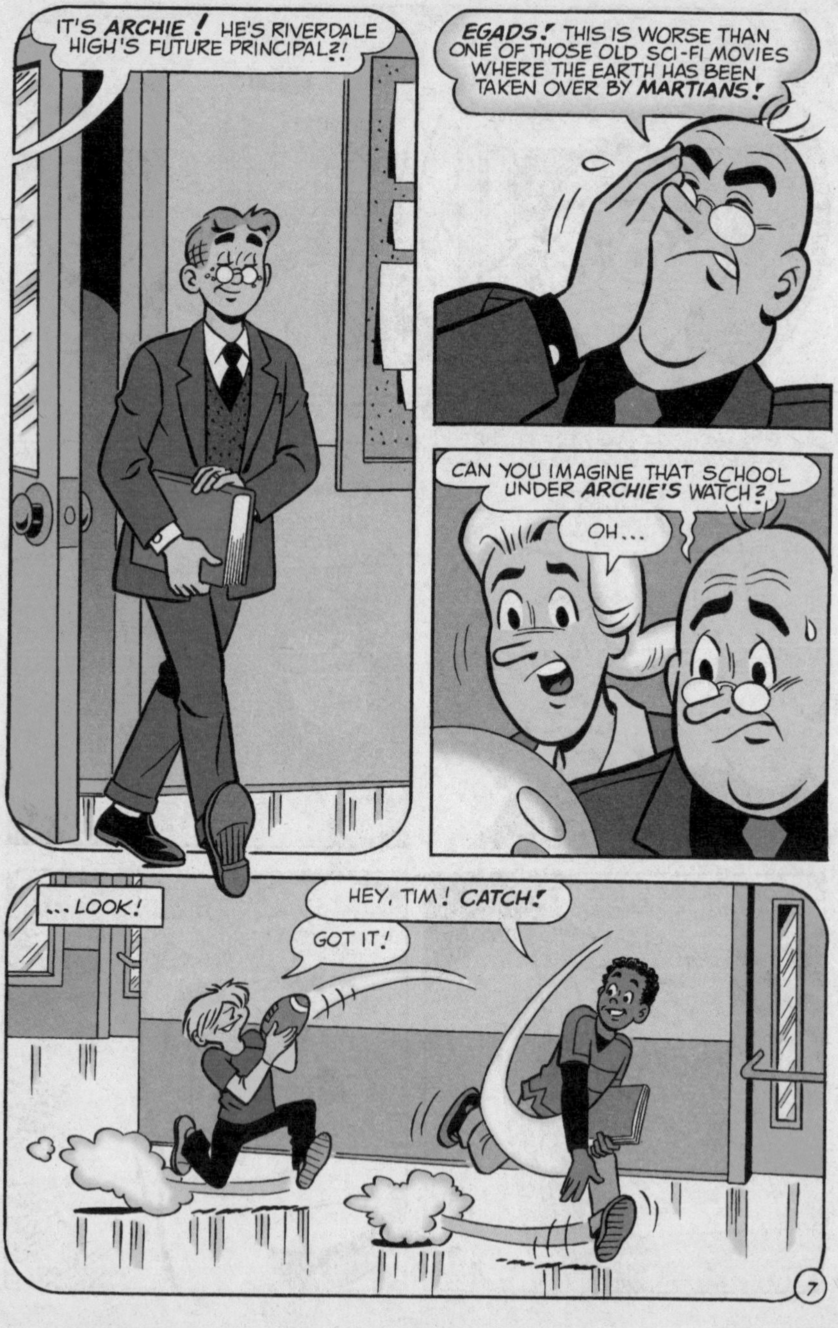
IT'S ARCHIE! HE'S RIVERDALE HIGH'S FUTURE PRINCIPAL?!
EGADS! THIS IS WORSE THAN ONE OF THOSE OLD SCI-FI MOVIES WHERE THE EARTH HAS BEEN TAKEN OVER BY MARTIANS!
CAN YOU IMAGINE THAT SCHOOL UNDER ARCHIE'S WATCH?
OH...
...LOOK!
HEY, TIM! CATCH!
GOT IT!
7

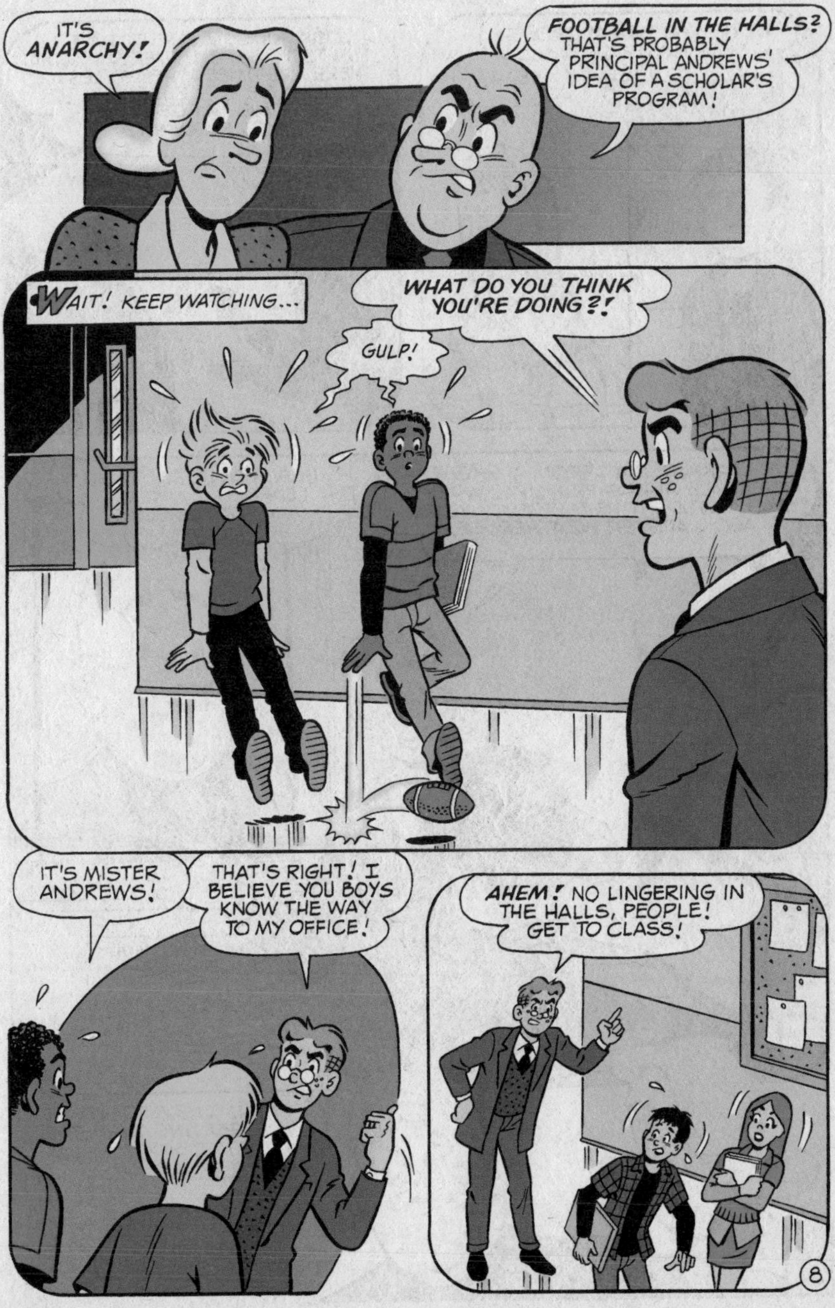
IT'S ANARCHY!
FOOTBALL IN THE HALLS? THAT'S PROBABLY PRINCIPAL ANDREWS' IDEA OF A SCHOLAR'S PROGRAM!
WAIT! KEEP WATCHING...
WHAT DO YOU THINK YOU'RE DOING?!
GULP!
IT'S MISTER ANDREWS!
THAT'S RIGHT! I BELIEVE YOU BOYS KNOW THE WAY TO MY OFFICE!
AHEM! NO LINGERING IN THE HALLS, PEOPLE! GET TO CLASS!
8

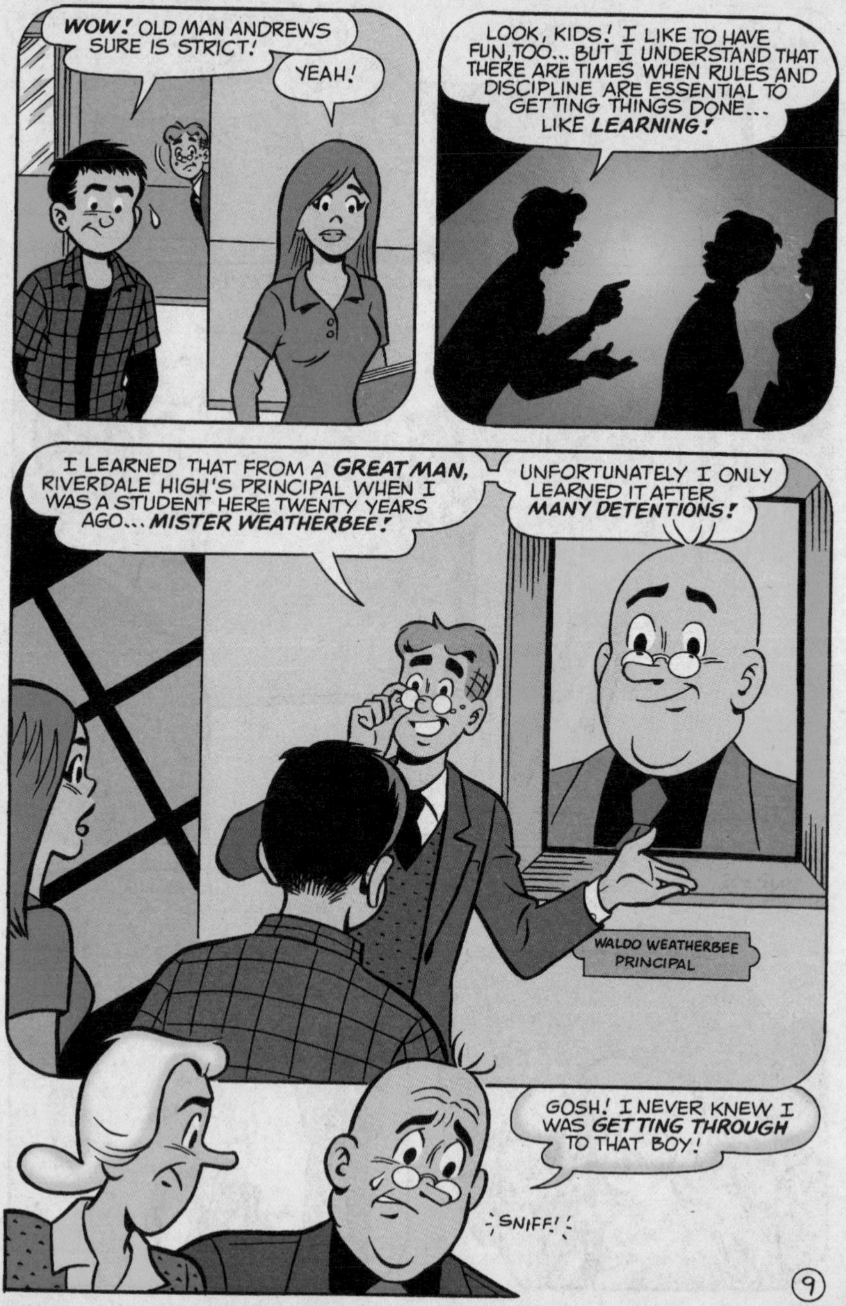
WOW! OLD MAN ANDREWS SURE IS STRICT!
YEAH!
LOOK, KIDS! I LIKE TO HAVE FUN, TOO... BUT I UNDERSTAND THAT THERE ARE TIMES WHEN RULES AND DISCIPLINE ARE ESSENTIAL TO GETTING THINGS DONE... LIKE LEARNING!
I LEARNED THAT FROM A GREAT MAN, RIVERDALE HIGH'S PRINCIPAL WHEN I WAS A STUDENT HERE TWENTY YEARS AGO... MISTER WEATHERBEE!
UNFORTUNATELY I ONLY LEARNED IT AFTER MANY DETENTIONS!
WALDO WEATHERBEE PRINCIPAL
GOSH! I NEVER KNEW I WAS GETTING THROUGH TO THAT BOY!
SNIFF!
9

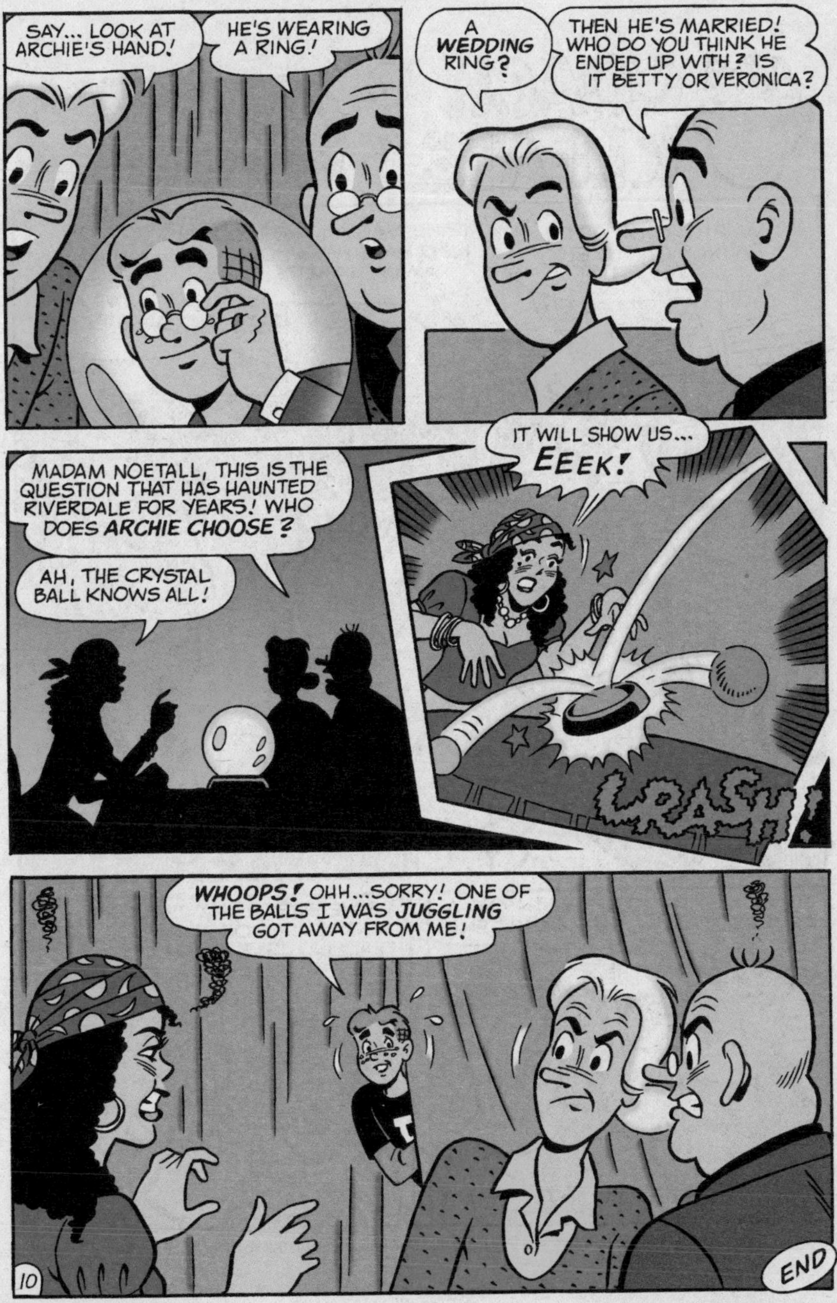
SAY... LOOK AT ARCHIE'S HAND!
HE'S WEARING A RING!
A WEDDING RING?
THEN HE'S MARRIED! WHO DO YOU THINK HE ENDED UP WITH? IS IT BETTY OR VERONICA?
MADAM NOETALL, THIS IS THE QUESTION THAT HAS HAUNTED RIVERDALE FOR YEARS! WHO DOES ARCHIE CHOOSE?
AH, THE CRYSTAL BALL KNOWS ALL!
IT WILL SHOW US... EEEK!
CRASH!
WHOOPS! OHH...SORRY! ONE OF THE BALLS I WAS JUGGLING GOT AWAY FROM ME!
10
END

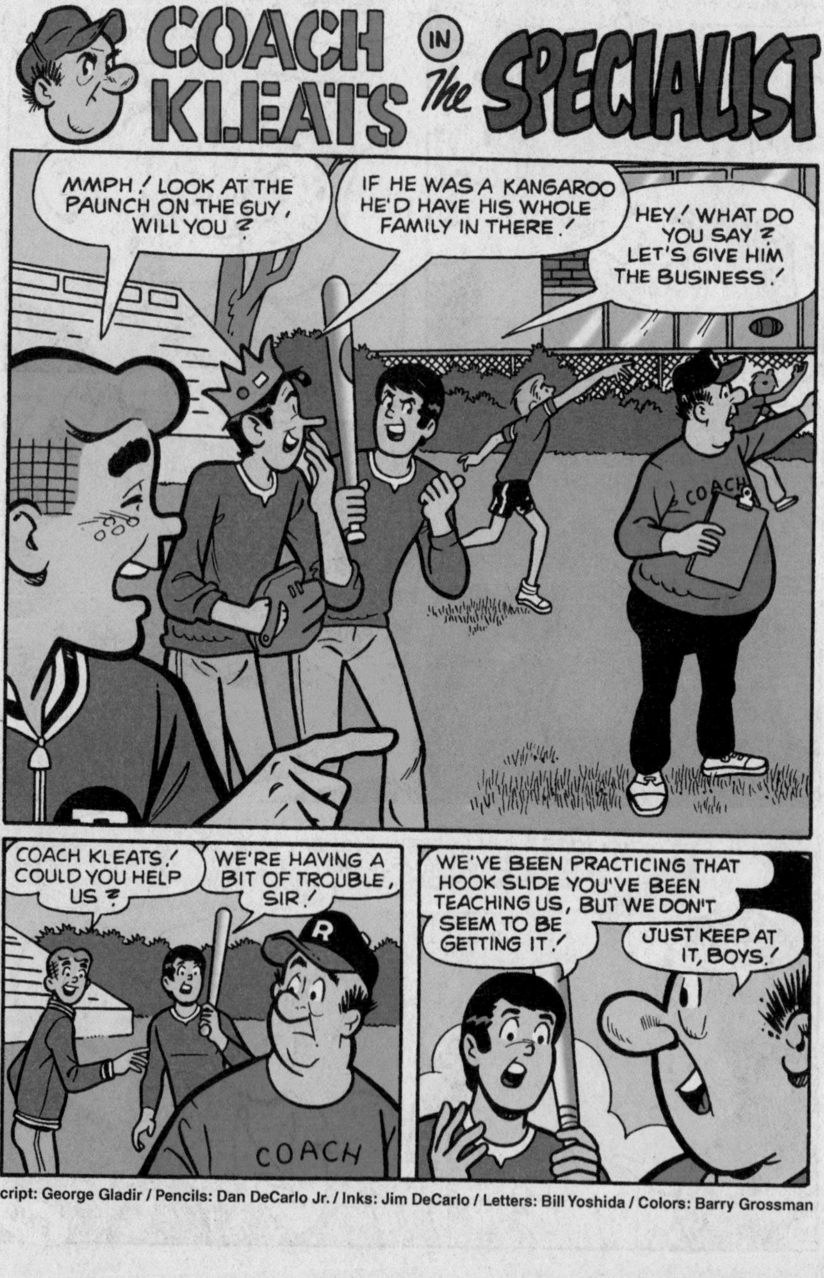
COACH KLEATS
IN
The SPECIALIST
MMPH! LOOK AT THE PAUNCH ON THE GUY, WILL YOU?
IF HE WAS A KANGAROO HE'D HAVE HIS WHOLE FAMILY IN THERE!
HEY! WHAT DO YOU SAY? LET'S GIVE HIM THE BUSINESS!
COACH
COACH KLEATS! COULD YOU HELP US?
WE'RE HAVING A BIT OF TROUBLE, SIR!
R
COACH
WE'VE BEEN PRACTICING THAT HOOK SLIDE YOU'VE BEEN TEACHING US, BUT WE DON'T SEEM TO BE GETTING IT!
JUST KEEP AT IT, BOYS!

Script: George Gladir / Pencils: Dan DeCarlo Jr. / Inks: Jim DeCarlo / Letters: Bill Yoshida / Colors: Barry Grossman

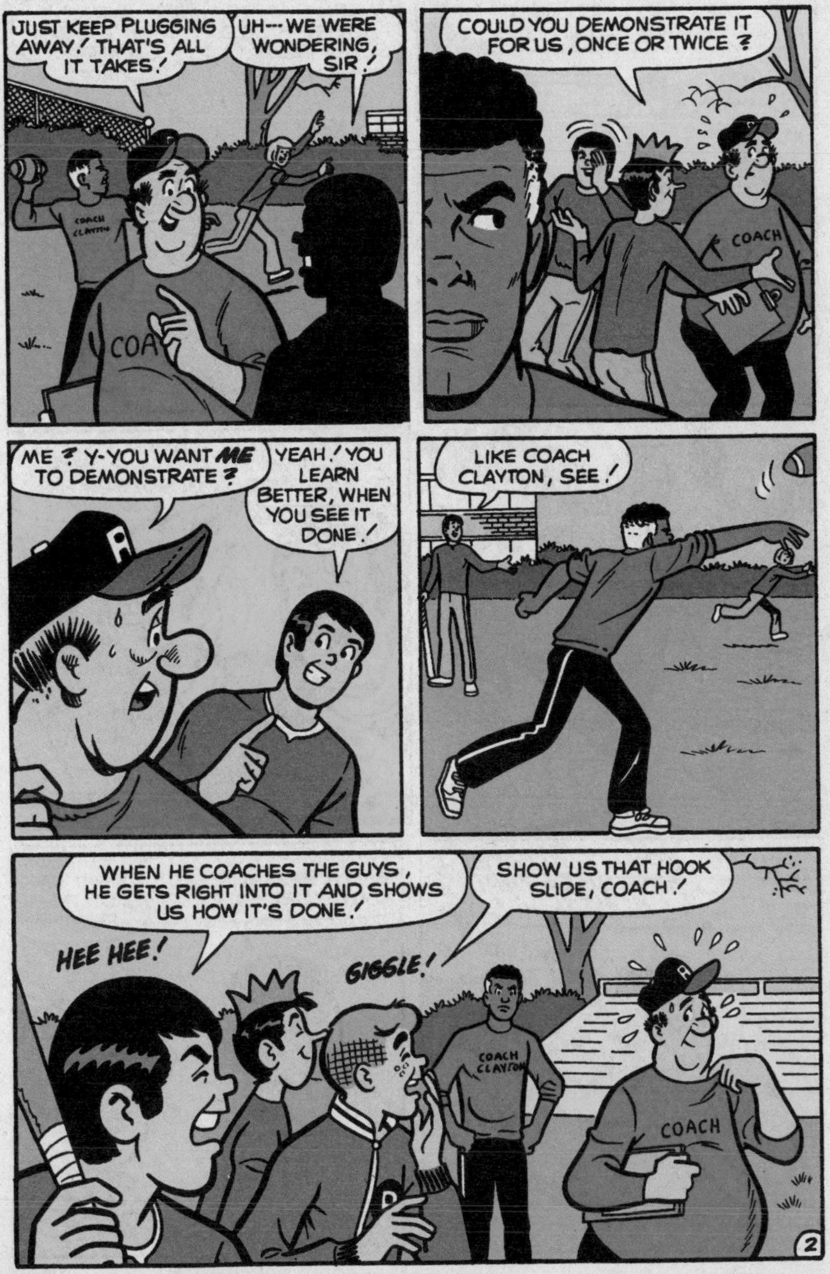
JUST KEEP PLUGGING AWAY! THAT'S ALL IT TAKES!
UH--- WE WERE WONDERING, SIR!
COACH CLAYTON
COA
COULD YOU DEMONSTRATE IT FOR US, ONCE OR TWICE ?
COACH
ME ? Y-YOU WANT ME TO DEMONSTRATE ?
YEAH! YOU LEARN BETTER, WHEN YOU SEE IT DONE!
LIKE COACH CLAYTON, SEE!
WHEN HE COACHES THE GUYS, HE GETS RIGHT INTO IT AND SHOWS US HOW IT'S DONE!
SHOW US THAT HOOK SLIDE, COACH!
HEE HEE!
GIGGLE!
COACH CLAYTON
COACH
2

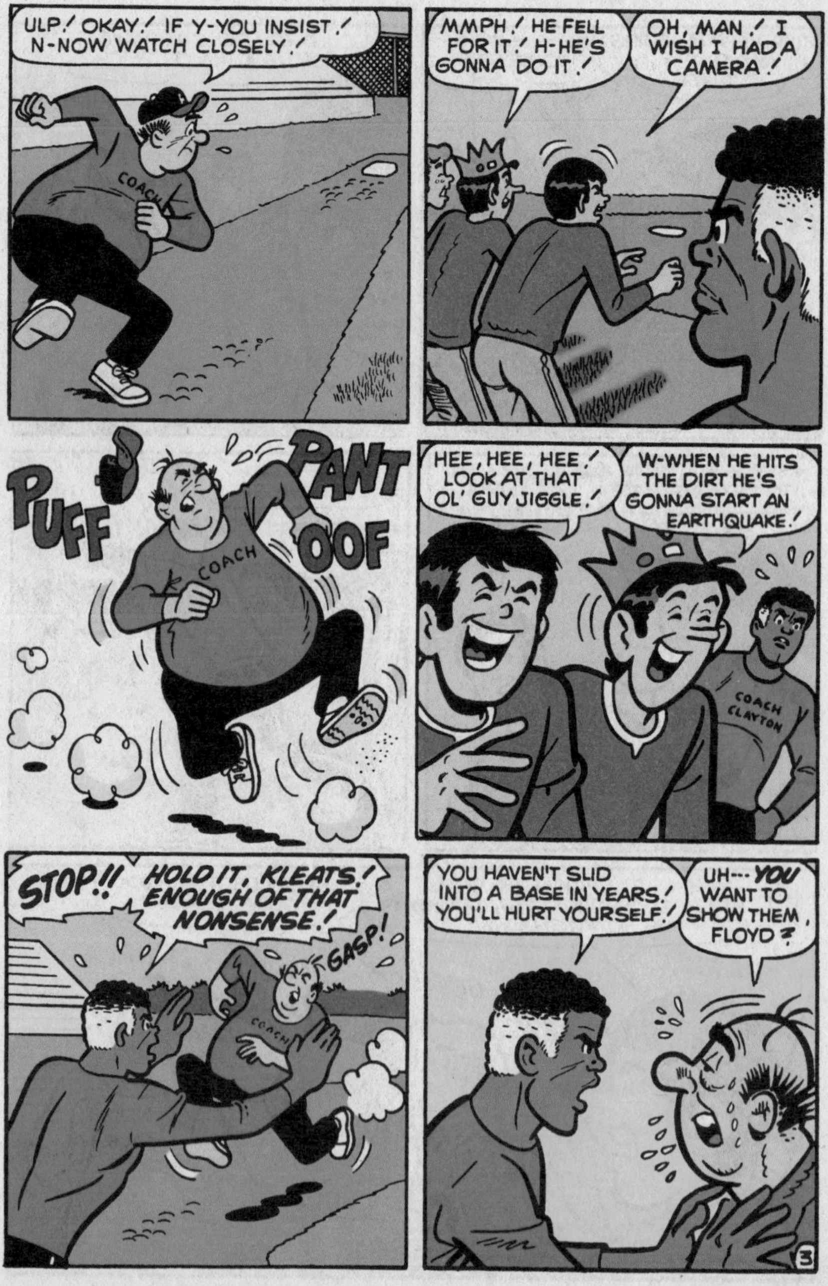

ULP! OKAY! IF Y-YOU INSIST! N-NOW WATCH CLOSELY!
COACH
MMPH! HE FELL FOR IT! H-HE'S GONNA DO IT!
OH, MAN! I WISH I HAD A CAMERA!
PUFF
PANT
OOF
COACH
HEE, HEE, HEE! LOOK AT THAT OL' GUY JIGGLE!
W-WHEN HE HITS THE DIRT HE'S GONNA START AN EARTHQUAKE!
COACH CLAYTON
STOP!!
HOLD IT, KLEATS! ENOUGH OF THAT NONSENSE!
GASP!
COACH
YOU HAVEN'T SLID INTO A BASE IN YEARS! YOU'LL HURT YOURSELF!
UH--- YOU WANT TO SHOW THEM, FLOYD?
3

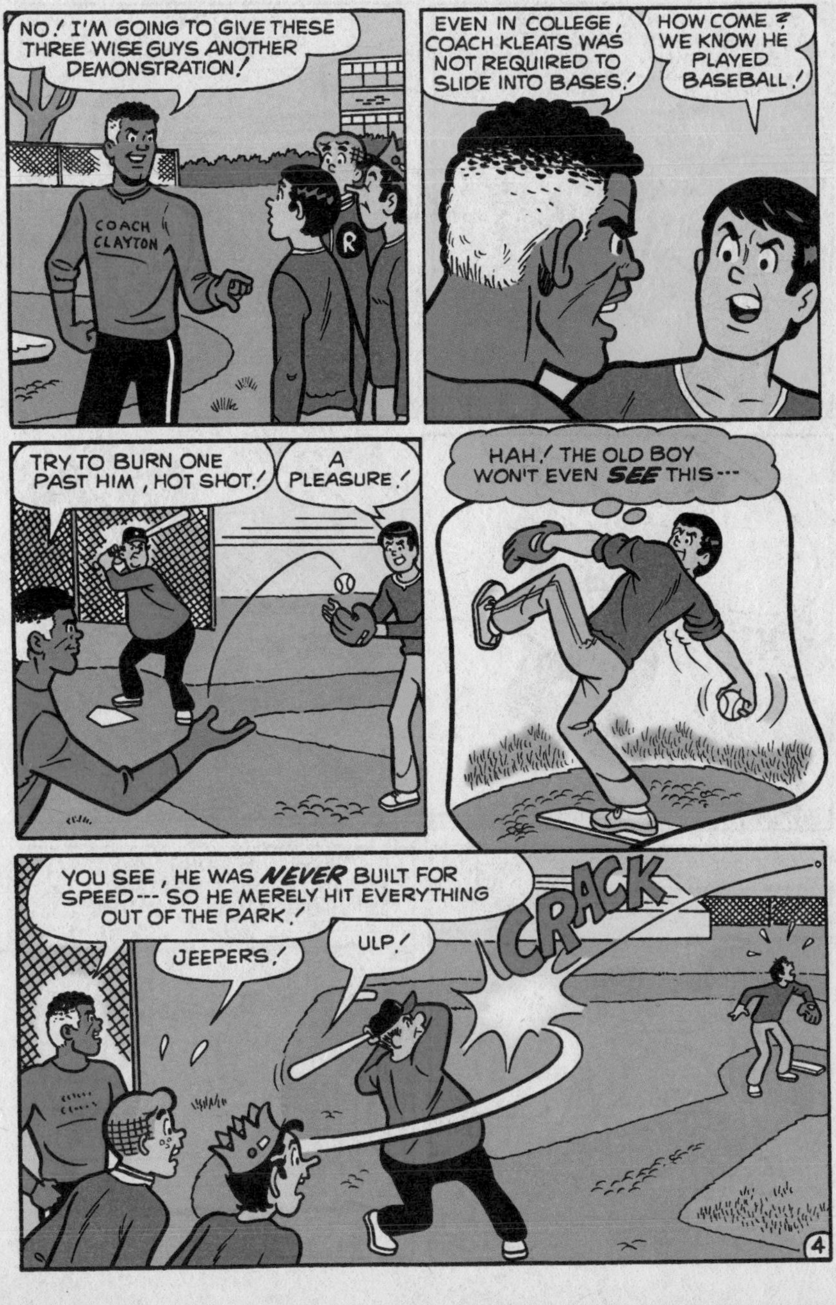
NO! I'M GOING TO GIVE THESE THREE WISE GUYS ANOTHER DEMONSTRATION!
COACH CLAYTON
R
EVEN IN COLLEGE, COACH KLEATS WAS NOT REQUIRED TO SLIDE INTO BASES!
HOW COME? WE KNOW HE PLAYED BASEBALL!
TRY TO BURN ONE PAST HIM, HOT SHOT!
A PLEASURE!
HAH! THE OLD BOY WON'T EVEN SEE THIS---
YOU SEE, HE WAS NEVER BUILT FOR SPEED--- SO HE MERELY HIT EVERYTHING OUT OF THE PARK!
JEEPERS!
ULP!
CRACK
4

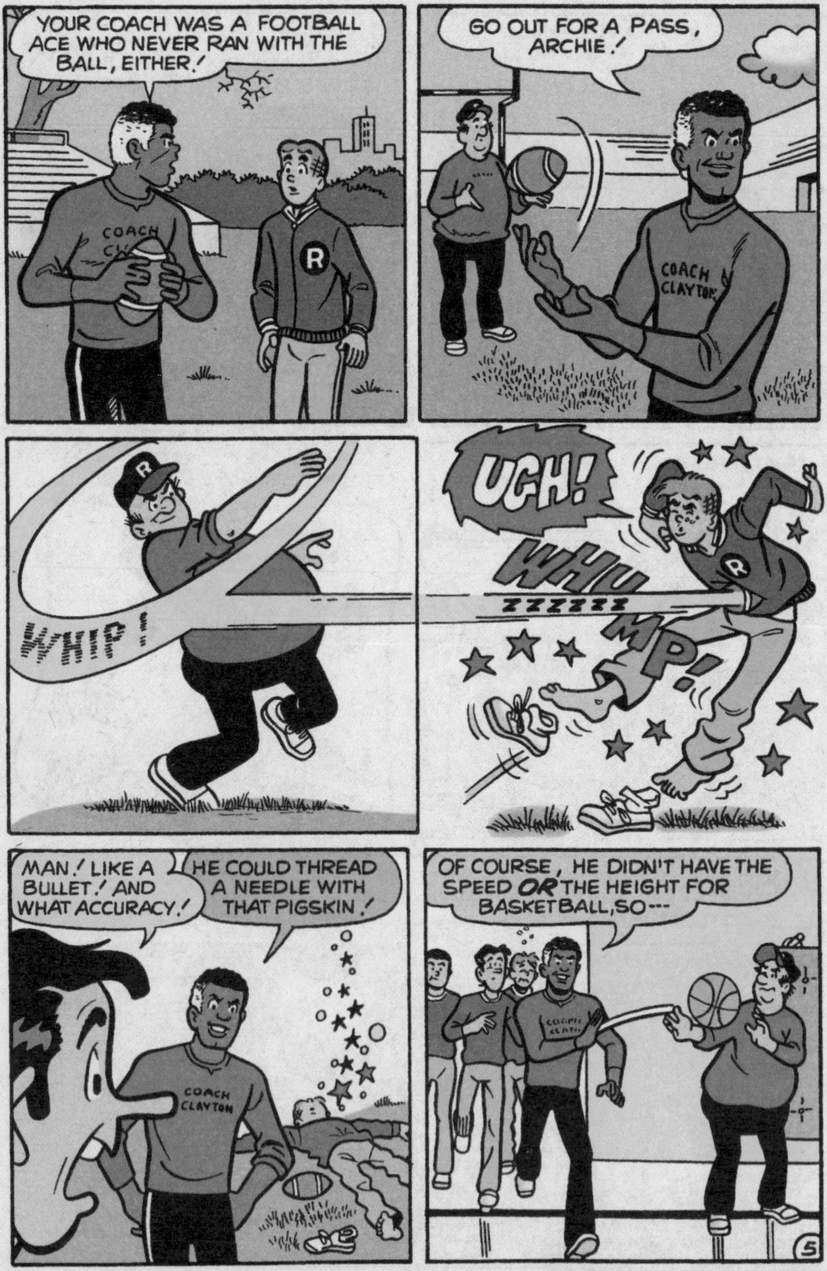
YOUR COACH WAS A FOOTBALL ACE WHO NEVER RAN WITH THE BALL, EITHER!
COACH CL
R
GO OUT FOR A PASS, ARCHIE!
COACH CLAYTON
WHIP!
R
UGH!
WHUMP!
ZZZZZZ
R
MAN! LIKE A BULLET! AND WHAT ACCURACY!
HE COULD THREAD A NEEDLE WITH THAT PIGSKIN!
COACH CLAYTON
OF COURSE, HE DIDN'T HAVE THE SPEED OR THE HEIGHT FOR BASKETBALL, SO---
5

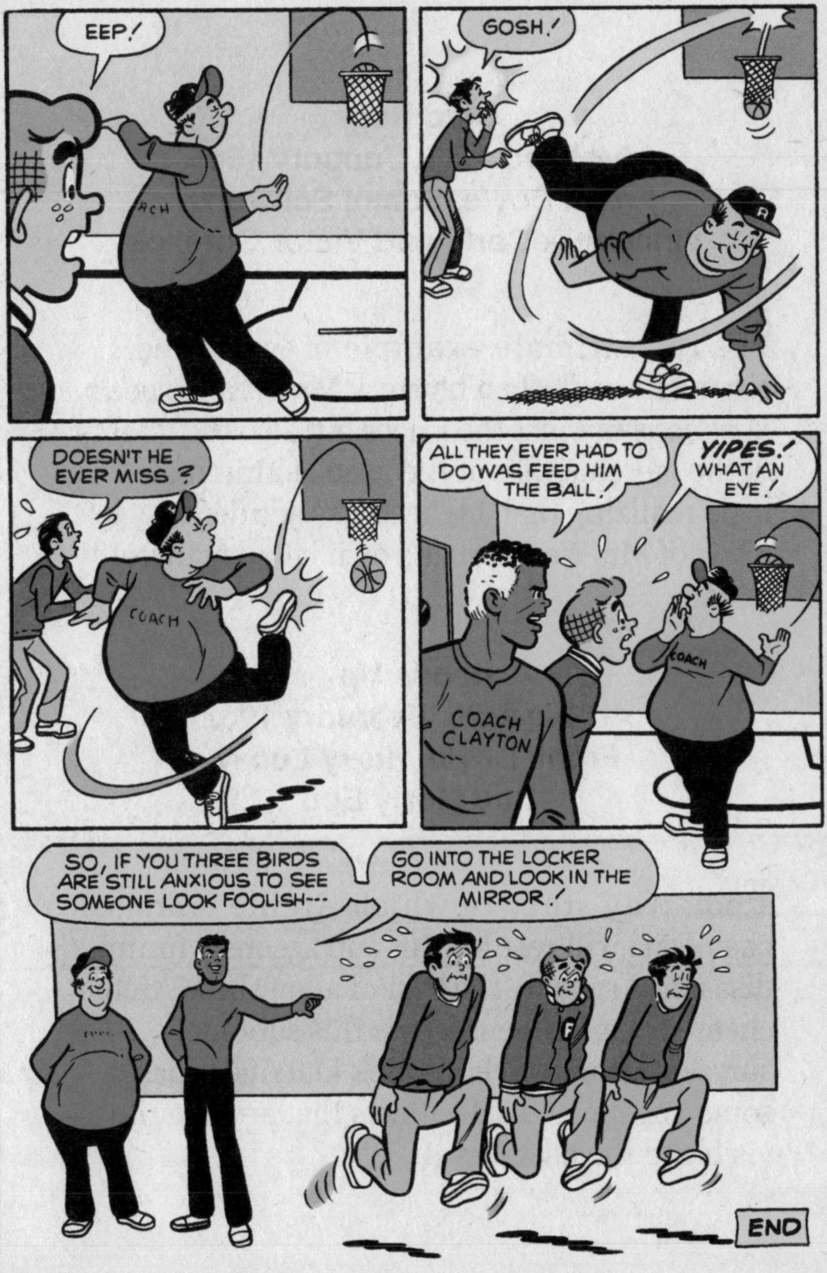
EEP!
ACH
GOSH!
DOESN'T HE EVER MISS ?
COACH
ALL THEY EVER HAD TO DO WAS FEED HIM THE BALL!
YIPES! WHAT AN EYE!
COACH CLAYTON
COACH
SO, IF YOU THREE BIRDS ARE STILL ANXIOUS TO SEE SOMEONE LOOK FOOLISH---
GO INTO THE LOCKER ROOM AND LOOK IN THE MIRROR!
END

Glad Rags
Jughead #116, January 1965
Frank Doyle, Samm Schwartz,
Vincent DeCarlo and Victor Gorelick

It's the ultimate example of "pomp and circumstance" when blustery Mr. Weatherbee questions not just the prices but also the quality of the merchandise at the used clothing sale... little realizing that Jughead has accidentally left a box of Mr. Weatherbee's own laundry there!

Heads Up
Archie #125, February 1962
Frank Doyle, Harry Lucey
and Marty Epp

Fact: Any story in which Archie is around chemicals will result in an outrageously funny disaster. Arguably the best of all of these Archie chemistry misadventures is this sublimely surreal tale in which Archie's klutziness has some unexpected side effects that aren't quite visible to the naked eye!

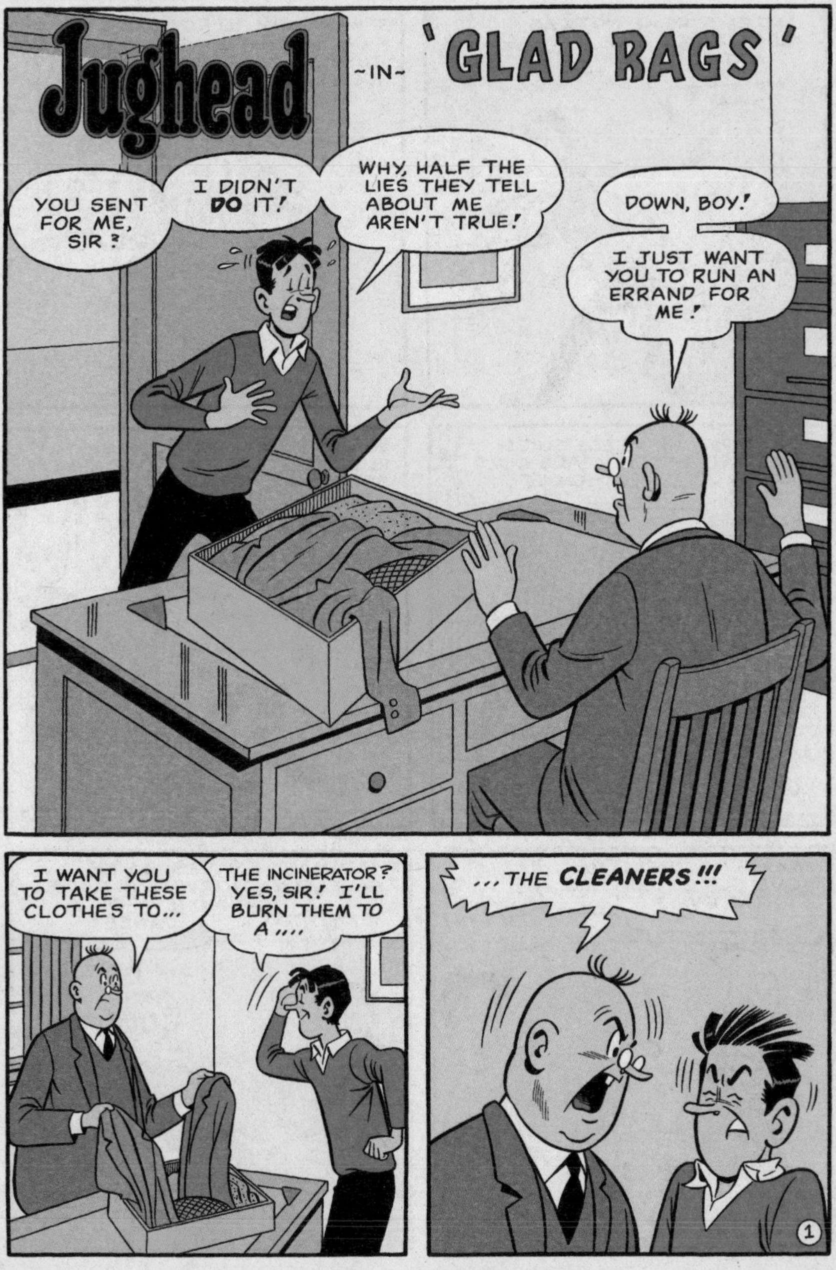
Jughead
~IN~
'GLAD RAGS'
YOU SENT FOR ME, SIR?
I DIDN'T DO IT!
WHY, HALF THE LIES THEY TELL ABOUT ME AREN'T TRUE!
DOWN, BOY!
I JUST WANT YOU TO RUN AN ERRAND FOR ME!
I WANT YOU TO TAKE THESE CLOTHES TO...
THE INCINERATOR? YES, SIR! I'LL BURN THEM TO A....
...THE CLEANERS!!!
1

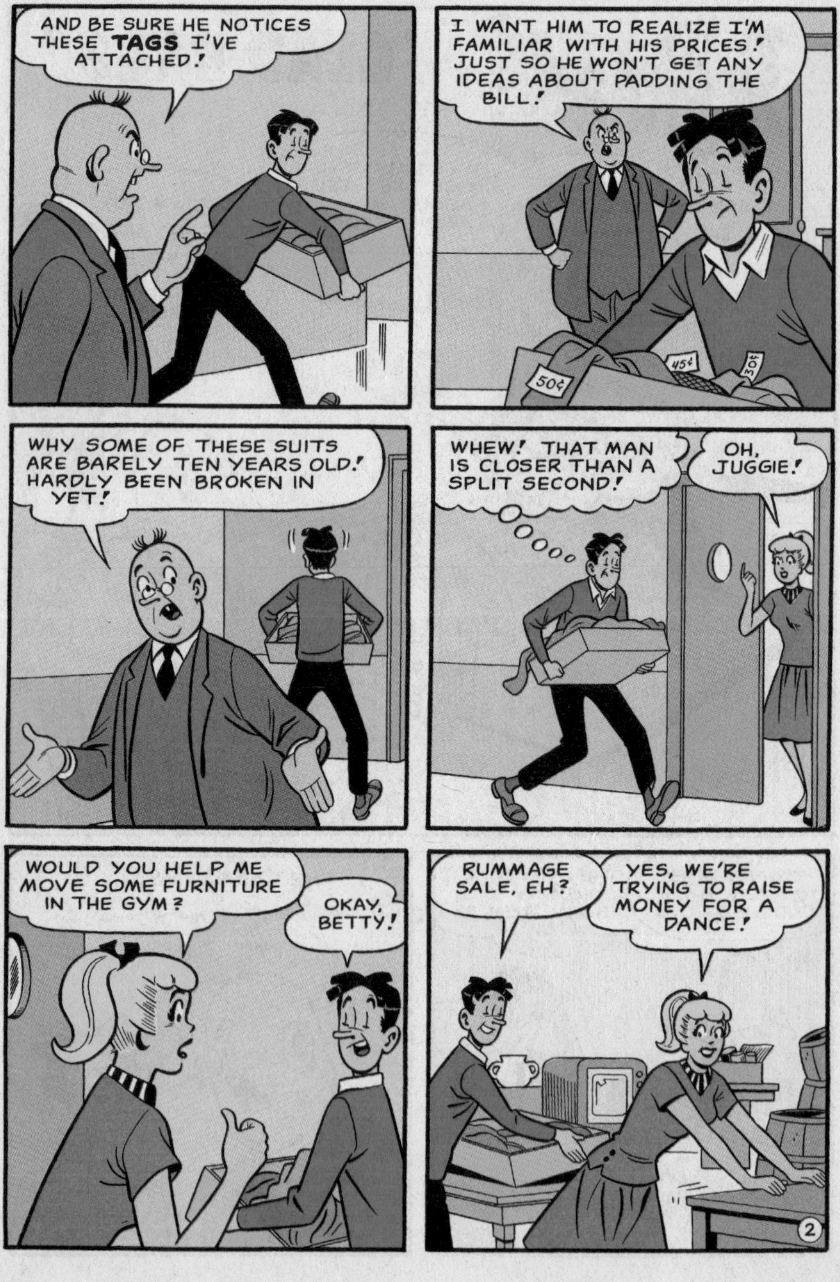
AND BE SURE HE NOTICES THESE **TAGS** I'VE ATTACHED!
I WANT HIM TO REALIZE I'M FAMILIAR WITH HIS PRICES! JUST SO HE WON'T GET ANY IDEAS ABOUT PADDING THE BILL!
50¢
45¢
30¢
WHY SOME OF THESE SUITS ARE BARELY TEN YEARS OLD! HARDLY BEEN BROKEN IN YET!
WHEW! THAT MAN IS CLOSER THAN A SPLIT SECOND!
OH, JUGGIE!
WOULD YOU HELP ME MOVE SOME FURNITURE IN THE GYM?
OKAY, BETTY!
RUMMAGE SALE, EH?
YES, WE'RE TRYING TO RAISE MONEY FOR A DANCE!
2

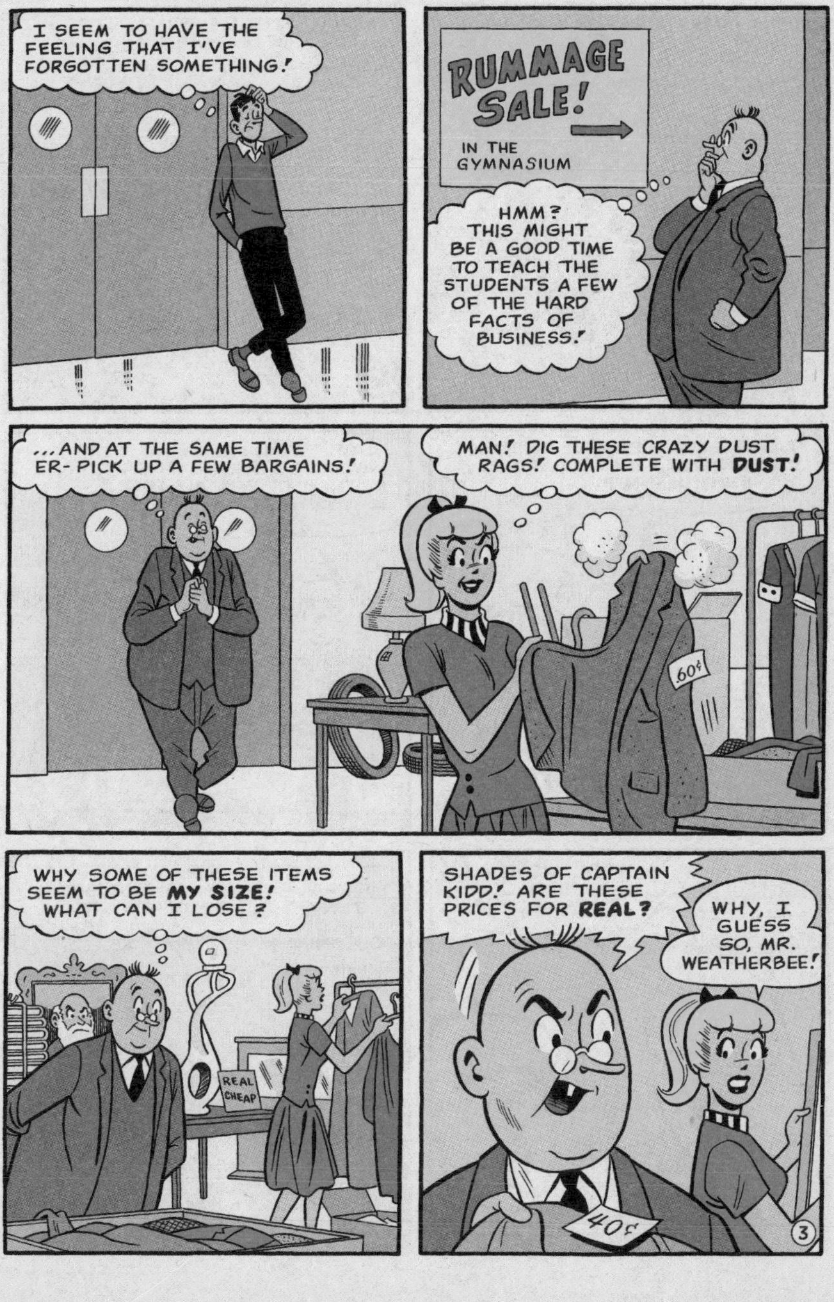
I SEEM TO HAVE THE FEELING THAT I'VE FORGOTTEN SOMETHING!
RUMMAGE SALE!
IN THE GYMNASIUM
HMM? THIS MIGHT BE A GOOD TIME TO TEACH THE STUDENTS A FEW OF THE HARD FACTS OF BUSINESS!
...AND AT THE SAME TIME ER- PICK UP A FEW BARGAINS!
MAN! DIG THESE CRAZY DUST RAGS! COMPLETE WITH DUST!
.60¢
WHY SOME OF THESE ITEMS SEEM TO BE MY SIZE! WHAT CAN I LOSE?
REAL CHEAP
SHADES OF CAPTAIN KIDD! ARE THESE PRICES FOR REAL?
WHY, I GUESS SO, MR. WEATHERBEE!
40¢
3

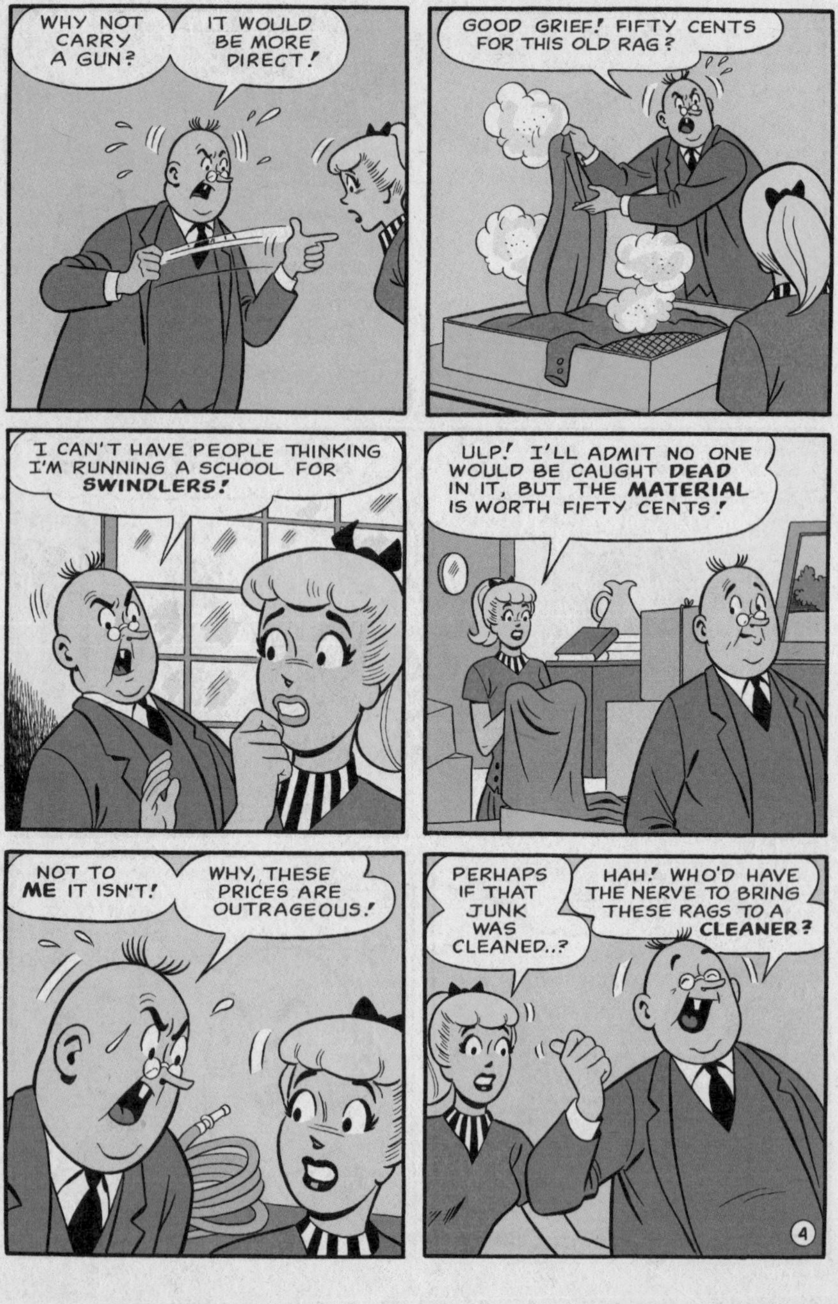
WHY NOT CARRY A GUN?
IT WOULD BE MORE DIRECT!
GOOD GRIEF! FIFTY CENTS FOR THIS OLD RAG?
I CAN'T HAVE PEOPLE THINKING I'M RUNNING A SCHOOL FOR **SWINDLERS!**
ULP! I'LL ADMIT NO ONE WOULD BE CAUGHT **DEAD** IN IT, BUT THE **MATERIAL** IS WORTH FIFTY CENTS!
NOT TO **ME** IT ISN'T!
WHY, THESE PRICES ARE OUTRAGEOUS!
PERHAPS IF THAT JUNK WAS CLEANED..?
HAH! WHO'D HAVE THE NERVE TO BRING THESE RAGS TO A **CLEANER?**
4

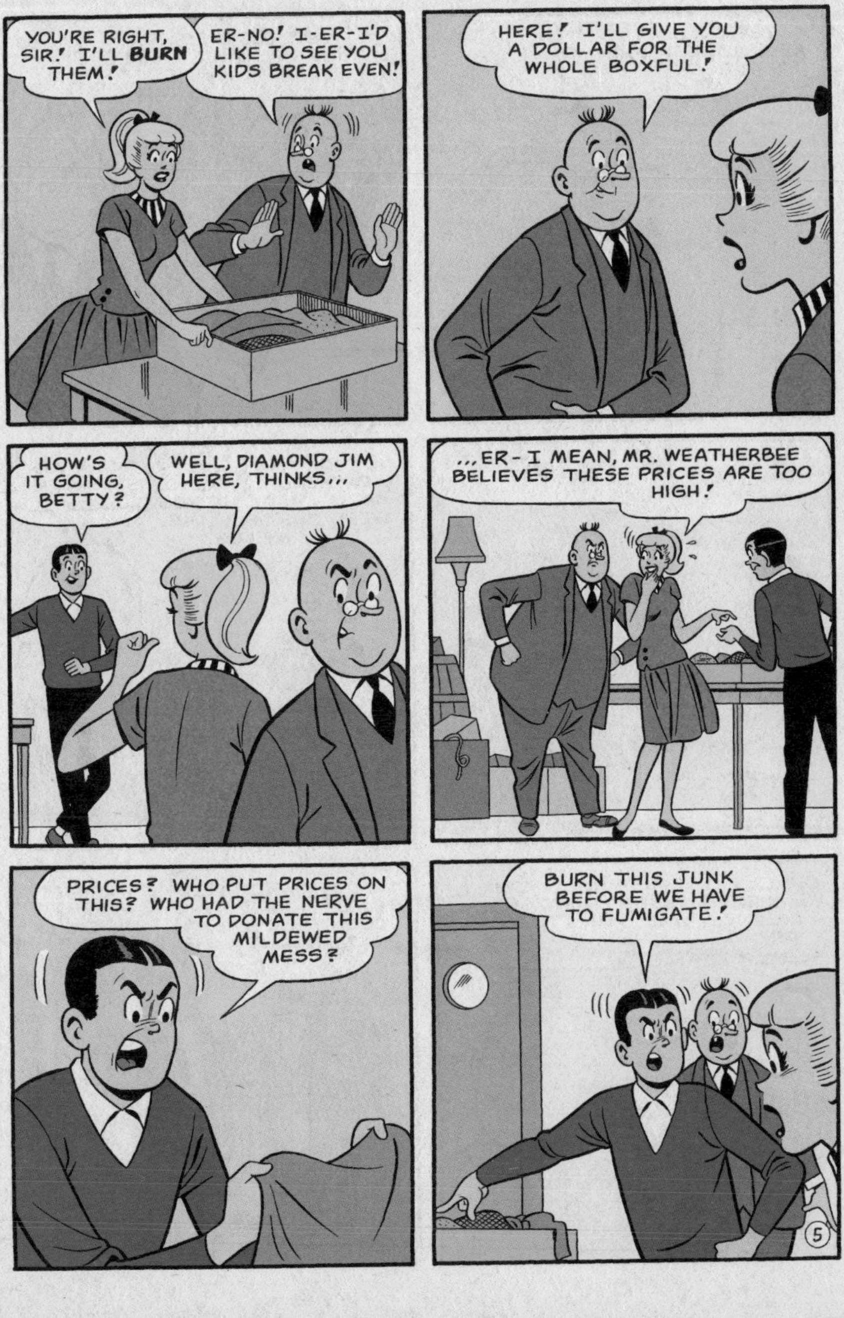
YOU'RE RIGHT, SIR! I'LL BURN THEM!
ER-NO! I-ER-I'D LIKE TO SEE YOU KIDS BREAK EVEN!
HERE! I'LL GIVE YOU A DOLLAR FOR THE WHOLE BOXFUL!
HOW'S IT GOING, BETTY?
WELL, DIAMOND JIM HERE, THINKS...
...ER- I MEAN, MR. WEATHERBEE BELIEVES THESE PRICES ARE TOO HIGH!
PRICES? WHO PUT PRICES ON THIS? WHO HAD THE NERVE TO DONATE THIS MILDEWED MESS?
BURN THIS JUNK BEFORE WE HAVE TO FUMIGATE!
5

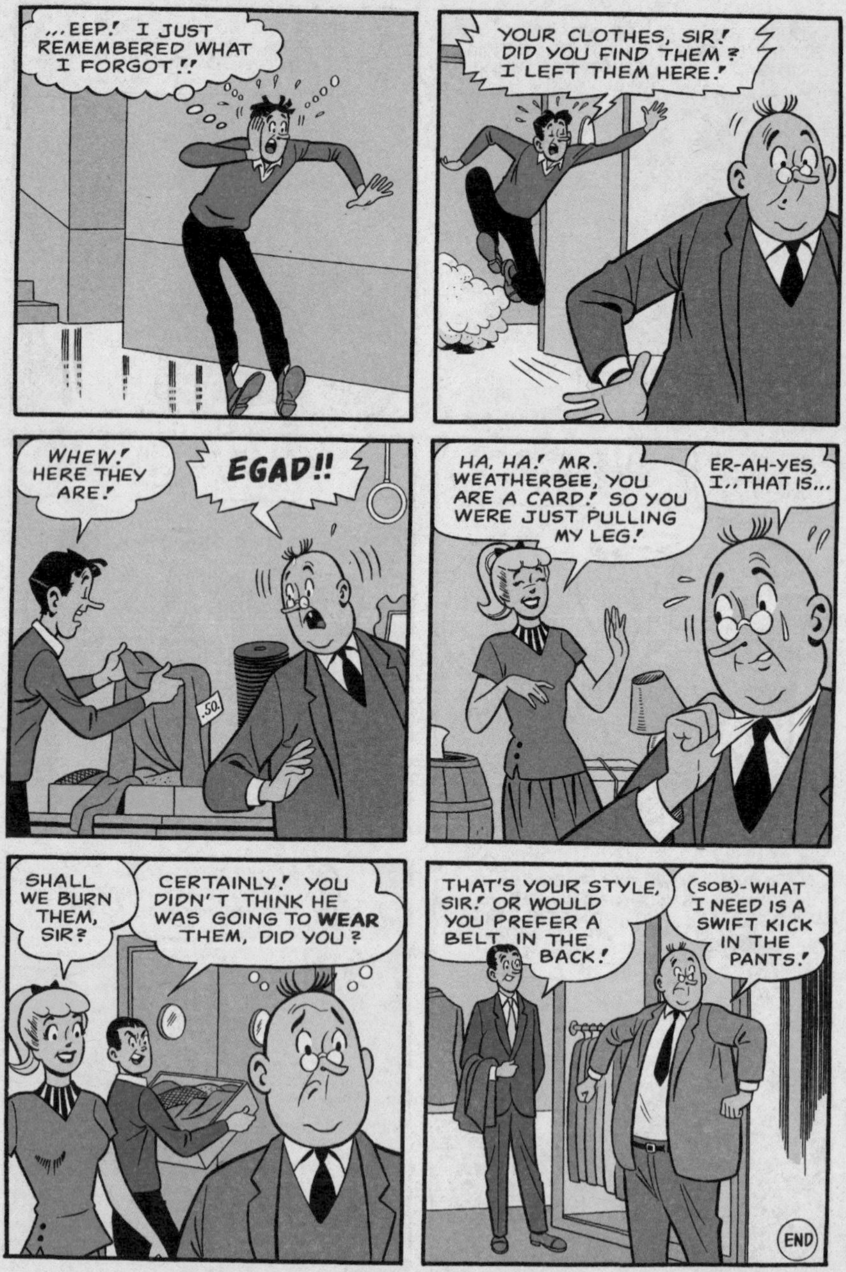
...EEP! I JUST REMEMBERED WHAT I FORGOT!!
YOUR CLOTHES, SIR! DID YOU FIND THEM? I LEFT THEM HERE!
WHEW! HERE THEY ARE!
EGAD!!
.50
HA, HA! MR. WEATHERBEE, YOU ARE A CARD! SO YOU WERE JUST PULLING MY LEG!
ER-AH-YES, I..THAT IS...
SHALL WE BURN THEM, SIR?
CERTAINLY! YOU DIDN'T THINK HE WAS GOING TO WEAR THEM, DID YOU?
THAT'S YOUR STYLE, SIR! OR WOULD YOU PREFER A BELT IN THE BACK!
(SOB)-WHAT I NEED IS A SWIFT KICK IN THE PANTS!
END

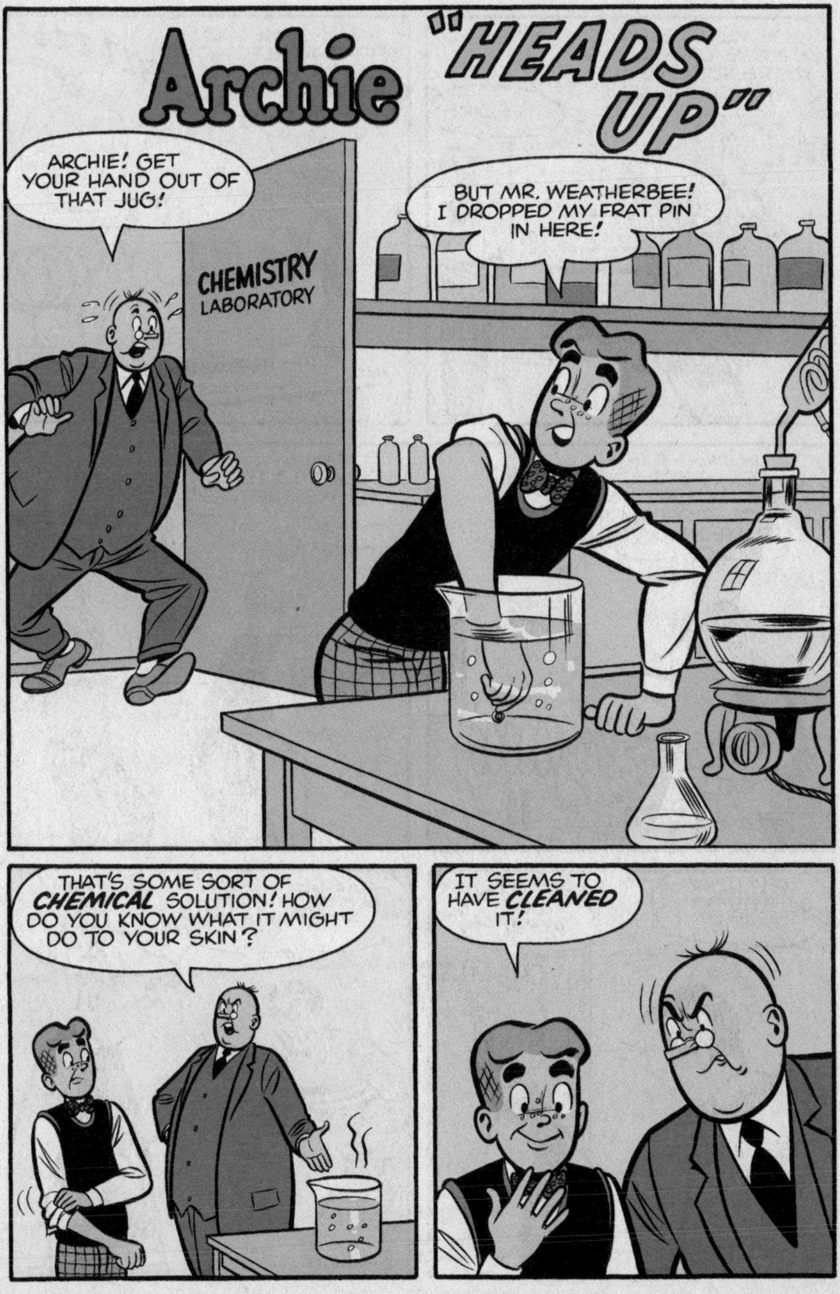
Archie
"HEADS UP"
ARCHIE! GET YOUR HAND OUT OF THAT JUG!
BUT MR. WEATHERBEE! I DROPPED MY FRAT PIN IN HERE!
CHEMISTRY LABORATORY
THAT'S SOME SORT OF CHEMICAL SOLUTION! HOW DO YOU KNOW WHAT IT MIGHT DO TO YOUR SKIN?
IT SEEMS TO HAVE CLEANED IT!

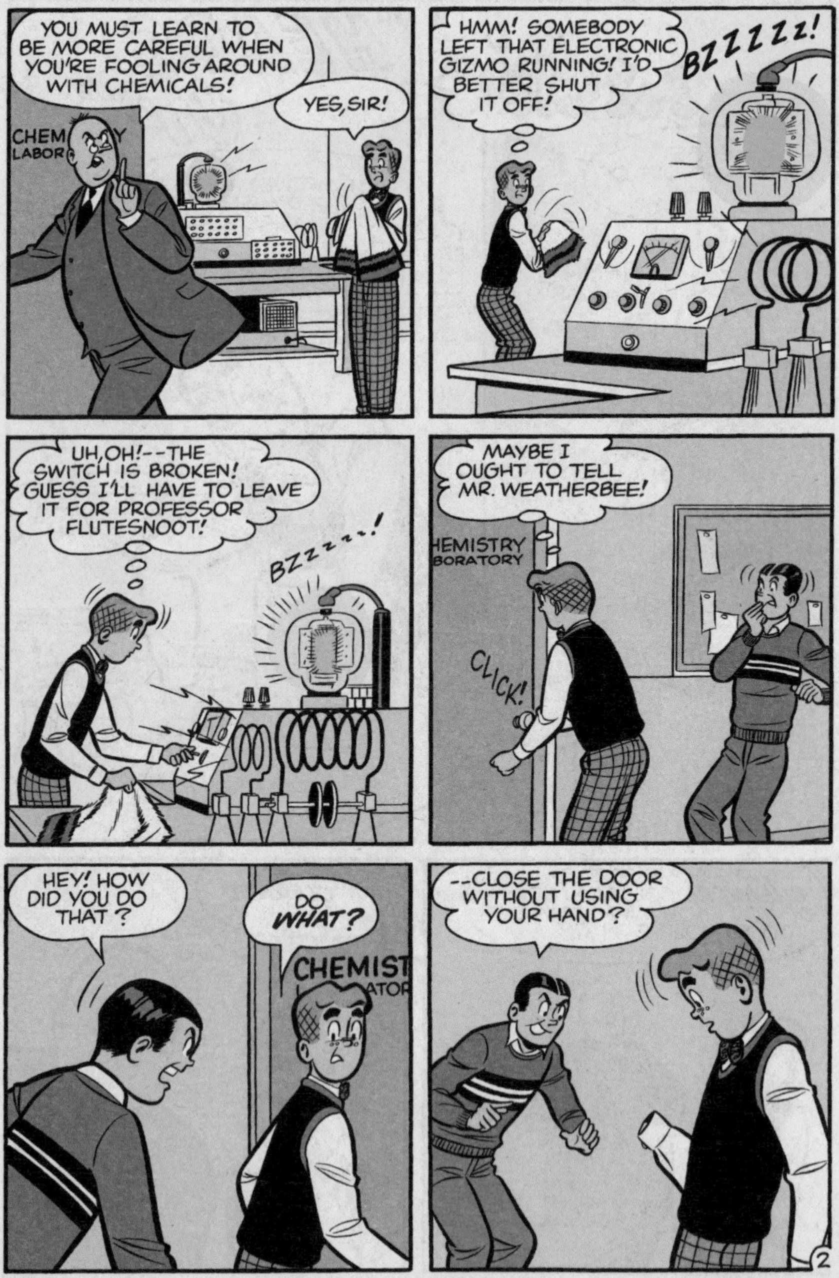
YOU MUST LEARN TO BE MORE CAREFUL WHEN YOU'RE FOOLING AROUND WITH CHEMICALS!
YES, SIR!
CHEM Y
LABOR
HMM! SOMEBODY LEFT THAT ELECTRONIC GIZMO RUNNING! I'D BETTER SHUT IT OFF!
BZZZZZz!
UH, OH!--THE SWITCH IS BROKEN! GUESS I'LL HAVE TO LEAVE IT FOR PROFESSOR FLUTESNOOT!
BZzzzz!
MAYBE I OUGHT TO TELL MR. WEATHERBEE!
HEMISTRY
BORATORY
CLICK!
HEY! HOW DID YOU DO THAT?
DO WHAT?
CHEMIST
ATOR
--CLOSE THE DOOR WITHOUT USING YOUR HAND?
2

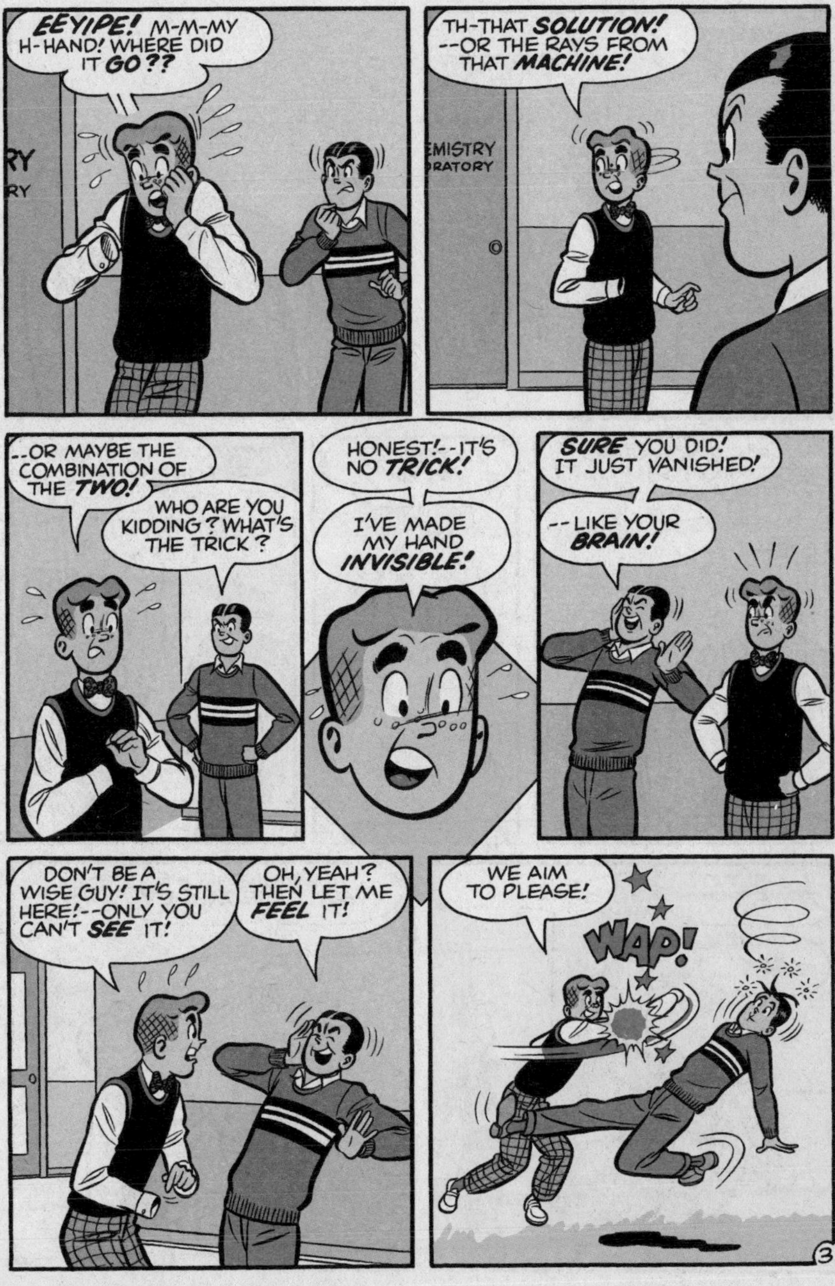
EEYIPE! M-M-MY H-HAND! WHERE DID IT GO??
TH-THAT SOLUTION! --OR THE RAYS FROM THAT MACHINE!
EMISTRY
RATORY
--OR MAYBE THE COMBINATION OF THE TWO!
WHO ARE YOU KIDDING? WHAT'S THE TRICK?
HONEST!--IT'S NO TRICK!
I'VE MADE MY HAND INVISIBLE!
SURE YOU DID! IT JUST VANISHED!
--LIKE YOUR BRAIN!
DON'T BE A WISE GUY! IT'S STILL HERE!--ONLY YOU CAN'T SEE IT!
OH, YEAH? THEN LET ME FEEL IT!
WE AIM TO PLEASE!
WAP!
3

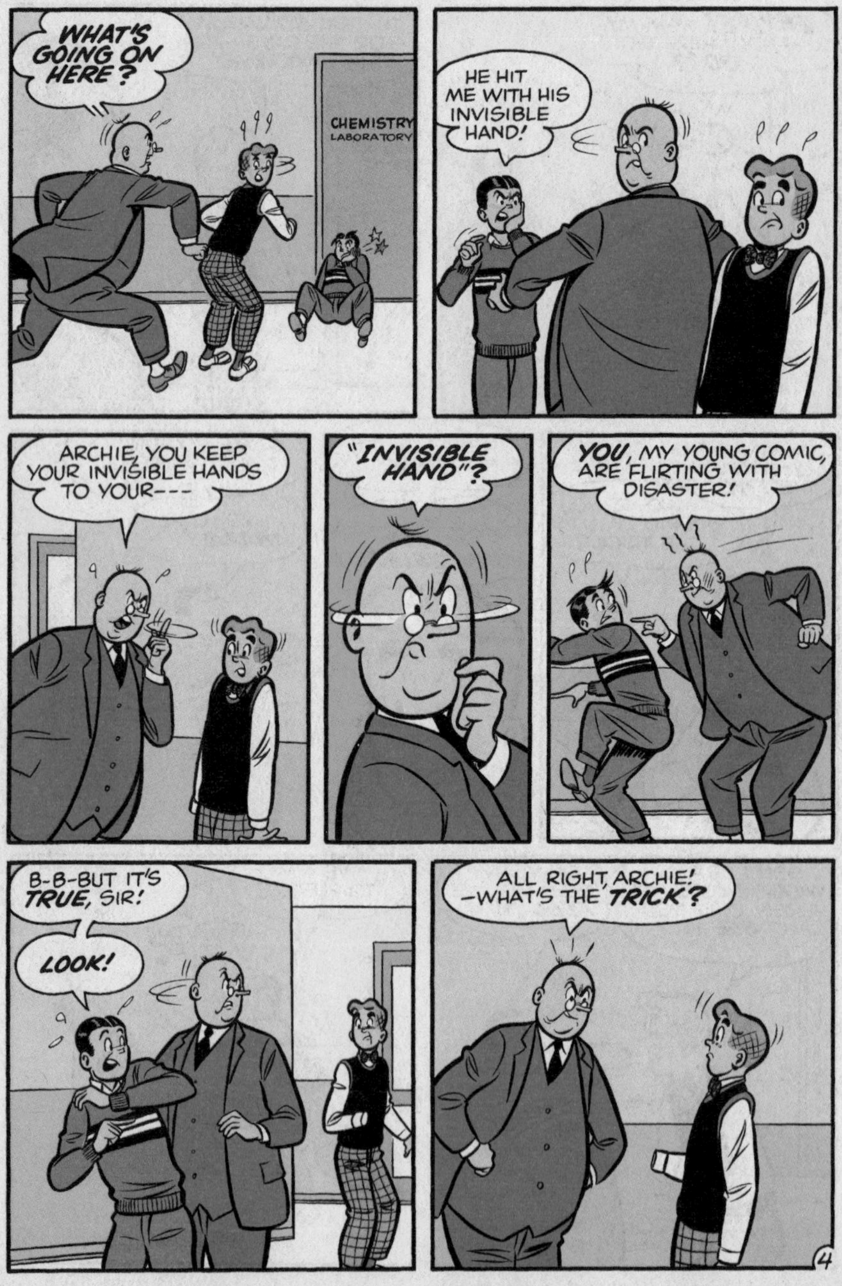
WHAT'S GOING ON HERE?
CHEMISTRY LABORATORY
HE HIT ME WITH HIS INVISIBLE HAND!
ARCHIE, YOU KEEP YOUR INVISIBLE HANDS TO YOUR---
"INVISIBLE HAND"?
YOU, MY YOUNG COMIC, ARE FLIRTING WITH DISASTER!
B-B-BUT IT'S TRUE, SIR!
LOOK!
ALL RIGHT, ARCHIE! -WHAT'S THE TRICK?
4

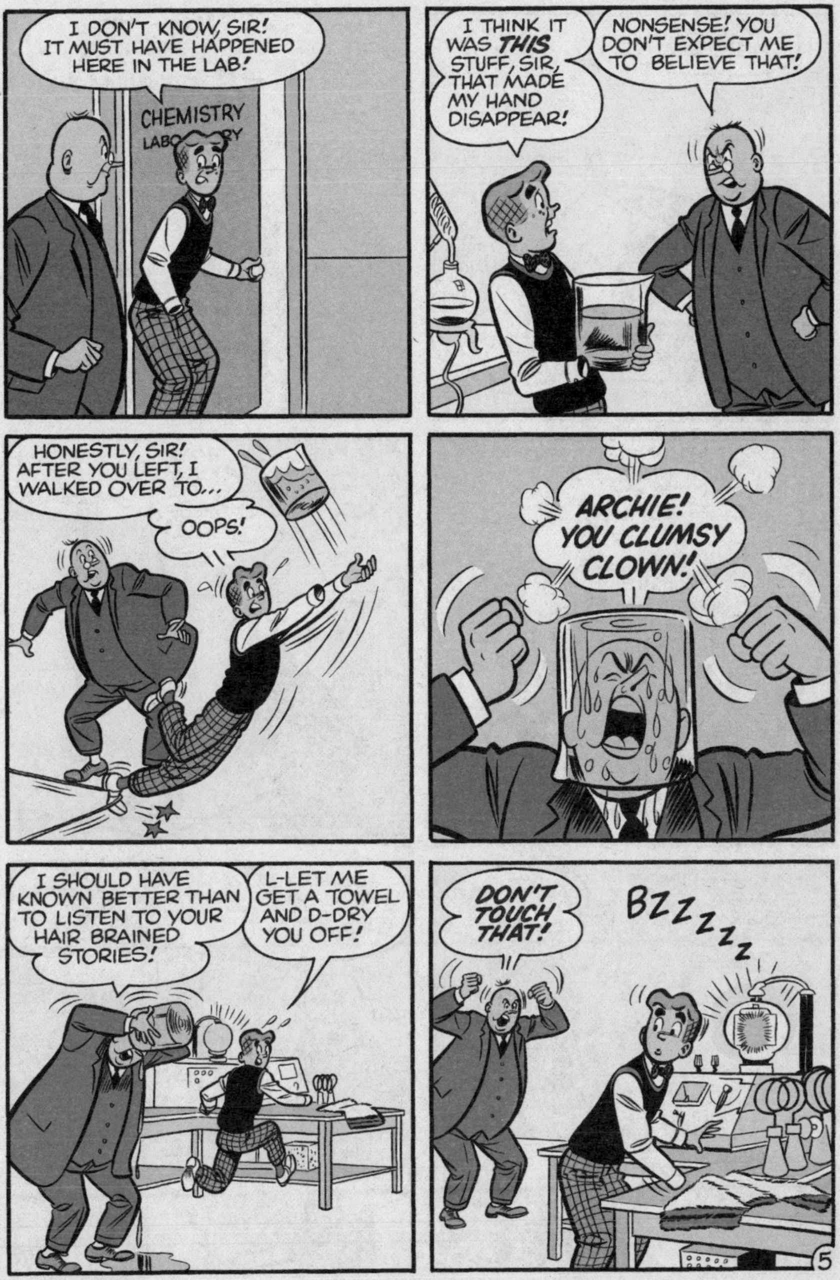

I DON'T KNOW, SIR! IT MUST HAVE HAPPENED HERE IN THE LAB!
CHEMISTRY LABORATORY
I THINK IT WAS THIS STUFF, SIR, THAT MADE MY HAND DISAPPEAR!
NONSENSE! YOU DON'T EXPECT ME TO BELIEVE THAT!
HONESTLY, SIR! AFTER YOU LEFT, I WALKED OVER TO...
OOPS!
ARCHIE! YOU CLUMSY CLOWN!
I SHOULD HAVE KNOWN BETTER THAN TO LISTEN TO YOUR HAIR BRAINED STORIES!
L-LET ME GET A TOWEL AND D-DRY YOU OFF!
DON'T TOUCH THAT!
BZZZZZ
5

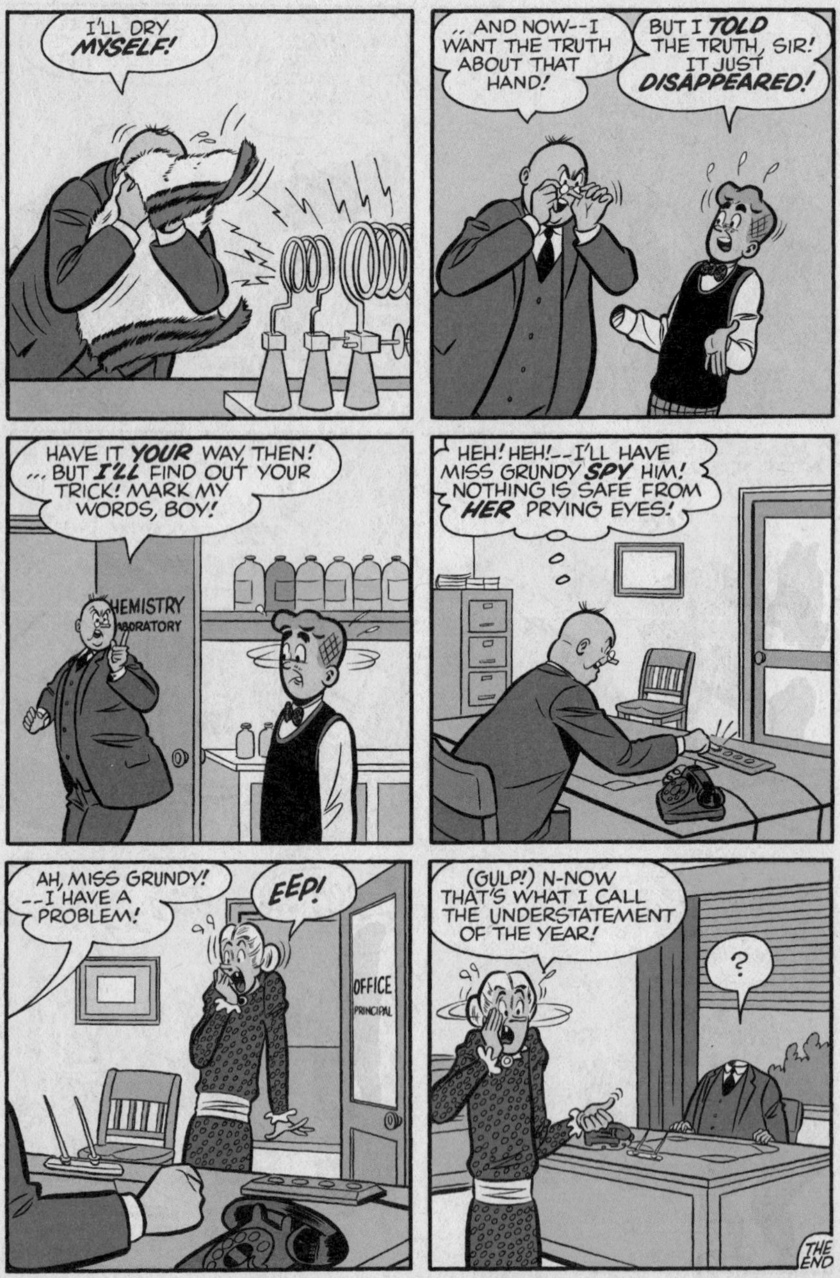
I'LL DRY MYSELF!
.. AND NOW--I WANT THE TRUTH ABOUT THAT HAND!
BUT I TOLD THE TRUTH, SIR! IT JUST DISAPPEARED!
HAVE IT YOUR WAY, THEN! ... BUT I'LL FIND OUT YOUR TRICK! MARK MY WORDS, BOY!
HEMISTRY
ABORATORY
HEH! HEH!--I'LL HAVE MISS GRUNDY SPY HIM! NOTHING IS SAFE FROM HER PRYING EYES!
AH, MISS GRUNDY! --I HAVE A PROBLEM!
EEP!
OFFICE
PRINCIPAL
(GULP!) N-NOW THAT'S WHAT I CALL THE UNDERSTATEMENT OF THE YEAR!
?
THE END

The Old School Spirit
Archie and Me #87, October 1976
Frank Doyle and Samm Schwartz

It's a case of "boo who?" when the Bee thinks he's seeing a ghost! Feeling homesick for Riverdale High over summer break, Mr. Weatherbee decides to look in on the place... not realizing Archie is there to clean the auditorium after theater practice!

Rivals?
Betty & Veronica #86, February 1963
Frank Doyle, Dan DeCarlo, Rudy Lapick and Vincent DeCarlo

Someone should tell the teachers at Riverdale High that eavesdropping is not a good example to set for the students! Alas, Miss Grundy and Mr. Weatherbee deliberately listen to a private conversation between Betty and Veronica and come up with the erroneous (and hilarious) conclusion that the girls have a crush on their principal.

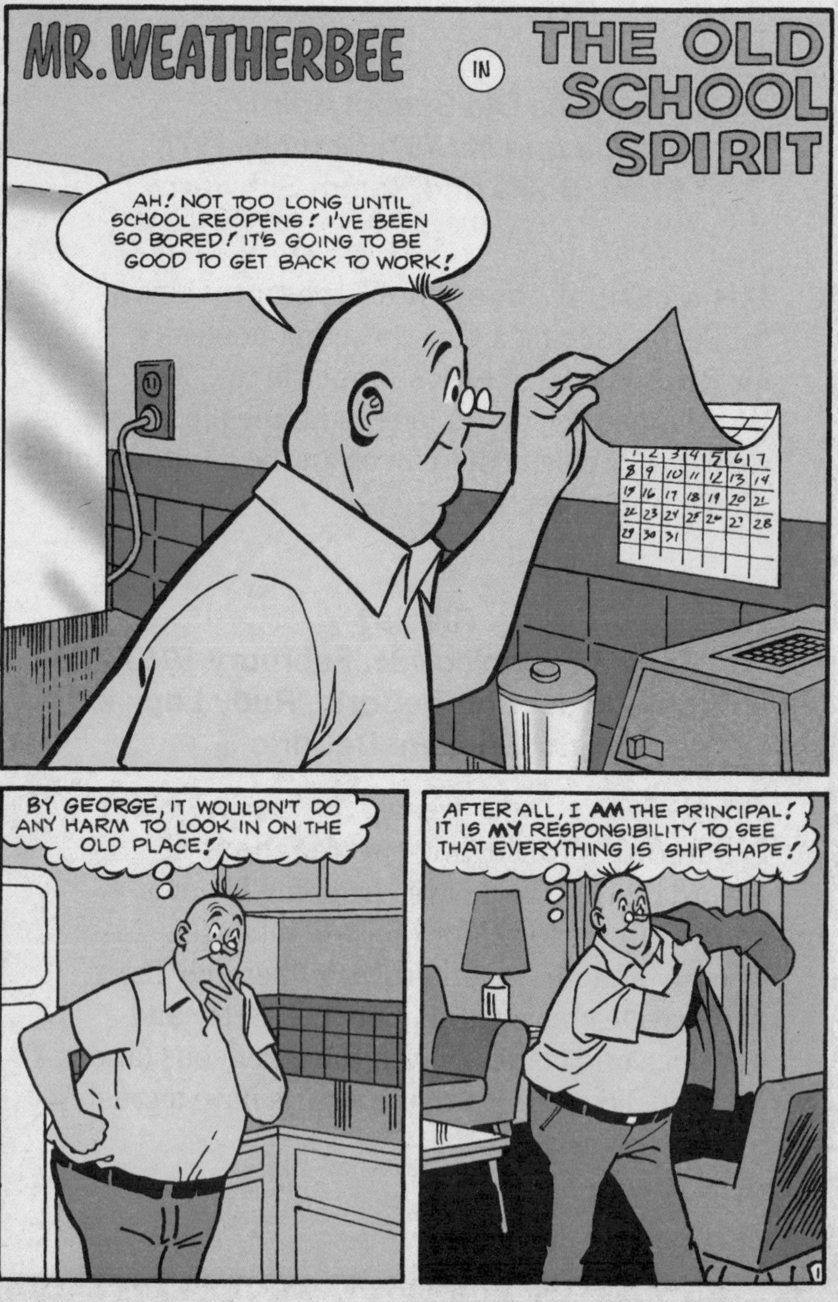
MR. WEATHERBEE
IN
THE OLD SCHOOL SPIRIT
AH! NOT TOO LONG UNTIL SCHOOL REOPENS! I'VE BEEN SO BORED! IT'S GOING TO BE GOOD TO GET BACK TO WORK!
BY GEORGE, IT WOULDN'T DO ANY HARM TO LOOK IN ON THE OLD PLACE!
AFTER ALL, I AM THE PRINCIPAL! IT IS MY RESPONSIBILITY TO SEE THAT EVERYTHING IS SHIPSHAPE!
1

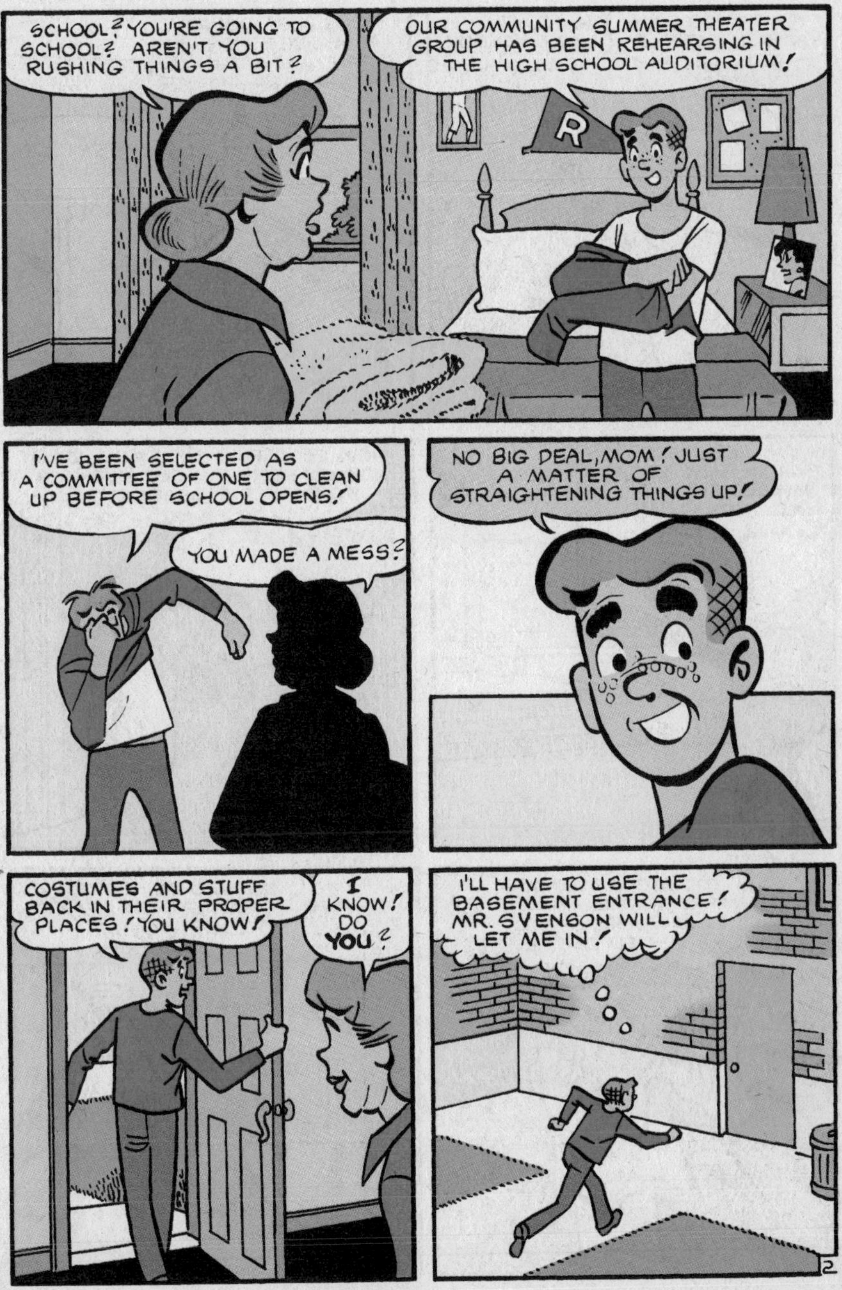
SCHOOL? YOU'RE GOING TO SCHOOL? AREN'T YOU RUSHING THINGS A BIT?
OUR COMMUNITY SUMMER THEATER GROUP HAS BEEN REHEARSING IN THE HIGH SCHOOL AUDITORIUM!
R
I'VE BEEN SELECTED AS A COMMITTEE OF ONE TO CLEAN UP BEFORE SCHOOL OPENS!
YOU MADE A MESS?
NO BIG DEAL, MOM! JUST A MATTER OF STRAIGHTENING THINGS UP!
COSTUMES AND STUFF BACK IN THEIR PROPER PLACES! YOU KNOW!
I KNOW! DO YOU?
I'LL HAVE TO USE THE BASEMENT ENTRANCE! MR. SVENSON WILL LET ME IN!
2

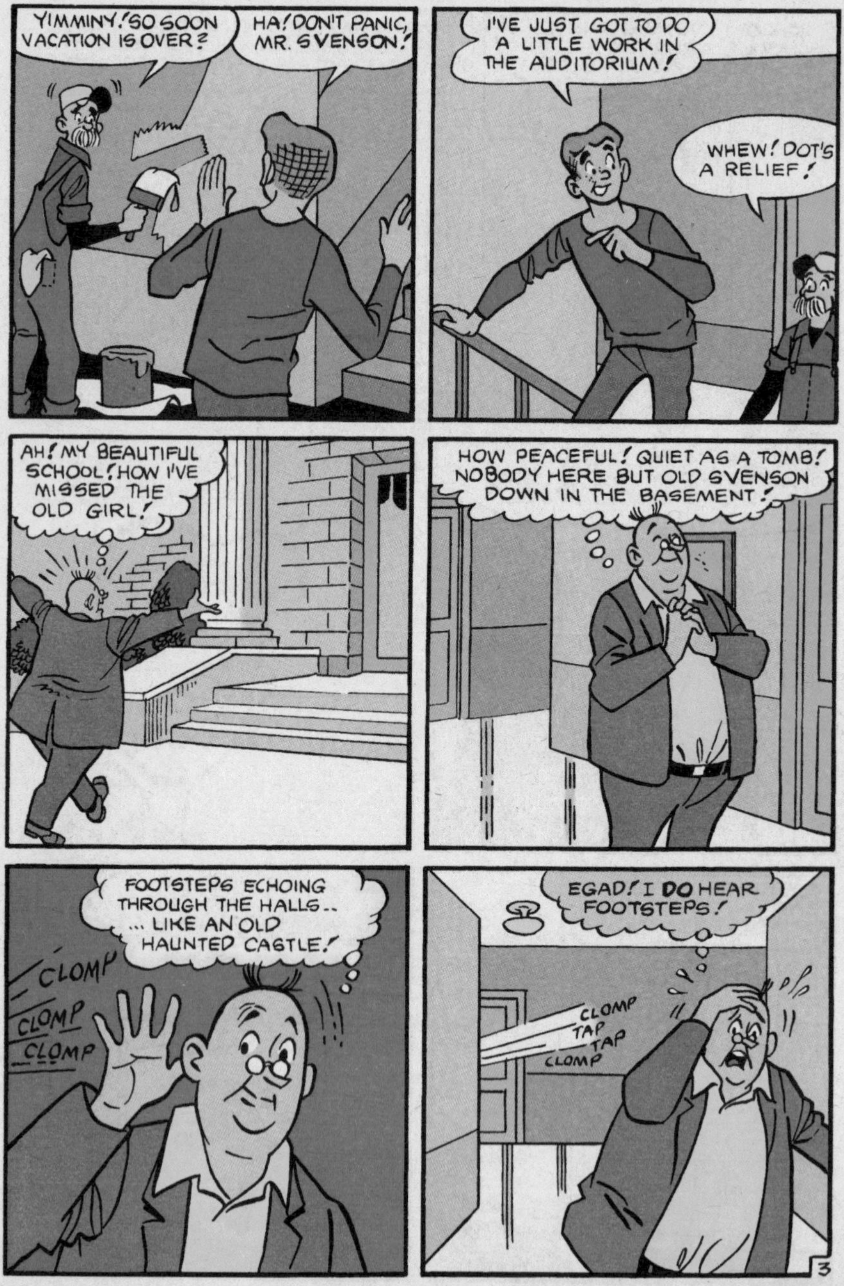
YIMMINY! SO SOON VACATION IS OVER?
HA! DON'T PANIC, MR. SVENSON!
I'VE JUST GOT TO DO A LITTLE WORK IN THE AUDITORIUM!
WHEW! DOT'S A RELIEF!
AH! MY BEAUTIFUL SCHOOL! HOW I'VE MISSED THE OLD GIRL!
HOW PEACEFUL! QUIET AS A TOMB! NOBODY HERE BUT OLD SVENSON DOWN IN THE BASEMENT!
FOOTSTEPS ECHOING THROUGH THE HALLS.. ... LIKE AN OLD HAUNTED CASTLE!
CLOMP
CLOMP
CLOMP
EGAD! I DO HEAR FOOTSTEPS!
CLOMP
TAP
TAP
CLOMP
3

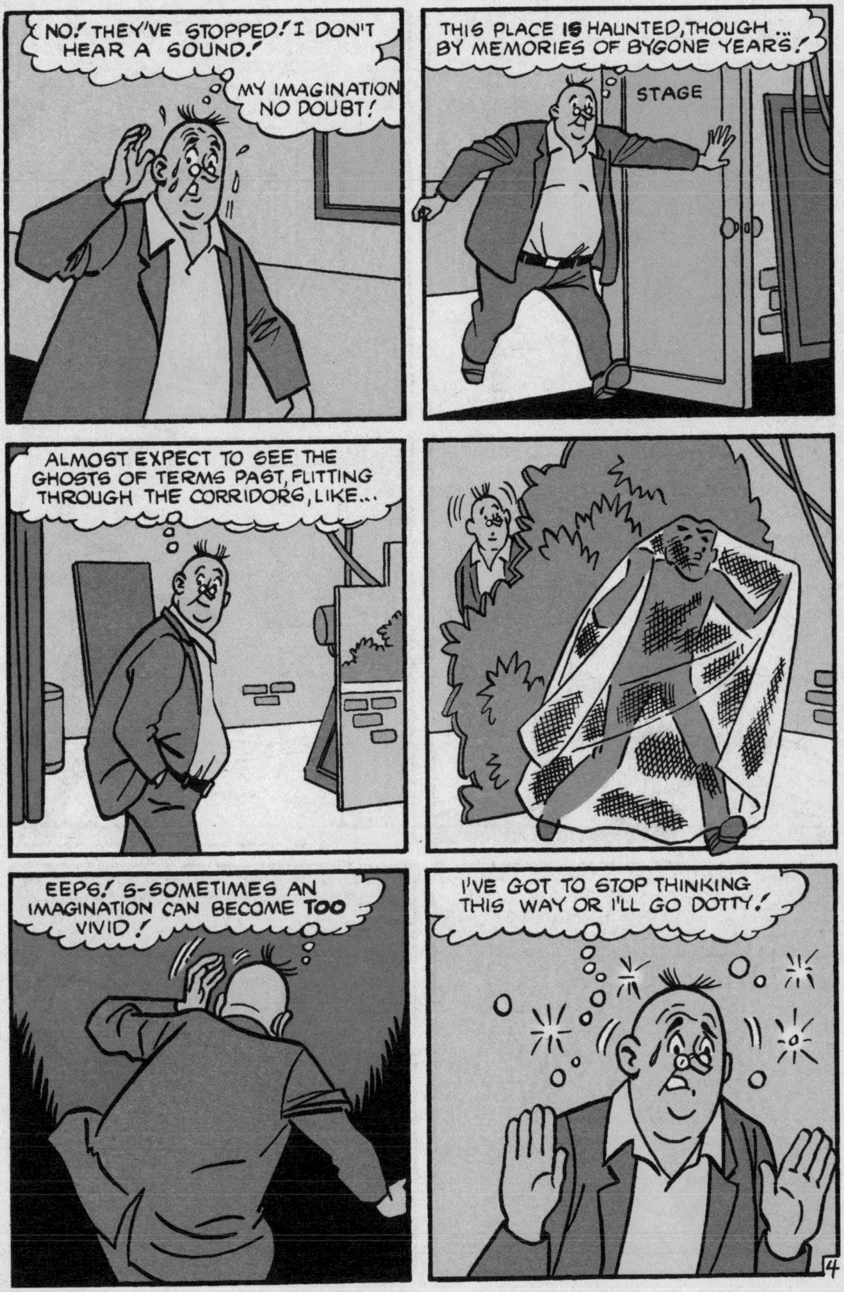
NO! THEY'VE STOPPED! I DON'T HEAR A SOUND!
MY IMAGINATION NO DOUBT!
THIS PLACE IS HAUNTED, THOUGH ... BY MEMORIES OF BYGONE YEARS!
STAGE
ALMOST EXPECT TO SEE THE GHOSTS OF TERMS PAST, FLITTING THROUGH THE CORRIDORS, LIKE...
EEPS! S-SOMETIMES AN IMAGINATION CAN BECOME TOO VIVID!
I'VE GOT TO STOP THINKING THIS WAY OR I'LL GO DOTTY!
4

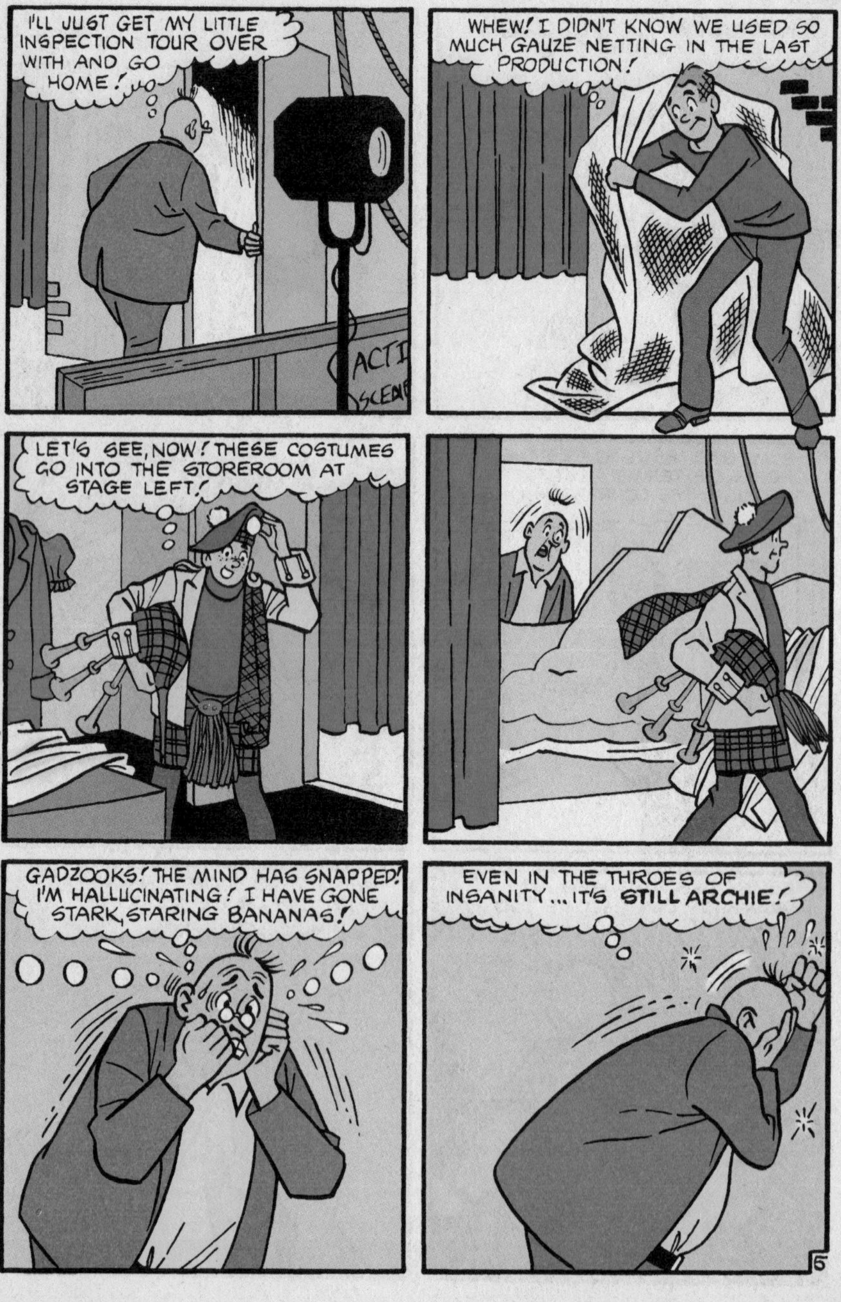
I'LL JUST GET MY LITTLE INSPECTION TOUR OVER WITH AND GO HOME!
WHEW! I DIDN'T KNOW WE USED SO MUCH GAUZE NETTING IN THE LAST PRODUCTION!
LET'S SEE, NOW! THESE COSTUMES GO INTO THE STOREROOM AT STAGE LEFT!
GADZOOKS! THE MIND HAS SNAPPED! I'M HALLUCINATING! I HAVE GONE STARK, STARING BANANAS!
EVEN IN THE THROES OF INSANITY... IT'S STILL ARCHIE!
5

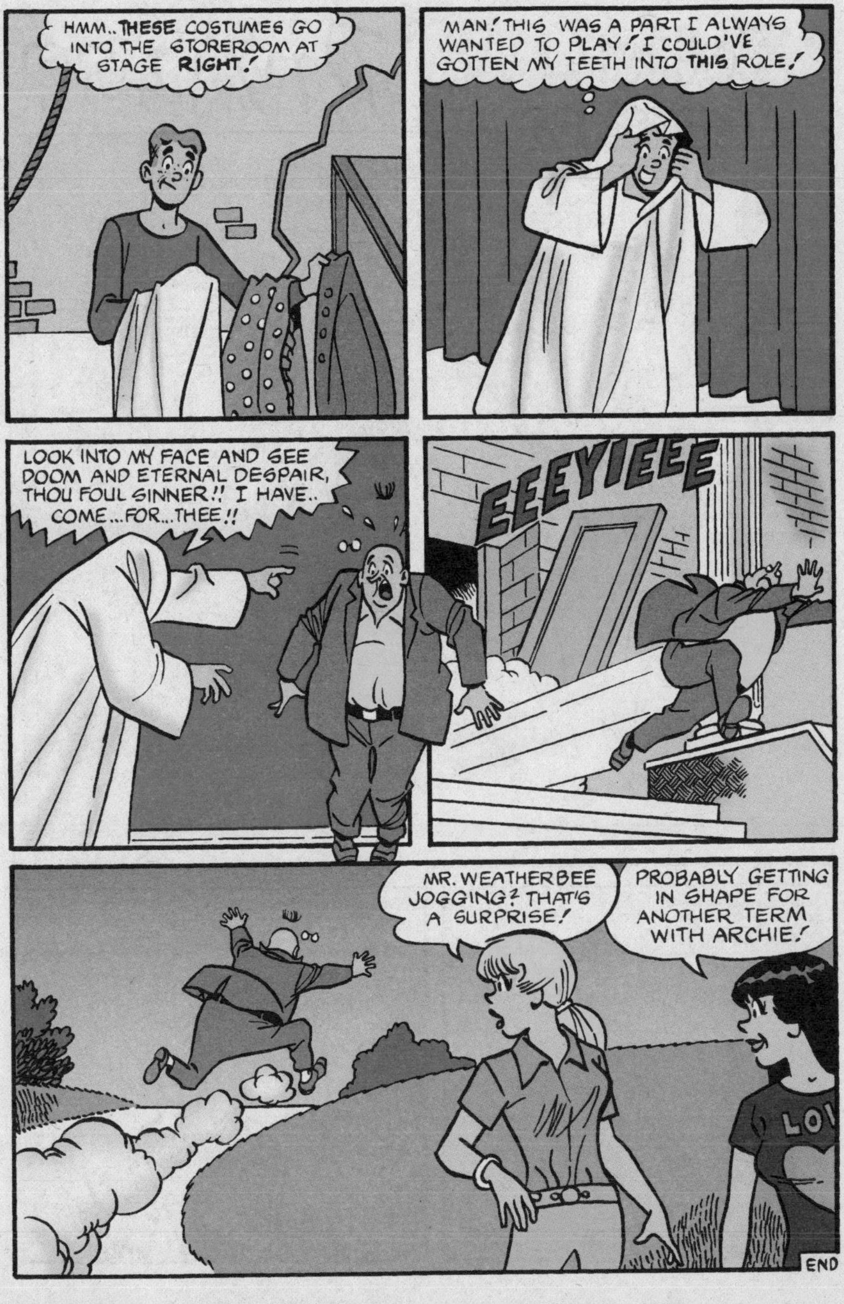
HMM.. THESE COSTUMES GO INTO THE STOREROOM AT STAGE RIGHT!
MAN! THIS WAS A PART I ALWAYS WANTED TO PLAY! I COULD'VE GOTTEN MY TEETH INTO THIS ROLE!
LOOK INTO MY FACE AND SEE DOOM AND ETERNAL DESPAIR, THOU FOUL SINNER!! I HAVE.. COME...FOR...THEE!!
EEEYIEEE
MR. WEATHERBEE JOGGING? THAT'S A SURPRISE!
PROBABLY GETTING IN SHAPE FOR ANOTHER TERM WITH ARCHIE!
LOV
END

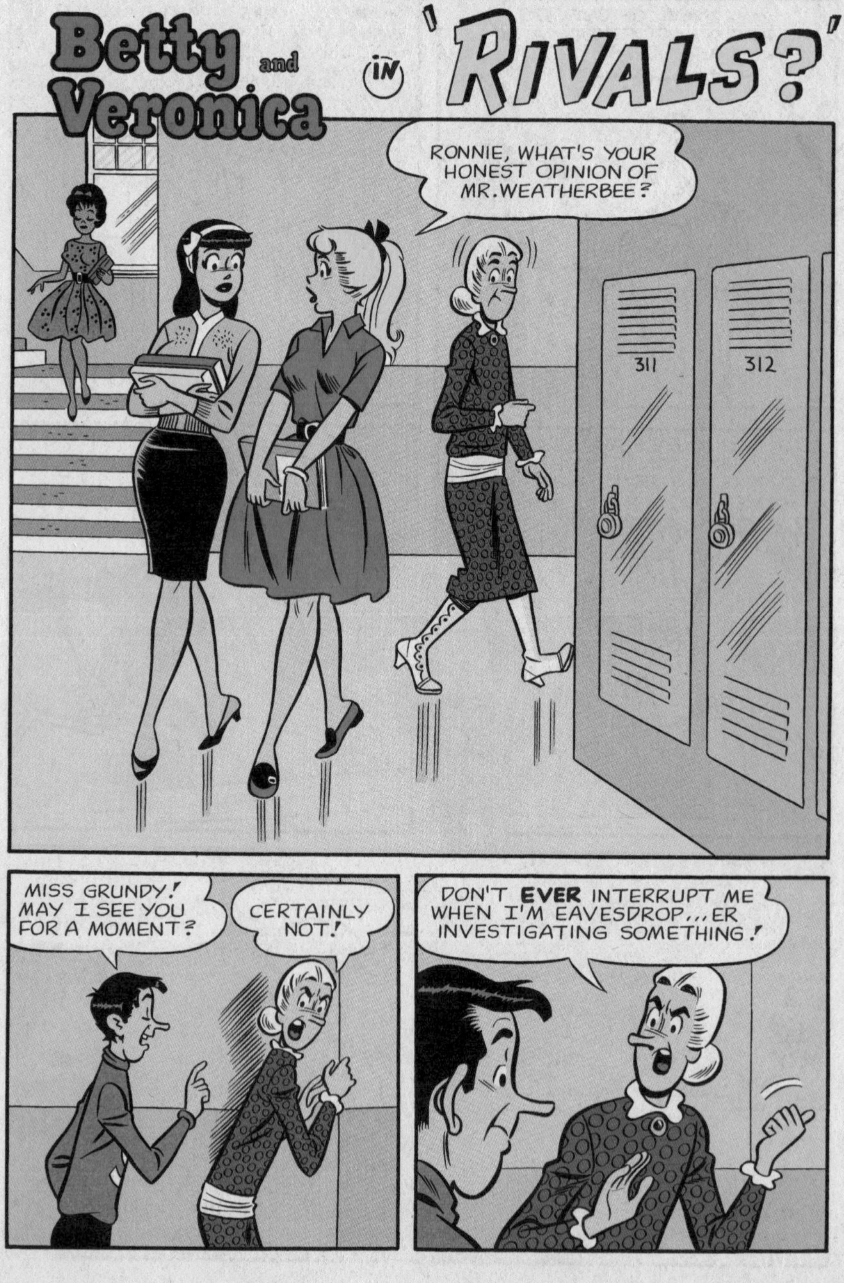
Betty and Veronica
IN
'RIVALS?'
RONNIE, WHAT'S YOUR HONEST OPINION OF MR. WEATHERBEE?
311
312
MISS GRUNDY! MAY I SEE YOU FOR A MOMENT?
CERTAINLY NOT!
DON'T EVER INTERRUPT ME WHEN I'M EAVESDROP... ER INVESTIGATING SOMETHING!

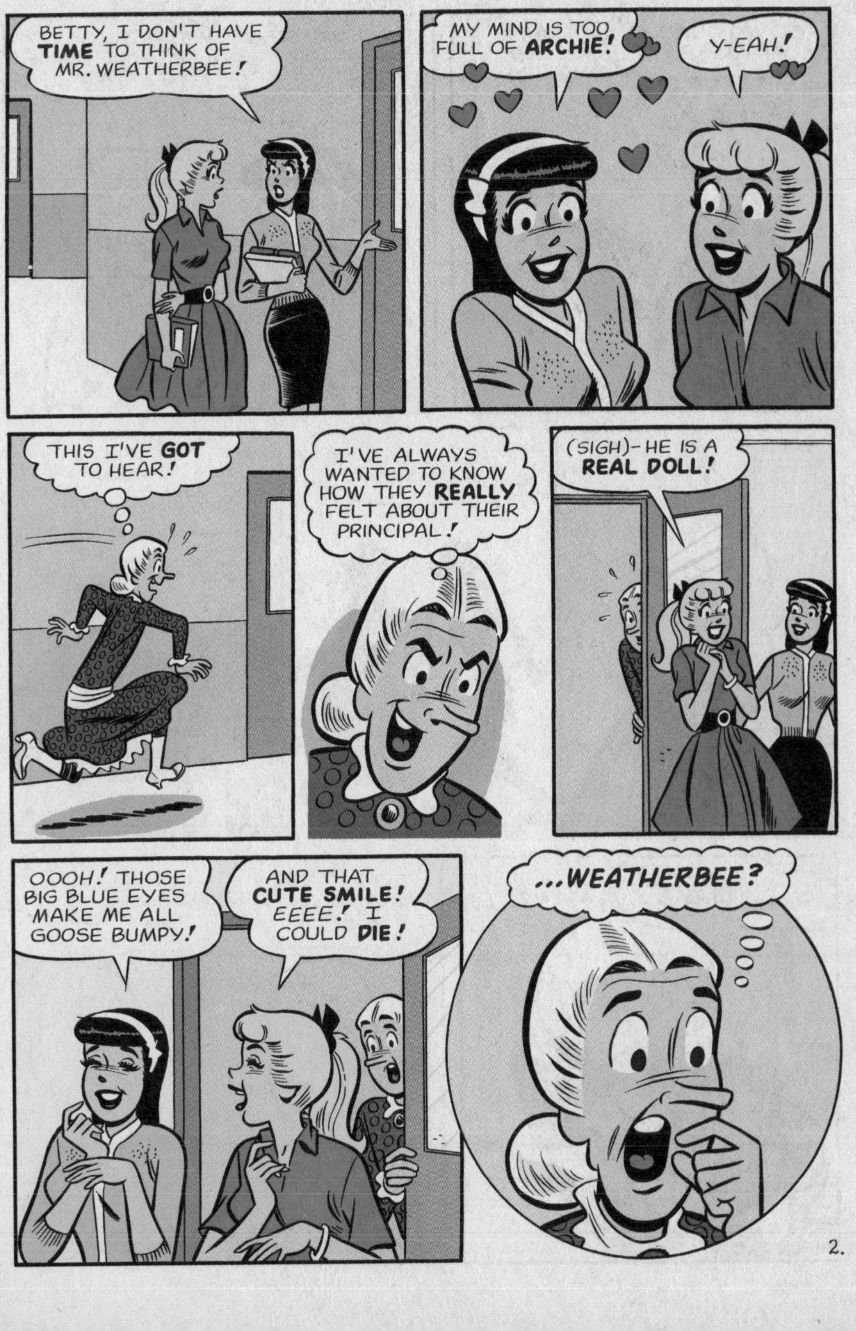
BETTY, I DON'T HAVE **TIME** TO THINK OF MR. WEATHERBEE!
MY MIND IS TOO FULL OF **ARCHIE**!
Y-EAH!
THIS I'VE **GOT** TO HEAR!
I'VE ALWAYS WANTED TO KNOW HOW THEY **REALLY** FELT ABOUT THEIR PRINCIPAL!
(SIGH)- HE IS A **REAL DOLL**!
OOOH! THOSE BIG BLUE EYES MAKE ME ALL GOOSE BUMPY!
AND THAT **CUTE SMILE**! EEEE! I COULD **DIE**!
...WEATHERBEE?
2.

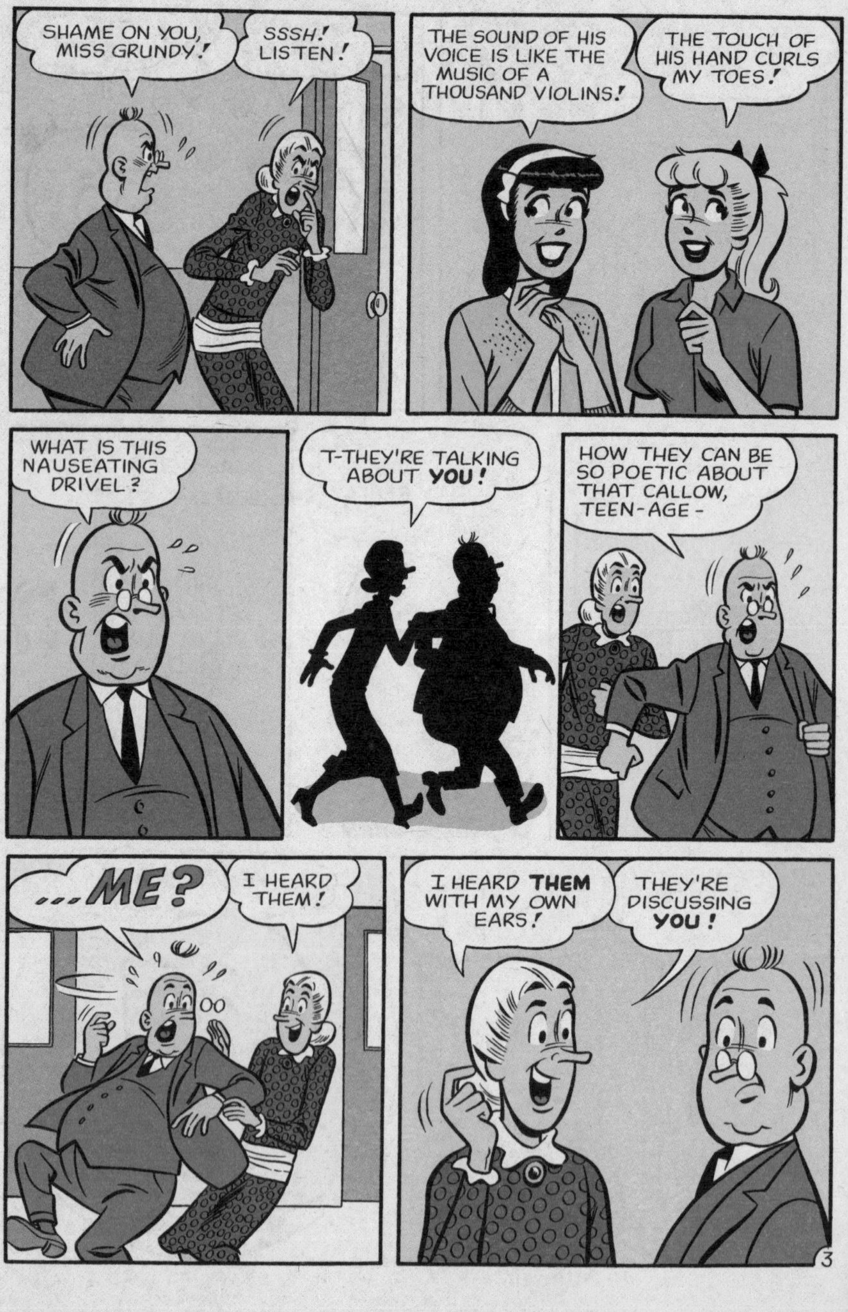
SHAME ON YOU, MISS GRUNDY!
SSSH! LISTEN!
THE SOUND OF HIS VOICE IS LIKE THE MUSIC OF A THOUSAND VIOLINS!
THE TOUCH OF HIS HAND CURLS MY TOES!
WHAT IS THIS NAUSEATING DRIVEL?
T-THEY'RE TALKING ABOUT **YOU**!
HOW THEY CAN BE SO POETIC ABOUT THAT CALLOW, TEEN-AGE -
...ME?
I HEARD THEM!
I HEARD **THEM** WITH MY OWN EARS!
THEY'RE DISCUSSING **YOU**!
3

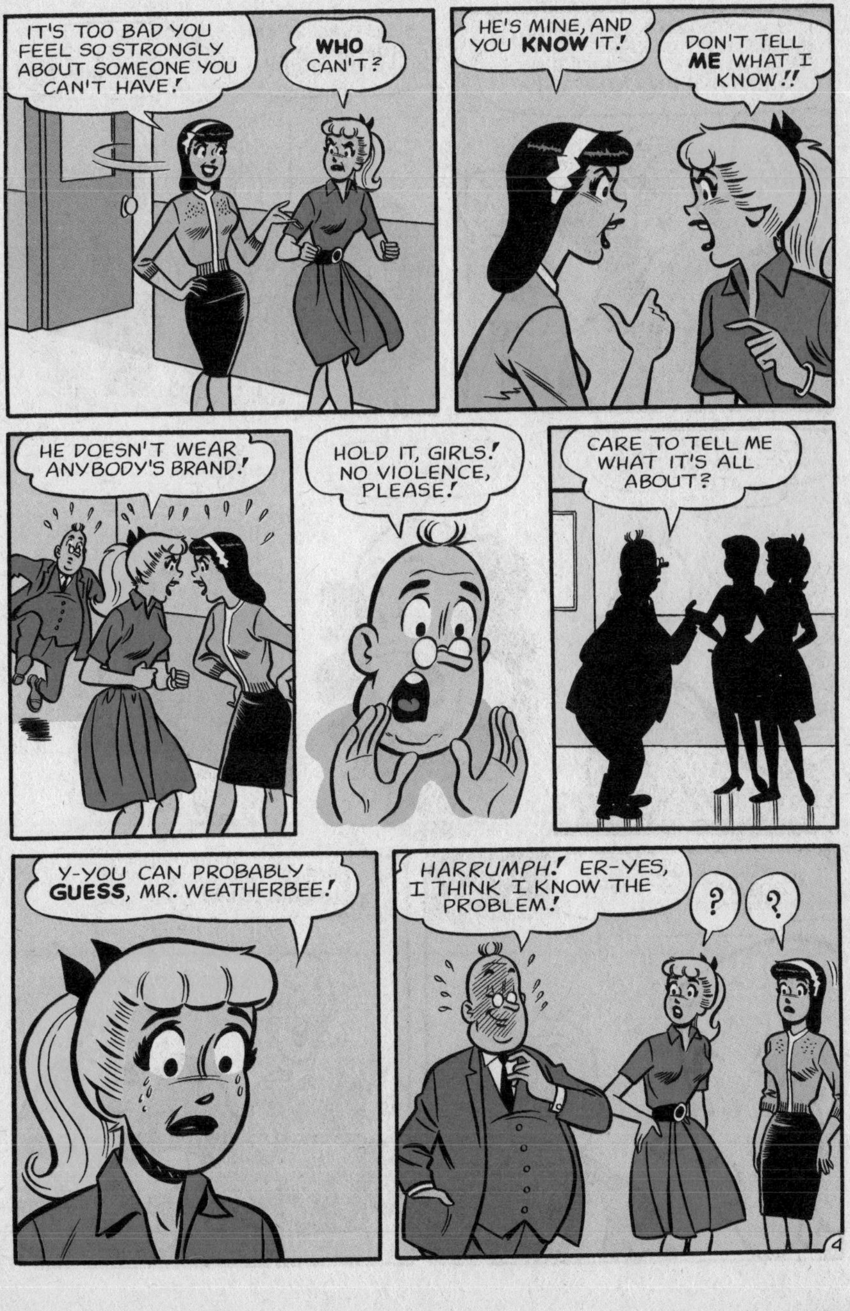
IT'S TOO BAD YOU FEEL SO STRONGLY ABOUT SOMEONE YOU CAN'T HAVE!
WHO CAN'T?
HE'S MINE, AND YOU KNOW IT!
DON'T TELL ME WHAT I KNOW!!
HE DOESN'T WEAR ANYBODY'S BRAND!
HOLD IT, GIRLS! NO VIOLENCE, PLEASE!
CARE TO TELL ME WHAT IT'S ALL ABOUT?
Y-YOU CAN PROBABLY GUESS, MR. WEATHERBEE!
HARRUMPH! ER-YES, I THINK I KNOW THE PROBLEM!
?
?
4

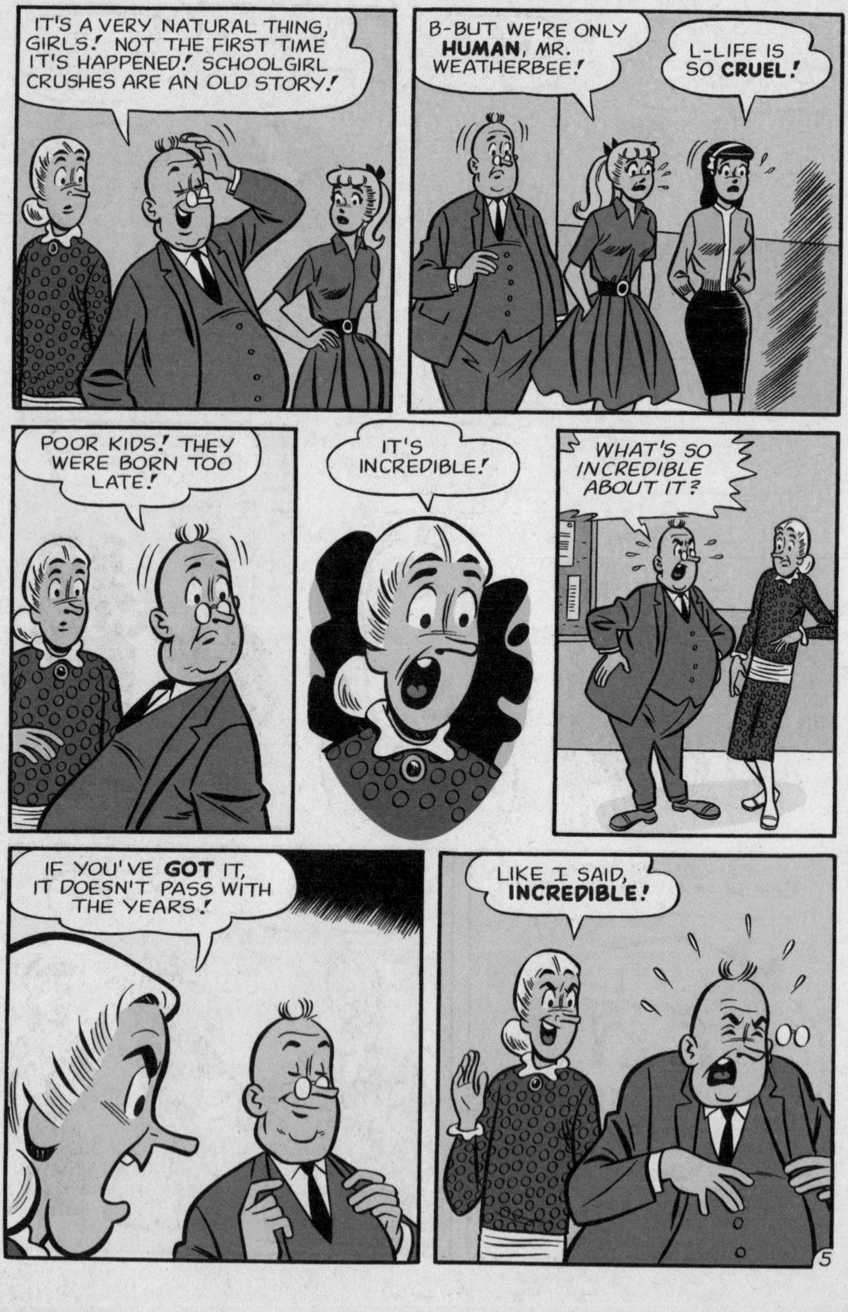
IT'S A VERY NATURAL THING, GIRLS! NOT THE FIRST TIME IT'S HAPPENED! SCHOOLGIRL CRUSHES ARE AN OLD STORY!
B-BUT WE'RE ONLY HUMAN, MR. WEATHERBEE!
L-LIFE IS SO CRUEL!
POOR KIDS! THEY WERE BORN TOO LATE!
IT'S SO INCREDIBLE!
WHAT'S SO INCREDIBLE ABOUT IT?
IF YOU'VE GOT IT, IT DOESN'T PASS WITH THE YEARS!
LIKE I SAID, INCREDIBLE!
5

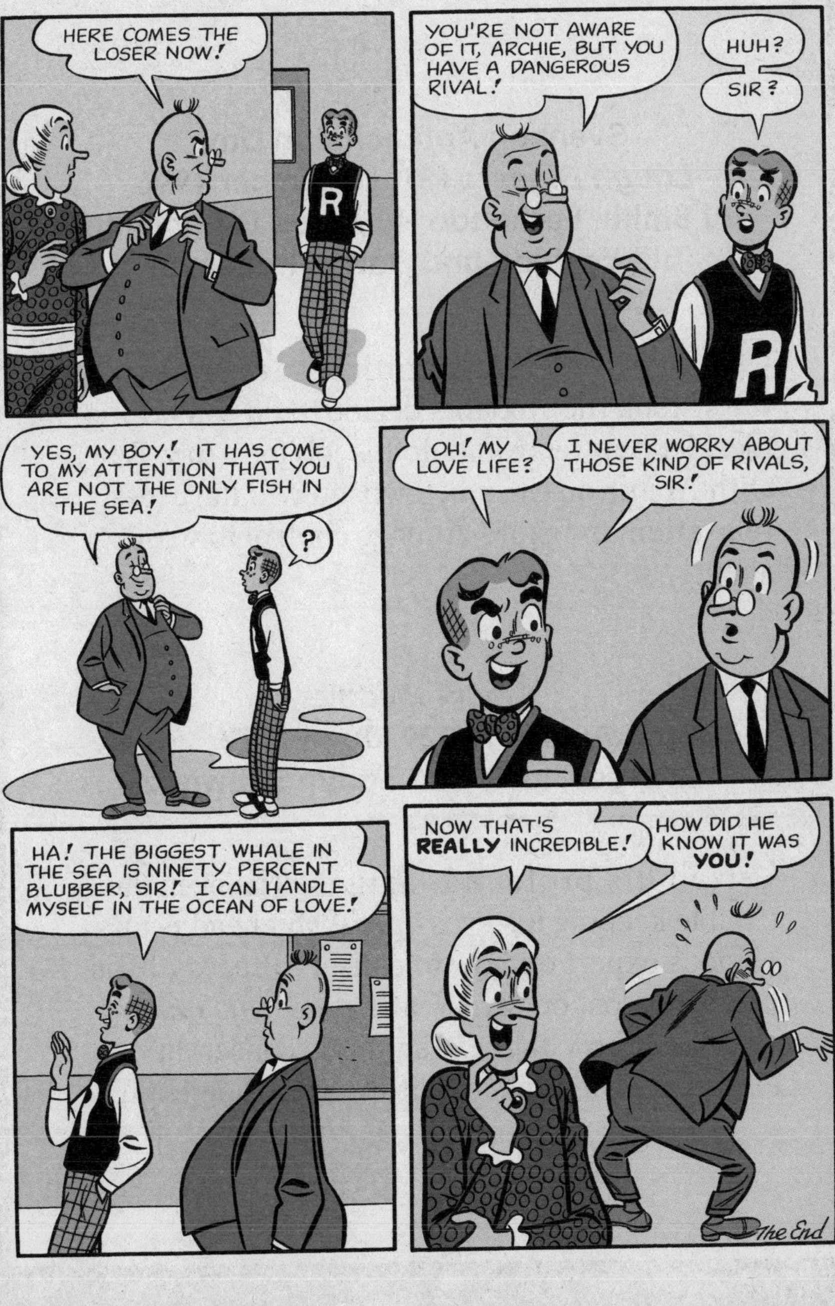
HERE COMES THE LOSER NOW!
R
YOU'RE NOT AWARE OF IT, ARCHIE, BUT YOU HAVE A DANGEROUS RIVAL!
HUH?
SIR?
R
YES, MY BOY! IT HAS COME TO MY ATTENTION THAT YOU ARE NOT THE ONLY FISH IN THE SEA!
?
OH! MY LOVE LIFE?
I NEVER WORRY ABOUT THOSE KIND OF RIVALS, SIR!
HA! THE BIGGEST WHALE IN THE SEA IS NINETY PERCENT BLUBBER, SIR! I CAN HANDLE MYSELF IN THE OCEAN OF LOVE!
NOW THAT'S **REALLY** INCREDIBLE!
HOW DID HE KNOW IT WAS **YOU**!
The End

Svenson Appreciation Day
Laugh Digest #131, December 1996
**Hal Smith, Fernando Ruiz, Jon D'Agostino,
Bill Yoshida and Barry Grossman**

On Svenson's 25th anniversary working at the school, the students decide to do something nice: let him relax and do his job for a day. But with Archie on the job, Svenson will have less relaxation and more damage control to worry about!

Model Muddle
Jughead #229, June 1974
George Gladir and Samm Schwartz

Given his profound laziness (he even has trouble keeping his eyes open!), Jughead is an obvious expert on how to conserve energy. This fact is not lost on Mr. Weatherbee, who quickly wearies of how Jughead's unique conservation efforts are catching on within Riverdale High.

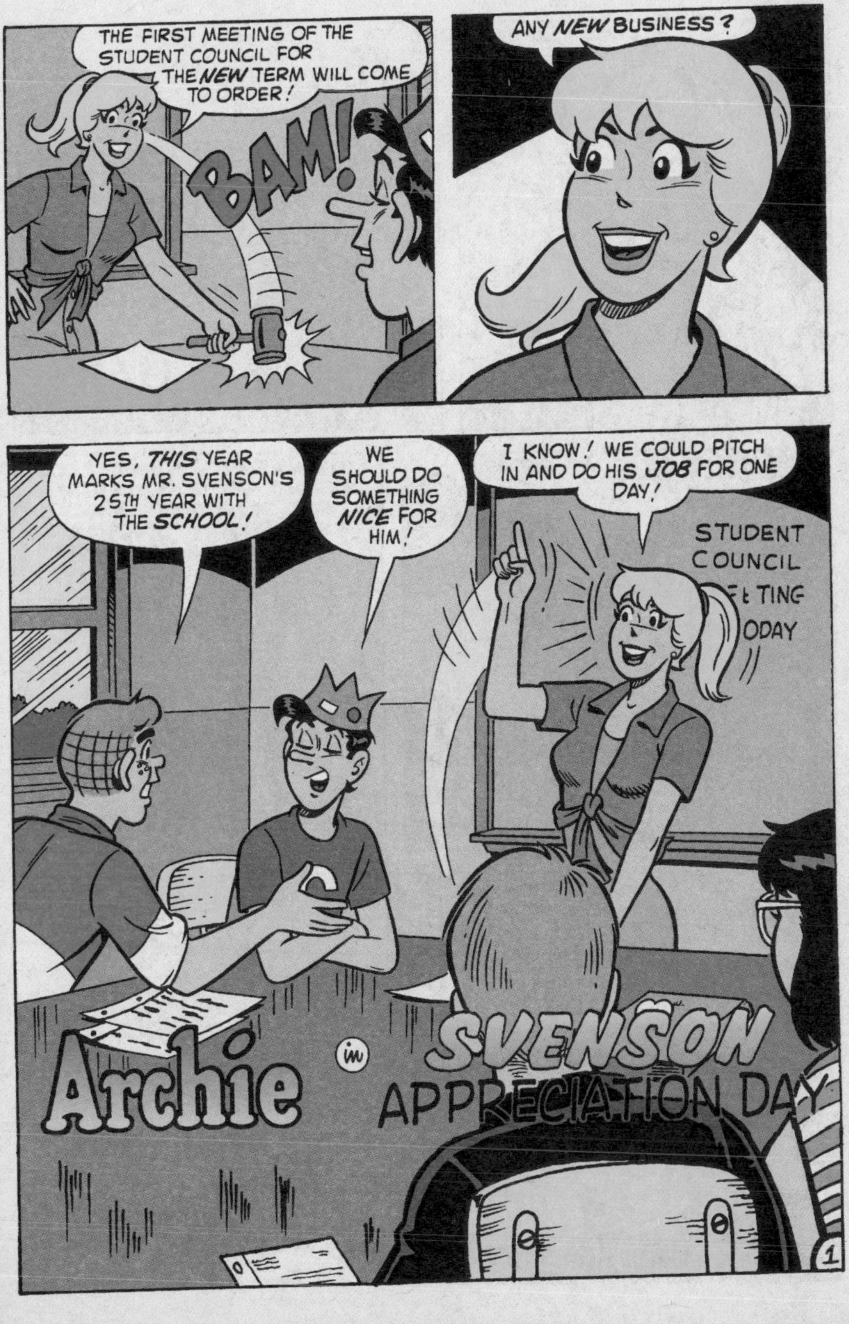
THE FIRST MEETING OF THE STUDENT COUNCIL FOR THE NEW TERM WILL COME TO ORDER!
BAM!
ANY NEW BUSINESS?
YES, THIS YEAR MARKS MR. SVENSON'S 25TH YEAR WITH THE SCHOOL!
WE SHOULD DO SOMETHING NICE FOR HIM!
I KNOW! WE COULD PITCH IN AND DO HIS JOB FOR ONE DAY!
STUDENT COUNCIL
Archie in SVENSON APPRECIATION DAY
1

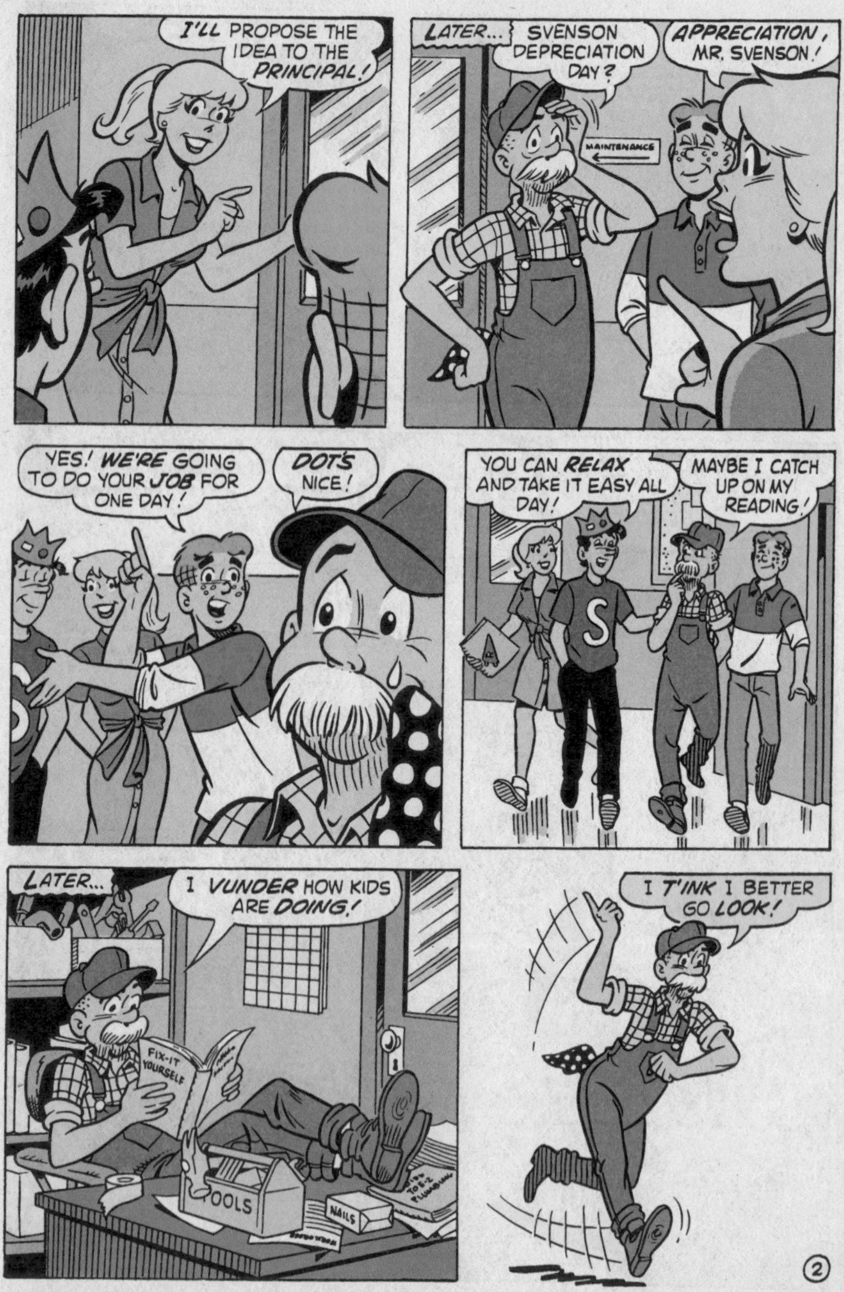
I'LL PROPOSE THE IDEA TO THE PRINCIPAL!
LATER...
SVENSON DEPRECIATION DAY?
APPRECIATION, MR. SVENSON!
MAINTENANCE
YES! WE'RE GOING TO DO YOUR JOB FOR ONE DAY!
DOT'S NICE!
YOU CAN RELAX AND TAKE IT EASY ALL DAY!
MAYBE I CATCH UP ON MY READING!
LATER...
I VUNDER HOW KIDS ARE DOING!
FIX-IT YOURSELF
TOOLS
NAILS
I T'INK I BETTER GO LOOK!
2

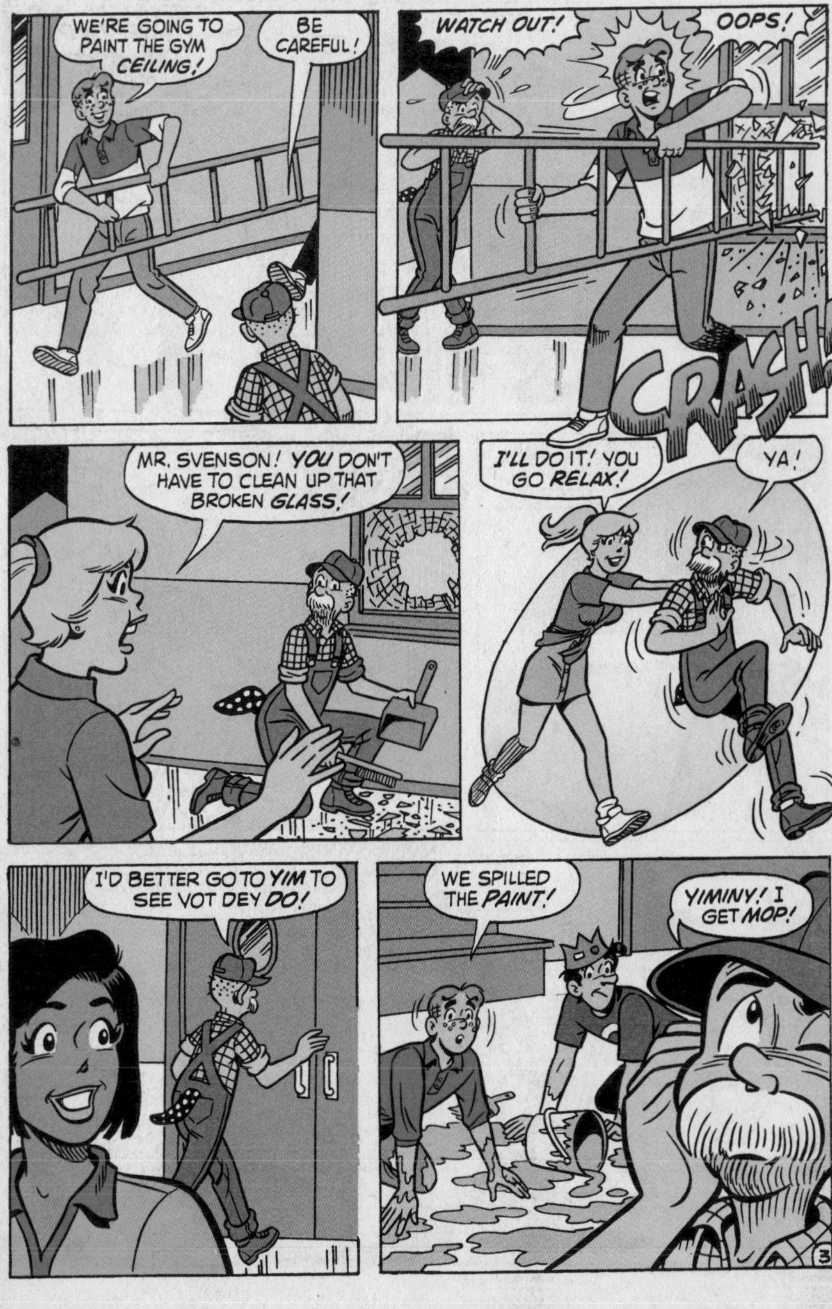
WE'RE GOING TO PAINT THE GYM CEILING!
BE CAREFUL!
WATCH OUT!
OOPS!
CRASH!
MR. SVENSON! YOU DON'T HAVE TO CLEAN UP THAT BROKEN GLASS!
I'LL DO IT! YOU GO RELAX!
YA!
I'D BETTER GO TO YIM TO SEE VOT DEY DO!
WE SPILLED THE PAINT!
YIMINY! I GET MOP!
3

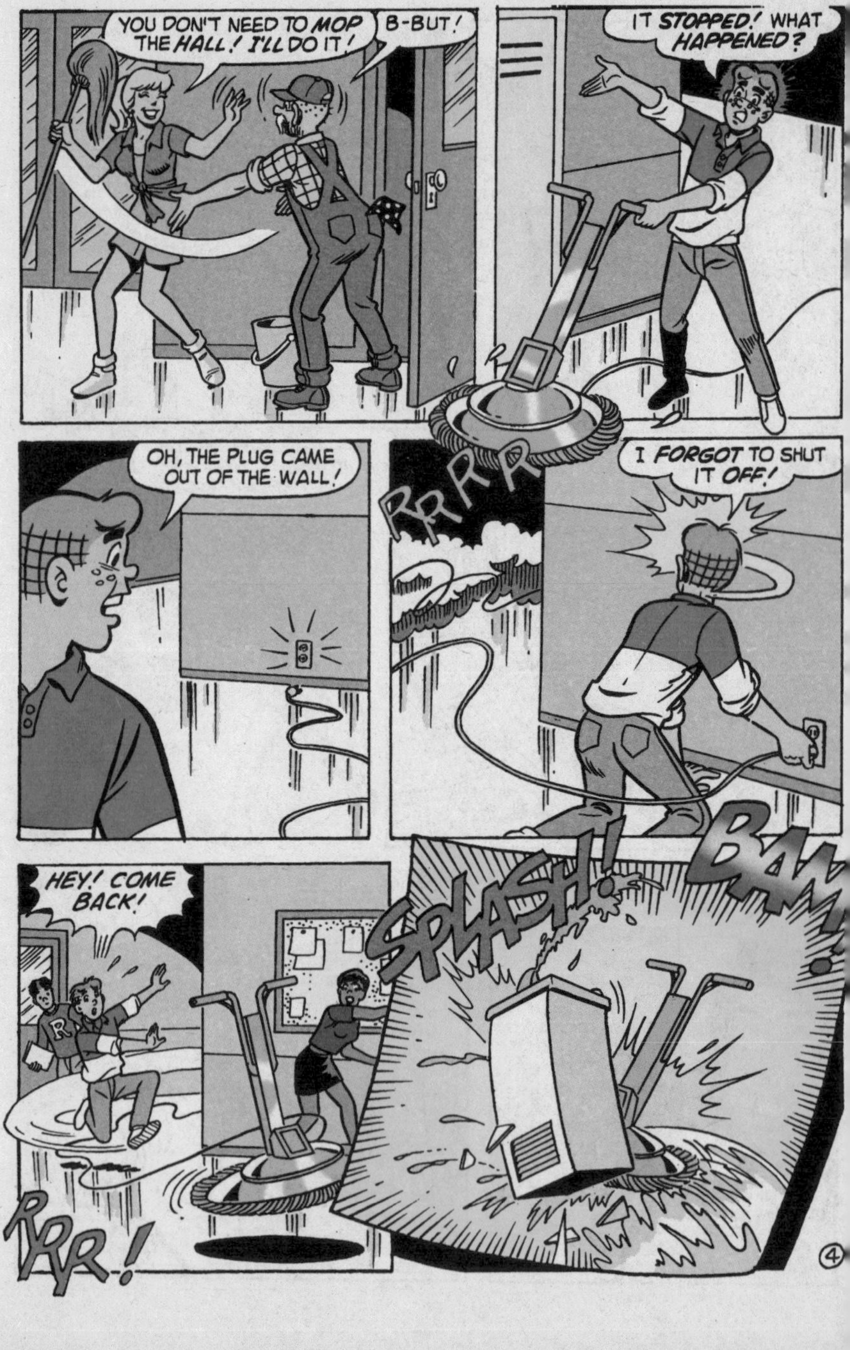
YOU DON'T NEED TO MOP THE HALL! I'LL DO IT!
B-BUT!
IT STOPPED! WHAT HAPPENED?
OH, THE PLUG CAME OUT OF THE WALL!
RRRR
I FORGOT TO SHUT IT OFF!
HEY! COME BACK!
RRR!
SPLASH!
BAM
4

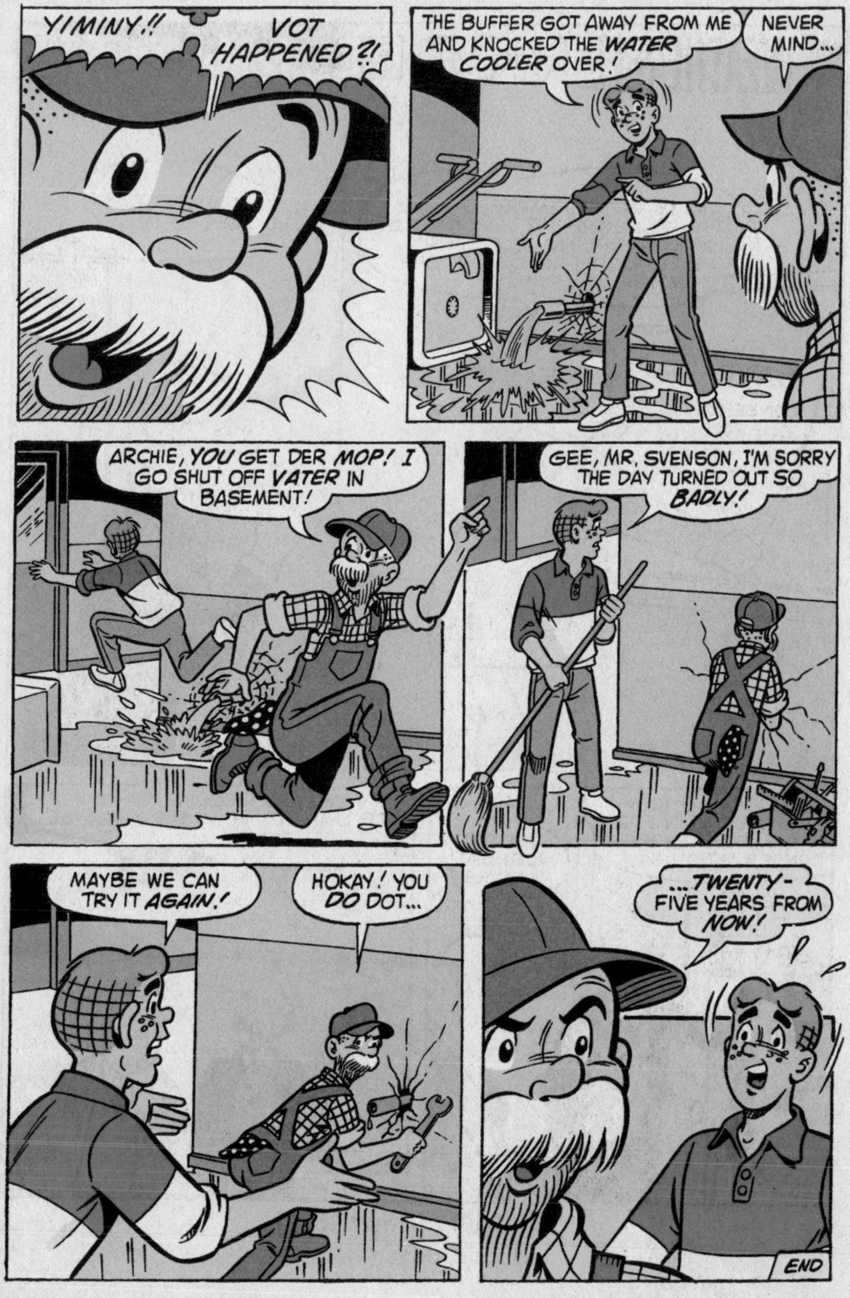
YIMINY!!
VOT HAPPENED?!
THE BUFFER GOT AWAY FROM ME AND KNOCKED THE WATER COOLER OVER!
NEVER MIND...
ARCHIE, YOU GET DER MOP! I GO SHUT OFF VATER IN BASEMENT!
GEE, MR. SVENSON, I'M SORRY THE DAY TURNED OUT SO BADLY!
MAYBE WE CAN TRY IT AGAIN!
HOKAY! YOU DO DOT...
...TWENTY-FIVE YEARS FROM NOW!
END

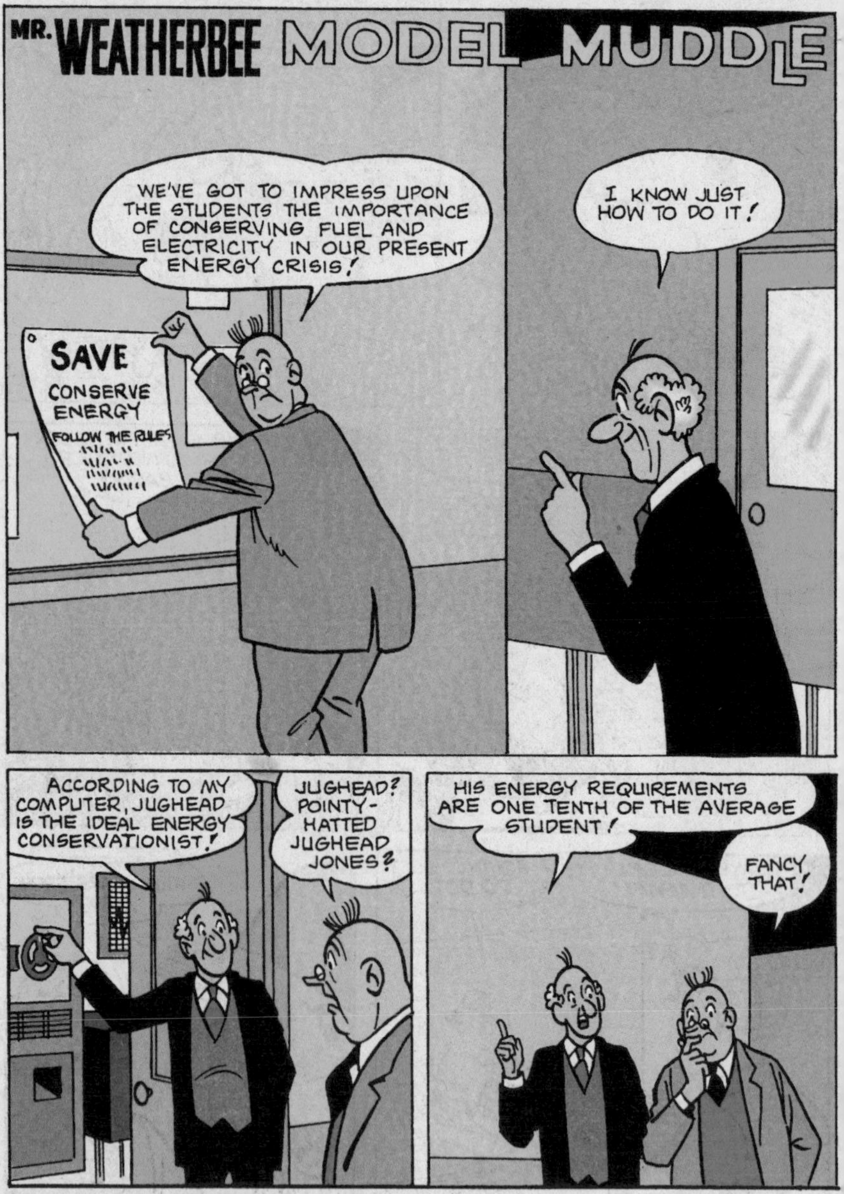
MR. WEATHERBEE MODEL MUDDLE
WE'VE GOT TO IMPRESS UPON THE STUDENTS THE IMPORTANCE OF CONSERVING FUEL AND ELECTRICITY IN OUR PRESENT ENERGY CRISIS!
SAVE
CONSERVE ENERGY
FOLLOW THE RULES
I KNOW JUST HOW TO DO IT!
ACCORDING TO MY COMPUTER, JUGHEAD IS THE IDEAL ENERGY CONSERVATIONIST!
JUGHEAD? POINTY-HATTED JUGHEAD JONES?
HIS ENERGY REQUIREMENTS ARE ONE TENTH OF THE AVERAGE STUDENT!
FANCY THAT!

Gladir / Schwartz

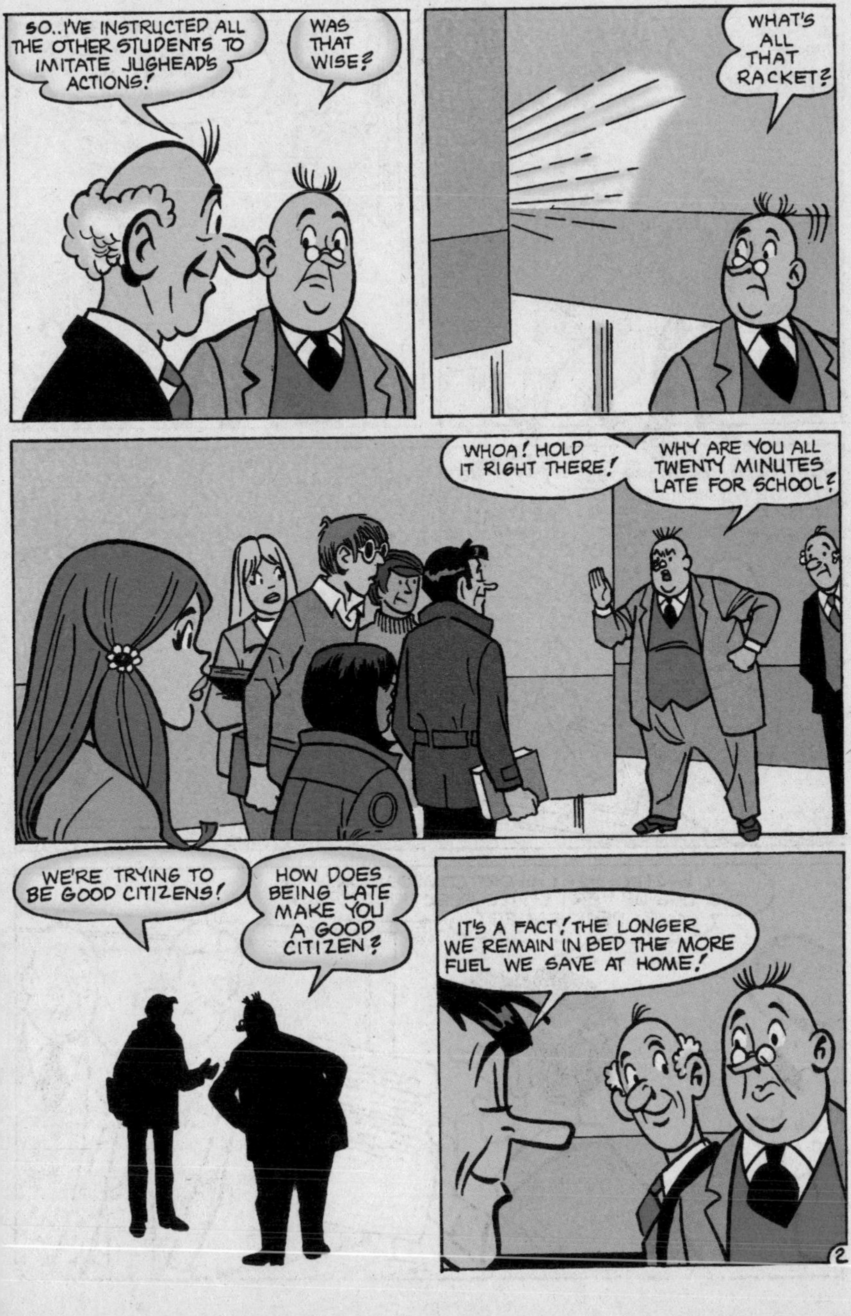
SO..I'VE INSTRUCTED ALL THE OTHER STUDENTS TO IMITATE JUGHEAD'S ACTIONS!
WAS THAT WISE?
WHAT'S ALL THAT RACKET?
WHOA! HOLD IT RIGHT THERE!
WHY ARE YOU ALL TWENTY MINUTES LATE FOR SCHOOL?
WE'RE TRYING TO BE GOOD CITIZENS!
HOW DOES BEING LATE MAKE YOU A GOOD CITIZEN?
IT'S A FACT! THE LONGER WE REMAIN IN BED THE MORE FUEL WE SAVE AT HOME!
2

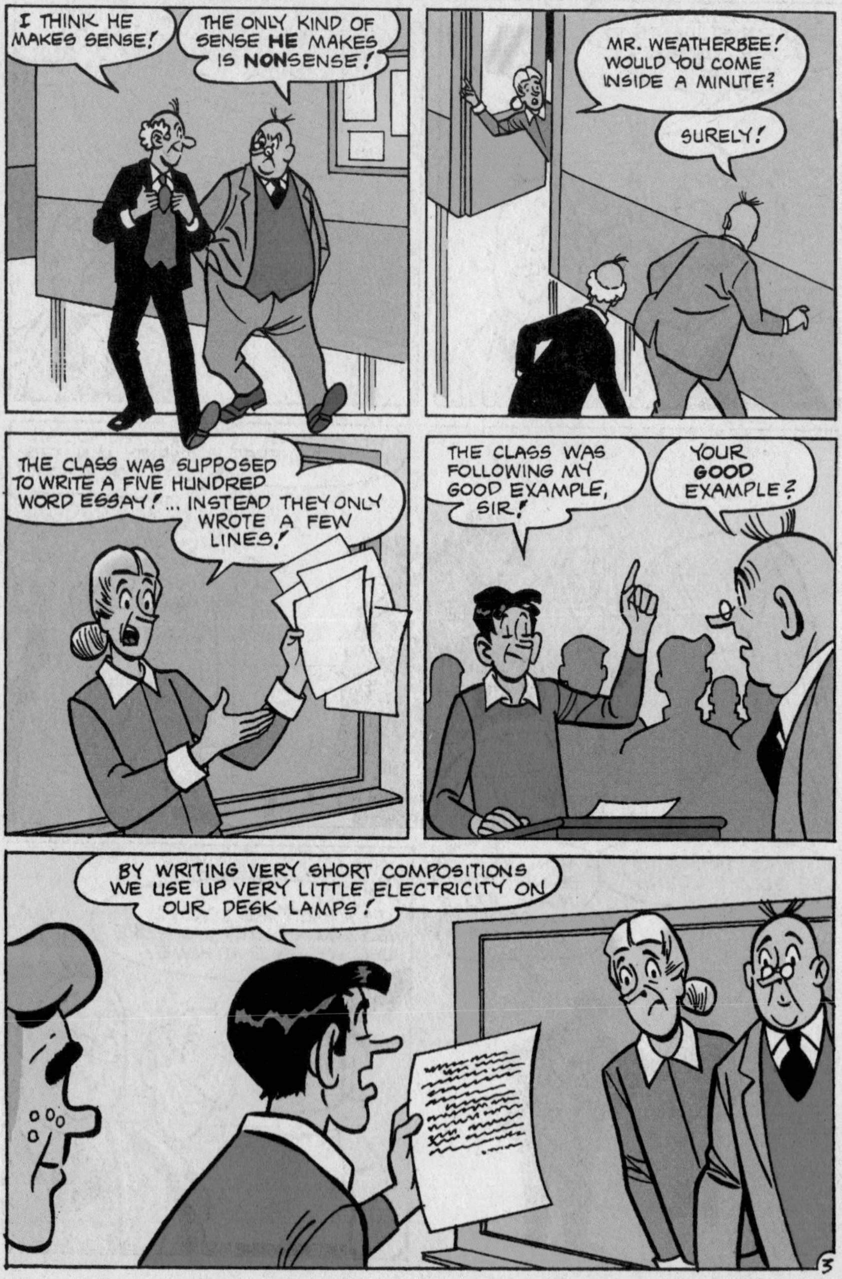
I THINK HE MAKES SENSE!
THE ONLY KIND OF SENSE HE MAKES IS NONSENSE!
MR. WEATHERBEE! WOULD YOU COME INSIDE A MINUTE?
SURELY!
THE CLASS WAS SUPPOSED TO WRITE A FIVE HUNDRED WORD ESSAY! ... INSTEAD THEY ONLY WROTE A FEW LINES!
THE CLASS WAS FOLLOWING MY GOOD EXAMPLE, SIR!
YOUR GOOD EXAMPLE?
BY WRITING VERY SHORT COMPOSITIONS WE USE UP VERY LITTLE ELECTRICITY ON OUR DESK LAMPS!
3

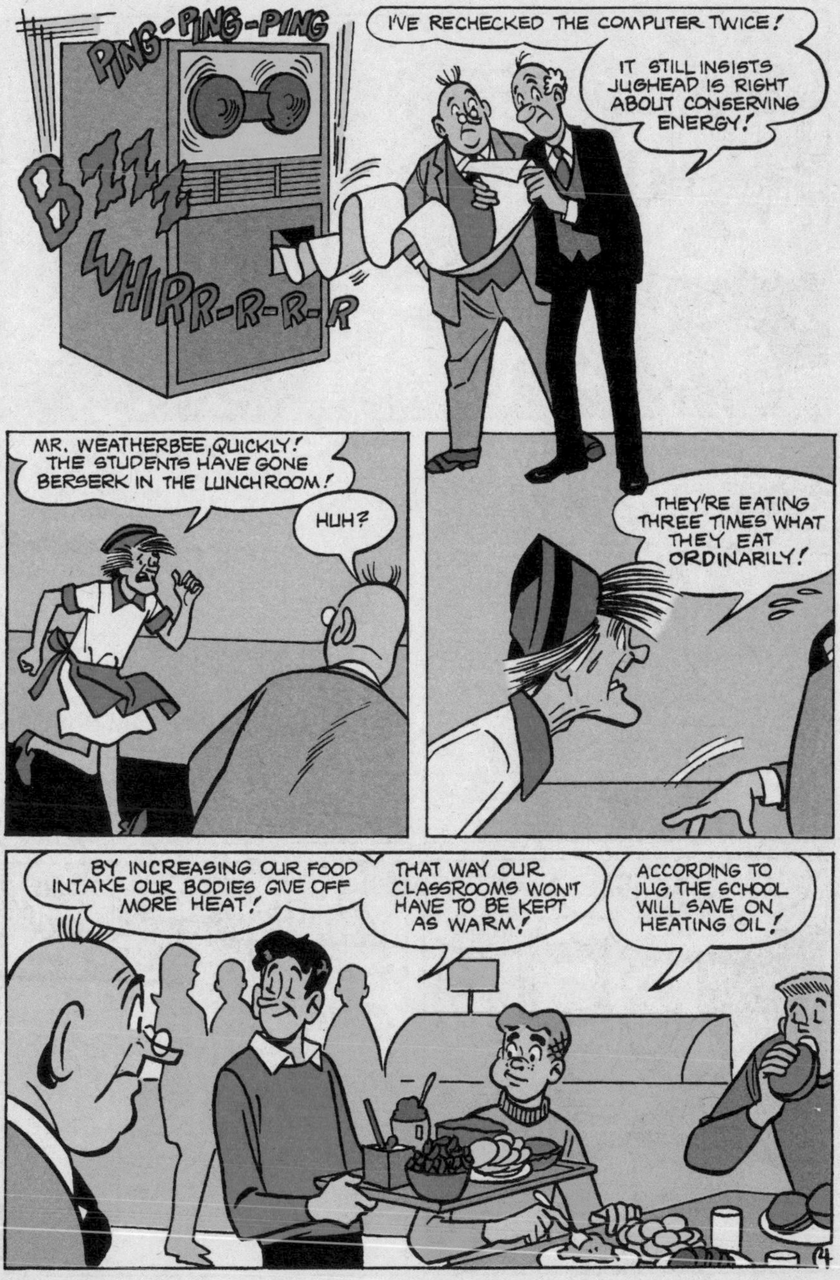
PING-PING-PING
BZZZZ
WHIRR-R-R-R
I'VE RECHECKED THE COMPUTER TWICE!
IT STILL INSISTS JUGHEAD IS RIGHT ABOUT CONSERVING ENERGY!
MR. WEATHERBEE, QUICKLY! THE STUDENTS HAVE GONE BERSERK IN THE LUNCHROOM!
HUH?
THEY'RE EATING THREE TIMES WHAT THEY EAT ORDINARILY!
BY INCREASING OUR FOOD INTAKE OUR BODIES GIVE OFF MORE HEAT!
THAT WAY OUR CLASSROOMS WON'T HAVE TO BE KEPT AS WARM!
ACCORDING TO JUG, THE SCHOOL WILL SAVE ON HEATING OIL!
14

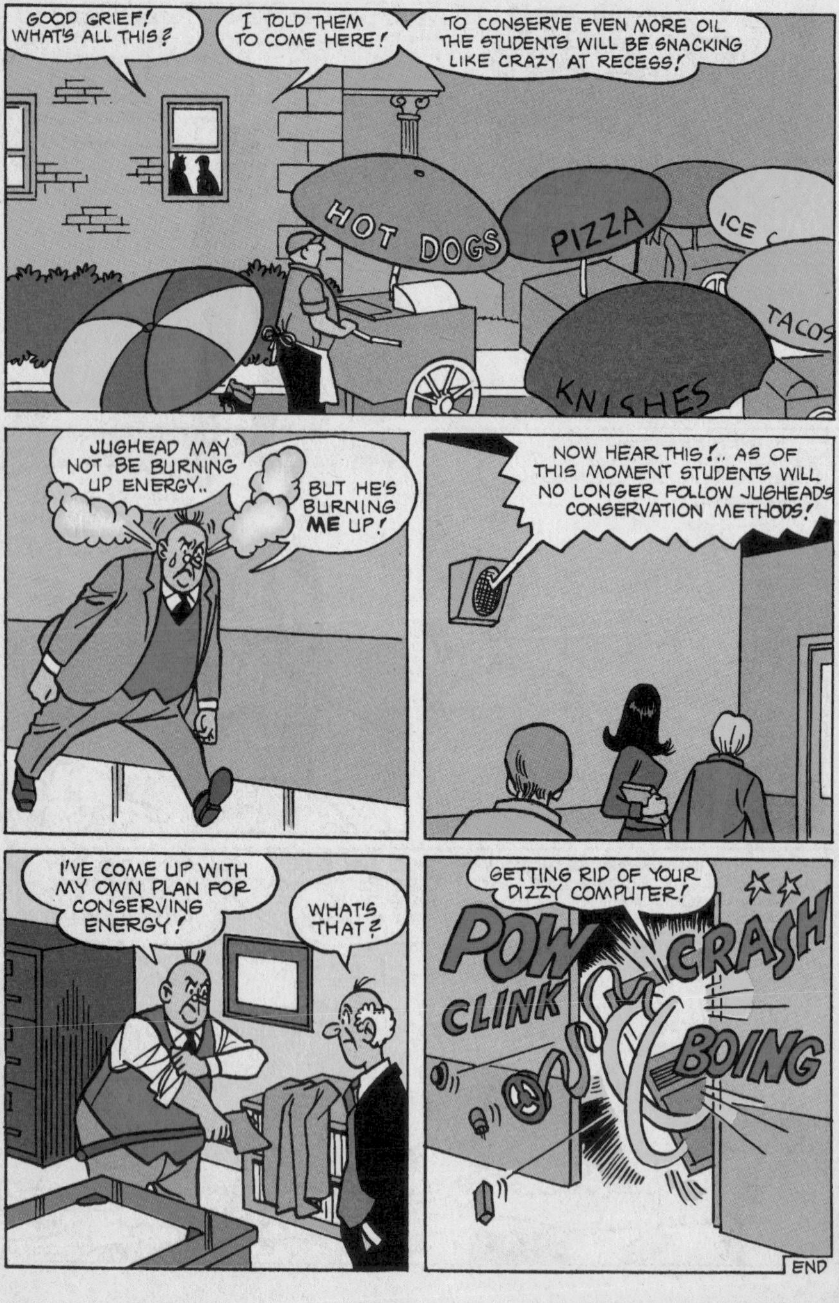
GOOD GRIEF! WHAT'S ALL THIS?
I TOLD THEM TO COME HERE!
TO CONSERVE EVEN MORE OIL THE STUDENTS WILL BE SNACKING LIKE CRAZY AT RECESS!
HOT DOGS
PIZZA
ICE C
TACOS
KNISHES
JUGHEAD MAY NOT BE BURNING UP ENERGY..
BUT HE'S BURNING **ME** UP!
NOW HEAR THIS!.. AS OF THIS MOMENT STUDENTS WILL NO LONGER FOLLOW JUGHEAD'S CONSERVATION METHODS!
I'VE COME UP WITH MY OWN PLAN FOR CONSERVING ENERGY!
WHAT'S THAT?
GETTING RID OF YOUR DIZZY COMPUTER!
POW
CRASH
CLINK
BOING
END

Archie's FAVORITE HIGH SCHOOL COMICS

AFTER SCHOOL SPECIALS

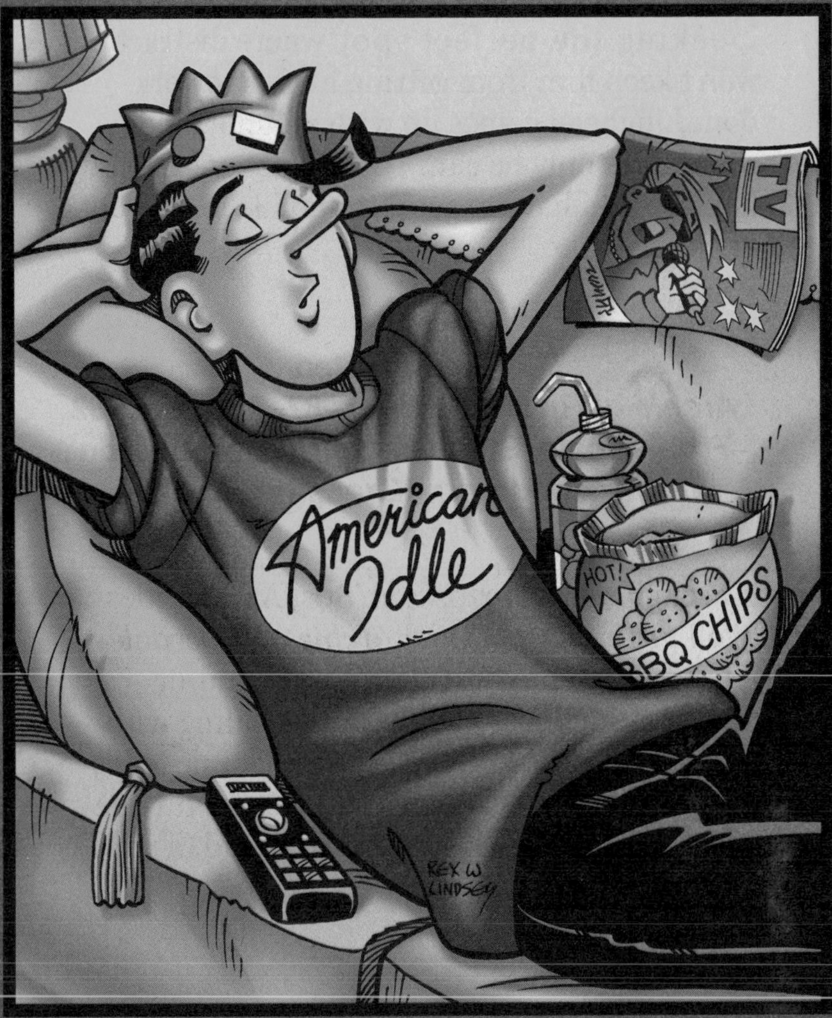
TV
American Idle
HOT!
BBQ CHIPS
REX W. LINDSEY

Soft Cell
Jughead #96, May 1963
Frank Doyle and Samm Schwartz

Seeking the perfect spot where distractions won't keep him from getting his homework done, Jughead comes up with an unorthodox solution as only he can. There's just one catch: he's going to have to get into trouble to stay out of trouble!

The Uninvited
Archie at Riverdale High #87, August 1982
Frank Doyle, Stan Goldberg, Bill Yoshida and Barry Grossman

Throughout the 1970s and '80s, Archie titles like *Life with Archie* and *Archie at Riverdale High* regularly featured adventure and/or topical stories that had the gang dealing with everything from kidnappers to a satanic teddy bear. From that era comes this wonderful tale of Archie and Chuck coming to the aid of a mysterious stranger.

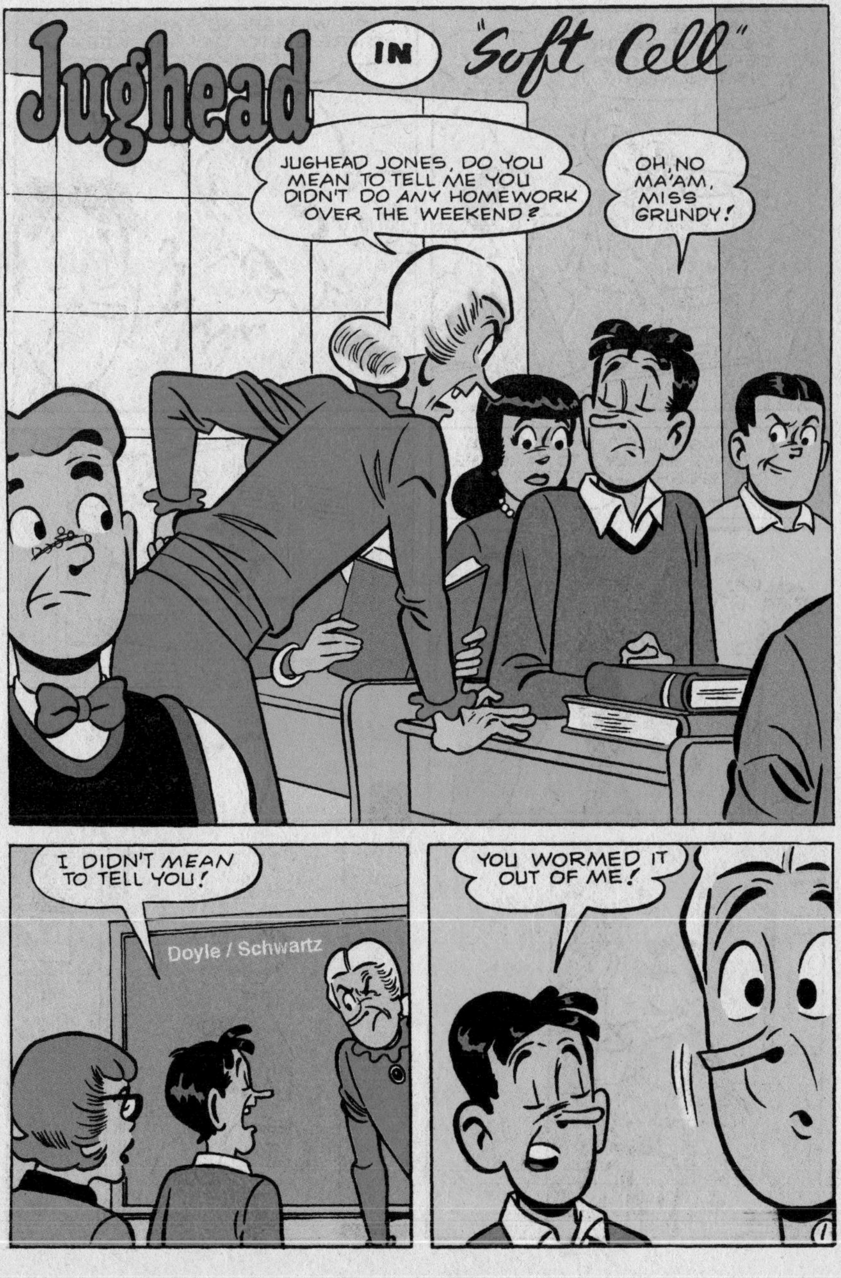
Jughead
IN
"Soft Cell"
JUGHEAD JONES, DO YOU MEAN TO TELL ME YOU DIDN'T DO ANY HOMEWORK OVER THE WEEKEND?
OH, NO MA'AM, MISS GRUNDY!
I DIDN'T MEAN TO TELL YOU!
Doyle / Schwartz
YOU WORMED IT OUT OF ME!

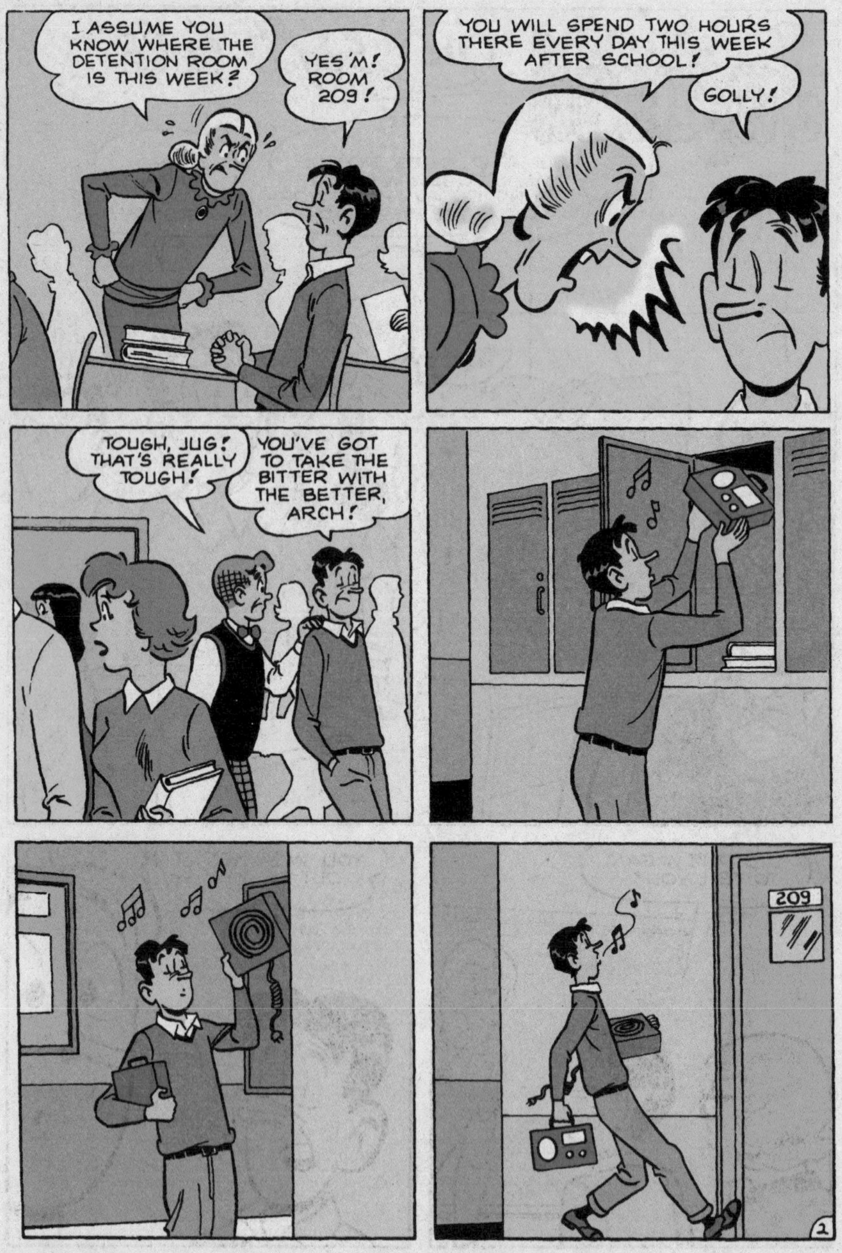
I ASSUME YOU KNOW WHERE THE DETENTION ROOM IS THIS WEEK?
YES'M! ROOM 209!
YOU WILL SPEND TWO HOURS THERE EVERY DAY THIS WEEK AFTER SCHOOL!
GOLLY!
TOUGH, JUG! THAT'S REALLY TOUGH!
YOU'VE GOT TO TAKE THE BITTER WITH THE BETTER, ARCH!
209
2

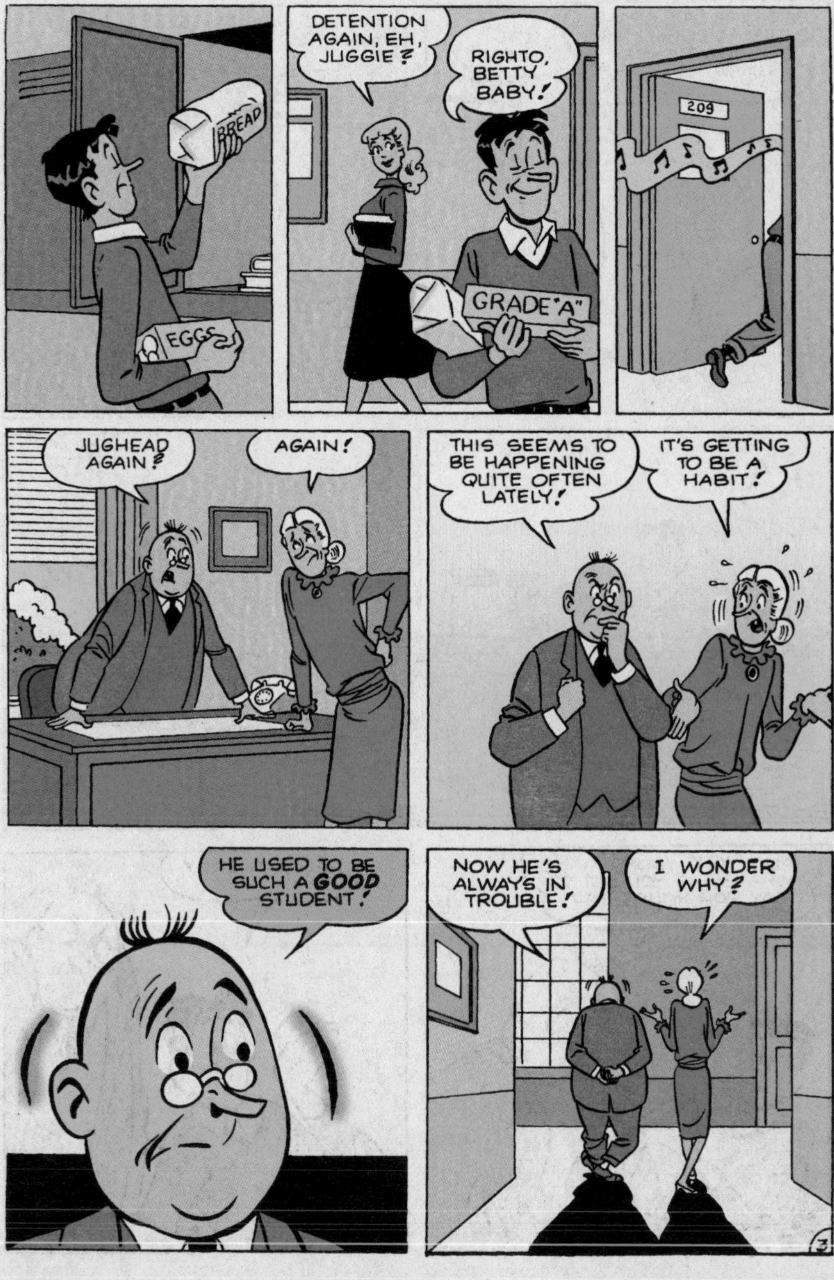
BREAD
EGGS
DETENTION AGAIN, EH, JUGGIE?
RIGHTO, BETTY BABY!
GRADE "A"
209
JUGHEAD AGAIN?
AGAIN!
THIS SEEMS TO BE HAPPENING QUITE OFTEN LATELY!
IT'S GETTING TO BE A HABIT!
HE USED TO BE SUCH A **GOOD** STUDENT!
NOW HE'S ALWAYS IN TROUBLE!
I WONDER WHY?
3

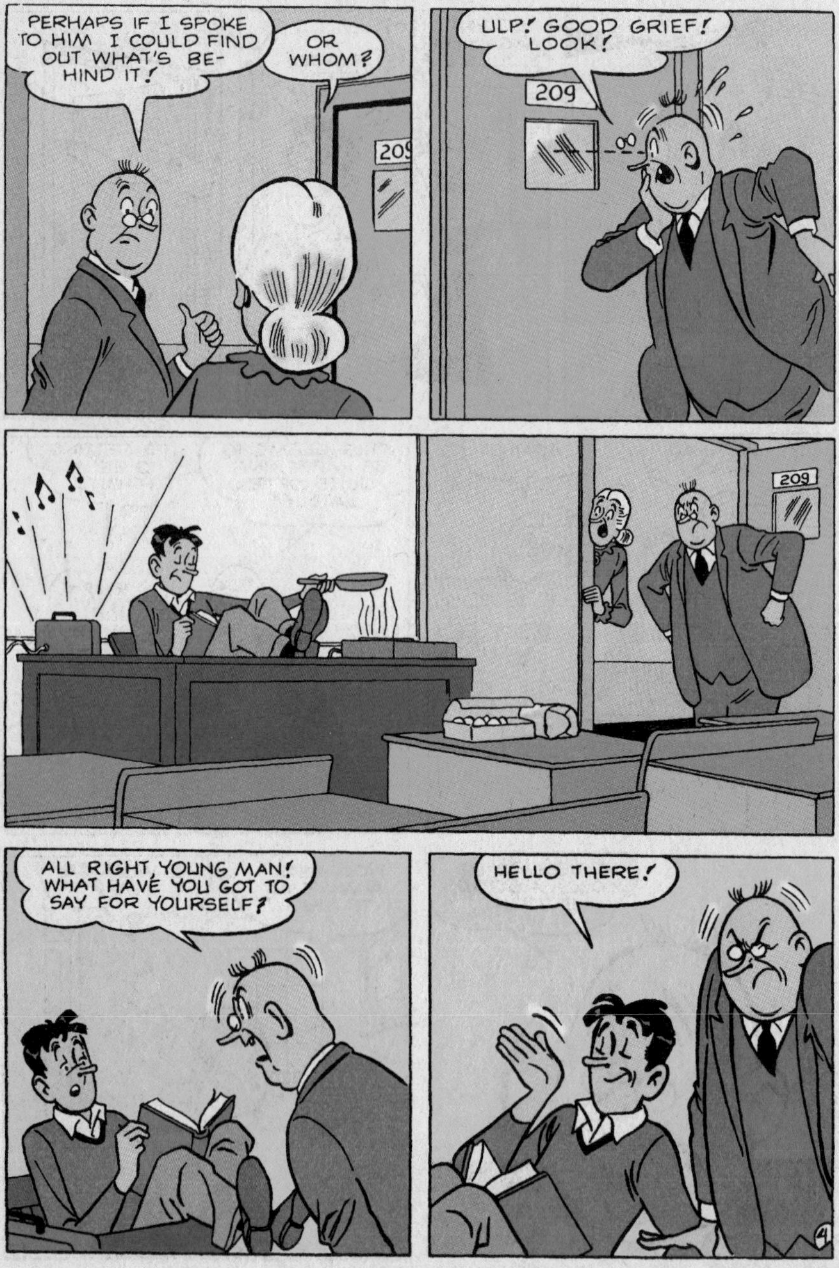
PERHAPS IF I SPOKE TO HIM I COULD FIND OUT WHAT'S BE- HIND IT!
OR WHOM?
ULP! GOOD GRIEF! LOOK!
209
209
209
ALL RIGHT, YOUNG MAN! WHAT HAVE YOU GOT TO SAY FOR YOURSELF?
HELLO THERE!
4

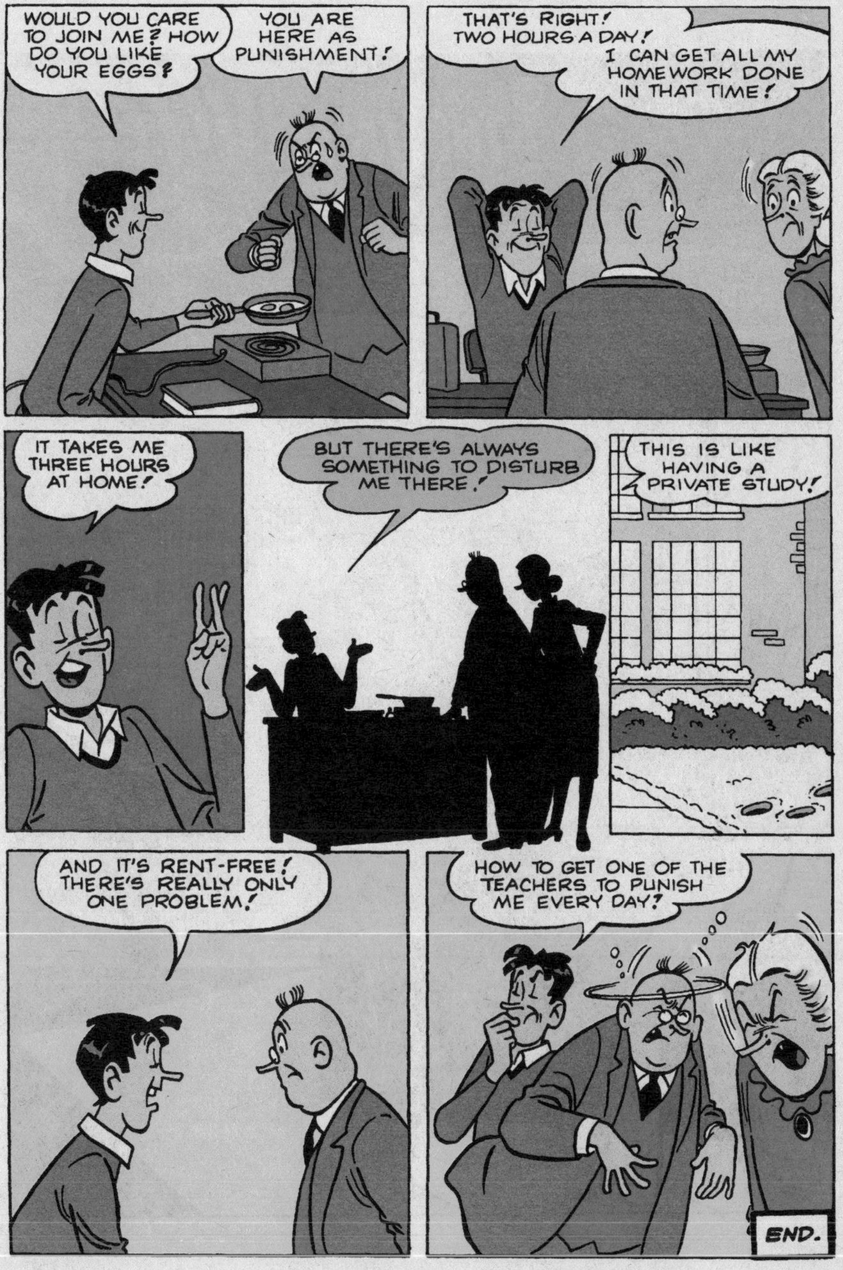
WOULD YOU CARE TO JOIN ME? HOW DO YOU LIKE YOUR EGGS?
YOU ARE HERE AS PUNISHMENT!
THAT'S RIGHT! TWO HOURS A DAY!
I CAN GET ALL MY HOMEWORK DONE IN THAT TIME!
IT TAKES ME THREE HOURS AT HOME!
BUT THERE'S ALWAYS SOMETHING TO DISTURB ME THERE!
THIS IS LIKE HAVING A PRIVATE STUDY!
AND IT'S RENT-FREE! THERE'S REALLY ONLY ONE PROBLEM!
HOW TO GET ONE OF THE TEACHERS TO PUNISH ME EVERY DAY?
END.

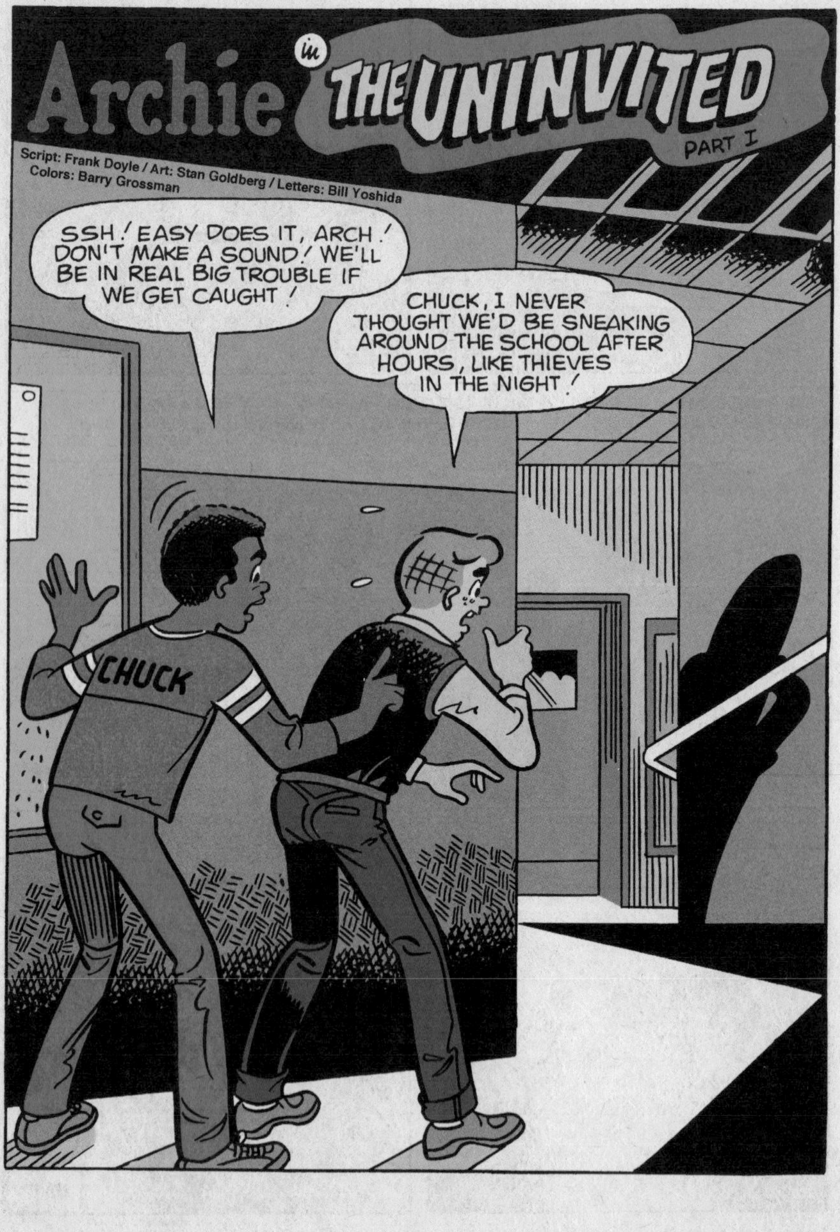
Archie in THE UNINVITED
PART I
Script: Frank Doyle / Art: Stan Goldberg / Letters: Bill Yoshida
Colors: Barry Grossman
SSH! EASY DOES IT, ARCH! DON'T MAKE A SOUND! WE'LL BE IN REAL BIG TROUBLE IF WE GET CAUGHT!
CHUCK, I NEVER THOUGHT WE'D BE SNEAKING AROUND THE SCHOOL AFTER HOURS, LIKE THIEVES IN THE NIGHT!
CHUCK

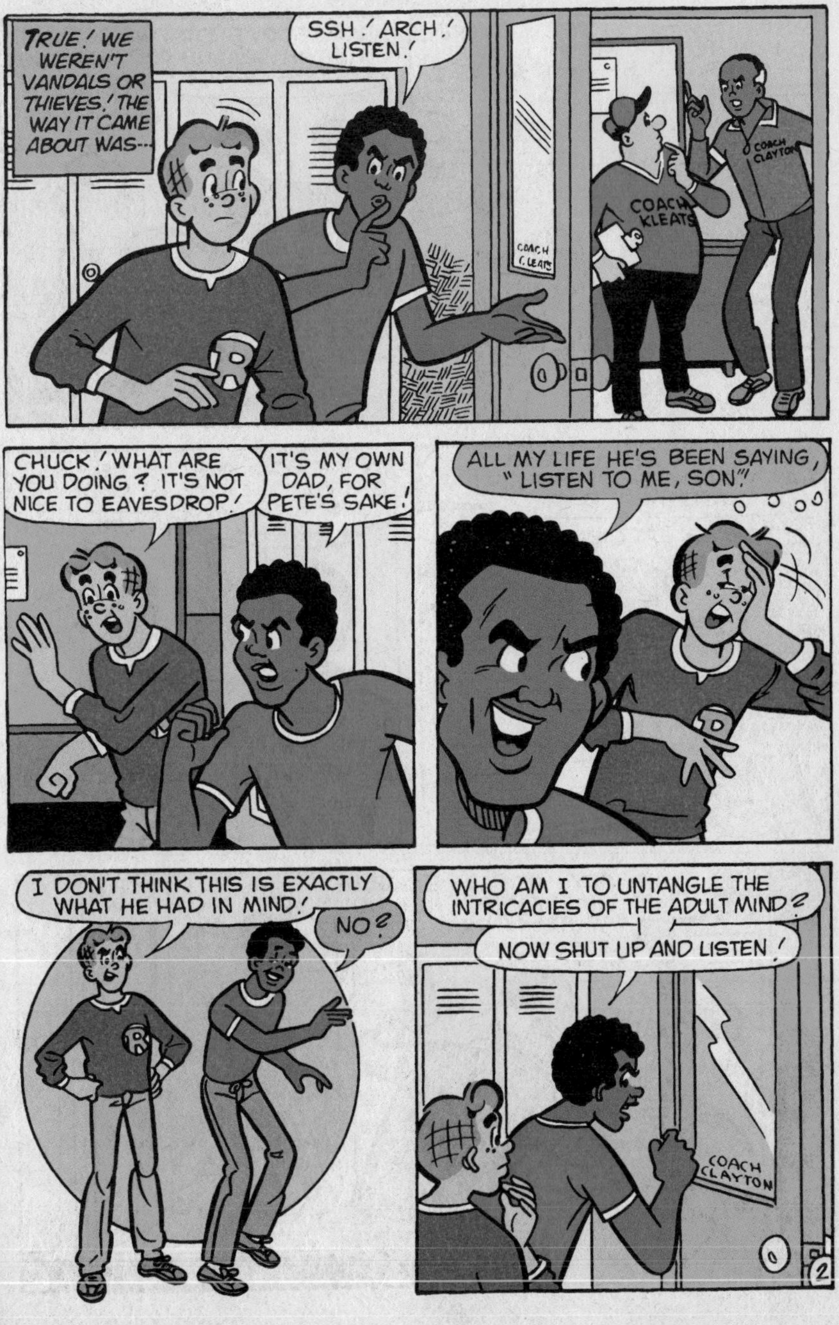
TRUE! WE WEREN'T VANDALS OR THIEVES! THE WAY IT CAME ABOUT WAS--
SSH! ARCH! LISTEN!
COACH KLEATS
COACH CLAYTON
COACH KLEATS
CHUCK! WHAT ARE YOU DOING? IT'S NOT NICE TO EAVESDROP!
IT'S MY OWN DAD, FOR PETE'S SAKE!
ALL MY LIFE HE'S BEEN SAYING, "LISTEN TO ME, SON"!
I DON'T THINK THIS IS EXACTLY WHAT HE HAD IN MIND!
NO?
WHO AM I TO UNTANGLE THE INTRICACIES OF THE ADULT MIND?
NOW SHUT UP AND LISTEN!
COACH CLAYTON
2

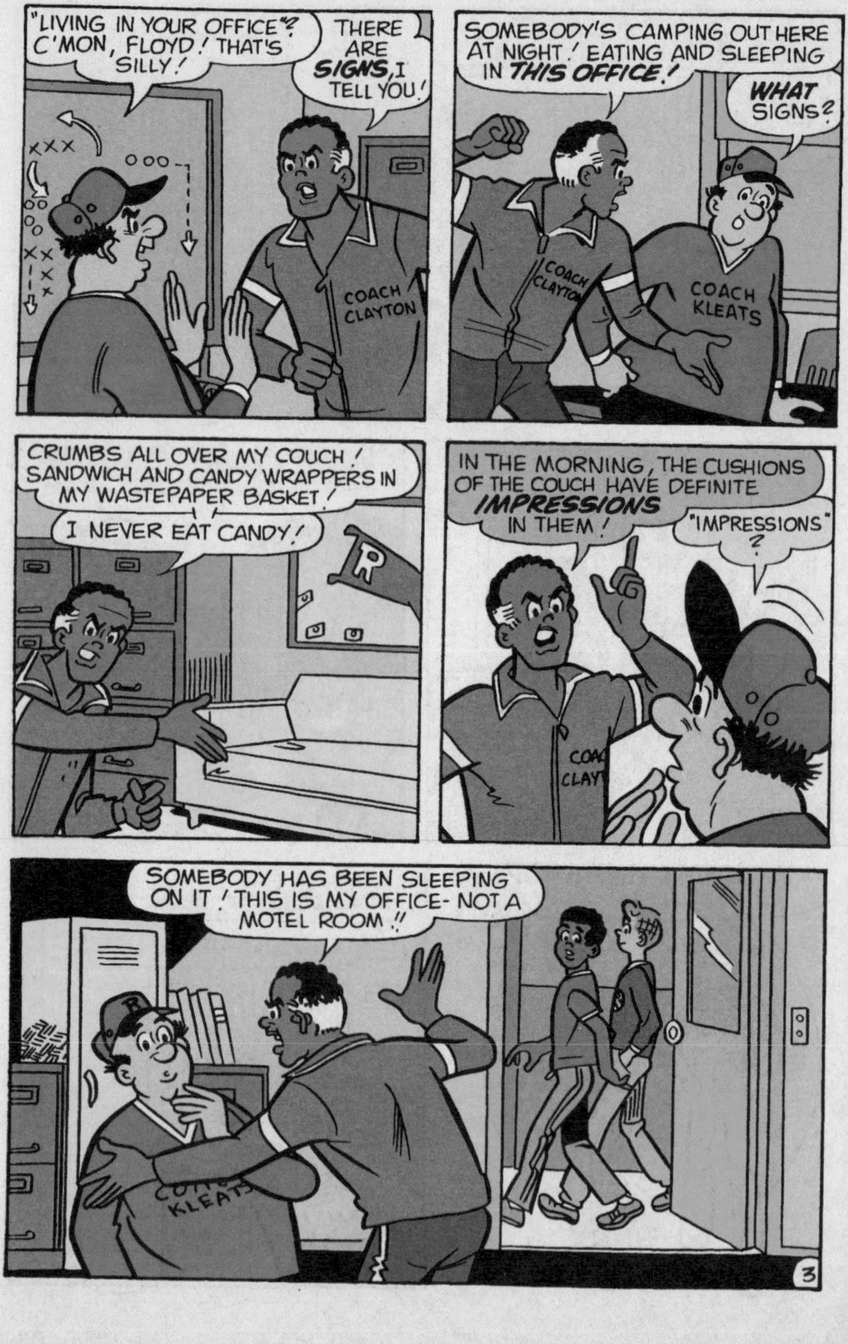
"LIVING IN YOUR OFFICE"? C'MON, FLOYD! THAT'S SILLY!
THERE ARE SIGNS, I TELL YOU!
SOMEBODY'S CAMPING OUT HERE AT NIGHT! EATING AND SLEEPING IN THIS OFFICE!
WHAT SIGNS?
COACH CLAYTON
COACH KLEATS
CRUMBS ALL OVER MY COUCH! SANDWICH AND CANDY WRAPPERS IN MY WASTEPAPER BASKET!
I NEVER EAT CANDY!
IN THE MORNING, THE CUSHIONS OF THE COUCH HAVE DEFINITE IMPRESSIONS IN THEM!
"IMPRESSIONS"?
SOMEBODY HAS BEEN SLEEPING ON IT! THIS IS MY OFFICE- NOT A MOTEL ROOM!!
3

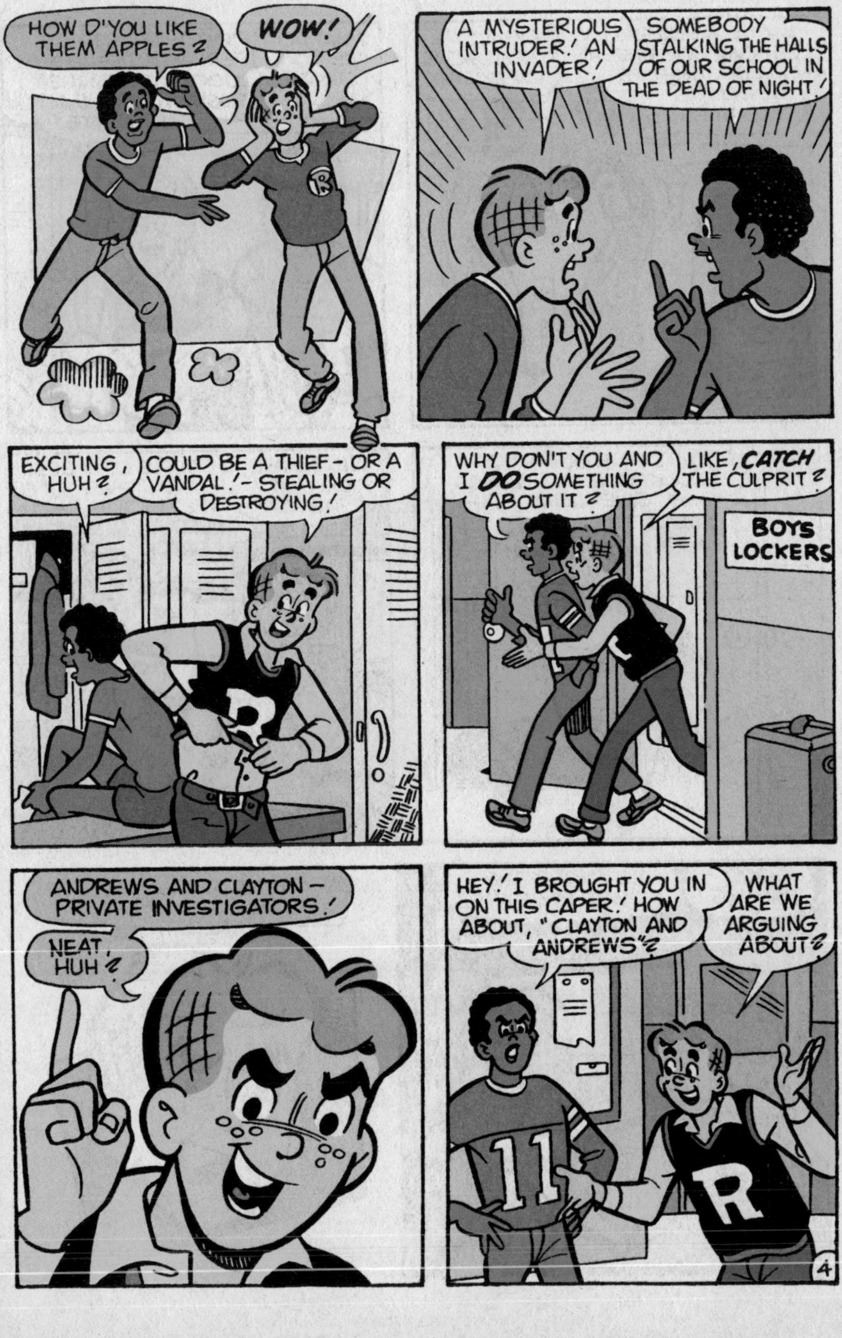
HOW D'YOU LIKE THEM APPLES?
WOW!
A MYSTERIOUS INTRUDER! AN INVADER!
SOMEBODY STALKING THE HALLS OF OUR SCHOOL IN THE DEAD OF NIGHT!
EXCITING, HUH?
COULD BE A THIEF - OR A VANDAL! - STEALING OR DESTROYING!
WHY DON'T YOU AND I DO SOMETHING ABOUT IT?
LIKE, CATCH THE CULPRIT?
BOYS LOCKERS
ANDREWS AND CLAYTON - PRIVATE INVESTIGATORS!
NEAT, HUH?
HEY! I BROUGHT YOU IN ON THIS CAPER! HOW ABOUT, "CLAYTON AND ANDREWS"?
WHAT ARE WE ARGUING ABOUT?
4

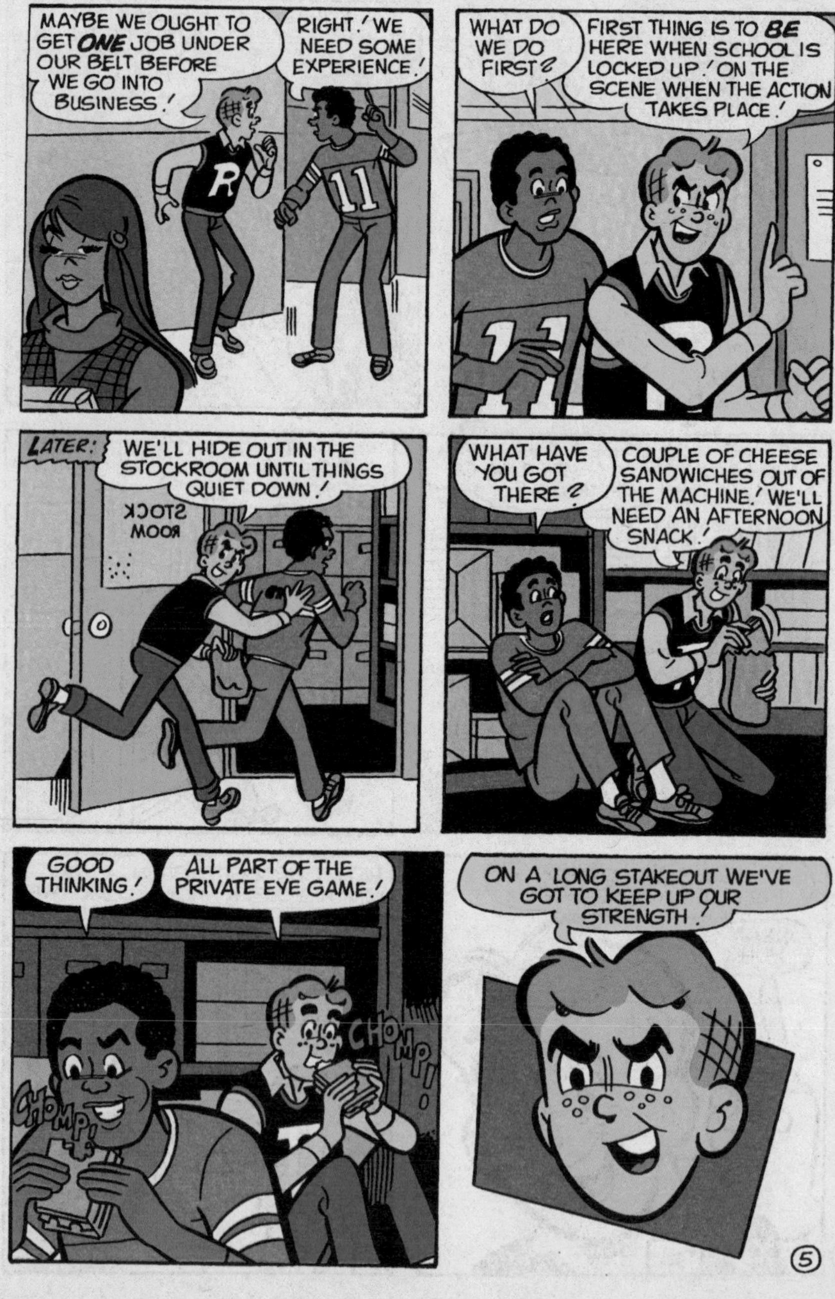
MAYBE WE OUGHT TO GET ONE JOB UNDER OUR BELT BEFORE WE GO INTO BUSINESS!
RIGHT! WE NEED SOME EXPERIENCE!
WHAT DO WE DO FIRST?
FIRST THING IS TO BE HERE WHEN SCHOOL IS LOCKED UP! ON THE SCENE WHEN THE ACTION TAKES PLACE!
LATER:
WE'LL HIDE OUT IN THE STOCKROOM UNTIL THINGS QUIET DOWN!
STOCK ROOM
WHAT HAVE YOU GOT THERE?
COUPLE OF CHEESE SANDWICHES OUT OF THE MACHINE! WE'LL NEED AN AFTERNOON SNACK!
GOOD THINKING!
ALL PART OF THE PRIVATE EYE GAME!
CHOMP!
CHOMP!
ON A LONG STAKEOUT WE'VE GOT TO KEEP UP OUR STRENGTH!
5

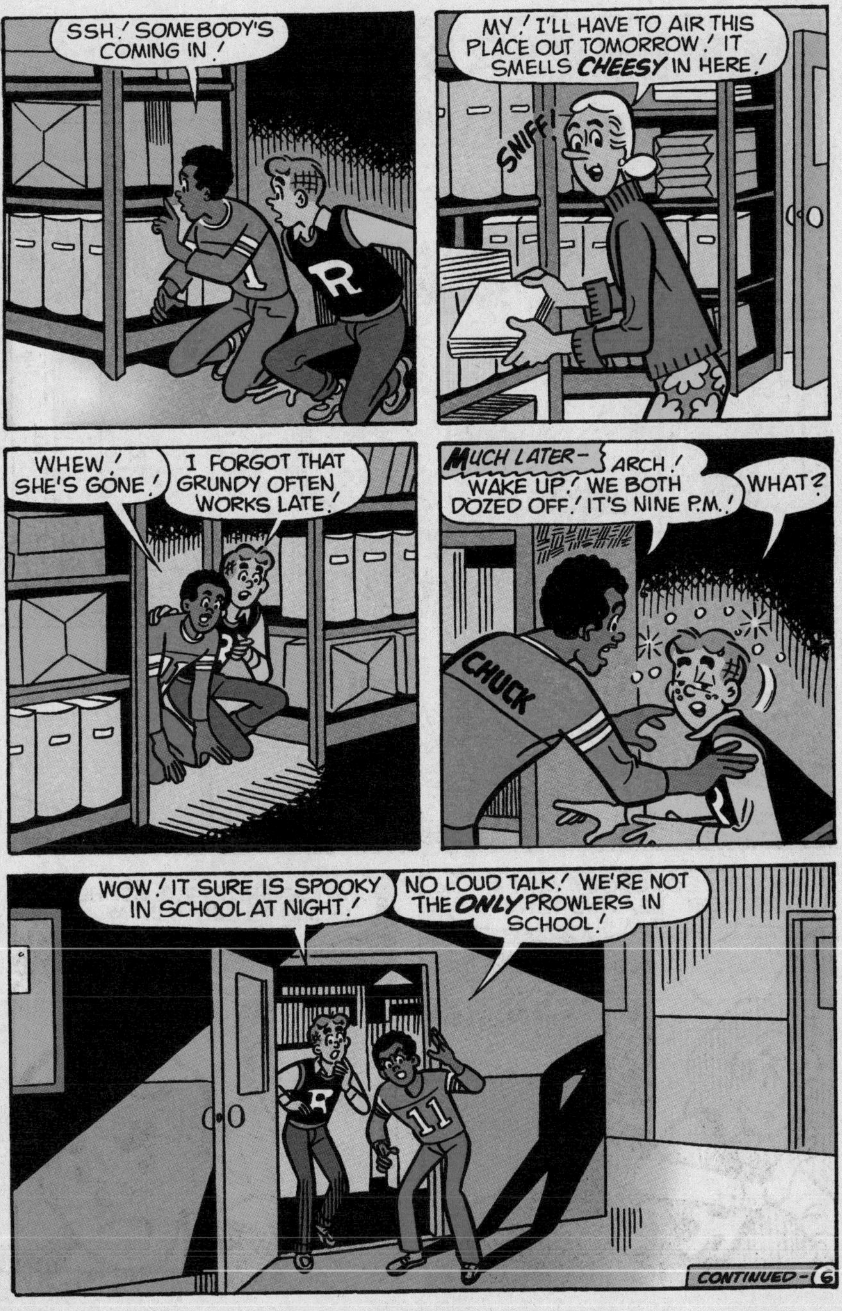
SSH! SOMEBODY'S COMING IN!
MY! I'LL HAVE TO AIR THIS PLACE OUT TOMORROW! IT SMELLS CHEESY IN HERE!
SNIFF!
WHEW! SHE'S GONE!
I FORGOT THAT GRUNDY OFTEN WORKS LATE!
MUCH LATER-
ARCH! WAKE UP! WE BOTH DOZED OFF! IT'S NINE P.M.!
WHAT?
CHUCK
WOW! IT SURE IS SPOOKY IN SCHOOL AT NIGHT!
NO LOUD TALK! WE'RE NOT THE ONLY PROWLERS IN SCHOOL!
CONTINUED-6

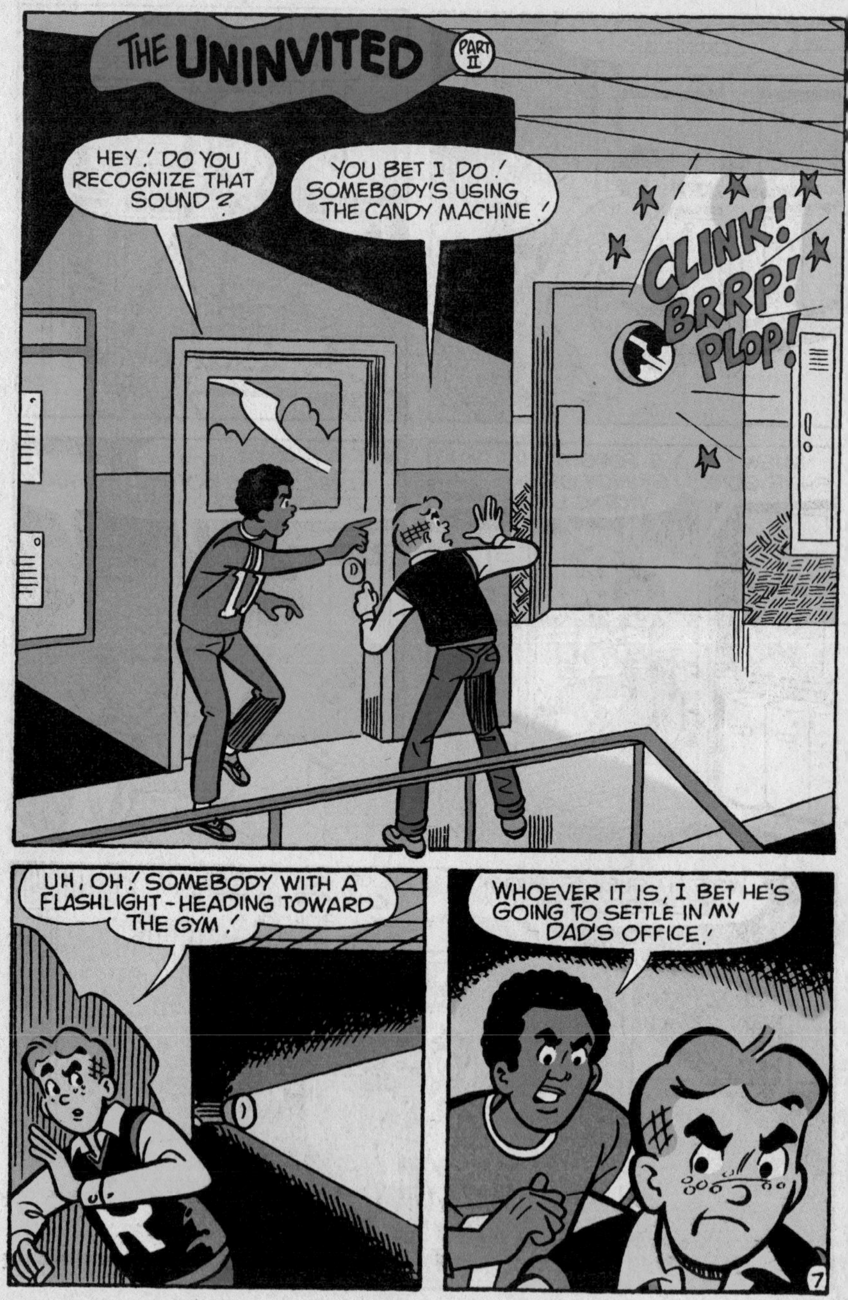
THE UNINVITED
PART II
HEY! DO YOU RECOGNIZE THAT SOUND?
YOU BET I DO! SOMEBODY'S USING THE CANDY MACHINE!
CLINK! BRRP! PLOP!
UH, OH! SOMEBODY WITH A FLASHLIGHT - HEADING TOWARD THE GYM!
WHOEVER IT IS, I BET HE'S GOING TO SETTLE IN MY DAD'S OFFICE!
7

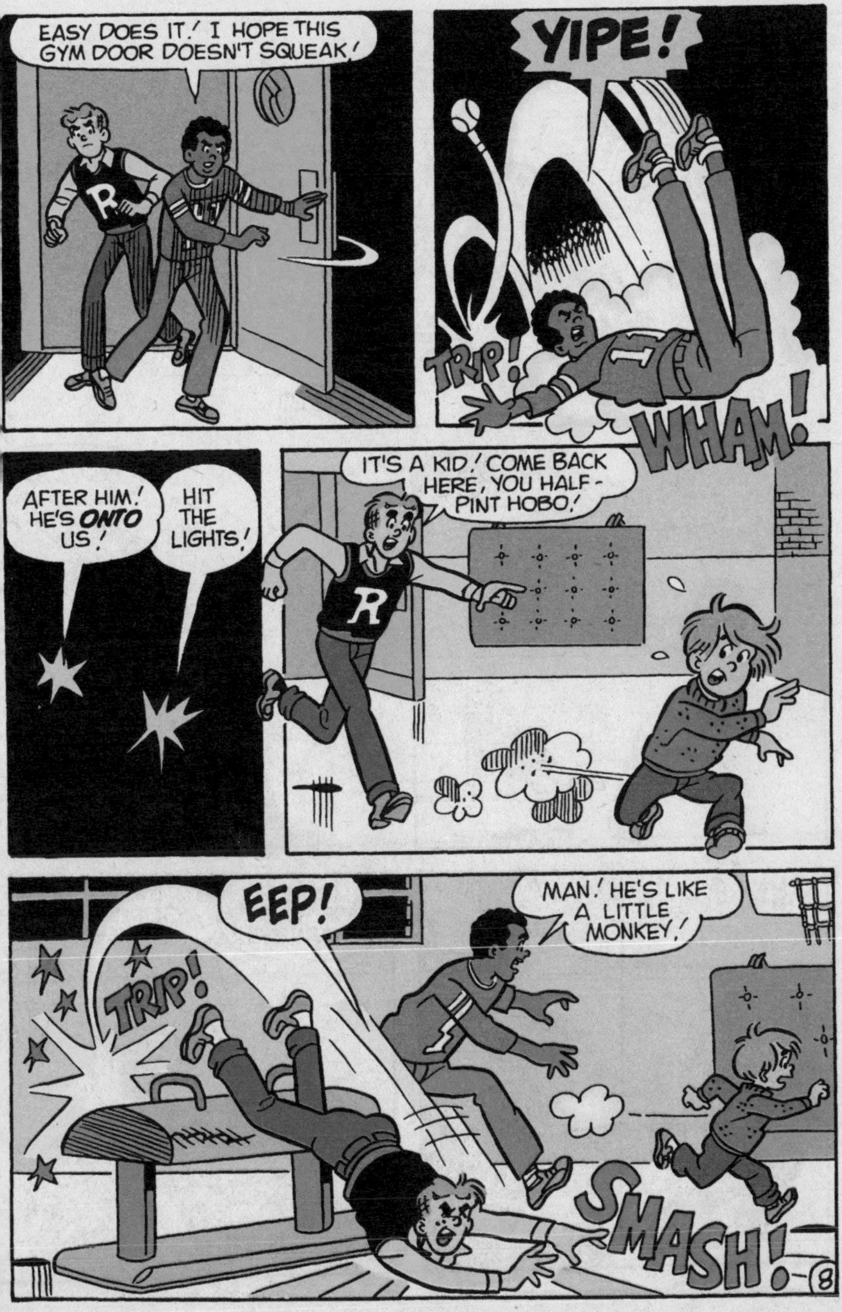
EASY DOES IT! I HOPE THIS GYM DOOR DOESN'T SQUEAK!
YIPE!
TRIP!
WHAM!
AFTER HIM! HE'S ONTO US!
HIT THE LIGHTS!
IT'S A KID! COME BACK HERE, YOU HALF-PINT HOBO!
EEP!
TRIP!
MAN! HE'S LIKE A LITTLE MONKEY!
SMASH!
8

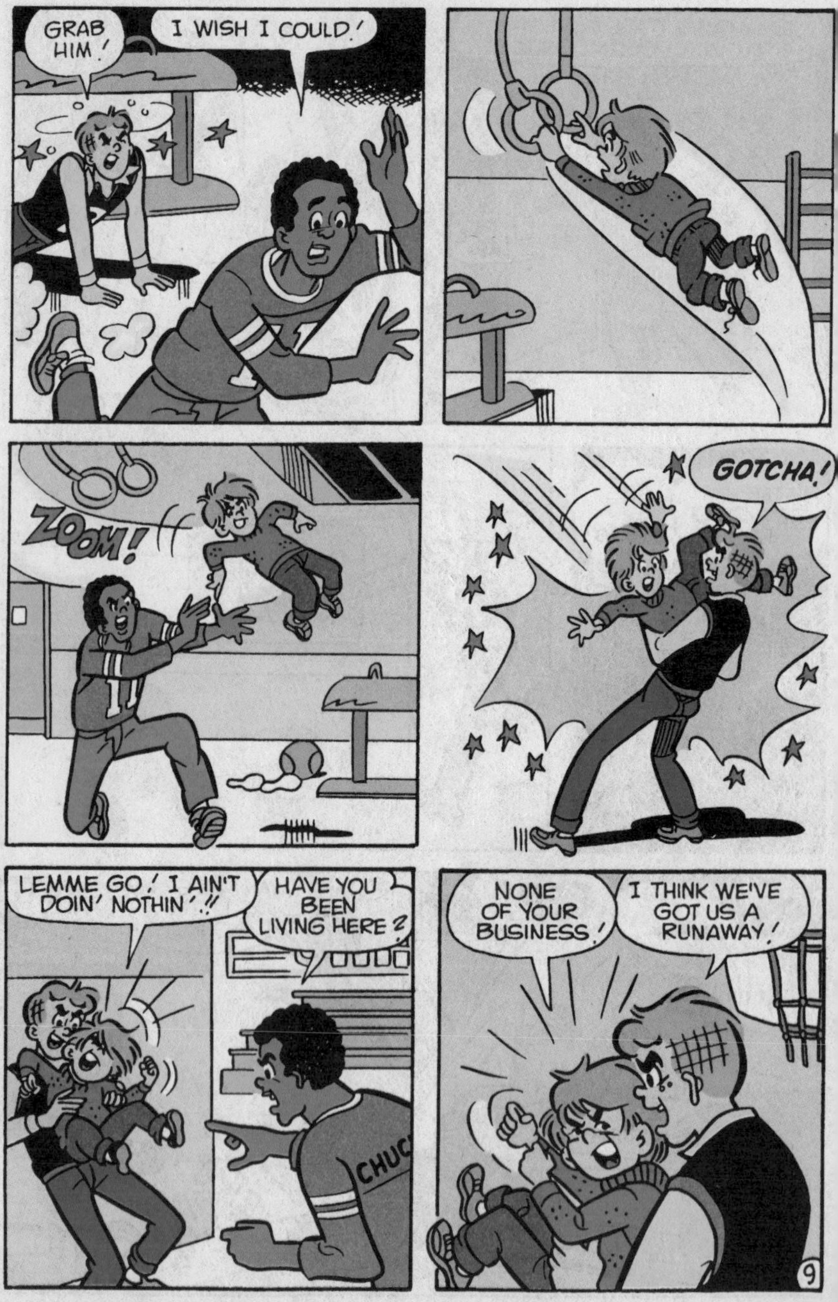
GRAB HIM!
I WISH I COULD!
ZOOM!
GOTCHA!
LEMME GO! I AIN'T DOIN' NOTHIN'!!
HAVE YOU BEEN LIVING HERE?
CHUC
NONE OF YOUR BUSINESS!
I THINK WE'VE GOT US A RUNAWAY!
9

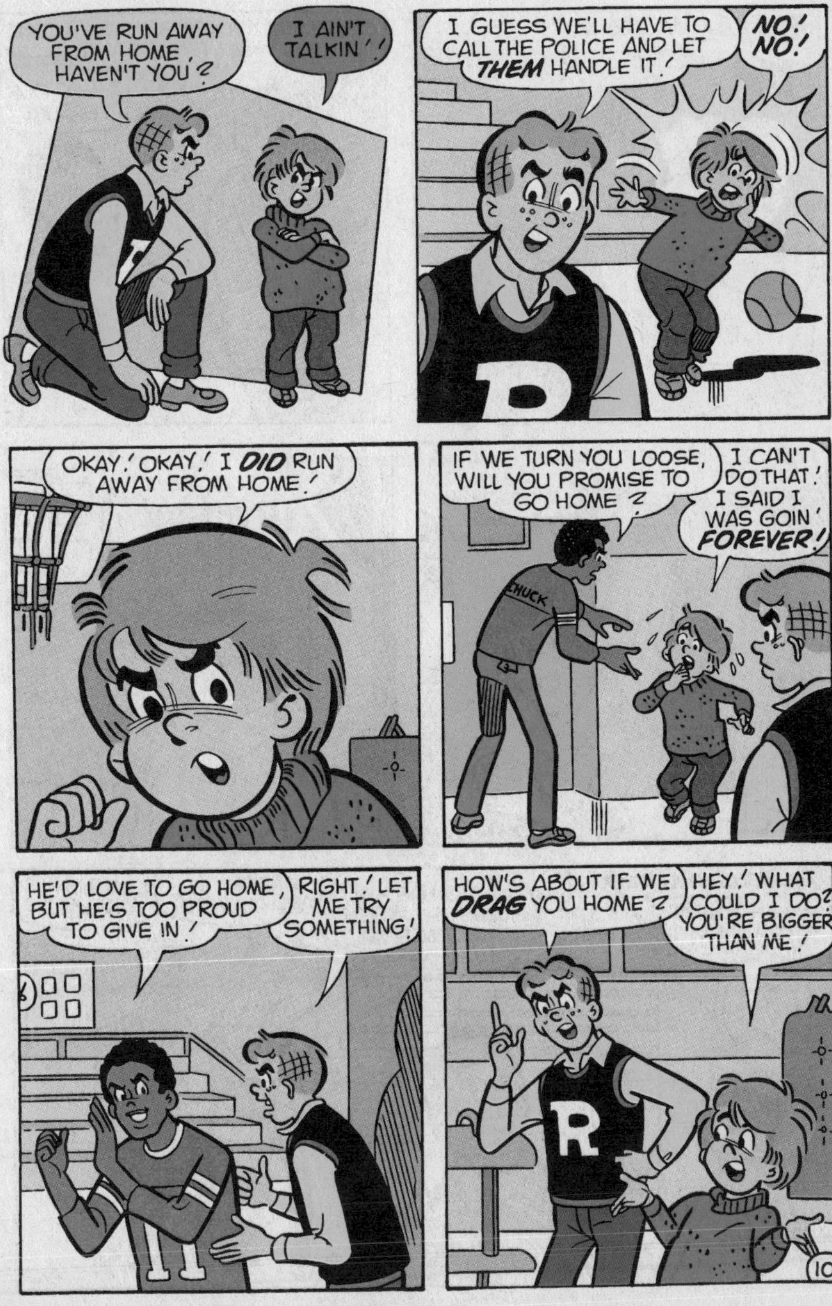
YOU'VE RUN AWAY FROM HOME, HAVEN'T YOU?
I AIN'T TALKIN'!
I GUESS WE'LL HAVE TO CALL THE POLICE AND LET THEM HANDLE IT!
NO! NO!
OKAY! OKAY! I DID RUN AWAY FROM HOME!
IF WE TURN YOU LOOSE, WILL YOU PROMISE TO GO HOME?
I CAN'T DO THAT! I SAID I WAS GOIN' FOREVER!
CHUCK
HE'D LOVE TO GO HOME, BUT HE'S TOO PROUD TO GIVE IN!
RIGHT! LET ME TRY SOMETHING!
HOW'S ABOUT IF WE DRAG YOU HOME?
HEY! WHAT COULD I DO? YOU'RE BIGGER THAN ME!
10

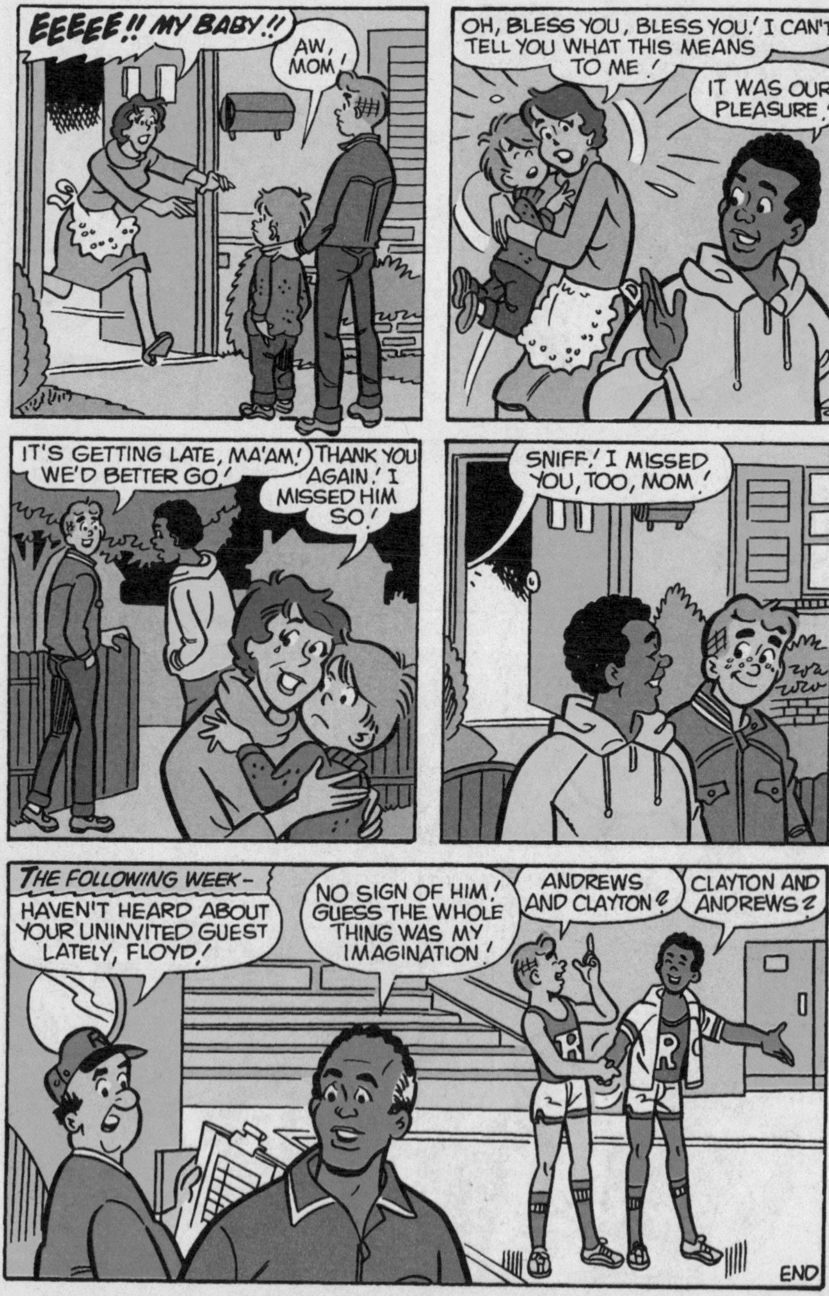
EEEEE!! MY BABY!!
AW, MOM!
OH, BLESS YOU, BLESS YOU! I CAN'T TELL YOU WHAT THIS MEANS TO ME!
IT WAS OUR PLEASURE!
IT'S GETTING LATE, MA'AM! WE'D BETTER GO!
THANK YOU AGAIN! I MISSED HIM SO!
SNIFF! I MISSED YOU, TOO, MOM!
THE FOLLOWING WEEK-
HAVEN'T HEARD ABOUT YOUR UNINVITED GUEST LATELY, FLOYD!
NO SIGN OF HIM! GUESS THE WHOLE THING WAS MY IMAGINATION!
ANDREWS AND CLAYTON?
CLAYTON AND ANDREWS?
END

Desk Jockey
Jughead #114, November 1964
**Frank Doyle, Samm Schwartz
and Vincent DeCarlo**

Along with his insatiable appetite, Jughead's best-known feature is his trademark hat. So when he accidentally forgets it in Mr. Weatherbee's office, his mission to retrieve it gets him stuck in a precarious situation—resulting in one of the strangest and silliest Archie stories ever.

Invention Day
Tales From Riverdale Digest #16,
January 2007
**Bill Golliher, Fernando Ruiz
and Al Nickerson**

Flutesnoot's students have an invention for everything! The perfect pizza slicer for Jughead, the surefire Archie detector for Betty... but of course, Dilton takes the prize with an invention that's useful for everyone... especially the faculty!

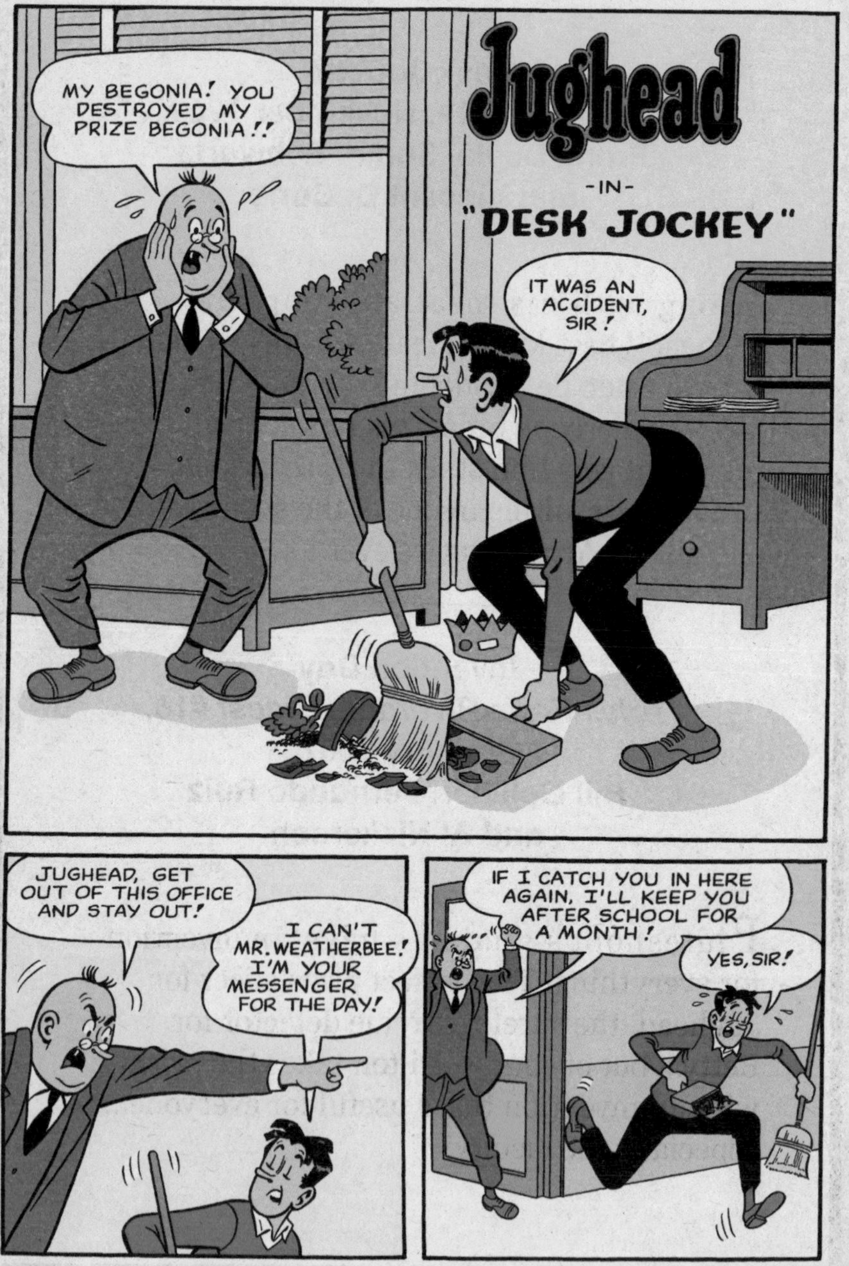
Jughead
-IN-
"DESK JOCKEY"
MY BEGONIA! YOU DESTROYED MY PRIZE BEGONIA!!
IT WAS AN ACCIDENT, SIR!
JUGHEAD, GET OUT OF THIS OFFICE AND STAY OUT!
I CAN'T MR. WEATHERBEE! I'M YOUR MESSENGER FOR THE DAY!
IF I CATCH YOU IN HERE AGAIN, I'LL KEEP YOU AFTER SCHOOL FOR A MONTH!
YES, SIR!

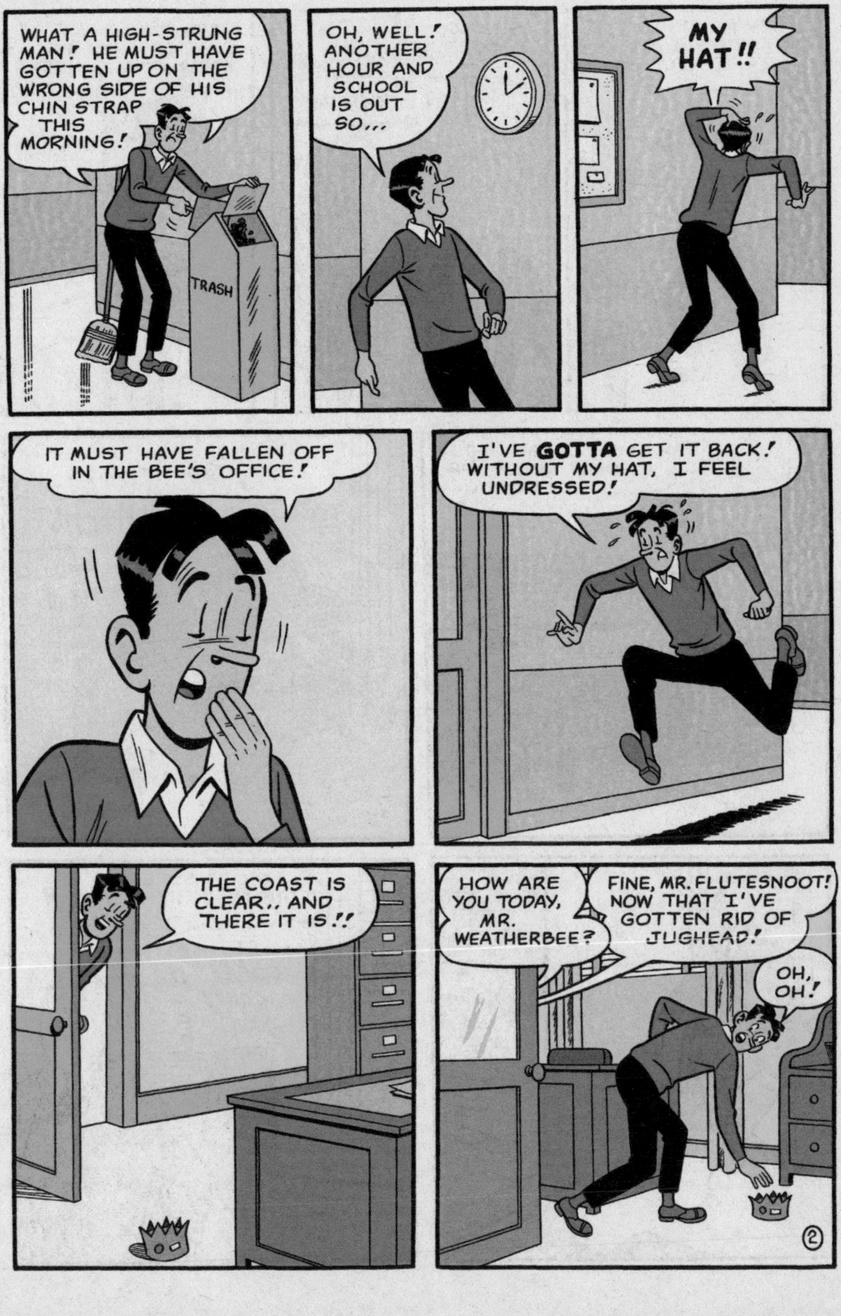
WHAT A HIGH-STRUNG MAN! HE MUST HAVE GOTTEN UP ON THE WRONG SIDE OF HIS CHIN STRAP THIS MORNING!
TRASH
OH, WELL! ANOTHER HOUR AND SCHOOL IS OUT SO...
MY HAT!!
IT MUST HAVE FALLEN OFF IN THE BEE'S OFFICE!
I'VE GOTTA GET IT BACK! WITHOUT MY HAT, I FEEL UNDRESSED!
THE COAST IS CLEAR.. AND THERE IT IS!!
HOW ARE YOU TODAY, MR. WEATHERBEE?
FINE, MR. FLUTESNOOT! NOW THAT I'VE GOTTEN RID OF JUGHEAD!
OH, OH!
2

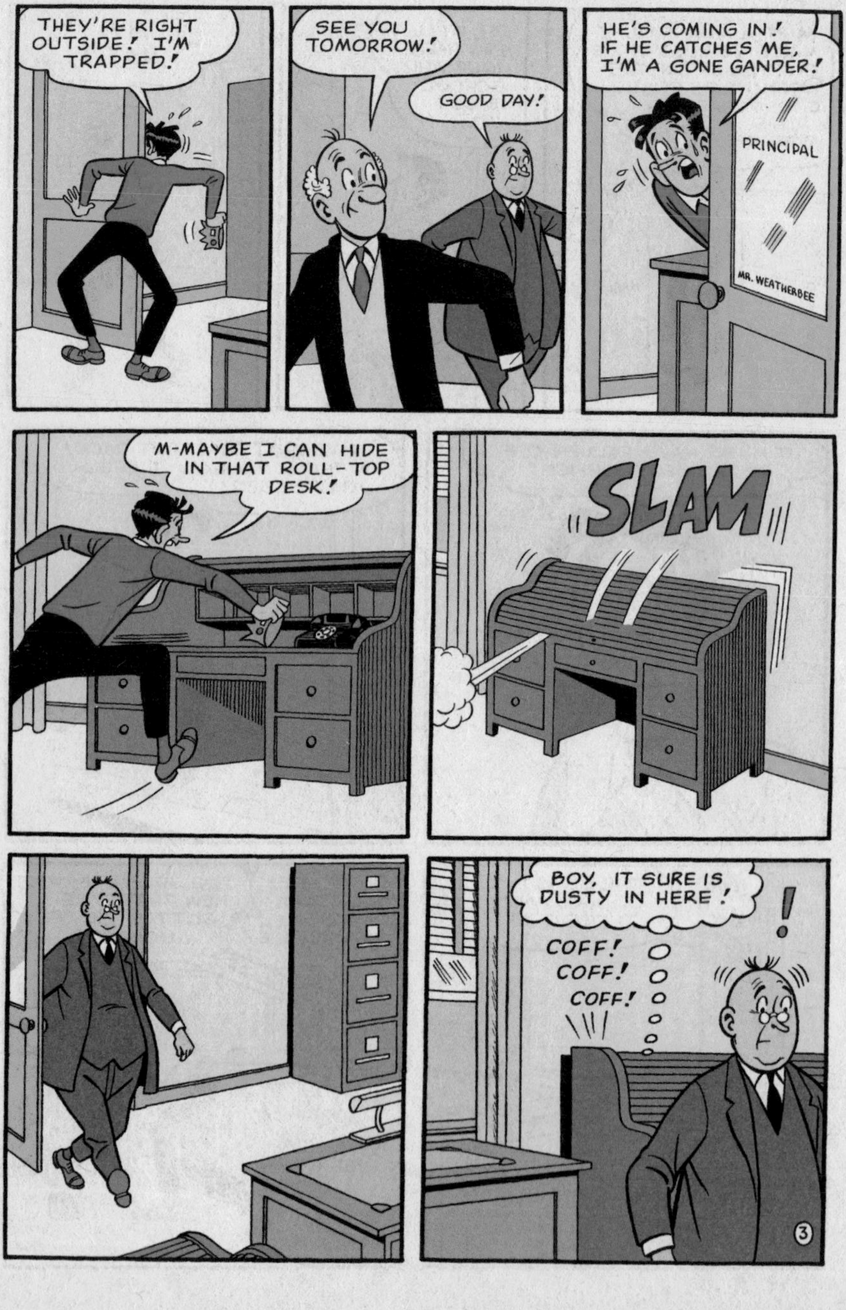
THEY'RE RIGHT OUTSIDE! I'M TRAPPED!
SEE YOU TOMORROW!
GOOD DAY!
HE'S COMING IN! IF HE CATCHES ME, I'M A GONE GANDER!
PRINCIPAL
MR. WEATHERBEE
M-MAYBE I CAN HIDE IN THAT ROLL-TOP DESK!
SLAM
BOY, IT SURE IS DUSTY IN HERE!
COFF! COFF! COFF!
!
3

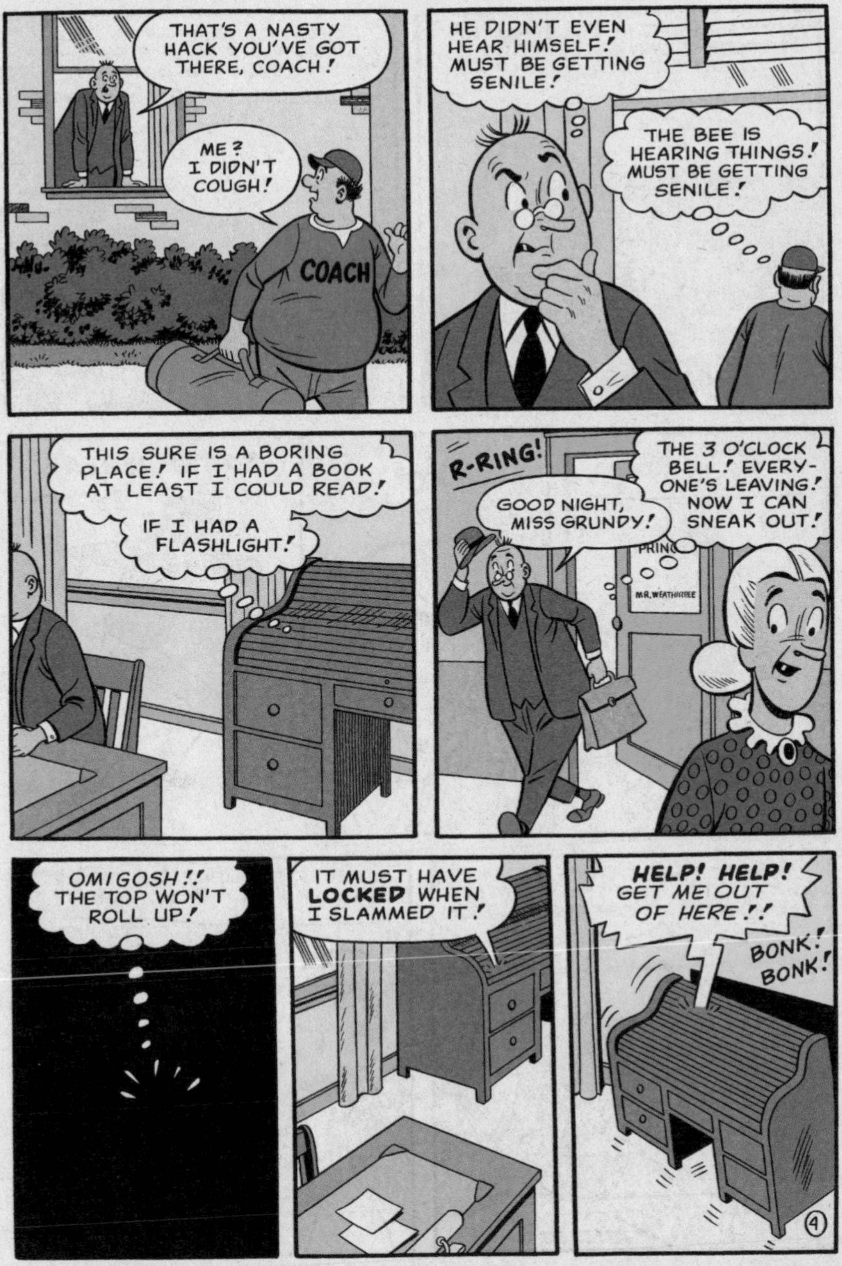
THAT'S A NASTY HACK YOU'VE GOT THERE, COACH!
ME? I DIDN'T COUGH!
COACH
HE DIDN'T EVEN HEAR HIMSELF! MUST BE GETTING SENILE!
THE BEE IS HEARING THINGS! MUST BE GETTING SENILE!
THIS SURE IS A BORING PLACE! IF I HAD A BOOK AT LEAST I COULD READ!
IF I HAD A FLASHLIGHT!
R-RING!
GOOD NIGHT, MISS GRUNDY!
THE 3 O'CLOCK BELL! EVERY-ONE'S LEAVING! NOW I CAN SNEAK OUT!
MR. WEATHERBEE
OMIGOSH!! THE TOP WON'T ROLL UP!
IT MUST HAVE **LOCKED** WHEN I SLAMMED IT!
HELP! HELP! GET ME OUT OF HERE!!
BONK! BONK!
4

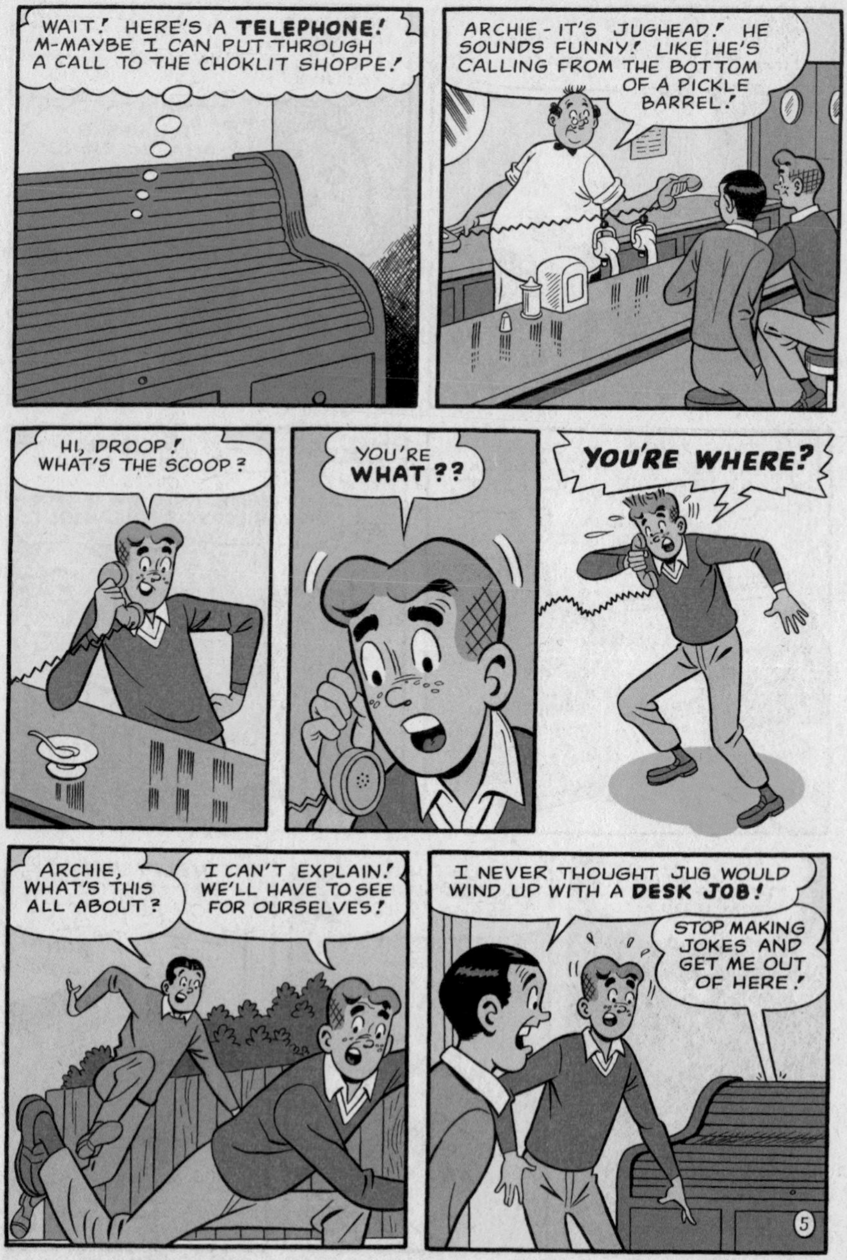
WAIT! HERE'S A TELEPHONE! M-MAYBE I CAN PUT THROUGH A CALL TO THE CHOKLIT SHOPPE!
ARCHIE - IT'S JUGHEAD! HE SOUNDS FUNNY! LIKE HE'S CALLING FROM THE BOTTOM OF A PICKLE BARREL!
HI, DROOP! WHAT'S THE SCOOP?
YOU'RE WHAT??
YOU'RE WHERE?
ARCHIE, WHAT'S THIS ALL ABOUT?
I CAN'T EXPLAIN! WE'LL HAVE TO SEE FOR OURSELVES!
I NEVER THOUGHT JUG WOULD WIND UP WITH A DESK JOB!
STOP MAKING JOKES AND GET ME OUT OF HERE!
5

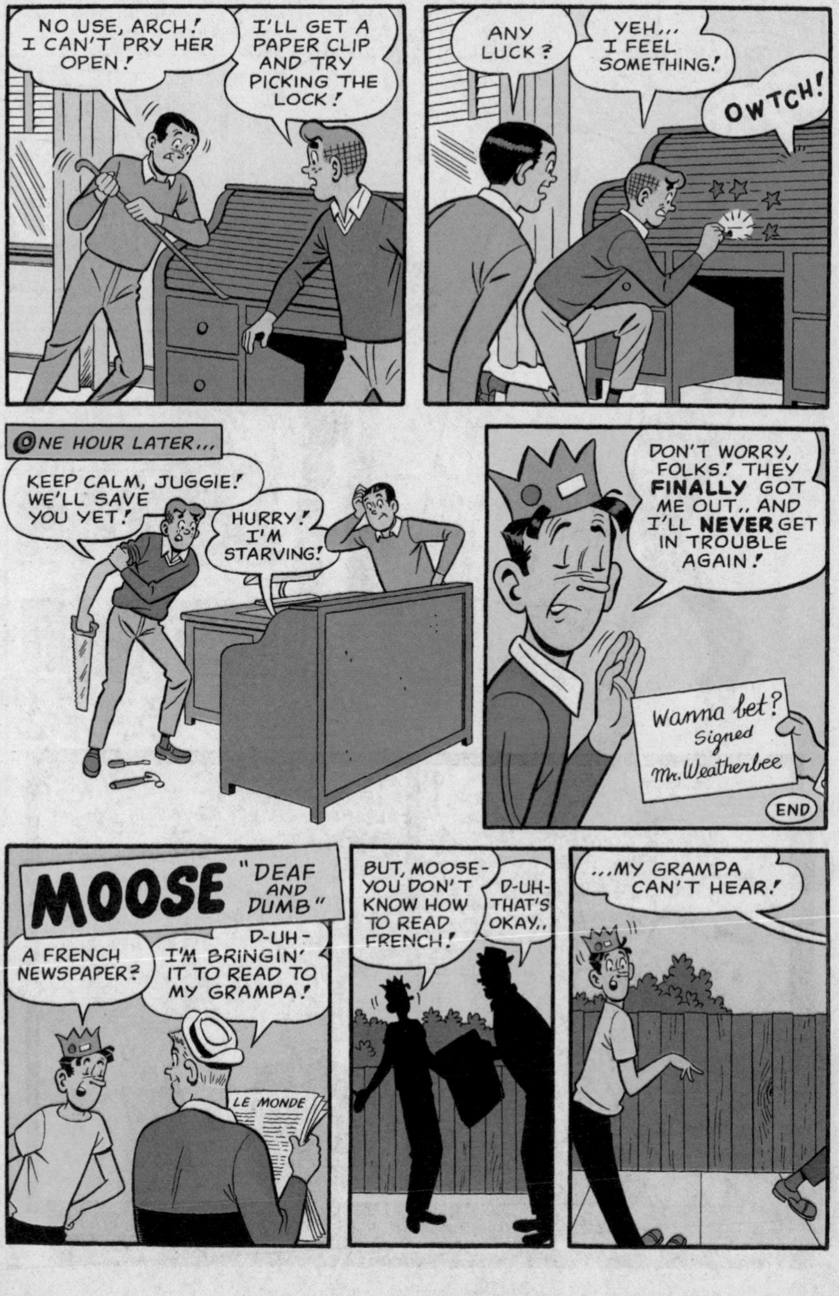
NO USE, ARCH! I CAN'T PRY HER OPEN!
I'LL GET A PAPER CLIP AND TRY PICKING THE LOCK!
ANY LUCK?
YEH,,, I FEEL SOMETHING!
OWTCH!
ONE HOUR LATER...
KEEP CALM, JUGGIE! WE'LL SAVE YOU YET!
HURRY! I'M STARVING!
DON'T WORRY, FOLKS! THEY FINALLY GOT ME OUT.. AND I'LL NEVER GET IN TROUBLE AGAIN!
Wanna bet? Signed Mr. Weatherbee
END
MOOSE "DEAF AND DUMB"
A FRENCH NEWSPAPER?
D-UH- I'M BRINGIN' IT TO READ TO MY GRAMPA!
LE MONDE
BUT, MOOSE- YOU DON'T KNOW HOW TO READ FRENCH!
D-UH- THAT'S OKAY..
...MY GRAMPA CAN'T HEAR!

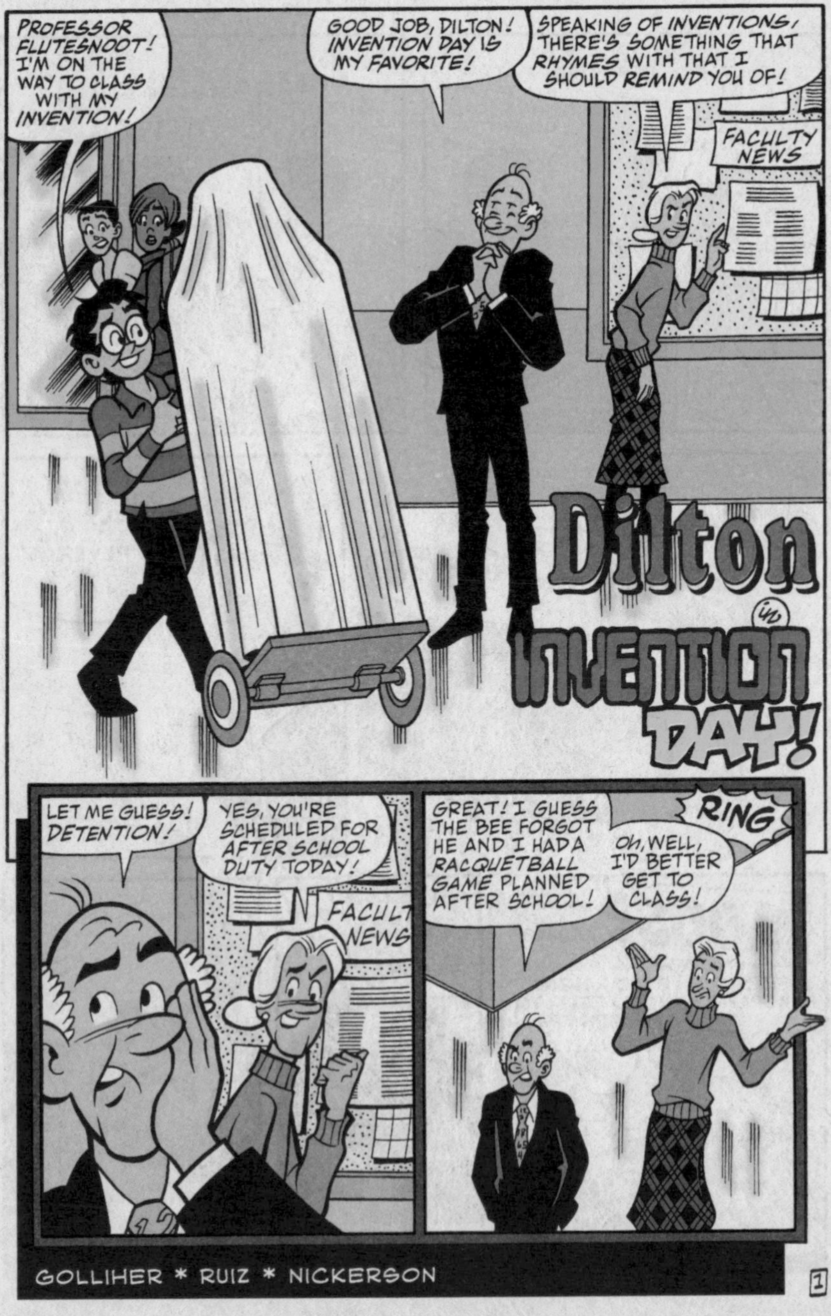
PROFESSOR FLUTESNOOT! I'M ON THE WAY TO CLASS WITH MY INVENTION!
GOOD JOB, DILTON! INVENTION DAY IS MY FAVORITE!
SPEAKING OF INVENTIONS, THERE'S SOMETHING THAT RHYMES WITH THAT I SHOULD REMIND YOU OF!
FACULTY NEWS
Dilton in INVENTION DAY!
LET ME GUESS! DETENTION!
YES, YOU'RE SCHEDULED FOR AFTER SCHOOL DUTY TODAY!
FACULT NEWS
GREAT! I GUESS THE BEE FORGOT HE AND I HAD A RACQUETBALL GAME PLANNED AFTER SCHOOL!
RING
Oh, WELL, I'D BETTER GET TO CLASS!
GOLLIHER * RUIZ * NICKERSON
1

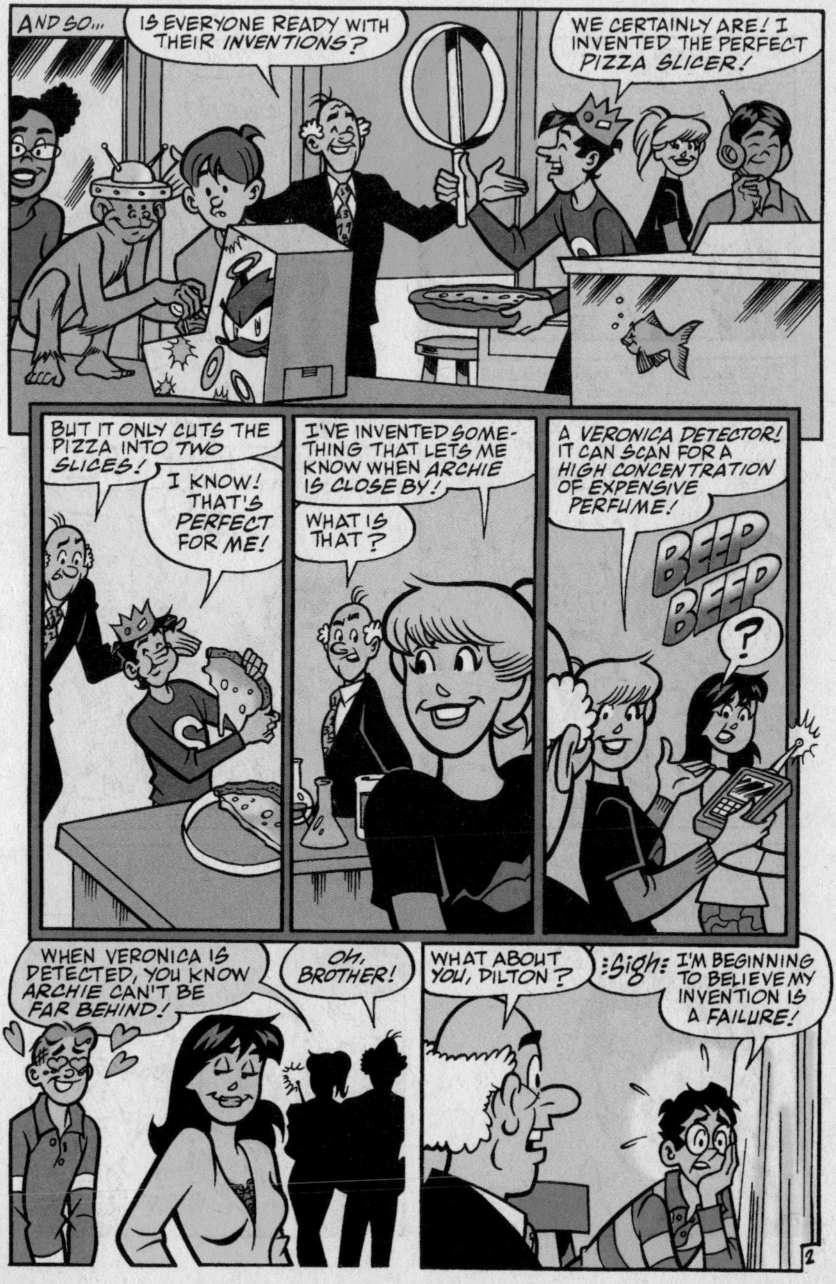
AND SO...
IS EVERYONE READY WITH THEIR INVENTIONS?
WE CERTAINLY ARE! I INVENTED THE PERFECT PIZZA SLICER!
BUT IT ONLY CUTS THE PIZZA INTO TWO SLICES!
I KNOW! THAT'S PERFECT FOR ME!
I'VE INVENTED SOMETHING THAT LETS ME KNOW WHEN ARCHIE IS CLOSE BY!
WHAT IS THAT?
A VERONICA DETECTOR! IT CAN SCAN FOR A HIGH CONCENTRATION OF EXPENSIVE PERFUME!
BEEP BEEP
?
WHEN VERONICA IS DETECTED, YOU KNOW ARCHIE CAN'T BE FAR BEHIND!
OH, BROTHER!
WHAT ABOUT YOU, DILTON?
:SIGH: I'M BEGINNING TO BELIEVE MY INVENTION IS A FAILURE!
2

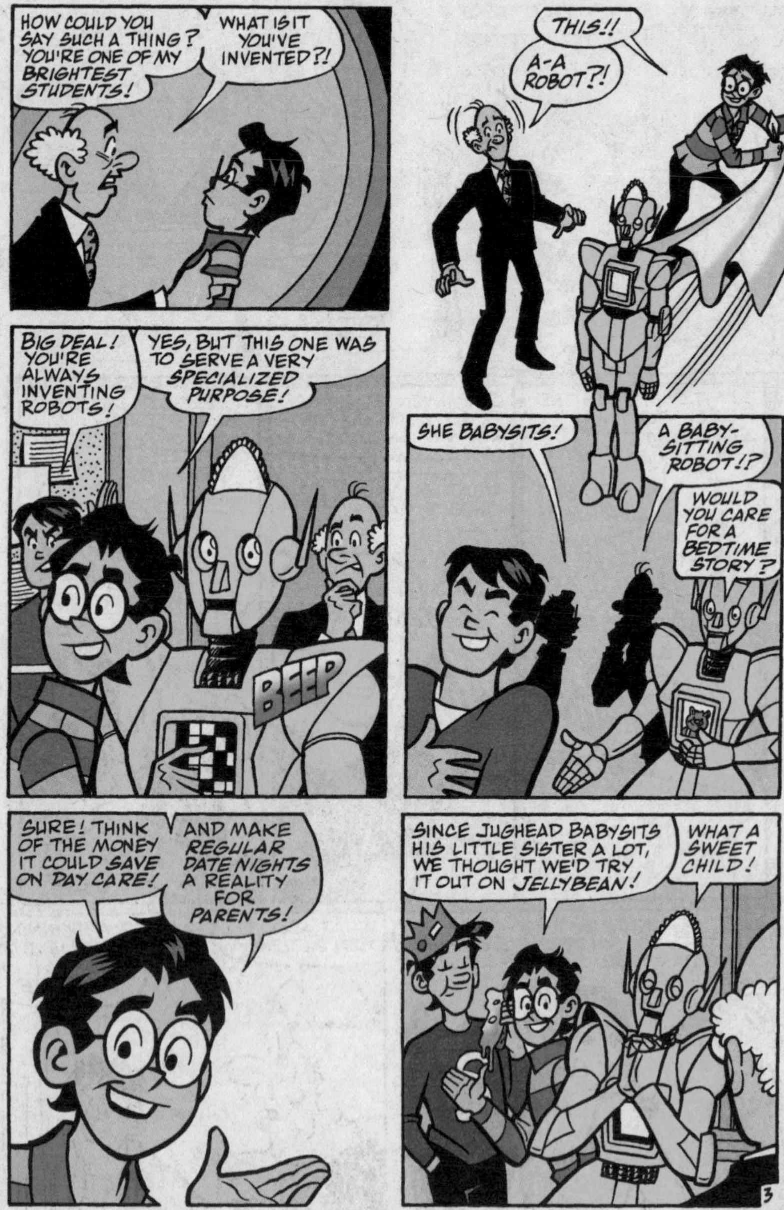
HOW COULD YOU SAY SUCH A THING? YOU'RE ONE OF MY BRIGHTEST STUDENTS!
WHAT IS IT YOU'VE INVENTED?!
THIS!!
A-A ROBOT?!
BIG DEAL! YOU'RE ALWAYS INVENTING ROBOTS!
YES, BUT THIS ONE WAS TO SERVE A VERY SPECIALIZED PURPOSE!
BEEP
SHE BABYSITS!
A BABY-SITTING ROBOT!?
WOULD YOU CARE FOR A BEDTIME STORY?
SURE! THINK OF THE MONEY IT COULD SAVE ON DAY CARE!
AND MAKE REGULAR DATE NIGHTS A REALITY FOR PARENTS!
SINCE JUGHEAD BABYSITS HIS LITTLE SISTER A LOT, WE THOUGHT WE'D TRY IT OUT ON JELLYBEAN!
WHAT A SWEET CHILD!
3

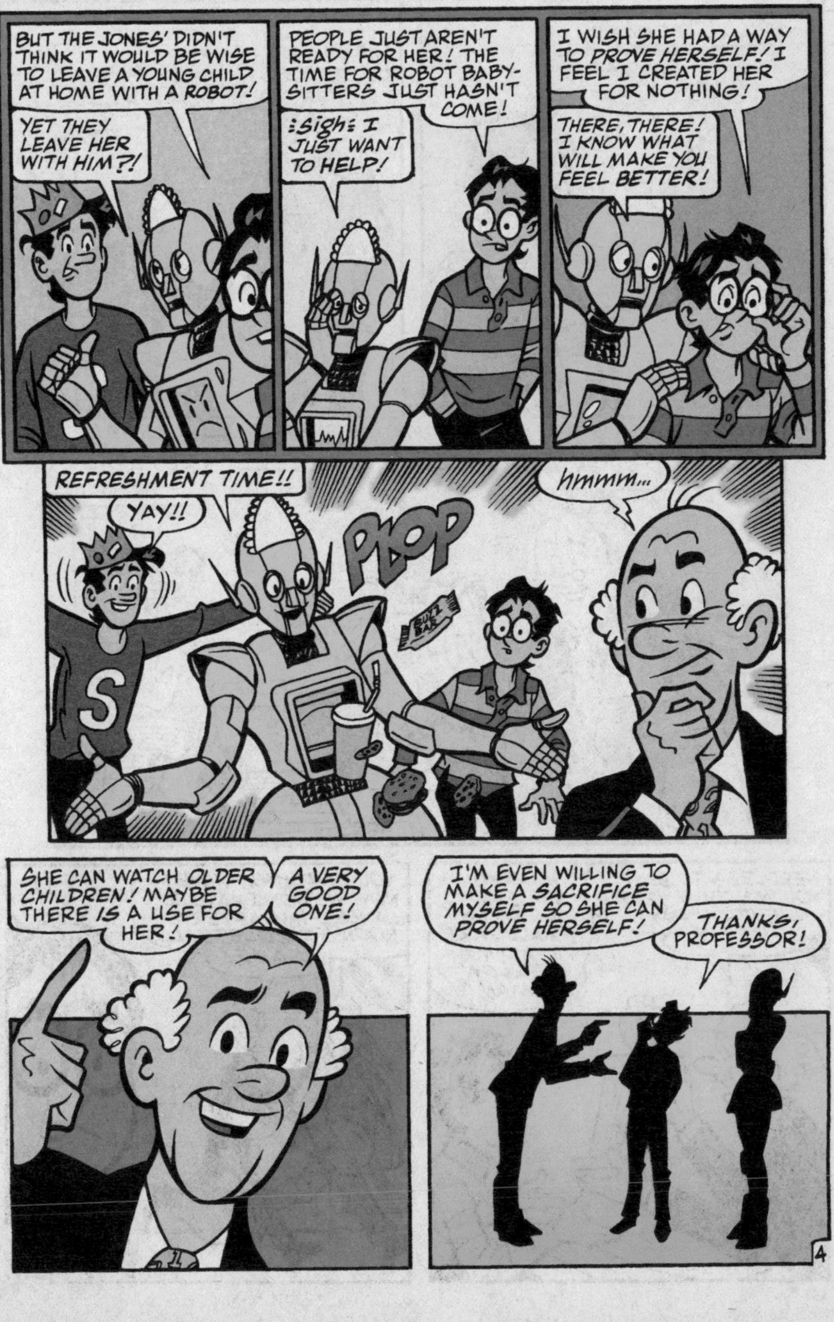
BUT THE JONES' DIDN'T THINK IT WOULD BE WISE TO LEAVE A YOUNG CHILD AT HOME WITH A ROBOT!
YET THEY LEAVE HER WITH HIM?!
PEOPLE JUST AREN'T READY FOR HER! THE TIME FOR ROBOT BABY-SITTERS JUST HASN'T COME!
:SIGH: I JUST WANT TO HELP!
I WISH SHE HAD A WAY TO PROVE HERSELF! I FEEL I CREATED HER FOR NOTHING!
THERE, THERE! I KNOW WHAT WILL MAKE YOU FEEL BETTER!
REFRESHMENT TIME!!
YAY!!
PLOP
hmmm...
SHE CAN WATCH OLDER CHILDREN! MAYBE THERE IS A USE FOR HER!
A VERY GOOD ONE!
I'M EVEN WILLING TO MAKE A SACRIFICE MYSELF SO SHE CAN PROVE HERSELF!
THANKS, PROFESSOR!
4

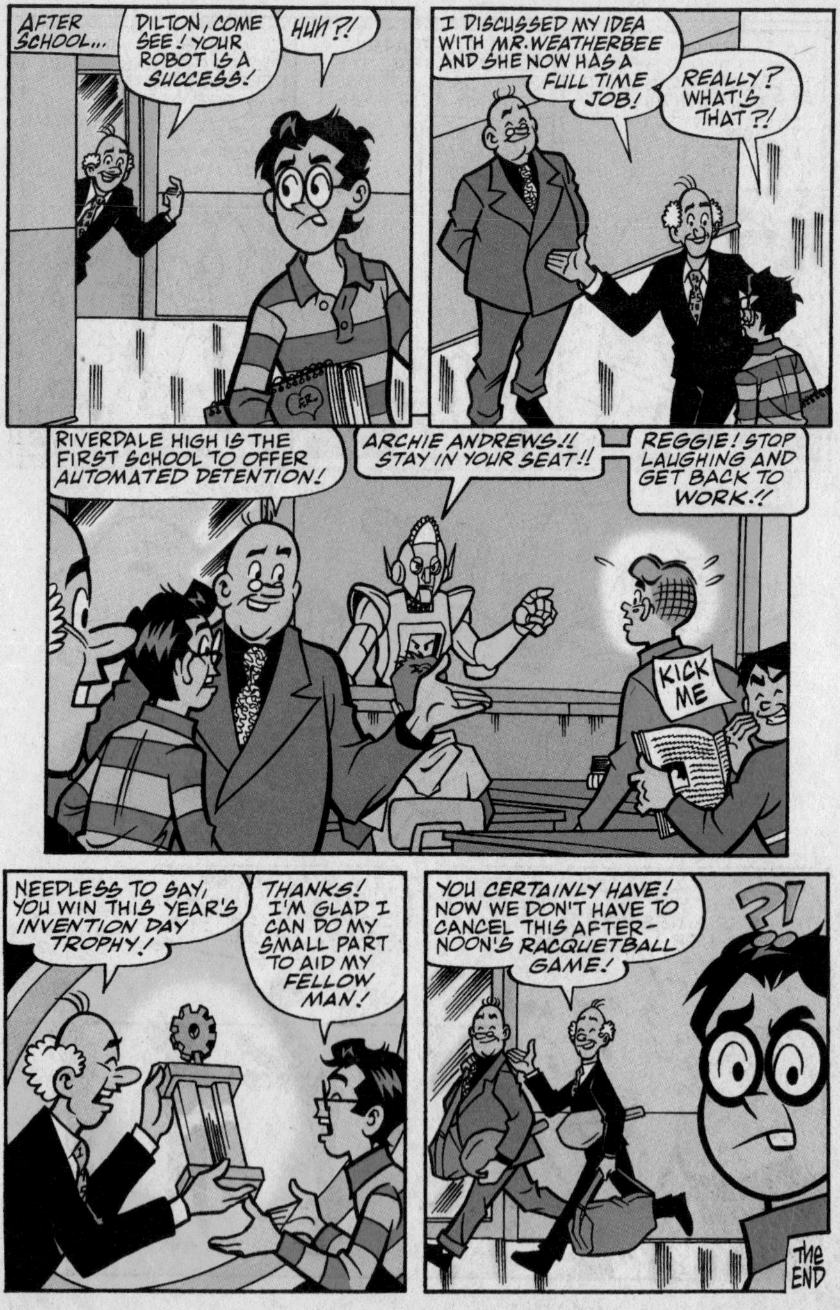
AFTER SCHOOL...
DILTON, COME SEE! YOUR ROBOT IS A SUCCESS!
HUH?!
I DISCUSSED MY IDEA WITH MR. WEATHERBEE AND SHE NOW HAS A FULL TIME JOB!
REALLY? WHAT'S THAT?!
RIVERDALE HIGH IS THE FIRST SCHOOL TO OFFER AUTOMATED DETENTION!
ARCHIE ANDREWS!! STAY IN YOUR SEAT!!
REGGIE! STOP LAUGHING AND GET BACK TO WORK!!
KICK ME
NEEDLESS TO SAY, YOU WIN THIS YEAR'S INVENTION DAY TROPHY!
THANKS! I'M GLAD I CAN DO MY SMALL PART TO AID MY FELLOW MAN!
YOU CERTAINLY HAVE! NOW WE DON'T HAVE TO CANCEL THIS AFTER-NOON'S RACQUETBALL GAME!
?!
THE END

Magic Mayhem
Archie #649, December 2013
Tom DeFalco, Bill Galvan, Rich Koslowski,
Jack Morelli and Digikore Studios

Since Archie first appeared in 1941,
his comics have regularly mirrored what was
happening in pop culture. Enter this thrilling
story which draws its inspiration from the
magic craze ignited by a certain boy wizard
that is highlighted by a return appearance from
Jughead nemesis Trula Twyst and the United
Girls Against Jughead!

**How to Get Ready for School
in Less Than 30 Seconds**
Original Printing Unknown
George Gladir and Gus Lemoine

Rube Goldberg has got nothing on
Jughead, as the crowned one demonstrates his
fool-proof method for getting to school on time.
But what if the fool in question is perpetually
tardy Archie?!

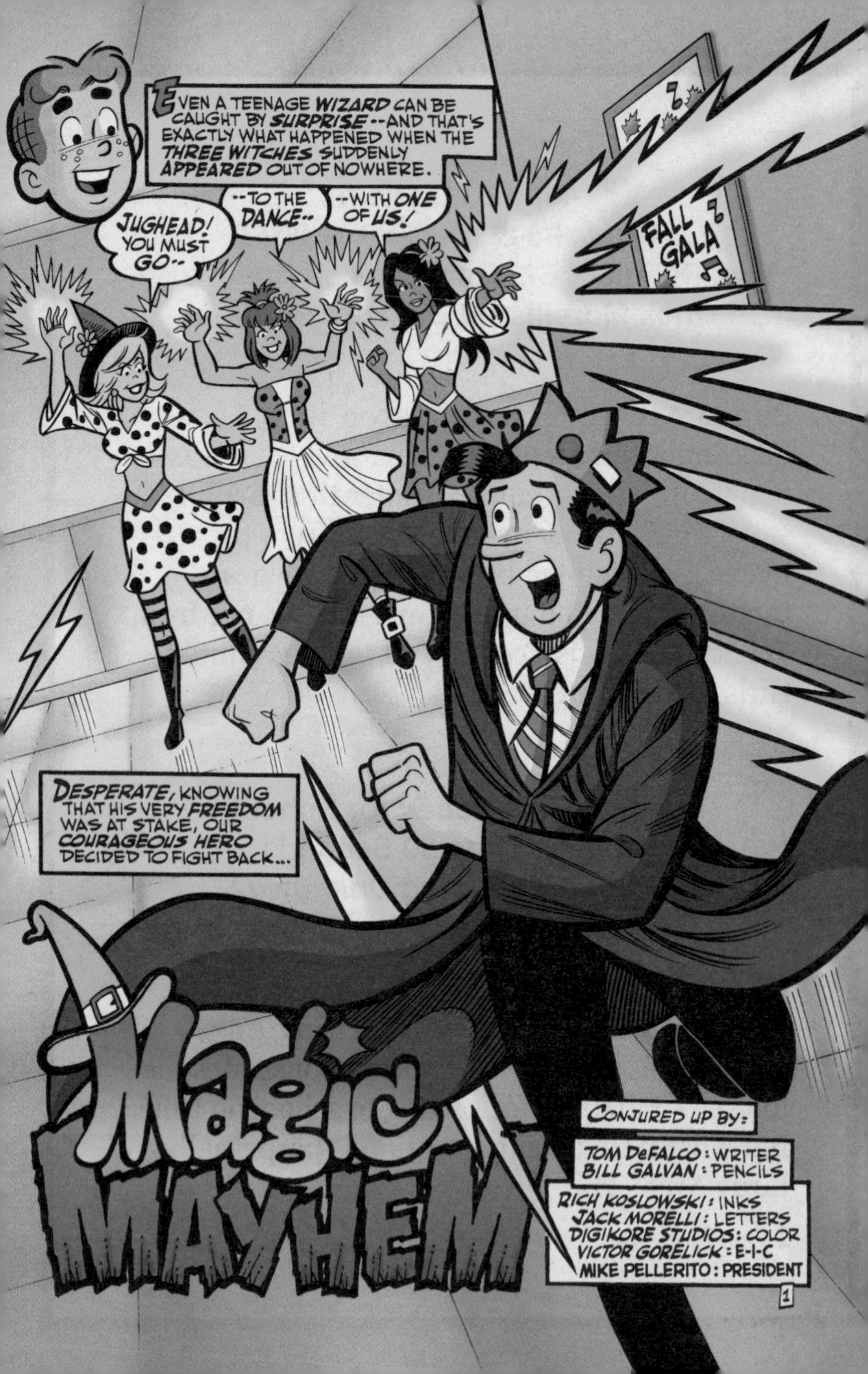
EVEN A TEENAGE WIZARD CAN BE CAUGHT BY SURPRISE --AND THAT'S EXACTLY WHAT HAPPENED WHEN THE THREE WITCHES SUDDENLY APPEARED OUT OF NOWHERE.
JUGHEAD! YOU MUST GO--
--TO THE DANCE--
--WITH ONE OF US!
FALL GALA
DESPERATE, KNOWING THAT HIS VERY FREEDOM WAS AT STAKE, OUR COURAGEOUS HERO DECIDED TO FIGHT BACK...
Magic MAYHEM
CONJURED UP BY:
TOM DeFALCO : WRITER
BILL GALVAN : PENCILS
RICH KOSLOWSKI : INKS
JACK MORELLI : LETTERS
DIGIKORE STUDIOS : COLOR
VICTOR GORELICK : E-I-C
MIKE PELLERITO : PRESIDENT
1

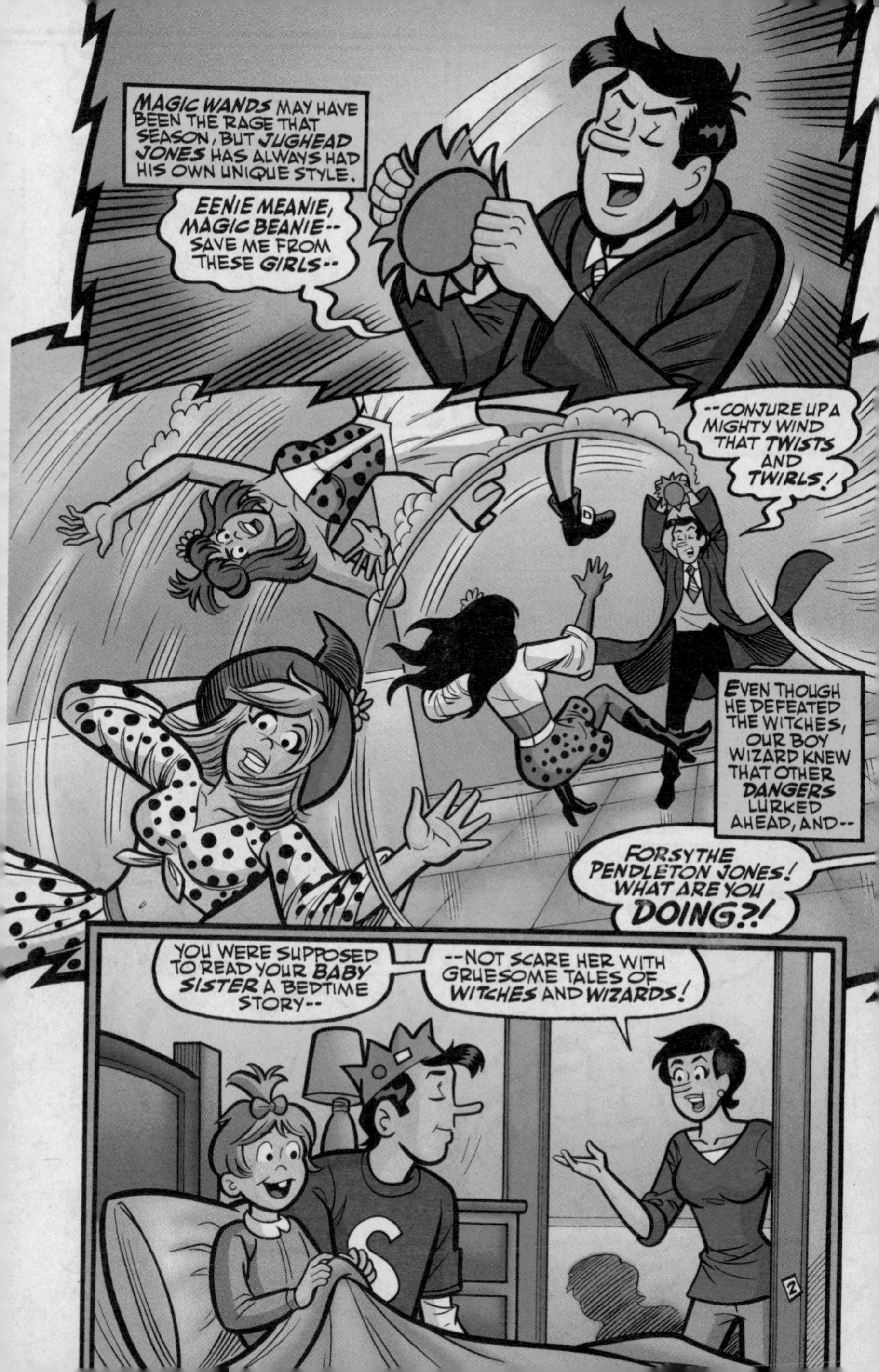

MAGIC WANDS MAY HAVE BEEN THE RAGE THAT SEASON, BUT JUGHEAD JONES HAS ALWAYS HAD HIS OWN UNIQUE STYLE.
EENIE MEANIE, MAGIC BEANIE-- SAVE ME FROM THESE GIRLS--
--CONJURE UP A MIGHTY WIND THAT TWISTS AND TWIRLS!
EVEN THOUGH HE DEFEATED THE WITCHES, OUR BOY WIZARD KNEW THAT OTHER DANGERS LURKED AHEAD, AND--
FORSYTHE PENDLETON JONES! WHAT ARE YOU DOING?!
YOU WERE SUPPOSED TO READ YOUR BABY SISTER A BEDTIME STORY--
--NOT SCARE HER WITH GRUESOME TALES OF WITCHES AND WIZARDS!
2

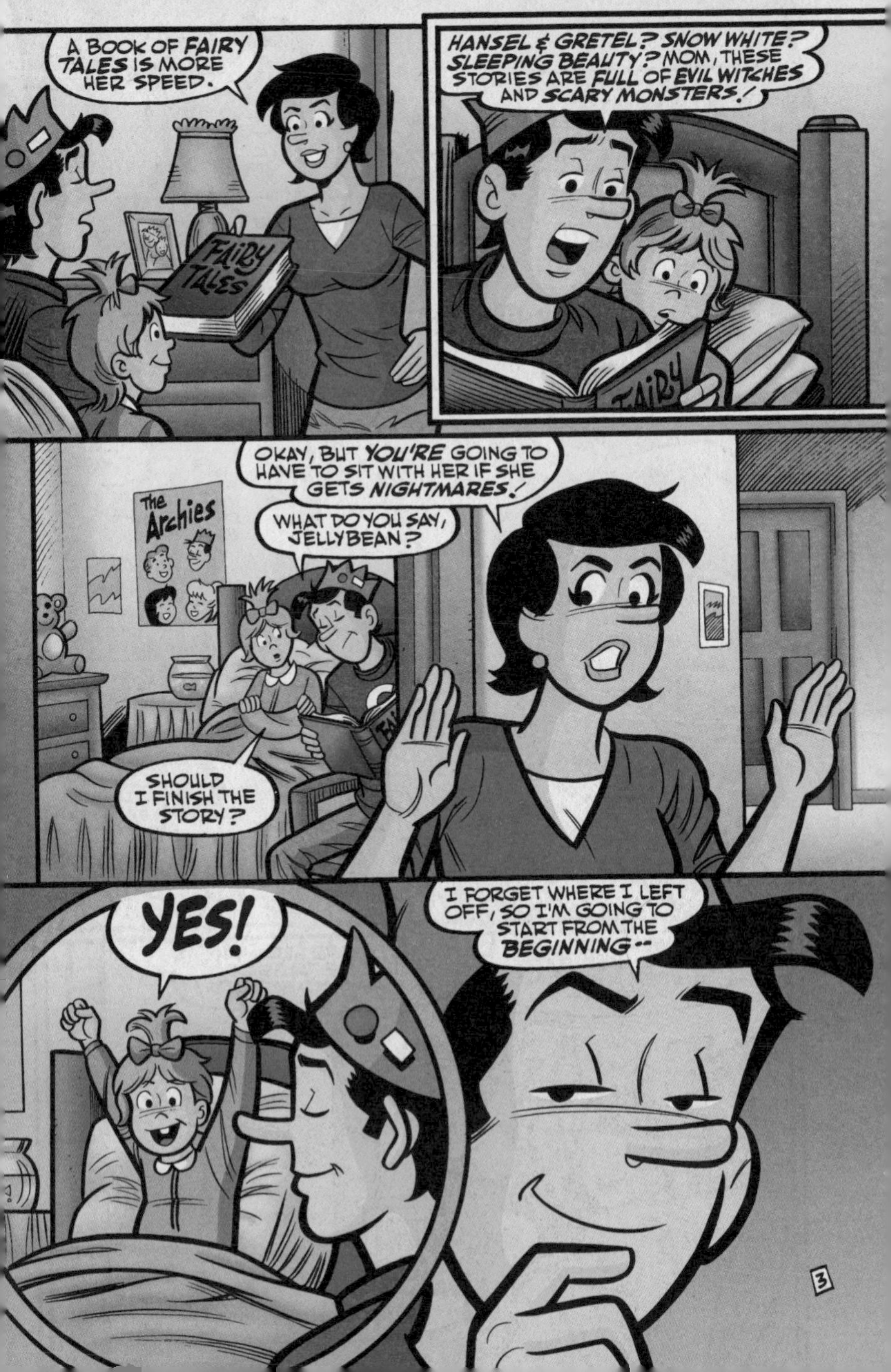

A BOOK OF FAIRY TALES IS MORE HER SPEED.
FAIRY TALES
HANSEL & GRETEL? SNOW WHITE? SLEEPING BEAUTY? MOM, THESE STORIES ARE FULL OF EVIL WITCHES AND SCARY MONSTERS!
FAIRY
The Archies
OKAY, BUT YOU'RE GOING TO HAVE TO SIT WITH HER IF SHE GETS NIGHTMARES!
WHAT DO YOU SAY, JELLYBEAN?
SHOULD I FINISH THE STORY?
YES!
I FORGET WHERE I LEFT OFF, SO I'M GOING TO START FROM THE BEGINNING--
3

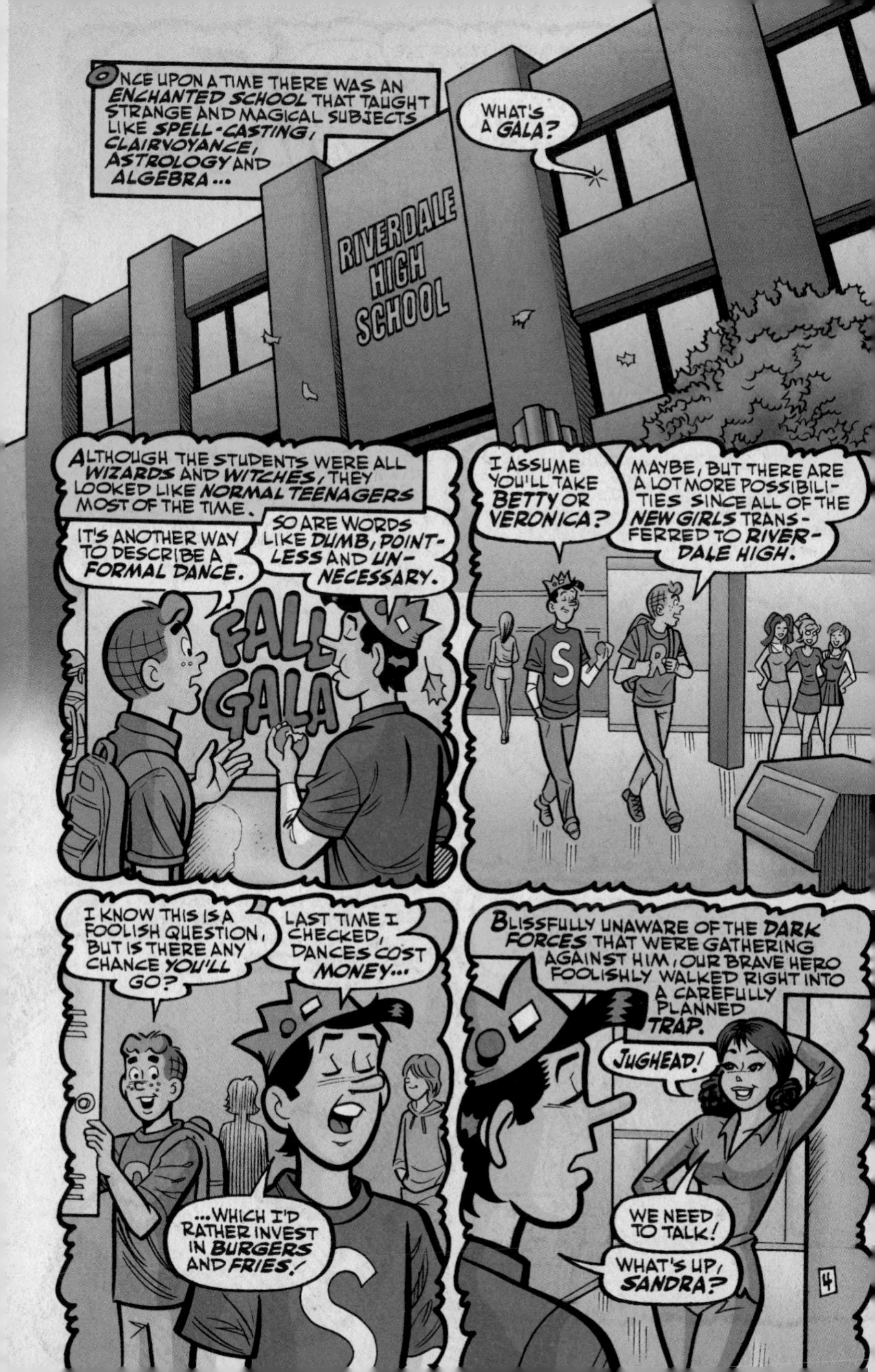
ONCE UPON A TIME THERE WAS AN ENCHANTED SCHOOL THAT TAUGHT STRANGE AND MAGICAL SUBJECTS LIKE SPELL-CASTING, CLAIRVOYANCE, ASTROLOGY AND ALGEBRA...
WHAT'S A GALA?
RIVERDALE HIGH SCHOOL
ALTHOUGH THE STUDENTS WERE ALL WIZARDS AND WITCHES, THEY LOOKED LIKE NORMAL TEENAGERS MOST OF THE TIME.
IT'S ANOTHER WAY TO DESCRIBE A FORMAL DANCE.
SO ARE WORDS LIKE DUMB, POINTLESS AND UNNECESSARY.
FALL GALA
I ASSUME YOU'LL TAKE BETTY OR VERONICA?
MAYBE, BUT THERE ARE A LOT MORE POSSIBILITIES SINCE ALL OF THE NEW GIRLS TRANSFERRED TO RIVERDALE HIGH.
I KNOW THIS IS A FOOLISH QUESTION, BUT IS THERE ANY CHANCE YOU'LL GO?
LAST TIME I CHECKED, DANCES COST MONEY...
...WHICH I'D RATHER INVEST IN BURGERS AND FRIES!
BLISSFULLY UNAWARE OF THE DARK FORCES THAT WERE GATHERING AGAINST HIM, OUR BRAVE HERO FOOLISHLY WALKED RIGHT INTO A CAREFULLY PLANNED TRAP.
JUGHEAD!
WE NEED TO TALK!
WHAT'S UP, SANDRA?
4

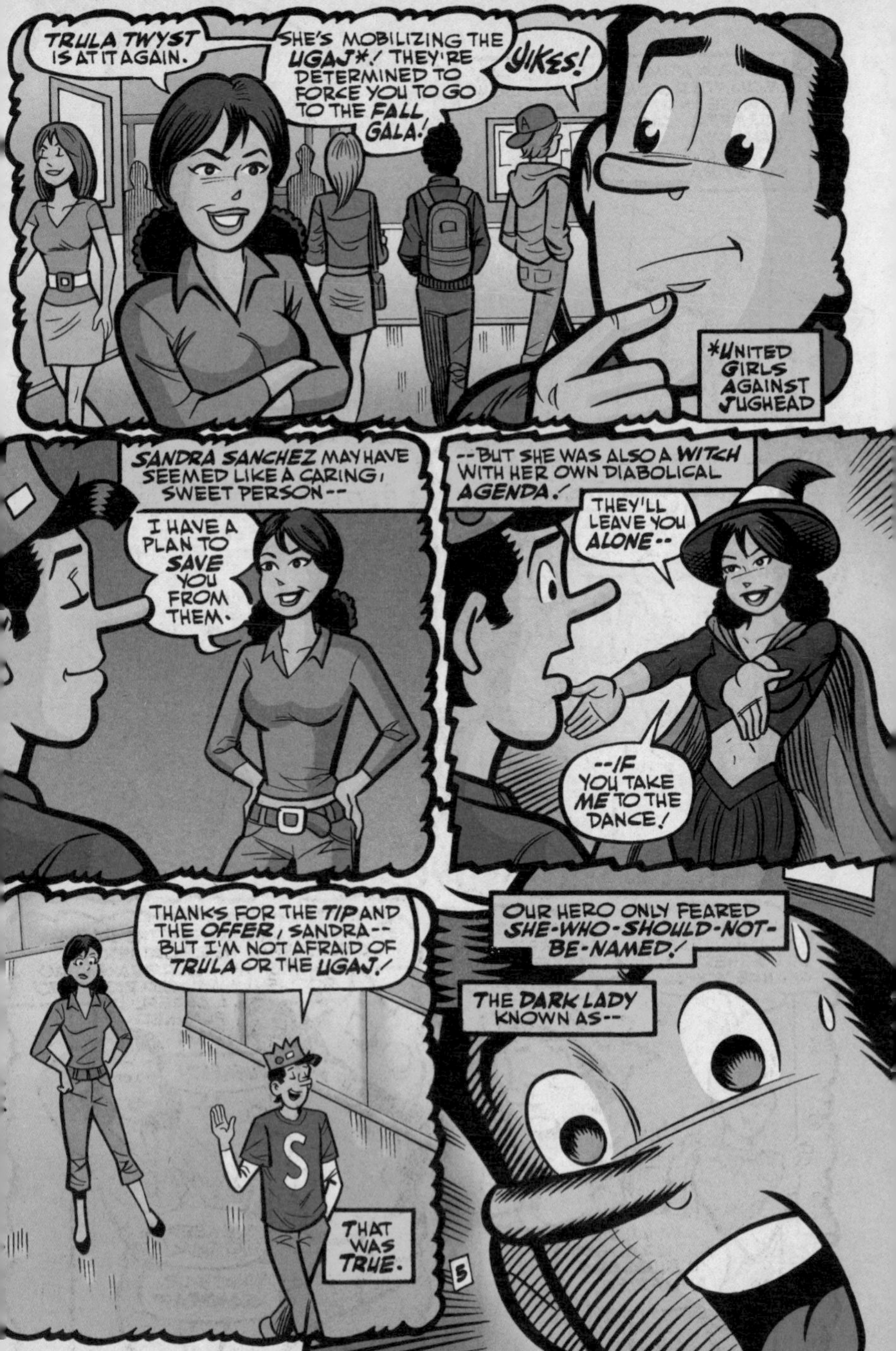
TRULA TWYST IS AT IT AGAIN.
SHE'S MOBILIZING THE UGAJ*! THEY'RE DETERMINED TO FORCE YOU TO GO TO THE FALL GALA!
YIKES!
*UNITED GIRLS AGAINST JUGHEAD
SANDRA SANCHEZ MAY HAVE SEEMED LIKE A CARING, SWEET PERSON--
I HAVE A PLAN TO SAVE YOU FROM THEM.
--BUT SHE WAS ALSO A WITCH WITH HER OWN DIABOLICAL AGENDA!
THEY'LL LEAVE YOU ALONE--
--IF YOU TAKE ME TO THE DANCE!
THANKS FOR THE TIP AND THE OFFER, SANDRA-- BUT I'M NOT AFRAID OF TRULA OR THE UGAJ!
THAT WAS TRUE.
OUR HERO ONLY FEARED SHE-WHO-SHOULD-NOT-BE-NAMED!
THE DARK LADY KNOWN AS--
5

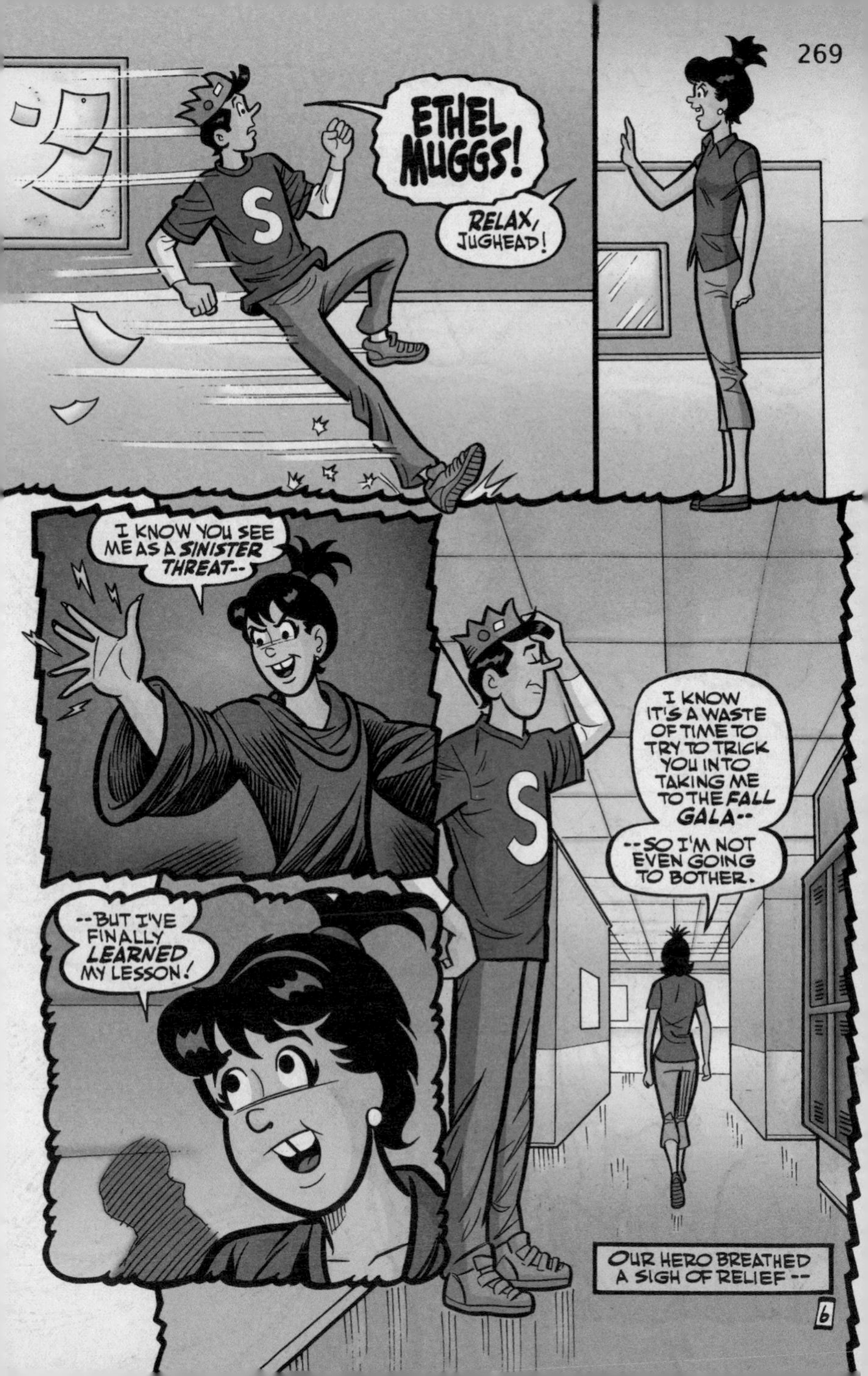
ETHEL MUGGS!
RELAX, JUGHEAD!
I KNOW YOU SEE ME AS A SINISTER THREAT--
--BUT I'VE FINALLY LEARNED MY LESSON!
I KNOW IT'S A WASTE OF TIME TO TRY TO TRICK YOU INTO TAKING ME TO THE FALL GALA--
--SO I'M NOT EVEN GOING TO BOTHER.
OUR HERO BREATHED A SIGH OF RELIEF --
6

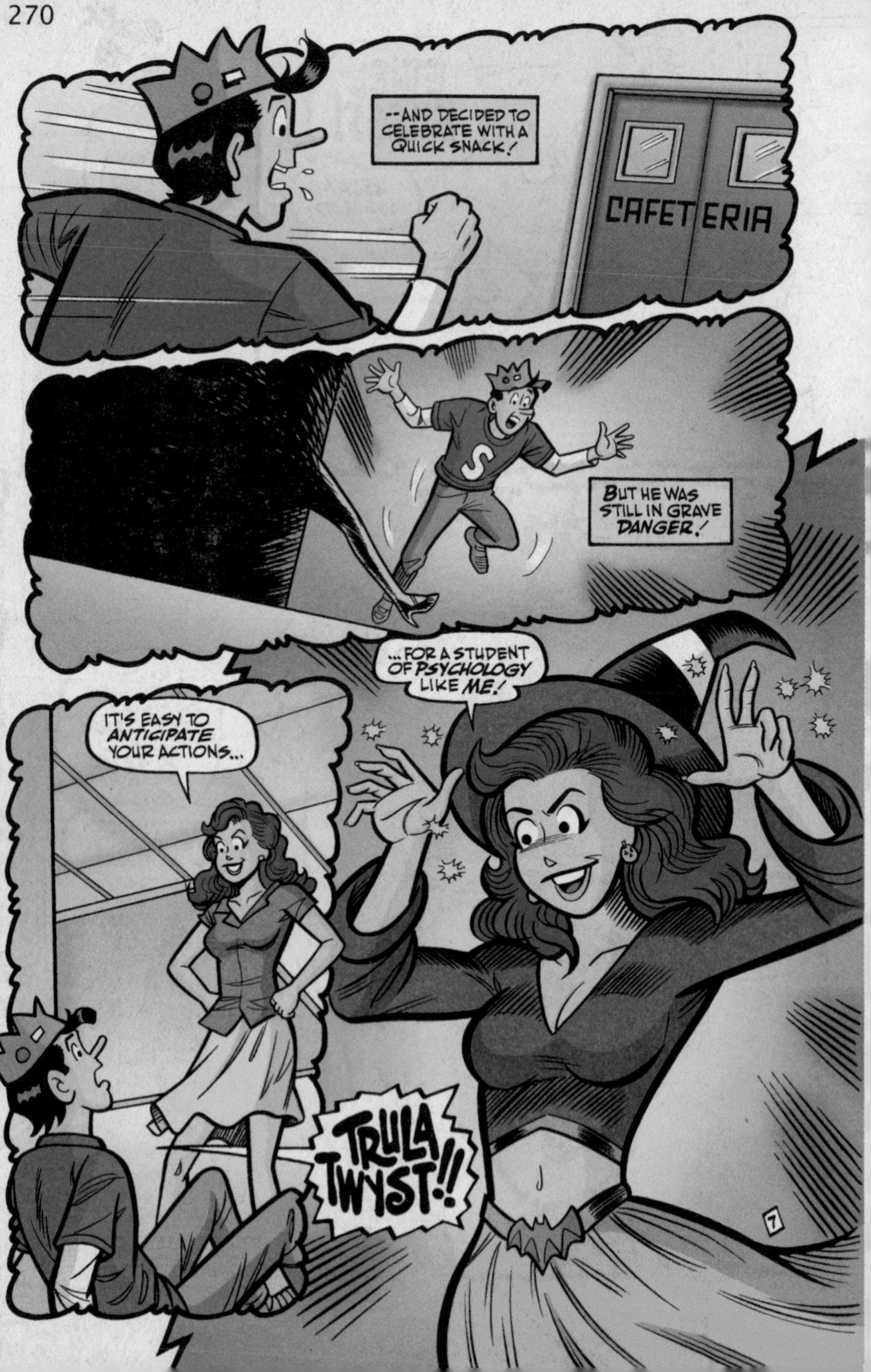
--AND DECIDED TO CELEBRATE WITH A QUICK SNACK!
CAFETERIA
BUT HE WAS STILL IN GRAVE DANGER!
IT'S EASY TO ANTICIPATE YOUR ACTIONS...
...FOR A STUDENT OF PSYCHOLOGY LIKE ME!
TRULA TWYST!!
7

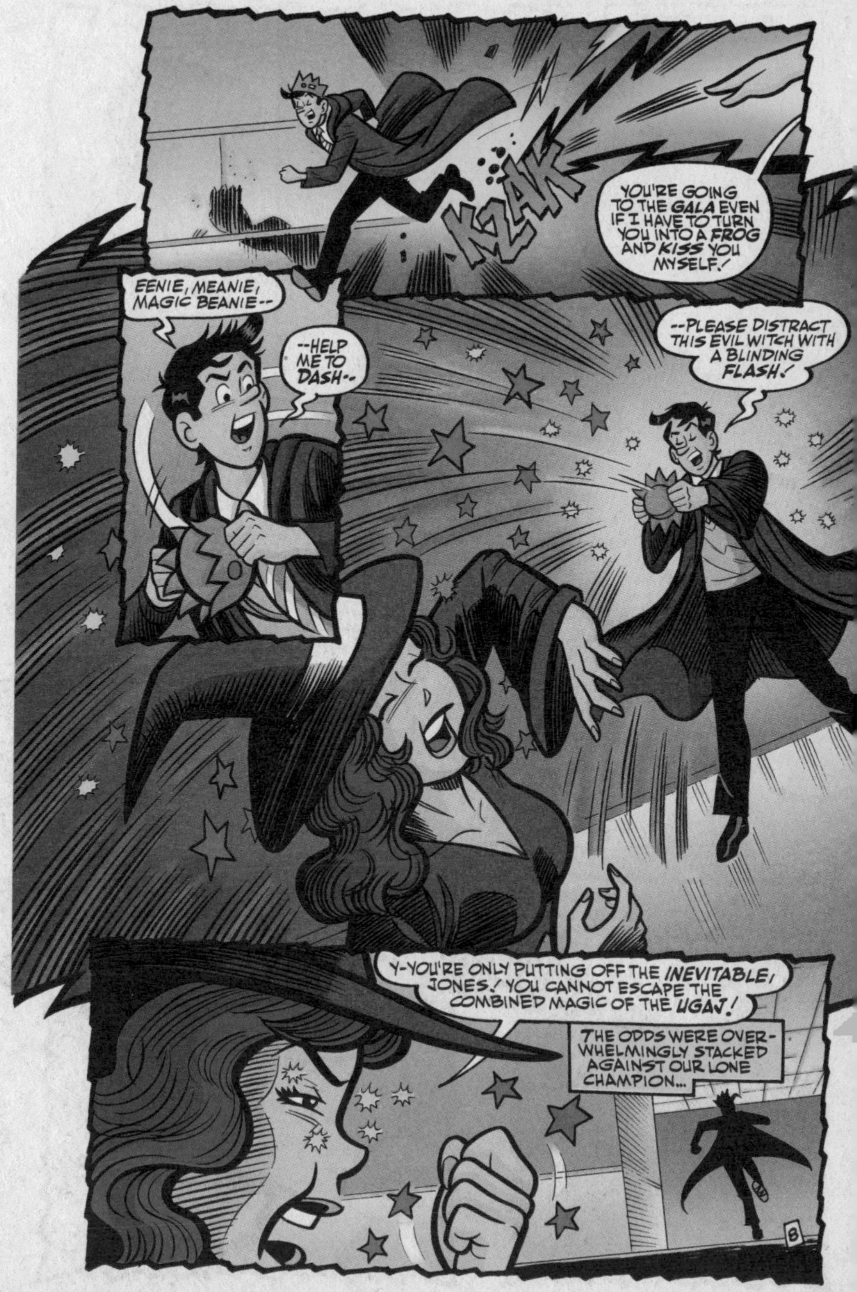

KZAK
YOU'RE GOING TO THE GALA EVEN IF I HAVE TO TURN YOU INTO A FROG AND KISS YOU MYSELF!
EENIE, MEANIE, MAGIC BEANIE--
--HELP ME TO DASH--
--PLEASE DISTRACT THIS EVIL WITCH WITH A BLINDING FLASH!
Y-YOU'RE ONLY PUTTING OFF THE INEVITABLE, JONES! YOU CANNOT ESCAPE THE COMBINED MAGIC OF THE UGAJ!
THE ODDS WERE OVERWHELMINGLY STACKED AGAINST OUR LONE CHAMPION...
8

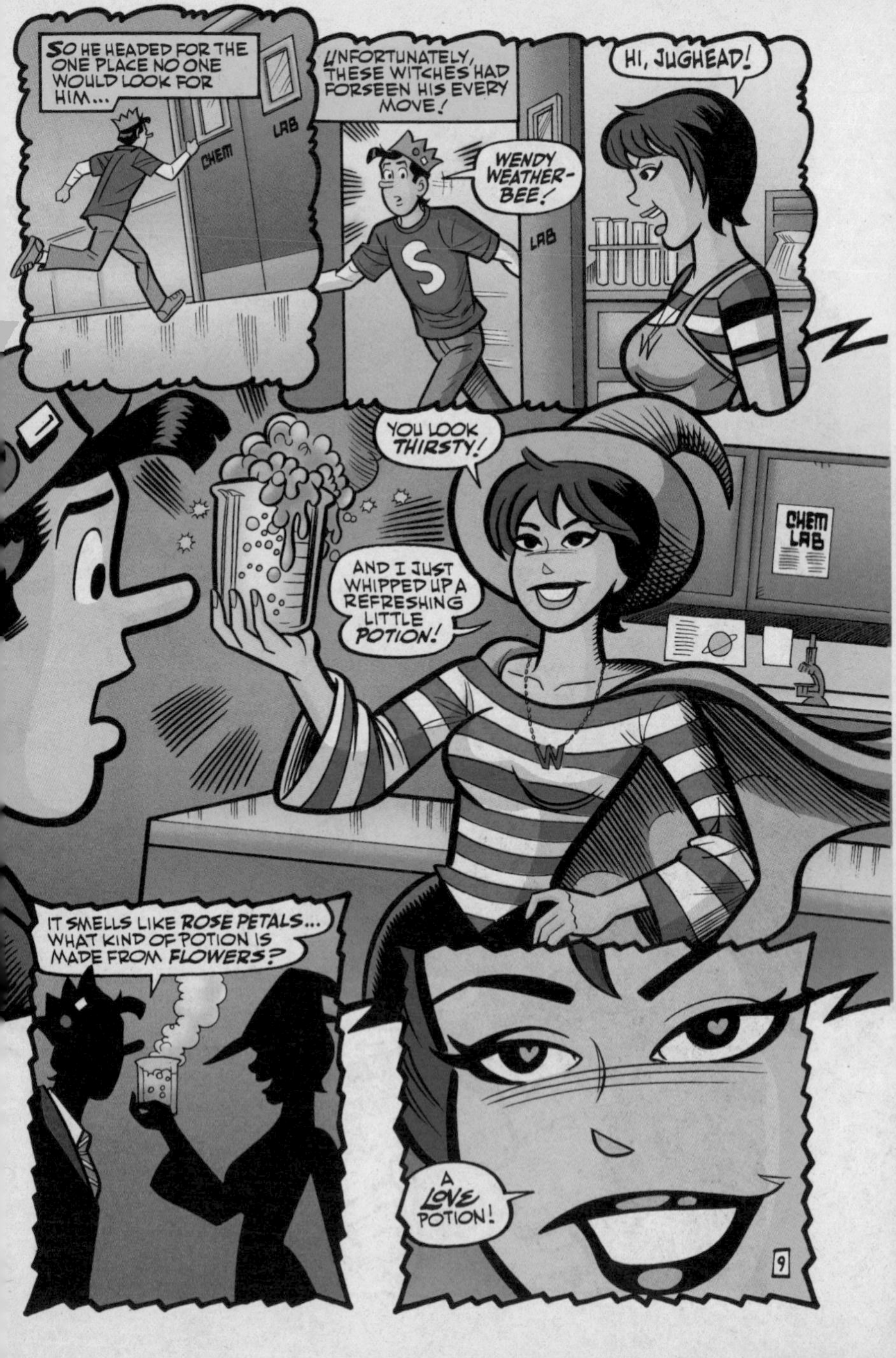
SO HE HEADED FOR THE ONE PLACE NO ONE WOULD LOOK FOR HIM...
CHEM
LAB
UNFORTUNATELY, THESE WITCHES HAD FORSEEN HIS EVERY MOVE!
WENDY WEATHER-BEE!
LAB
HI, JUGHEAD!
YOU LOOK THIRSTY!
AND I JUST WHIPPED UP A REFRESHING LITTLE POTION!
CHEM LAB
IT SMELLS LIKE ROSE PETALS... WHAT KIND OF POTION IS MADE FROM FLOWERS?
A LOVE POTION!
9

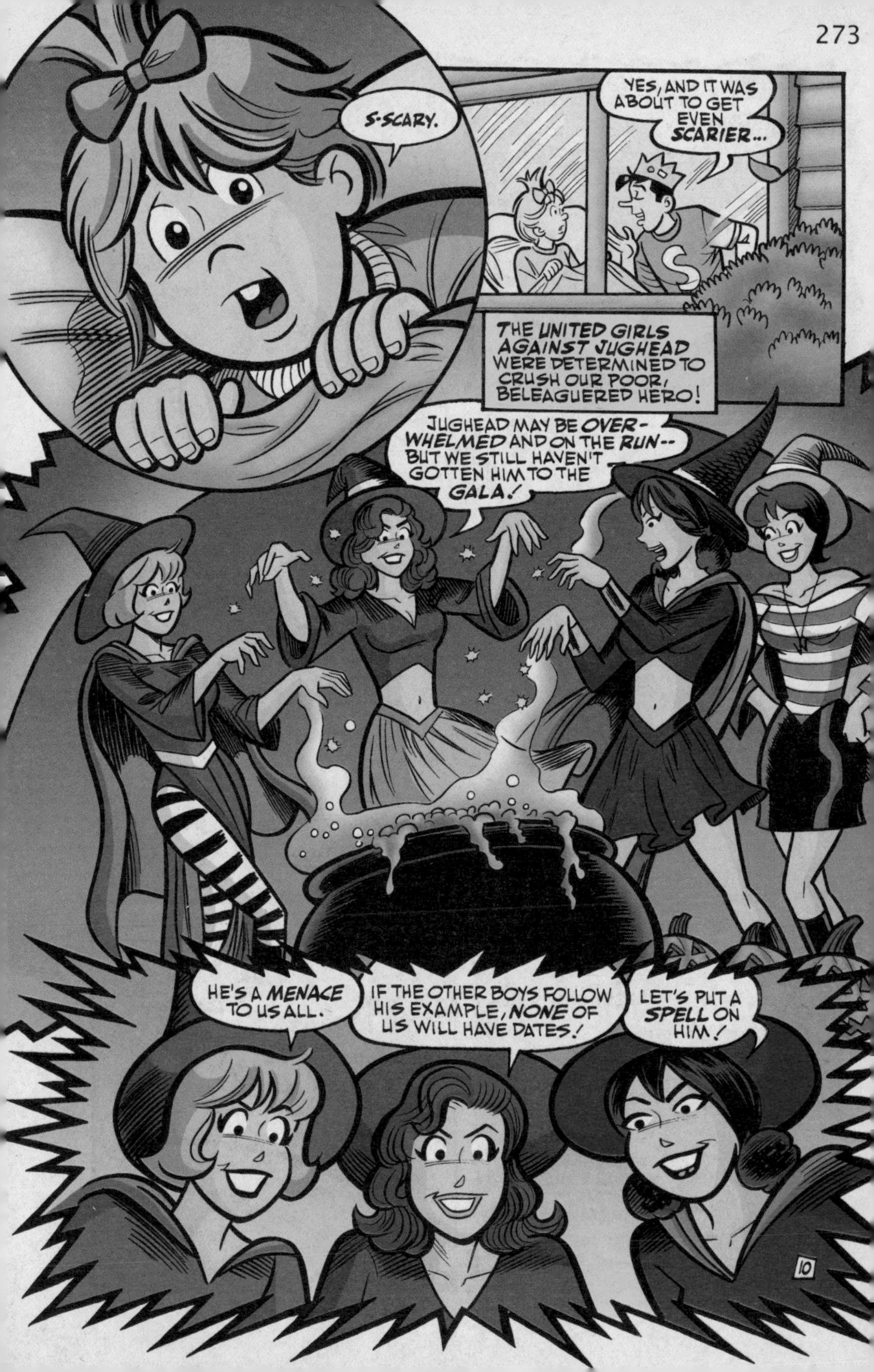
S-SCARY.
YES, AND IT WAS ABOUT TO GET EVEN SCARIER...
THE UNITED GIRLS AGAINST JUGHEAD WERE DETERMINED TO CRUSH OUR POOR, BELEAGUERED HERO!
JUGHEAD MAY BE OVER-WHELMED AND ON THE RUN-- BUT WE STILL HAVEN'T GOTTEN HIM TO THE GALA!
HE'S A MENACE TO US ALL.
IF THE OTHER BOYS FOLLOW HIS EXAMPLE, NONE OF US WILL HAVE DATES!
LET'S PUT A SPELL ON HIM!
10

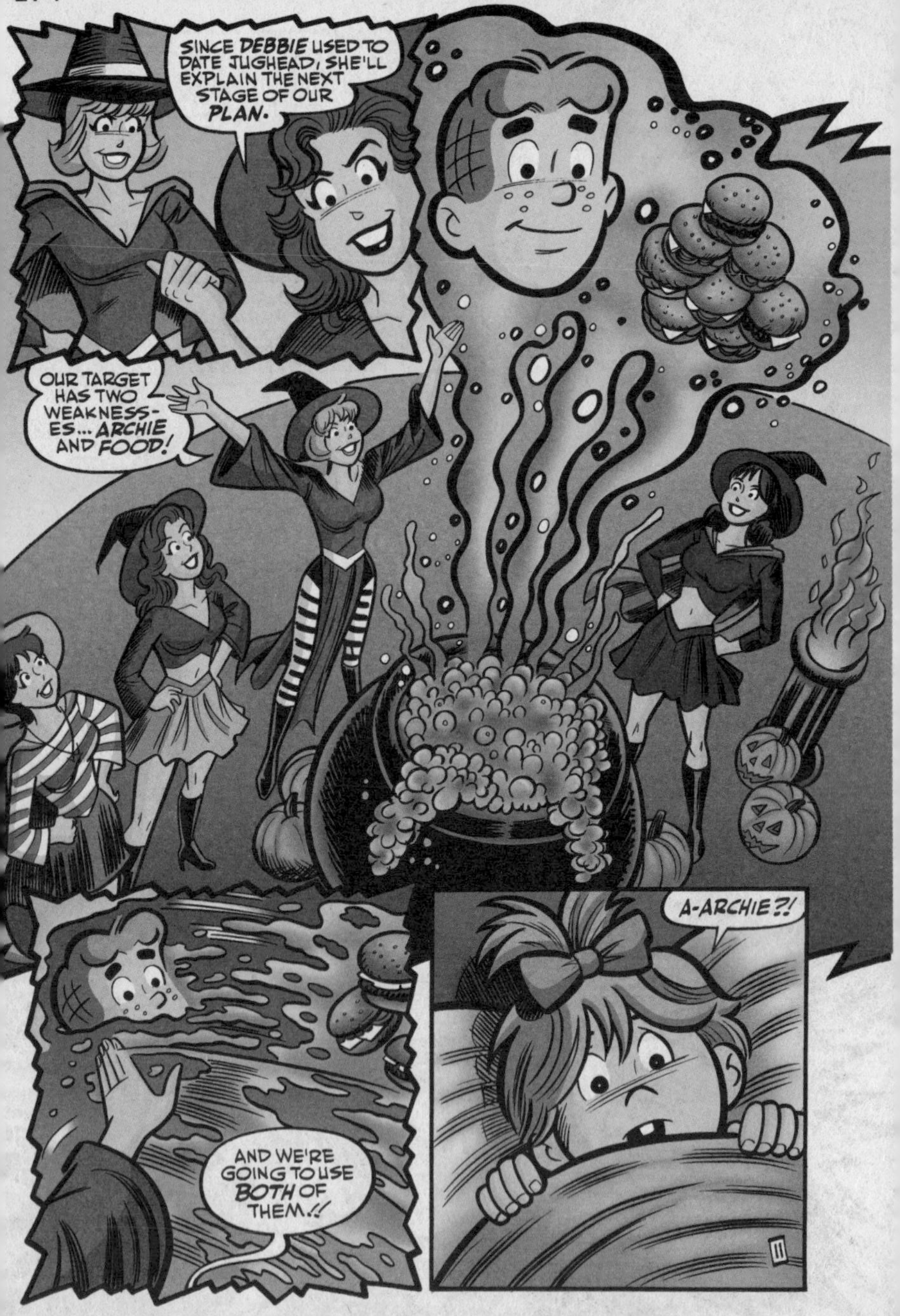
SINCE DEBBIE USED TO DATE JUGHEAD, SHE'LL EXPLAIN THE NEXT STAGE OF OUR PLAN.
OUR TARGET HAS TWO WEAKNESS-ES... ARCHIE AND FOOD!
AND WE'RE GOING TO USE BOTH OF THEM!!
A-ARCHIE?!

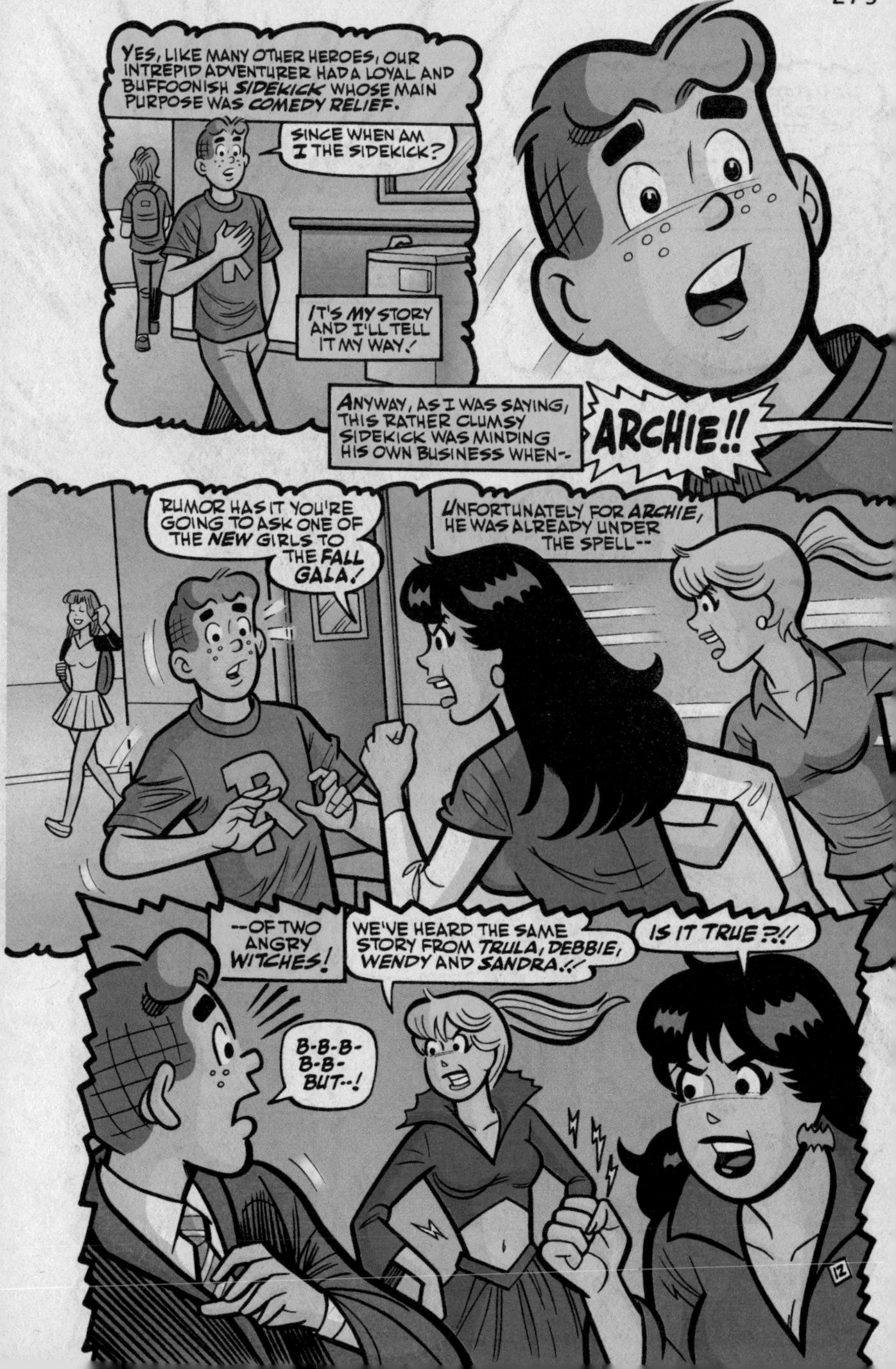
YES, LIKE MANY OTHER HEROES, OUR INTREPID ADVENTURER HAD A LOYAL AND BUFFOONISH SIDEKICK WHOSE MAIN PURPOSE WAS COMEDY RELIEF.
SINCE WHEN AM I THE SIDEKICK?
IT'S MY STORY AND I'LL TELL IT MY WAY!
ANYWAY, AS I WAS SAYING, THIS RATHER CLUMSY SIDEKICK WAS MINDING HIS OWN BUSINESS WHEN--
ARCHIE!!
RUMOR HAS IT YOU'RE GOING TO ASK ONE OF THE NEW GIRLS TO THE FALL GALA!
UNFORTUNATELY FOR ARCHIE, HE WAS ALREADY UNDER THE SPELL--
--OF TWO ANGRY WITCHES!
WE'VE HEARD THE SAME STORY FROM TRULA, DEBBIE, WENDY AND SANDRA!!
IS IT TRUE?!!
B-B-B-B-B-BUT--!
12

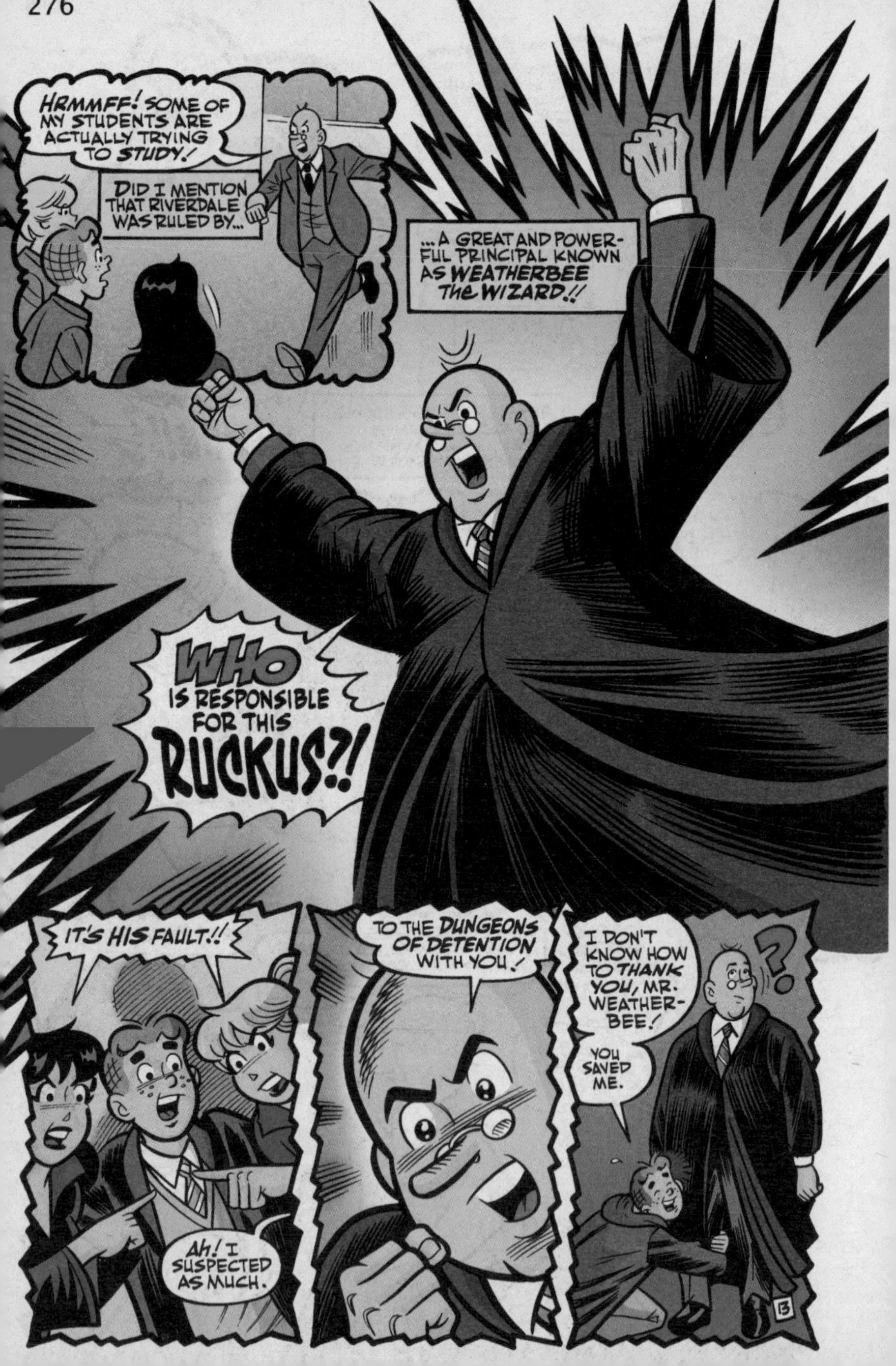
HRMMFF! SOME OF MY STUDENTS ARE ACTUALLY TRYING TO STUDY!
DID I MENTION THAT RIVERDALE WAS RULED BY...
...A GREAT AND POWERFUL PRINCIPAL KNOWN AS WEATHERBEE THE WIZARD!!
WHO IS RESPONSIBLE FOR THIS RUCKUS?!
IT'S HIS FAULT!!
AH! I SUSPECTED AS MUCH.
TO THE DUNGEONS OF DETENTION WITH YOU!
I DON'T KNOW HOW TO THANK YOU, MR. WEATHERBEE!
YOU SAVED ME.
?
13

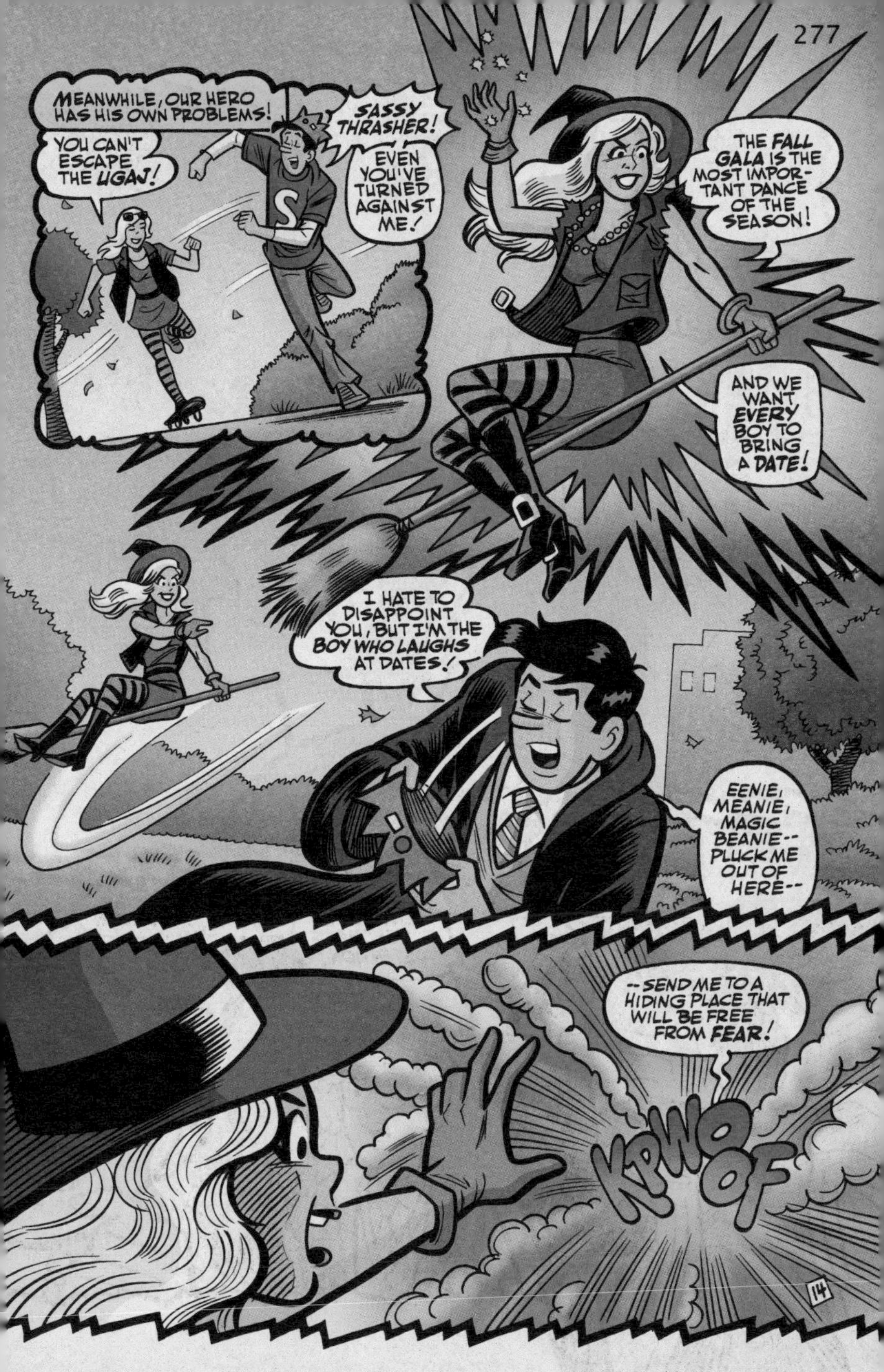
MEANWHILE, OUR HERO HAS HIS OWN PROBLEMS!
YOU CAN'T ESCAPE THE UGAJ!
SASSY THRASHER!
EVEN YOU'VE TURNED AGAINST ME!
THE FALL GALA IS THE MOST IMPORTANT DANCE OF THE SEASON!
AND WE WANT EVERY BOY TO BRING A DATE!
I HATE TO DISAPPOINT YOU, BUT I'M THE BOY WHO LAUGHS AT DATES!
EENIE, MEANIE, MAGIC BEANIE-- PLUCK ME OUT OF HERE--
--SEND ME TO A HIDING PLACE THAT WILL BE FREE FROM FEAR!
KPWOOF
14

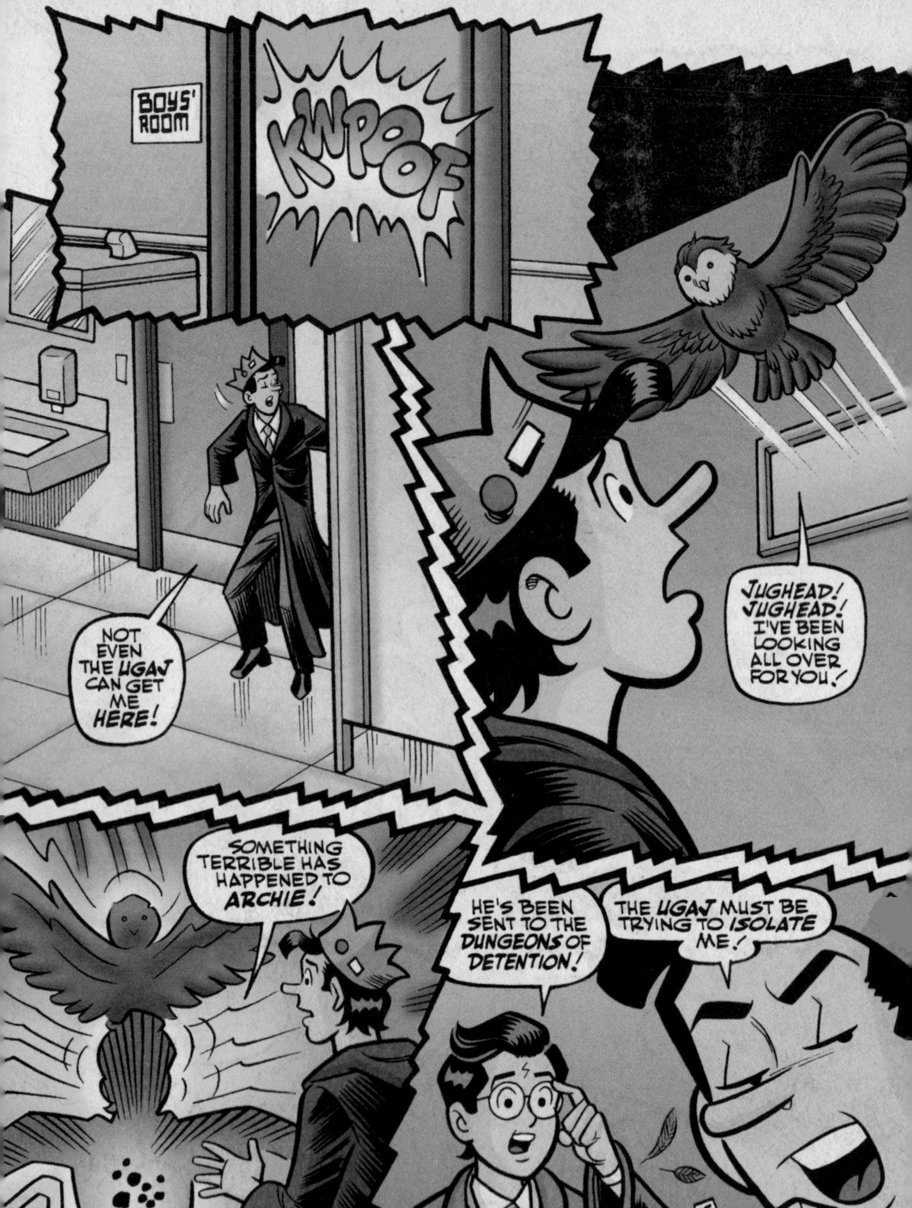
BOYS' ROOM
KWPOOF
NOT EVEN THE UGAJ CAN GET ME HERE!
JUGHEAD! JUGHEAD! I'VE BEEN LOOKING ALL OVER FOR YOU!
SOMETHING TERRIBLE HAS HAPPENED TO ARCHIE!
HE'S BEEN SENT TO THE DUNGEONS OF DETENTION!
THE UGAJ MUST BE TRYING TO ISOLATE ME!
15

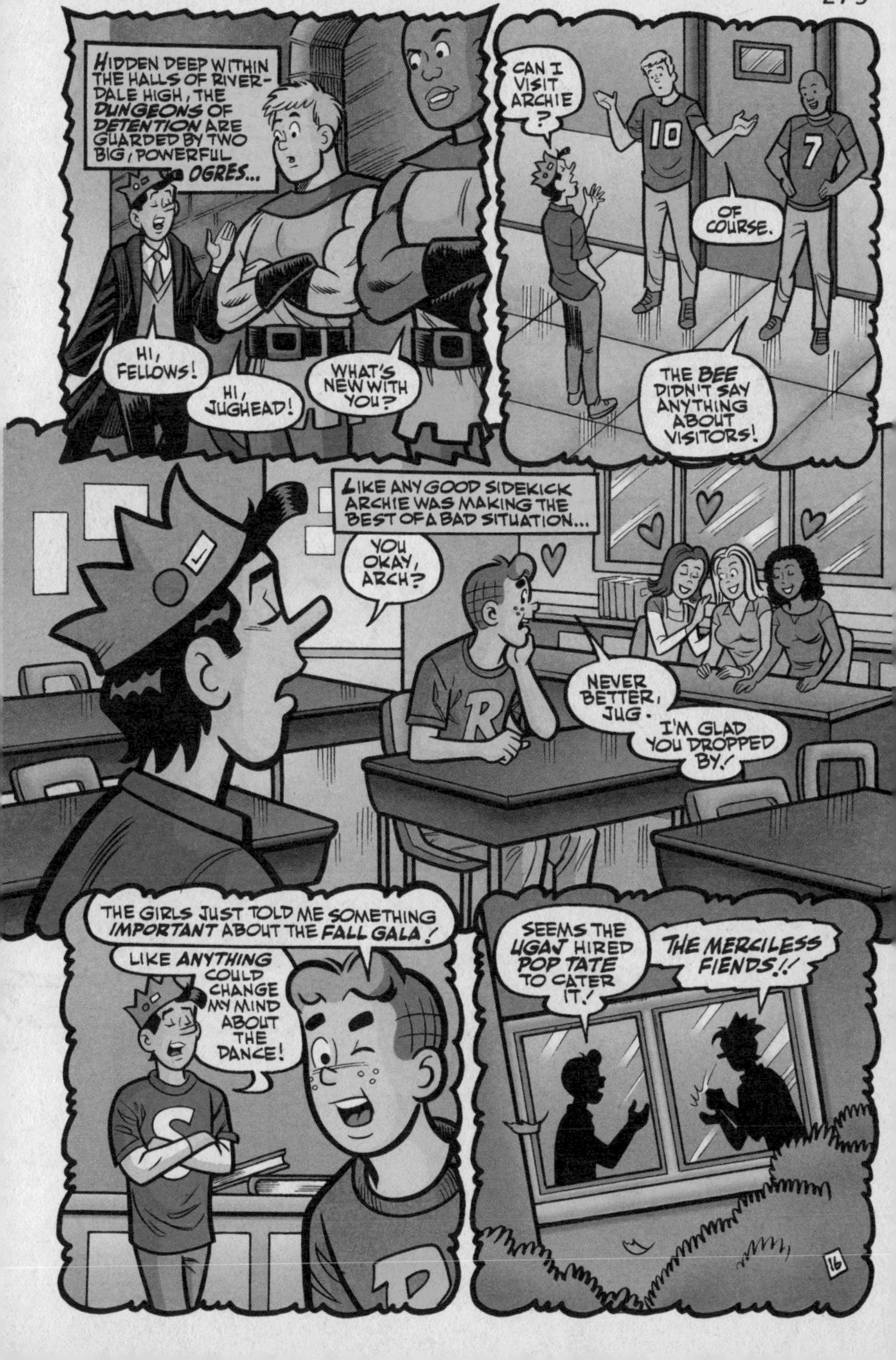
HIDDEN DEEP WITHIN THE HALLS OF RIVERDALE HIGH, THE DUNGEONS OF DETENTION ARE GUARDED BY TWO BIG, POWERFUL OGRES...
HI, FELLOWS!
HI, JUGHEAD!
WHAT'S NEW WITH YOU?
CAN I VISIT ARCHIE?
OF COURSE.
THE BEE DIDN'T SAY ANYTHING ABOUT VISITORS!
LIKE ANY GOOD SIDEKICK ARCHIE WAS MAKING THE BEST OF A BAD SITUATION...
YOU OKAY, ARCH?
NEVER BETTER, JUG.
I'M GLAD YOU DROPPED BY!
THE GIRLS JUST TOLD ME SOMETHING IMPORTANT ABOUT THE FALL GALA!
LIKE ANYTHING COULD CHANGE MY MIND ABOUT THE DANCE!
SEEMS THE UGAJ HIRED POP TATE TO CATER IT!
THE MERCILESS FIENDS!!
16

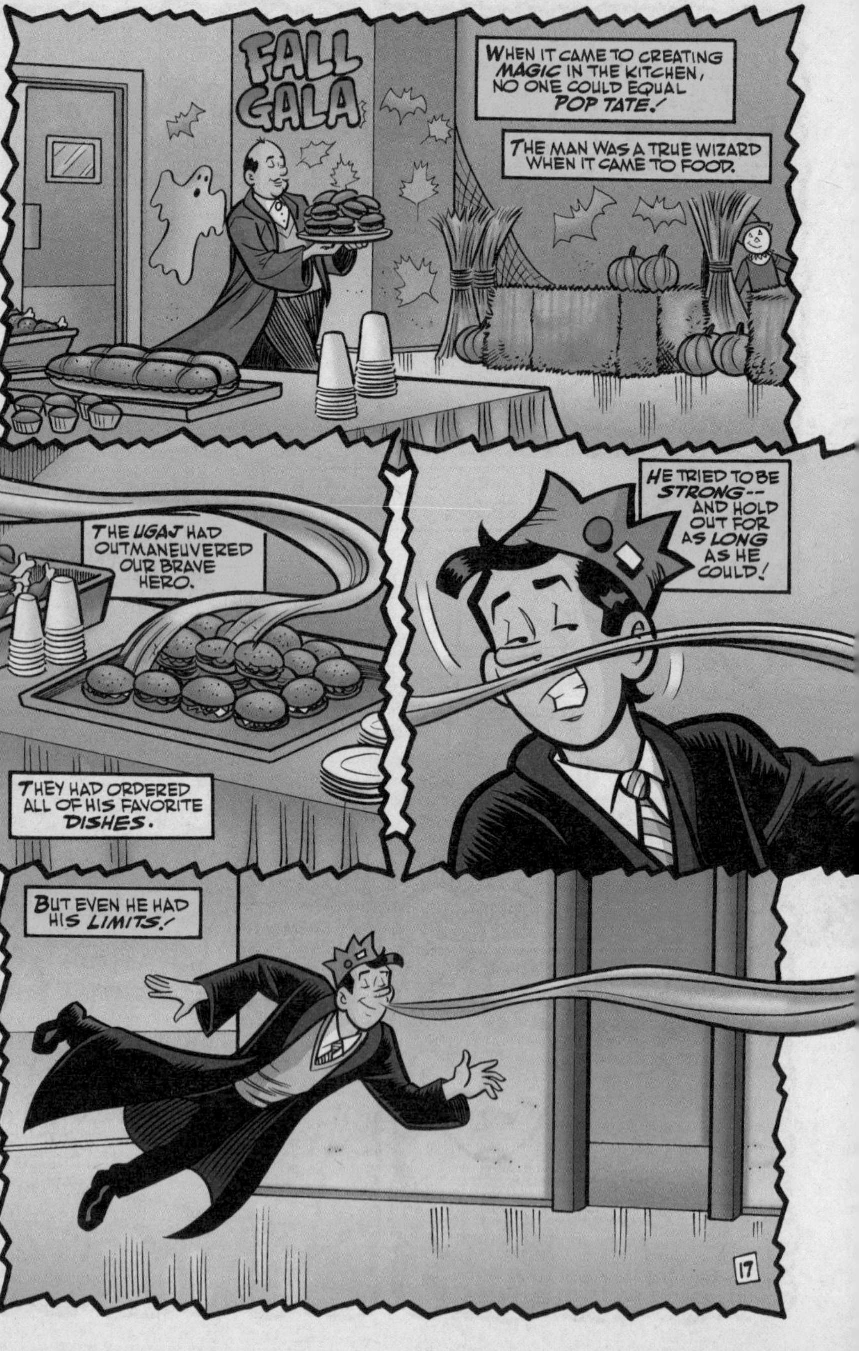
FALL GALA
WHEN IT CAME TO CREATING MAGIC IN THE KITCHEN, NO ONE COULD EQUAL POP TATE!
THE MAN WAS A TRUE WIZARD WHEN IT CAME TO FOOD.
THE UGAJ HAD OUTMANEUVERED OUR BRAVE HERO.
THEY HAD ORDERED ALL OF HIS FAVORITE DISHES.
HE TRIED TO BE STRONG-- AND HOLD OUT FOR AS LONG AS HE COULD!
BUT EVEN HE HAD HIS LIMITS!
17

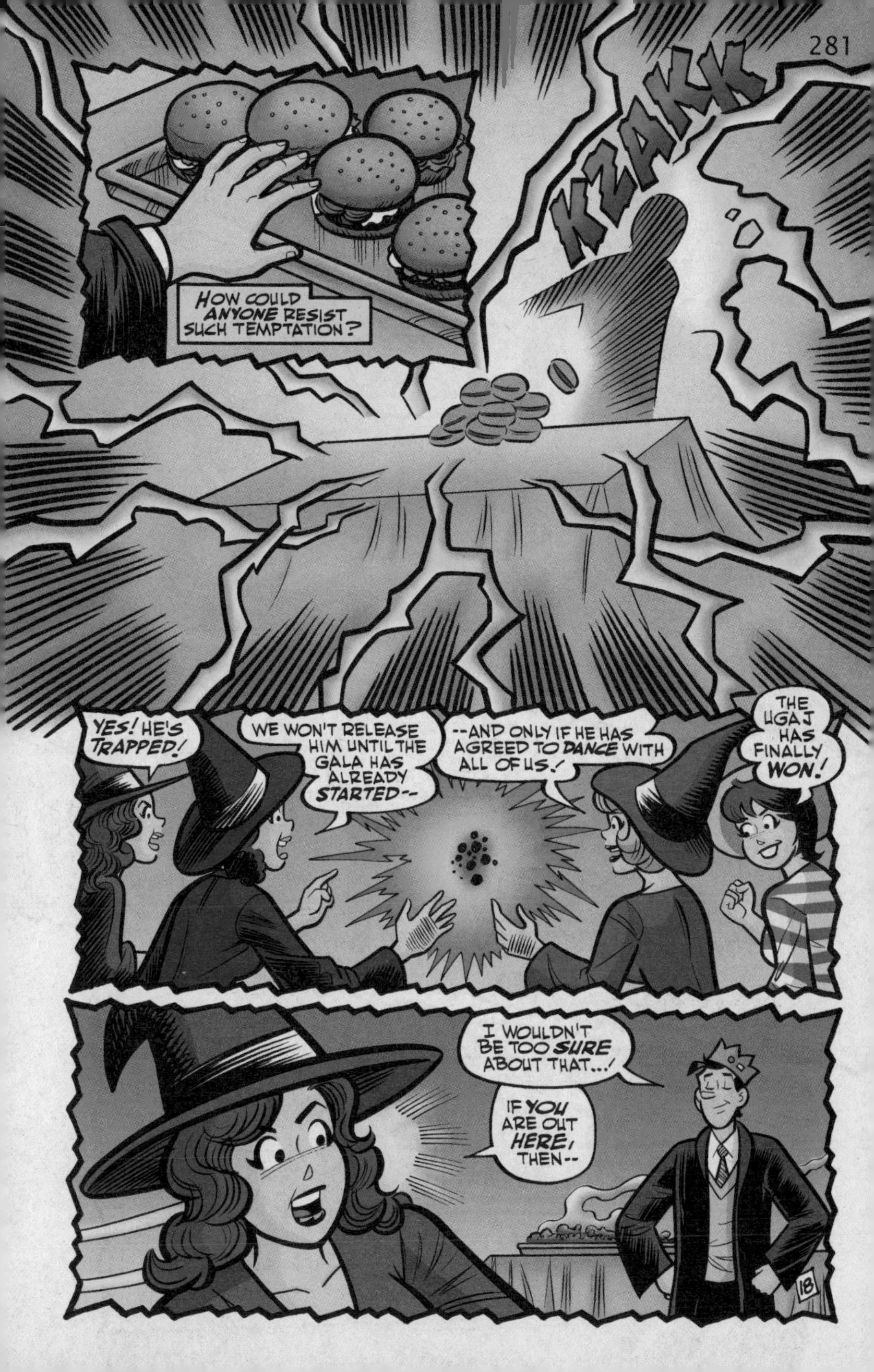

HOW COULD ANYONE RESIST SUCH TEMPTATION?
KZAKK
YES! HE'S TRAPPED!
WE WON'T RELEASE HIM UNTIL THE GALA HAS ALREADY STARTED--
--AND ONLY IF HE HAS AGREED TO DANCE WITH ALL OF US.!
THE UGAJ HAS FINALLY WON!
I WOULDN'T BE TOO SURE ABOUT THAT...!
IF YOU ARE OUT HERE, THEN--
18

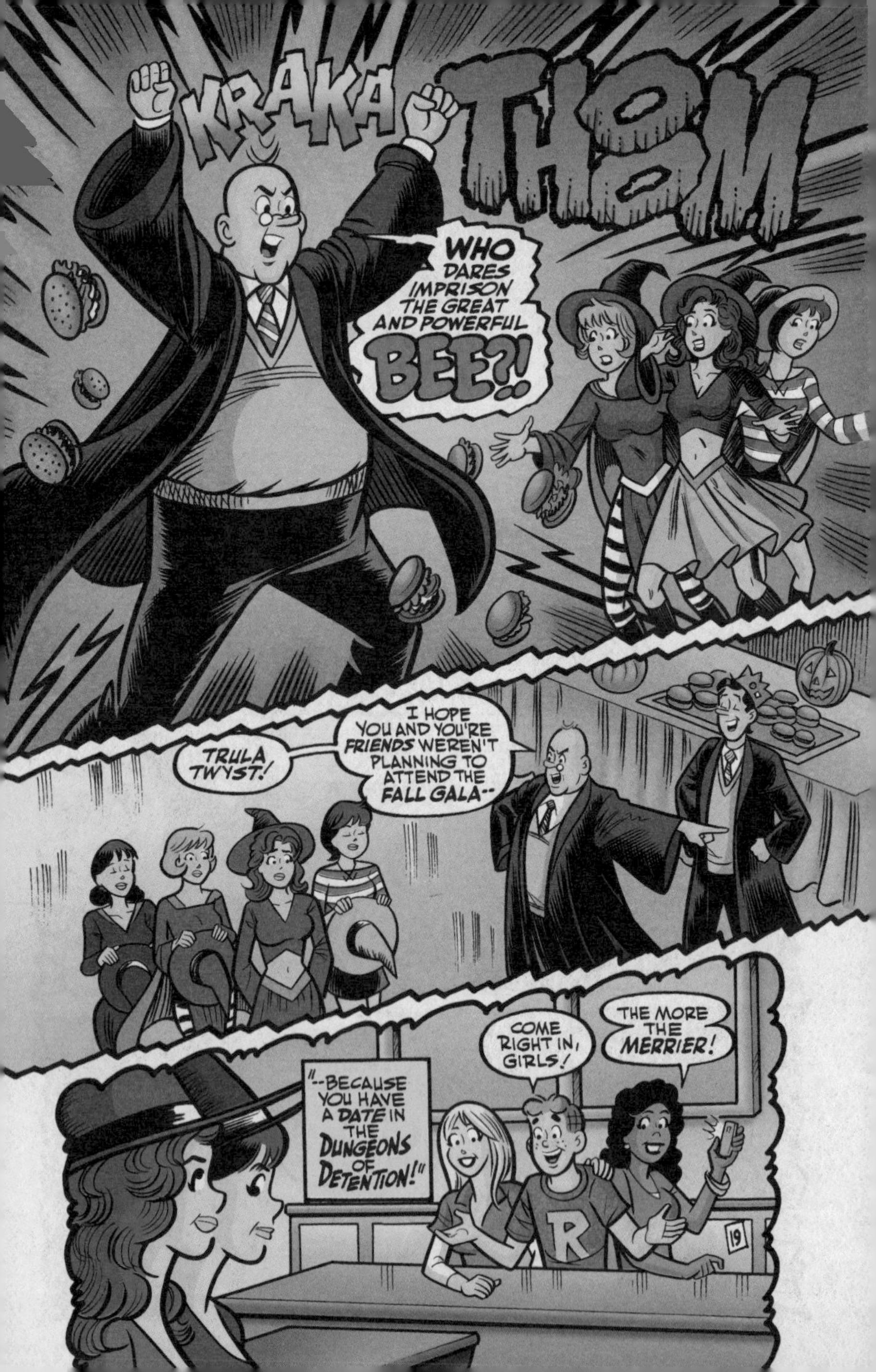
KRAKA THOOM
WHO DARES IMPRISON THE GREAT AND POWERFUL BEE?!
TRULA TWYST!
I HOPE YOU AND YOU'RE FRIENDS WEREN'T PLANNING TO ATTEND THE FALL GALA--
"--BECAUSE YOU HAVE A DATE IN THE DUNGEONS OF DETENTION!"
COME RIGHT IN, GIRLS!
THE MORE THE MERRIER!
19

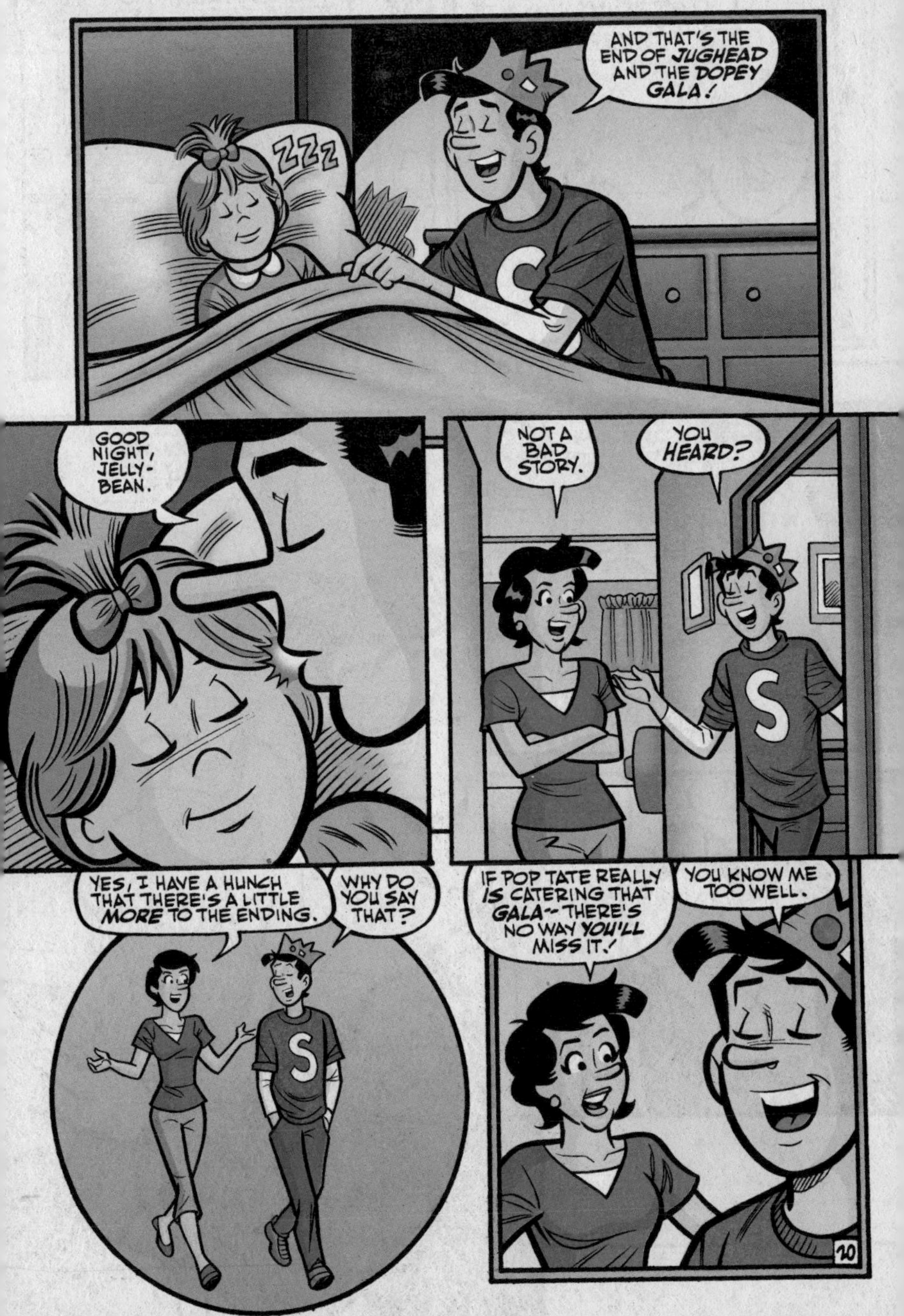
AND THAT'S THE END OF JUGHEAD AND THE DOPEY GALA!
ZZZ
GOOD NIGHT, JELLY-BEAN.
NOT A BAD STORY.
YOU HEARD?
YES, I HAVE A HUNCH THAT THERE'S A LITTLE MORE TO THE ENDING.
WHY DO YOU SAY THAT?
IF POP TATE REALLY IS CATERING THAT GALA-- THERE'S NO WAY YOU'LL MISS IT.!
YOU KNOW ME TOO WELL.
20

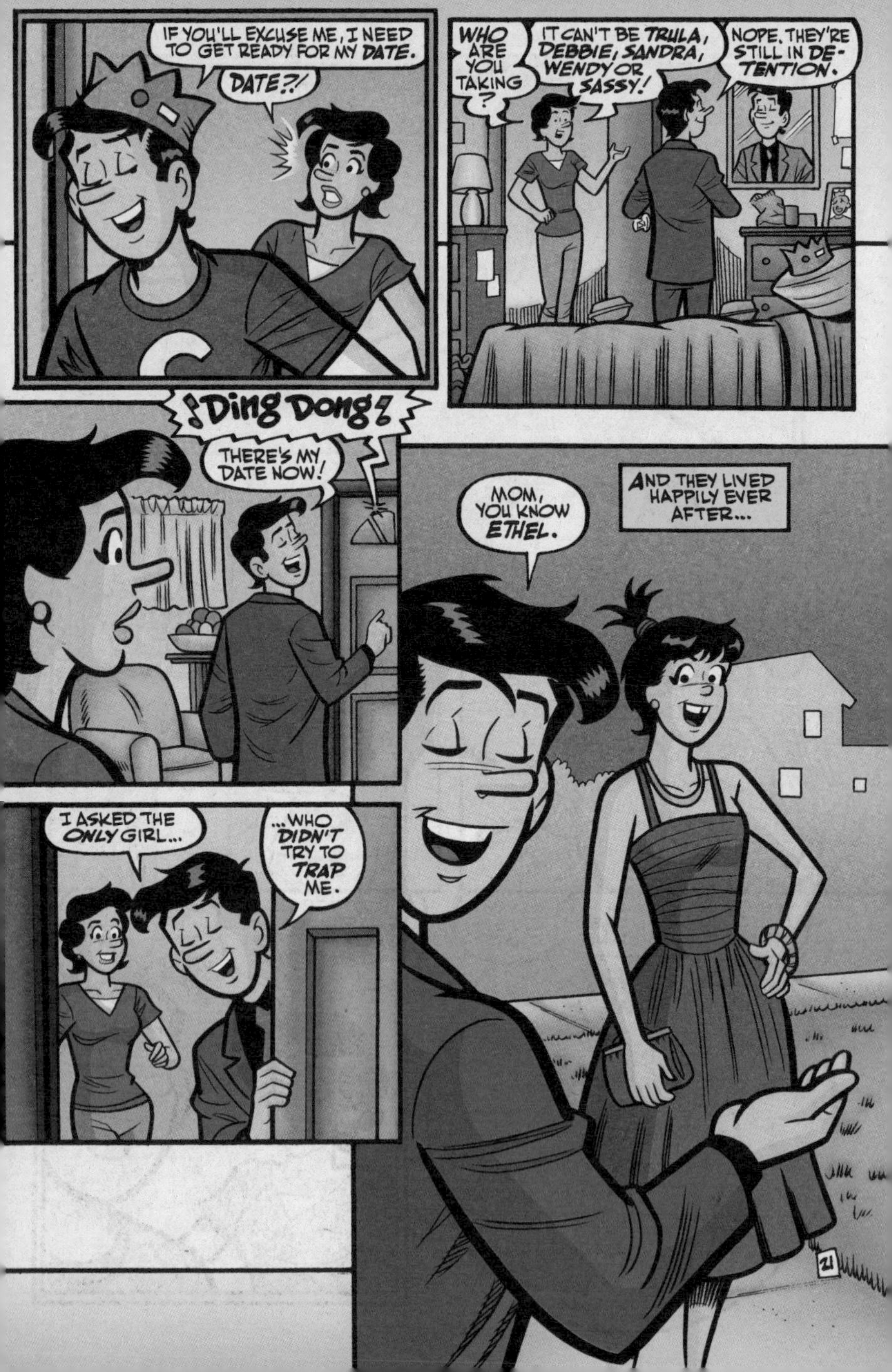
IF YOU'LL EXCUSE ME, I NEED TO GET READY FOR MY DATE.
DATE?!
WHO ARE YOU TAKING?
IT CAN'T BE TRULA, DEBBIE, SANDRA, WENDY OR SASSY!
NOPE. THEY'RE STILL IN DETENTION.
Ding Dong
THERE'S MY DATE NOW!
I ASKED THE ONLY GIRL...
...WHO DIDN'T TRY TO TRAP ME.
MOM, YOU KNOW ETHEL.
AND THEY LIVED HAPPILY EVER AFTER...
21

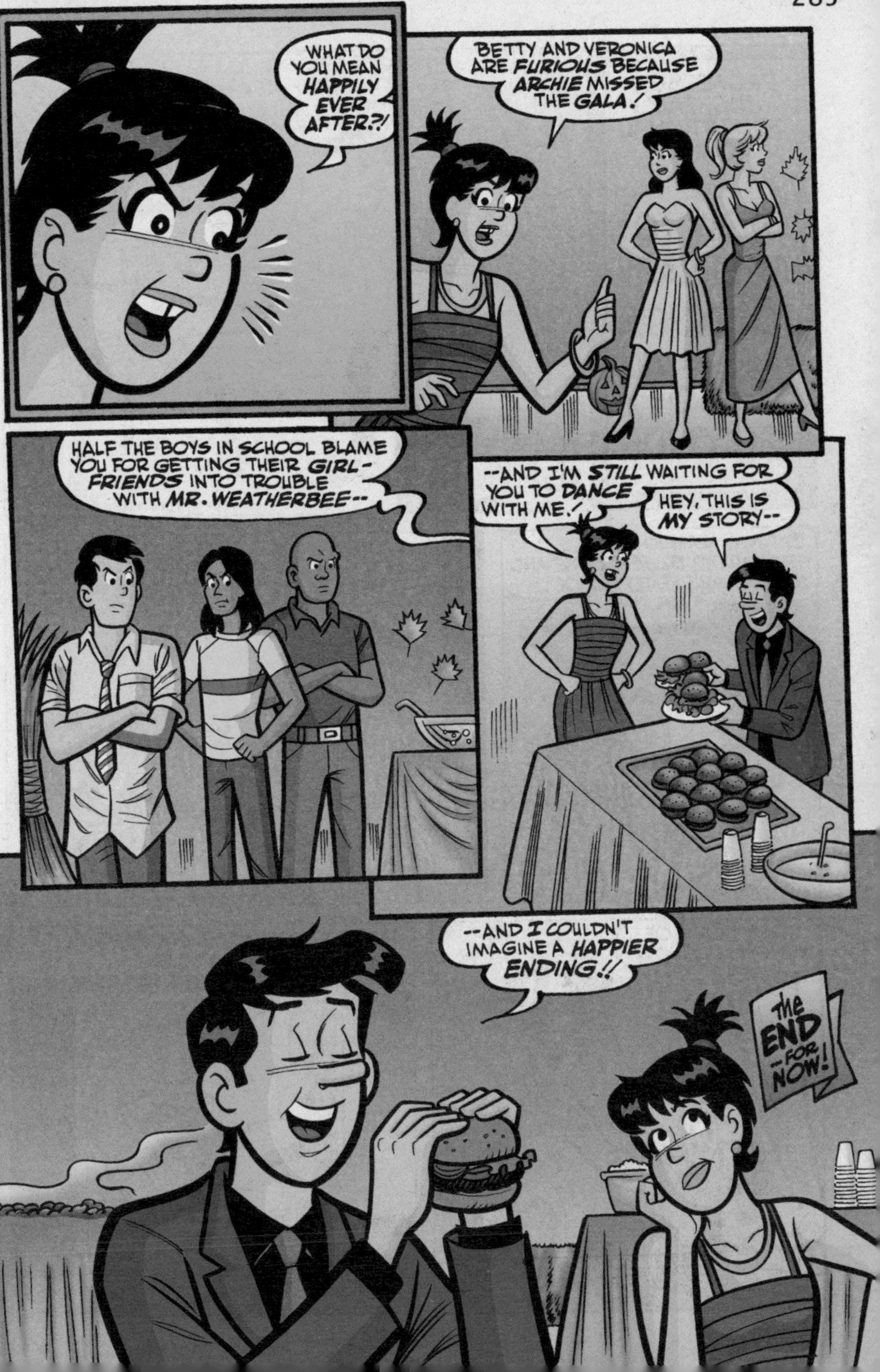
WHAT DO YOU MEAN HAPPILY EVER AFTER?!
BETTY AND VERONICA ARE FURIOUS BECAUSE ARCHIE MISSED THE GALA!
HALF THE BOYS IN SCHOOL BLAME YOU FOR GETTING THEIR GIRL-FRIENDS INTO TROUBLE WITH MR. WEATHERBEE--
--AND I'M STILL WAITING FOR YOU TO DANCE WITH ME!
HEY, THIS IS MY STORY--
--AND I COULDN'T IMAGINE A HAPPIER ENDING!!
THE END --FOR NOW!

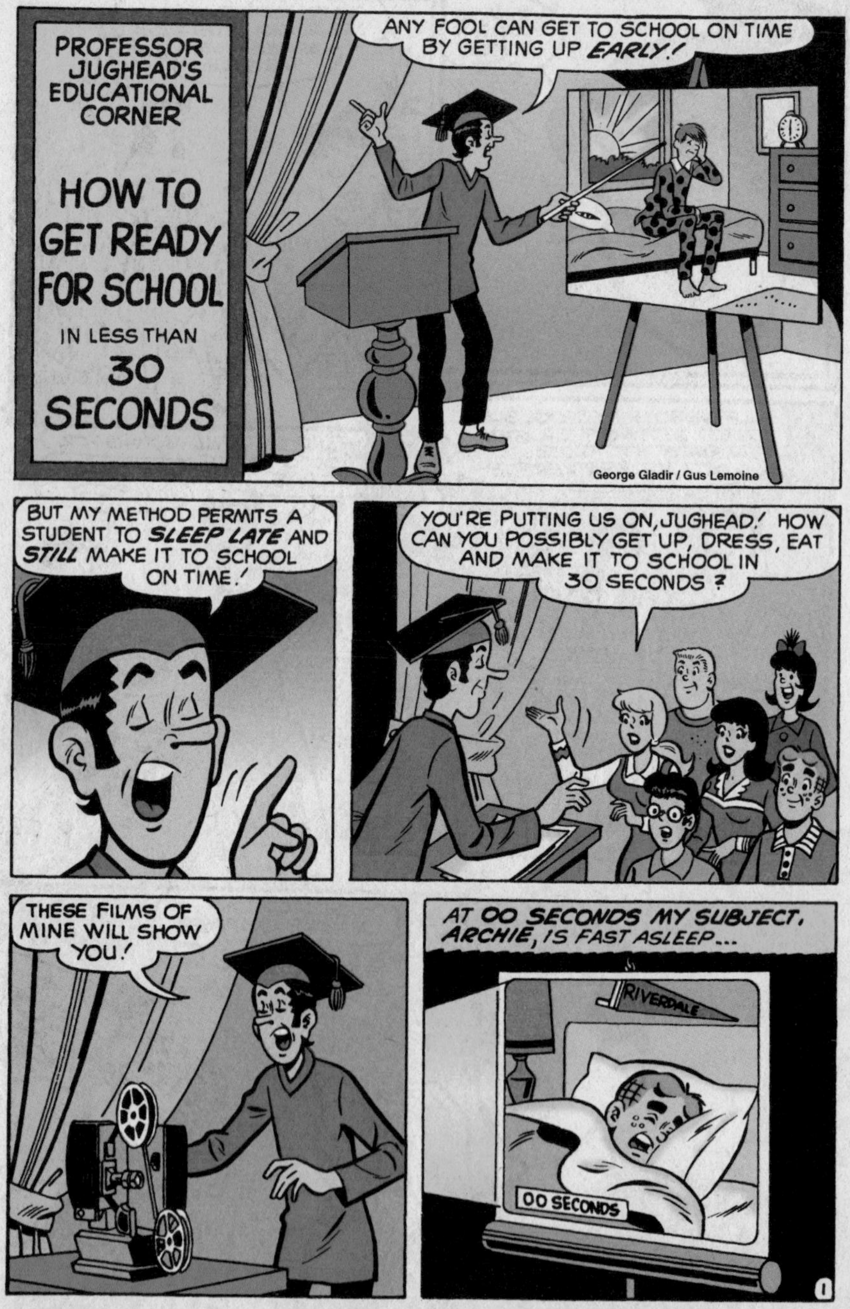
PROFESSOR JUGHEAD'S EDUCATIONAL CORNER
HOW TO GET READY FOR SCHOOL IN LESS THAN 30 SECONDS
ANY FOOL CAN GET TO SCHOOL ON TIME BY GETTING UP EARLY!
George Gladir / Gus Lemoine
BUT MY METHOD PERMITS A STUDENT TO SLEEP LATE AND STILL MAKE IT TO SCHOOL ON TIME!
YOU'RE PUTTING US ON, JUGHEAD! HOW CAN YOU POSSIBLY GET UP, DRESS, EAT AND MAKE IT TO SCHOOL IN 30 SECONDS?
THESE FILMS OF MINE WILL SHOW YOU!
AT 00 SECONDS MY SUBJECT, ARCHIE, IS FAST ASLEEP...
RIVERDALE
00 SECONDS
1

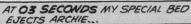

AT 03 SECONDS MY SPECIAL BED EJECTS ARCHIE...
SPRONG
...INTO HIS TROUSERS AND SHOES...
05 SECONDS
HE THEN HEADS FOR AN OPEN WINDOW, GRABBING HIS BOOKS AND BREAK - FAST TRAY EN ROUTE...
09 SECONDS
HE FINISHES HIS BREAKFAST WHILE SLIDING DOWN...
12 SECONDS
...TO AN AWAITING SKATEBOARD...
15 SECONDS
...THAT TAKES HIM TO THE SCHOOL BUS..
SCHOOL
SCHOOL BUS
23 SECONDS
2

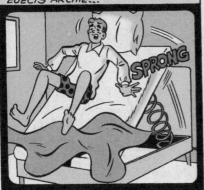

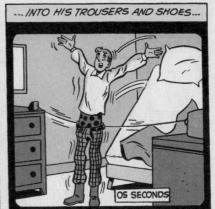

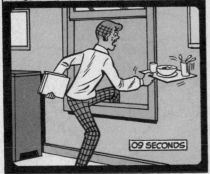

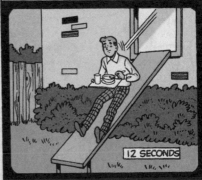

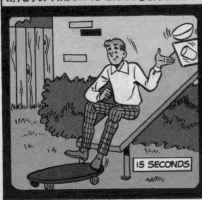

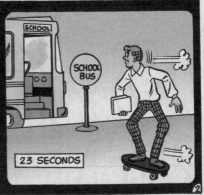

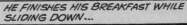

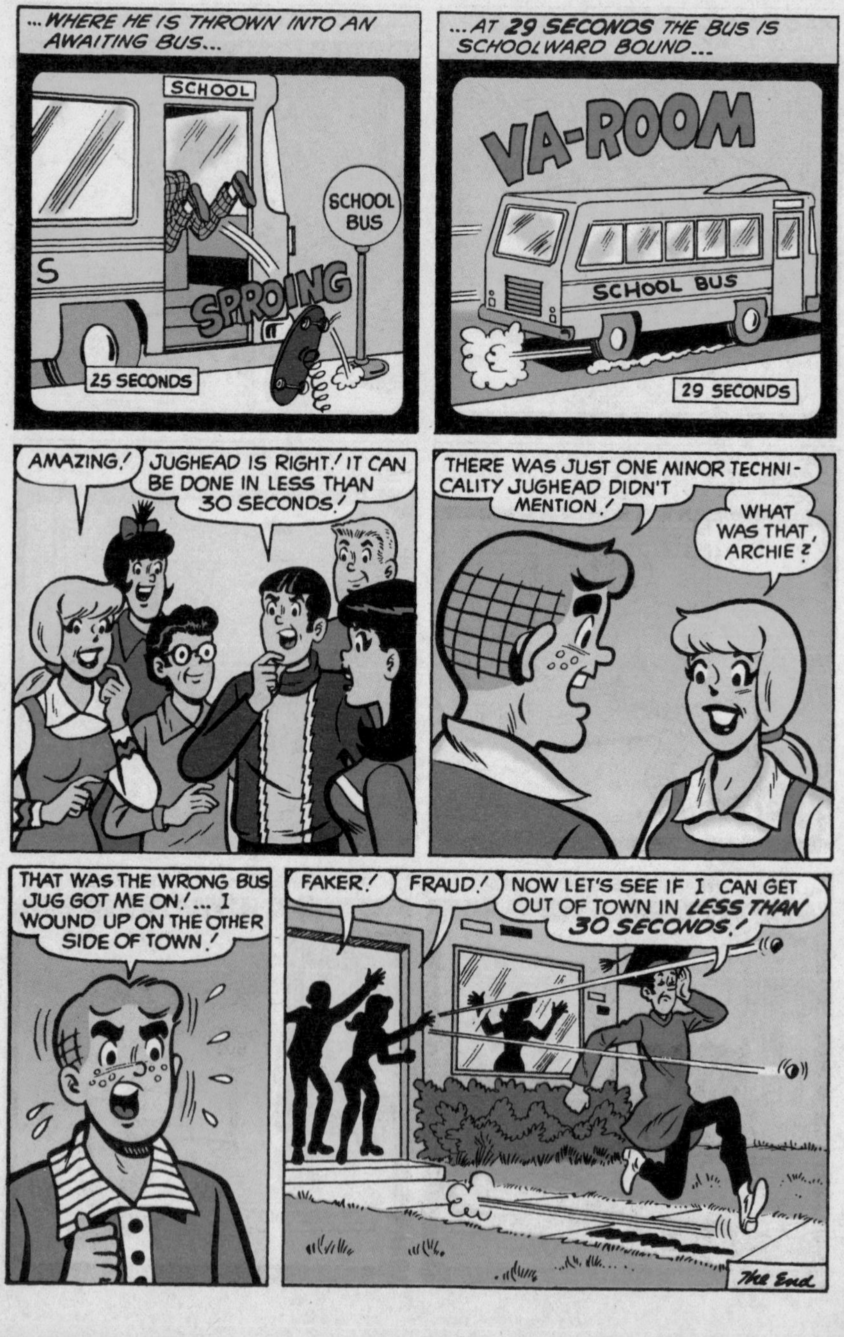
...WHERE HE IS THROWN INTO AN AWAITING BUS...
SCHOOL
SCHOOL BUS
S
SPROING
25 SECONDS
...AT 29 SECONDS THE BUS IS SCHOOLWARD BOUND...
VA-ROOM
SCHOOL BUS
29 SECONDS
AMAZING!
JUGHEAD IS RIGHT! IT CAN BE DONE IN LESS THAN 30 SECONDS!
THERE WAS JUST ONE MINOR TECHNICALITY JUGHEAD DIDN'T MENTION!
WHAT WAS THAT, ARCHIE?
THAT WAS THE WRONG BUS JUG GOT ME ON!... I WOUND UP ON THE OTHER SIDE OF TOWN!
FAKER!
FRAUD!
NOW LET'S SEE IF I CAN GET OUT OF TOWN IN LESS THAN 30 SECONDS!
The End

The Prom
Archie #146, June 1964
Frank Doyle and Harry Lucey

A night of fun and romance at the Riverdale High School Prom is threatened when Archie's jalopy gets a flat. Determined to get Veronica to the dance, Archie enlists the help of some creative transportation options that will get the pair to their date in offbeat style.

The Quitter
Archie at Riverdale High #18, August 1974
Frank Doyle, Stan Goldberg, Jon D'Agostino, Bill Yoshida and Barry Grossman

It's no runs, no hits, and all errors when Riverdale High's baseball team strikes out big time on the ball field. Can the team stick it out, or will they have to hang up their mitts for good? Can Coach Kleats juggle both his job and a losing record? Time to put on your rally cap and root for the home team!

Bonus: **Newspaper Strip, March 4, 2001 Craig Boldman and Henry Scarpelli**

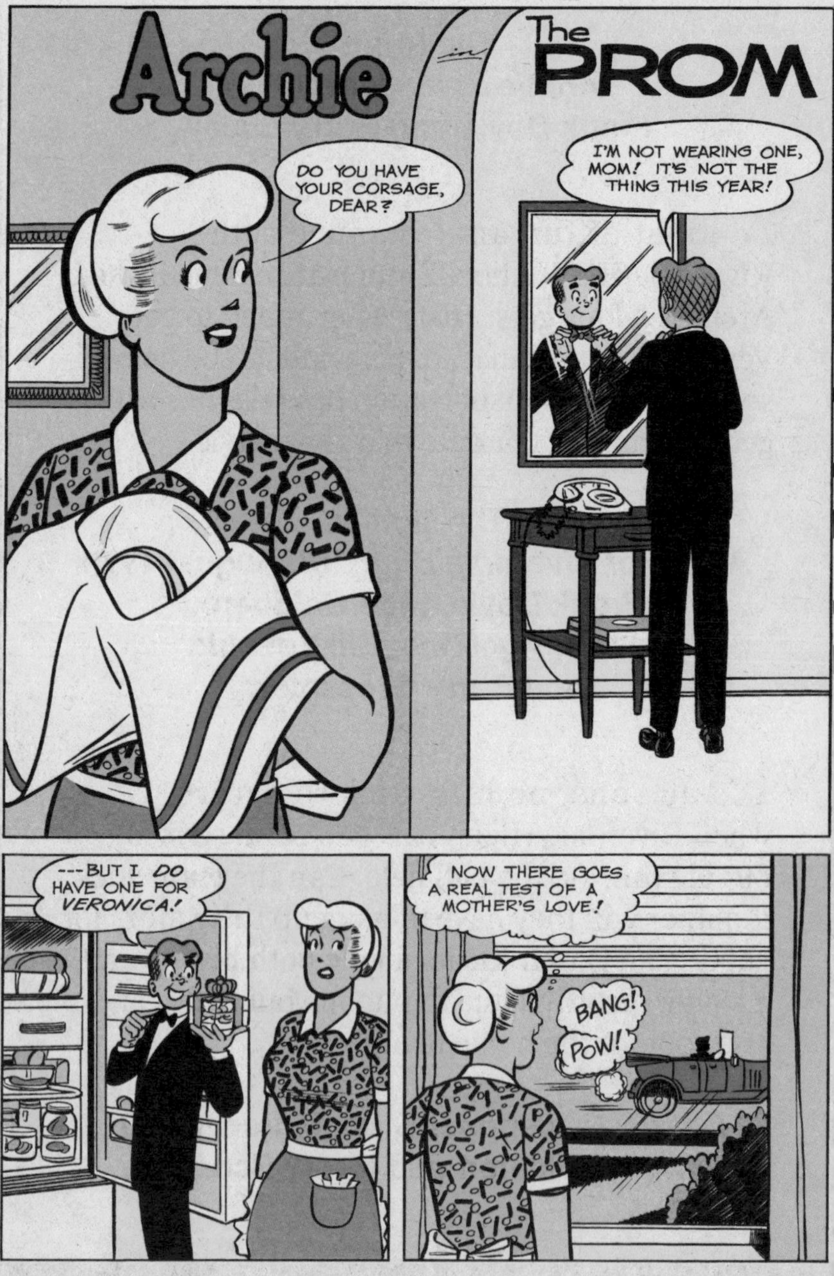
Archie in The PROM
DO YOU HAVE YOUR CORSAGE, DEAR?
I'M NOT WEARING ONE, MOM! IT'S NOT THE THING THIS YEAR!
---BUT I DO HAVE ONE FOR VERONICA!
NOW THERE GOES A REAL TEST OF A MOTHER'S LOVE!
BANG!
POW!

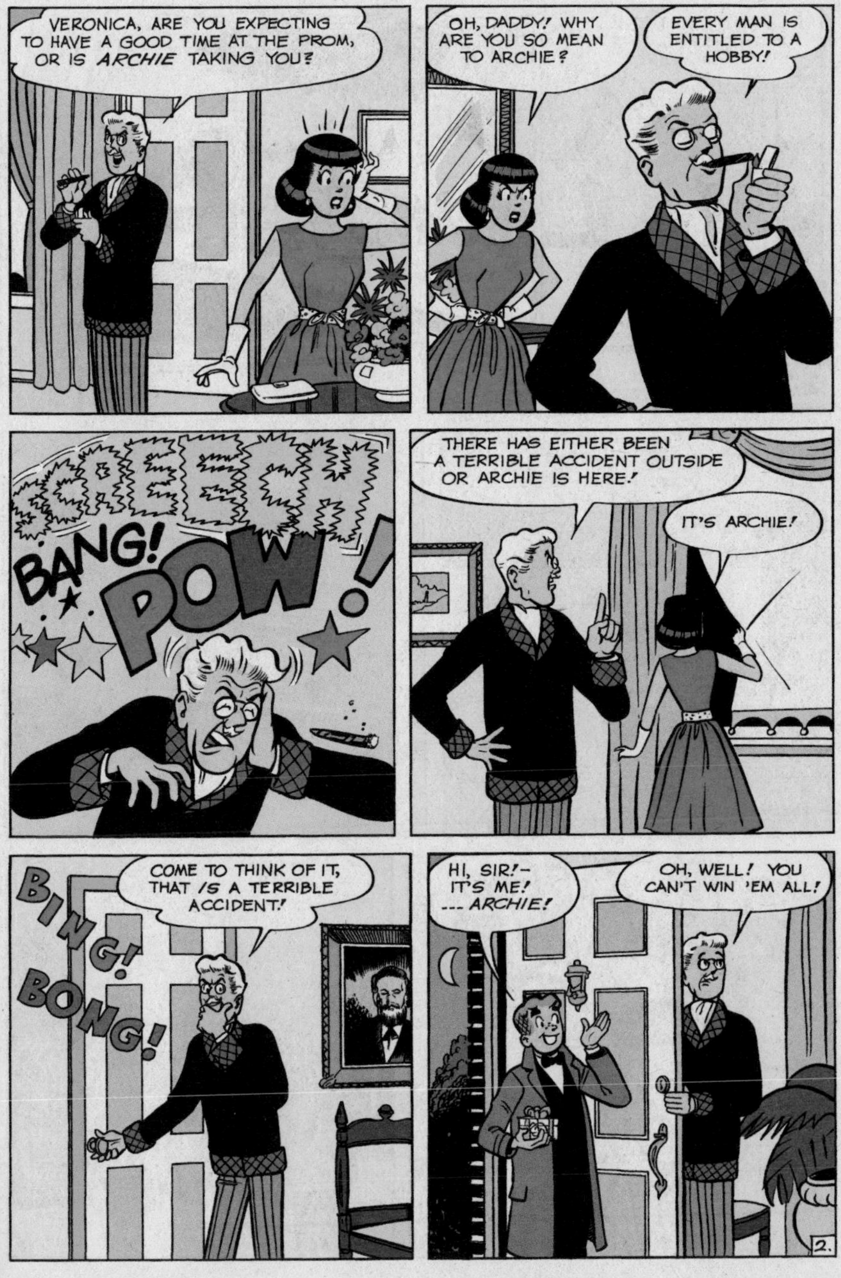
VERONICA, ARE YOU EXPECTING TO HAVE A GOOD TIME AT THE PROM, OR IS ARCHIE TAKING YOU?
OH, DADDY! WHY ARE YOU SO MEAN TO ARCHIE?
EVERY MAN IS ENTITLED TO A HOBBY!
SCREECH!
BANG!
POW!
THERE HAS EITHER BEEN A TERRIBLE ACCIDENT OUTSIDE OR ARCHIE IS HERE!
IT'S ARCHIE!
BING! BONG!
COME TO THINK OF IT, THAT IS A TERRIBLE ACCIDENT!
HI, SIR!— IT'S ME! --- ARCHIE!
OH, WELL! YOU CAN'T WIN 'EM ALL!
2.

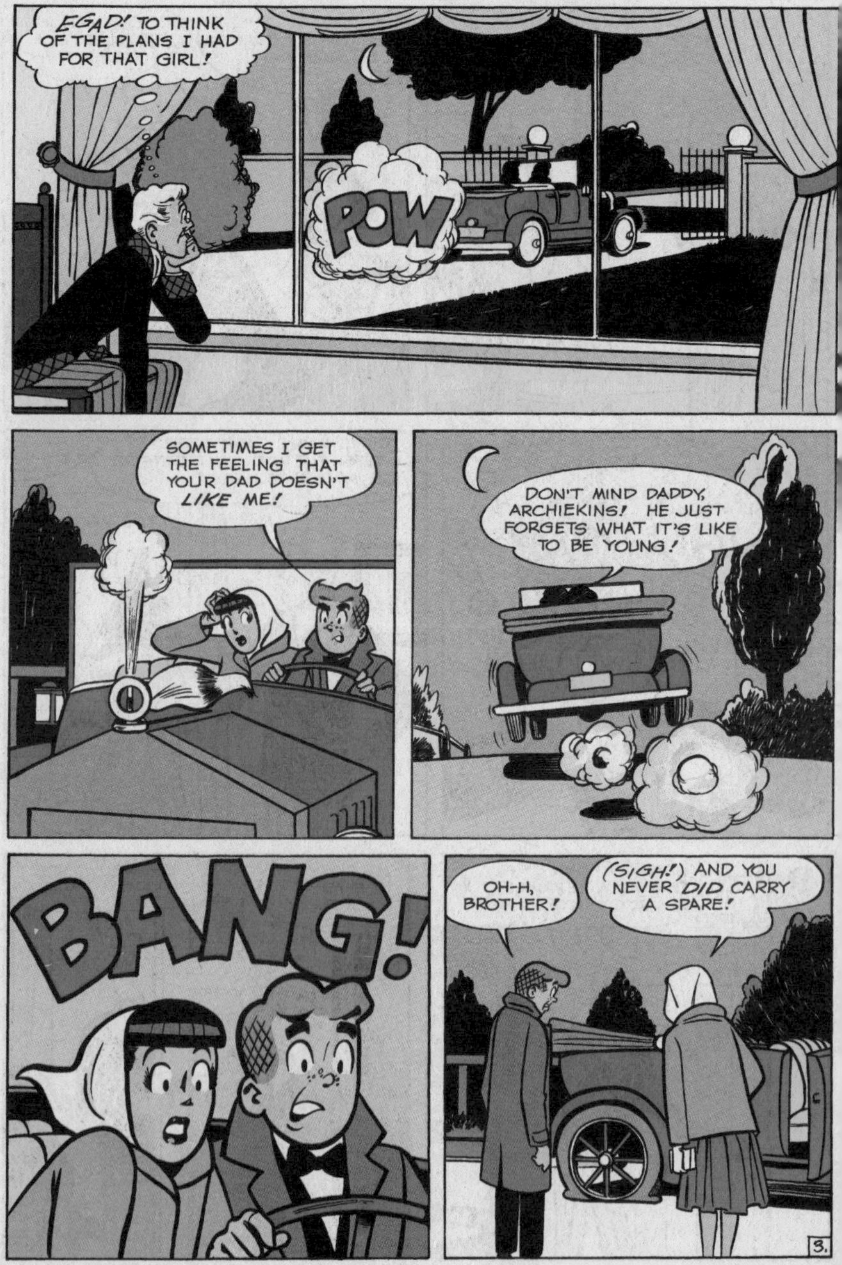
EGAD! TO THINK OF THE PLANS I HAD FOR THAT GIRL!
POW
SOMETIMES I GET THE FEELING THAT YOUR DAD DOESN'T LIKE ME!
DON'T MIND DADDY, ARCHIEKINS! HE JUST FORGETS WHAT IT'S LIKE TO BE YOUNG!
BANG!
OH-H, BROTHER!
(SIGH!) AND YOU NEVER DID CARRY A SPARE!
3.

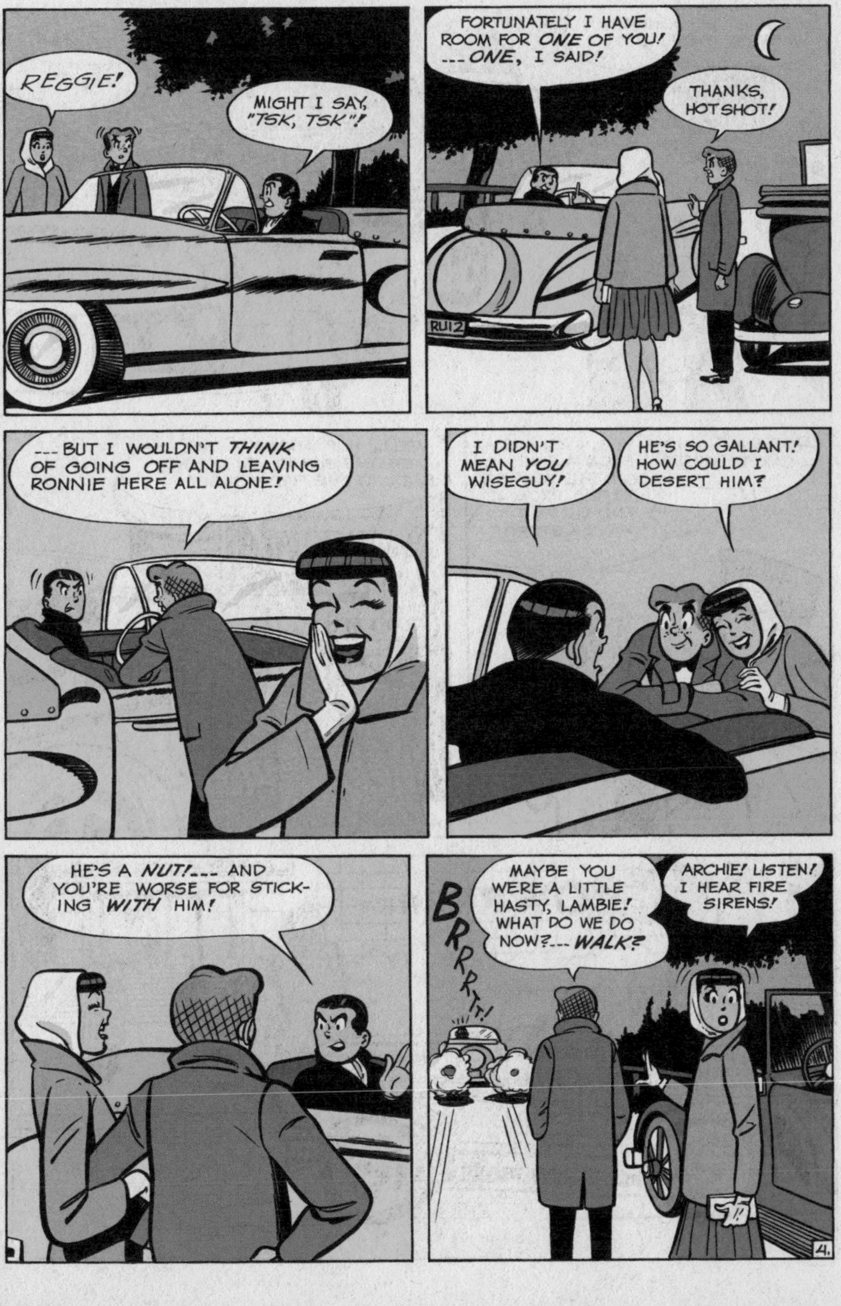
REGGIE!
MIGHT I SAY, "TSK, TSK"!
FORTUNATELY I HAVE ROOM FOR ONE OF YOU! --- ONE, I SAID!
THANKS, HOTSHOT!
RU12
--- BUT I WOULDN'T THINK OF GOING OFF AND LEAVING RONNIE HERE ALL ALONE!
I DIDN'T MEAN YOU WISEGUY!
HE'S SO GALLANT! HOW COULD I DESERT HIM?
HE'S A NUT!--- AND YOU'RE WORSE FOR STICKING WITH HIM!
BRRRTTT!
MAYBE YOU WERE A LITTLE HASTY, LAMBIE! WHAT DO WE DO NOW?--- WALK?
ARCHIE! LISTEN! I HEAR FIRE SIRENS!
4.

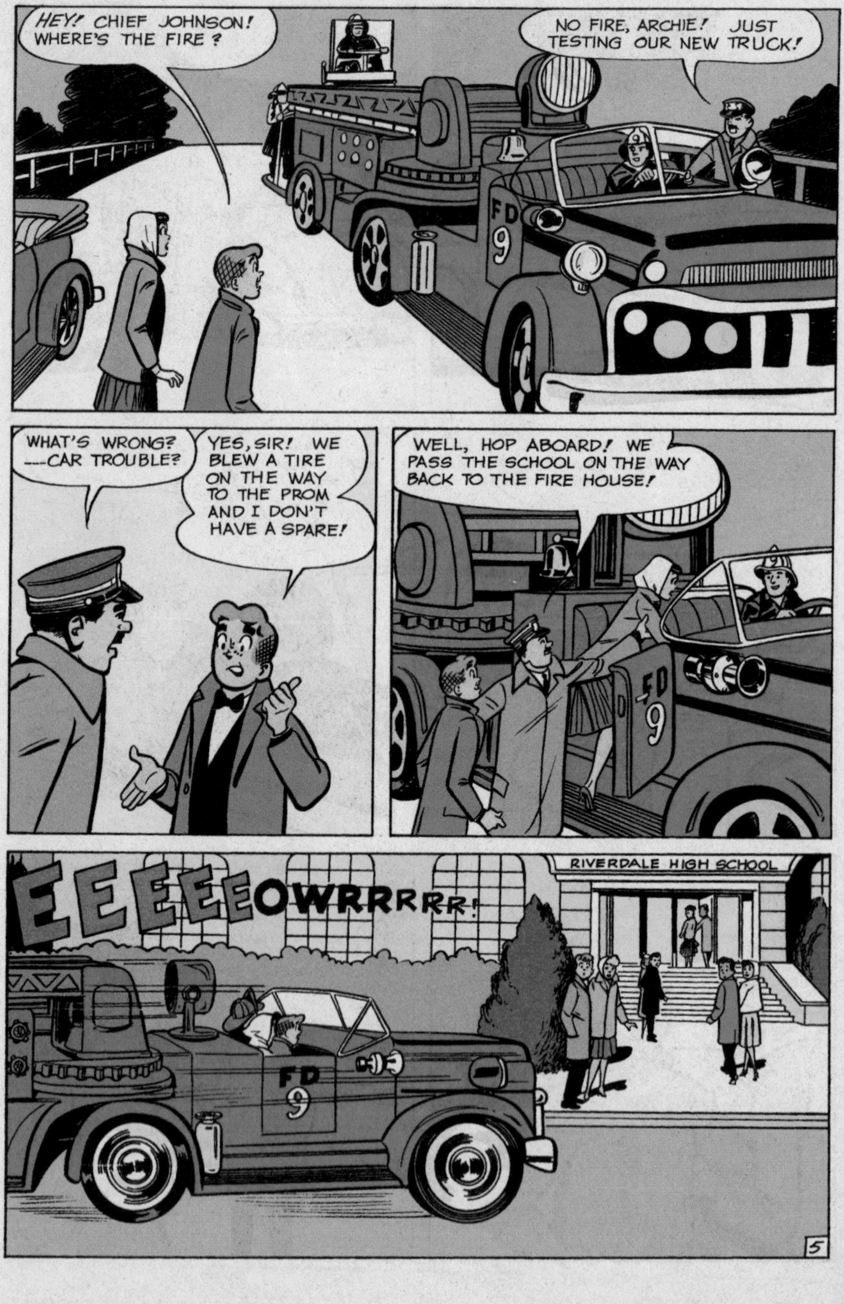
HEY! CHIEF JOHNSON! WHERE'S THE FIRE ?
NO FIRE, ARCHIE! JUST TESTING OUR NEW TRUCK!
FD 9
WHAT'S WRONG? ---CAR TROUBLE?
YES, SIR! WE BLEW A TIRE ON THE WAY TO THE PROM AND I DON'T HAVE A SPARE!
WELL, HOP ABOARD! WE PASS THE SCHOOL ON THE WAY BACK TO THE FIRE HOUSE!
FD 9
EEEEEOWRRRRRR!
RIVERDALE HIGH SCHOOL
FD 9
5

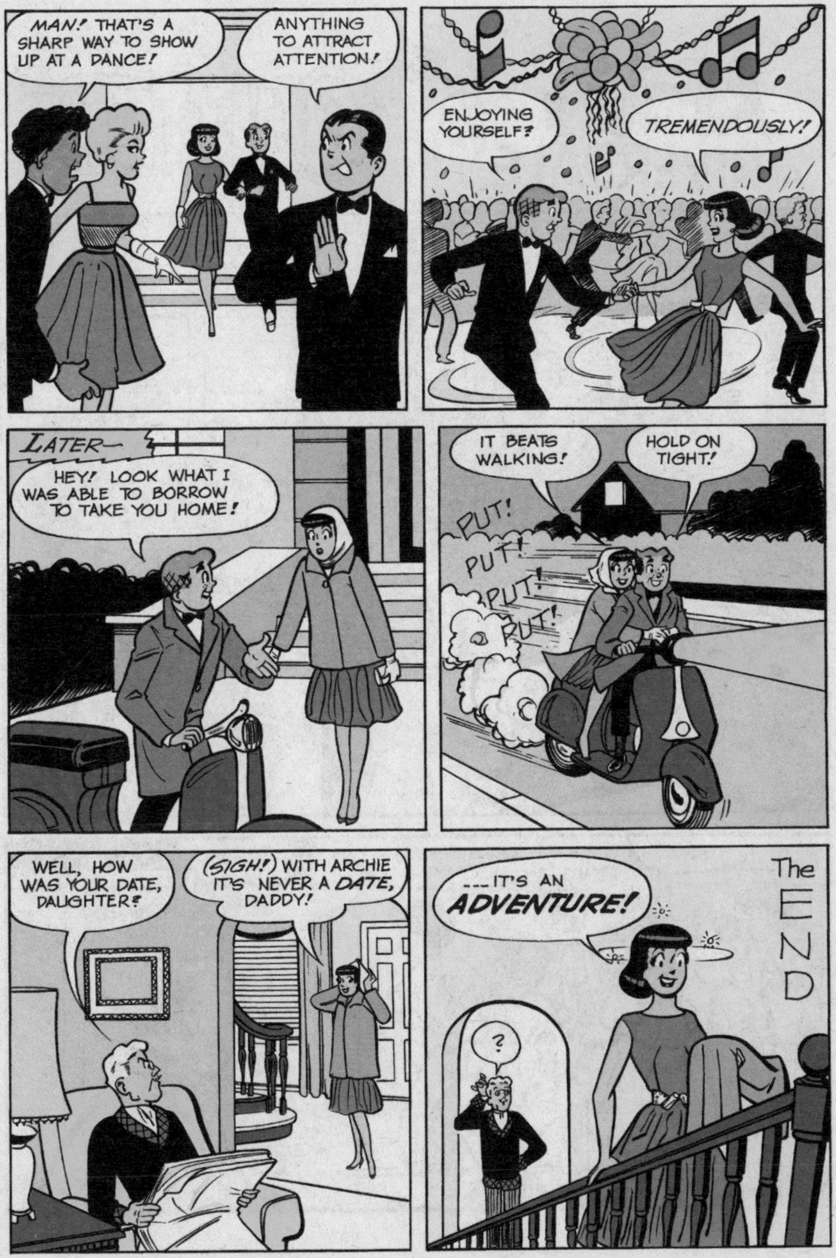
MAN! THAT'S A SHARP WAY TO SHOW UP AT A DANCE!
ANYTHING TO ATTRACT ATTENTION!
ENJOYING YOURSELF?
TREMENDOUSLY!
LATER—
HEY! LOOK WHAT I WAS ABLE TO BORROW TO TAKE YOU HOME!
IT BEATS WALKING!
HOLD ON TIGHT!
PUT! PUT! PUT! PUT!
WELL, HOW WAS YOUR DATE, DAUGHTER?
(SIGH!) WITH ARCHIE IT'S NEVER A DATE, DADDY!
---IT'S AN ADVENTURE!
?
The END

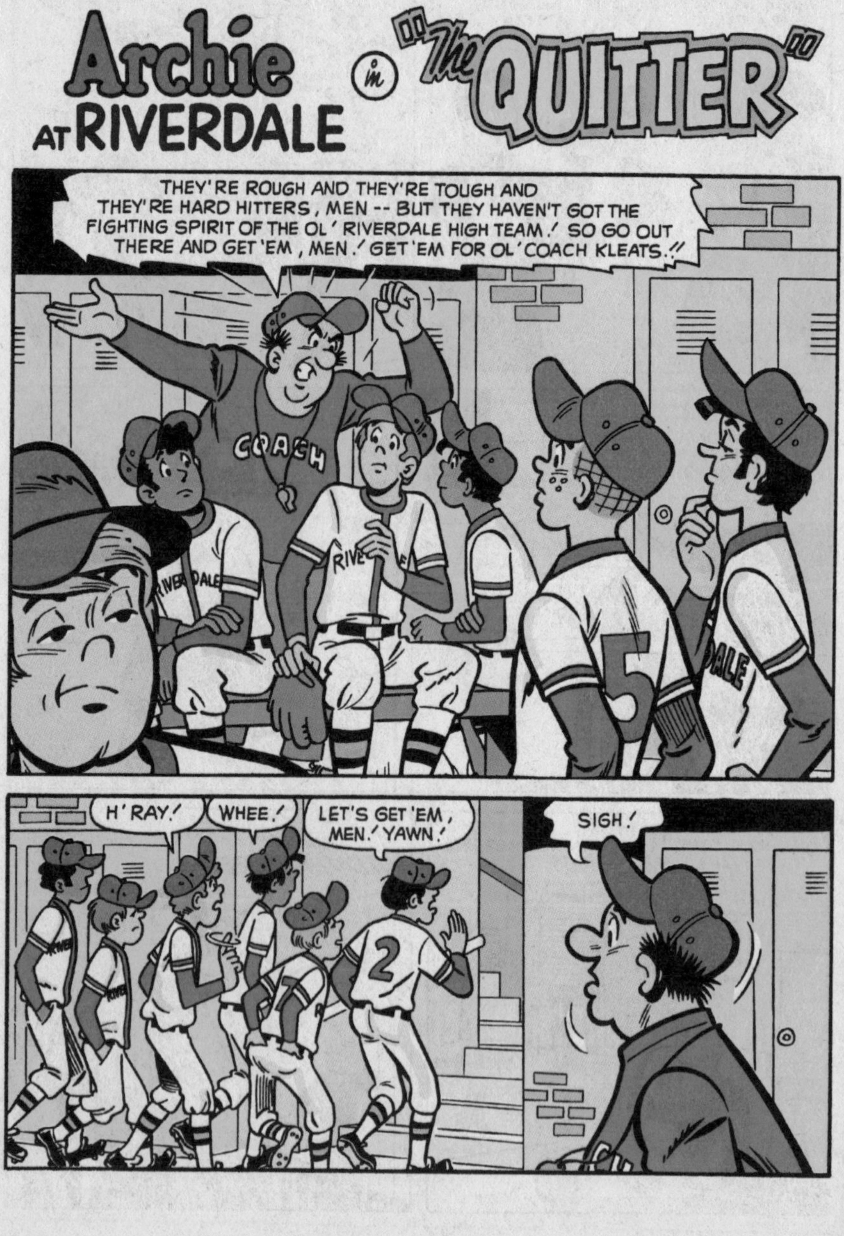
Archie AT RIVERDALE in "The QUITTER"
THEY'RE ROUGH AND THEY'RE TOUGH AND THEY'RE HARD HITTERS, MEN -- BUT THEY HAVEN'T GOT THE FIGHTING SPIRIT OF THE OL' RIVERDALE HIGH TEAM.! SO GO OUT THERE AND GET 'EM, MEN.! GET 'EM FOR OL' COACH KLEATS.!!
COACH
RIVERDALE
H' RAY!
WHEE.!
LET'S GET 'EM, MEN.! YAWN.!
SIGH!

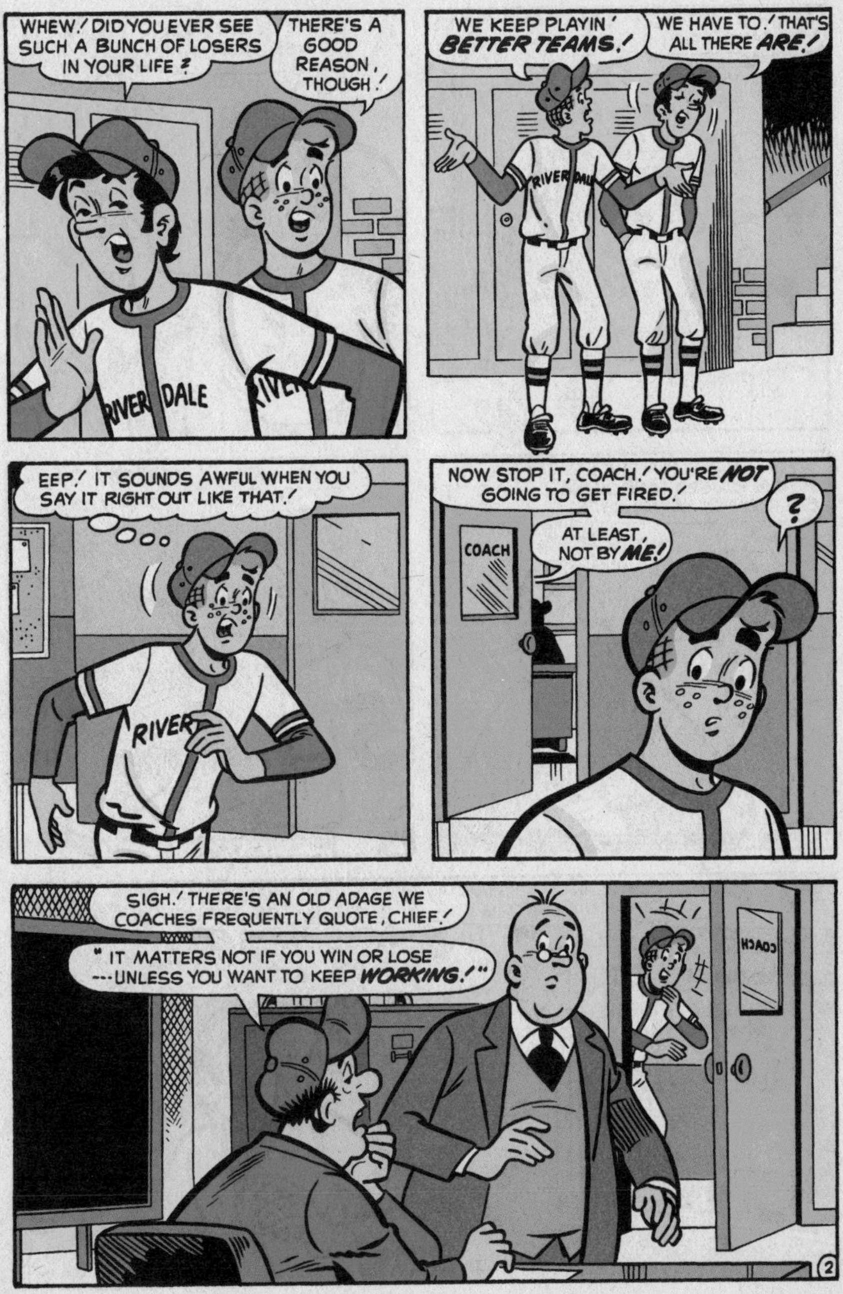
WHEW! DID YOU EVER SEE SUCH A BUNCH OF LOSERS IN YOUR LIFE?
THERE'S A GOOD REASON, THOUGH!
RIVERDALE
WE KEEP PLAYIN' BETTER TEAMS!
WE HAVE TO! THAT'S ALL THERE ARE!
RIVERDALE
EEP! IT SOUNDS AWFUL WHEN YOU SAY IT RIGHT OUT LIKE THAT!
RIVER
NOW STOP IT, COACH! YOU'RE NOT GOING TO GET FIRED!
COACH
AT LEAST, NOT BY ME!
?
SIGH! THERE'S AN OLD ADAGE WE COACHES FREQUENTLY QUOTE, CHIEF!
" IT MATTERS NOT IF YOU WIN OR LOSE ---UNLESS YOU WANT TO KEEP WORKING!"
COACH
2

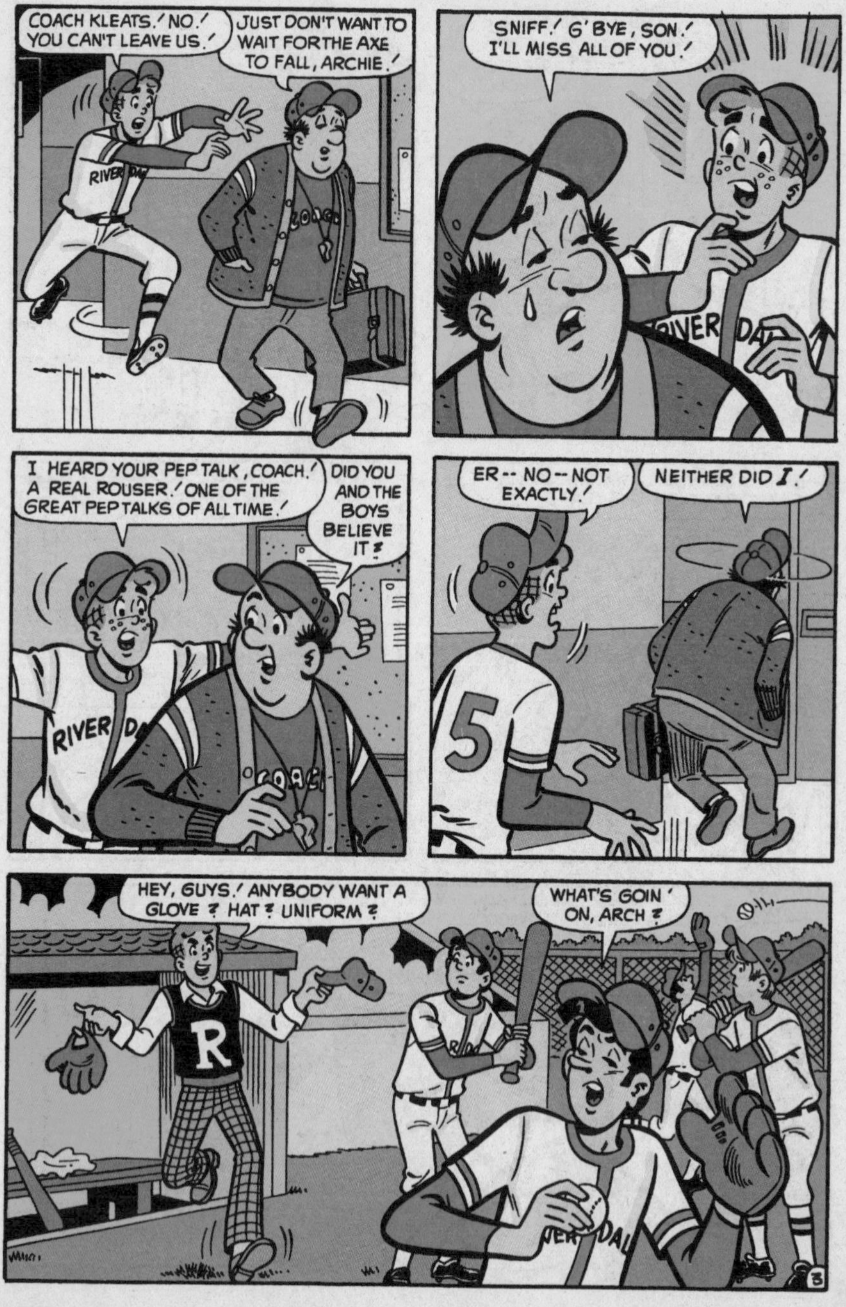
COACH KLEATS! NO! YOU CAN'T LEAVE US!
JUST DON'T WANT TO WAIT FOR THE AXE TO FALL, ARCHIE!
RIVERDALE
COACH
SNIFF! G'BYE, SON! I'LL MISS ALL OF YOU!
RIVERDALE
I HEARD YOUR PEP TALK, COACH! A REAL ROUSER! ONE OF THE GREAT PEP TALKS OF ALL TIME!
DID YOU AND THE BOYS BELIEVE IT?
RIVERDALE
COACH
ER -- NO -- NOT EXACTLY!
NEITHER DID I!
5
HEY, GUYS! ANYBODY WANT A GLOVE? HAT? UNIFORM?
WHAT'S GOIN' ON, ARCH?
R
3

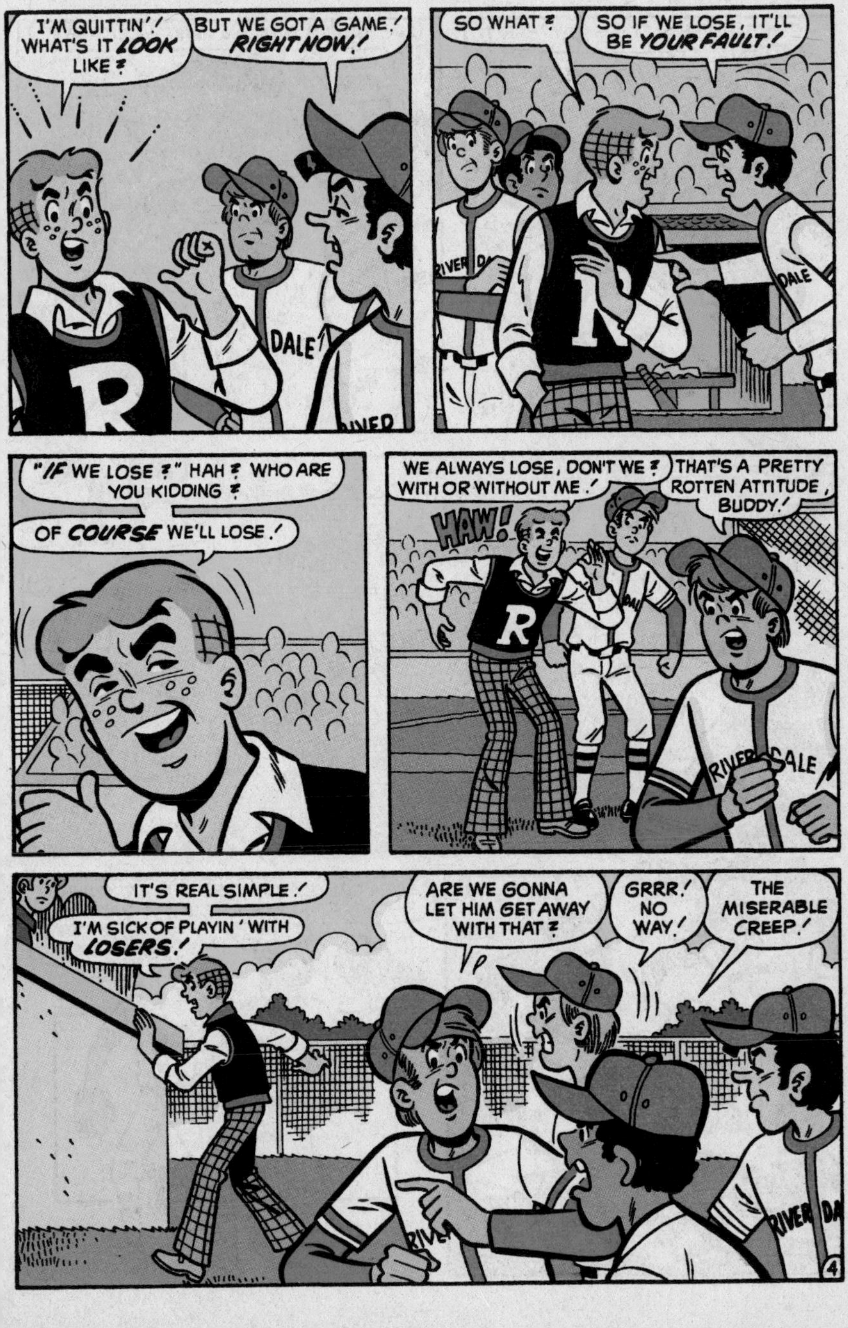
I'M QUITTIN'! WHAT'S IT LOOK LIKE?
BUT WE GOT A GAME! RIGHT NOW!
SO WHAT?
SO IF WE LOSE, IT'LL BE YOUR FAULT!
"IF WE LOSE?" HAH? WHO ARE YOU KIDDING?
OF COURSE WE'LL LOSE!
HAW!
WE ALWAYS LOSE, DON'T WE? WITH OR WITHOUT ME!
THAT'S A PRETTY ROTTEN ATTITUDE, BUDDY!
IT'S REAL SIMPLE!
I'M SICK OF PLAYIN' WITH LOSERS!
ARE WE GONNA LET HIM GET AWAY WITH THAT?
GRRR! NO WAY!
THE MISERABLE CREEP!
4

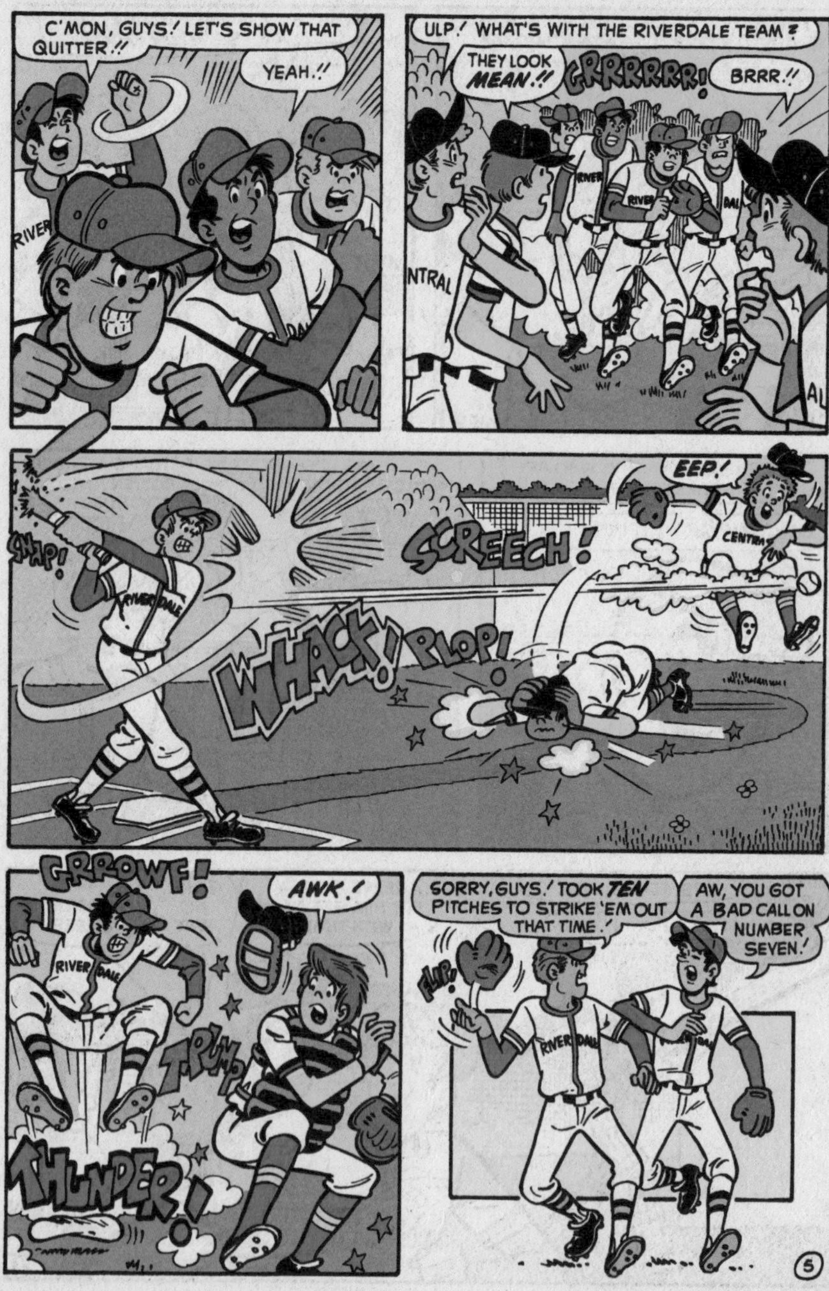
C'MON, GUYS! LET'S SHOW THAT QUITTER!!
YEAH!!
ULP! WHAT'S WITH THE RIVERDALE TEAM?
THEY LOOK MEAN!!
GRRRRRR!
BRRR!!
SNAP!
SCREECH!
EEP!
WHACK!
PLOP!
GRROWF!
AWK!
TRUMP
THUNDER!
SORRY, GUYS! TOOK TEN PITCHES TO STRIKE 'EM OUT THAT TIME!
AW, YOU GOT A BAD CALL ON NUMBER SEVEN!
FLIP!
5

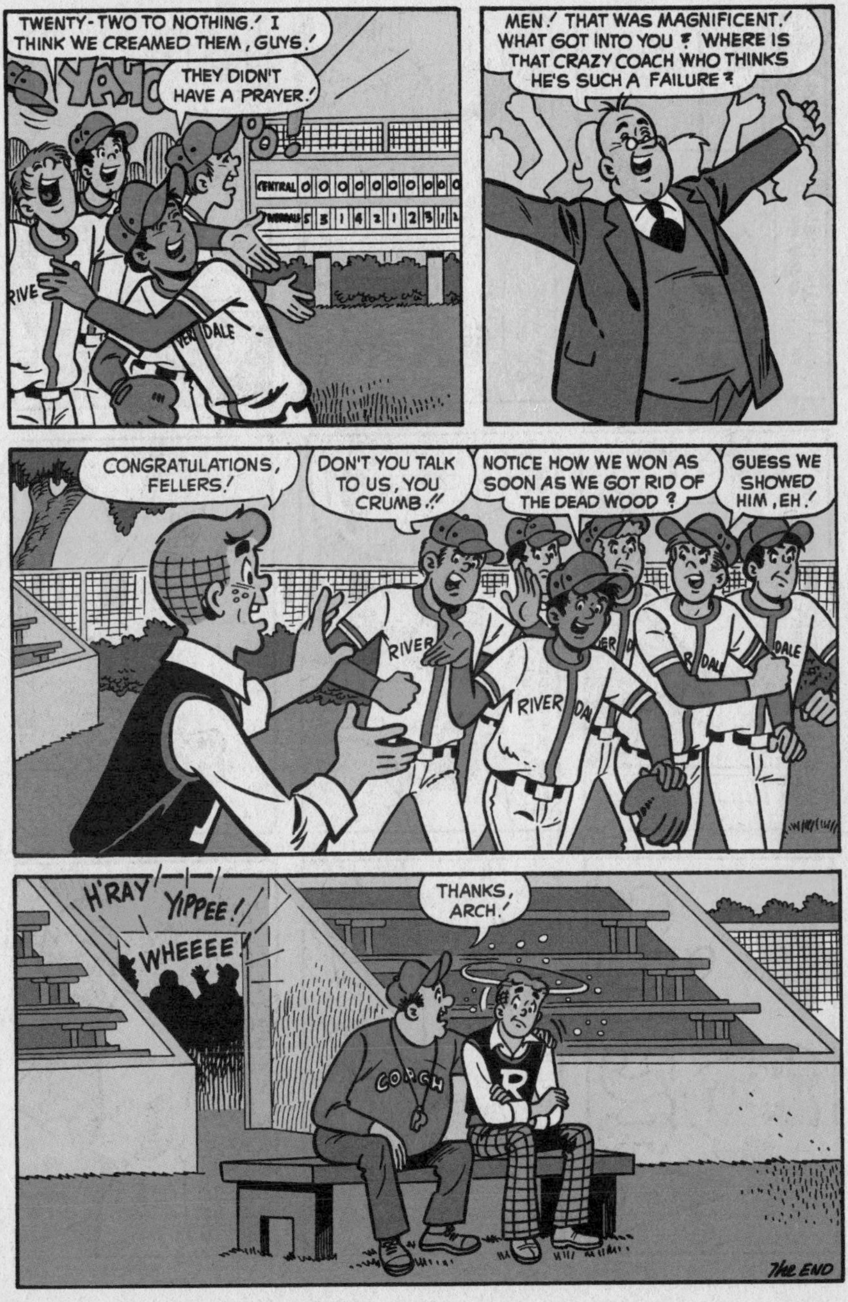
TWENTY-TWO TO NOTHING! I THINK WE CREAMED THEM, GUYS!
YAHOO!
THEY DIDN'T HAVE A PRAYER!
CENTRAL
MEN! THAT WAS MAGNIFICENT! WHAT GOT INTO YOU? WHERE IS THAT CRAZY COACH WHO THINKS HE'S SUCH A FAILURE?
CONGRATULATIONS, FELLERS!
DON'T YOU TALK TO US, YOU CRUMB!!
NOTICE HOW WE WON AS SOON AS WE GOT RID OF THE DEAD WOOD?
GUESS WE SHOWED HIM, EH!
H'RAY
YIPPEE!
WHEEEE!
THANKS, ARCH!
COACH
The END

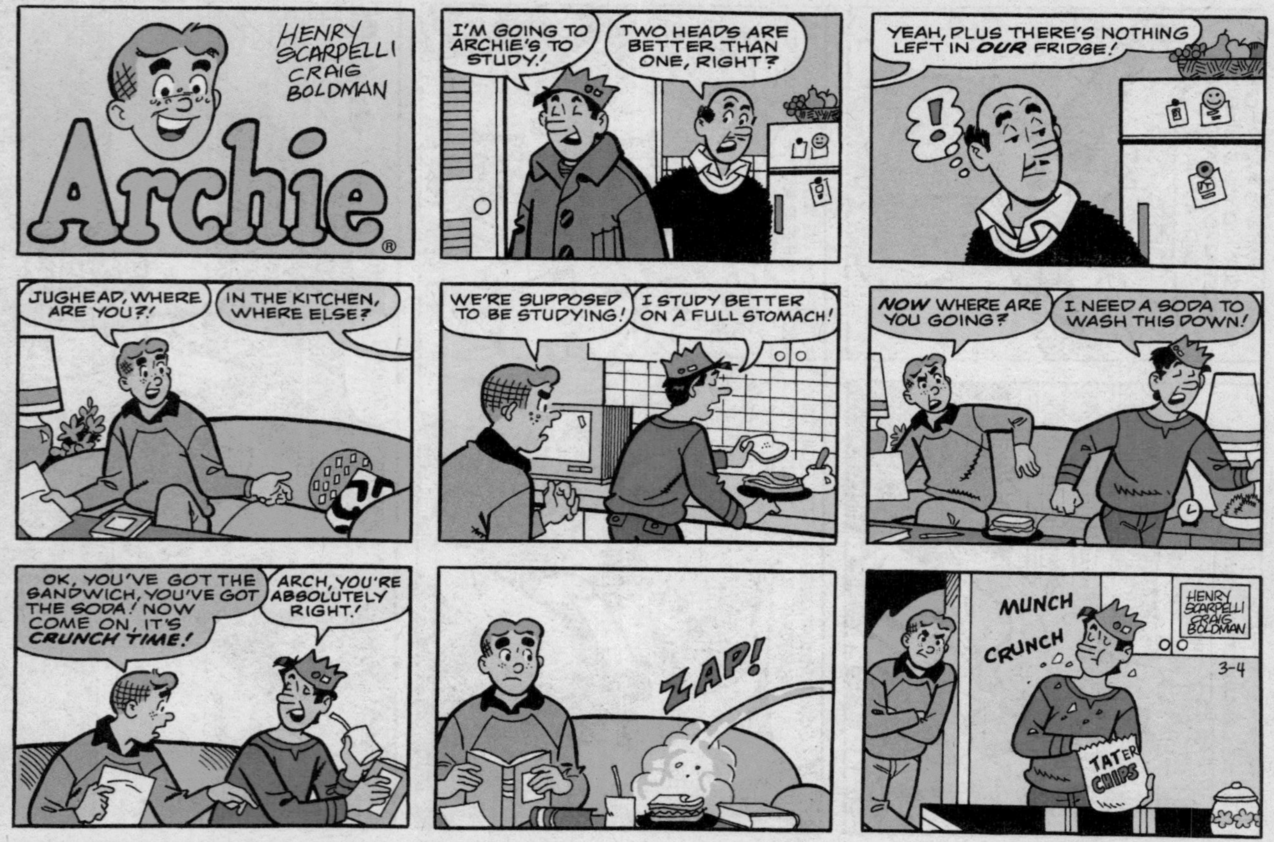
Archie®
HENRY SCARPELLI
CRAIG BOLDMAN
I'M GOING TO ARCHIE'S TO STUDY!
TWO HEADS ARE BETTER THAN ONE, RIGHT?
YEAH, PLUS THERE'S NOTHING LEFT IN **OUR** FRIDGE!
!
JUGHEAD, WHERE ARE YOU?!
IN THE KITCHEN, WHERE ELSE?
WE'RE SUPPOSED TO BE STUDYING!
I STUDY BETTER ON A FULL STOMACH!
NOW WHERE ARE YOU GOING?
I NEED A SODA TO WASH THIS DOWN!
OK, YOU'VE GOT THE SANDWICH, YOU'VE GOT THE SODA! NOW COME ON, IT'S **CRUNCH TIME!**
ARCH, YOU'RE ABSOLUTELY RIGHT!
ZAP!
MUNCH
CRUNCH
HENRY SCARPELLI CRAIG BOLDMAN
3-4
TATER CHIPS

Archie's FAVORITE HIGH SCHOOL COMICS

BEST FRENEMIES

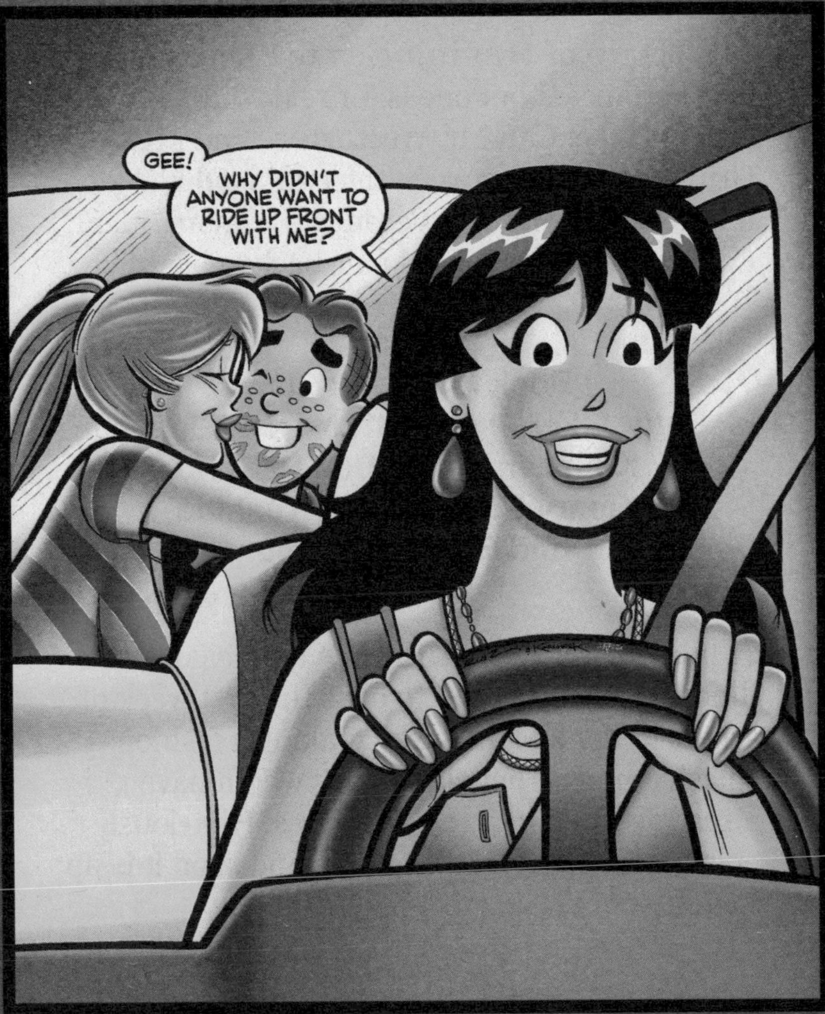
GEE!
WHY DIDN'T ANYONE WANT TO RIDE UP FRONT WITH ME?

School of Hard Knocks
***Betty & Veronica* #282, June 1979**
Frank Doyle, Dan DeCarlo, Rudy Lapick,
Bill Yoshida and Barry Grossman

It's a tale of two injuries for Betty and Veronica... but one is for real while the other is fake! Can Mr. Weatherbee and Miss Grundy discern between the two? And how does it reflect on Betty and Veronica's personalities? Can Archie nurse his gal pals back to health?

Back to School Blues
***Betty & Veronica* #153, November 2000**
Kathleen Webb, Dan DeCarlo,
Henry Scarpelli, Bill Yoshida
and Barry Grossman

Always the opportunist, Veronica uses an illness that caused her to miss the first week of school to her advantage by making a fashion splash amongst her classmates whom have already settled into their routines. Hilariously enough, things don't go to plan and soon it is up to Betty to once again save the day.

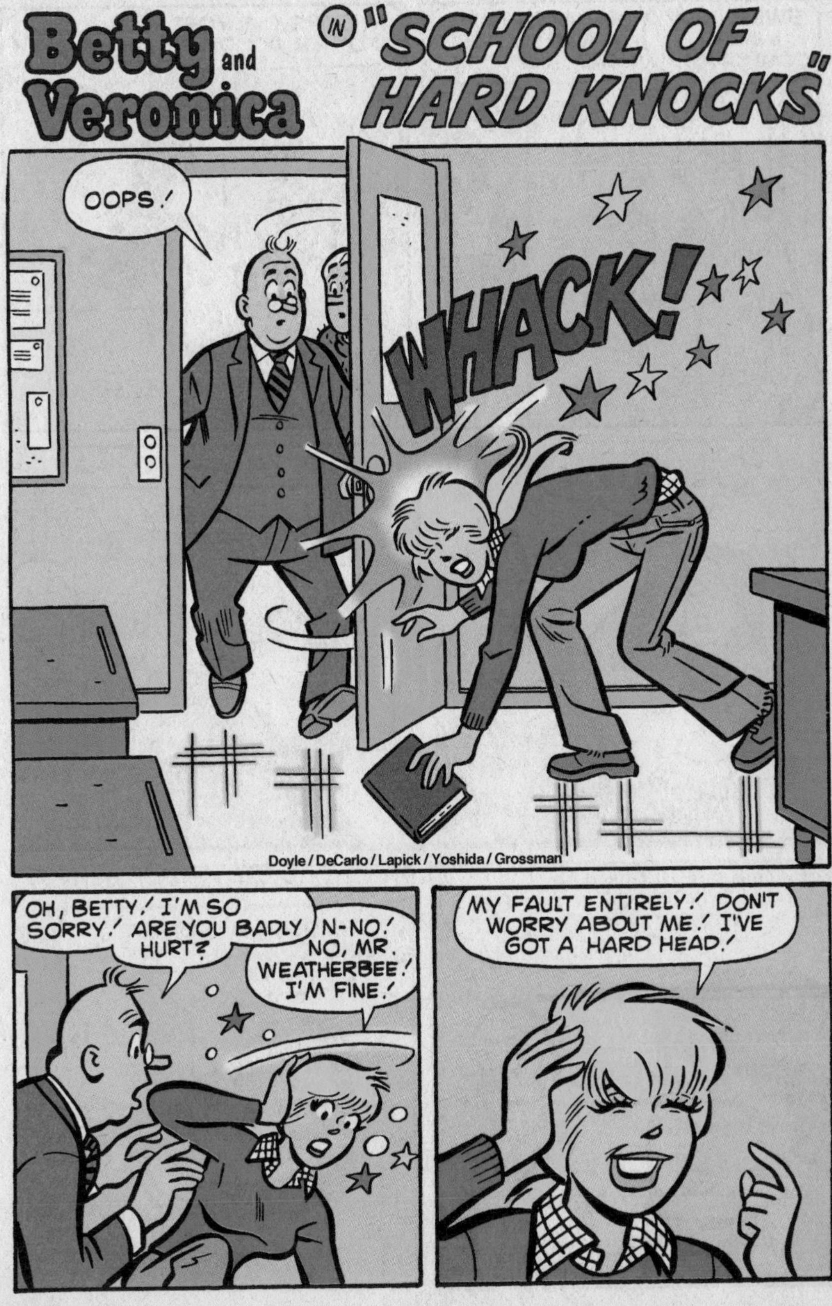
Betty and Veronica
IN "SCHOOL OF HARD KNOCKS"
OOPS!
WHACK!
Doyle / DeCarlo / Lapick / Yoshida / Grossman
OH, BETTY! I'M SO SORRY! ARE YOU BADLY HURT?
N-NO! NO, MR. WEATHERBEE! I'M FINE!
MY FAULT ENTIRELY! DON'T WORRY ABOUT ME! I'VE GOT A HARD HEAD!

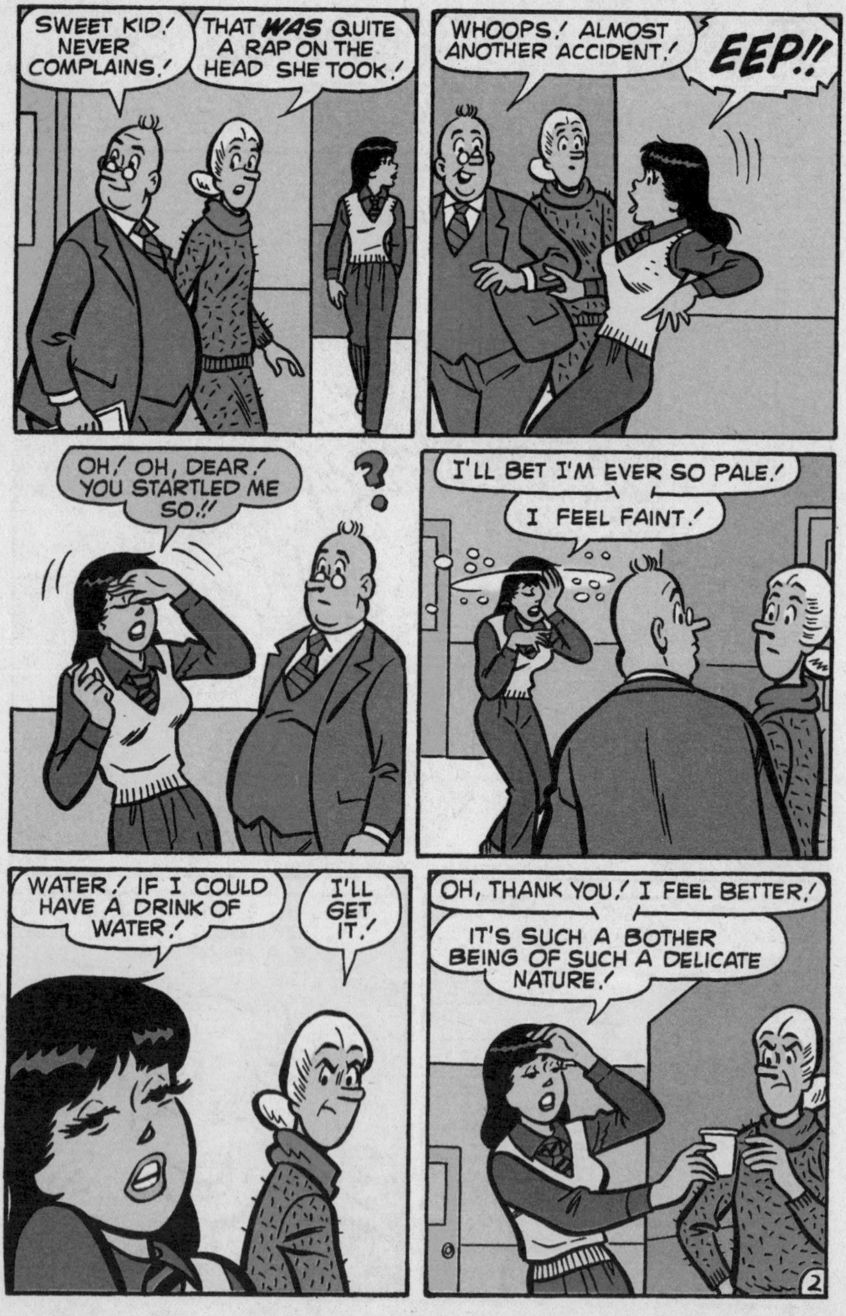
SWEET KID! NEVER COMPLAINS!
THAT WAS QUITE A RAP ON THE HEAD SHE TOOK!
WHOOPS! ALMOST ANOTHER ACCIDENT!
EEP!!
OH! OH, DEAR! YOU STARTLED ME SO!!
?
I'LL BET I'M EVER SO PALE!
I FEEL FAINT!
WATER! IF I COULD HAVE A DRINK OF WATER!
I'LL GET IT!
OH, THANK YOU! I FEEL BETTER!
IT'S SUCH A BOTHER BEING OF SUCH A DELICATE NATURE!
2

QUITE A DIFFERENCE BETWEEN BETTY AND VERONICA, ISN'T THERE?

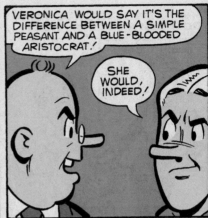

VERONICA WOULD SAY IT'S THE DIFFERENCE BETWEEN A SIMPLE PEASANT AND A BLUE-BLOODED ARISTOCRAT!

SHE WOULD, INDEED!

THE WAY I SEE IT, ONE IS HONEST AND THE OTHER A BIG FAKER!

I'LL BUY THAT!

BUT BETTY'S HEAD INJURY WAS NOT AS SIMPLE AS SHE PRETENDED---

OOOH, I FEEL DIZZY!

BETTY! WHAT'S WRONG?

WHAT'S GOING ON HERE?

BETTY DOESN'T FEEL WELL!

3

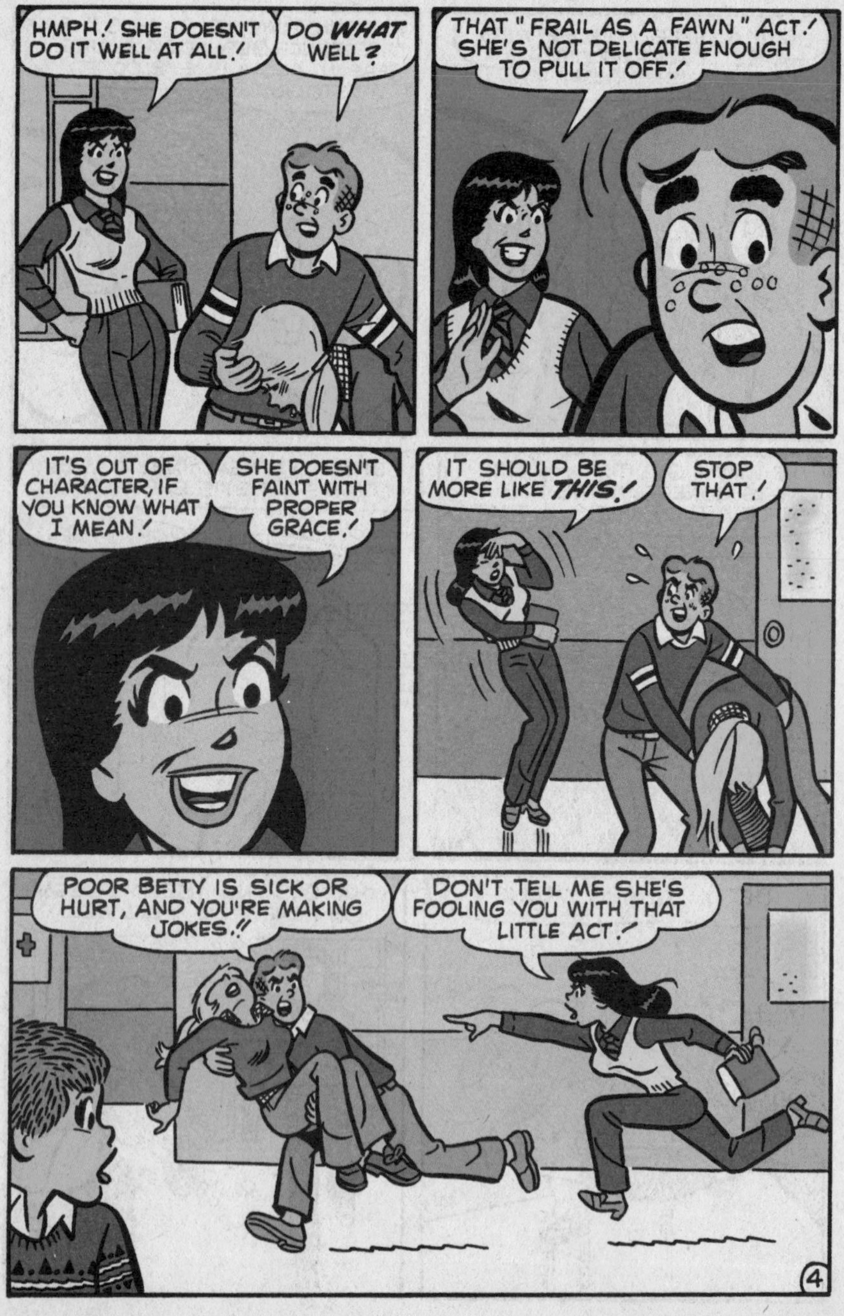
HMPH! SHE DOESN'T DO IT WELL AT ALL!
DO WHAT WELL?
THAT "FRAIL AS A FAWN" ACT! SHE'S NOT DELICATE ENOUGH TO PULL IT OFF!
IT'S OUT OF CHARACTER, IF YOU KNOW WHAT I MEAN!
SHE DOESN'T FAINT WITH PROPER GRACE!
IT SHOULD BE MORE LIKE THIS!
STOP THAT!
POOR BETTY IS SICK OR HURT, AND YOU'RE MAKING JOKES!!
DON'T TELL ME SHE'S FOOLING YOU WITH THAT LITTLE ACT!
4

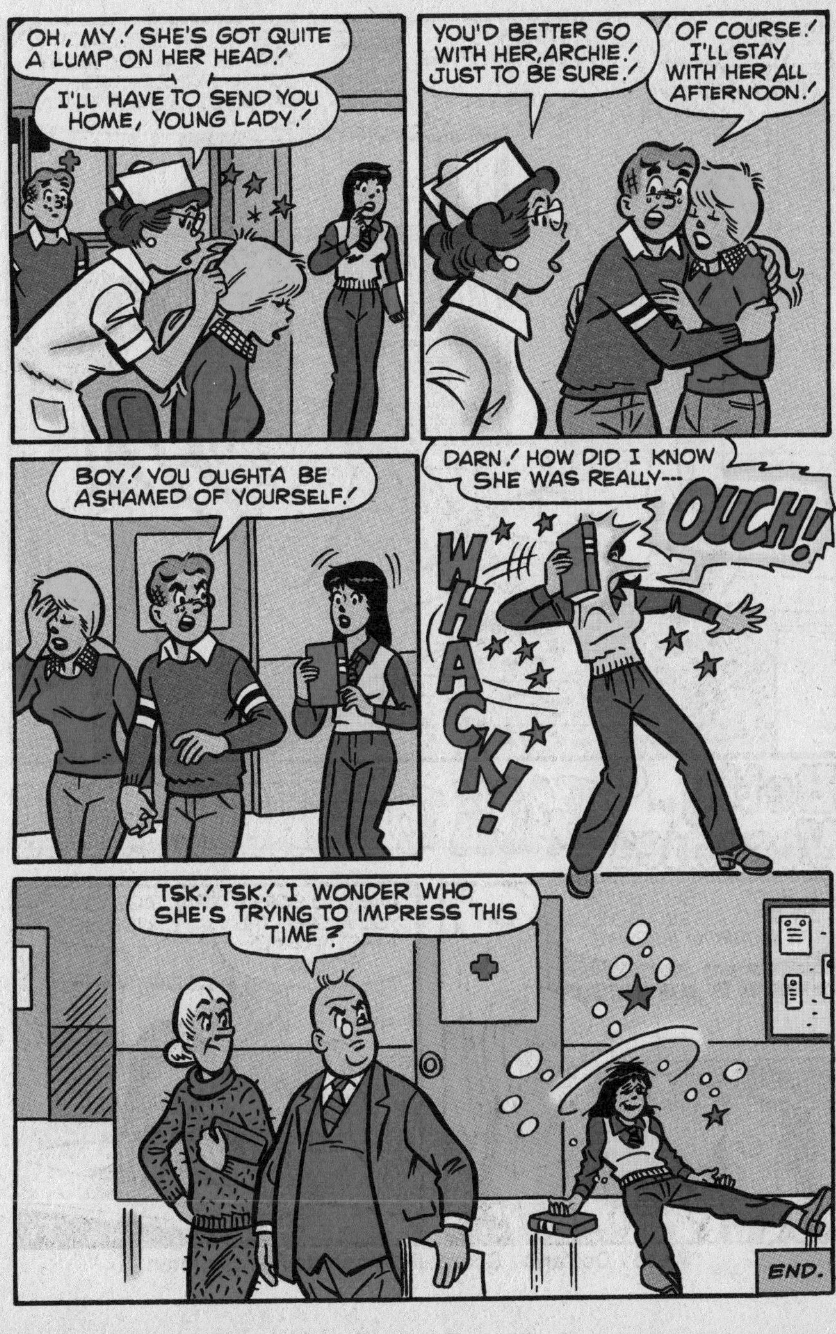
OH, MY! SHE'S GOT QUITE A LUMP ON HER HEAD!
I'LL HAVE TO SEND YOU HOME, YOUNG LADY!
YOU'D BETTER GO WITH HER, ARCHIE! JUST TO BE SURE!
OF COURSE! I'LL STAY WITH HER ALL AFTERNOON!
BOY! YOU OUGHTA BE ASHAMED OF YOURSELF!
DARN! HOW DID I KNOW SHE WAS REALLY---
OUCH!
WHACK!
TSK! TSK! I WONDER WHO SHE'S TRYING TO IMPRESS THIS TIME?
END.

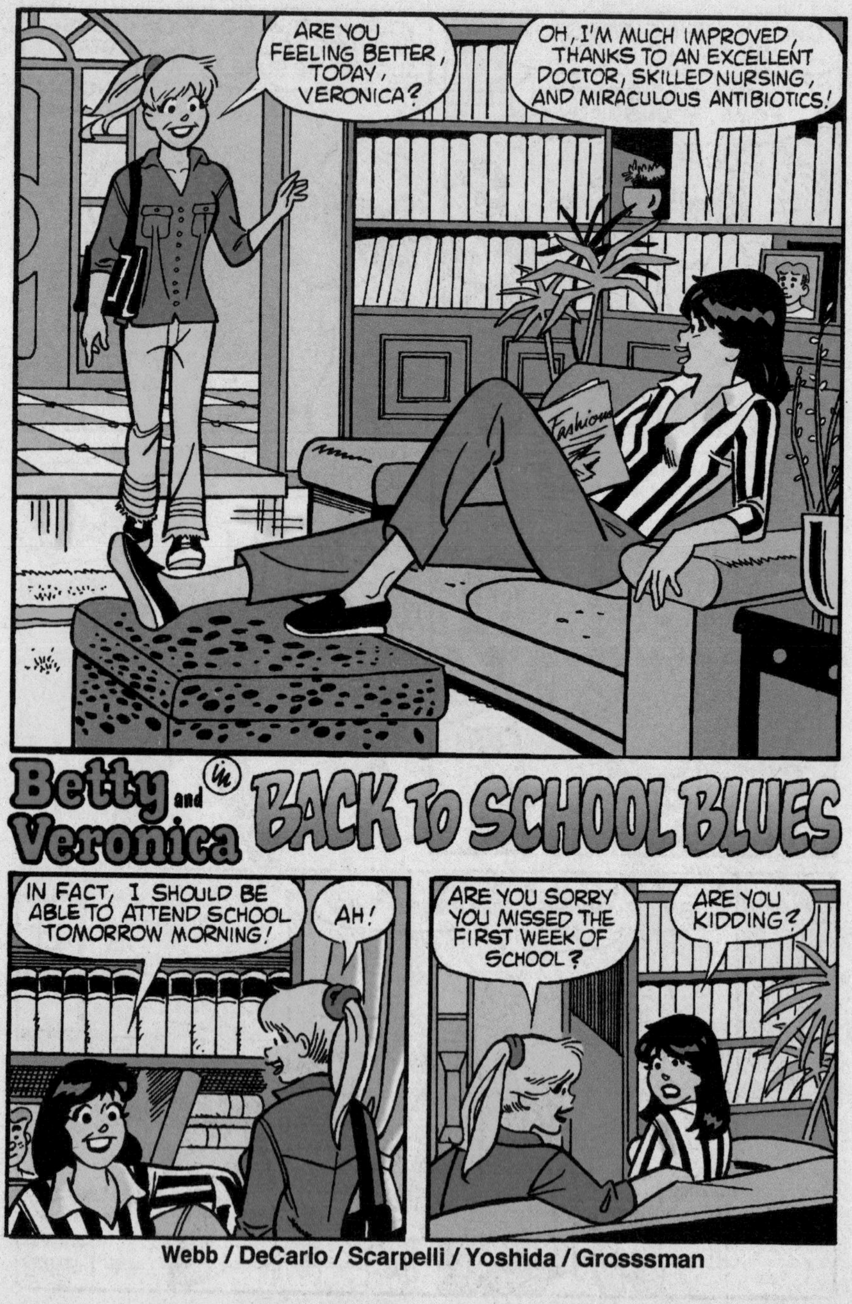
ARE YOU FEELING BETTER, TODAY, VERONICA?
OH, I'M MUCH IMPROVED, THANKS TO AN EXCELLENT DOCTOR, SKILLED NURSING, AND MIRACULOUS ANTIBIOTICS!
Fashions
Betty and Veronica in
BACK TO SCHOOL BLUES
IN FACT, I SHOULD BE ABLE TO ATTEND SCHOOL TOMORROW MORNING!
AH!
ARE YOU SORRY YOU MISSED THE FIRST WEEK OF SCHOOL?
ARE YOU KIDDING?

Webb / DeCarlo / Scarpelli / Yoshida / Grosssman

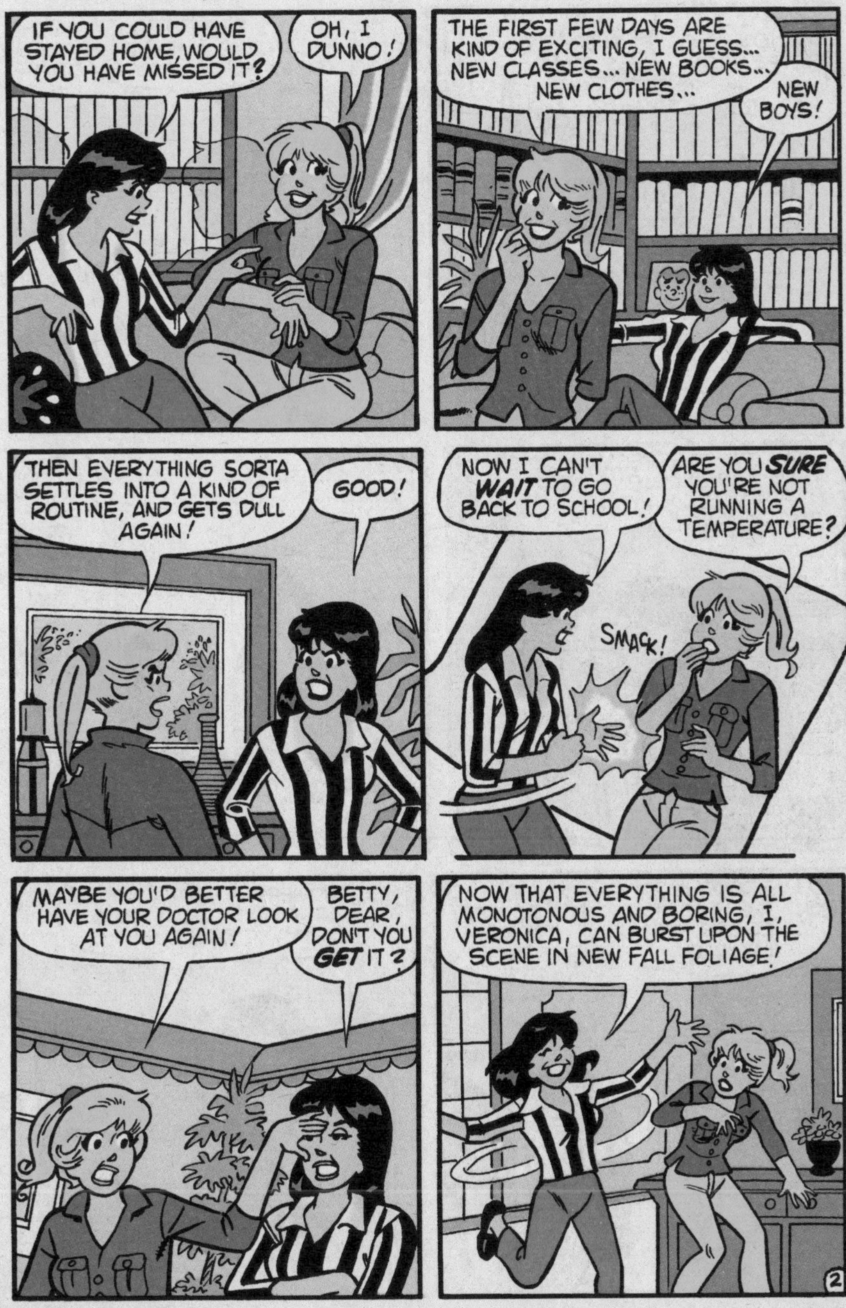
IF YOU COULD HAVE STAYED HOME, WOULD YOU HAVE MISSED IT?
OH, I DUNNO!
THE FIRST FEW DAYS ARE KIND OF EXCITING, I GUESS... NEW CLASSES... NEW BOOKS... NEW CLOTHES...
NEW BOYS!
THEN EVERYTHING SORTA SETTLES INTO A KIND OF ROUTINE, AND GETS DULL AGAIN!
GOOD!
NOW I CAN'T WAIT TO GO BACK TO SCHOOL!
ARE YOU SURE YOU'RE NOT RUNNING A TEMPERATURE?
SMACK!
MAYBE YOU'D BETTER HAVE YOUR DOCTOR LOOK AT YOU AGAIN!
BETTY, DEAR, DON'T YOU GET IT?
NOW THAT EVERYTHING IS ALL MONOTONOUS AND BORING, I, VERONICA, CAN BURST UPON THE SCENE IN NEW FALL FOLIAGE!
2

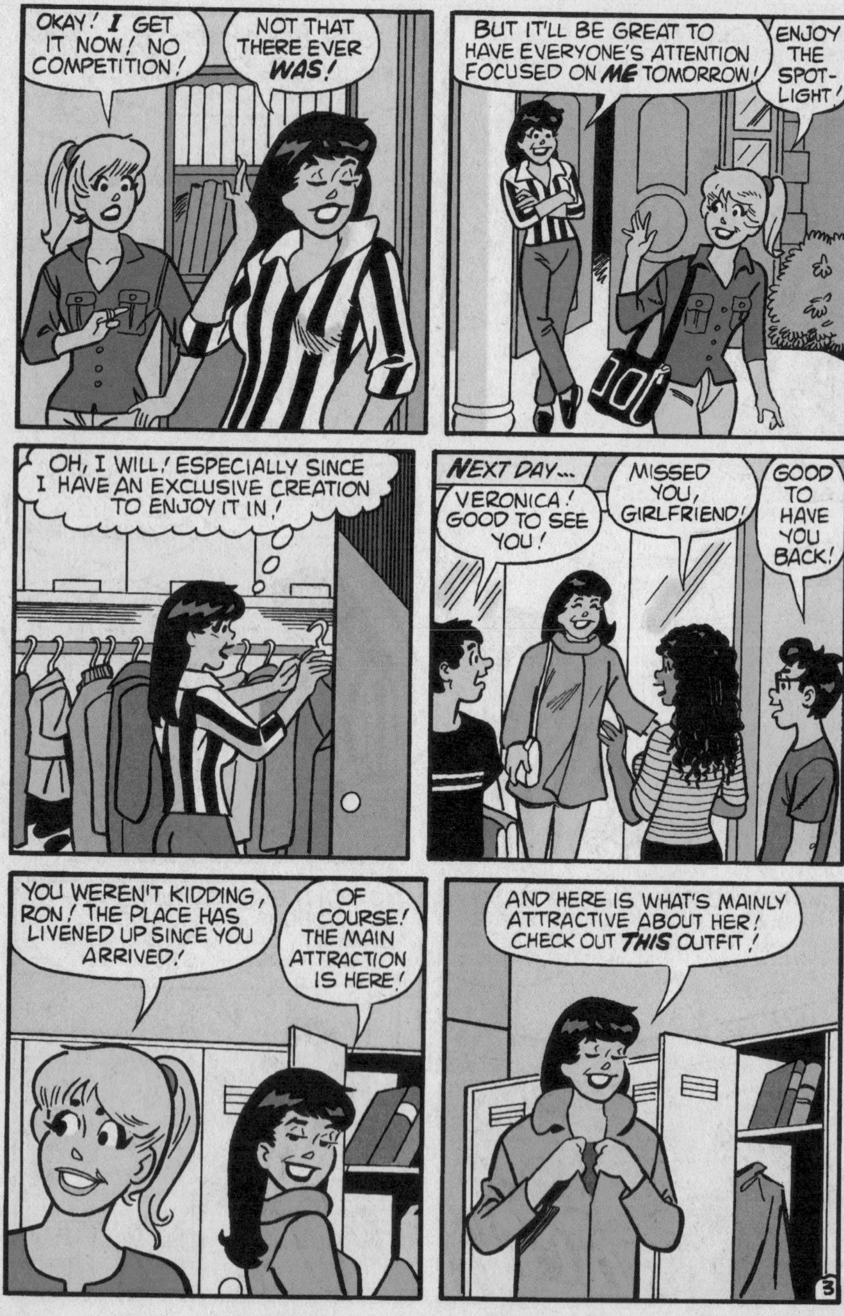
OKAY! I GET IT NOW! NO COMPETITION!
NOT THAT THERE EVER WAS!
BUT IT'LL BE GREAT TO HAVE EVERYONE'S ATTENTION FOCUSED ON ME TOMORROW!
ENJOY THE SPOT-LIGHT!
OH, I WILL! ESPECIALLY SINCE I HAVE AN EXCLUSIVE CREATION TO ENJOY IT IN!
NEXT DAY...
VERONICA! GOOD TO SEE YOU!
MISSED YOU, GIRLFRIEND!
GOOD TO HAVE YOU BACK!
YOU WEREN'T KIDDING, RON! THE PLACE HAS LIVENED UP SINCE YOU ARRIVED!
OF COURSE! THE MAIN ATTRACTION IS HERE!
AND HERE IS WHAT'S MAINLY ATTRACTIVE ABOUT HER! CHECK OUT THIS OUTFIT!
3

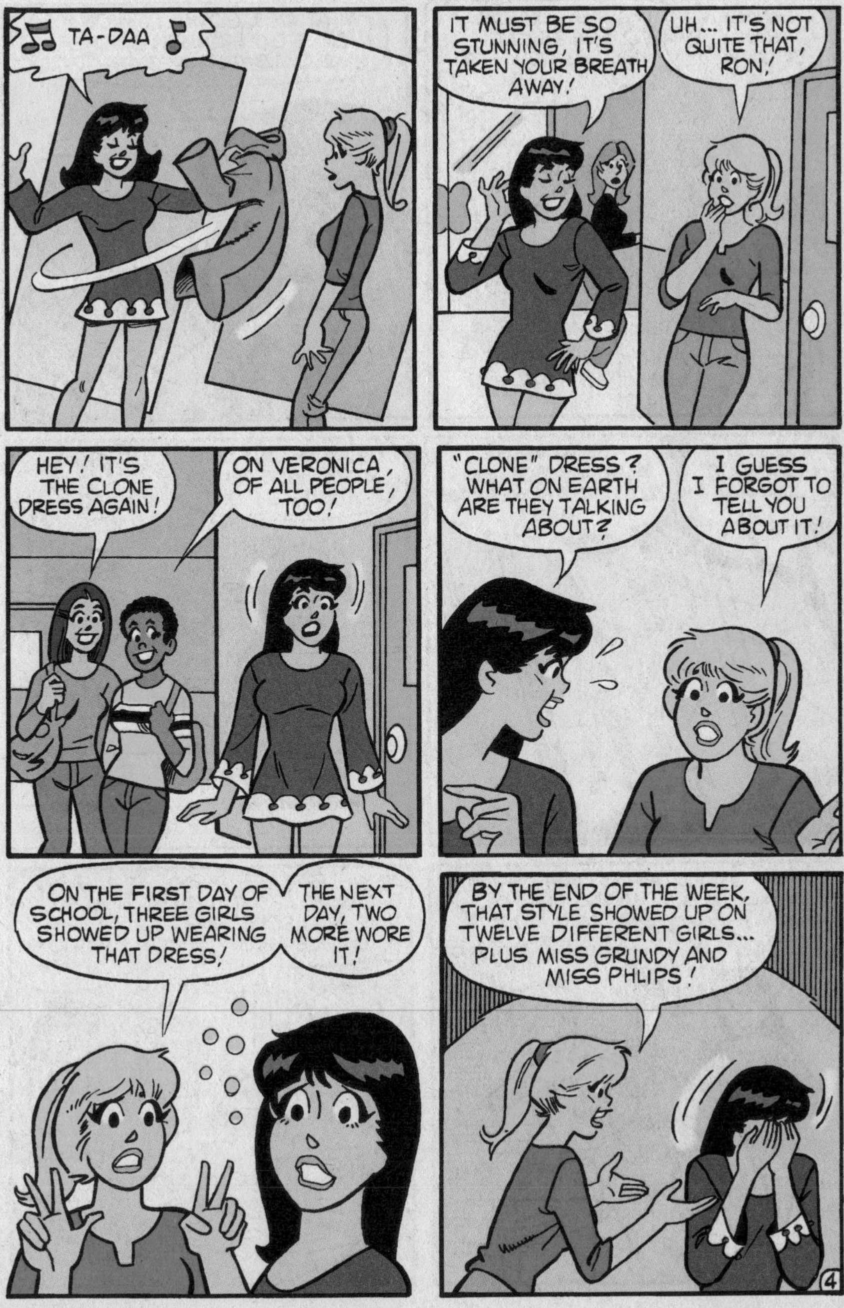
TA-DAA
IT MUST BE SO STUNNING, IT'S TAKEN YOUR BREATH AWAY!
UH... IT'S NOT QUITE THAT, RON!
HEY! IT'S THE CLONE DRESS AGAIN!
ON VERONICA, OF ALL PEOPLE, TOO!
"CLONE" DRESS? WHAT ON EARTH ARE THEY TALKING ABOUT?
I GUESS I FORGOT TO TELL YOU ABOUT IT!
ON THE FIRST DAY OF SCHOOL, THREE GIRLS SHOWED UP WEARING THAT DRESS!
THE NEXT DAY, TWO MORE WORE IT!
BY THE END OF THE WEEK, THAT STYLE SHOWED UP ON TWELVE DIFFERENT GIRLS... PLUS MISS GRUNDY AND MISS PHLIPS!
4

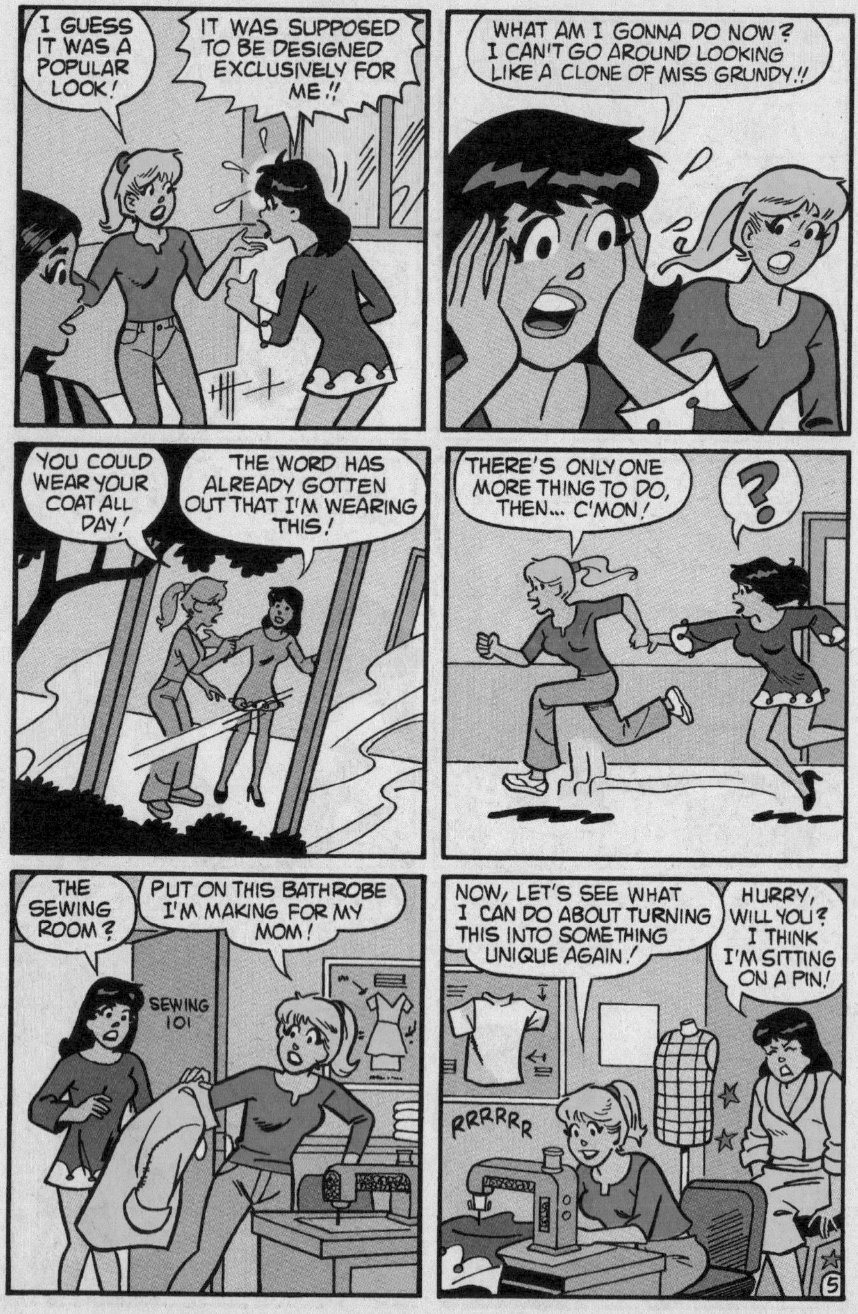
I GUESS IT WAS A POPULAR LOOK!
IT WAS SUPPOSED TO BE DESIGNED EXCLUSIVELY FOR ME!!
WHAT AM I GONNA DO NOW? I CAN'T GO AROUND LOOKING LIKE A CLONE OF MISS GRUNDY!!
YOU COULD WEAR YOUR COAT ALL DAY!
THE WORD HAS ALREADY GOTTEN OUT THAT I'M WEARING THIS!
THERE'S ONLY ONE MORE THING TO DO, THEN... C'MON!
?
THE SEWING ROOM?
PUT ON THIS BATHROBE I'M MAKING FOR MY MOM!
SEWING 101
NOW, LET'S SEE WHAT I CAN DO ABOUT TURNING THIS INTO SOMETHING UNIQUE AGAIN!
HURRY, WILL YOU? I THINK I'M SITTING ON A PIN!
RRRRRR
5

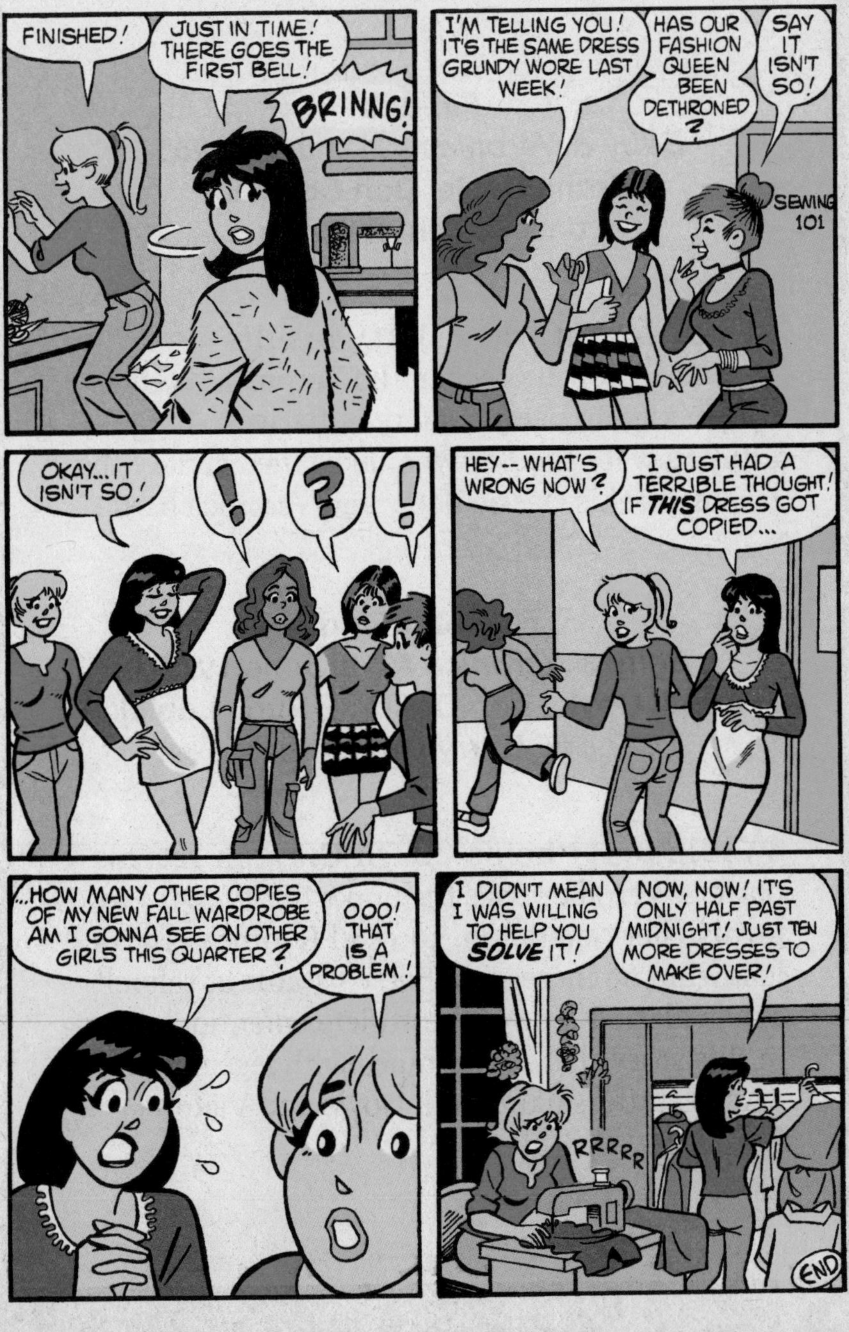
FINISHED!
JUST IN TIME! THERE GOES THE FIRST BELL!
BRINNG!
I'M TELLING YOU! IT'S THE SAME DRESS GRUNDY WORE LAST WEEK!
HAS OUR FASHION QUEEN BEEN DETHRONED?
SAY IT ISN'T SO!
SEWING 101
OKAY... IT ISN'T SO!
!
?
!
HEY-- WHAT'S WRONG NOW?
I JUST HAD A TERRIBLE THOUGHT! IF THIS DRESS GOT COPIED...
...HOW MANY OTHER COPIES OF MY NEW FALL WARDROBE AM I GONNA SEE ON OTHER GIRLS THIS QUARTER?
OOO! THAT IS A PROBLEM!
I DIDN'T MEAN I WAS WILLING TO HELP YOU SOLVE IT!
NOW, NOW! IT'S ONLY HALF PAST MIDNIGHT! JUST TEN MORE DRESSES TO MAKE OVER!
RRRRRR
END

Fireball
Betty & Veronica #114, June 1965
Frank Doyle, Dan DeCarlo
and Vincent DeCarlo

It's tit for tat when Betty insults Veronica's new headwear and Veronica retaliates by sabotaging Betty's safety initiatives. But ultimately it's the Bee who takes the brunt of the brouhaha this classic Betty and Veronica battle!

Five Star Final
Betty & Veronica #258, June 1977
Frank Doyle, Dan DeCarlo, Rudy Lapick
and Barry Grossman

While Betty helps Coach Clayton rate his players, Veronica uses the opportunity to try to tarnish her reputation. Too bad Ronnie's efforts just wind up increasing Betty's status at school! Trivia alert: Some of the athletes mentioned in this story share last names with legendary Archie staffers like Frank Doyle and Victor Gorelick.

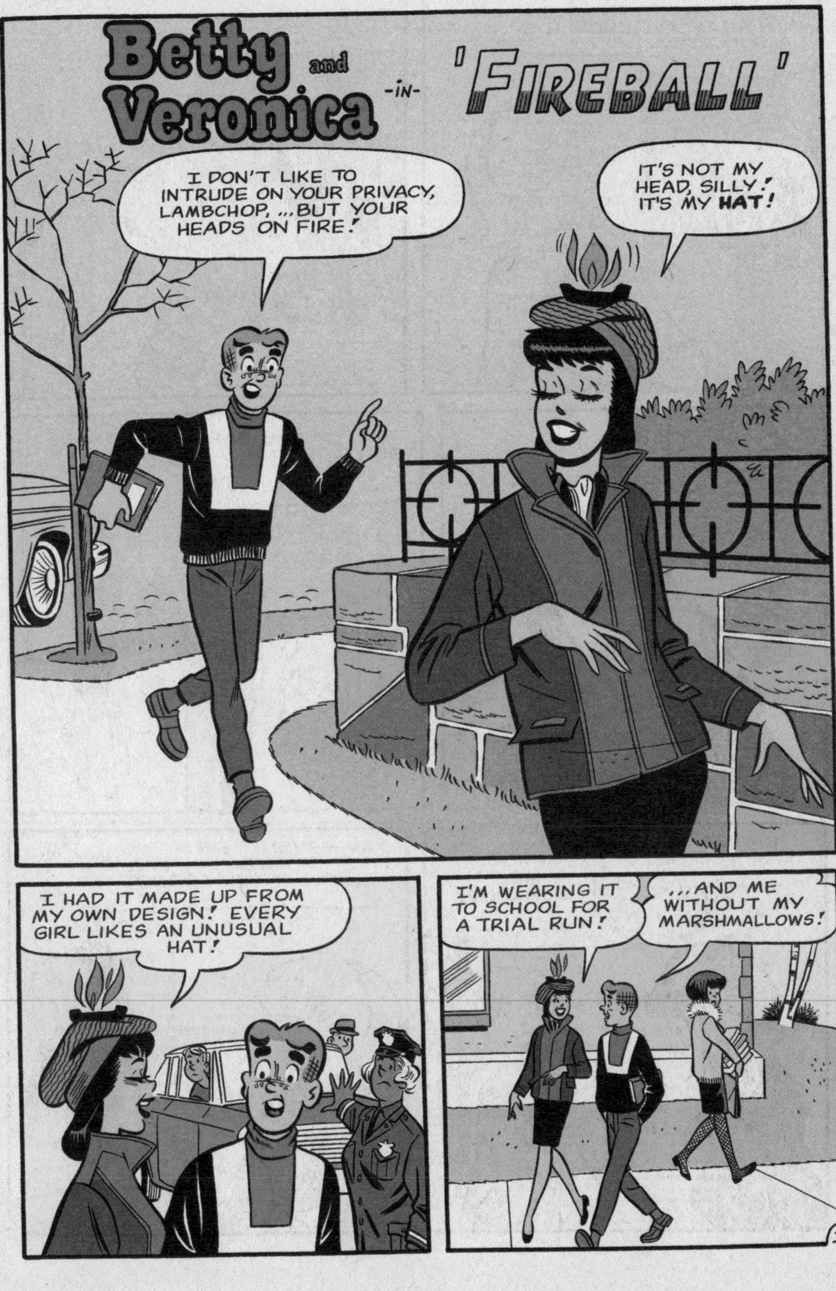
Betty and Veronica -IN- 'FIREBALL'
I DON'T LIKE TO INTRUDE ON YOUR PRIVACY, LAMBCHOP, ...BUT YOUR HEADS ON FIRE!
IT'S NOT MY HEAD, SILLY! IT'S MY HAT!
I HAD IT MADE UP FROM MY OWN DESIGN! EVERY GIRL LIKES AN UNUSUAL HAT!
I'M WEARING IT TO SCHOOL FOR A TRIAL RUN!
...AND ME WITHOUT MY MARSHMALLOWS!
1

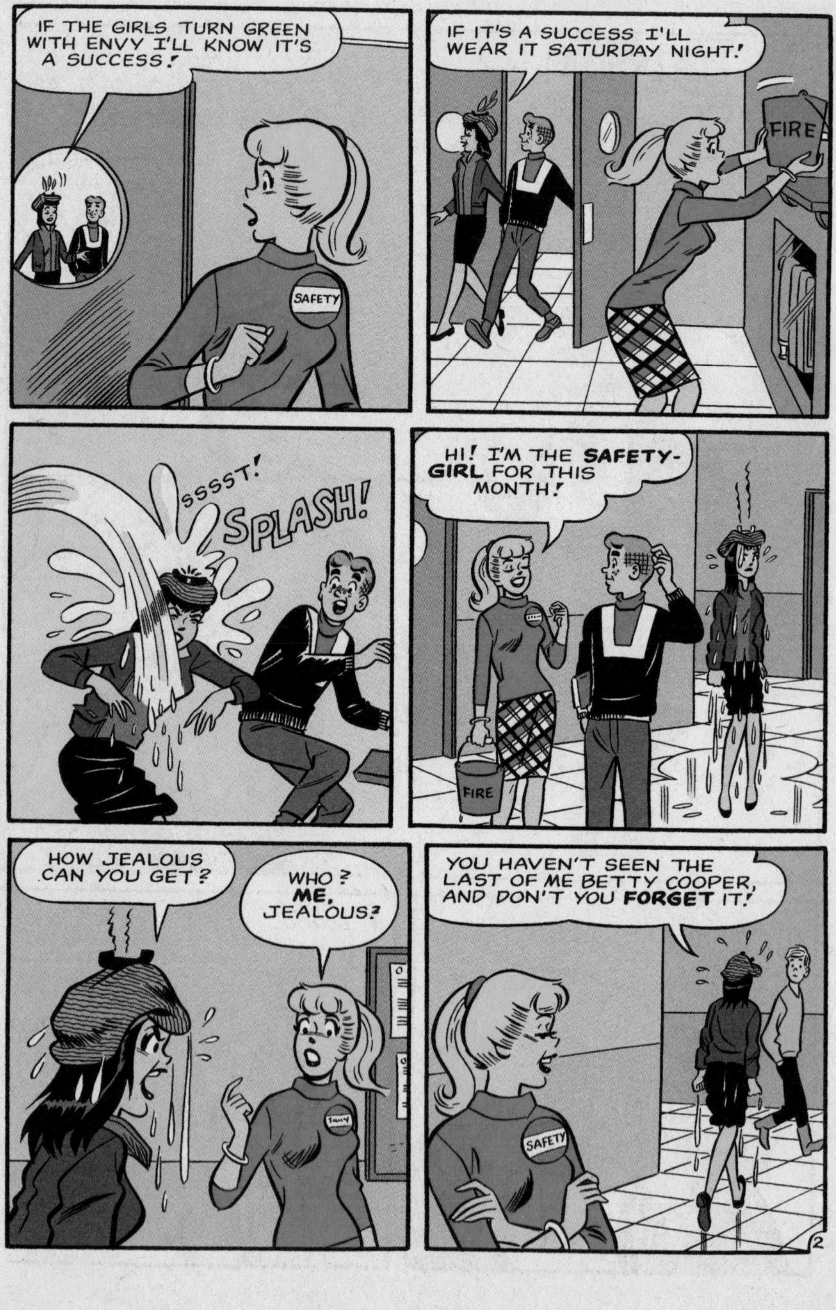
IF THE GIRLS TURN GREEN WITH ENVY I'LL KNOW IT'S A SUCCESS!
SAFETY
IF IT'S A SUCCESS I'LL WEAR IT SATURDAY NIGHT!
FIRE
SSSST!
SPLASH!
HI! I'M THE **SAFETY-GIRL** FOR THIS MONTH!
FIRE
HOW JEALOUS CAN YOU GET?
WHO? **ME**, JEALOUS?
YOU HAVEN'T SEEN THE LAST OF ME BETTY COOPER, AND DON'T YOU **FORGET** IT!
SAFETY
2

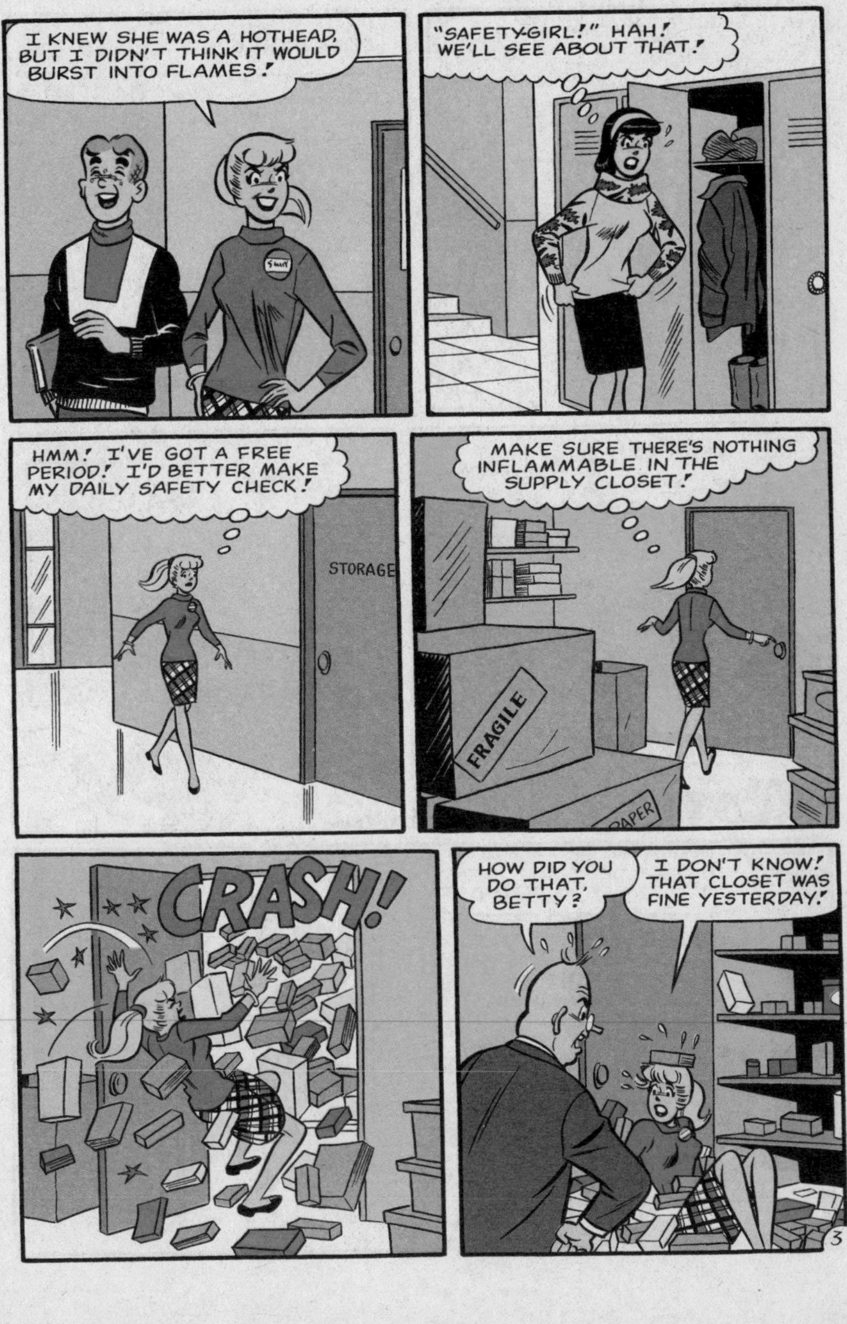
I KNEW SHE WAS A HOTHEAD, BUT I DIDN'T THINK IT WOULD BURST INTO FLAMES!
"SAFETY-GIRL!" HAH! WE'LL SEE ABOUT THAT!
HMM! I'VE GOT A FREE PERIOD! I'D BETTER MAKE MY DAILY SAFETY CHECK!
STORAGE
MAKE SURE THERE'S NOTHING INFLAMMABLE IN THE SUPPLY CLOSET!
FRAGILE
CRASH!
HOW DID YOU DO THAT, BETTY?
I DON'T KNOW! THAT CLOSET WAS FINE YESTERDAY!
3

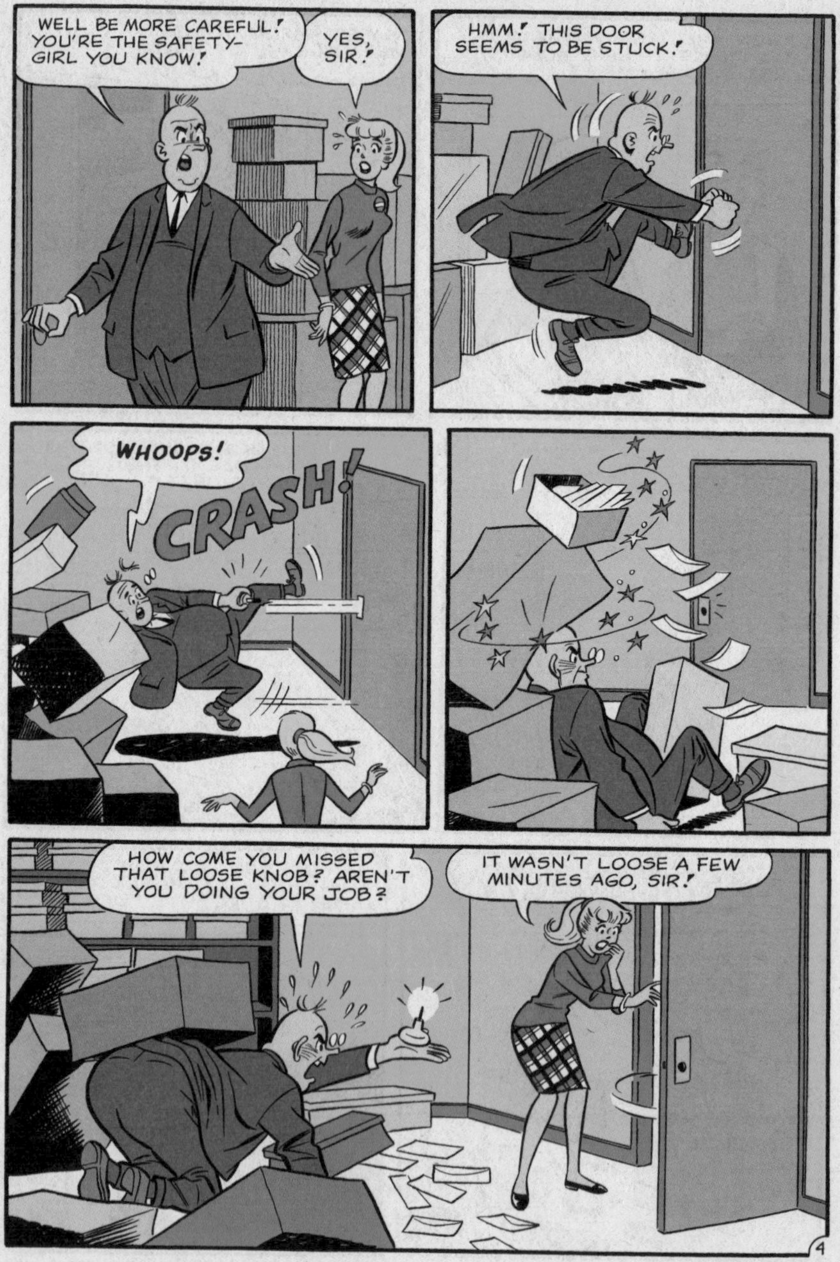
WELL BE MORE CAREFUL! YOU'RE THE SAFETY-GIRL YOU KNOW!
YES, SIR!
HMM! THIS DOOR SEEMS TO BE STUCK!
WHOOPS!
CRASH!
HOW COME YOU MISSED THAT LOOSE KNOB? AREN'T YOU DOING YOUR JOB?
IT WASN'T LOOSE A FEW MINUTES AGO, SIR!
4

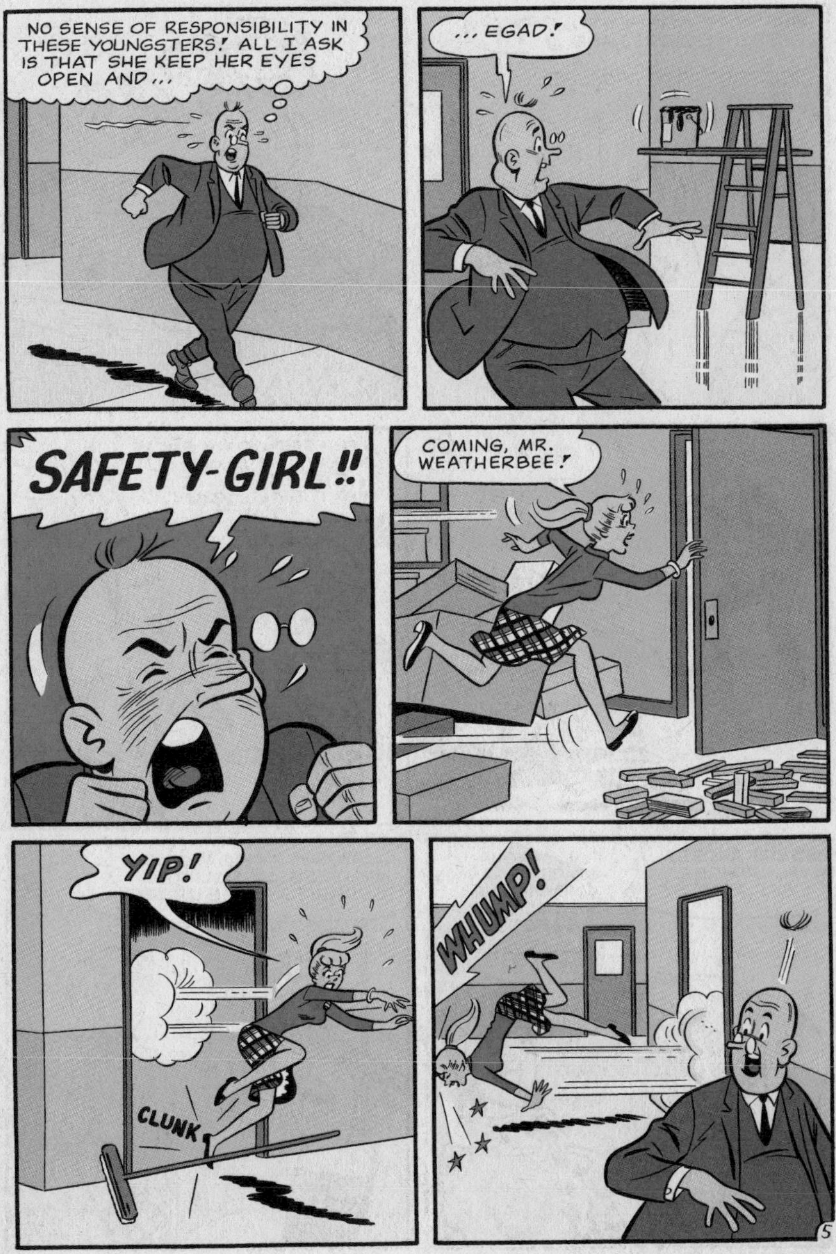
NO SENSE OF RESPONSIBILITY IN THESE YOUNGSTERS! ALL I ASK IS THAT SHE KEEP HER EYES OPEN AND...
...EGAD!
SAFETY-GIRL!!
COMING, MR. WEATHERBEE!
YIP!
CLUNK
WHUMP!
5

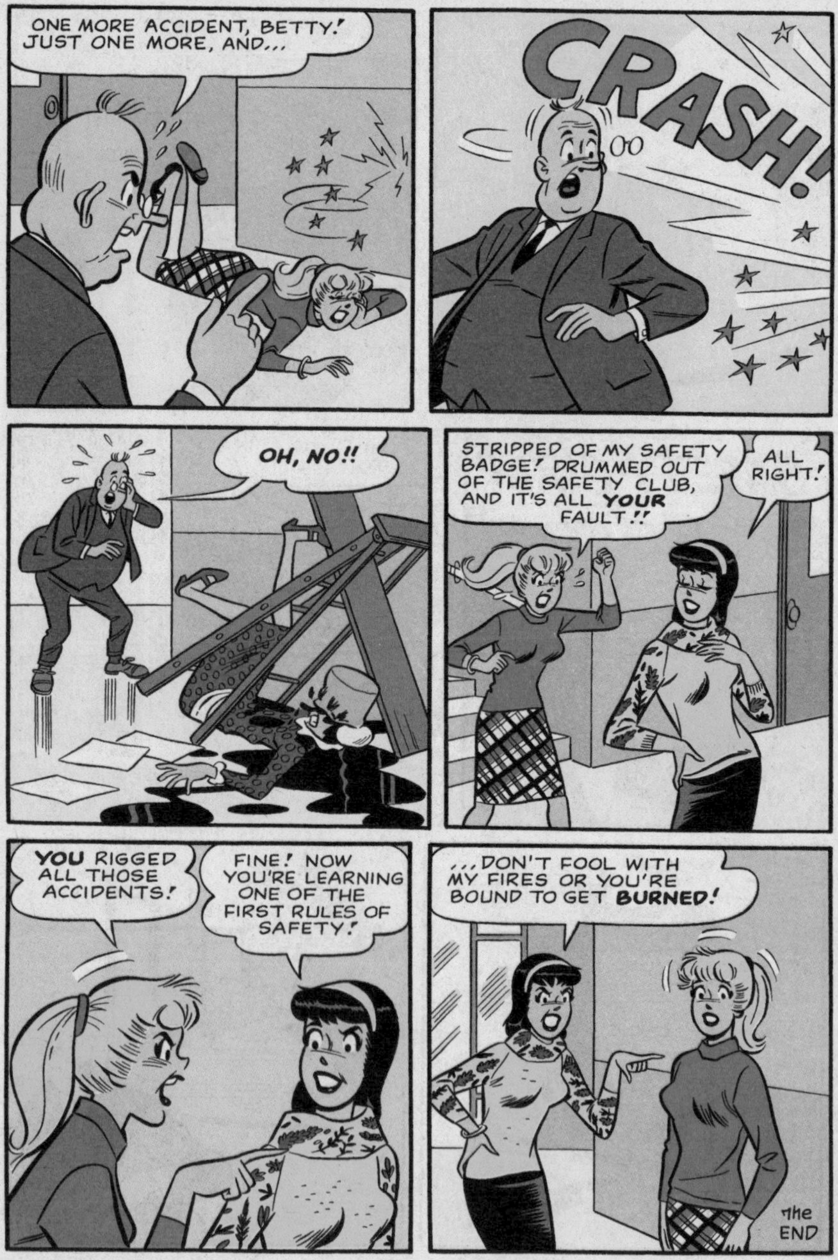
ONE MORE ACCIDENT, BETTY! JUST ONE MORE, AND...
CRASH!
OH, NO!!
STRIPPED OF MY SAFETY BADGE! DRUMMED OUT OF THE SAFETY CLUB, AND IT'S ALL YOUR FAULT!!
ALL RIGHT!
YOU RIGGED ALL THOSE ACCIDENTS!
FINE! NOW YOU'RE LEARNING ONE OF THE FIRST RULES OF SAFETY!
...DON'T FOOL WITH MY FIRES OR YOU'RE BOUND TO GET BURNED!
The END

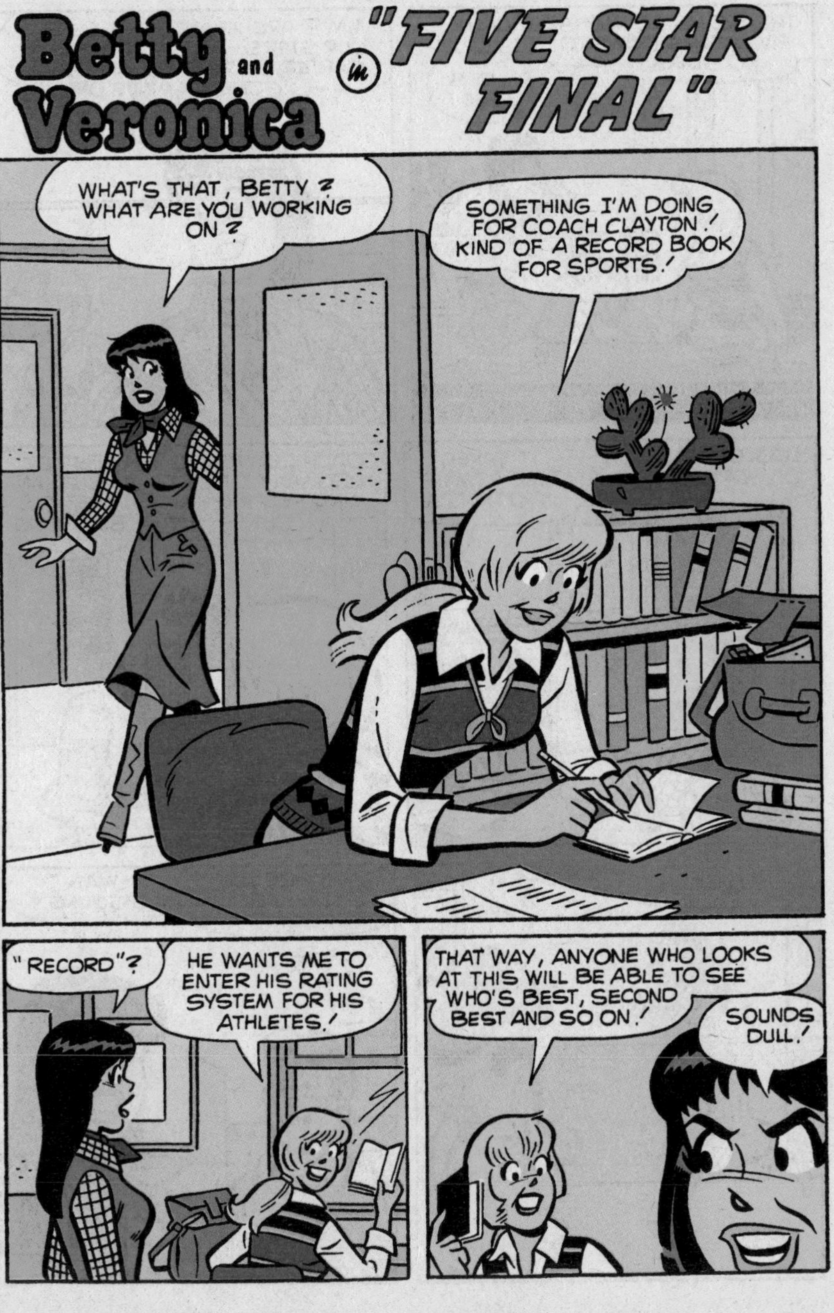

Betty and Veronica in "FIVE STAR FINAL"
WHAT'S THAT, BETTY? WHAT ARE YOU WORKING ON?
SOMETHING I'M DOING FOR COACH CLAYTON! KIND OF A RECORD BOOK FOR SPORTS!
"RECORD"?
HE WANTS ME TO ENTER HIS RATING SYSTEM FOR HIS ATHLETES!
THAT WAY, ANYONE WHO LOOKS AT THIS WILL BE ABLE TO SEE WHO'S BEST, SECOND BEST AND SO ON!
SOUNDS DULL!

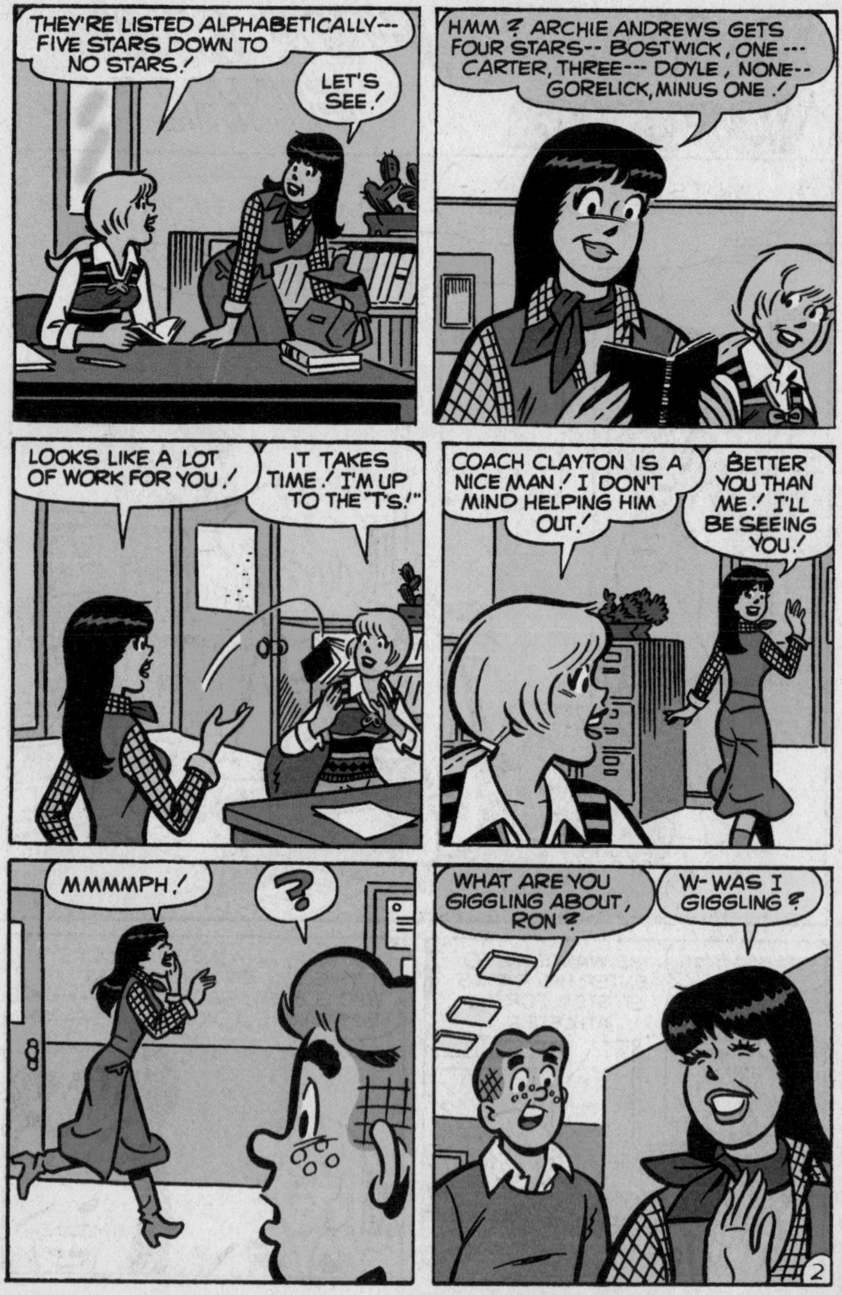
THEY'RE LISTED ALPHABETICALLY--- FIVE STARS DOWN TO NO STARS!
LET'S SEE!
HMM ? ARCHIE ANDREWS GETS FOUR STARS-- BOSTWICK, ONE --- CARTER, THREE--- DOYLE, NONE-- GORELICK, MINUS ONE!
LOOKS LIKE A LOT OF WORK FOR YOU!
IT TAKES TIME! I'M UP TO THE "T'S!"
COACH CLAYTON IS A NICE MAN! I DON'T MIND HELPING HIM OUT!
BETTER YOU THAN ME! I'LL BE SEEING YOU!
MMMMPH!
?
WHAT ARE YOU GIGGLING ABOUT, RON ?
W-WAS I GIGGLING ?
2

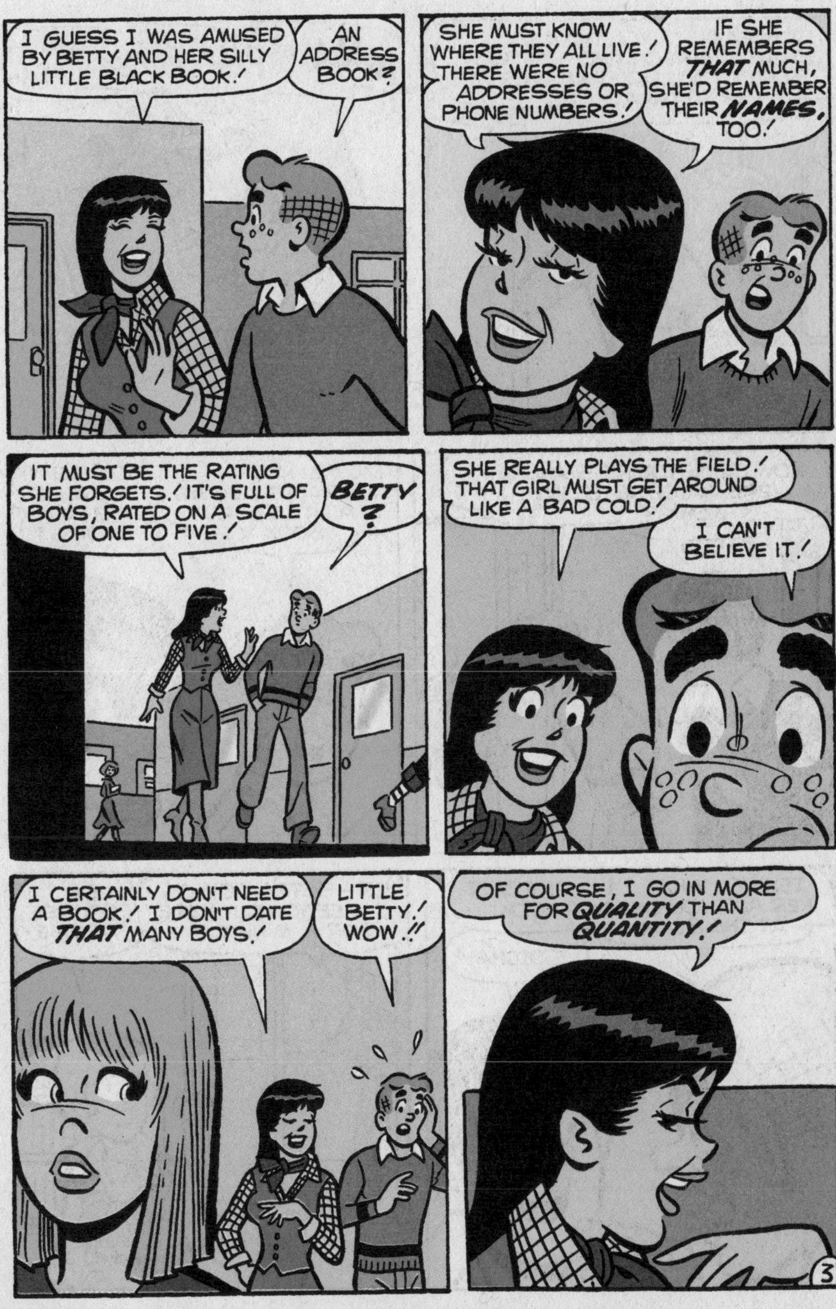
I GUESS I WAS AMUSED BY BETTY AND HER SILLY LITTLE BLACK BOOK!
AN ADDRESS BOOK?
SHE MUST KNOW WHERE THEY ALL LIVE! THERE WERE NO ADDRESSES OR PHONE NUMBERS!
IF SHE REMEMBERS THAT MUCH, SHE'D REMEMBER THEIR NAMES, TOO!
IT MUST BE THE RATING SHE FORGETS! IT'S FULL OF BOYS, RATED ON A SCALE OF ONE TO FIVE!
BETTY?
SHE REALLY PLAYS THE FIELD! THAT GIRL MUST GET AROUND LIKE A BAD COLD!
I CAN'T BELIEVE IT!
I CERTAINLY DON'T NEED A BOOK! I DON'T DATE THAT MANY BOYS!
LITTLE BETTY! WOW!!
OF COURSE, I GO IN MORE FOR QUALITY THAN QUANTITY!
3

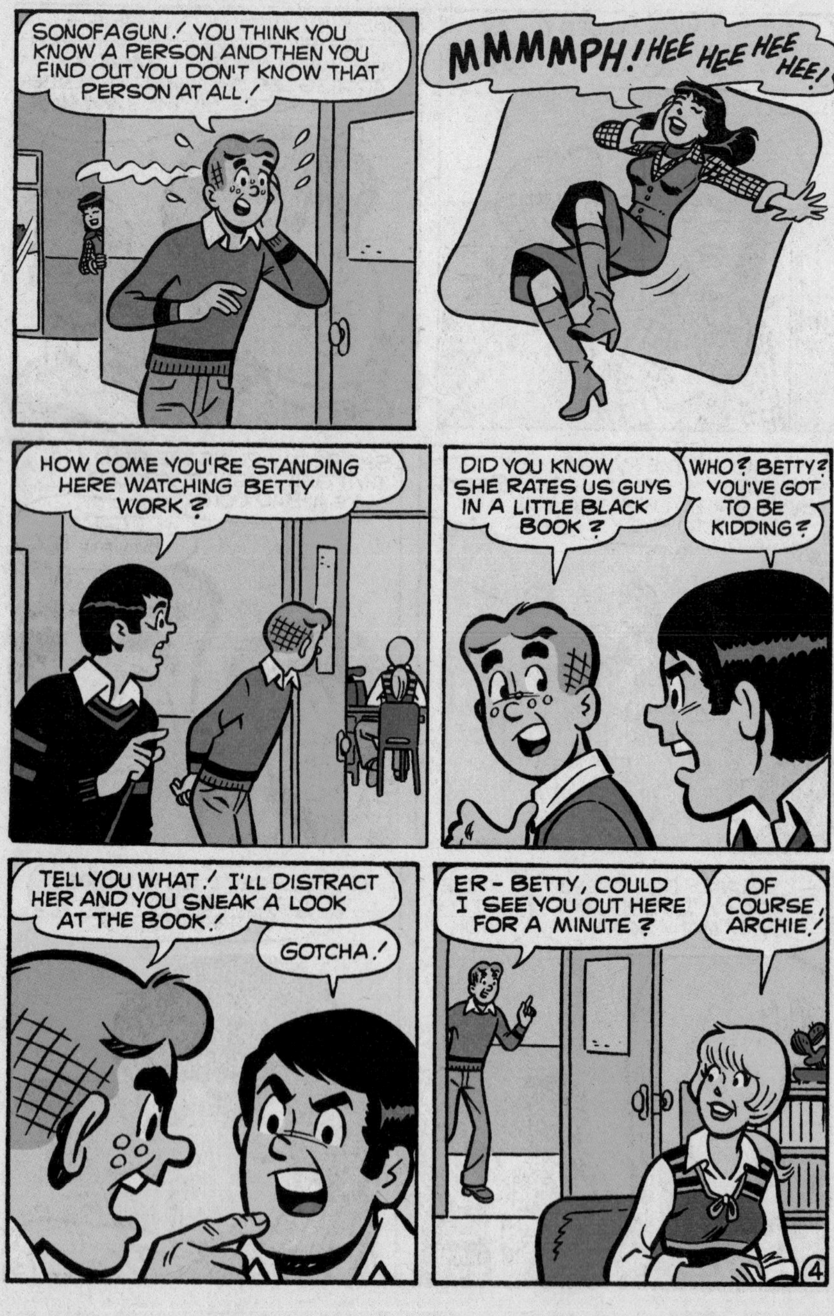
SONOFAGUN! YOU THINK YOU KNOW A PERSON AND THEN YOU FIND OUT YOU DON'T KNOW THAT PERSON AT ALL!
MMMMPH! HEE HEE HEE HEE!
HOW COME YOU'RE STANDING HERE WATCHING BETTY WORK?
DID YOU KNOW SHE RATES US GUYS IN A LITTLE BLACK BOOK?
WHO? BETTY? YOU'VE GOT TO BE KIDDING?
TELL YOU WHAT! I'LL DISTRACT HER AND YOU SNEAK A LOOK AT THE BOOK!
GOTCHA!
ER - BETTY, COULD I SEE YOU OUT HERE FOR A MINUTE?
OF COURSE, ARCHIE!
4

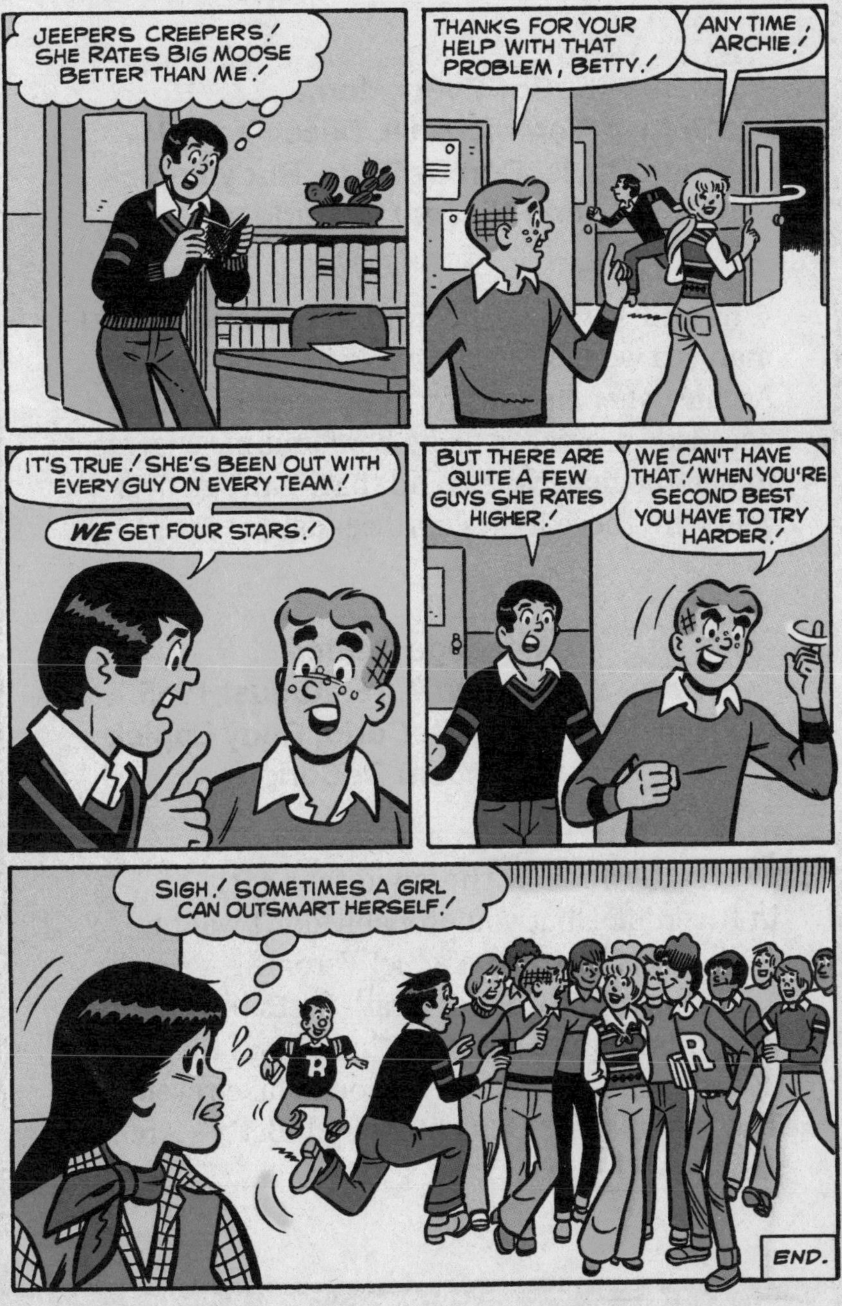
JEEPERS CREEPERS! SHE RATES BIG MOOSE BETTER THAN ME!
THANKS FOR YOUR HELP WITH THAT PROBLEM, BETTY!
ANY TIME, ARCHIE!
IT'S TRUE! SHE'S BEEN OUT WITH EVERY GUY ON EVERY TEAM!
WE GET FOUR STARS!
BUT THERE ARE QUITE A FEW GUYS SHE RATES HIGHER!
WE CAN'T HAVE THAT! WHEN YOU'RE SECOND BEST YOU HAVE TO TRY HARDER!
SIGH! SOMETIMES A GIRL CAN OUTSMART HERSELF!
R
R
END.

For Every Man…
Betty & Veronica #84, December 1962
**Frank Doyle, Dan DeCarlo, Rudy Lapick
and Vincent DeCarlo**

The old saying, "behind every successful man is a woman" gets a workout… and so does Archie, when he runs for class president! That's because Veronica is using her feminine charms to win the male vote… and that's can't go over well with those males' girlfriends!

Message Center
Betty & Veronica #116, August 1965
**Frank Doyle, Dan DeCarlo, Rudy Lapick
and Vincent DeCarlo**

Betty Cooper is the sweetest girl in Riverdale…but you probably don't want to get between her and Archie! Veronica experiences the Cooper wrath firsthand after she pulls a prank on Betty that causes the usually mild-mannered blonde to take revenge. The lesson here? Don't mess with Betty's Archie time.

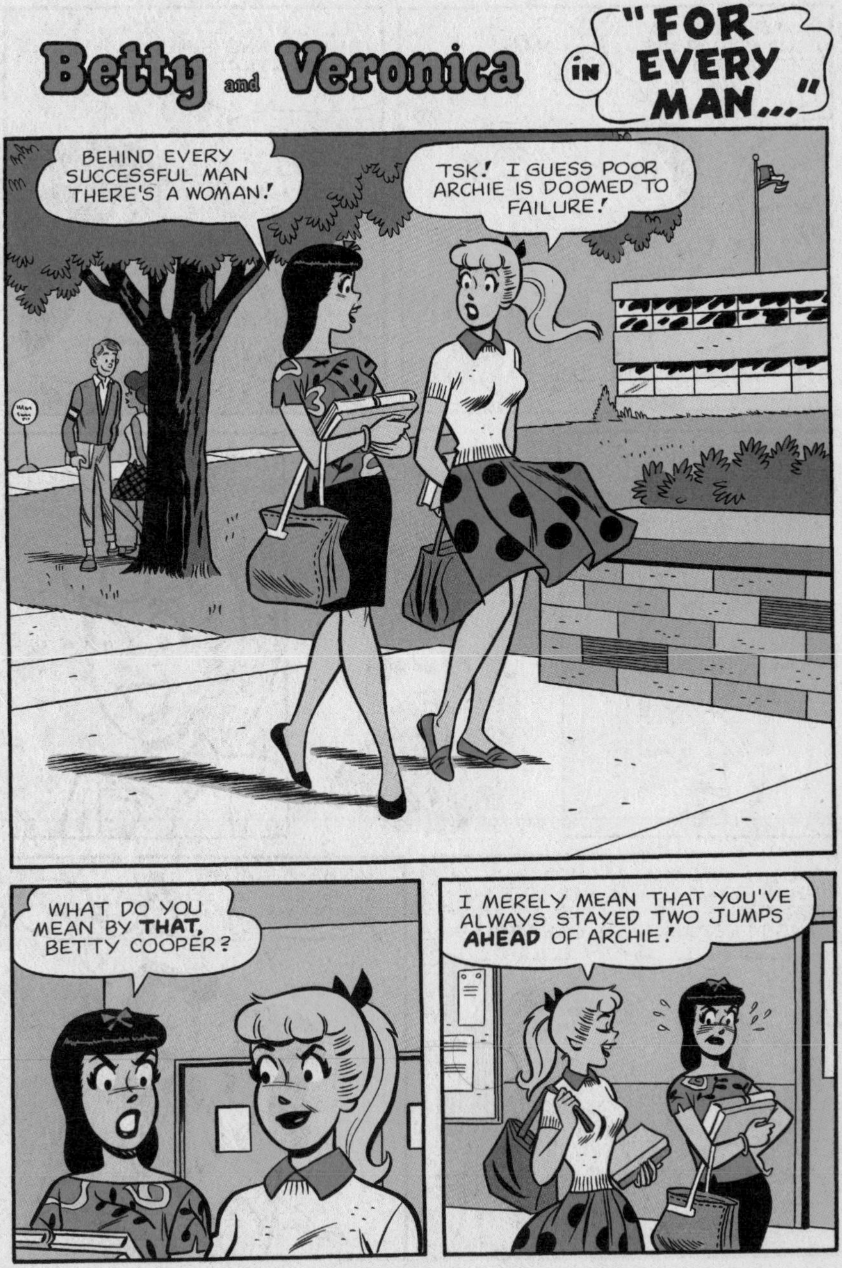
Betty and Veronica
IN "FOR EVERY MAN..."
BEHIND EVERY SUCCESSFUL MAN THERE'S A WOMAN!
TSK! I GUESS POOR ARCHIE IS DOOMED TO FAILURE!
WHAT DO YOU MEAN BY THAT, BETTY COOPER?
I MERELY MEAN THAT YOU'VE ALWAYS STAYED TWO JUMPS AHEAD OF ARCHIE!

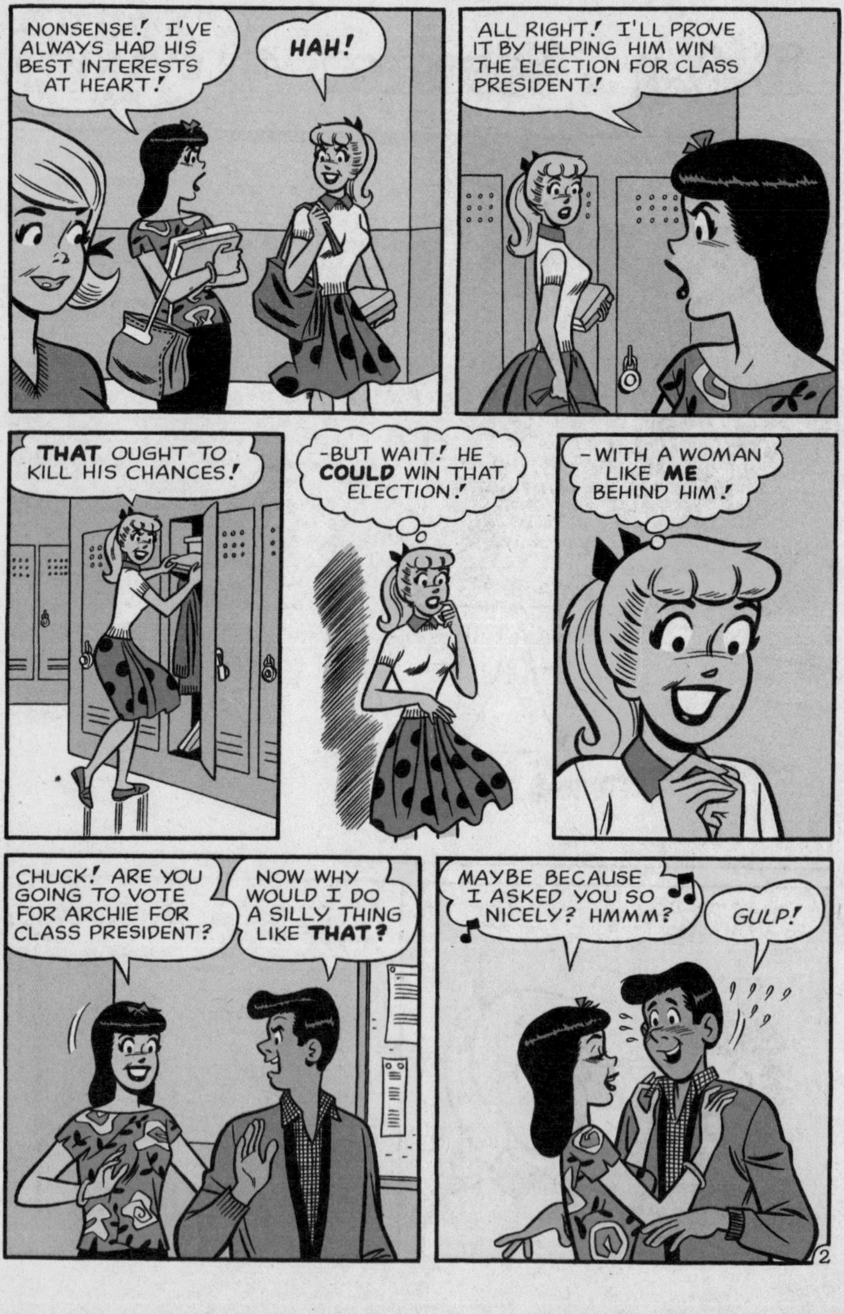
NONSENSE! I'VE ALWAYS HAD HIS BEST INTERESTS AT HEART!
HAH!
ALL RIGHT! I'LL PROVE IT BY HELPING HIM WIN THE ELECTION FOR CLASS PRESIDENT!
THAT OUGHT TO KILL HIS CHANCES!
-BUT WAIT! HE COULD WIN THAT ELECTION!
-WITH A WOMAN LIKE ME BEHIND HIM!
CHUCK! ARE YOU GOING TO VOTE FOR ARCHIE FOR CLASS PRESIDENT?
NOW WHY WOULD I DO A SILLY THING LIKE THAT?
MAYBE BECAUSE I ASKED YOU SO NICELY? HMMM?
GULP!
2

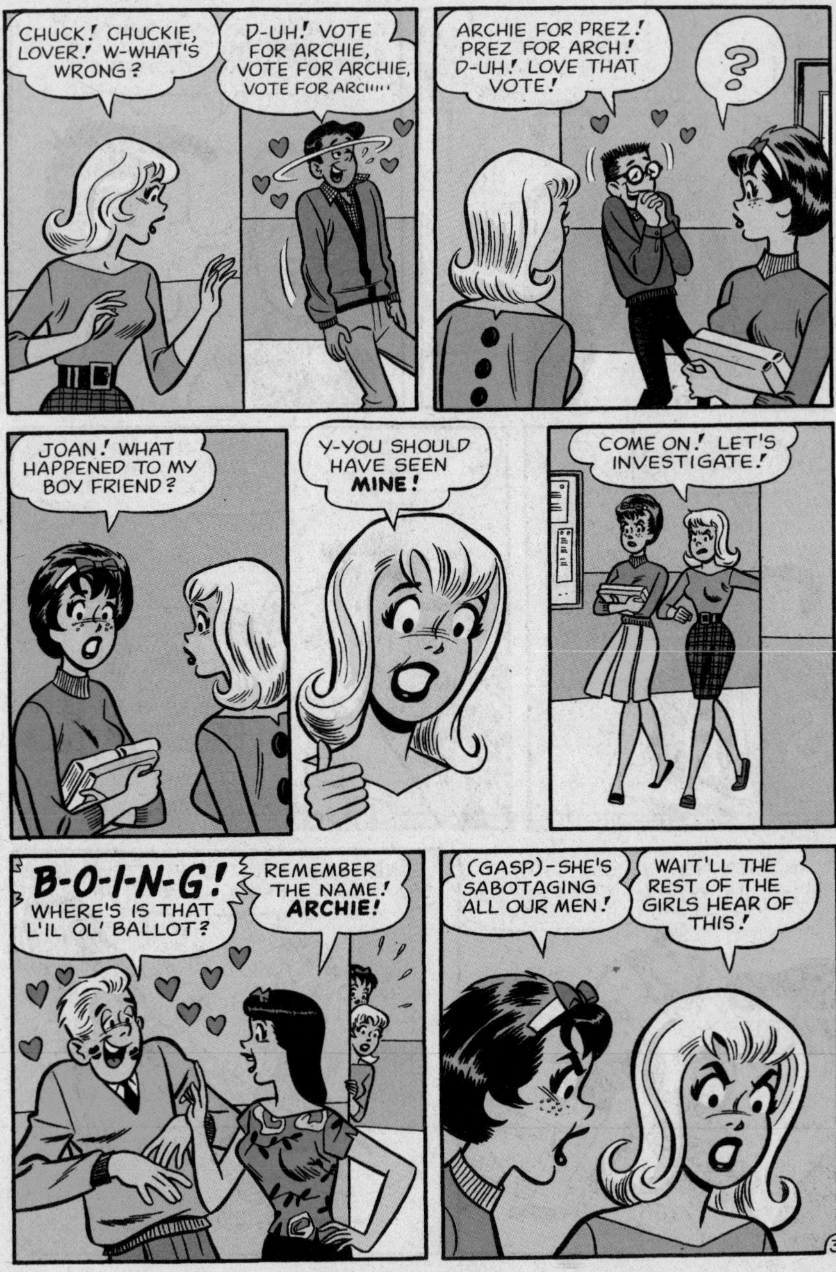
CHUCK! CHUCKIE, LOVER! W-WHAT'S WRONG?
D-UH! VOTE FOR ARCHIE, VOTE FOR ARCHIE, VOTE FOR ARC!!!!!
ARCHIE FOR PREZ! PREZ FOR ARCH! D-UH! LOVE THAT VOTE!
?
JOAN! WHAT HAPPENED TO MY BOY FRIEND?
Y-YOU SHOULD HAVE SEEN MINE!
COME ON! LET'S INVESTIGATE!
B-O-I-N-G! WHERE'S IS THAT L'IL OL' BALLOT?
REMEMBER THE NAME! ARCHIE!
(GASP)-SHE'S SABOTAGING ALL OUR MEN!
WAIT'LL THE REST OF THE GIRLS HEAR OF THIS!
3

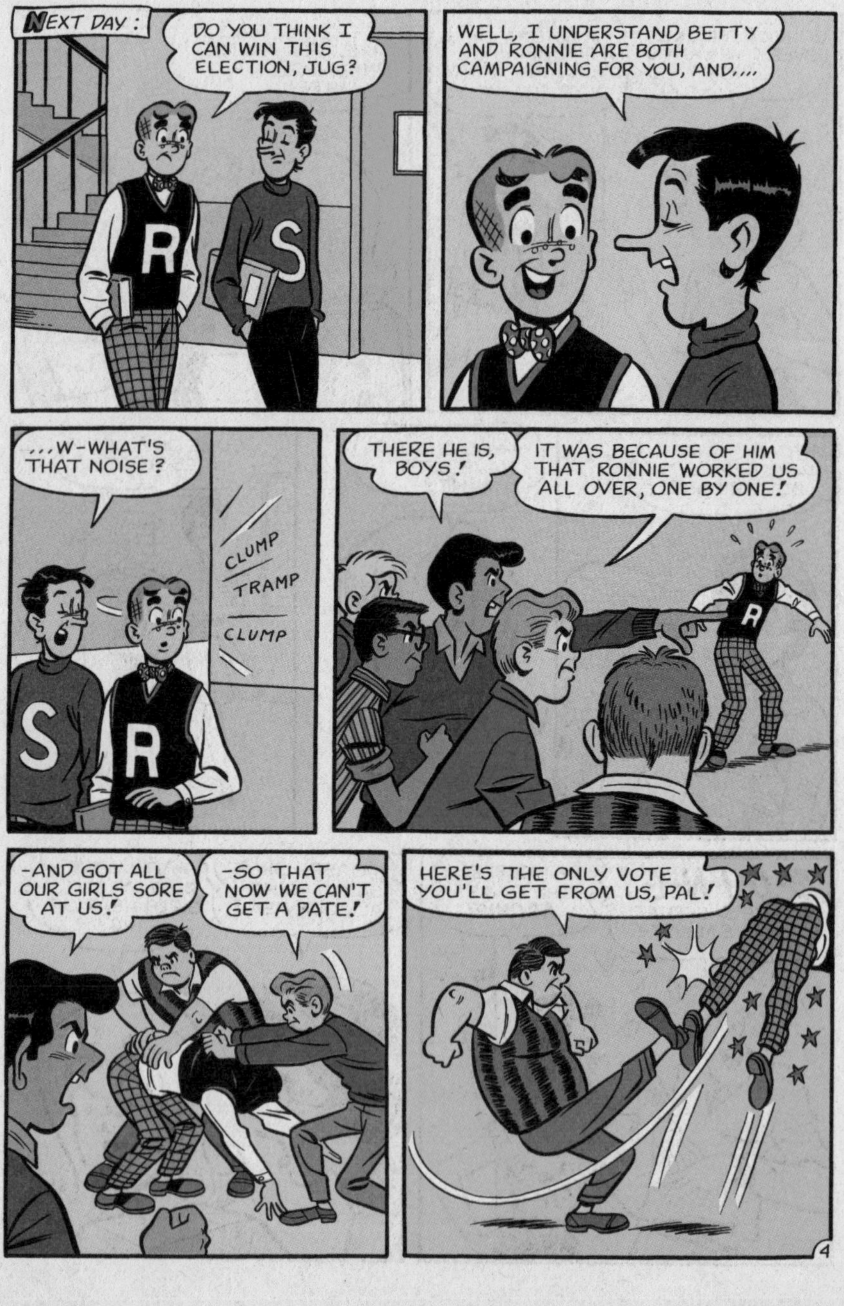
NEXT DAY :
DO YOU THINK I CAN WIN THIS ELECTION, JUG?
WELL, I UNDERSTAND BETTY AND RONNIE ARE BOTH CAMPAIGNING FOR YOU, AND....
...W-WHAT'S THAT NOISE ?
CLUMP
TRAMP
CLUMP
THERE HE IS, BOYS!
IT WAS BECAUSE OF HIM THAT RONNIE WORKED US ALL OVER, ONE BY ONE!
-AND GOT ALL OUR GIRLS SORE AT US!
-SO THAT NOW WE CAN'T GET A DATE!
HERE'S THE ONLY VOTE YOU'LL GET FROM US, PAL!
4

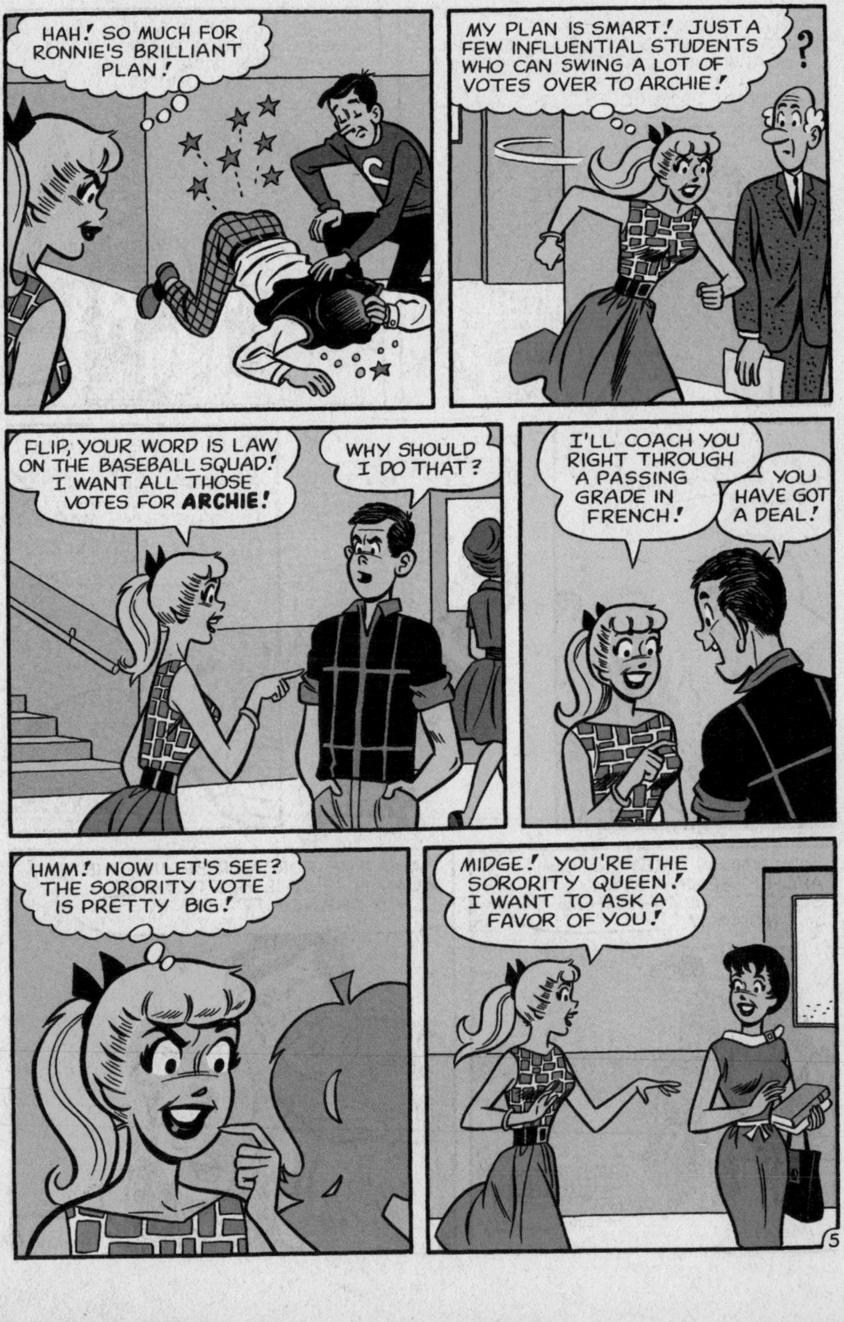
HAH! SO MUCH FOR RONNIE'S BRILLIANT PLAN!
MY PLAN IS SMART! JUST A FEW INFLUENTIAL STUDENTS WHO CAN SWING A LOT OF VOTES OVER TO ARCHIE!
?
FLIP, YOUR WORD IS LAW ON THE BASEBALL SQUAD! I WANT ALL THOSE VOTES FOR **ARCHIE**!
WHY SHOULD I DO THAT?
I'LL COACH YOU RIGHT THROUGH A PASSING GRADE IN FRENCH!
YOU HAVE GOT A DEAL!
HMM! NOW LET'S SEE? THE SORORITY VOTE IS PRETTY BIG!
MIDGE! YOU'RE THE SORORITY QUEEN! I WANT TO ASK A FAVOR OF YOU!
5

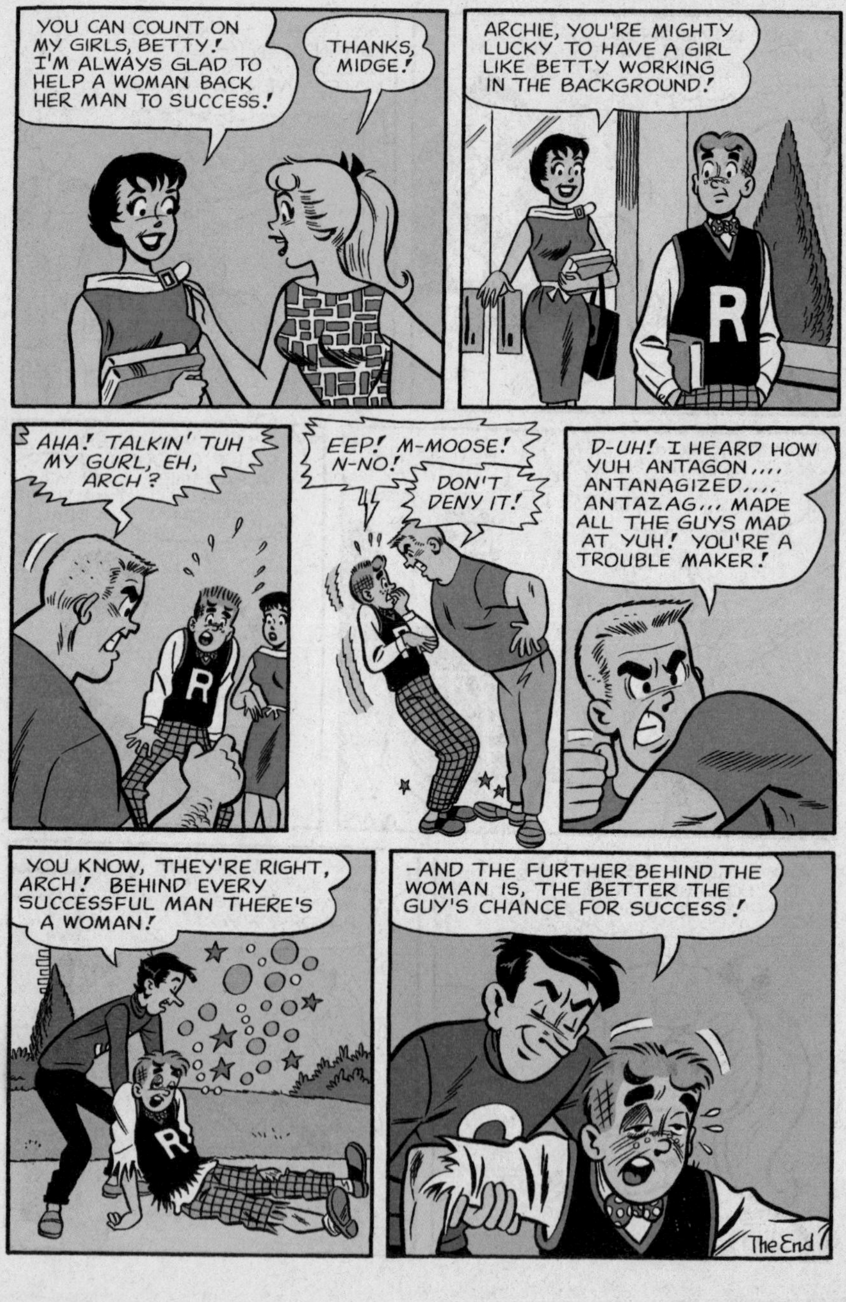
YOU CAN COUNT ON MY GIRLS, BETTY! I'M ALWAYS GLAD TO HELP A WOMAN BACK HER MAN TO SUCCESS!
THANKS, MIDGE!
ARCHIE, YOU'RE MIGHTY LUCKY TO HAVE A GIRL LIKE BETTY WORKING IN THE BACKGROUND!
AHA! TALKIN' TUH MY GURL, EH, ARCH?
EEP! M-MOOSE! N-NO!
DON'T DENY IT!
D-UH! I HEARD HOW YUH ANTAGON.... ANTANAGIZED.... ANTAZAG... MADE ALL THE GUYS MAD AT YUH! YOU'RE A TROUBLE MAKER!
YOU KNOW, THEY'RE RIGHT, ARCH! BEHIND EVERY SUCCESSFUL MAN THERE'S A WOMAN!
-AND THE FURTHER BEHIND THE WOMAN IS, THE BETTER THE GUY'S CHANCE FOR SUCCESS!
The End

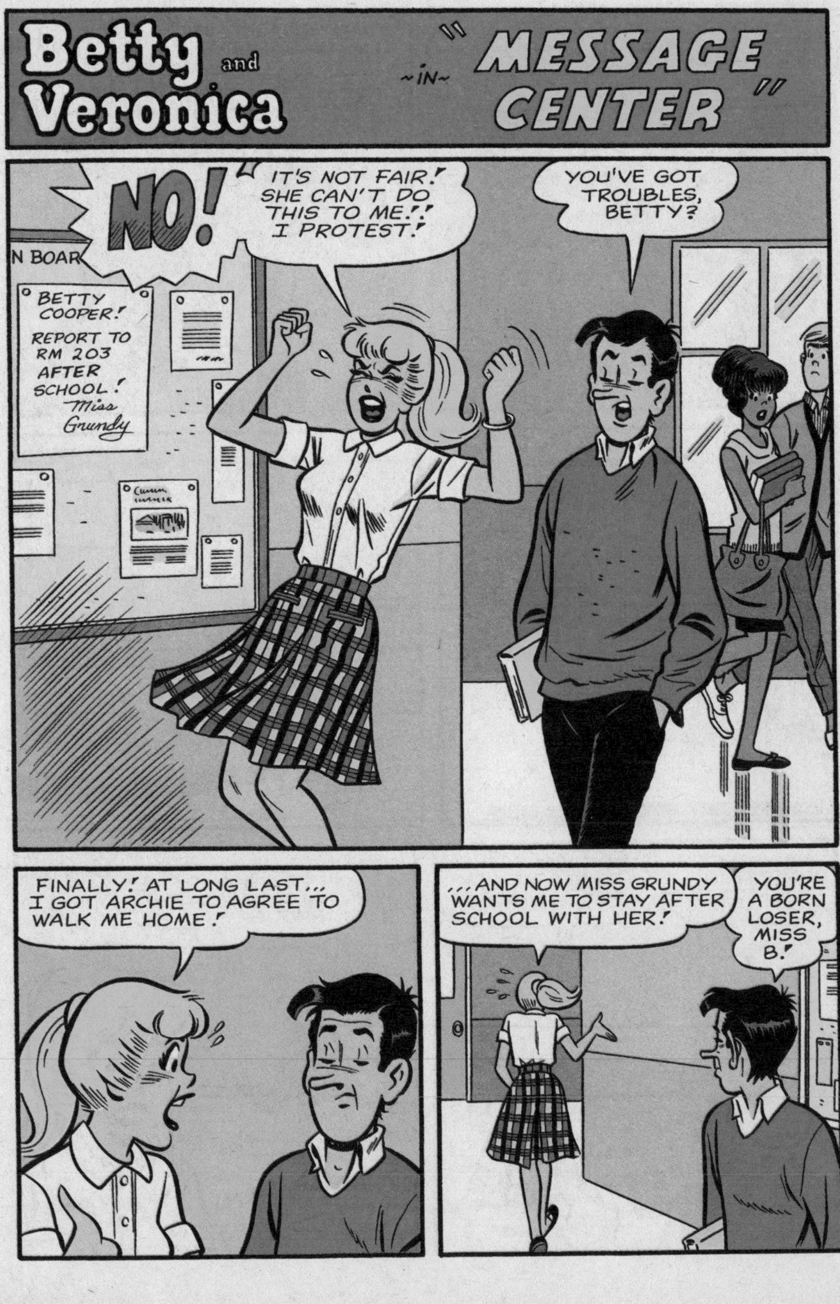
Betty and Veronica
~in~ "MESSAGE CENTER"
NO!
IT'S NOT FAIR! SHE CAN'T DO THIS TO ME!! I PROTEST!
N BOAR
BETTY COOPER!
REPORT TO RM 203 AFTER SCHOOL! Miss Grundy
YOU'VE GOT TROUBLES, BETTY?
FINALLY! AT LONG LAST... I GOT ARCHIE TO AGREE TO WALK ME HOME!
...AND NOW MISS GRUNDY WANTS ME TO STAY AFTER SCHOOL WITH HER!
YOU'RE A BORN LOSER, MISS B.!

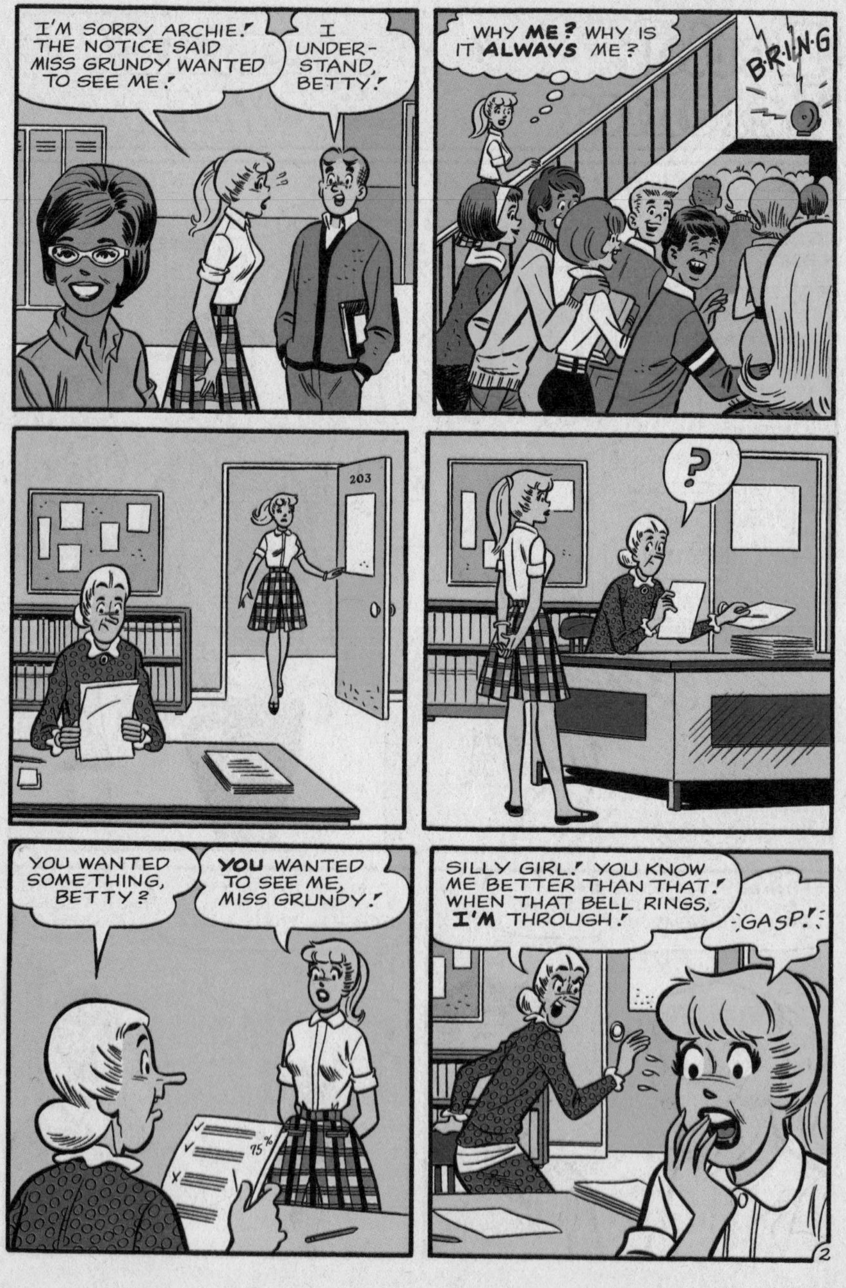
I'M SORRY ARCHIE! THE NOTICE SAID MISS GRUNDY WANTED TO SEE ME!
I UNDERSTAND, BETTY!
WHY ME? WHY IS IT ALWAYS ME?
B-R-I-N-G
203
?
YOU WANTED SOMETHING, BETTY?
YOU WANTED TO SEE ME, MISS GRUNDY!
75%
SILLY GIRL! YOU KNOW ME BETTER THAN THAT! WHEN THAT BELL RINGS, I'M THROUGH!
GASP!
2

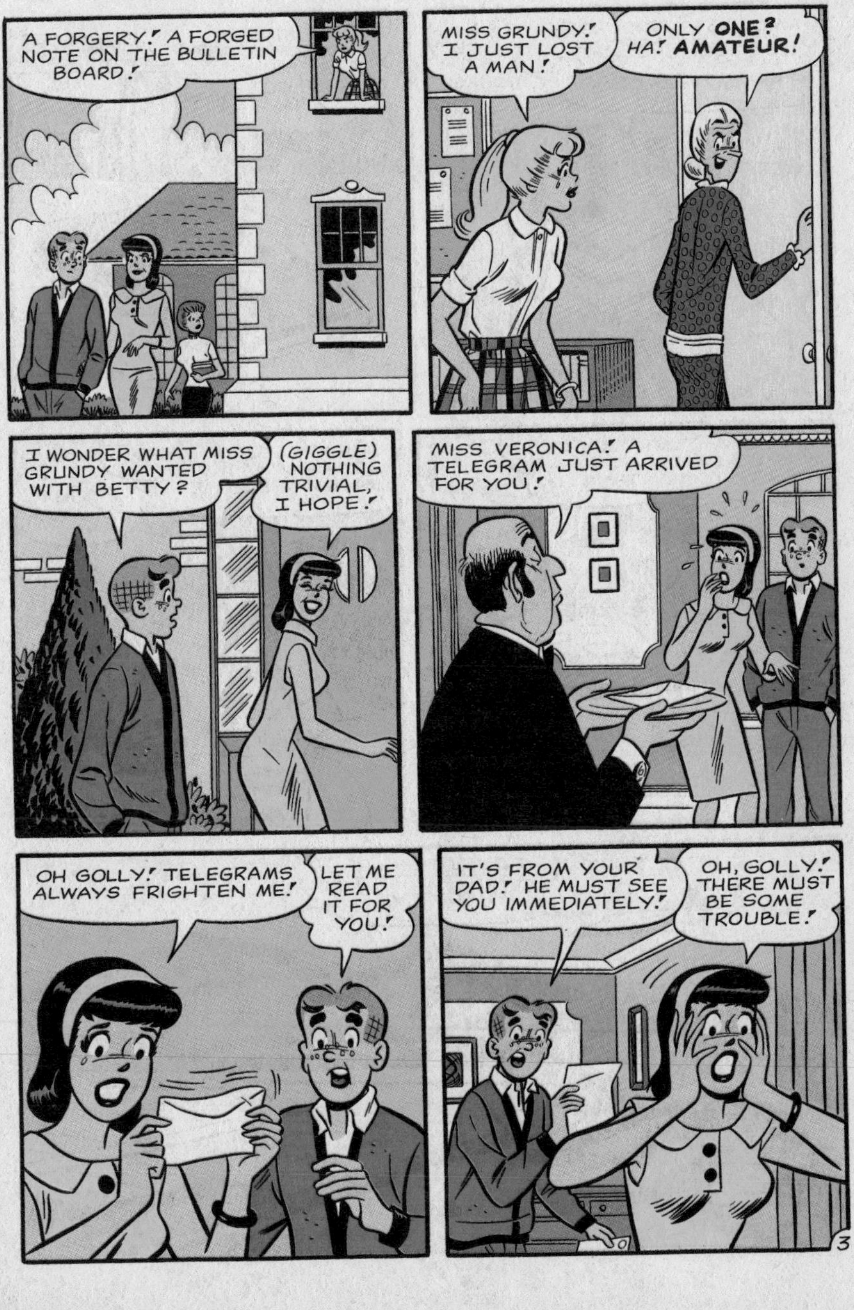
A FORGERY! A FORGED NOTE ON THE BULLETIN BOARD!
MISS GRUNDY! I JUST LOST A MAN!
ONLY ONE? HA! AMATEUR!
I WONDER WHAT MISS GRUNDY WANTED WITH BETTY?
(GIGGLE) NOTHING TRIVIAL, I HOPE!
MISS VERONICA! A TELEGRAM JUST ARRIVED FOR YOU!
OH GOLLY! TELEGRAMS ALWAYS FRIGHTEN ME!
LET ME READ IT FOR YOU!
IT'S FROM YOUR DAD! HE MUST SEE YOU IMMEDIATELY!
OH, GOLLY! THERE MUST BE SOME TROUBLE!
3

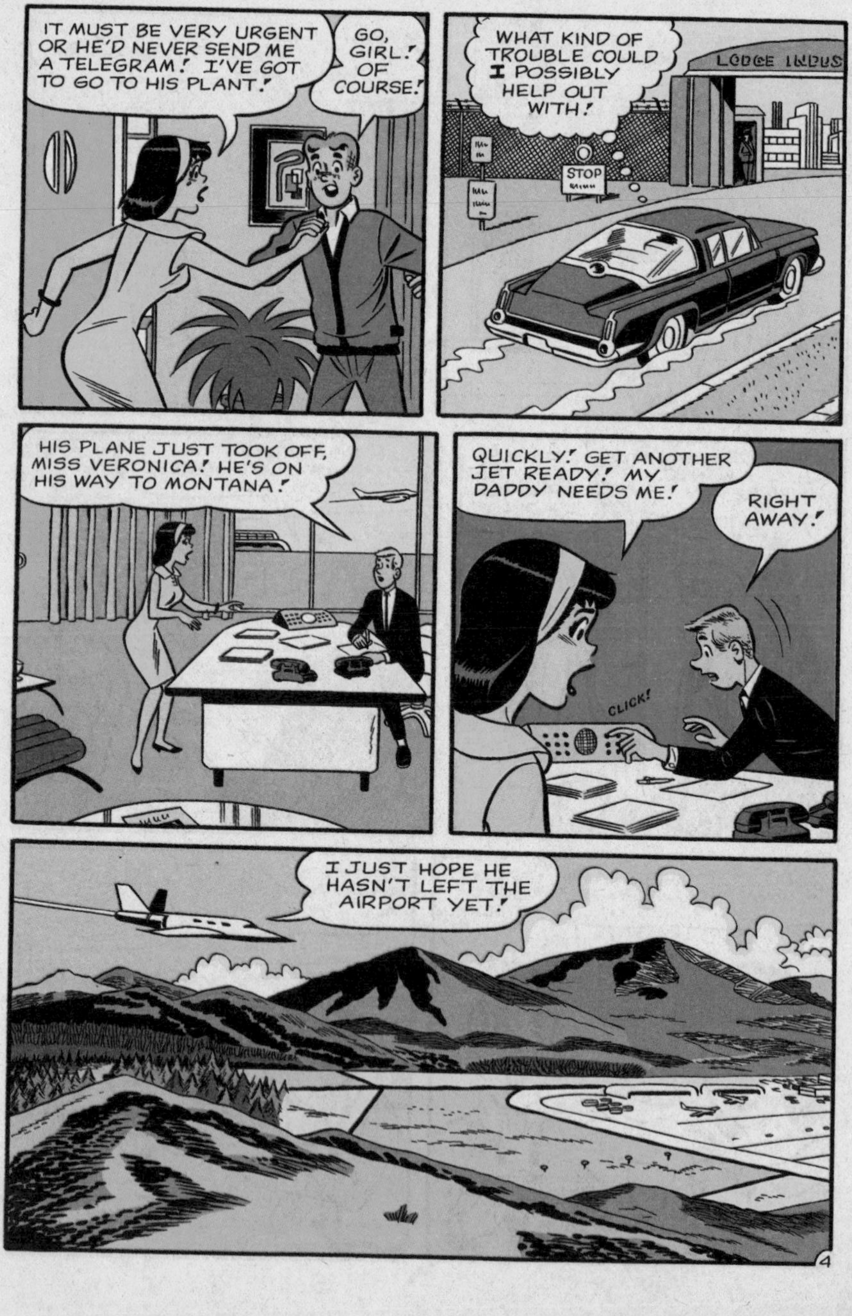
IT MUST BE VERY URGENT OR HE'D NEVER SEND ME A TELEGRAM! I'VE GOT TO GO TO HIS PLANT!
GO, GIRL! OF COURSE!
WHAT KIND OF TROUBLE COULD I POSSIBLY HELP OUT WITH!
LODGE INDUS
STOP
HIS PLANE JUST TOOK OFF, MISS VERONICA! HE'S ON HIS WAY TO MONTANA!
QUICKLY! GET ANOTHER JET READY! MY DADDY NEEDS ME!
RIGHT AWAY!
CLICK!
I JUST HOPE HE HASN'T LEFT THE AIRPORT YET!
4

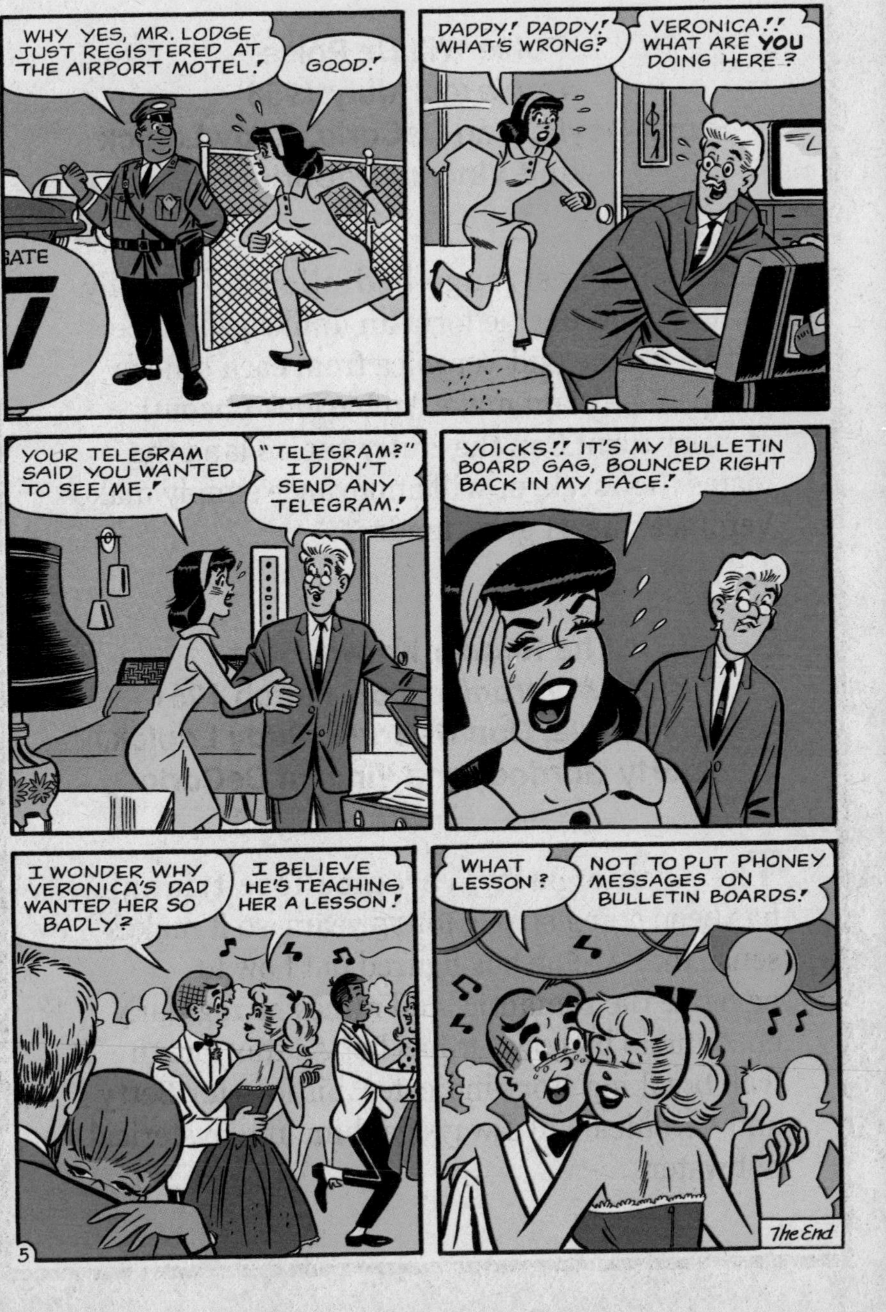
WHY YES, MR. LODGE JUST REGISTERED AT THE AIRPORT MOTEL!
GOOD!
GATE
DADDY! DADDY! WHAT'S WRONG?
VERONICA!! WHAT ARE YOU DOING HERE?
YOUR TELEGRAM SAID YOU WANTED TO SEE ME!
"TELEGRAM?" I DIDN'T SEND ANY TELEGRAM!
YOICKS!! IT'S MY BULLETIN BOARD GAG, BOUNCED RIGHT BACK IN MY FACE!
I WONDER WHY VERONICA'S DAD WANTED HER SO BADLY?
I BELIEVE HE'S TEACHING HER A LESSON!
WHAT LESSON?
NOT TO PUT PHONEY MESSAGES ON BULLETIN BOARDS!
The End
5

Poise Will Be Poise
Archie #93, July 1958
Frank Doyle, Dan DeCarlo, Rudy Lapick
and Vincent DeCarlo

Love makes strange bedfellows... literally, as Betty and Reggie form an unlikely alliance to free Archie and Veronica from each other's grasps. The plan: make Archie look uncouth at every turn! Can the crafty cupids land the mates they seek, or will annoyance simply make Veronica's heart grow fonder?

The Reader Knows Best
Betty & Veronica #63, March 1961
Frank Doyle, Dan DeCarlo, Rudy Lapick,
Marty Gardner and Vincent DeCarlo

The Archie/Betty/Veronica love triangle has been going strong for 75 years, so it makes sense that Archie has figured out how to navigate the romantic land mines he regularly encounters by now. Or has he? As this fourth wall breaking story indicates, his love for Betty and Veronica will always get him into hysterical hot water.

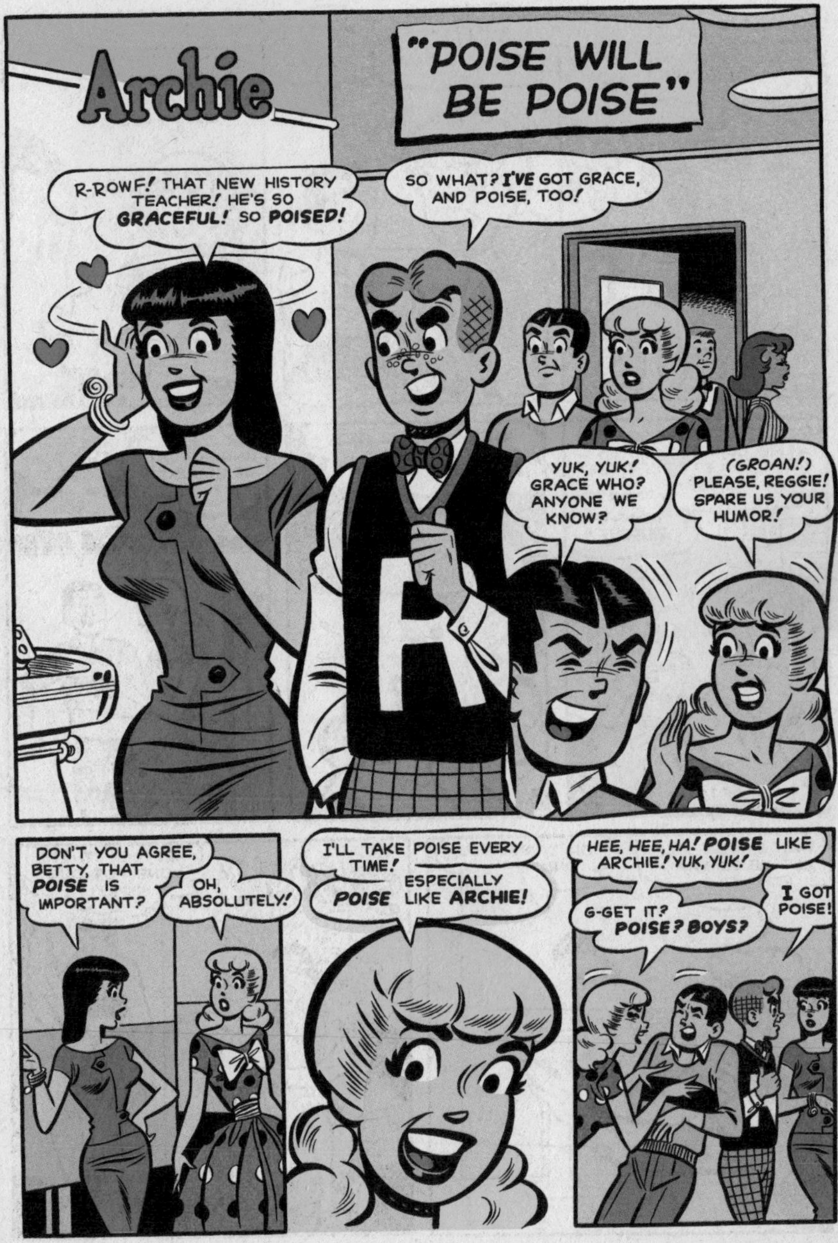
Archie
"POISE WILL BE POISE"
R-ROWF! THAT NEW HISTORY TEACHER! HE'S SO GRACEFUL! SO POISED!
SO WHAT? I'VE GOT GRACE, AND POISE, TOO!
YUK, YUK! GRACE WHO? ANYONE WE KNOW?
(GROAN!) PLEASE, REGGIE! SPARE US YOUR HUMOR!
DON'T YOU AGREE, BETTY, THAT POISE IS IMPORTANT?
OH, ABSOLUTELY!
I'LL TAKE POISE EVERY TIME!
ESPECIALLY POISE LIKE ARCHIE!
HEE, HEE, HA! POISE LIKE ARCHIE! YUK, YUK!
G-GET IT? POISE? BOYS?
I GOT POISE!

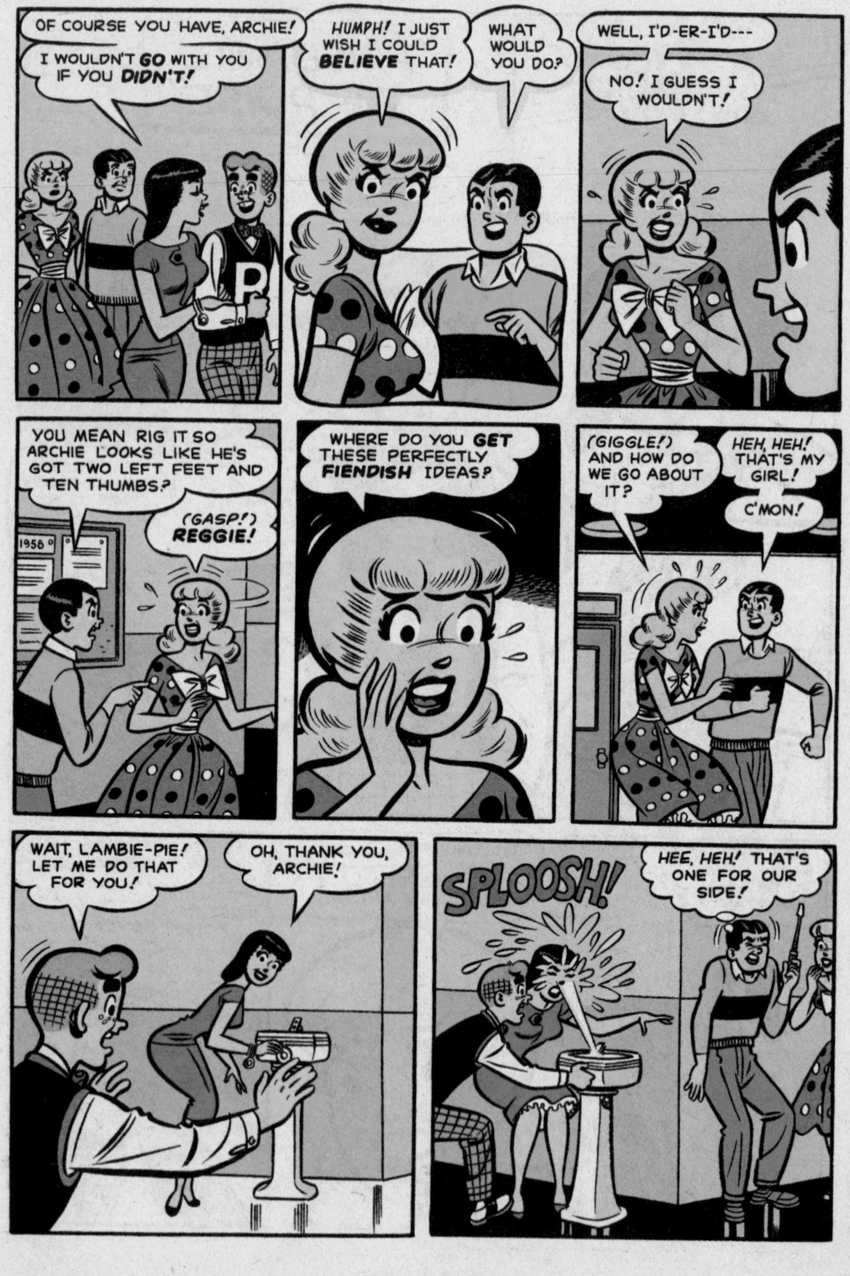
OF COURSE YOU HAVE, ARCHIE!
I WOULDN'T GO WITH YOU IF YOU DIDN'T!
HUMPH! I JUST WISH I COULD BELIEVE THAT!
WHAT WOULD YOU DO?
WELL, I'D-ER-I'D---
NO! I GUESS I WOULDN'T!
YOU MEAN RIG IT SO ARCHIE LOOKS LIKE HE'S GOT TWO LEFT FEET AND TEN THUMBS?
(GASP!) REGGIE!
1958
WHERE DO YOU GET THESE PERFECTLY FIENDISH IDEAS?
(GIGGLE!) AND HOW DO WE GO ABOUT IT?
HEH, HEH! THAT'S MY GIRL!
C'MON!
WAIT, LAMBIE-PIE! LET ME DO THAT FOR YOU!
OH, THANK YOU, ARCHIE!
SPLOOSH!
HEE, HEH! THAT'S ONE FOR OUR SIDE!

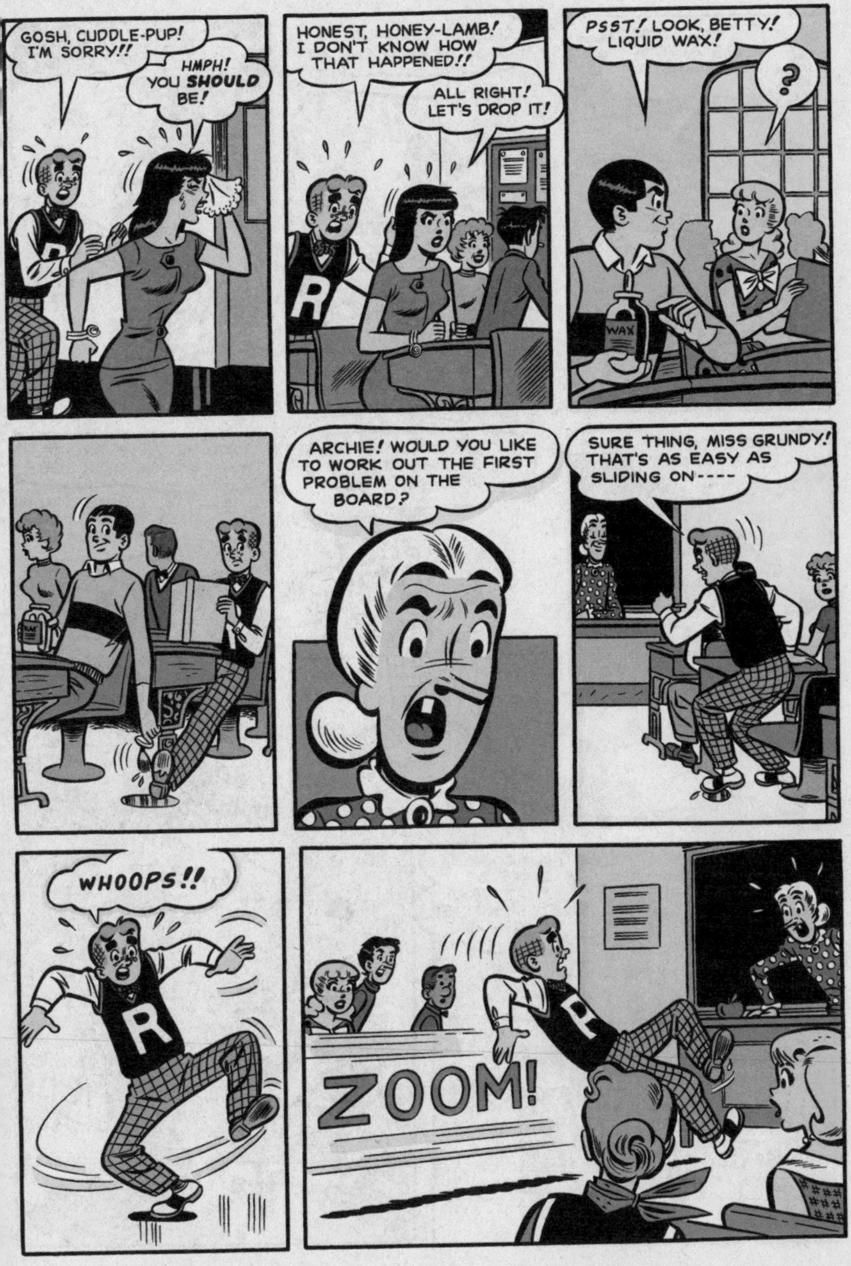
GOSH, CUDDLE-PUP! I'M SORRY!!
HMPH! YOU SHOULD BE!
HONEST, HONEY-LAMB! I DON'T KNOW HOW THAT HAPPENED!!
ALL RIGHT! LET'S DROP IT!
PSST! LOOK, BETTY! LIQUID WAX!
?
WAX
ARCHIE! WOULD YOU LIKE TO WORK OUT THE FIRST PROBLEM ON THE BOARD?
SURE THING, MISS GRUNDY! THAT'S AS EASY AS SLIDING ON----
WHOOPS!!
ZOOM!

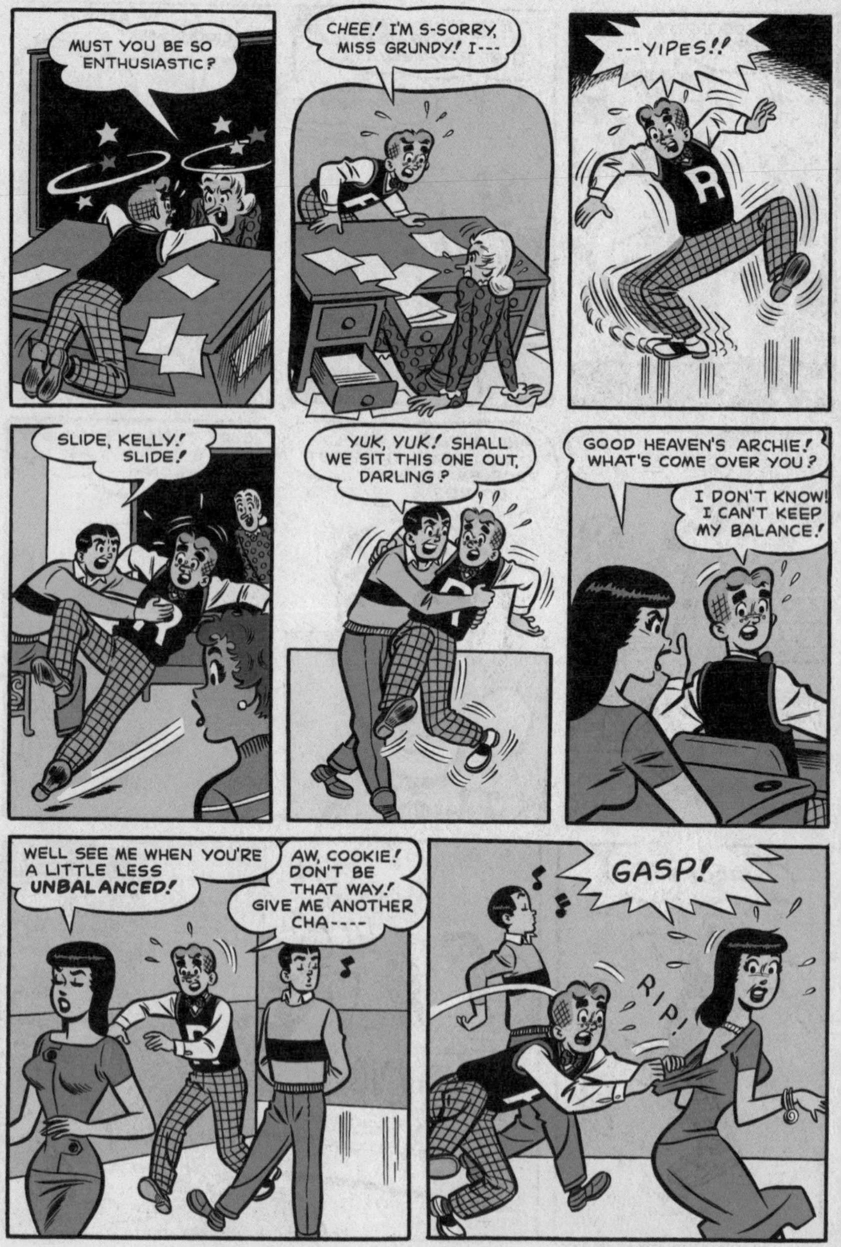
MUST YOU BE SO ENTHUSIASTIC?
CHEE! I'M S-SORRY, MISS GRUNDY! I---
---YIPES!!
SLIDE, KELLY! SLIDE!
YUK, YUK! SHALL WE SIT THIS ONE OUT, DARLING?
GOOD HEAVEN'S ARCHIE! WHAT'S COME OVER YOU?
I DON'T KNOW! I CAN'T KEEP MY BALANCE!
WELL SEE ME WHEN YOU'RE A LITTLE LESS UNBALANCED!
AW, COOKIE! DON'T BE THAT WAY! GIVE ME ANOTHER CHA----
GASP!
RIP!

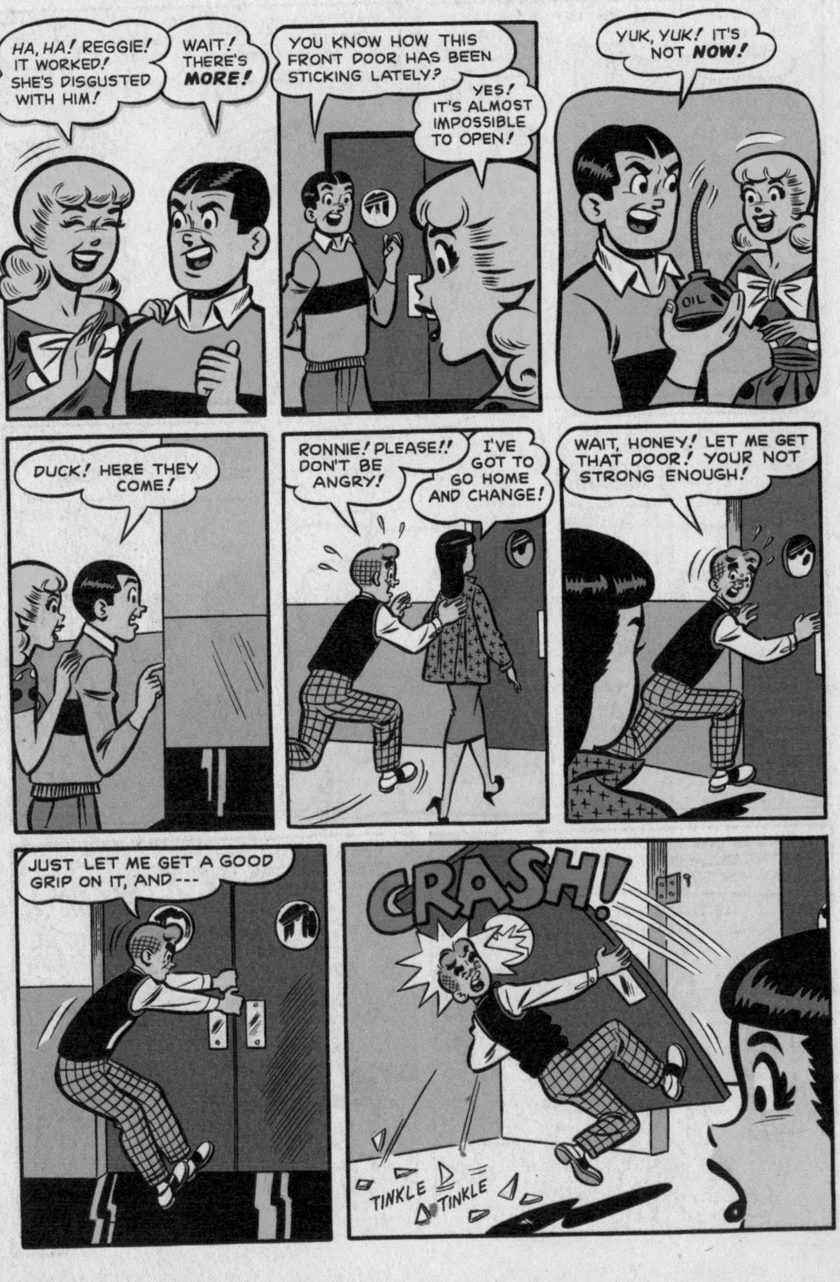
HA, HA! REGGIE! IT WORKED! SHE'S DISGUSTED WITH HIM!
WAIT! THERE'S **MORE!**
YOU KNOW HOW THIS FRONT DOOR HAS BEEN STICKING LATELY?
YES! IT'S ALMOST IMPOSSIBLE TO OPEN!
YUK, YUK! IT'S NOT **NOW!**
OIL
DUCK! HERE THEY COME!
RONNIE! PLEASE!! DON'T BE ANGRY!
I'VE GOT TO GO HOME AND CHANGE!
WAIT, HONEY! LET ME GET THAT DOOR! YOUR NOT STRONG ENOUGH!
JUST LET ME GET A GOOD GRIP ON IT, AND ---
CRASH!
TINKLE TINKLE

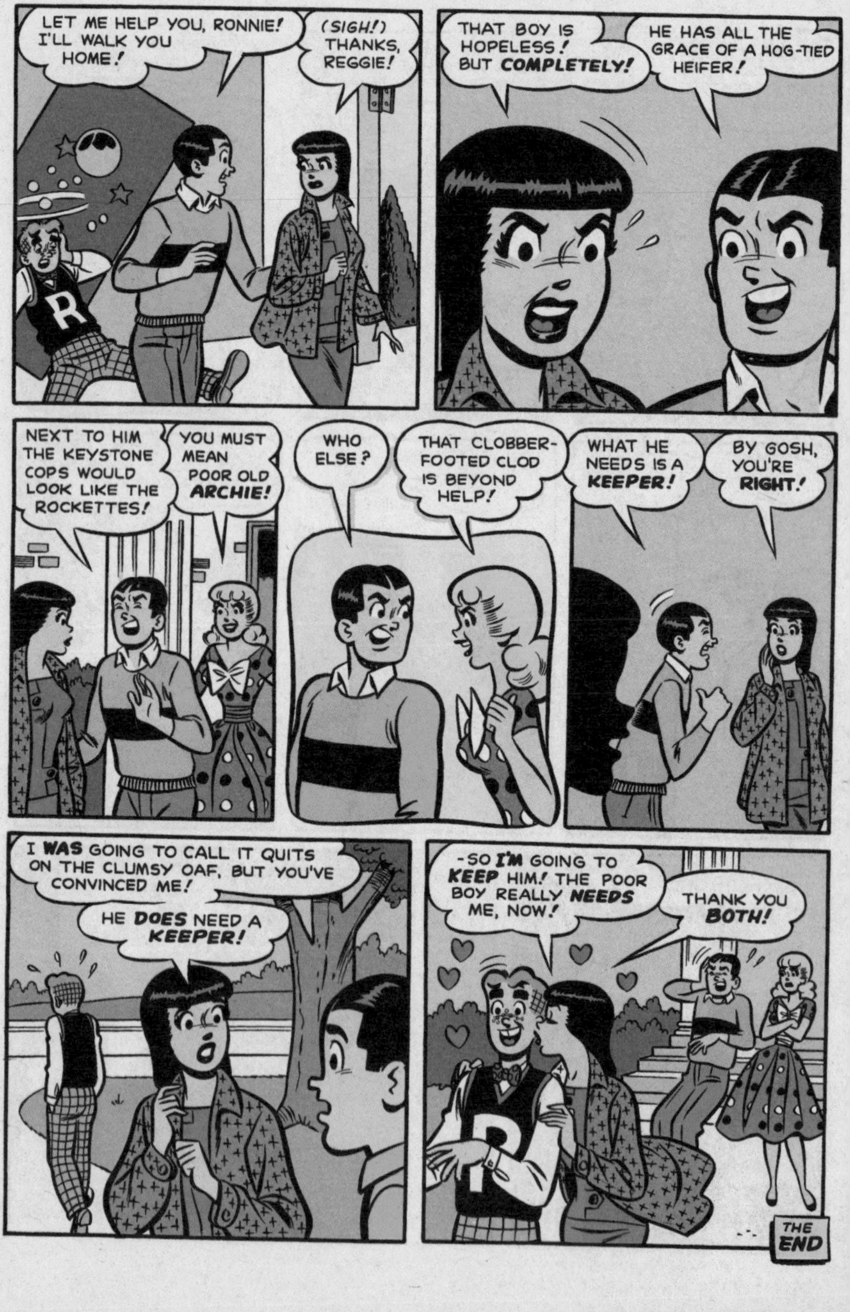
LET ME HELP YOU, RONNIE! I'LL WALK YOU HOME!
(SIGH!) THANKS, REGGIE!
THAT BOY IS HOPELESS! BUT COMPLETELY!
HE HAS ALL THE GRACE OF A HOG-TIED HEIFER!
NEXT TO HIM THE KEYSTONE COPS WOULD LOOK LIKE THE ROCKETTES!
YOU MUST MEAN POOR OLD ARCHIE!
WHO ELSE?
THAT CLOBBER-FOOTED CLOD IS BEYOND HELP!
WHAT HE NEEDS IS A KEEPER!
BY GOSH, YOU'RE RIGHT!
I WAS GOING TO CALL IT QUITS ON THE CLUMSY OAF, BUT YOU'VE CONVINCED ME!
HE DOES NEED A KEEPER!
-SO I'M GOING TO KEEP HIM! THE POOR BOY REALLY NEEDS ME, NOW!
THANK YOU BOTH!
THE END

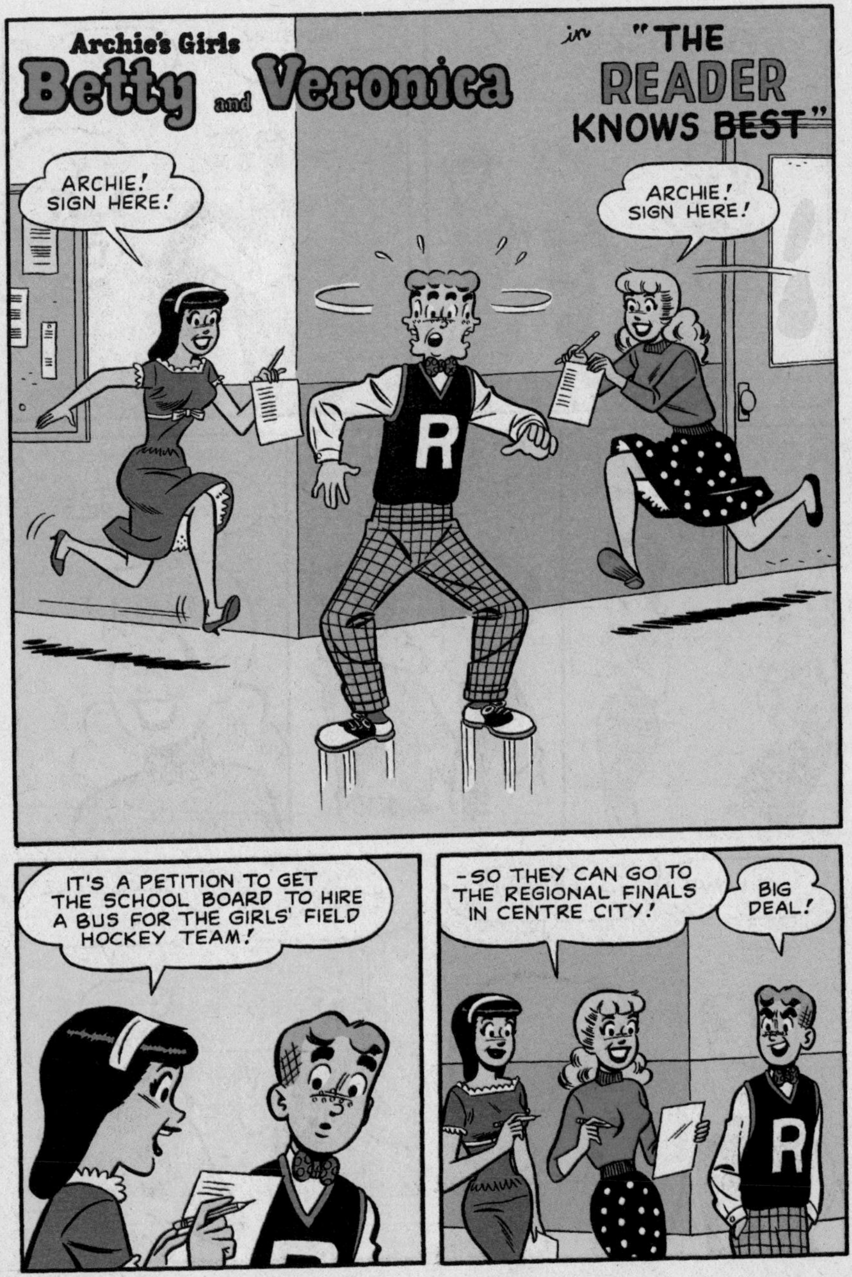
Archie's Girls
Betty and Veronica
in "THE READER KNOWS BEST"
ARCHIE! SIGN HERE!
ARCHIE! SIGN HERE!
IT'S A PETITION TO GET THE SCHOOL BOARD TO HIRE A BUS FOR THE GIRLS' FIELD HOCKEY TEAM!
-SO THEY CAN GO TO THE REGIONAL FINALS IN CENTRE CITY!
BIG DEAL!

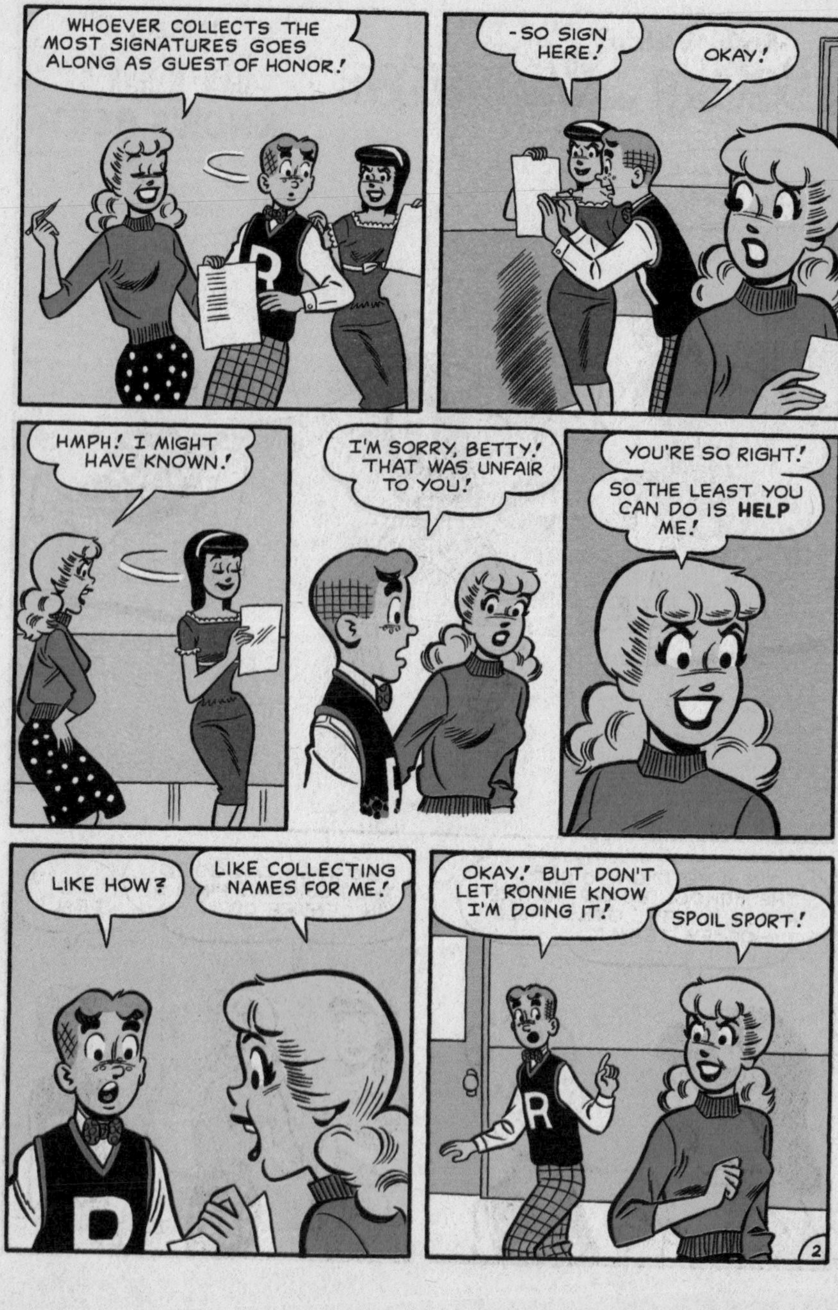
WHOEVER COLLECTS THE MOST SIGNATURES GOES ALONG AS GUEST OF HONOR!
-SO SIGN HERE!
OKAY!
HMPH! I MIGHT HAVE KNOWN!
I'M SORRY, BETTY! THAT WAS UNFAIR TO YOU!
YOU'RE SO RIGHT!
SO THE LEAST YOU CAN DO IS **HELP** ME!
LIKE HOW?
LIKE COLLECTING NAMES FOR ME!
OKAY! BUT DON'T LET RONNIE KNOW I'M DOING IT!
SPOIL SPORT!
2

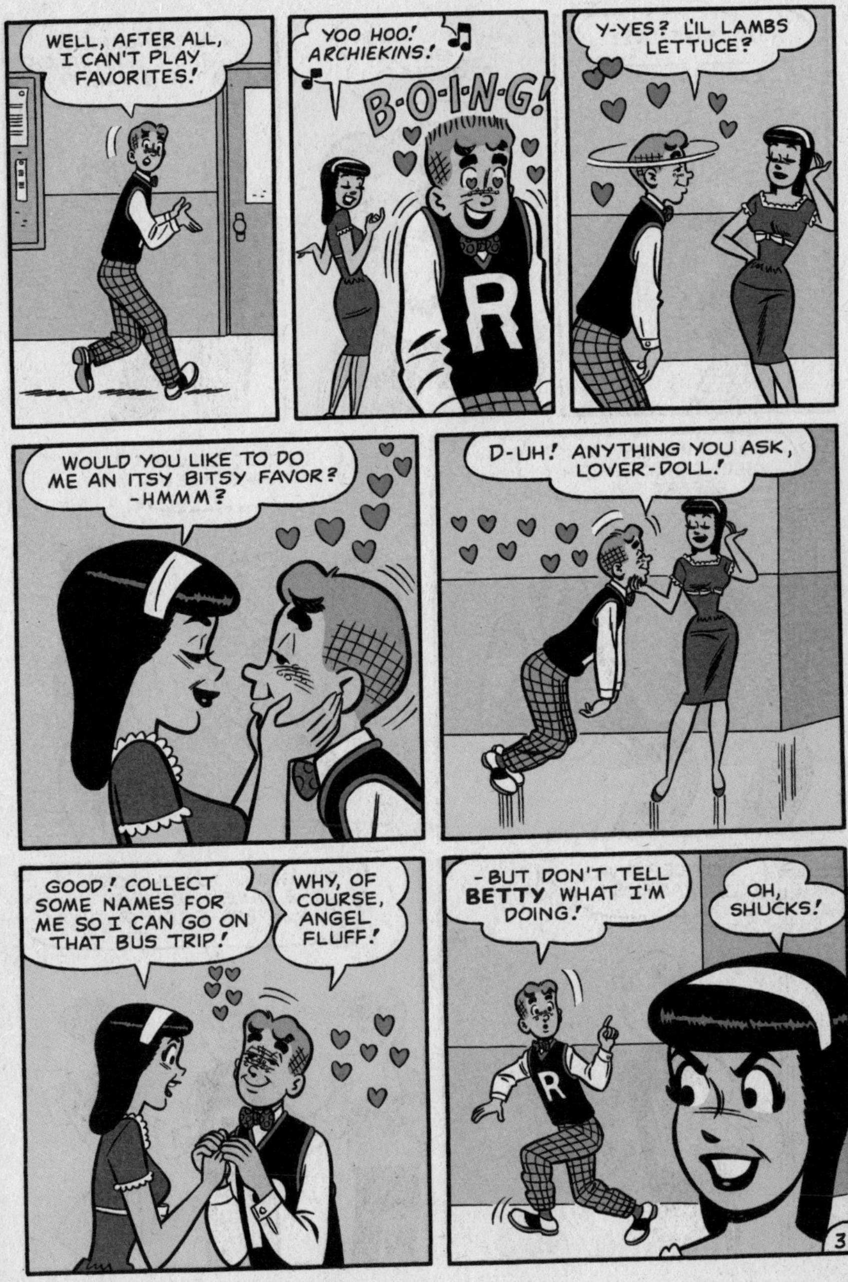
WELL, AFTER ALL, I CAN'T PLAY FAVORITES!
YOO HOO! ARCHIEKINS!
B-O-I-N-G!
Y-YES? L'IL LAMBS LETTUCE?
WOULD YOU LIKE TO DO ME AN ITSY BITSY FAVOR? -HMMM?
D-UH! ANYTHING YOU ASK, LOVER-DOLL!
GOOD! COLLECT SOME NAMES FOR ME SO I CAN GO ON THAT BUS TRIP!
WHY, OF COURSE, ANGEL FLUFF!
-BUT DON'T TELL BETTY WHAT I'M DOING!
OH, SHUCKS!
3

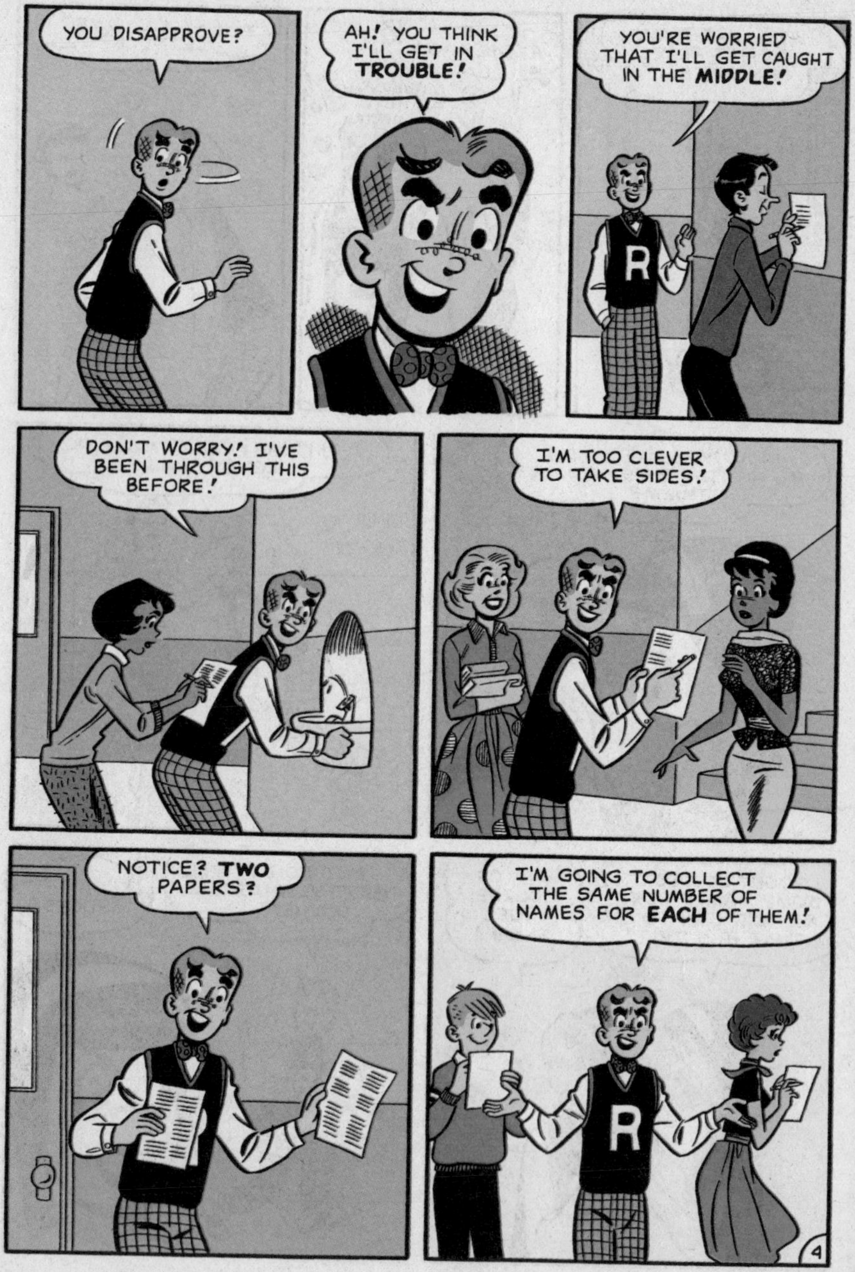
YOU DISAPPROVE?
AH! YOU THINK I'LL GET IN TROUBLE!
YOU'RE WORRIED THAT I'LL GET CAUGHT IN THE MIDDLE!
DON'T WORRY! I'VE BEEN THROUGH THIS BEFORE!
I'M TOO CLEVER TO TAKE SIDES!
NOTICE? TWO PAPERS?
I'M GOING TO COLLECT THE SAME NUMBER OF NAMES FOR EACH OF THEM!
4

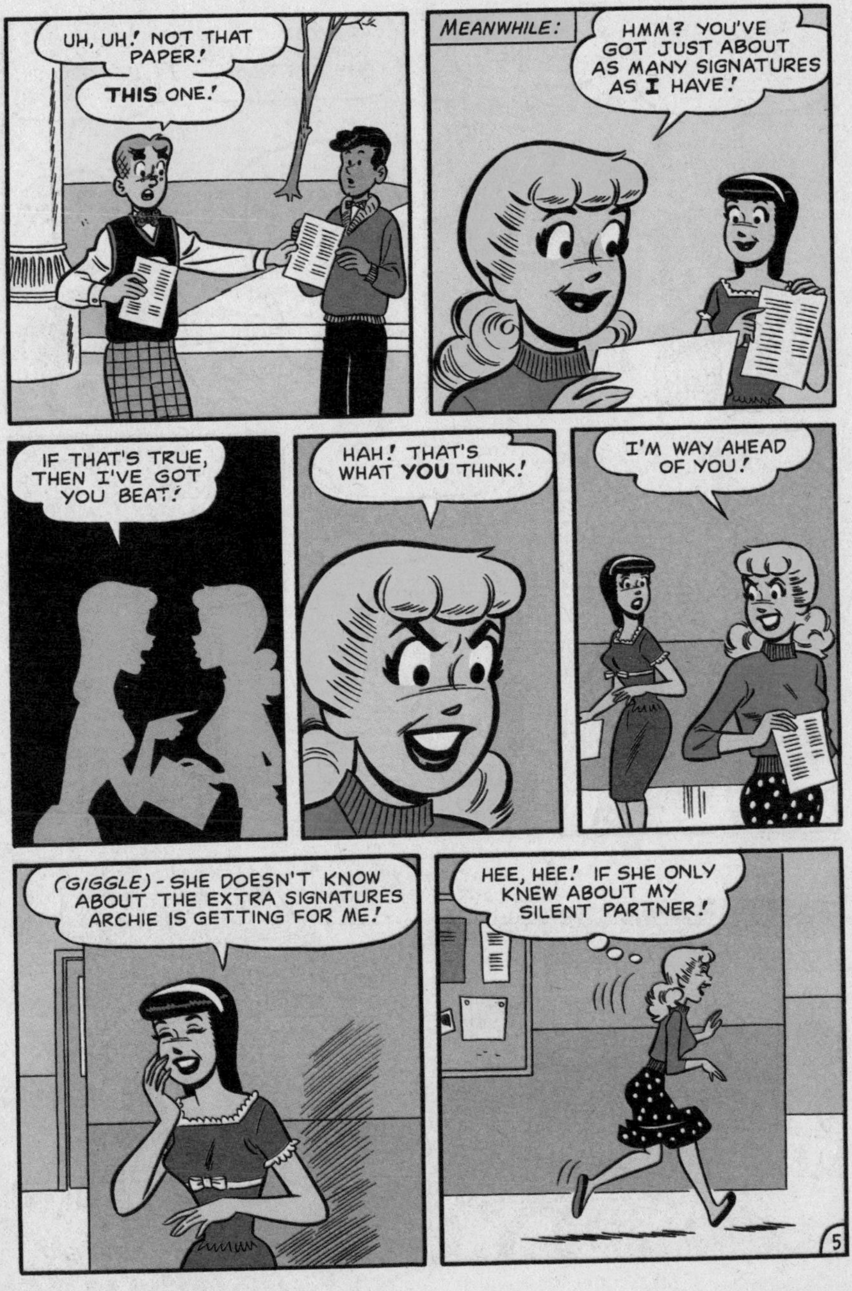
UH, UH! NOT THAT PAPER!
THIS ONE!
MEANWHILE:
HMM? YOU'VE GOT JUST ABOUT AS MANY SIGNATURES AS I HAVE!
IF THAT'S TRUE, THEN I'VE GOT YOU BEAT!
HAH! THAT'S WHAT YOU THINK!
I'M WAY AHEAD OF YOU!
(GIGGLE) - SHE DOESN'T KNOW ABOUT THE EXTRA SIGNATURES ARCHIE IS GETTING FOR ME!
HEE, HEE! IF SHE ONLY KNEW ABOUT MY SILENT PARTNER!
5

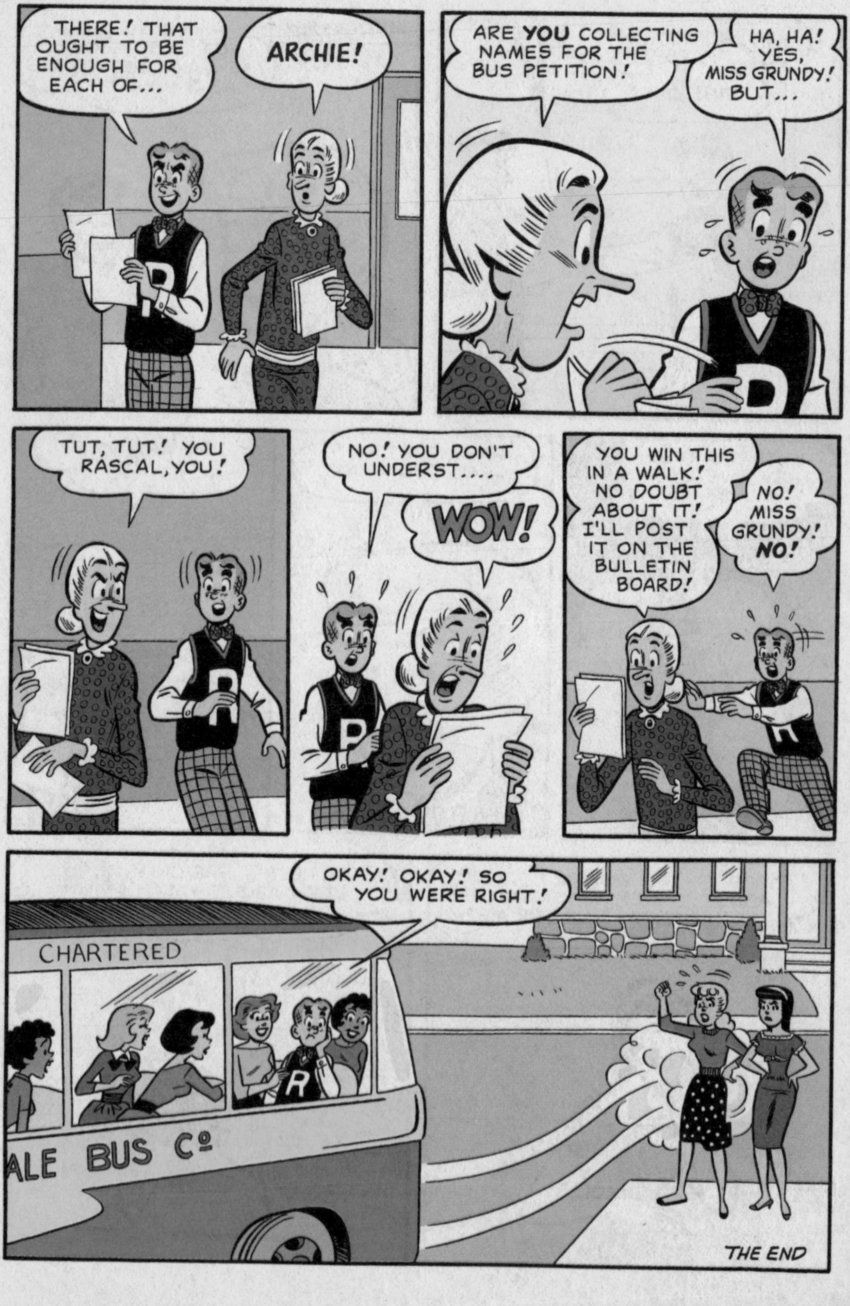
THERE! THAT OUGHT TO BE ENOUGH FOR EACH OF...
ARCHIE!
ARE YOU COLLECTING NAMES FOR THE BUS PETITION!
HA, HA! YES, MISS GRUNDY! BUT...
TUT, TUT! YOU RASCAL, YOU!
NO! YOU DON'T UNDERST....
WOW!
YOU WIN THIS IN A WALK! NO DOUBT ABOUT IT! I'LL POST IT ON THE BULLETIN BOARD!
NO! MISS GRUNDY! NO!
OKAY! OKAY! SO YOU WERE RIGHT!
CHARTERED
ALE BUS Cº
THE END

Sound Off
Betty & Veronica #144, December 1967
Frank Doyle, Dan DeCarlo, Rudy Lapick,
Bill Yoshida and Sal Contrera

Another in the time-honored tradition of Archie "pantomime" stories. For generations, the "eternal love triangle" between Archie, Betty and Veronica has left readers speechless... and in this special story, the love-struck teens are speechless, too!

She's Got Class
Veronica #151, June 2004
Bill Golliher, Dan Parent, Jon D'Agostino,
Vickie Williams and Barry Grossman

Jealous of the attention Betty is getting for helping tutor students in algebra, Veronica decides that she can share her knowledge as well. She promptly sets up a tutoring session focusing on romance tips—and creates a monster when the female population of Riverdale High uses her own tactics to try to woo Archie!

Bonus: Newspaper Strip, February 12, 2006
Craig Boldman and Henry Scarpelli

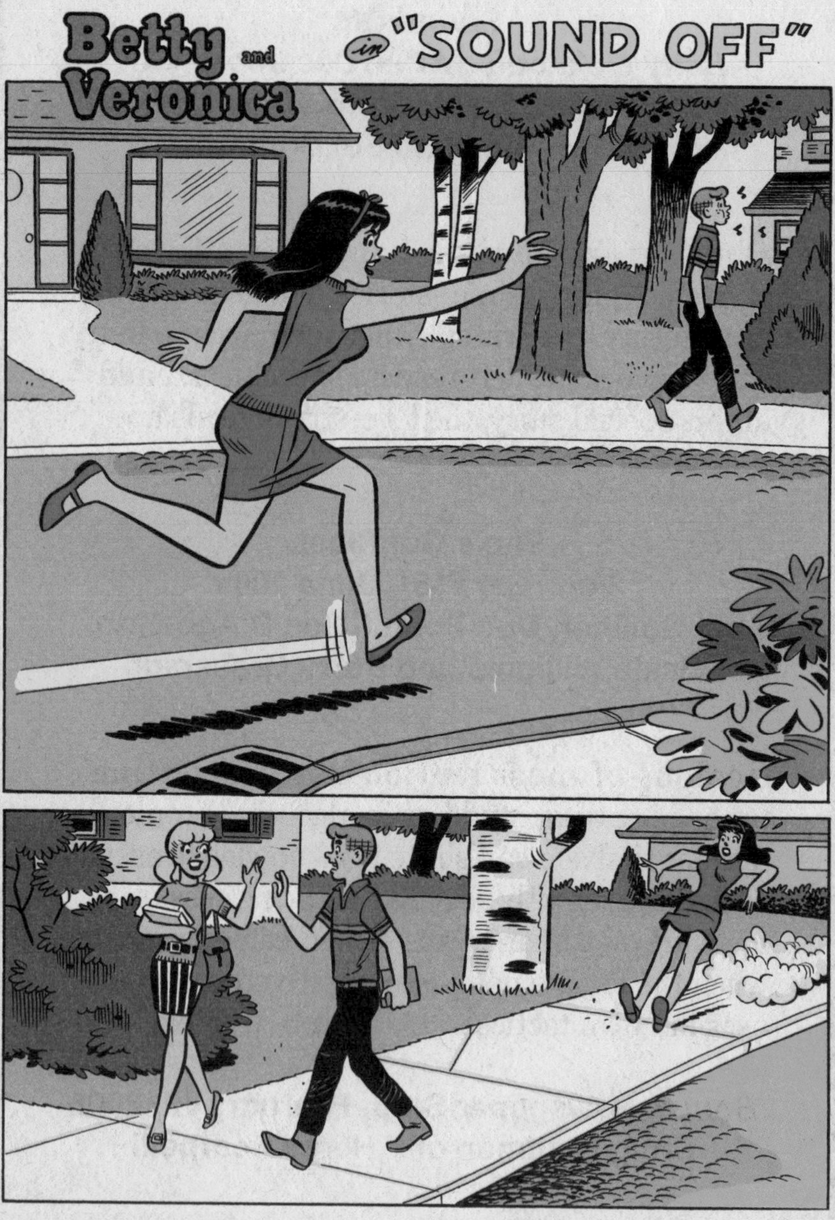
Betty and Veronica
in "SOUND OFF"

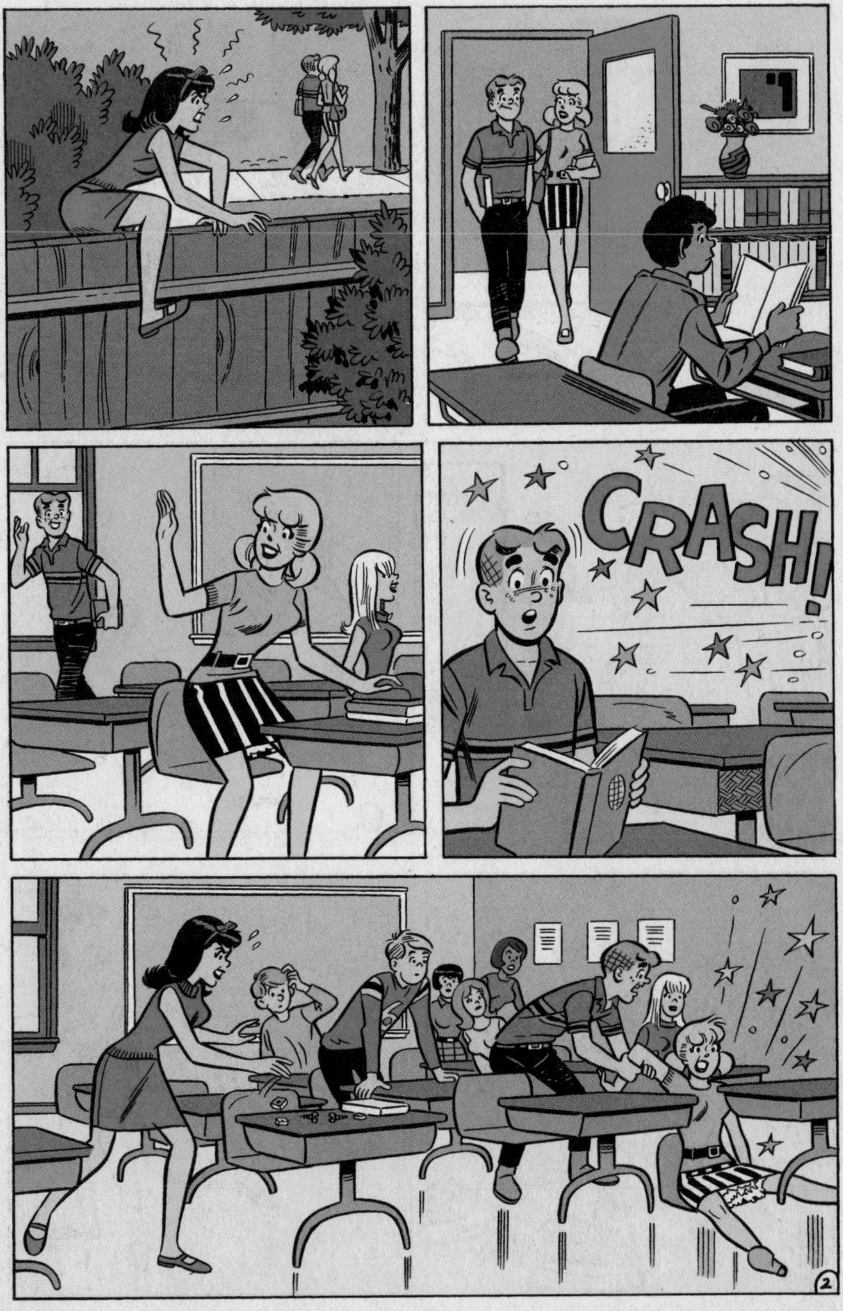
CRASH!
2

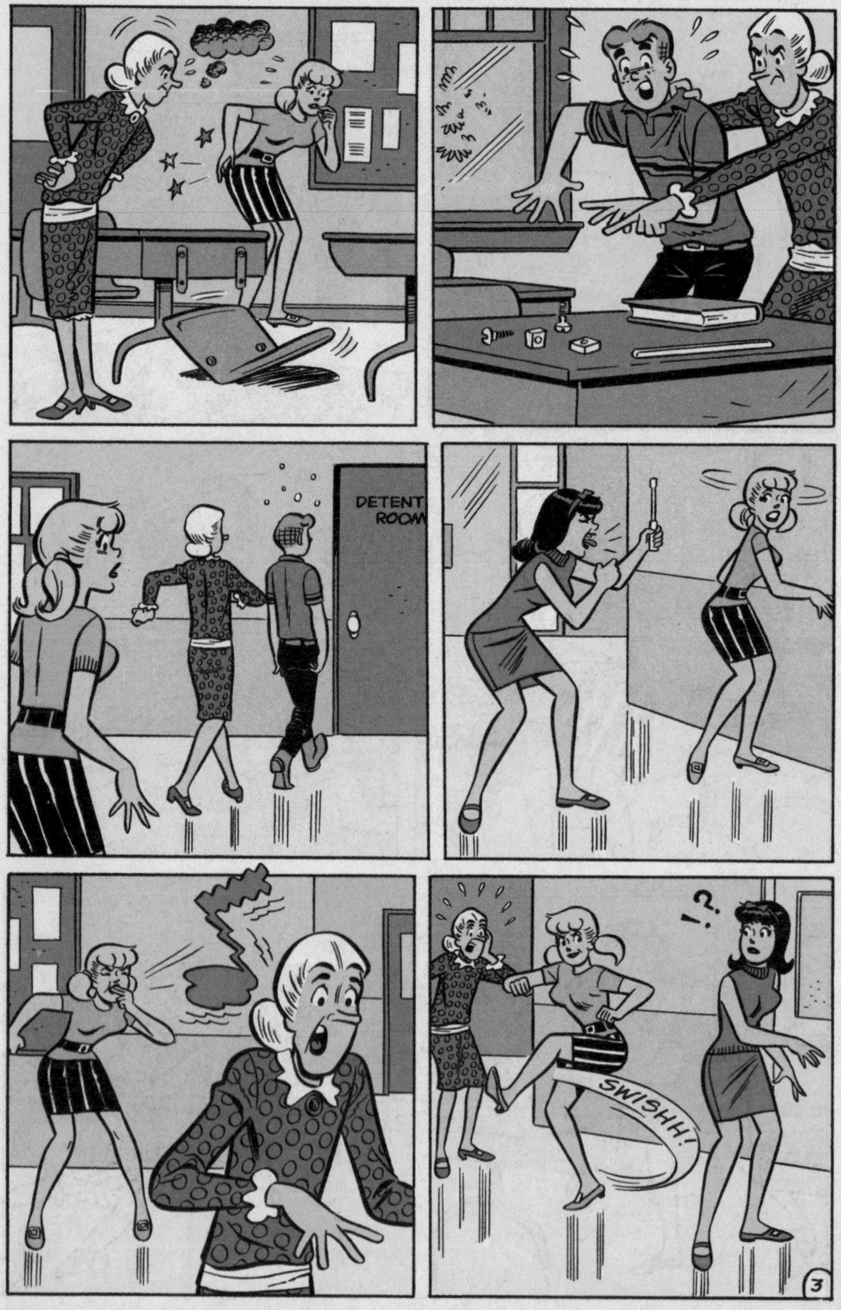
DETENT
ROOM
SWISHH!
3

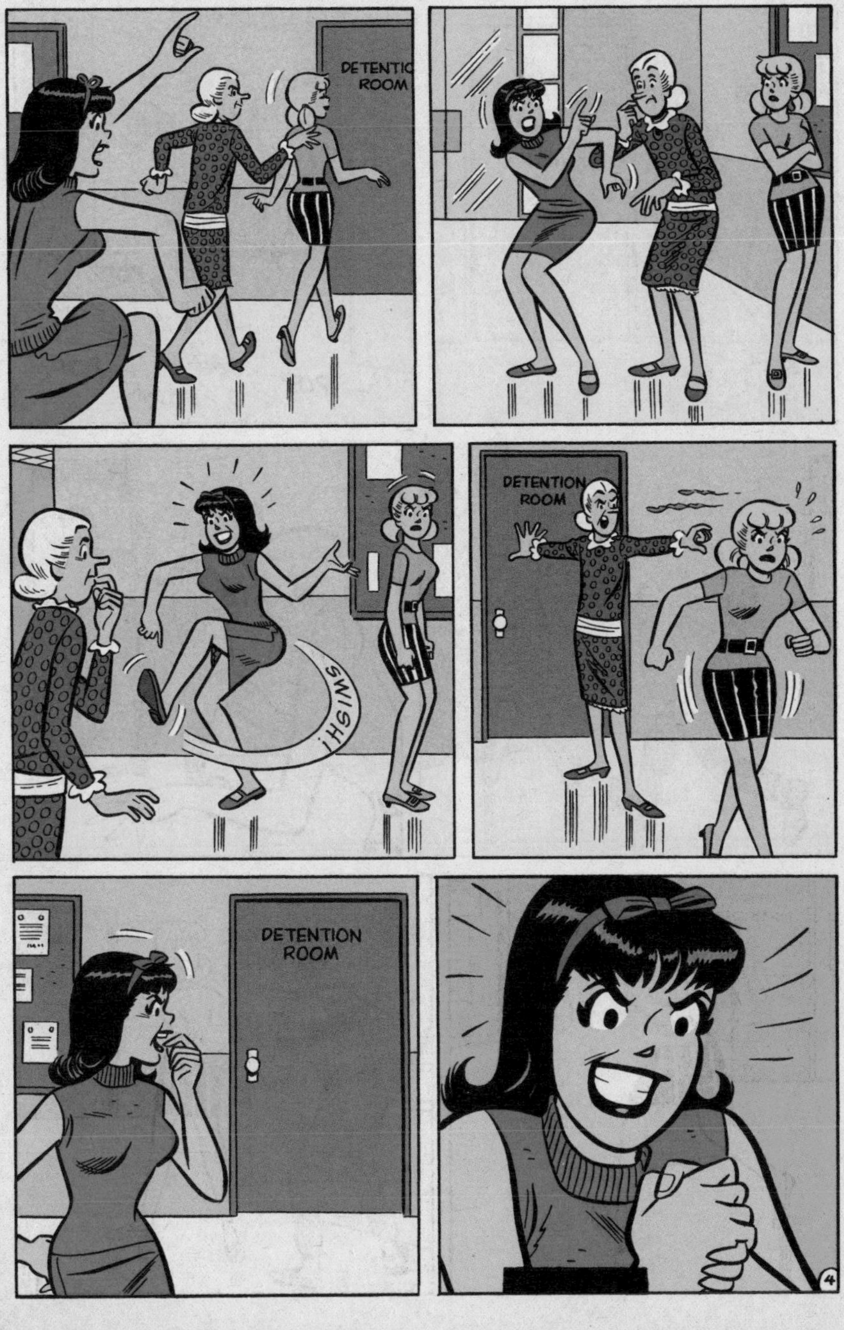
DETENTION ROOM
SWISH!
DETENTION ROOM
DETENTION ROOM

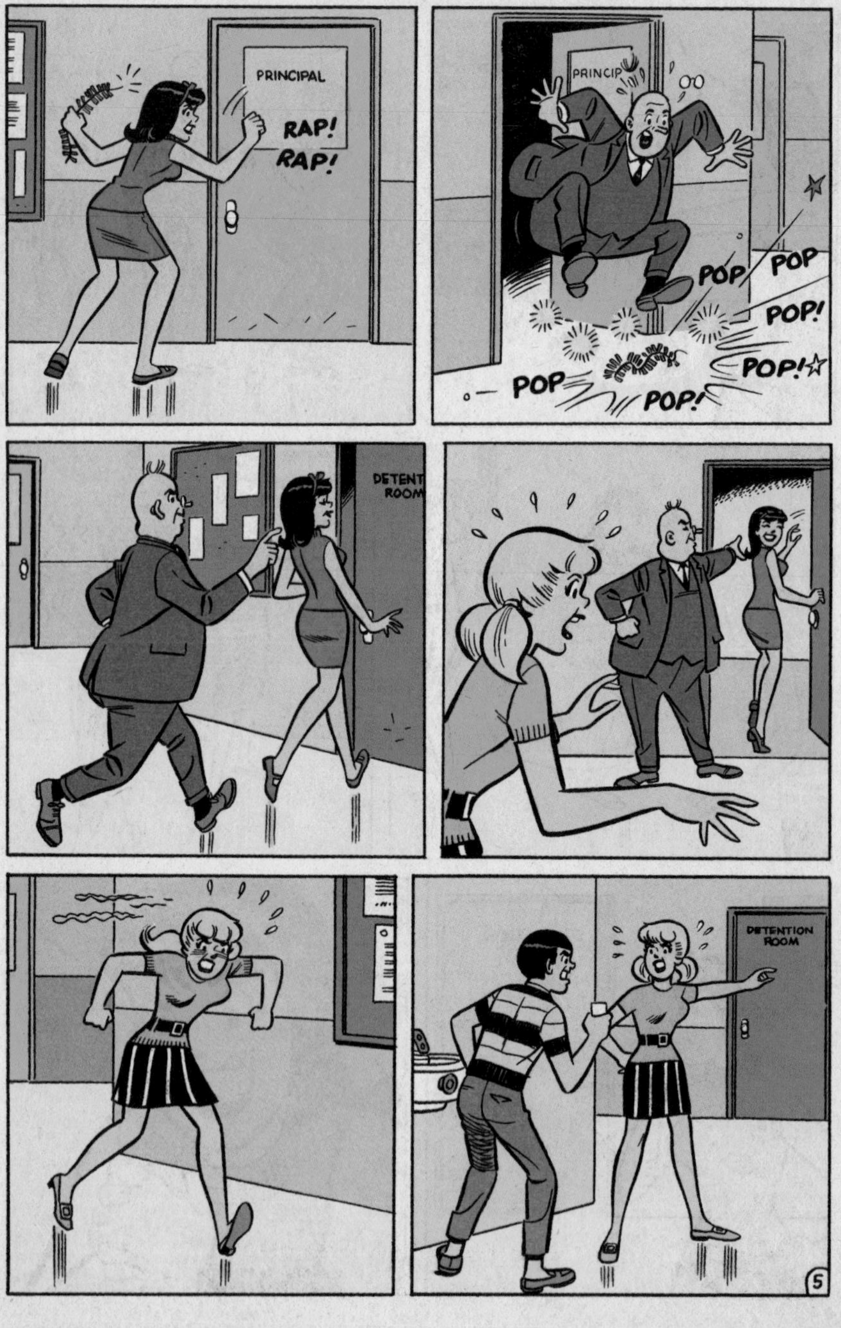
PRINCIPAL
RAP!
RAP!
PRINCIP
POP
POP
POP!
POP
POP!
POP!
DETENT
ROOM
DETENTION
ROOM
5

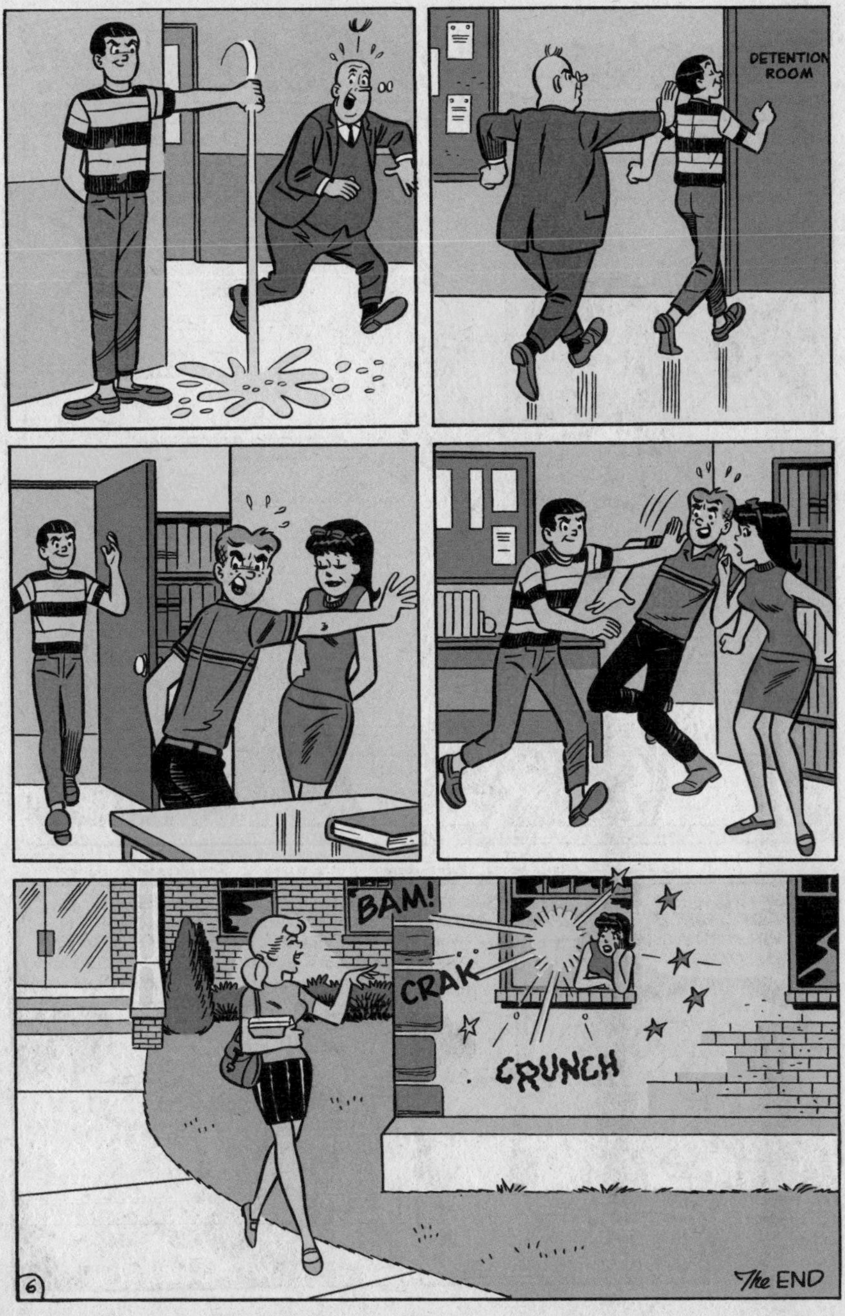
DETENTION ROOM
BAM!
CRAK
CRUNCH
6
The END

Veronica® She's Got Class!

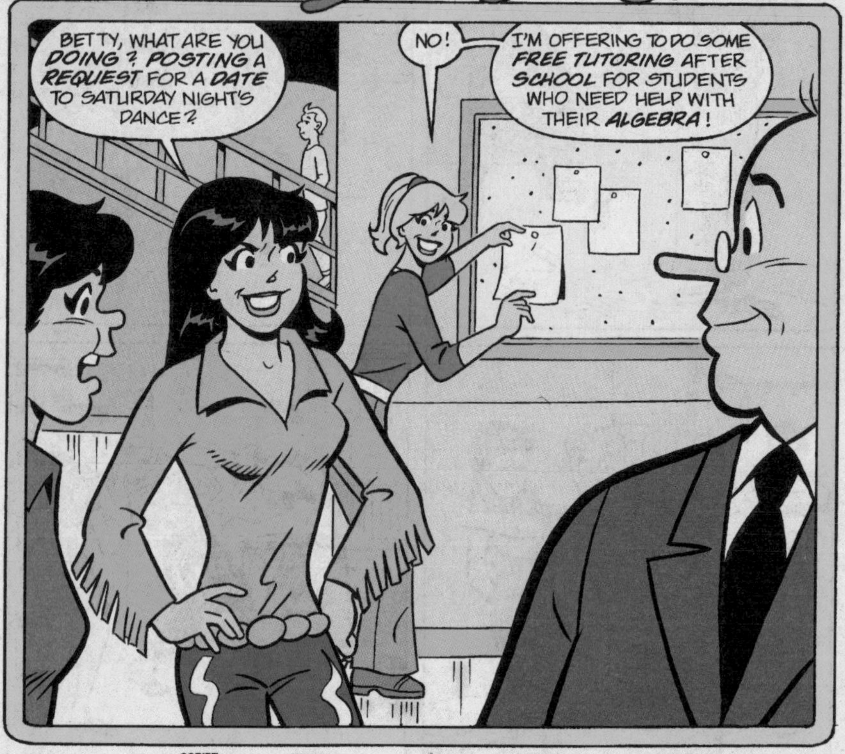
BETTY, WHAT ARE YOU DOING? POSTING A REQUEST FOR A DATE TO SATURDAY NIGHT'S DANCE?
NO!
I'M OFFERING TO DO SOME FREE TUTORING AFTER SCHOOL FOR STUDENTS WHO NEED HELP WITH THEIR ALGEBRA!

SCRIPT: BILL GOLLIHER PENCILS: DAN PARENT INKING: JON D'AGOSTINO LETTERING: VICKIE WILLIAMS COLORING: BARRY GROSSMAN

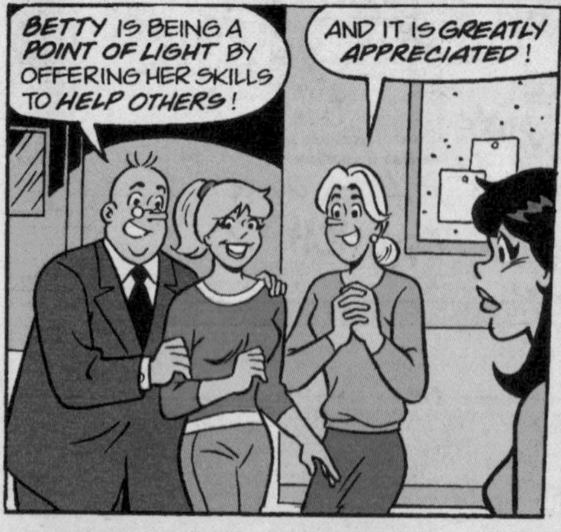
BETTY IS BEING A POINT OF LIGHT BY OFFERING HER SKILLS TO HELP OTHERS!
AND IT IS GREATLY APPRECIATED!

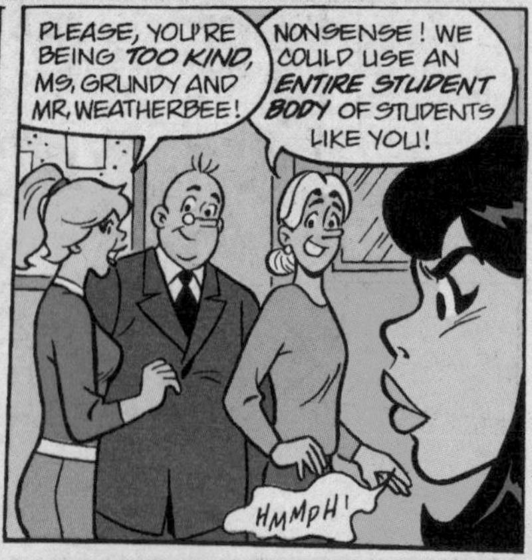
PLEASE, YOU'RE BEING TOO KIND, MS. GRUNDY AND MR. WEATHERBEE!
NONSENSE! WE COULD USE AN ENTIRE STUDENT BODY OF STUDENTS LIKE YOU!
HMMPH!

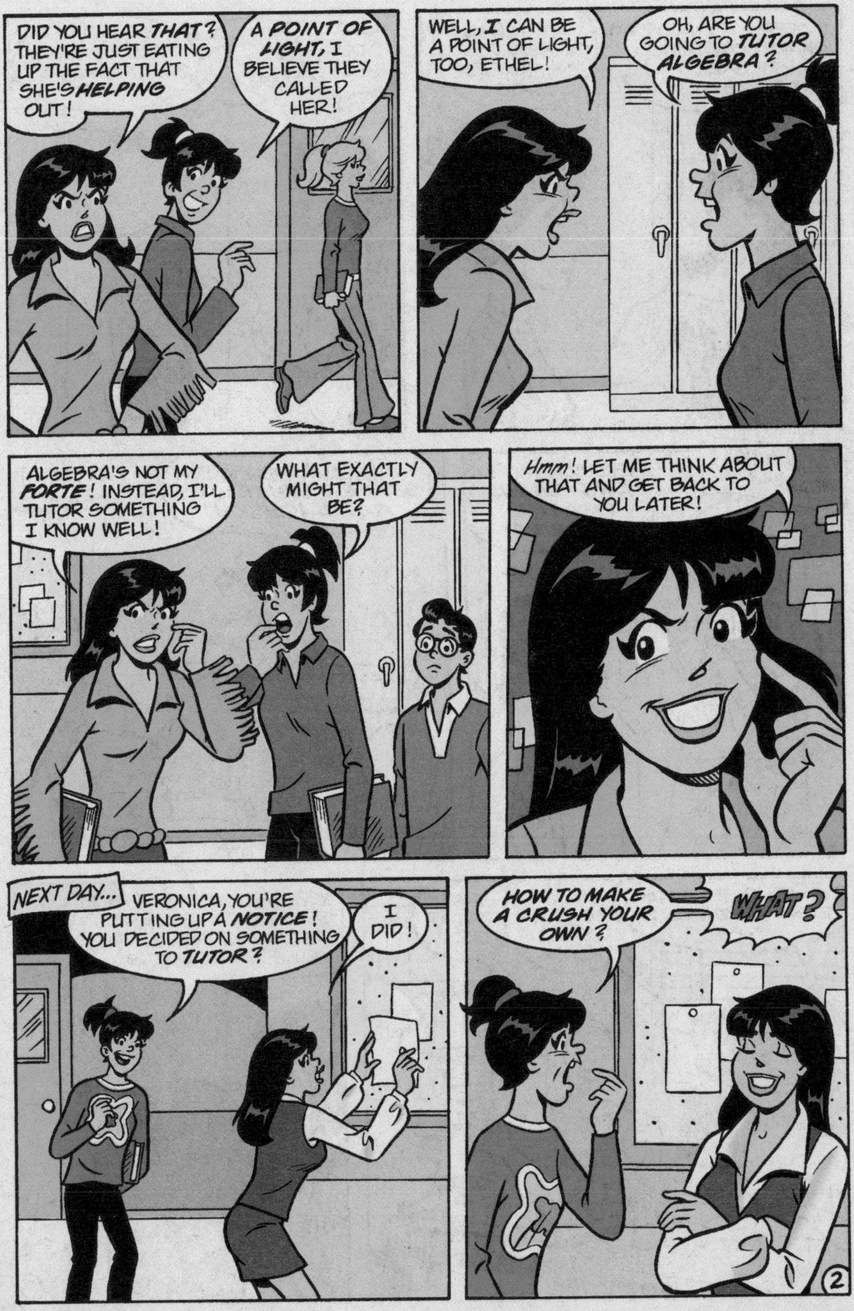
DID YOU HEAR THAT? THEY'RE JUST EATING UP THE FACT THAT SHE'S HELPING OUT!
A POINT OF LIGHT, I BELIEVE THEY CALLED HER!
WELL, I CAN BE A POINT OF LIGHT, TOO, ETHEL!
OH, ARE YOU GOING TO TUTOR ALGEBRA?
ALGEBRA'S NOT MY FORTE! INSTEAD, I'LL TUTOR SOMETHING I KNOW WELL!
WHAT EXACTLY MIGHT THAT BE?
Hmm! LET ME THINK ABOUT THAT AND GET BACK TO YOU LATER!
NEXT DAY...
VERONICA, YOU'RE PUTTING UP A NOTICE! YOU DECIDED ON SOMETHING TO TUTOR?
I DID!
HOW TO MAKE A CRUSH YOUR OWN?
WHAT?
2

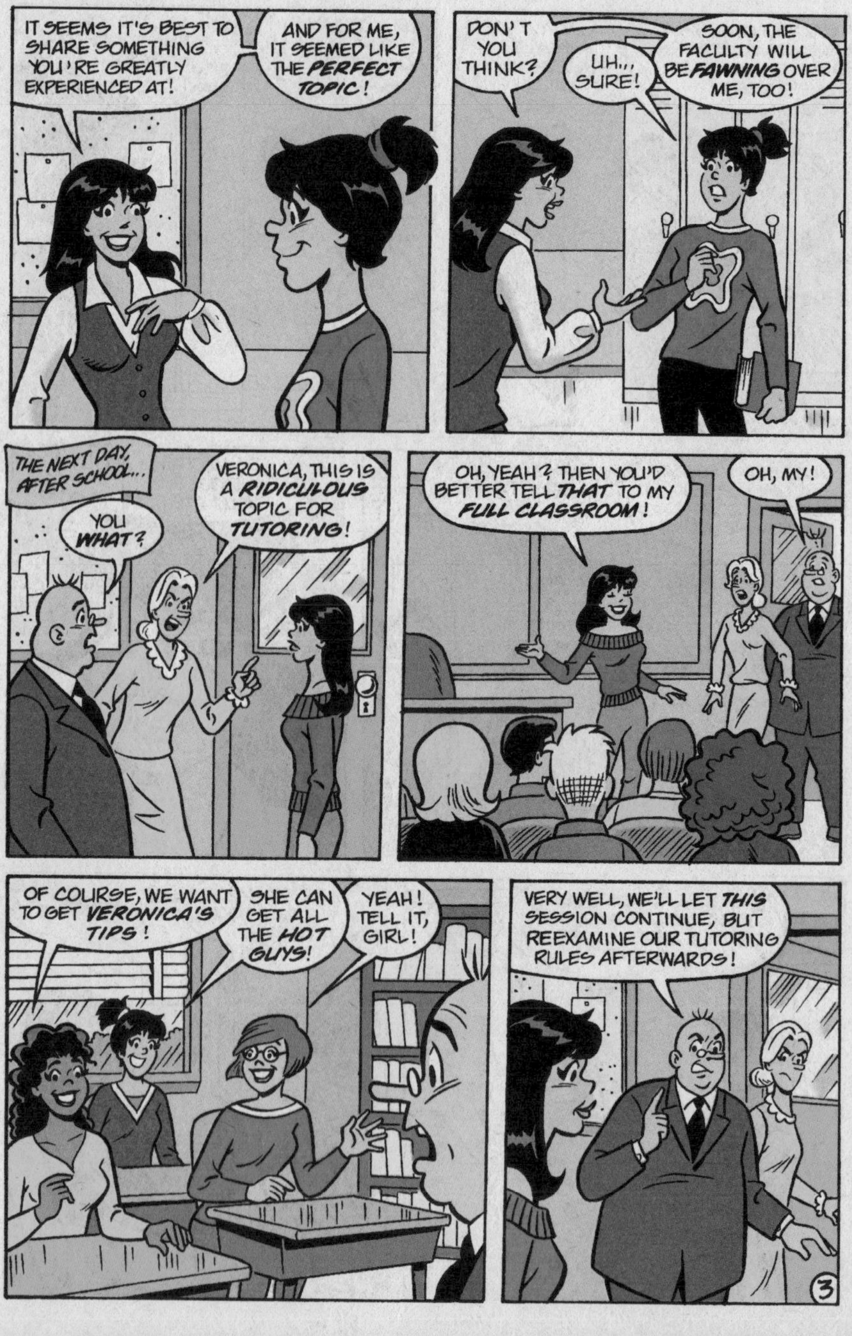
IT SEEMS IT'S BEST TO SHARE SOMETHING YOU'RE GREATLY EXPERIENCED AT!
AND FOR ME, IT SEEMED LIKE THE PERFECT TOPIC!
DON'T YOU THINK?
UH... SURE!
SOON, THE FACULTY WILL BE FAWNING OVER ME, TOO!
THE NEXT DAY, AFTER SCHOOL...
VERONICA, THIS IS A RIDICULOUS TOPIC FOR TUTORING!
YOU WHAT?
OH, YEAH? THEN YOU'D BETTER TELL THAT TO MY FULL CLASSROOM!
OH, MY!
OF COURSE, WE WANT TO GET VERONICA'S TIPS!
SHE CAN GET ALL THE HOT GUYS!
YEAH! TELL IT, GIRL!
VERY WELL, WE'LL LET THIS SESSION CONTINUE, BUT REEXAMINE OUR TUTORING RULES AFTERWARDS!
3

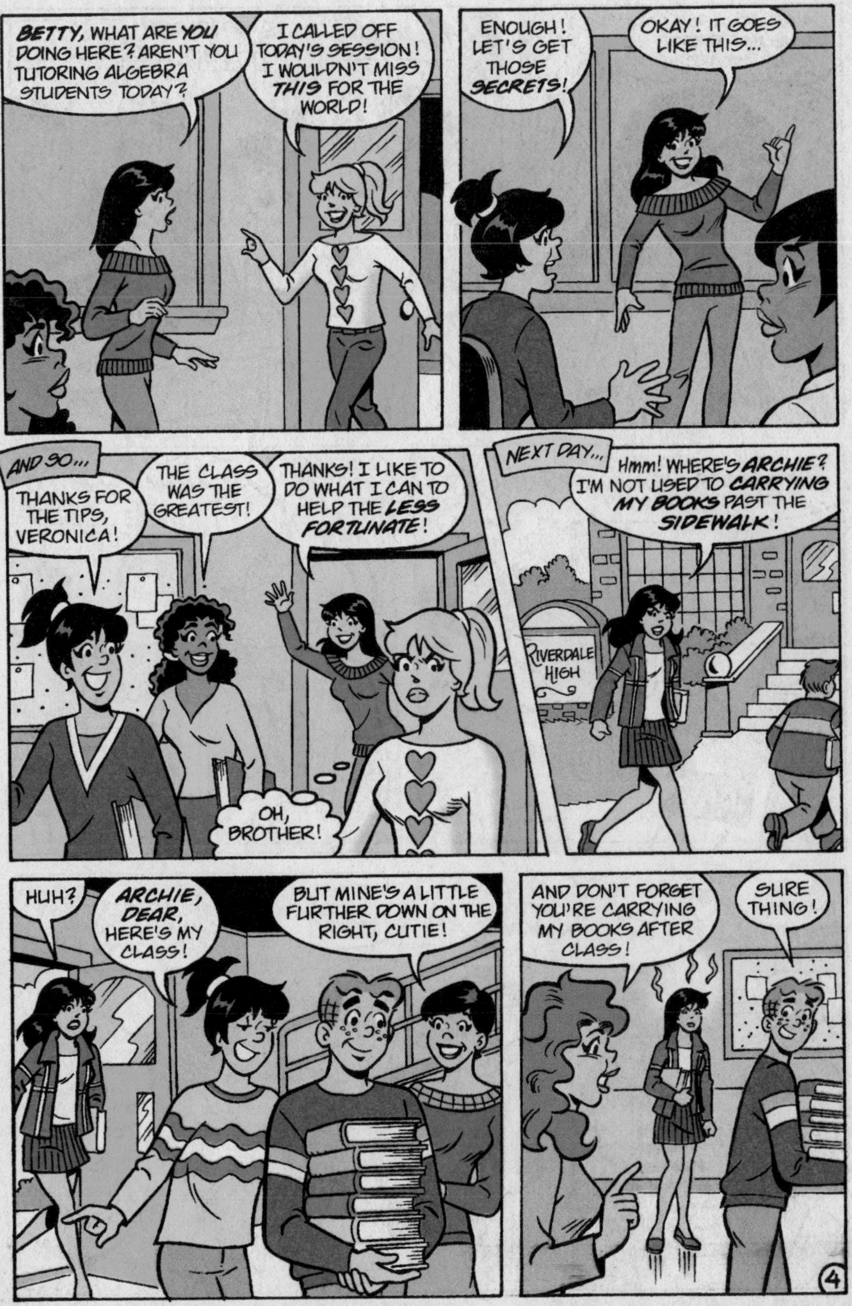
BETTY, WHAT ARE YOU DOING HERE? AREN'T YOU TUTORING ALGEBRA STUDENTS TODAY?
I CALLED OFF TODAY'S SESSION! I WOULDN'T MISS THIS FOR THE WORLD!
ENOUGH! LET'S GET THOSE SECRETS!
OKAY! IT GOES LIKE THIS...
AND SO...
THANKS FOR THE TIPS, VERONICA!
THE CLASS WAS THE GREATEST!
THANKS! I LIKE TO DO WHAT I CAN TO HELP THE LESS FORTUNATE!
OH, BROTHER!
NEXT DAY...
Hmm! WHERE'S ARCHIE? I'M NOT USED TO CARRYING MY BOOKS PAST THE SIDEWALK!
RIVERDALE HIGH
HUH?
ARCHIE, DEAR, HERE'S MY CLASS!
BUT MINE'S A LITTLE FURTHER DOWN ON THE RIGHT, CUTIE!
AND DON'T FORGET YOU'RE CARRYING MY BOOKS AFTER CLASS!
SURE THING!
4

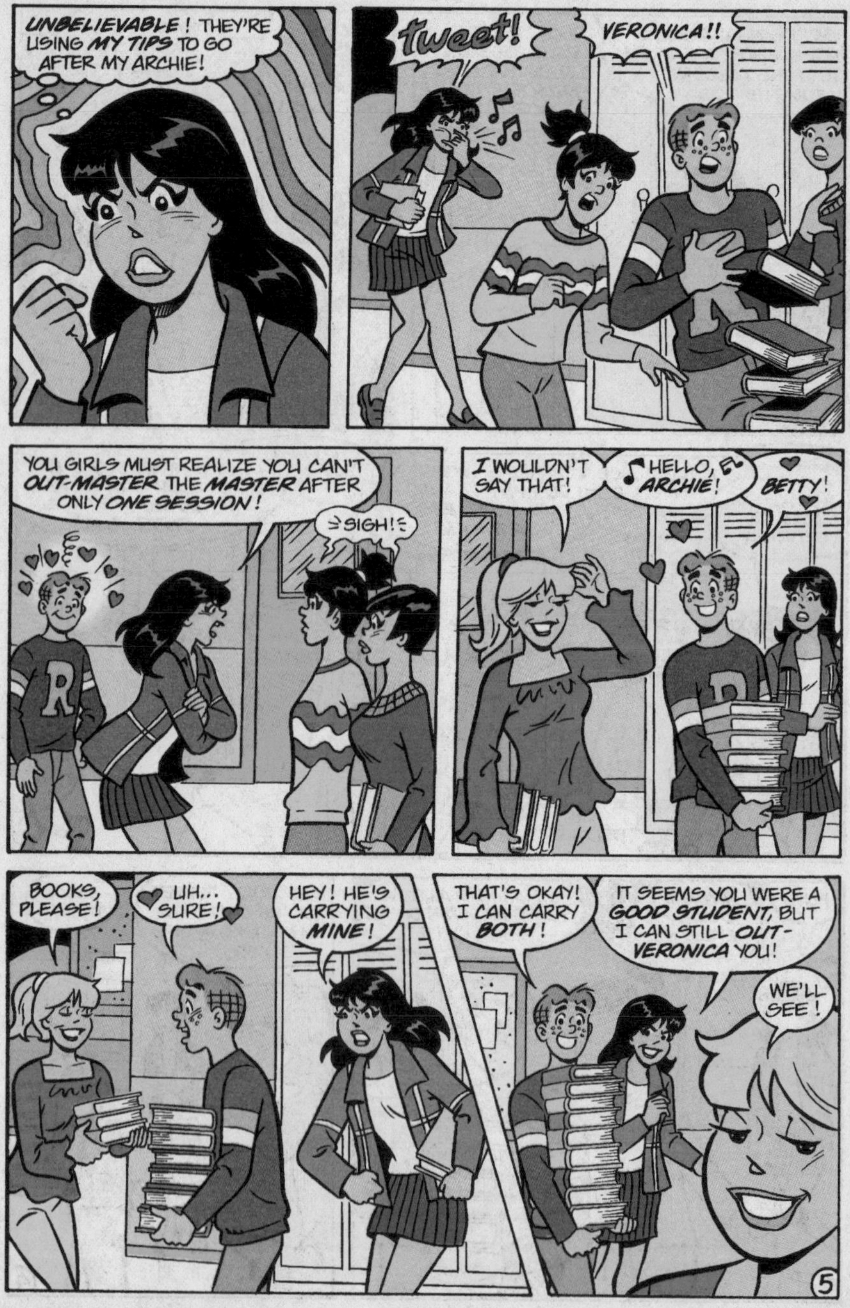
UNBELIEVABLE! THEY'RE USING MY TIPS TO GO AFTER MY ARCHIE!
tweet!
VERONICA!!
YOU GIRLS MUST REALIZE YOU CAN'T OUT-MASTER THE MASTER AFTER ONLY ONE SESSION!
SIGH!
I WOULDN'T SAY THAT!
HELLO, ARCHIE!
BETTY!
BOOKS, PLEASE!
UH... SURE!
HEY! HE'S CARRYING MINE!
THAT'S OKAY! I CAN CARRY BOTH!
IT SEEMS YOU WERE A GOOD STUDENT, BUT I CAN STILL OUT-VERONICA YOU!
WE'LL SEE!
5

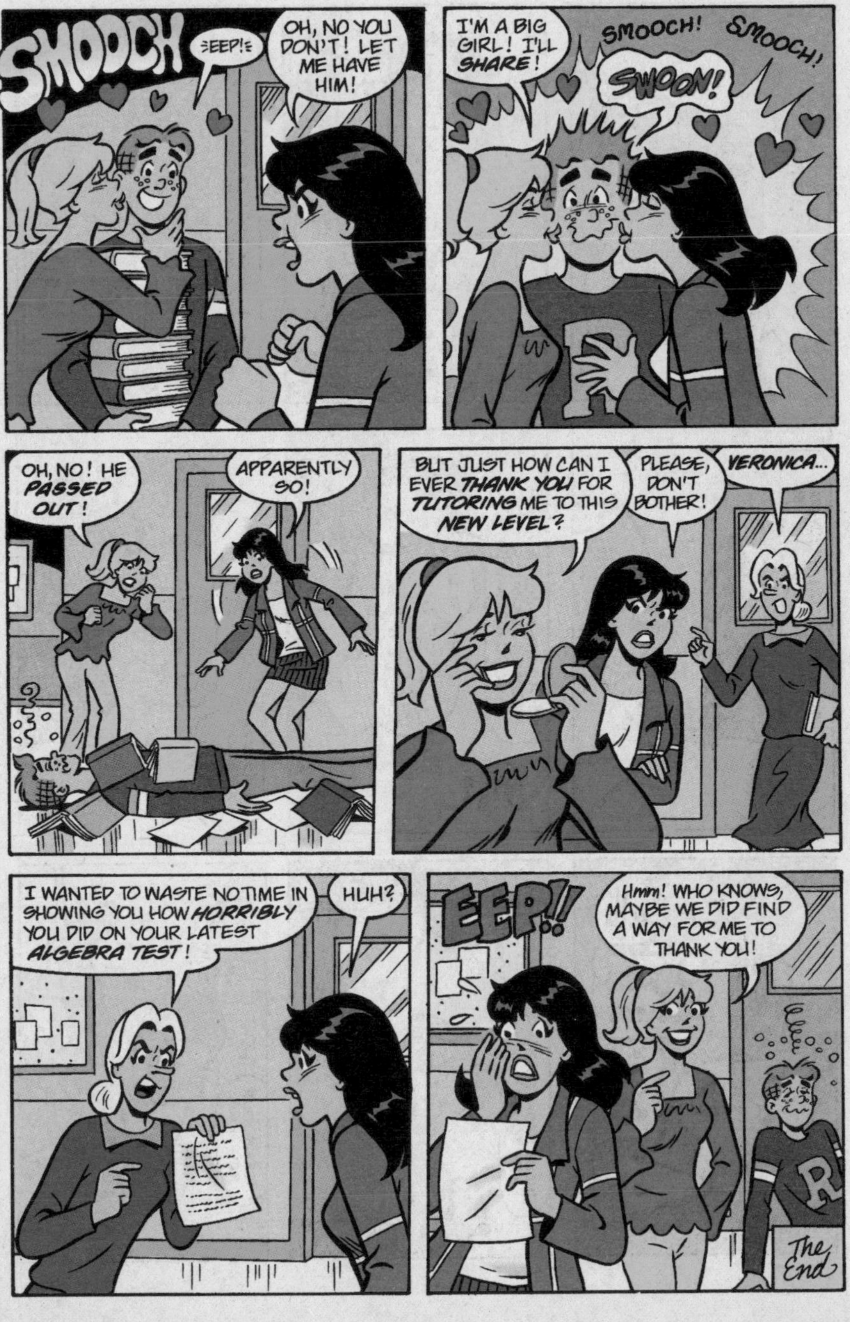
SMOOCH
EEP!
OH, NO YOU DON'T! LET ME HAVE HIM!
I'M A BIG GIRL! I'LL SHARE!
SMOOCH!
SMOOCH!
SWOON!
OH, NO! HE PASSED OUT!
APPARENTLY SO!
BUT JUST HOW CAN I EVER THANK YOU FOR TUTORING ME TO THIS NEW LEVEL?
PLEASE, DON'T BOTHER!
VERONICA...
I WANTED TO WASTE NO TIME IN SHOWING YOU HOW HORRIBLY YOU DID ON YOUR LATEST ALGEBRA TEST!
HUH?
EEP!!
Hmm! WHO KNOWS, MAYBE WE DID FIND A WAY FOR ME TO THANK YOU!
The End

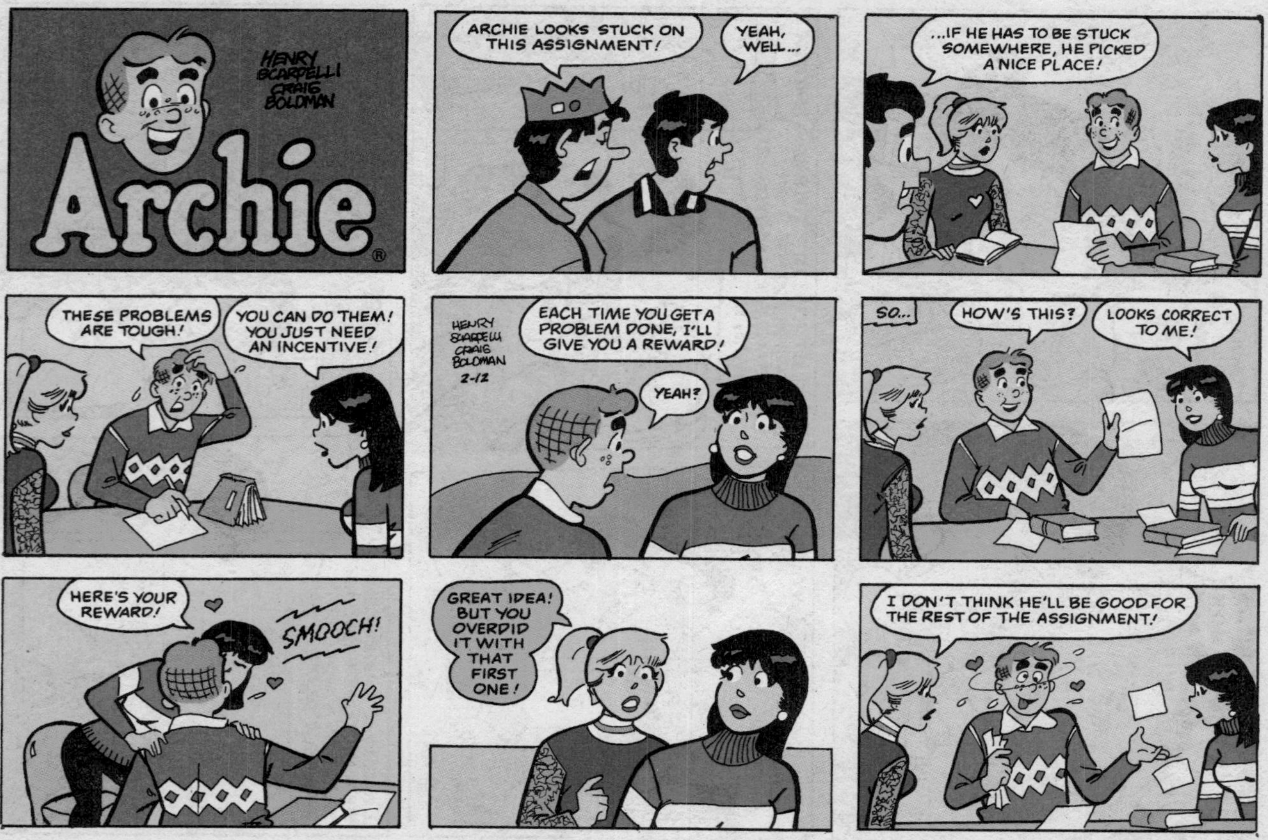
Archie
HENRY SCARPELLI CRAIG BOLDMAN
ARCHIE LOOKS STUCK ON THIS ASSIGNMENT!
YEAH, WELL...
...IF HE HAS TO BE STUCK SOMEWHERE, HE PICKED A NICE PLACE!
THESE PROBLEMS ARE TOUGH!
YOU CAN DO THEM! YOU JUST NEED AN INCENTIVE!
HENRY SCARPELLI CRAIG BOLDMAN 2-12
EACH TIME YOU GET A PROBLEM DONE, I'LL GIVE YOU A REWARD!
YEAH?
SO...
HOW'S THIS?
LOOKS CORRECT TO ME!
HERE'S YOUR REWARD!
SMOOCH!
GREAT IDEA! BUT YOU OVERDID IT WITH THAT FIRST ONE!
I DON'T THINK HE'LL BE GOOD FOR THE REST OF THE ASSIGNMENT!

Archie's FAVORITE HIGH SCHOOL COMICS

PALS 'N' GALS

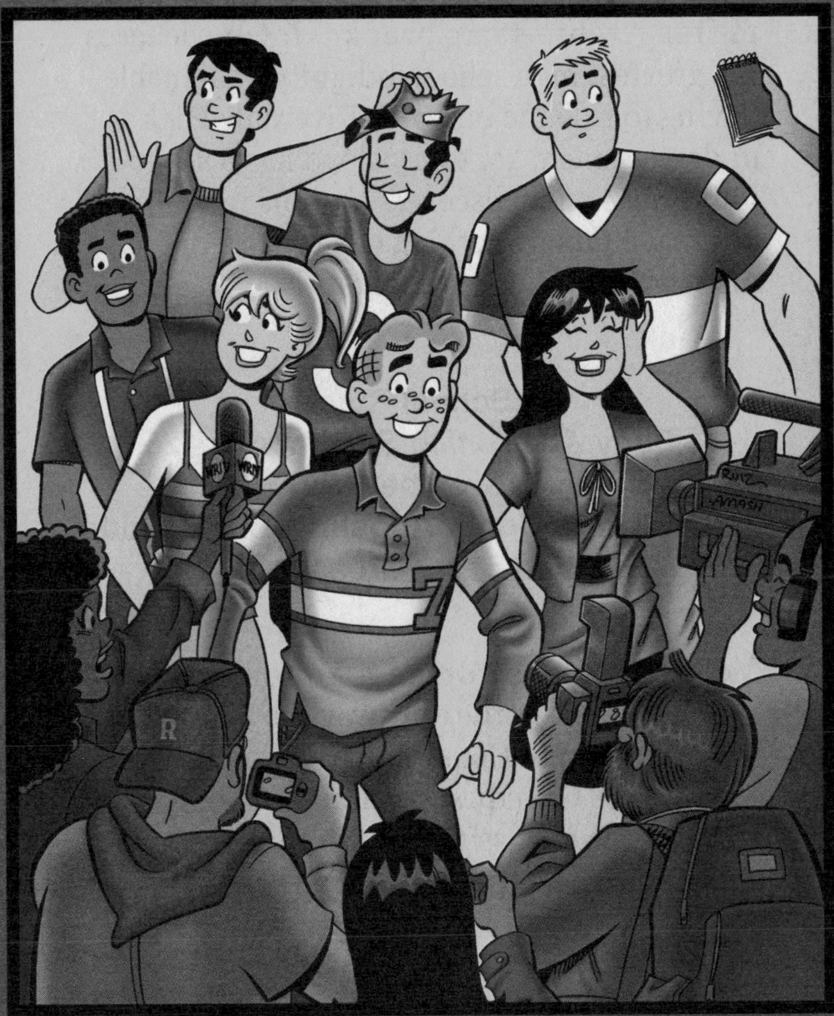

WRIV
WRIV
R

School Bus-ted
Archie Double Digest #249, April 2014
Fernando Ruiz, Al Nickerson,
Vickie Williams and Barry Grossman

After Archie's car breaks down, he faces
the greatest high school indignity imaginable–
having to ride the bus with Riverdale High's
underclassmen. Yet every cloud has a silver
lining, as Archie discovers that his reputation
has made him something of a celebrity amongst
his school's younger students.

School Rules
Betty & Veronica Spectacular #26,
November 1997
Dan Parent, Jon D'Agostino, Bill Yoshida
and Barry Grossman

Veronica spins "Bring a Young Friend
to School Day" in the only way she knows how:
by paying off her Cousin Leroy to join her! Of
course Miss Grundy sees through the charade
and extends the assignment so the cousins can
truly bond... she can dream, can't she?

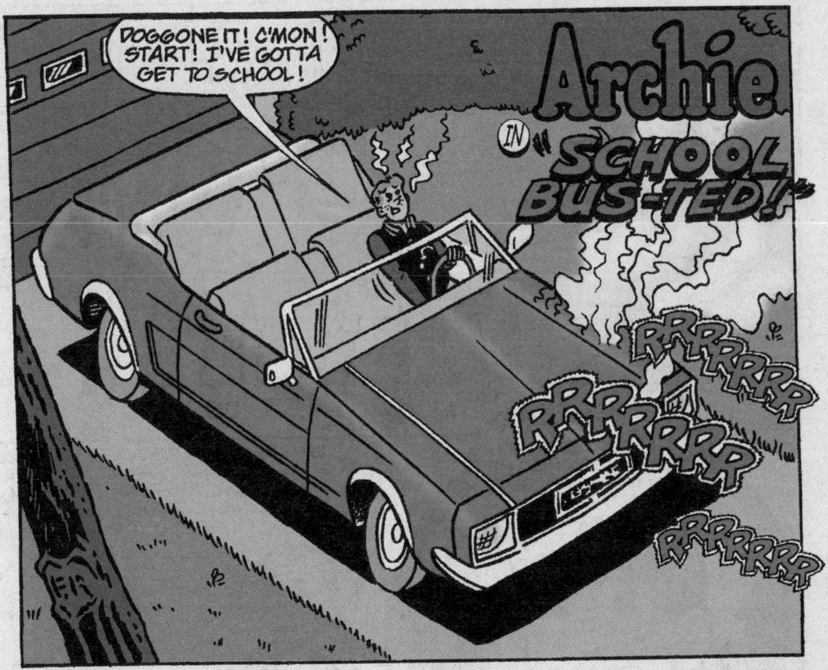
DOGGONE IT! C'MON! START! I'VE GOTTA GET TO SCHOOL!
Archie
IN "SCHOOL BUS-TED!"
RRRRRRRRR
RRRRRRRRR
RRRRRRRR

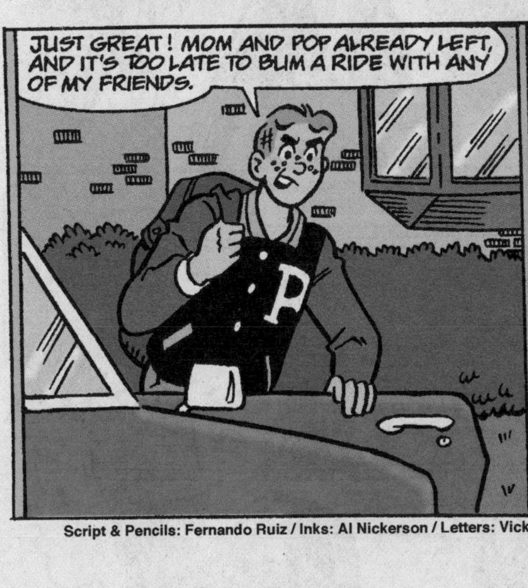
JUST GREAT! MOM AND POP ALREADY LEFT, AND IT'S TOO LATE TO BUM A RIDE WITH ANY OF MY FRIENDS.

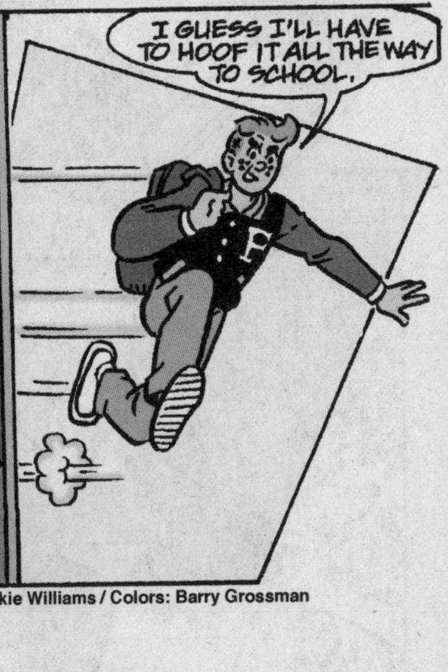
I GUESS I'LL HAVE TO HOOF IT ALL THE WAY TO SCHOOL.

Script & Pencils: Fernando Ruiz / Inks: Al Nickerson / Letters: Vickie Williams / Colors: Barry Grossman

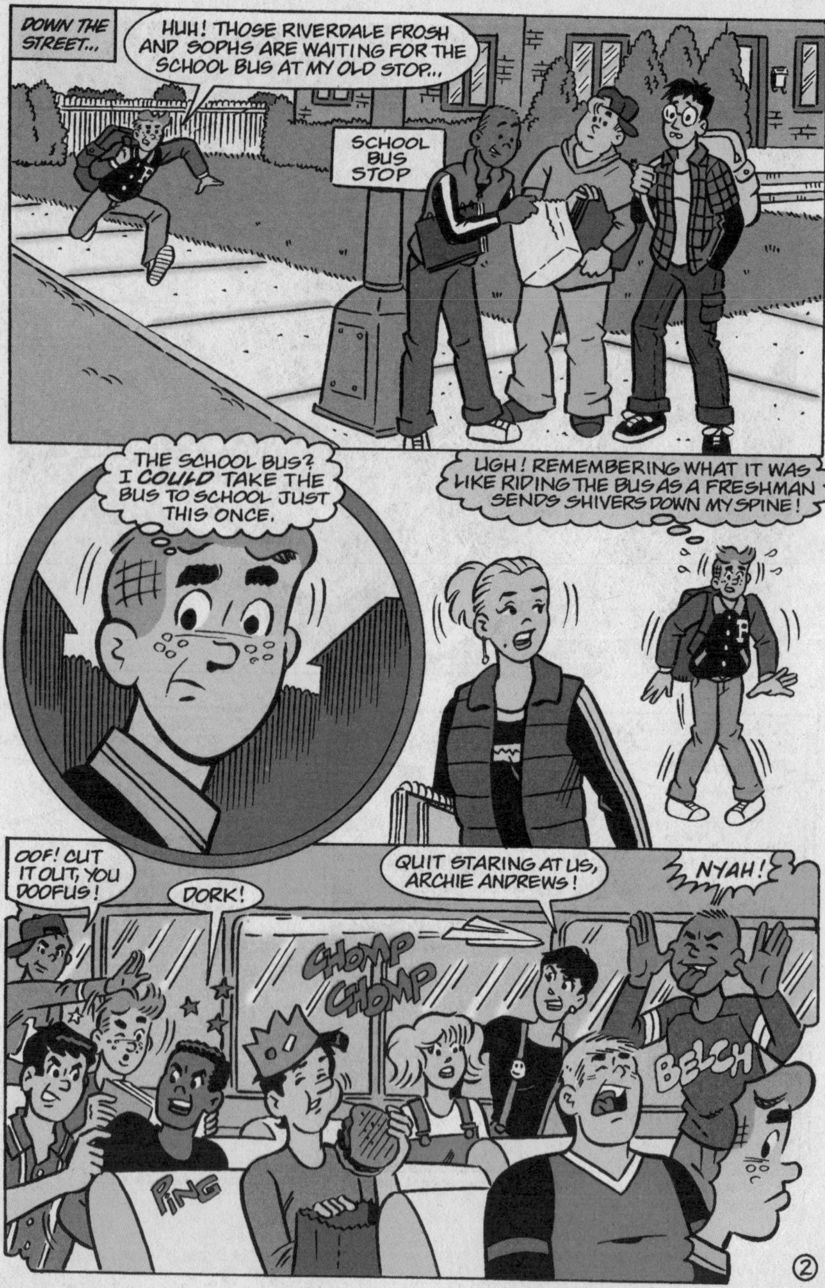
DOWN THE STREET...
HUH! THOSE RIVERDALE FROSH AND SOPHS ARE WAITING FOR THE SCHOOL BUS AT MY OLD STOP...
SCHOOL BUS STOP
THE SCHOOL BUS? I COULD TAKE THE BUS TO SCHOOL JUST THIS ONCE.
UGH! REMEMBERING WHAT IT WAS LIKE RIDING THE BUS AS A FRESHMAN SENDS SHIVERS DOWN MY SPINE!
OOF! CUT IT OUT, YOU DOOFUS!
DORK!
QUIT STARING AT US, ARCHIE ANDREWS!
NYAH!
CHOMP CHOMP
BELCH
PING
2

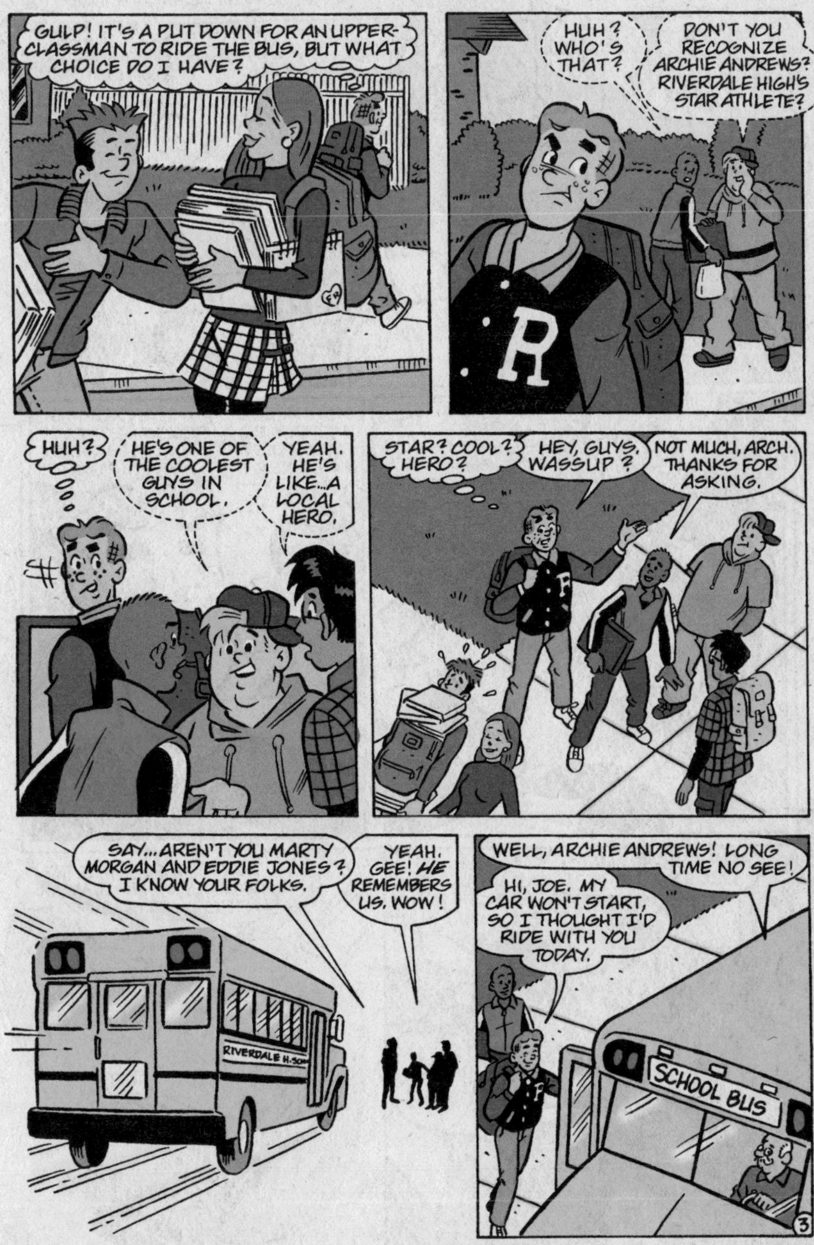
GULP! IT'S A PUT DOWN FOR AN UPPER-CLASSMAN TO RIDE THE BUS, BUT WHAT CHOICE DO I HAVE?
HUH? WHO'S THAT?
DON'T YOU RECOGNIZE ARCHIE ANDREWS? RIVERDALE HIGH'S STAR ATHLETE?
HUH?
HE'S ONE OF THE COOLEST GUYS IN SCHOOL.
YEAH. HE'S LIKE...A LOCAL HERO.
STAR? COOL? HERO?
HEY, GUYS, WASSUP?
NOT MUCH, ARCH. THANKS FOR ASKING.
SAY... AREN'T YOU MARTY MORGAN AND EDDIE JONES? I KNOW YOUR FOLKS.
YEAH. GEE! HE REMEMBERS US. WOW!
RIVERDALE H. SCH
WELL, ARCHIE ANDREWS! LONG TIME NO SEE!
HI, JOE. MY CAR WON'T START, SO I THOUGHT I'D RIDE WITH YOU TODAY.
SCHOOL BUS
3

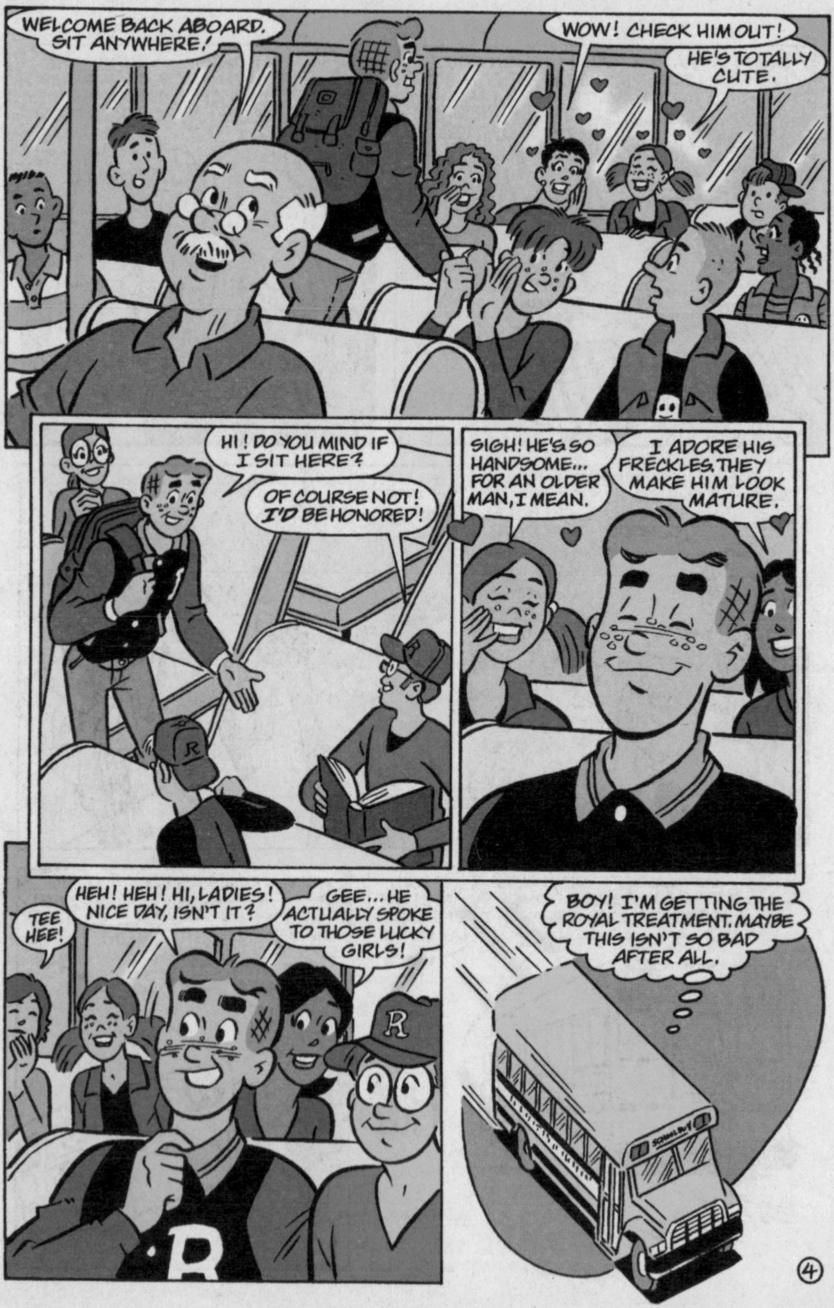
WELCOME BACK ABOARD. SIT ANYWHERE!
WOW! CHECK HIM OUT!
HE'S TOTALLY CUTE.
HI! DO YOU MIND IF I SIT HERE?
OF COURSE NOT! I'D BE HONORED!
SIGH! HE'S SO HANDSOME... FOR AN OLDER MAN, I MEAN.
I ADORE HIS FRECKLES. THEY MAKE HIM LOOK MATURE.
TEE HEE!
HEH! HEH! HI, LADIES! NICE DAY, ISN'T IT?
GEE... HE ACTUALLY SPOKE TO THOSE LUCKY GIRLS!
BOY! I'M GETTING THE ROYAL TREATMENT. MAYBE THIS ISN'T SO BAD AFTER ALL.
4

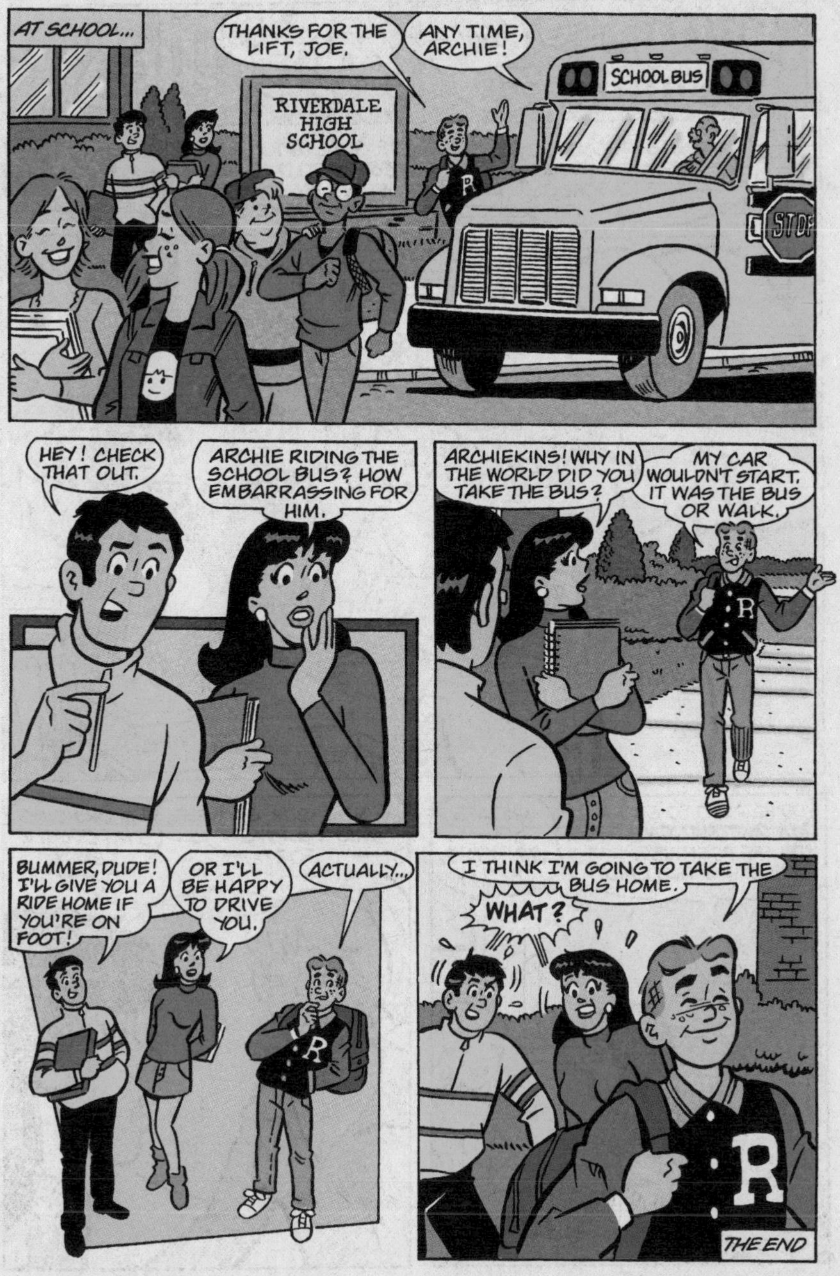
AT SCHOOL...
THANKS FOR THE LIFT, JOE.
ANY TIME, ARCHIE!
RIVERDALE HIGH SCHOOL
SCHOOL BUS
STOP
HEY! CHECK THAT OUT.
ARCHIE RIDING THE SCHOOL BUS? HOW EMBARRASSING FOR HIM.
ARCHIEKINS! WHY IN THE WORLD DID YOU TAKE THE BUS?
MY CAR WOULDN'T START. IT WAS THE BUS OR WALK.
BUMMER, DUDE! I'LL GIVE YOU A RIDE HOME IF YOU'RE ON FOOT!
OR I'LL BE HAPPY TO DRIVE YOU.
ACTUALLY...
I THINK I'M GOING TO TAKE THE BUS HOME.
WHAT?
THE END

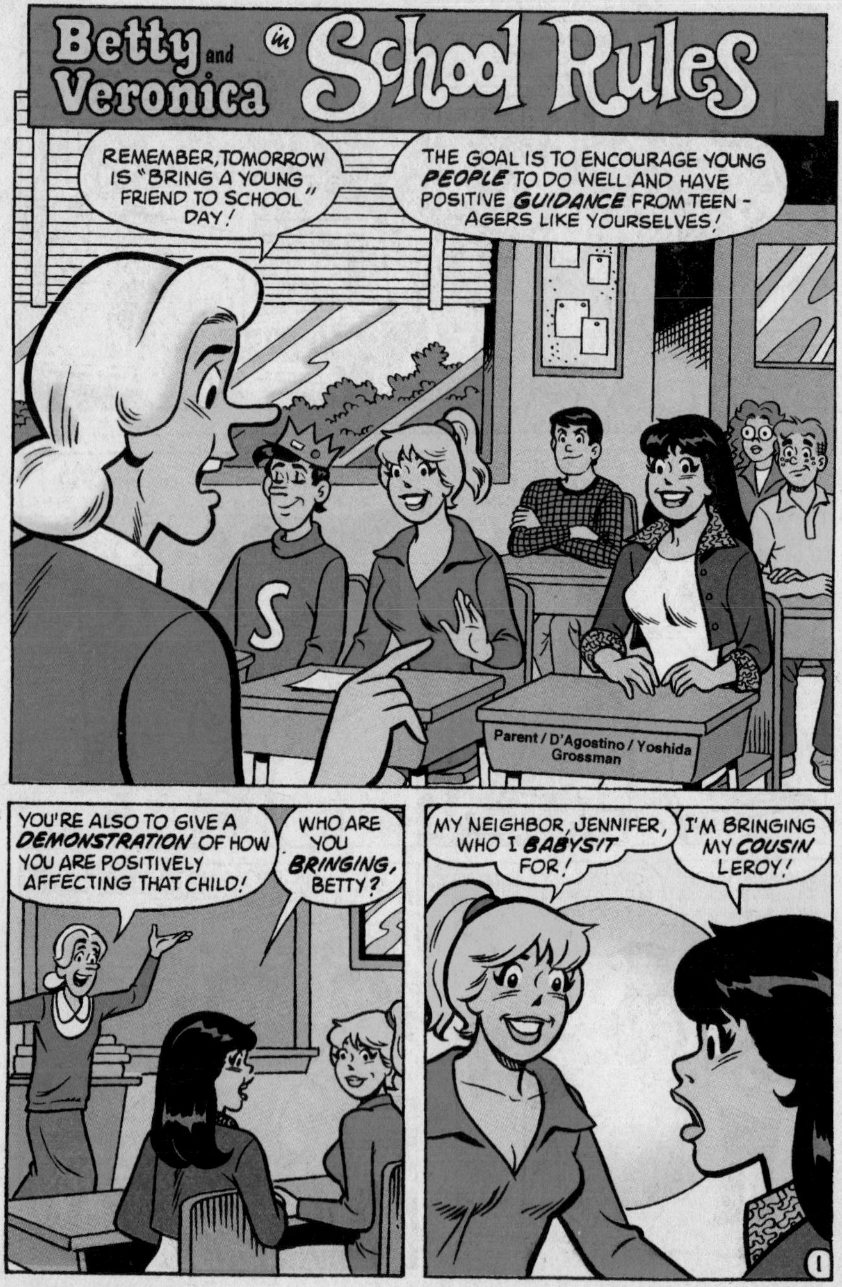
Betty and Veronica in School Rules
REMEMBER, TOMORROW IS "BRING A YOUNG FRIEND TO SCHOOL" DAY!
THE GOAL IS TO ENCOURAGE YOUNG PEOPLE TO DO WELL AND HAVE POSITIVE GUIDANCE FROM TEEN-AGERS LIKE YOURSELVES!
Parent / D'Agostino / Yoshida
Grossman
YOU'RE ALSO TO GIVE A DEMONSTRATION OF HOW YOU ARE POSITIVELY AFFECTING THAT CHILD!
WHO ARE YOU BRINGING, BETTY?
MY NEIGHBOR, JENNIFER, WHO I BABYSIT FOR!
I'M BRINGING MY COUSIN LEROY!
1

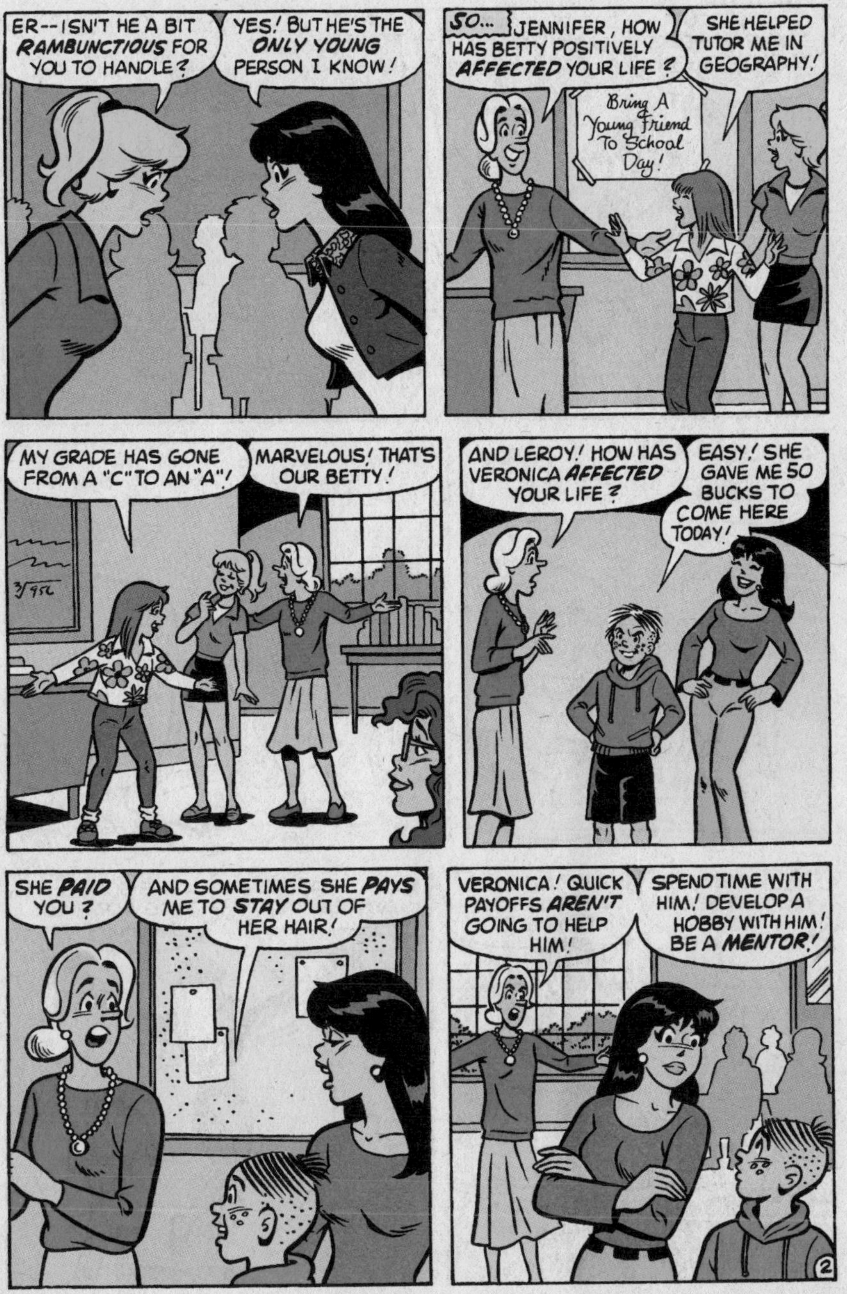
ER--ISN'T HE A BIT RAMBUNCTIOUS FOR YOU TO HANDLE?
YES! BUT HE'S THE ONLY YOUNG PERSON I KNOW!
SO...
JENNIFER, HOW HAS BETTY POSITIVELY AFFECTED YOUR LIFE?
Bring A Young Friend To School Day!
SHE HELPED TUTOR ME IN GEOGRAPHY!
MY GRADE HAS GONE FROM A "C" TO AN "A"!
MARVELOUS! THAT'S OUR BETTY!
AND LEROY! HOW HAS VERONICA AFFECTED YOUR LIFE?
EASY! SHE GAVE ME 50 BUCKS TO COME HERE TODAY!
SHE PAID YOU?
AND SOMETIMES SHE PAYS ME TO STAY OUT OF HER HAIR!
VERONICA! QUICK PAYOFFS AREN'T GOING TO HELP HIM!
SPEND TIME WITH HIM! DEVELOP A HOBBY WITH HIM! BE A MENTOR!
2

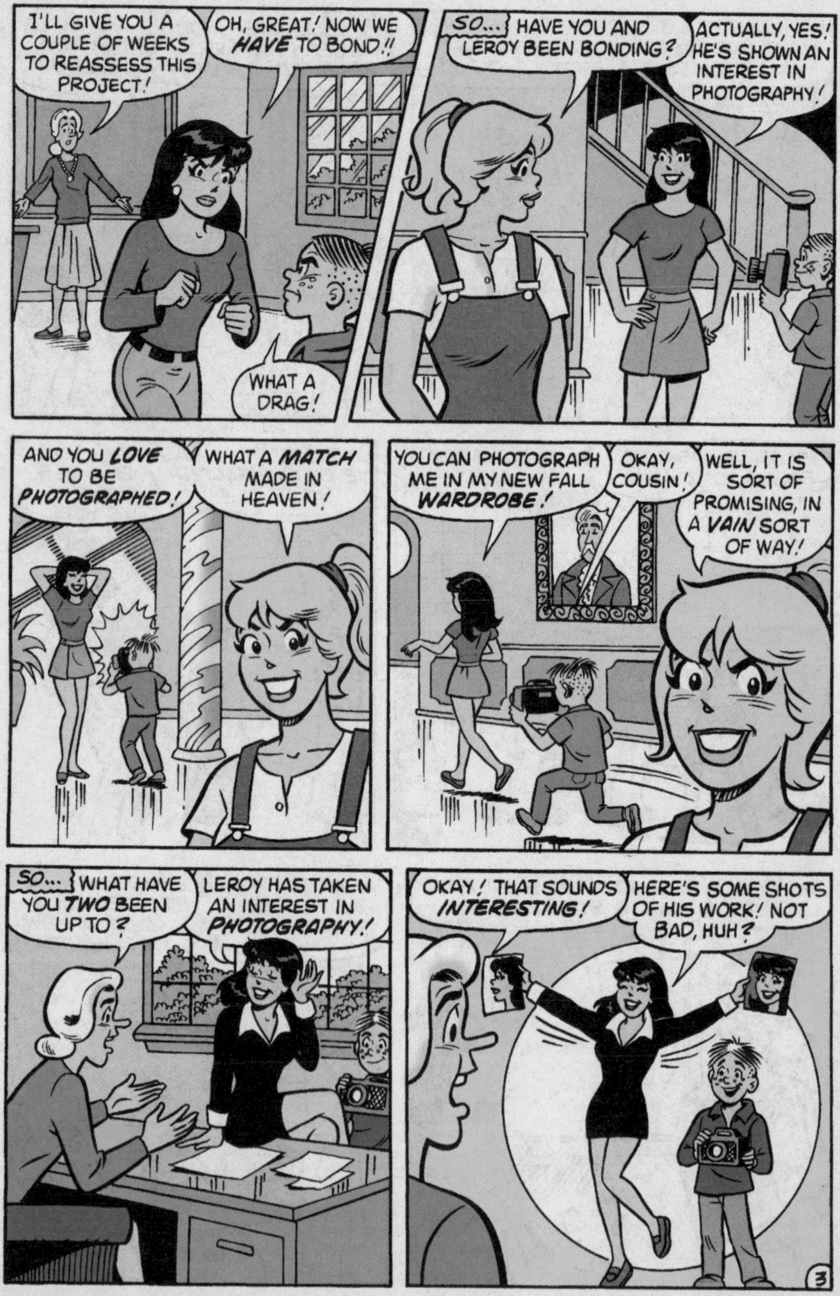
I'LL GIVE YOU A COUPLE OF WEEKS TO REASSESS THIS PROJECT!
OH, GREAT! NOW WE HAVE TO BOND!!
WHAT A DRAG!
SO... HAVE YOU AND LEROY BEEN BONDING?
ACTUALLY, YES! HE'S SHOWN AN INTEREST IN PHOTOGRAPHY!
AND YOU LOVE TO BE PHOTOGRAPHED!
WHAT A MATCH MADE IN HEAVEN!
YOU CAN PHOTOGRAPH ME IN MY NEW FALL WARDROBE!
OKAY, COUSIN!
WELL, IT IS SORT OF PROMISING, IN A VAIN SORT OF WAY!
SO... WHAT HAVE YOU TWO BEEN UP TO?
LEROY HAS TAKEN AN INTEREST IN PHOTOGRAPHY!
OKAY! THAT SOUNDS INTERESTING!
HERE'S SOME SHOTS OF HIS WORK! NOT BAD, HUH?
3

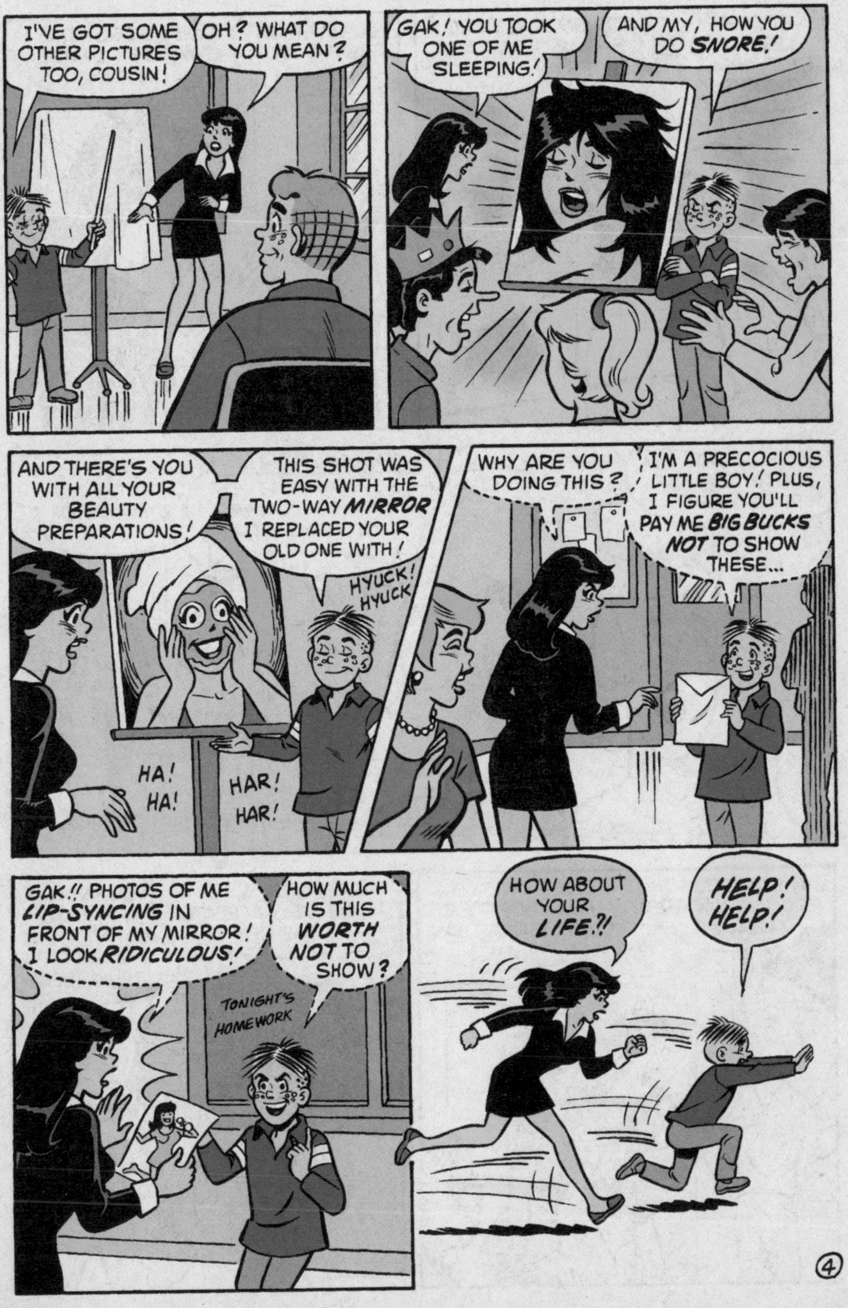
I'VE GOT SOME OTHER PICTURES TOO, COUSIN!
OH? WHAT DO YOU MEAN?
GAK! YOU TOOK ONE OF ME SLEEPING!
AND MY, HOW YOU DO SNORE!
AND THERE'S YOU WITH ALL YOUR BEAUTY PREPARATIONS!
THIS SHOT WAS EASY WITH THE TWO-WAY MIRROR I REPLACED YOUR OLD ONE WITH!
HYUCK! HYUCK!
HA! HA!
HAR! HAR!
WHY ARE YOU DOING THIS?
I'M A PRECOCIOUS LITTLE BOY! PLUS, I FIGURE YOU'LL PAY ME BIG BUCKS NOT TO SHOW THESE...
GAK!! PHOTOS OF ME LIP-SYNCING IN FRONT OF MY MIRROR! I LOOK RIDICULOUS!
HOW MUCH IS THIS WORTH NOT TO SHOW?
TONIGHT'S HOMEWORK
HOW ABOUT YOUR LIFE?!
HELP! HELP!
4

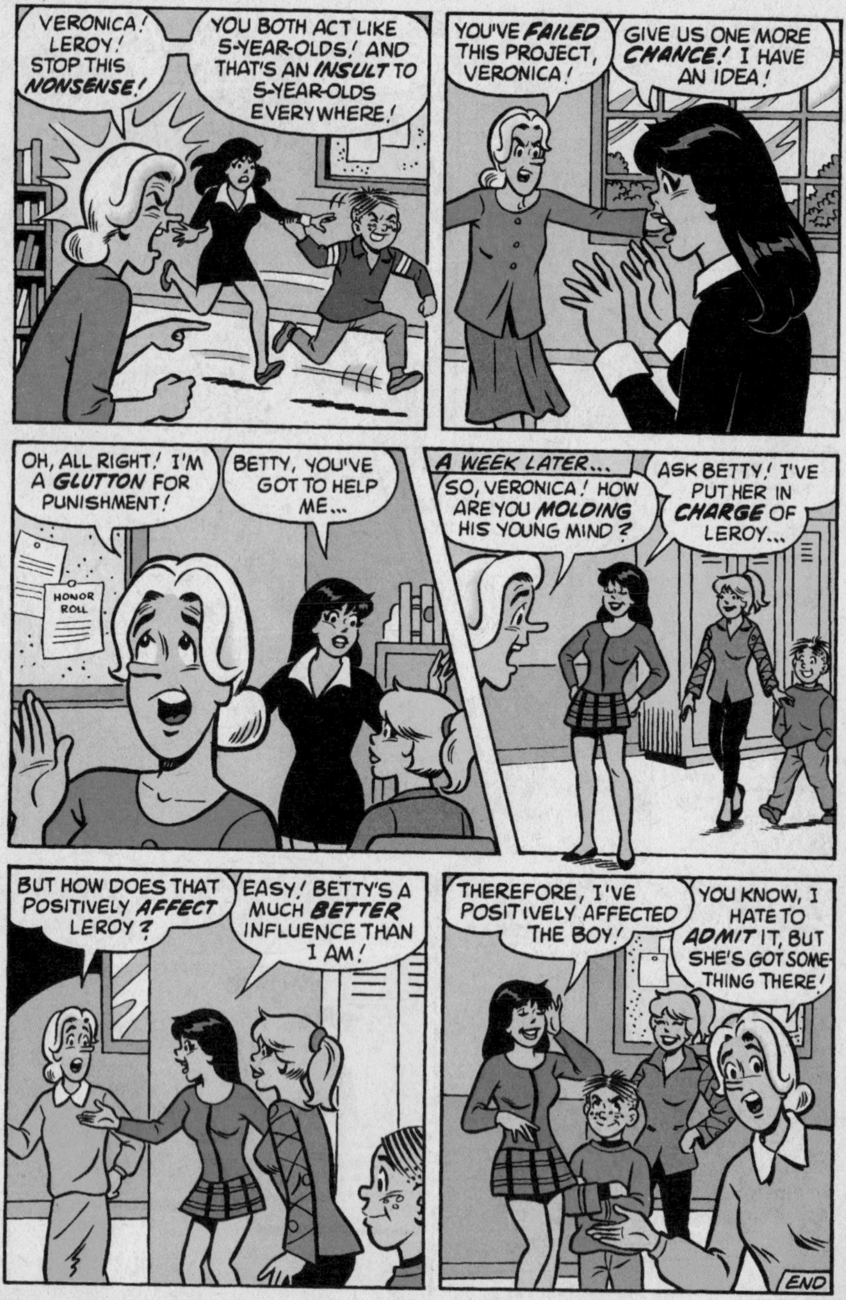

VERONICA! LEROY! STOP THIS NONSENSE!
YOU BOTH ACT LIKE 5-YEAR-OLDS! AND THAT'S AN INSULT TO 5-YEAR-OLDS EVERYWHERE!
YOU'VE FAILED THIS PROJECT, VERONICA!
GIVE US ONE MORE CHANCE! I HAVE AN IDEA!
OH, ALL RIGHT! I'M A GLUTTON FOR PUNISHMENT!
BETTY, YOU'VE GOT TO HELP ME...
HONOR ROLL
A WEEK LATER...
SO, VERONICA! HOW ARE YOU MOLDING HIS YOUNG MIND?
ASK BETTY! I'VE PUT HER IN CHARGE OF LEROY...
BUT HOW DOES THAT POSITIVELY AFFECT LEROY?
EASY! BETTY'S A MUCH BETTER INFLUENCE THAN I AM!
THEREFORE, I'VE POSITIVELY AFFECTED THE BOY!
YOU KNOW, I HATE TO ADMIT IT, BUT SHE'S GOT SOMETHING THERE!
END

The First Day of School
Pep #403, November 1985
George Gladir, Hy Eisman, Rudy Lapick,
Bill Yoshida and Barry Grossman

Going back to school is one of the most stressful things teenagers have to endure. For Archie, returning to Riverdale High becomes a comedy of errors... one that isn't making him laugh one bit. Fortunately for our red-headed hero, Veronica Lodge is there when he needs her the most!

The Welcoming Committee
Betty & Veronica #280, April 1979
Frank Doyle, Dan DeCarlo and Rudy Lapick

When Betty and Veronica spot a pair of nervous freshman girls, they decide to welcome the new students and treat them to fried chicken. Skeptical of upperclassmen and suspicious of the gesture, the new girls don't know what to do with the gift... until Jughead wanders by...

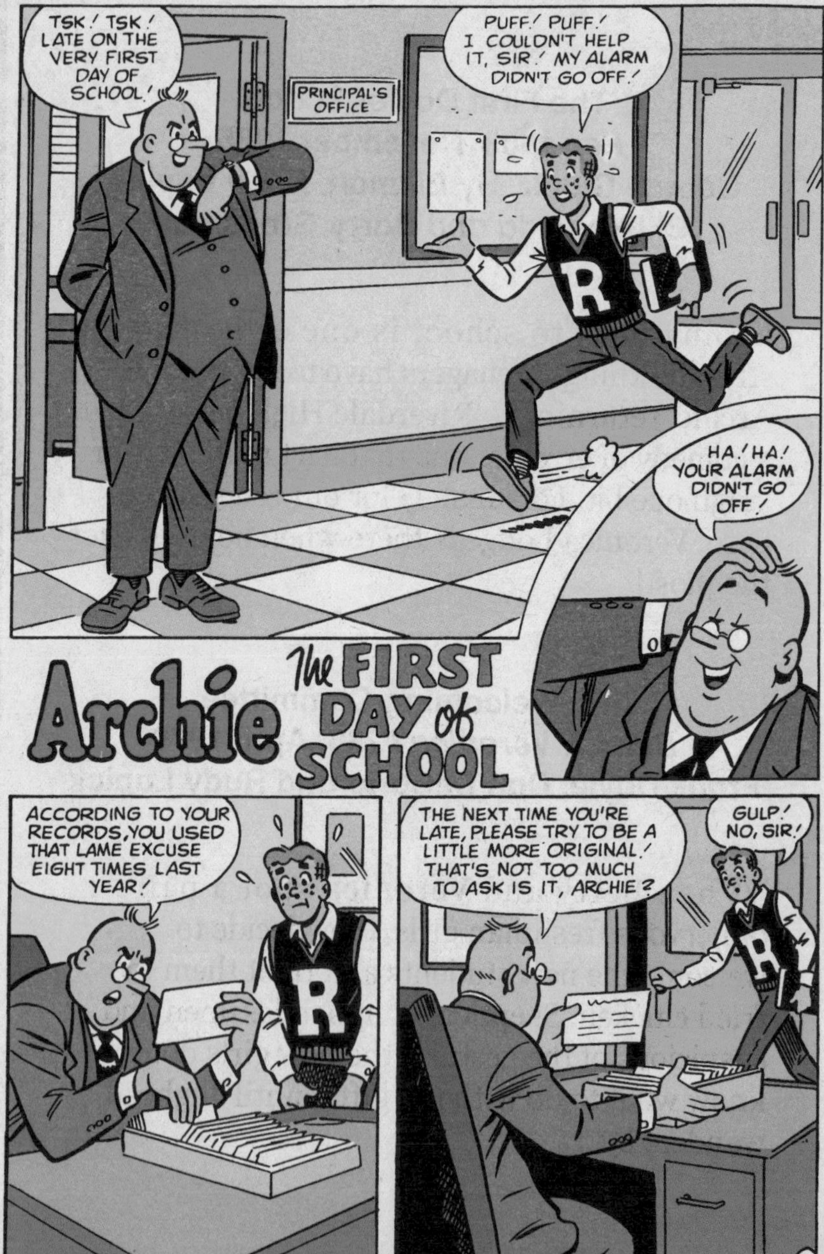
TSK! TSK! LATE ON THE VERY FIRST DAY OF SCHOOL!
PRINCIPAL'S OFFICE
PUFF! PUFF! I COULDN'T HELP IT, SIR! MY ALARM DIDN'T GO OFF!
HA! HA! YOUR ALARM DIDN'T GO OFF!
Archie
The FIRST DAY of SCHOOL
ACCORDING TO YOUR RECORDS, YOU USED THAT LAME EXCUSE EIGHT TIMES LAST YEAR!
THE NEXT TIME YOU'RE LATE, PLEASE TRY TO BE A LITTLE MORE ORIGINAL! THAT'S NOT TOO MUCH TO ASK IS IT, ARCHIE?
GULP! NO, SIR!
1

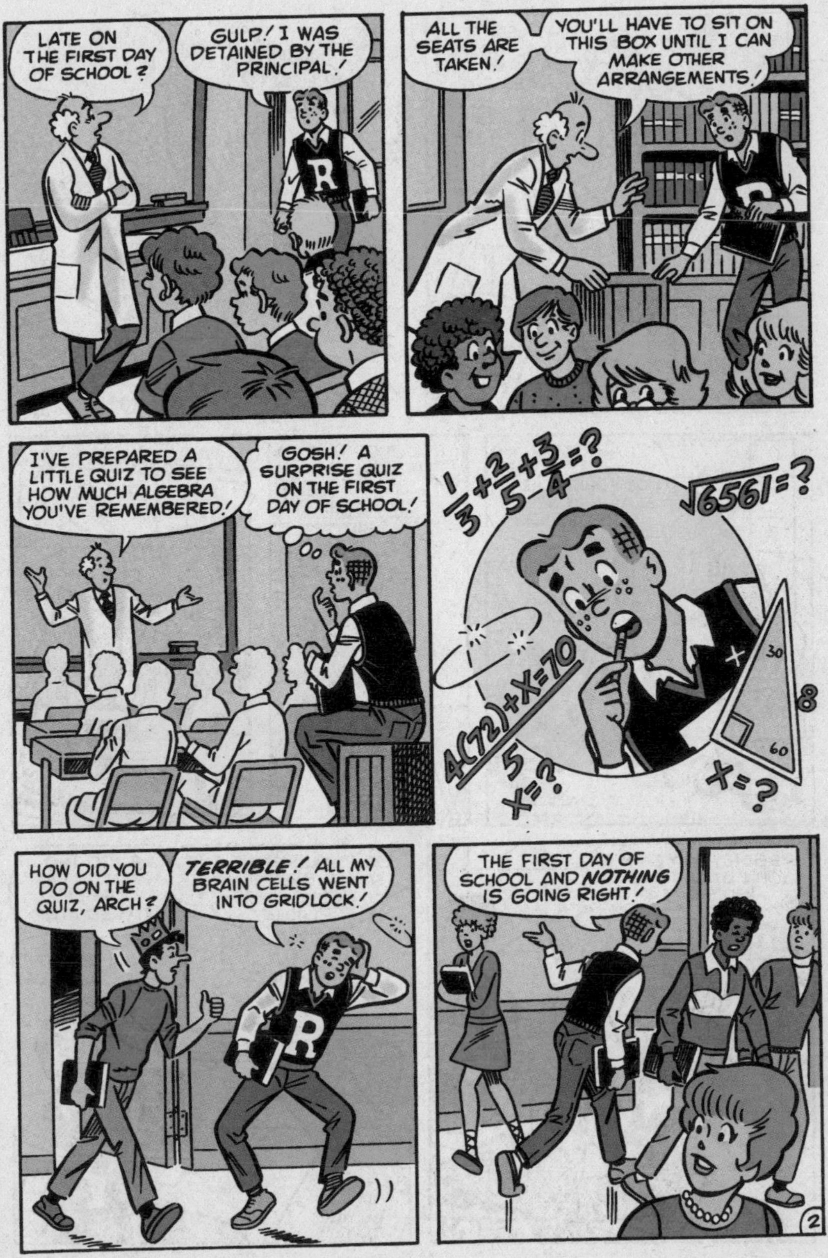
LATE ON THE FIRST DAY OF SCHOOL?
GULP! I WAS DETAINED BY THE PRINCIPAL!
ALL THE SEATS ARE TAKEN!
YOU'LL HAVE TO SIT ON THIS BOX UNTIL I CAN MAKE OTHER ARRANGEMENTS!
I'VE PREPARED A LITTLE QUIZ TO SEE HOW MUCH ALGEBRA YOU'VE REMEMBERED!
GOSH! A SURPRISE QUIZ ON THE FIRST DAY OF SCHOOL!
1/3 + 2/5 + 3/4 = ?
√6561 = ?
4(72)+X=70 / 5
X=?
30
8
60
X=?
HOW DID YOU DO ON THE QUIZ, ARCH?
TERRIBLE! ALL MY BRAIN CELLS WENT INTO GRIDLOCK!
THE FIRST DAY OF SCHOOL AND NOTHING IS GOING RIGHT!
2

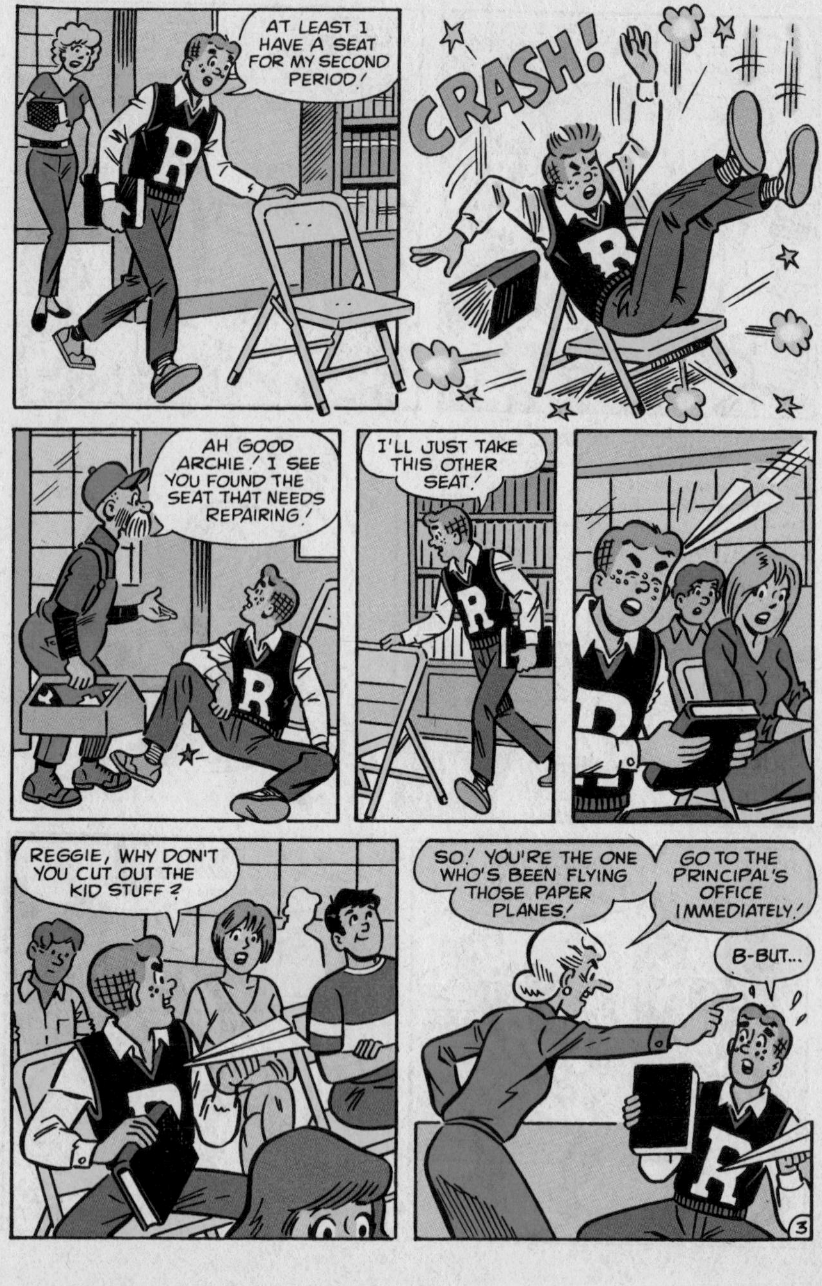
AT LEAST I HAVE A SEAT FOR MY SECOND PERIOD!
CRASH!
AH GOOD ARCHIE! I SEE YOU FOUND THE SEAT THAT NEEDS REPAIRING!
I'LL JUST TAKE THIS OTHER SEAT!
REGGIE, WHY DON'T YOU CUT OUT THE KID STUFF?
SO! YOU'RE THE ONE WHO'S BEEN FLYING THOSE PAPER PLANES!
GO TO THE PRINCIPAL'S OFFICE IMMEDIATELY!
B-BUT...
3

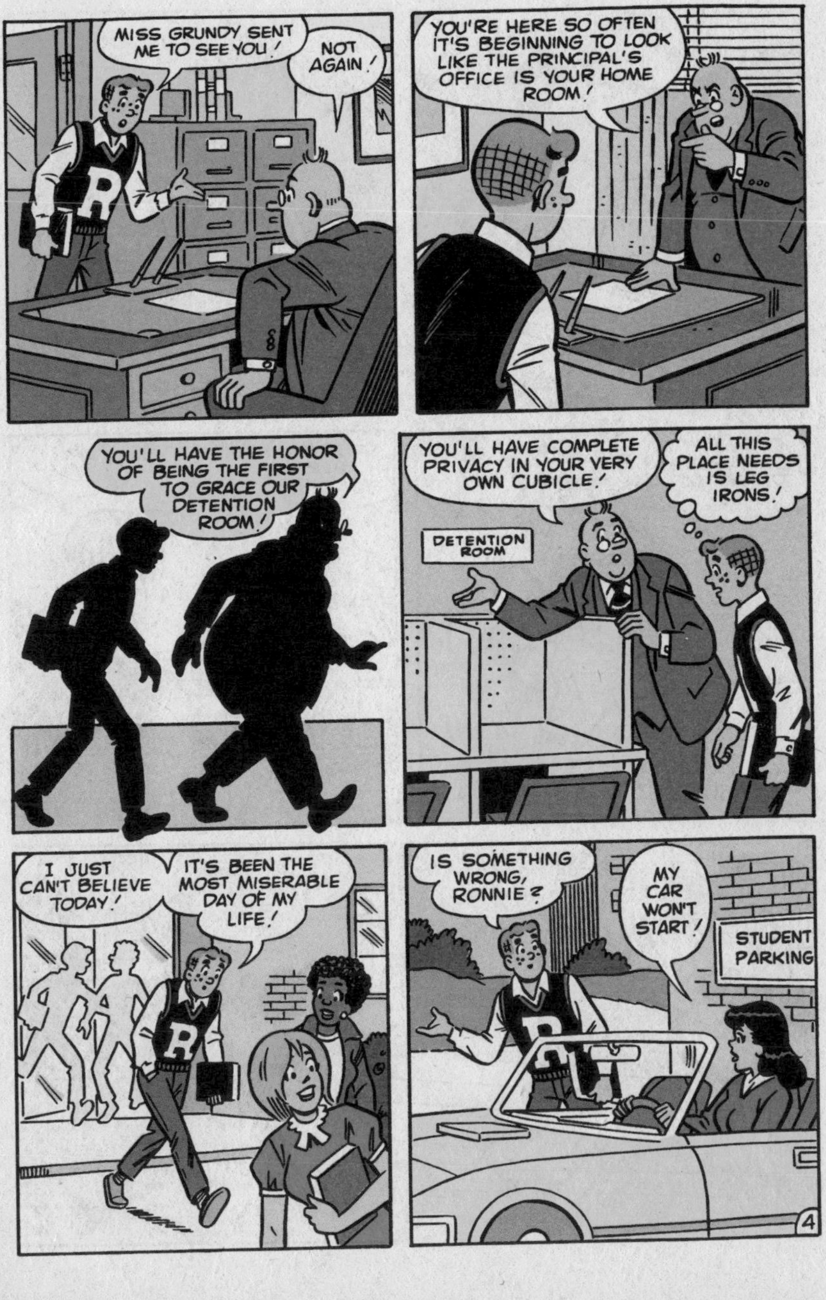
MISS GRUNDY SENT ME TO SEE YOU!
NOT AGAIN!
YOU'RE HERE SO OFTEN IT'S BEGINNING TO LOOK LIKE THE PRINCIPAL'S OFFICE IS YOUR HOME ROOM!
YOU'LL HAVE THE HONOR OF BEING THE FIRST TO GRACE OUR DETENTION ROOM!
YOU'LL HAVE COMPLETE PRIVACY IN YOUR VERY OWN CUBICLE!
ALL THIS PLACE NEEDS IS LEG IRONS!
DETENTION ROOM
I JUST CAN'T BELIEVE TODAY!
IT'S BEEN THE MOST MISERABLE DAY OF MY LIFE!
IS SOMETHING WRONG, RONNIE?
MY CAR WON'T START!
STUDENT PARKING
4

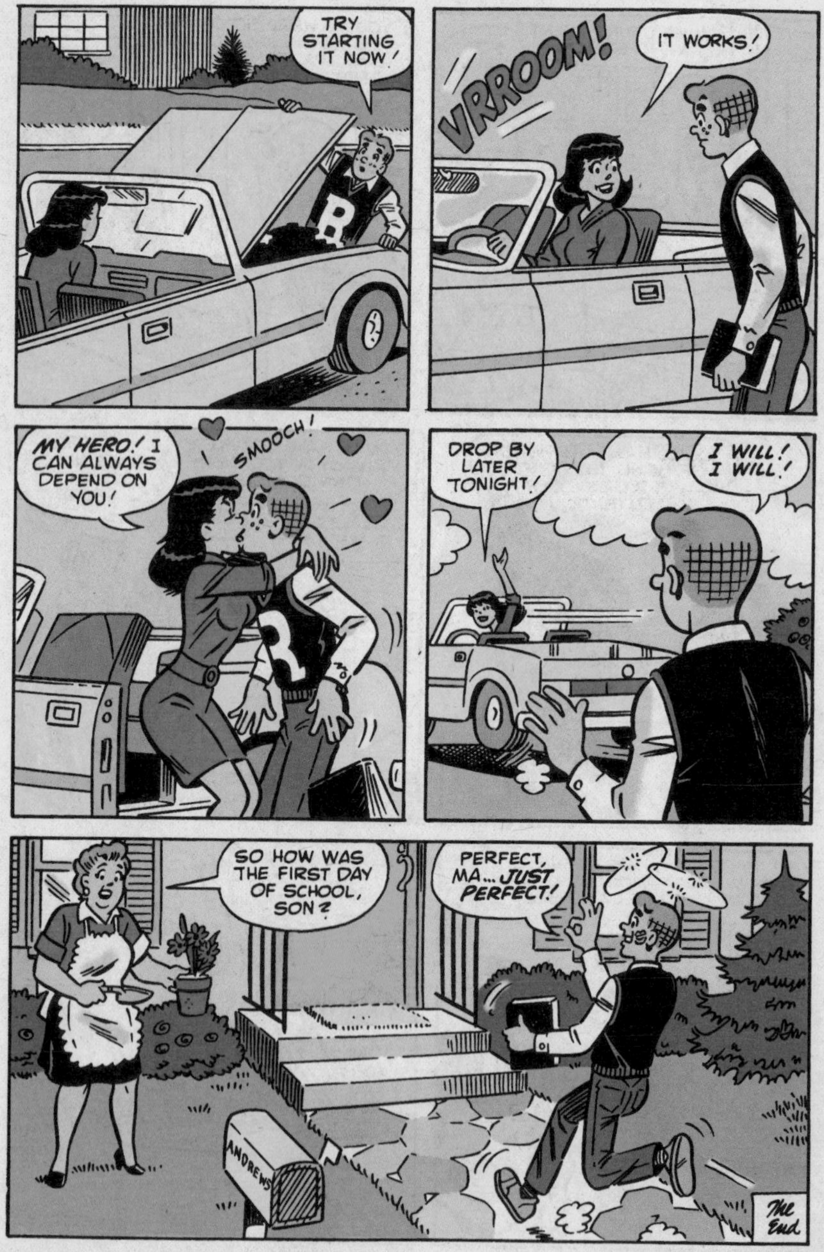
TRY STARTING IT NOW!
VRROOM!
IT WORKS!
MY HERO! I CAN ALWAYS DEPEND ON YOU!
SMOOCH!
DROP BY LATER TONIGHT!
I WILL! I WILL!
SO HOW WAS THE FIRST DAY OF SCHOOL, SON?
PERFECT, MA... JUST PERFECT!
ANDREWS
The End

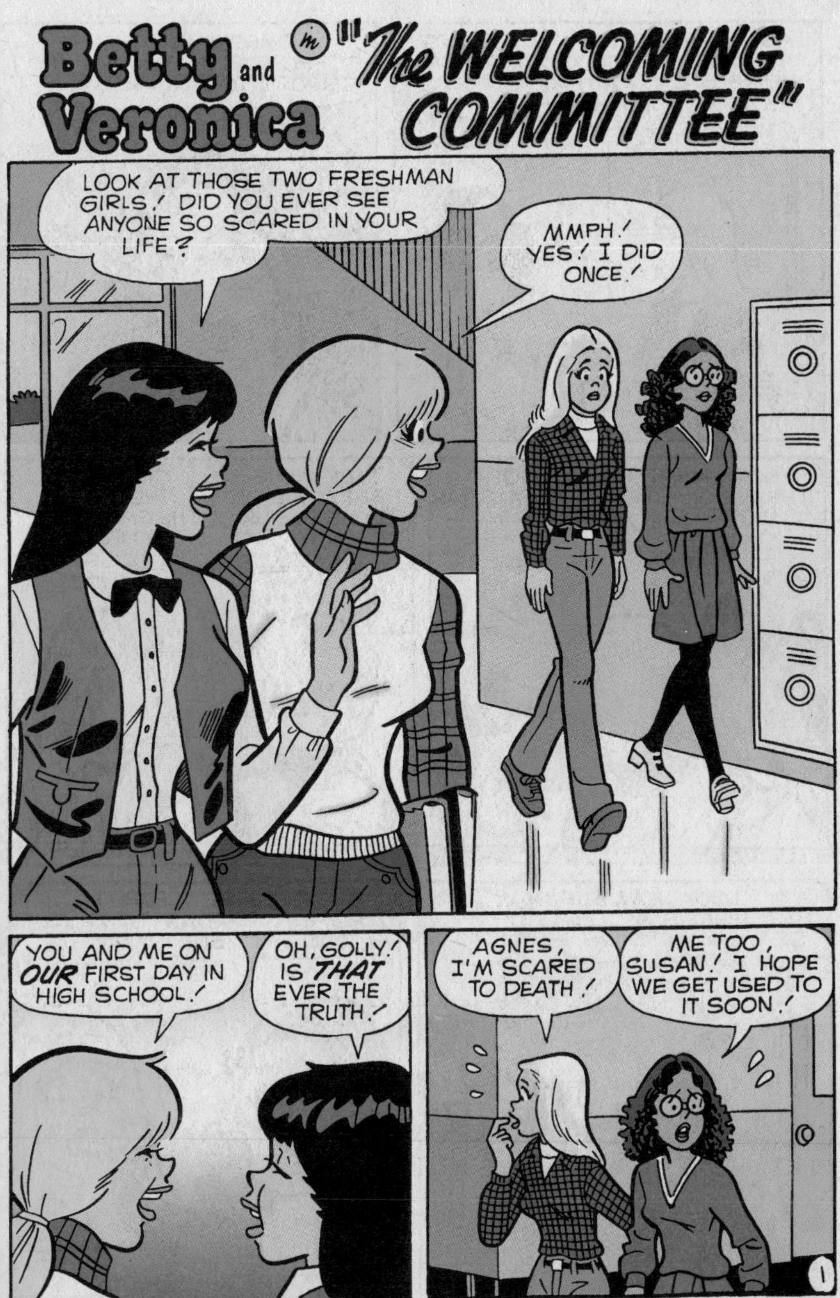
Betty and Veronica
in "The WELCOMING COMMITTEE"
LOOK AT THOSE TWO FRESHMAN GIRLS! DID YOU EVER SEE ANYONE SO SCARED IN YOUR LIFE?
MMPH! YES! I DID ONCE!
YOU AND ME ON OUR FIRST DAY IN HIGH SCHOOL!
OH, GOLLY! IS THAT EVER THE TRUTH!
AGNES, I'M SCARED TO DEATH!
ME TOO, SUSAN! I HOPE WE GET USED TO IT SOON!
1

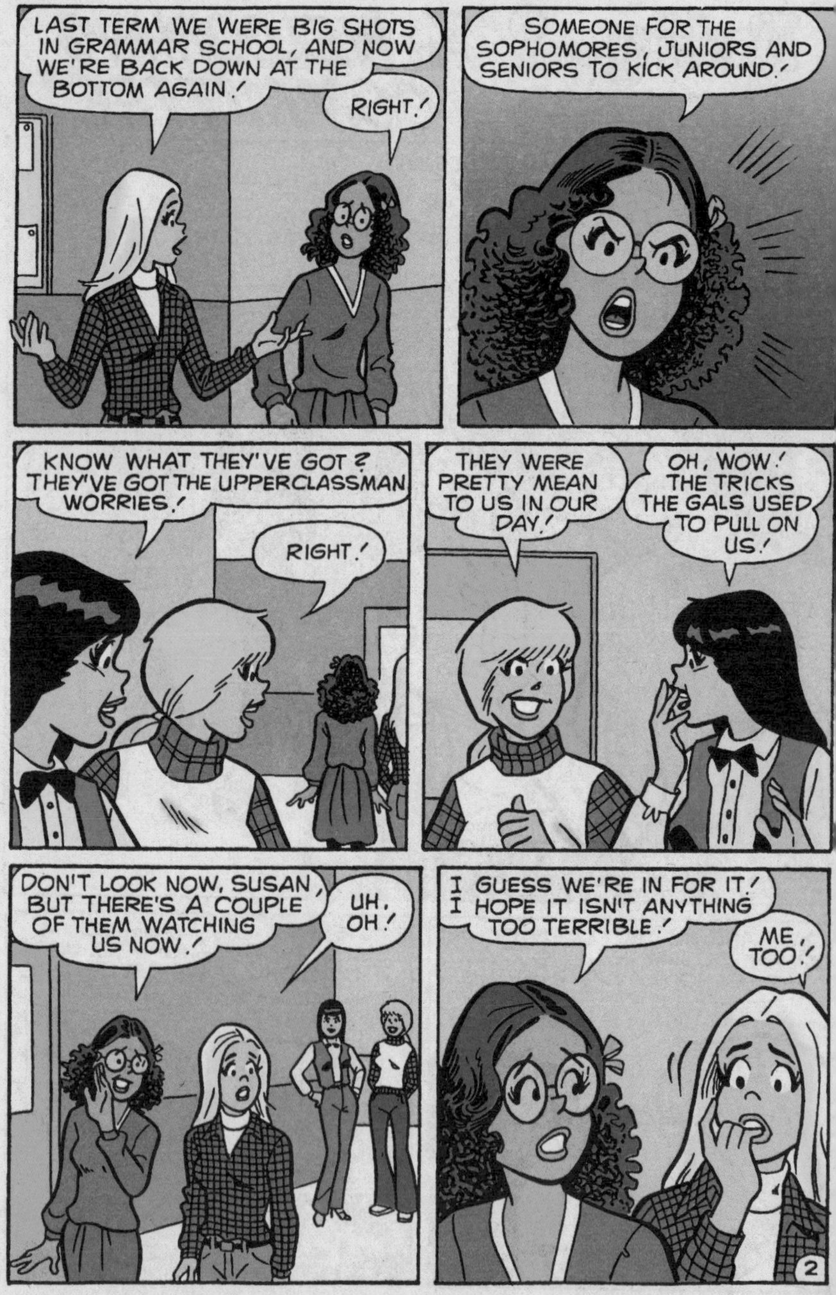
LAST TERM WE WERE BIG SHOTS IN GRAMMAR SCHOOL, AND NOW WE'RE BACK DOWN AT THE BOTTOM AGAIN!
RIGHT!
SOMEONE FOR THE SOPHOMORES, JUNIORS AND SENIORS TO KICK AROUND!
KNOW WHAT THEY'VE GOT? THEY'VE GOT THE UPPERCLASSMAN WORRIES!
RIGHT!
THEY WERE PRETTY MEAN TO US IN OUR DAY!
OH, WOW! THE TRICKS THE GALS USED TO PULL ON US!
DON'T LOOK NOW, SUSAN, BUT THERE'S A COUPLE OF THEM WATCHING US NOW!
UH, OH!
I GUESS WE'RE IN FOR IT! I HOPE IT ISN'T ANYTHING TOO TERRIBLE!
ME, TOO!
2

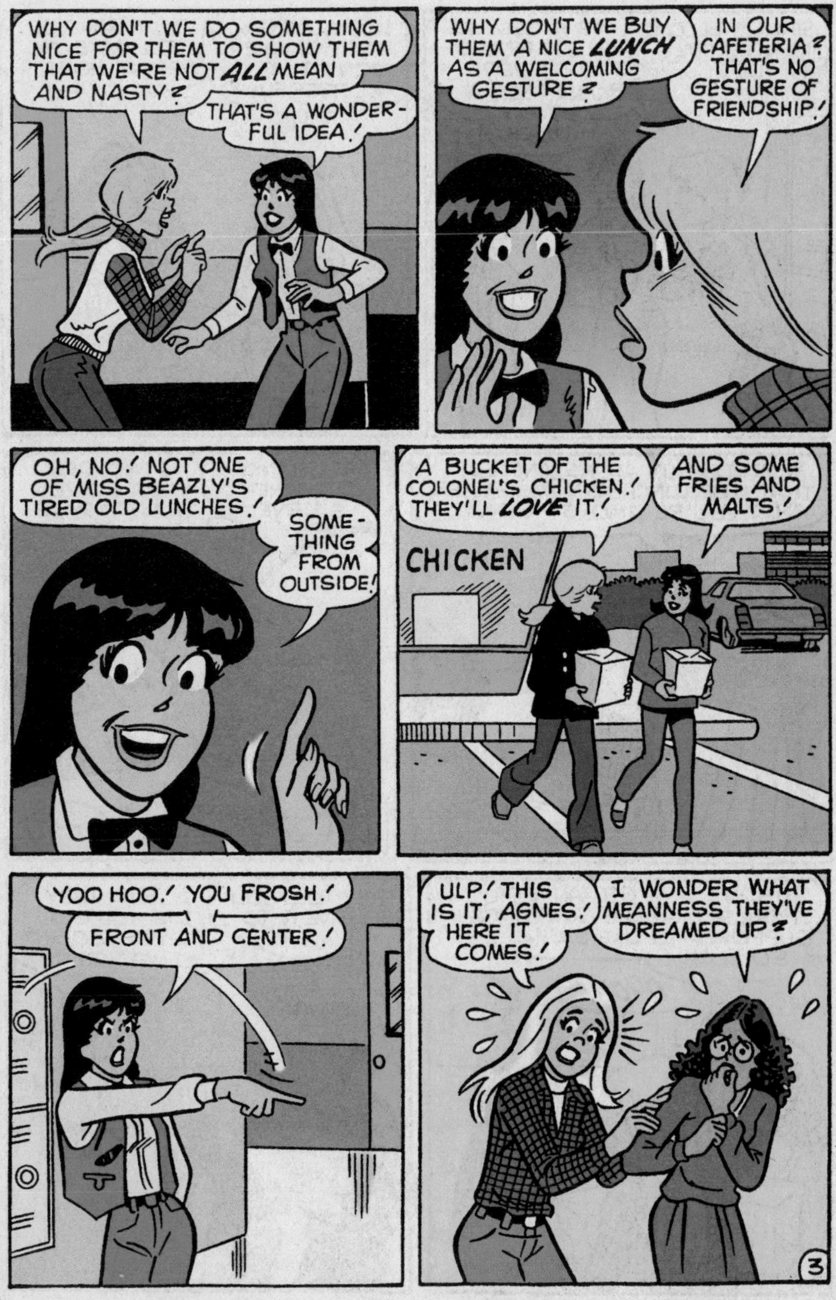
WHY DON'T WE DO SOMETHING NICE FOR THEM TO SHOW THEM THAT WE'RE NOT ALL MEAN AND NASTY?
THAT'S A WONDERFUL IDEA!
WHY DON'T WE BUY THEM A NICE LUNCH AS A WELCOMING GESTURE?
IN OUR CAFETERIA? THAT'S NO GESTURE OF FRIENDSHIP!
OH, NO! NOT ONE OF MISS BEAZLY'S TIRED OLD LUNCHES!
SOMETHING FROM OUTSIDE!
A BUCKET OF THE COLONEL'S CHICKEN! THEY'LL LOVE IT!
AND SOME FRIES AND MALTS!
CHICKEN
YOO HOO! YOU FROSH!
FRONT AND CENTER!
ULP! THIS IS IT, AGNES! HERE IT COMES!
I WONDER WHAT MEANNESS THEY'VE DREAMED UP?
3

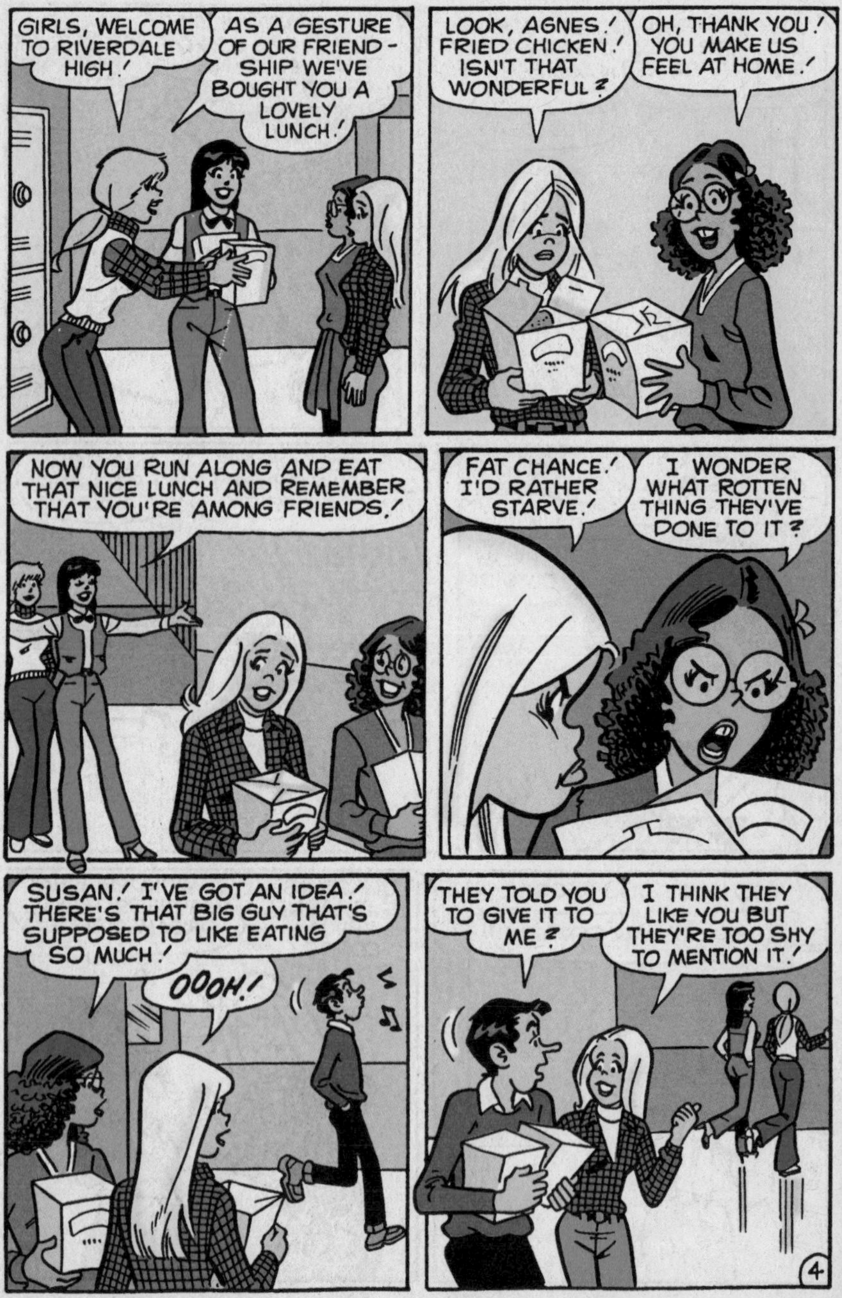
GIRLS, WELCOME TO RIVERDALE HIGH!
AS A GESTURE OF OUR FRIEND-SHIP WE'VE BOUGHT YOU A LOVELY LUNCH!
LOOK, AGNES! FRIED CHICKEN! ISN'T THAT WONDERFUL?
OH, THANK YOU! YOU MAKE US FEEL AT HOME!
NOW YOU RUN ALONG AND EAT THAT NICE LUNCH AND REMEMBER THAT YOU'RE AMONG FRIENDS!
FAT CHANCE! I'D RATHER STARVE!
I WONDER WHAT ROTTEN THING THEY'VE DONE TO IT?
SUSAN! I'VE GOT AN IDEA! THERE'S THAT BIG GUY THAT'S SUPPOSED TO LIKE EATING SO MUCH!
OOOH!
THEY TOLD YOU TO GIVE IT TO ME?
I THINK THEY LIKE YOU BUT THEY'RE TOO SHY TO MENTION IT!
4

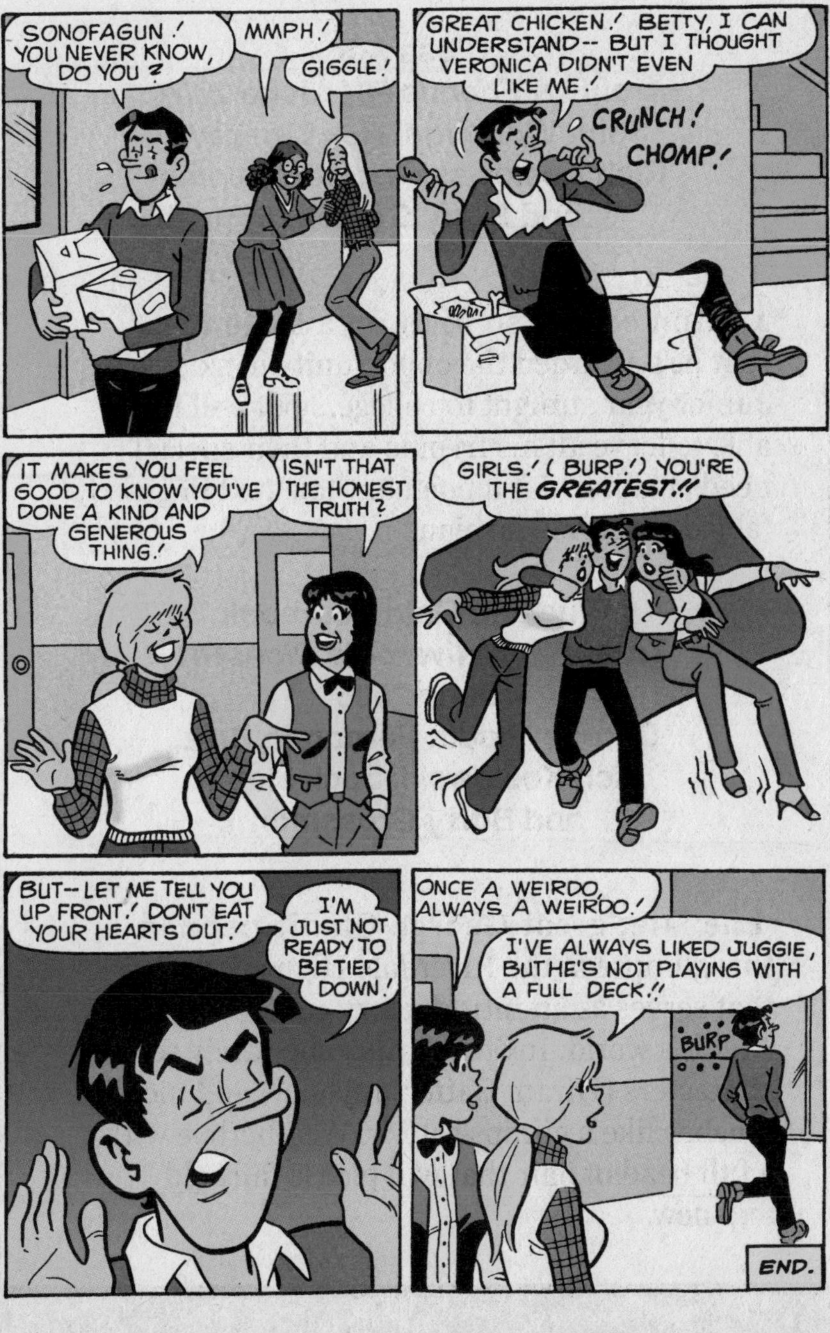
SONOFAGUN! YOU NEVER KNOW, DO YOU?
MMPH!
GIGGLE!
GREAT CHICKEN! BETTY, I CAN UNDERSTAND-- BUT I THOUGHT VERONICA DIDN'T EVEN LIKE ME!
CRUNCH!
CHOMP!
IT MAKES YOU FEEL GOOD TO KNOW YOU'VE DONE A KIND AND GENEROUS THING!
ISN'T THAT THE HONEST TRUTH?
GIRLS! (BURP!) YOU'RE THE GREATEST!!
BUT-- LET ME TELL YOU UP FRONT! DON'T EAT YOUR HEARTS OUT!
I'M JUST NOT READY TO BE TIED DOWN!
ONCE A WEIRDO, ALWAYS A WEIRDO!
I'VE ALWAYS LIKED JUGGIE, BUT HE'S NOT PLAYING WITH A FULL DECK!!
BURP
END.

Class Act
Archie & Friends #81, June 2004
**John Workman, Rex Lindsey,
Rich Koslowski, Vickie Williams
and Barry Grossman**

Dilton scores so high on a state test
that he's awarded the opportunity to skip from
Junior year straight to college... but will he be
able to leave all his friends and their special
needs behind? It's a poignant tale told in grand,
fabled Riverdale fashion.

Blue and Gold Yearbook
Tales From Riverdale Digest #1,
**June 2005
George Gladir, Fernando Ruiz,
Rich Koslowski, Jack Morelli
and Barry Grossman**

The late, great George Gladir penned
this glimpse at the Riverdale High yearbook
that serves as an introductory course for
Archie's world. Included are some rarely seen
characters (Hiram Gaffer, anyone?) and nice
touches like a glimpse at Mr. Weatherbee with
a full head of hair that will please fans old
and new.

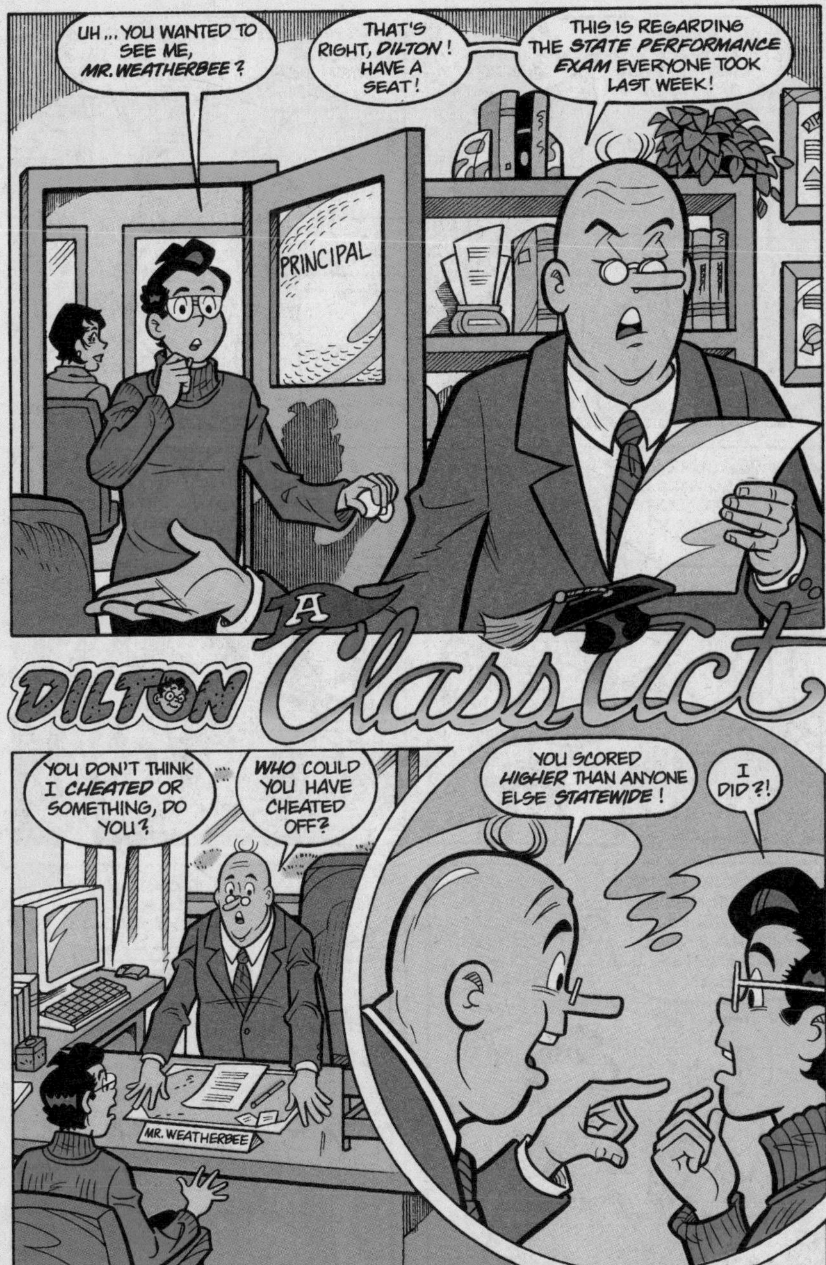
UH ... YOU WANTED TO SEE ME, MR. WEATHERBEE ?
THAT'S RIGHT, DILTON ! HAVE A SEAT !
THIS IS REGARDING THE STATE PERFORMANCE EXAM EVERYONE TOOK LAST WEEK!
PRINCIPAL
A
DILTON
Class Act
YOU DON'T THINK I CHEATED OR SOMETHING, DO YOU?
WHO COULD YOU HAVE CHEATED OFF?
MR. WEATHERBEE
YOU SCORED HIGHER THAN ANYONE ELSE STATEWIDE !
I DID?!

SCRIPT: JOHN WORKMAN PENCILS: REX LINDSEY INKING: RICH KOSLOWSKI LETTERING: VICKIE WILLIAMS COLORING: BARRY GROSSMAN

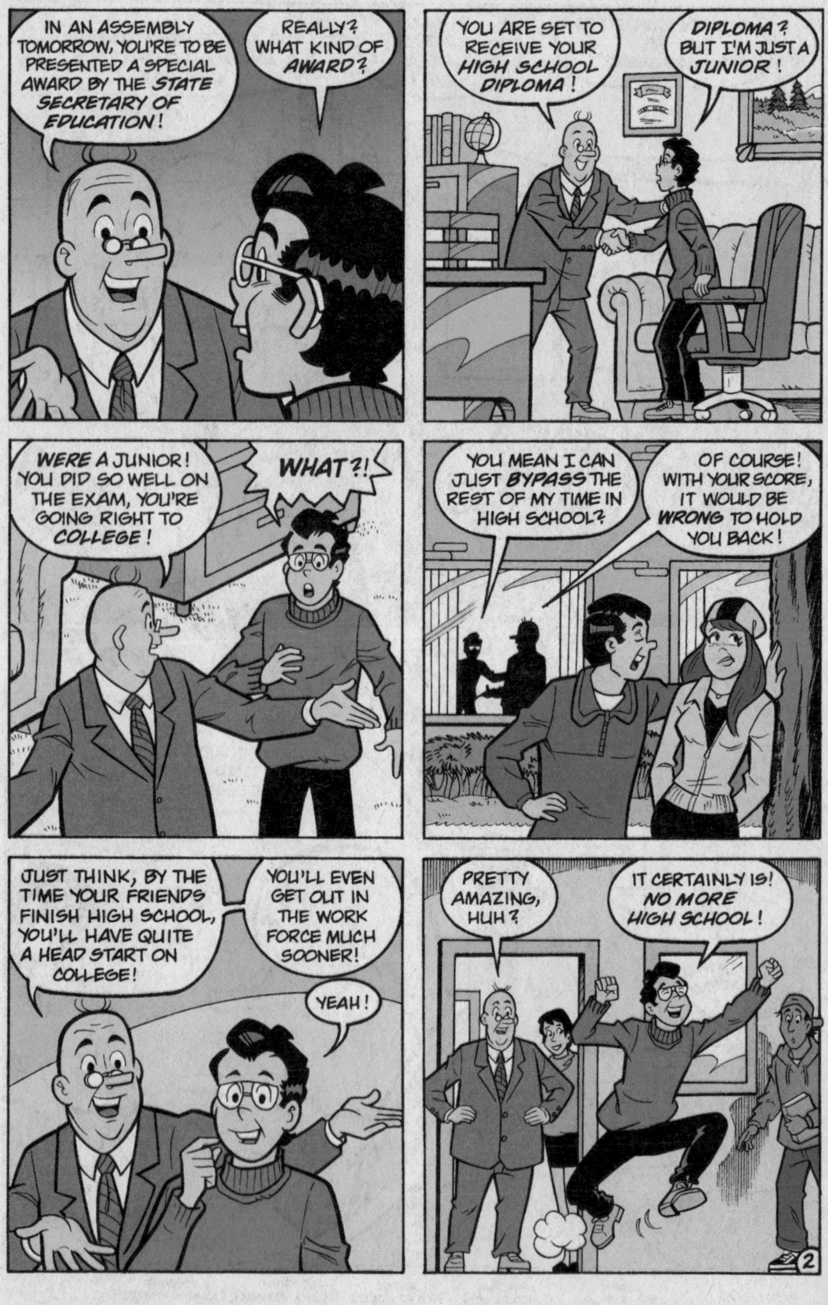
IN AN ASSEMBLY TOMORROW, YOU'RE TO BE PRESENTED A SPECIAL AWARD BY THE STATE SECRETARY OF EDUCATION!
REALLY? WHAT KIND OF AWARD?
YOU ARE SET TO RECEIVE YOUR HIGH SCHOOL DIPLOMA!
DIPLOMA? BUT I'M JUST A JUNIOR!
WERE A JUNIOR! YOU DID SO WELL ON THE EXAM, YOU'RE GOING RIGHT TO COLLEGE!
WHAT?!
YOU MEAN I CAN JUST BYPASS THE REST OF MY TIME IN HIGH SCHOOL?
OF COURSE! WITH YOUR SCORE, IT WOULD BE WRONG TO HOLD YOU BACK!
JUST THINK, BY THE TIME YOUR FRIENDS FINISH HIGH SCHOOL, YOU'LL HAVE QUITE A HEAD START ON COLLEGE!
YOU'LL EVEN GET OUT IN THE WORK FORCE MUCH SOONER!
YEAH!
PRETTY AMAZING, HUH?
IT CERTAINLY IS! NO MORE HIGH SCHOOL!
2

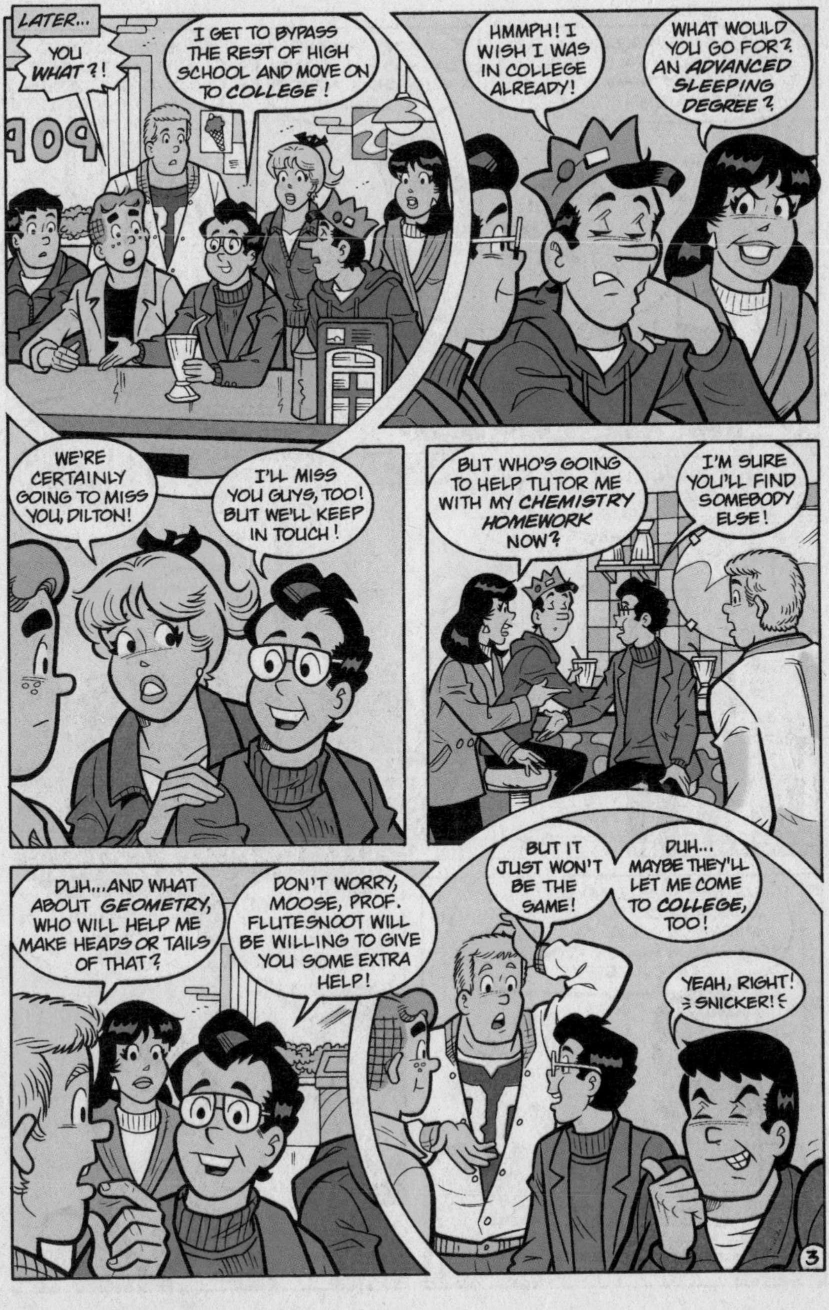
LATER...
YOU WHAT?!
I GET TO BYPASS THE REST OF HIGH SCHOOL AND MOVE ON TO COLLEGE!
POP
HMMPH! I WISH I WAS IN COLLEGE ALREADY!
WHAT WOULD YOU GO FOR? AN ADVANCED SLEEPING DEGREE?
WE'RE CERTAINLY GOING TO MISS YOU, DILTON!
I'LL MISS YOU GUYS, TOO! BUT WE'LL KEEP IN TOUCH!
BUT WHO'S GOING TO HELP TUTOR ME WITH MY CHEMISTRY HOMEWORK NOW?
I'M SURE YOU'LL FIND SOMEBODY ELSE!
DUH...AND WHAT ABOUT GEOMETRY, WHO WILL HELP ME MAKE HEADS OR TAILS OF THAT?
DON'T WORRY, MOOSE, PROF. FLUTESNOOT WILL BE WILLING TO GIVE YOU SOME EXTRA HELP!
BUT IT JUST WON'T BE THE SAME!
DUH... MAYBE THEY'LL LET ME COME TO COLLEGE, TOO!
YEAH, RIGHT! SNICKER!
3

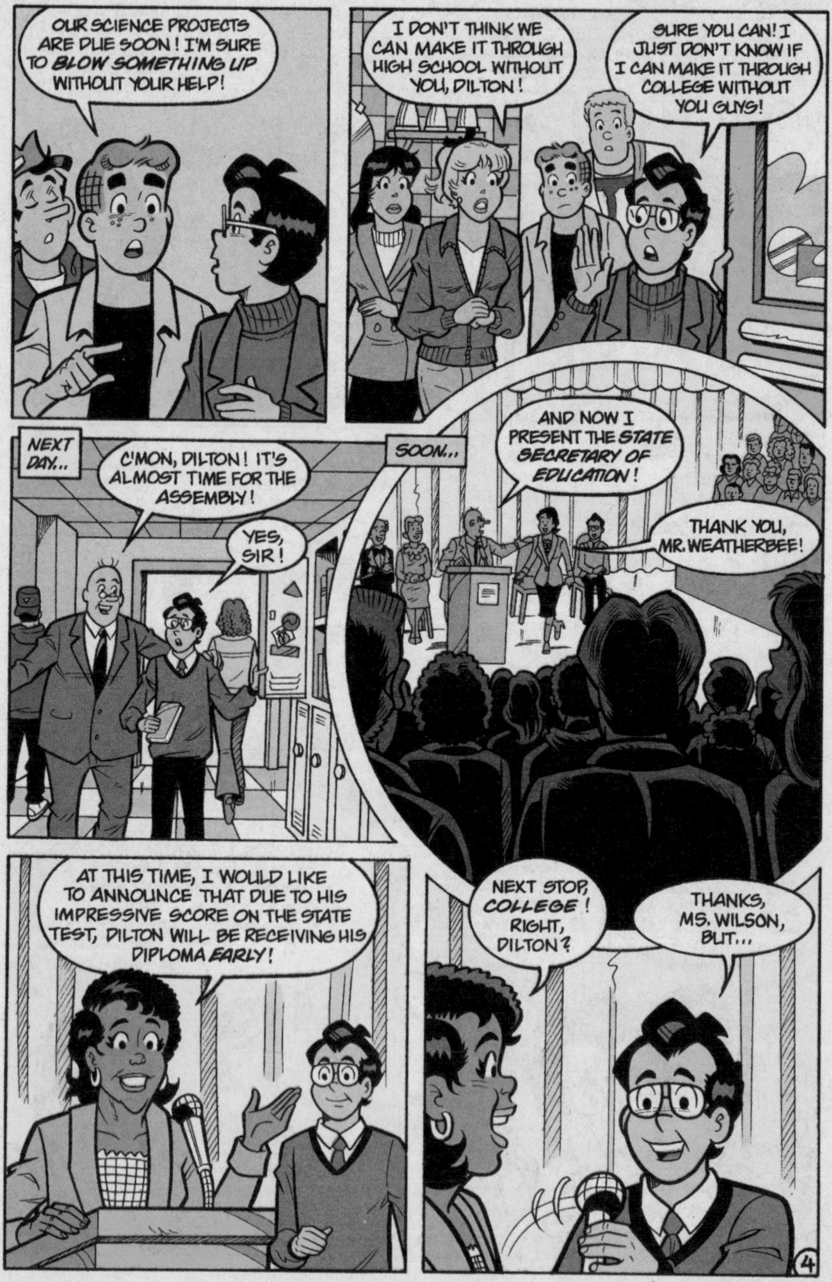
OUR SCIENCE PROJECTS ARE DUE SOON! I'M SURE TO BLOW SOMETHING UP WITHOUT YOUR HELP!
I DON'T THINK WE CAN MAKE IT THROUGH HIGH SCHOOL WITHOUT YOU, DILTON!
SURE YOU CAN! I JUST DON'T KNOW IF I CAN MAKE IT THROUGH COLLEGE WITHOUT YOU GUYS!
NEXT DAY...
C'MON, DILTON! IT'S ALMOST TIME FOR THE ASSEMBLY!
YES, SIR!
SOON...
AND NOW I PRESENT THE STATE SECRETARY OF EDUCATION!
THANK YOU, MR. WEATHERBEE!
AT THIS TIME, I WOULD LIKE TO ANNOUNCE THAT DUE TO HIS IMPRESSIVE SCORE ON THE STATE TEST, DILTON WILL BE RECEIVING HIS DIPLOMA EARLY!
NEXT STOP, COLLEGE! RIGHT, DILTON?
THANKS, MS. WILSON, BUT...
4

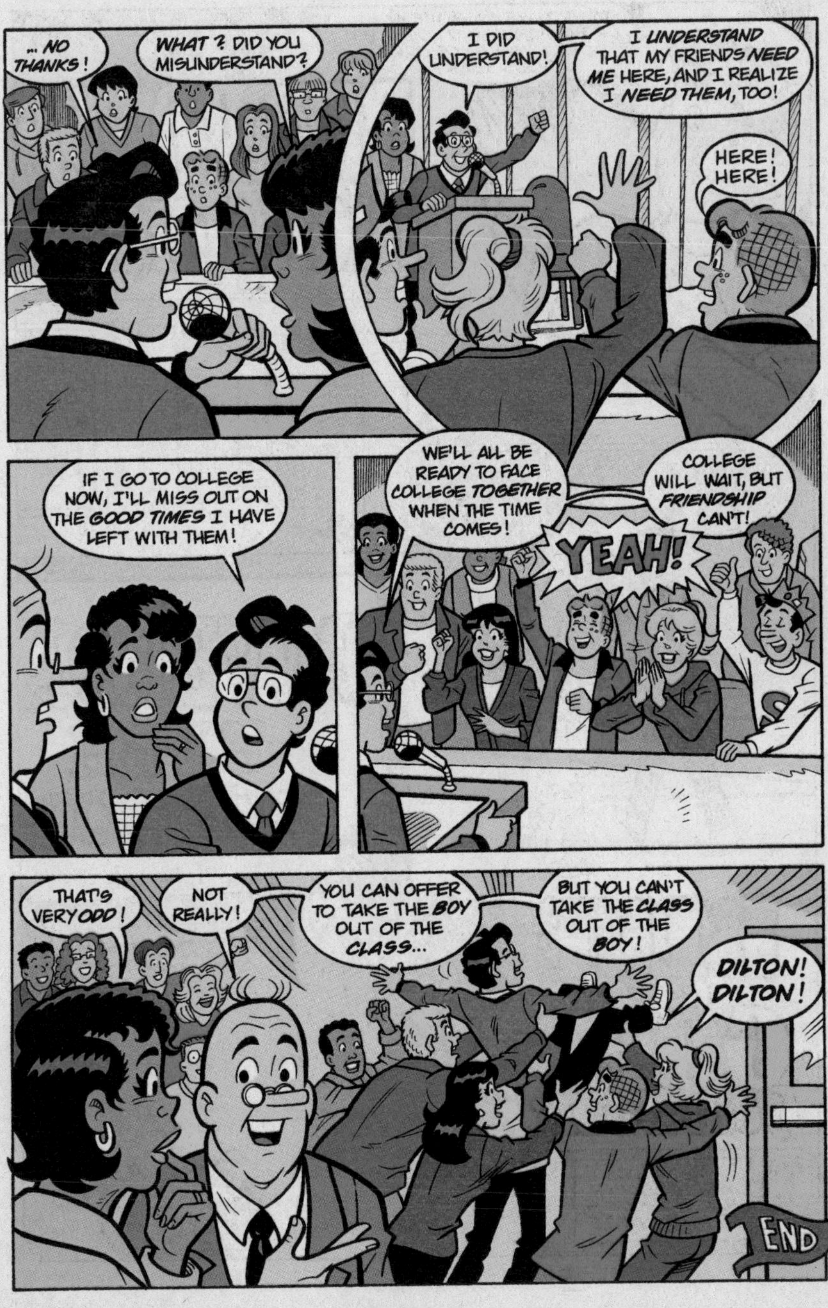
... NO THANKS!
WHAT? DID YOU MISUNDERSTAND?
I DID UNDERSTAND!
I UNDERSTAND THAT MY FRIENDS NEED ME HERE, AND I REALIZE I NEED THEM, TOO!
HERE! HERE!
IF I GO TO COLLEGE NOW, I'LL MISS OUT ON THE GOOD TIMES I HAVE LEFT WITH THEM!
WE'LL ALL BE READY TO FACE COLLEGE TOGETHER WHEN THE TIME COMES!
COLLEGE WILL WAIT, BUT FRIENDSHIP CAN'T!
YEAH!
THAT'S VERY ODD!
NOT REALLY!
YOU CAN OFFER TO TAKE THE BOY OUT OF THE CLASS...
BUT YOU CAN'T TAKE THE CLASS OUT OF THE BOY!
DILTON! DILTON!
END

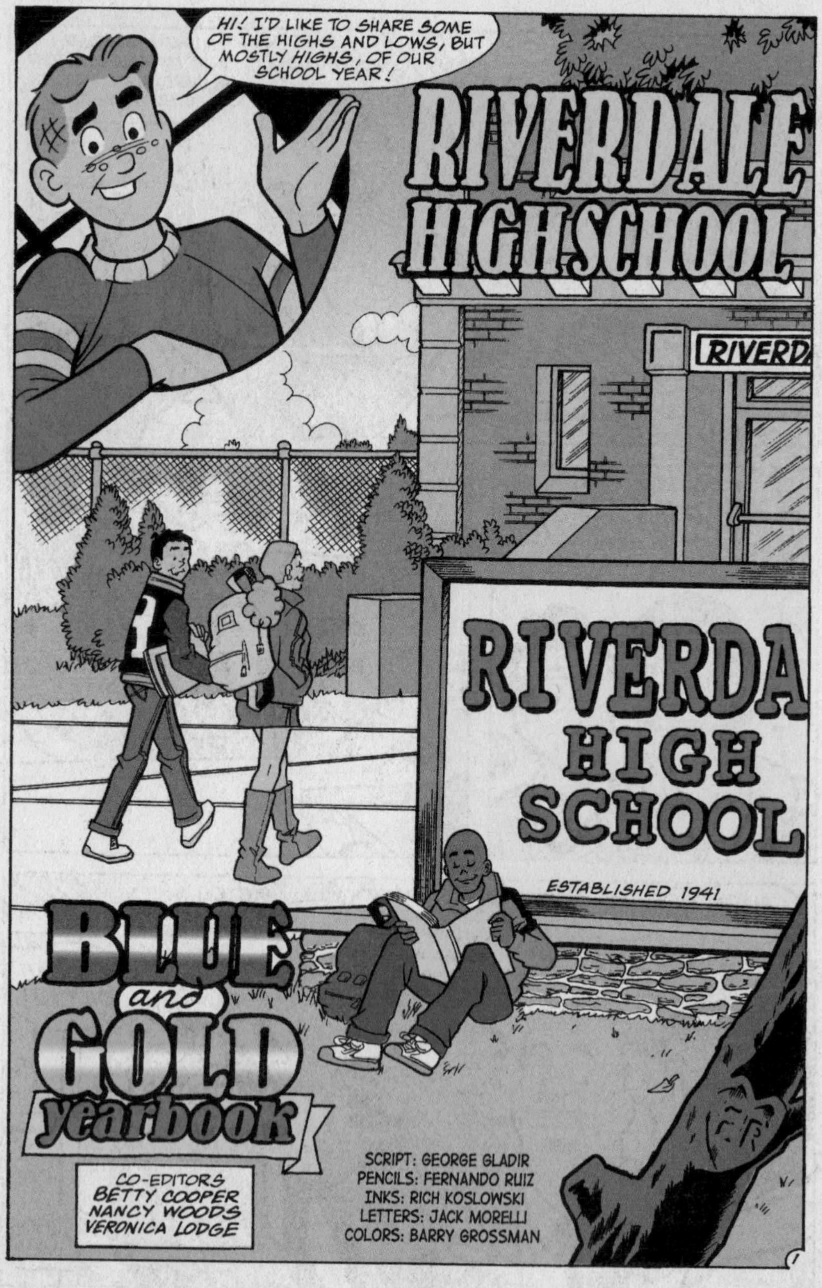
HI! I'D LIKE TO SHARE SOME OF THE HIGHS AND LOWS, BUT MOSTLY HIGHS, OF OUR SCHOOL YEAR!
RIVERDALE HIGH SCHOOL
RIVERD
RIVERDA HIGH SCHOOL
ESTABLISHED 1941
BLUE and GOLD yearbook
CO-EDITORS
BETTY COOPER
NANCY WOODS
VERONICA LODGE
SCRIPT: GEORGE GLADIR
PENCILS: FERNANDO RUIZ
INKS: RICH KOSLOWSKI
LETTERS: JACK MORELLI
COLORS: BARRY GROSSMAN
1

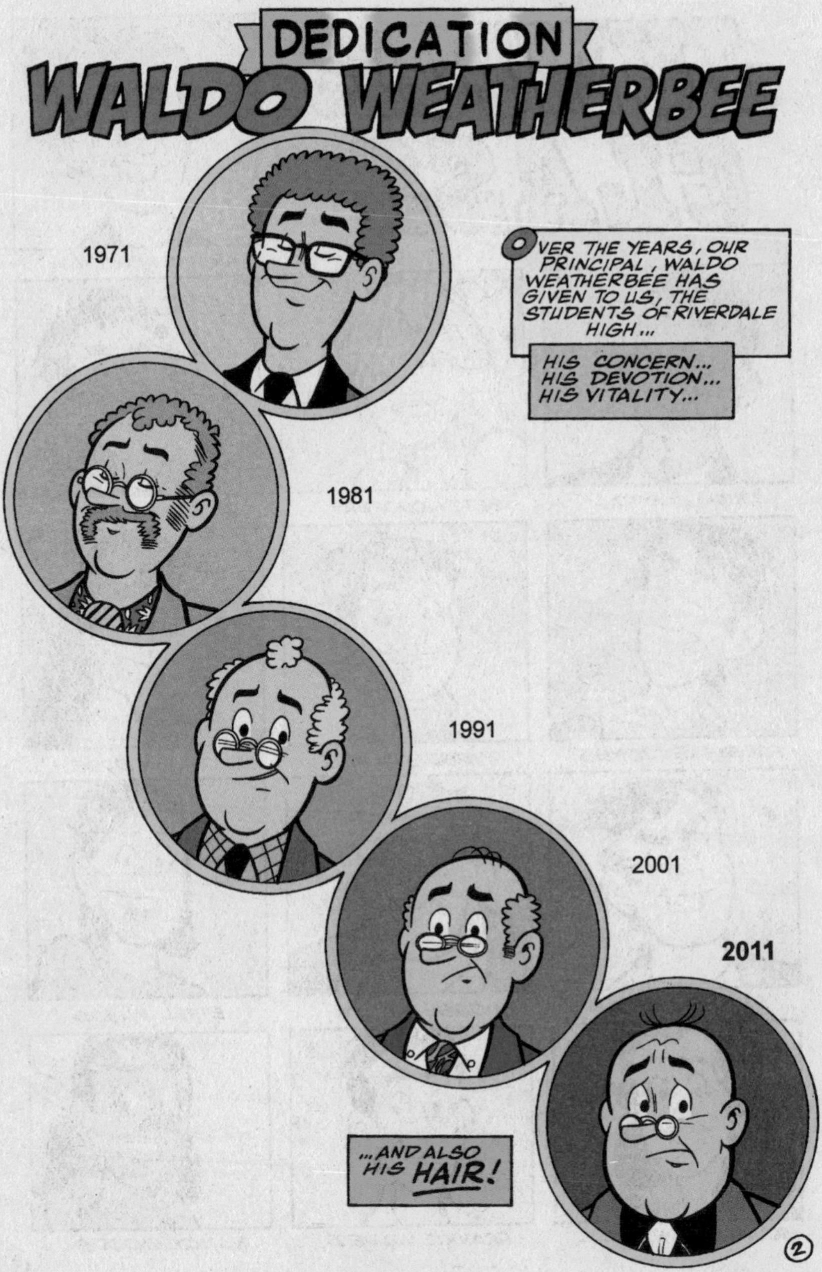
DEDICATION
WALDO WEATHERBEE
1971
OVER THE YEARS, OUR PRINCIPAL, WALDO WEATHERBEE HAS GIVEN TO US, THE STUDENTS OF RIVERDALE HIGH...
HIS CONCERN... HIS DEVOTION... HIS VITALITY...
1981
1991
2001
2011
...AND ALSO HIS HAIR!
2

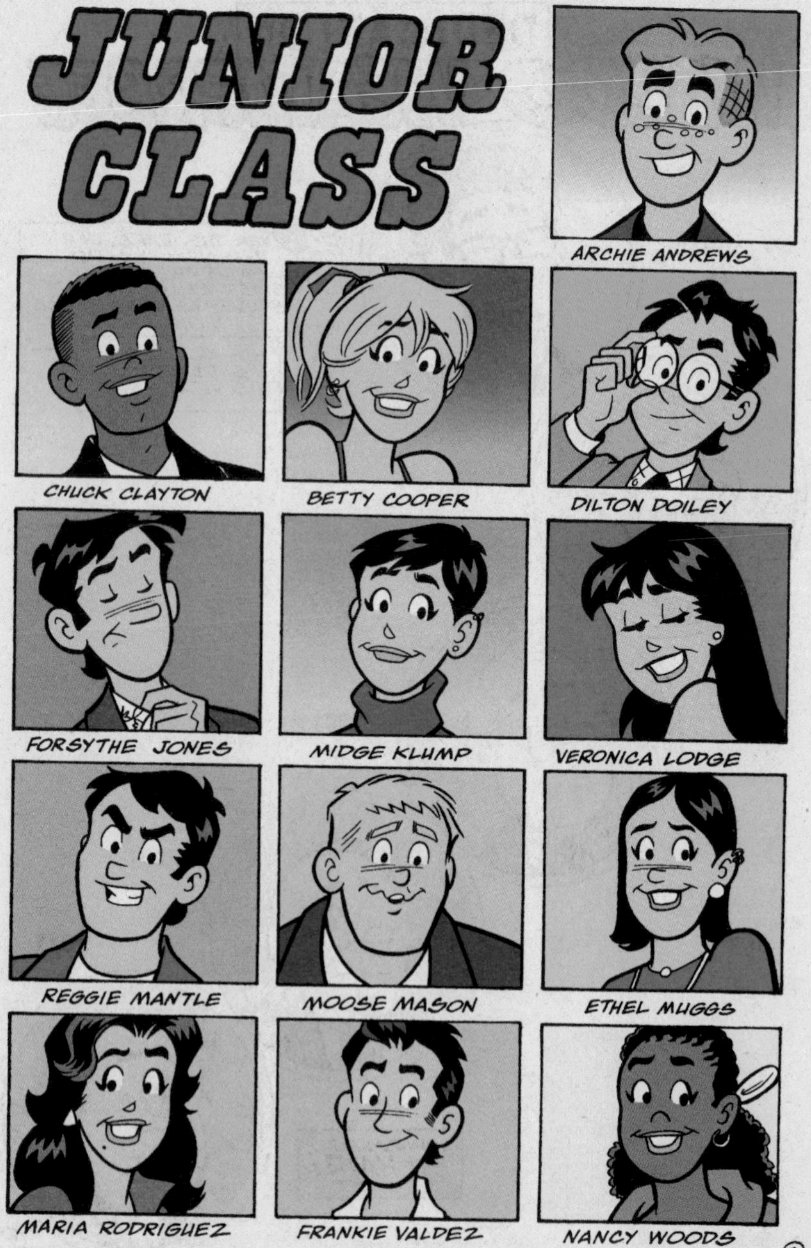
JUNIOR CLASS
ARCHIE ANDREWS
CHUCK CLAYTON
BETTY COOPER
DILTON DOILEY
FORSYTHE JONES
MIDGE KLUMP
VERONICA LODGE
REGGIE MANTLE
MOOSE MASON
ETHEL MUGGS
MARIA RODRIGUEZ
FRANKIE VALDEZ
NANCY WOODS
3

SCHOOL FACULTY & STAFF

PRINCIPAL WALDO WEATHERBEE

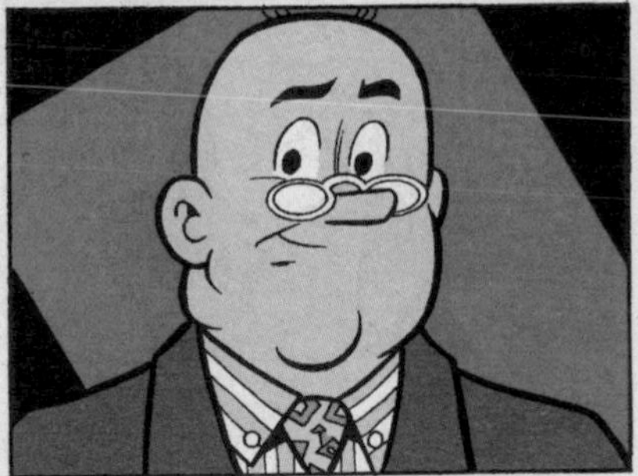

PROBLEM STUDENTS USED TO GET IN HIS HAIR... BUT NOT ANYMORE!

VICE PRINCIPAL PATTON HOWITZER

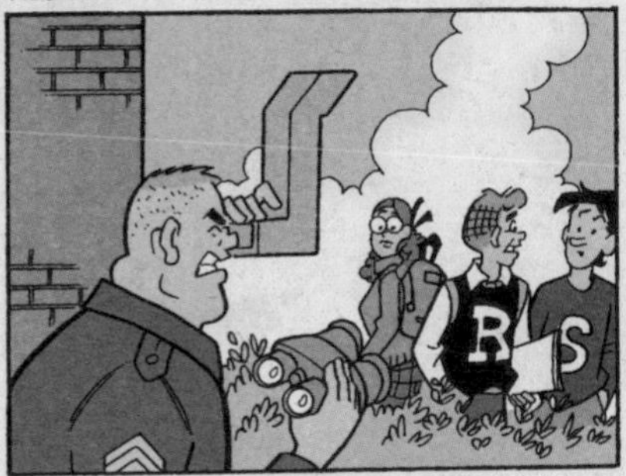
R
S

IT'S NOT TRUE HE ORDERED SIX BLOODHOUNDS TO KEEP TRACK OF CLASS DITCHERS... HE SAYS HE ORDERED ONLY **TWO**.

MRS. HARRIET BURBLE : GUIDANCE COUNSELOR

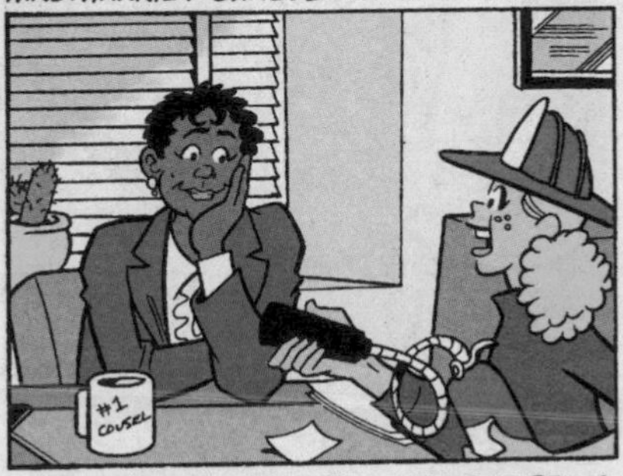
#1 COUSEL

STUDENTS BELIEVE HER WHEN SHE TELLS THEM THEY CAN BE ANYTHING THEY WISH!

MR. HARRY CLAYTON: HISTORY & BASKETBALL

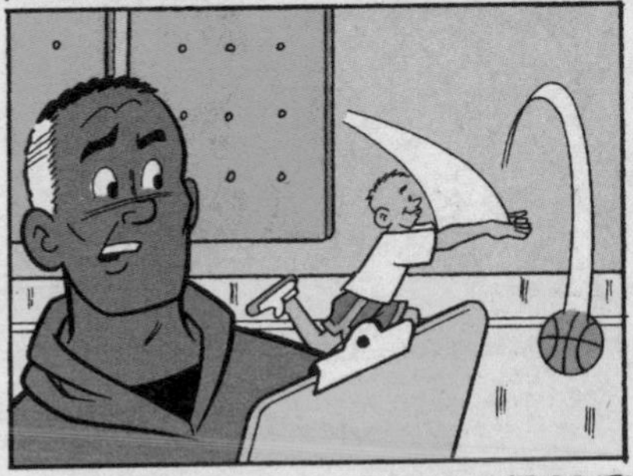

BELIEVES EDUCATION ENABLES STUDENTS TO GROW... AND HE WISHES THAT HIS BASKETBALL PLAYERS **WOULD**!

MR. MICHAEL DEE : SCHOOL LIBRARIAN-MEDIA SPECIALIST

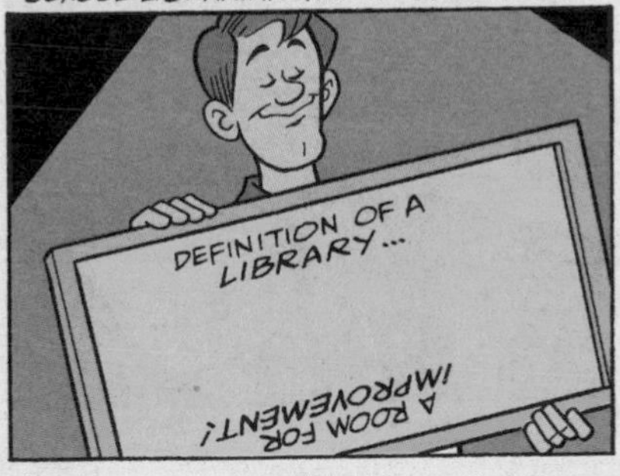
DEFINITION OF A LIBRARY...
A ROOM FOR IMPROVEMENT!

MR. RAUL FLORES: MATHEMATICS & COMPUTER SCIENCE

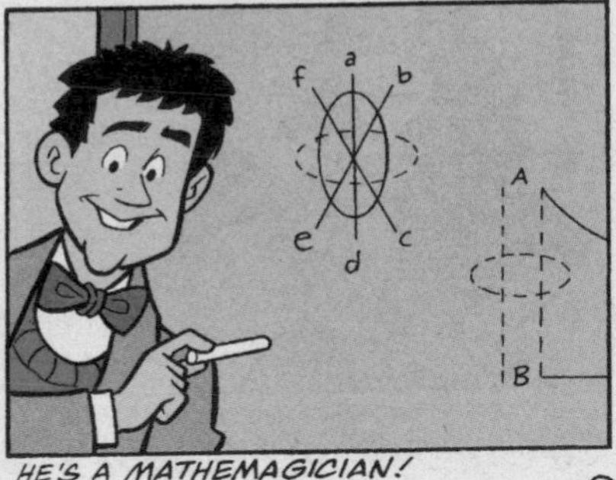
a
b
c
d
e
f
A
B

HE'S A MATHEMAGICIAN!

MR. FLUTESNOOT
CHEMISTRY

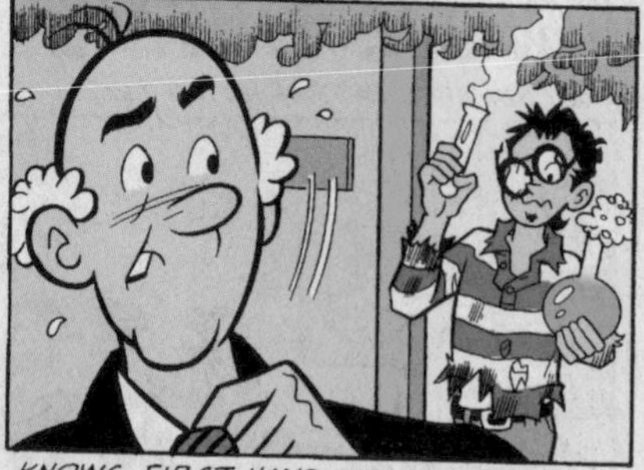

KNOWS FIRST HAND HIS STUDENTS DON'T HAVE TO PARTY TO HAVE A BLAST!

MS. GRETA GRAPPLER
PHYSICAL EDUCATION

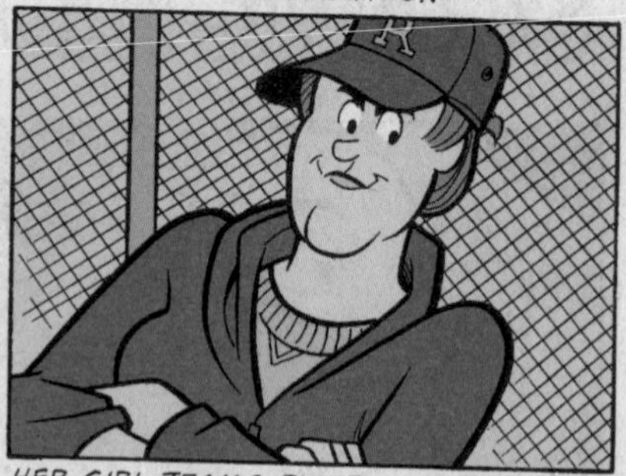

HER GIRL TEAMS FIGHT HARD... ESPECIALLY AGAINST THE BOY TEAMS THAT TRY TO HOG THE PRACTICE FIELDS!

MR. PUTNAM GRIMLEY
DRIVER EDUCATION

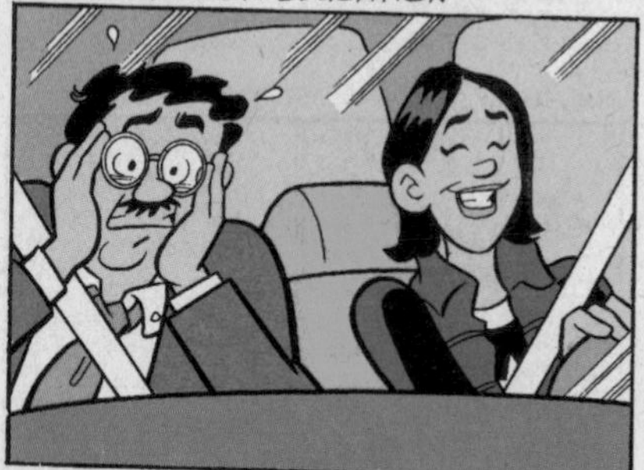

HE TELLS STUDENTS TO RELAX WHILE DRIVING... HE ONLY WISHES HE COULD TAKE HIS OWN ADVICE!

MISS GERALDINE GRUNDY
ENGLISH

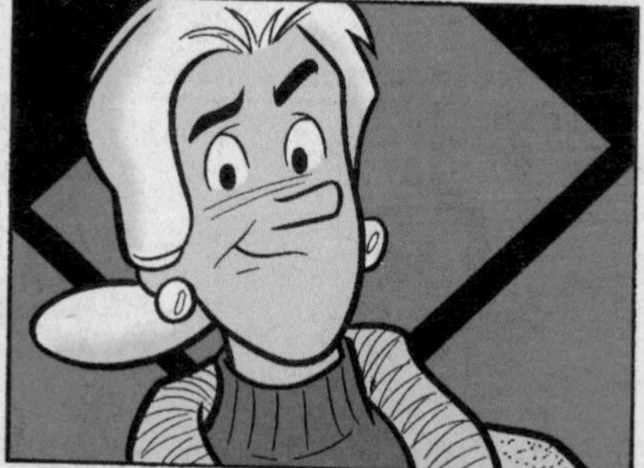

STUDENTS CAN DEPEND ON MISS GRUNDY. THEY CAN DEPEND ON HER TO GIVE PLENTY OF HOMEWORK AND TESTS!

MRS. OPHELIA HAMMLY
DRAMA & LITERATURE

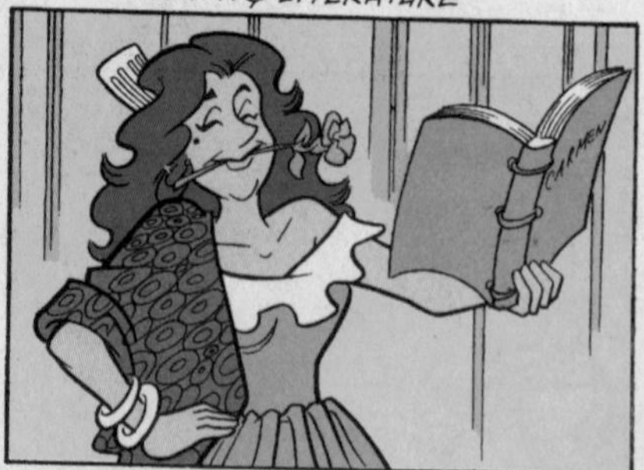
CARMEN

SHE NEVER HAS TROUBLE FILLING HER PLAYS WITH A CAST OF CHARACTERS, RIVERDALE HIGH HAS CHARACTERS GALORE!

COACH KLEATS
PHYSICAL EDUCATION

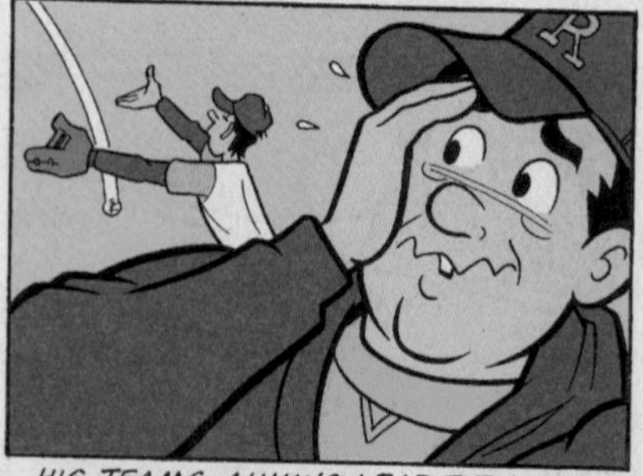

HIS TEAMS ALWAYS LEAD THE LEAGUE ...IN ERRORS, FUMBLES, AND LOSSES!

MRS. BERNICE BEAZLY
CAFETERIA SUPERVISOR & STAFF
STUDENTS REGARD MISS BEAZLY AND STAFF AS THE SCHOOL'S MOST COURAGEOUS EMPLOYEES... BECAUSE THEY ACTUALLY EAT THE FOOD THAT THEY SERVE!

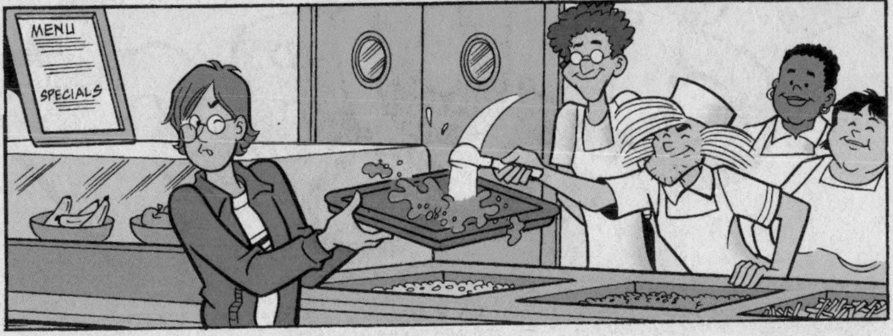
MENU
SPECIALS

MR. HIRAM GAFFER
SCHOOL CROSSING GUARD
HE MAKES SURE IT'S SAFE TO CROSS FOR BOTH STUDENTS AND NON-STUDENTS!

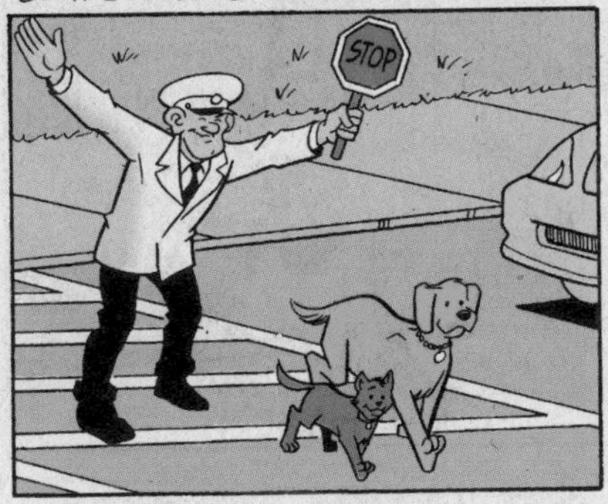
STOP

MISS PHLIPS
THE PRINCIPAL'S SECRETARY
SHE'S CAREFUL TO FILE **ALL** OF HER BOSS'S THINGS!

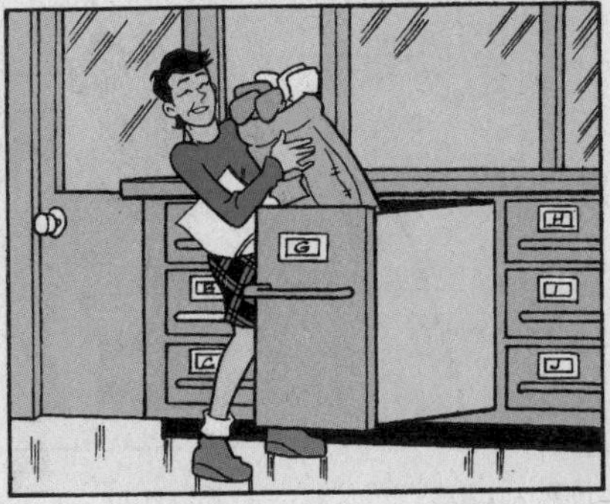
G

MR. SVENSON
SCHOOL CUSTODIAN

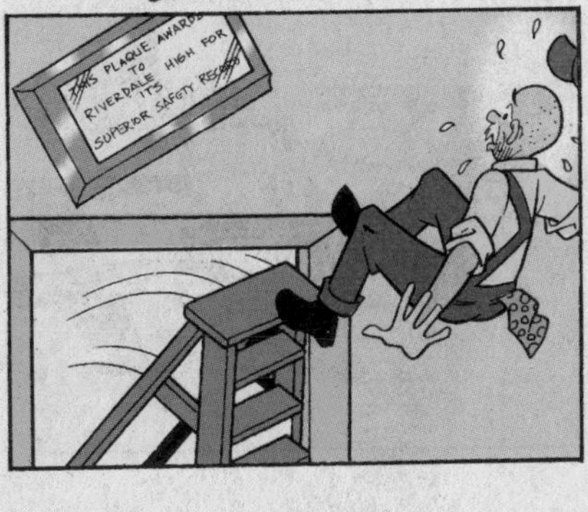
PLAQUE AWARDED TO RIVERDALE HIGH FOR ITS SUPERIOR SAFETY RECORD

MRS. WANDA WHEELER
SCHOOL BUS DRIVER
SHE'S THINKING OF SWITCHING TO A LESS STRESSFUL JOB -- LIKE LION TAMER!

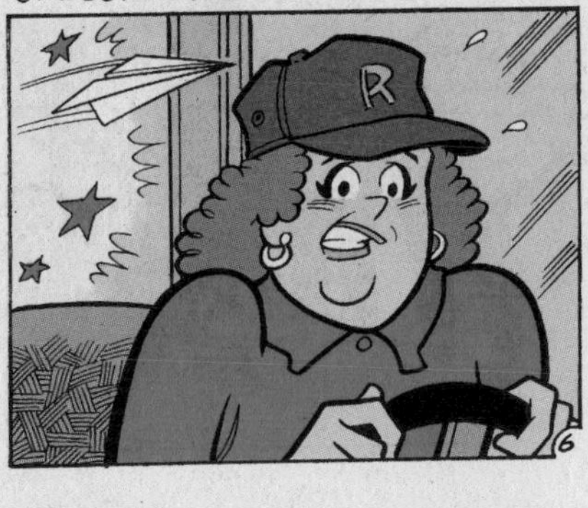
R
6

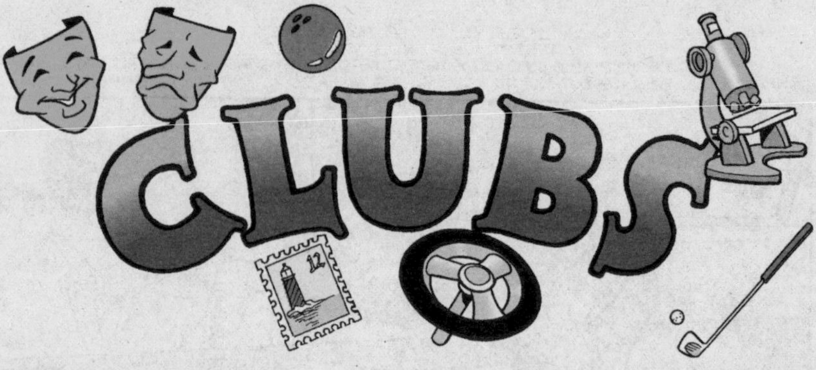
CLUBS

DRAMA CLUB: MISS OPHELIA HAMMLY'S DRAMA CLUB DRESSES IN AUTHENTIC SHAKESPEARIAN COSTUMES WHEN DISCUSSING THE BARD. THAT'S JUGHEAD CONSUMING PORRIDGE, A MUTTON BURGER AND A MEAD COLA.

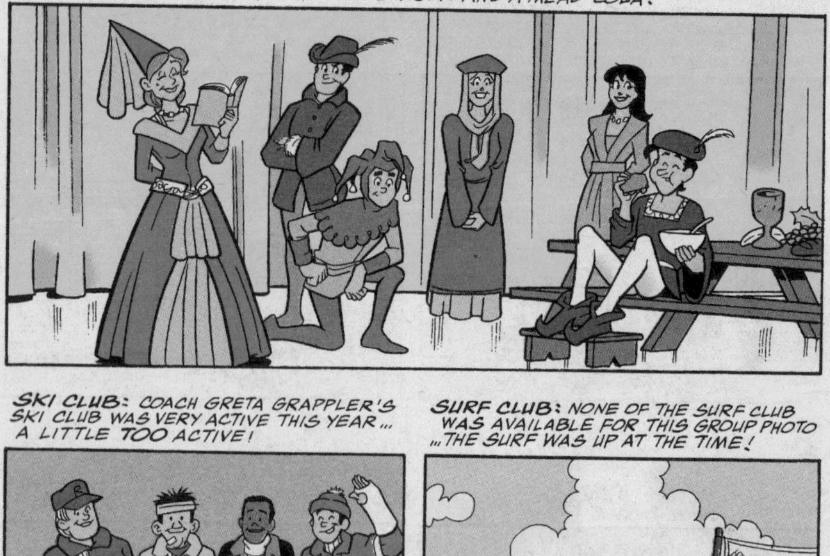

SKI CLUB: COACH GRETA GRAPPLER'S SKI CLUB WAS VERY ACTIVE THIS YEAR... A LITTLE TOO ACTIVE!

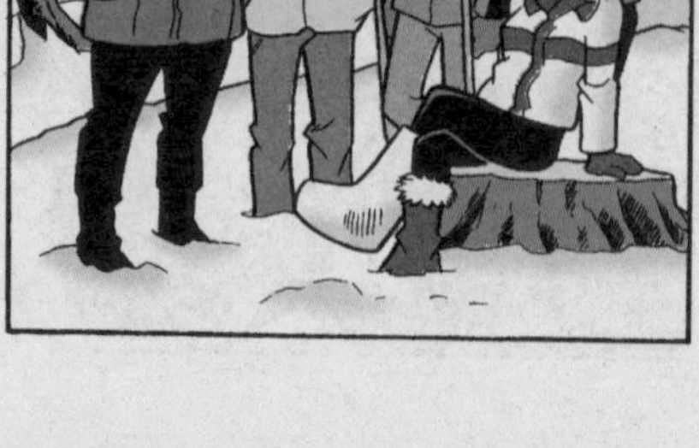

SURF CLUB: NONE OF THE SURF CLUB WAS AVAILABLE FOR THIS GROUP PHOTO ...THE SURF WAS UP AT THE TIME!

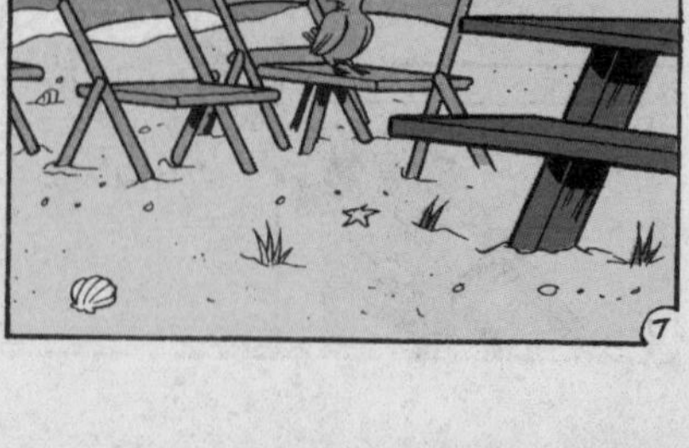

MATH CLUB: MATH CLUB MEMBERS DILTON DOILEY AND MOOSE MASON TACKLE A DIFFICULT PROBEM TOGETHER... DILTON DID THE WRITING, MOOSE THE ERASING.

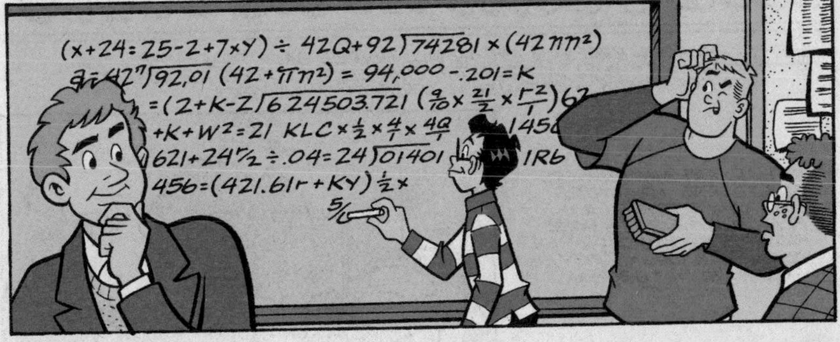

SHEET METAL CLUB: HAPPY MEMBERS OF THIS CLUB ARE THE ONLY STUDENTS WHO NEVER HAVE A PROBLEM OPENING A JAMMED LOCKER.

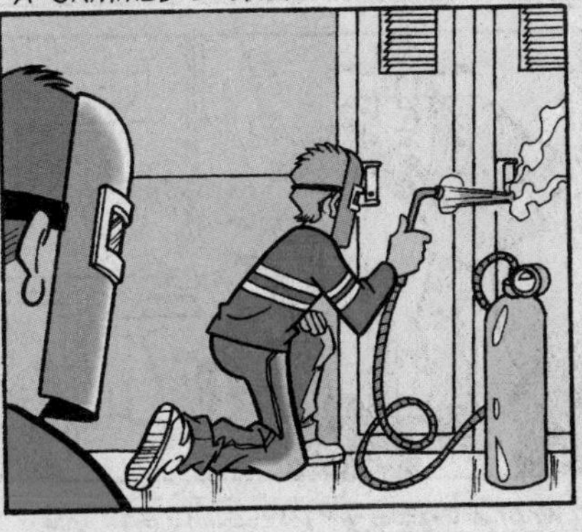

HALL MONITOR S' CLUB: CLUB SUPERVISOR, VICE PRINCIPAL PATTON HOWITZER, SHOWS CLUB MEMBERS HOW TO CHECK HALL PASSES FOR FORGERIES.

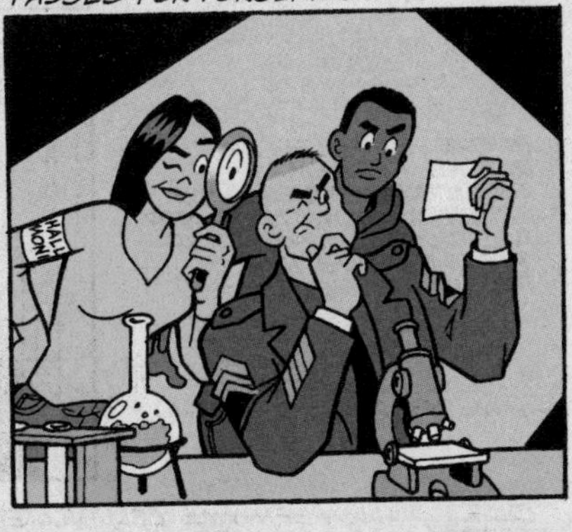

SCIENCE CLUB: SCIENCE CLUB MEMBERS HAD JUST CONCLUDED A DELICATE CHEM EXPERIMENT WHEN THIS PHOTO WAS TAKEN. SEVERAL CLUB MEMBERS WERE UNAVAILABLE FOR THIS PHOTO, BUT ARE RECOVERING NICELY.

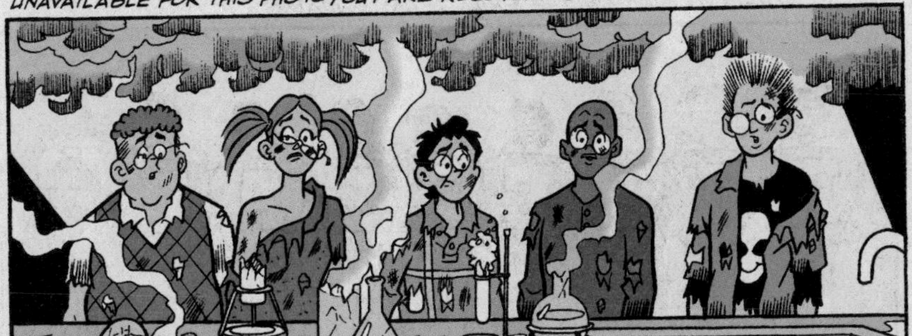

THE YEAR IN REVIEW

SEPT.: SCHOOL REOPENS AND WE ALL TRUDGE BACK TO SCHOOL... THE FACULTY DOES MOST OF THE TRUDGING. WE ALSO WELCOME THE FRESHMEN IN OUR USUAL "FRIENDLY" MANNER!

NOT ALL FRESHMEN WERE SUBJECT TO INDIGNITIES LIKE HAVING TO PUSH A PEANUT WITH ONE'S NOSE. PICTURE SHOWS AN UPPER-CLASSMAN TAKING PITY ON FROSH "HULK" GROGAN.

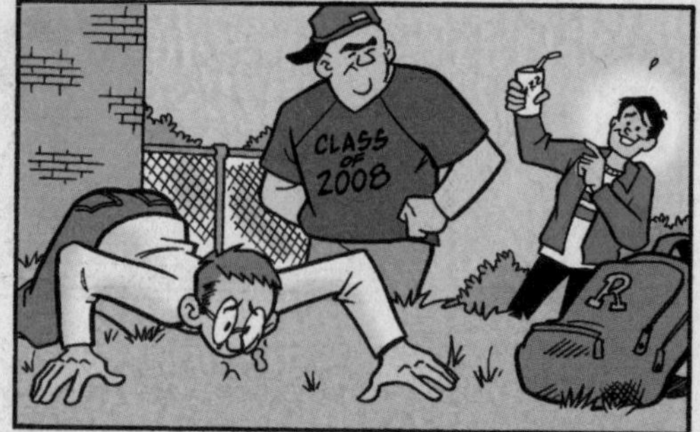
CLASS OF 2008
R

IN ONE FUN-FILLED SKIT DURING FRESHMAN ORIENTATION WEEK, VICE PRINCIPAL HOWITZER AND A STUDENT JOKE ABOUT THE SCHOOL'S NEW DISCIPLINE POLICY.

...HEY! WE HOPE THEY WERE JUST JOKING!

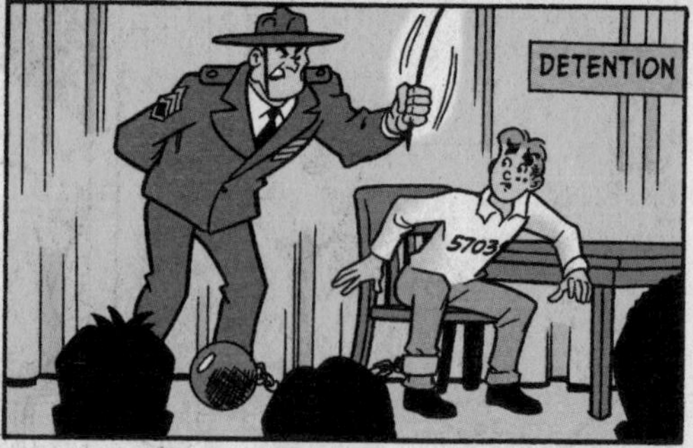
DETENTION
5703

OCT.: HALLOWEEN WAS CELEBRATED WITH A DRESS-UP DAY. SOME SAY THE SCARIEST PART OF THE DAY WAS MR. FLORES' GEOMETRY EXAM!

NOV.: WE CELEBRATE HOMECOMING DAY. HIGHLIGHT OF THE EVENT WAS THE HOMECOMING DAY PARADE. EVERYONE WAS EXCITED, ESPECIALLY THE END GIRL ON THE DRILL TEAM SQUAD!

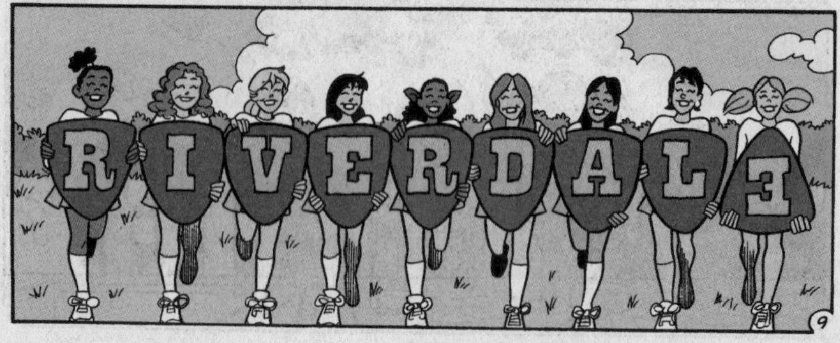
R I V E R D A L Ǝ

NOV.: (CONT.) THIS THANKSGIVING WE ALL HAD A LOT TO BE THANKFUL FOR... ESPECIALLY THE FOOTBALL TEAM... ITS LONG LOSING SEASON WAS FINALLY OVER!

DEC.: WE CELEBRATE CHRISTMAS. WE'RE NOT SAYING PRINCIPAL WEATHERBEE GAINED WEIGHT, BUT THIS YEAR HE DID NOT NEED A PILLOW TO COMPLETE HIS SANTA CLAUS DISGUISE!

OUR NEW SNOW PLOWS ENABLED RIVERDALE HIGH TO STAY OPEN DESPITE HEAVY SNOWS. FOR SOME STRANGE REASON, STUDENTS DIDN'T SEEM OVERLY HAPPY ABOUT THIS DEVELOPMENT.

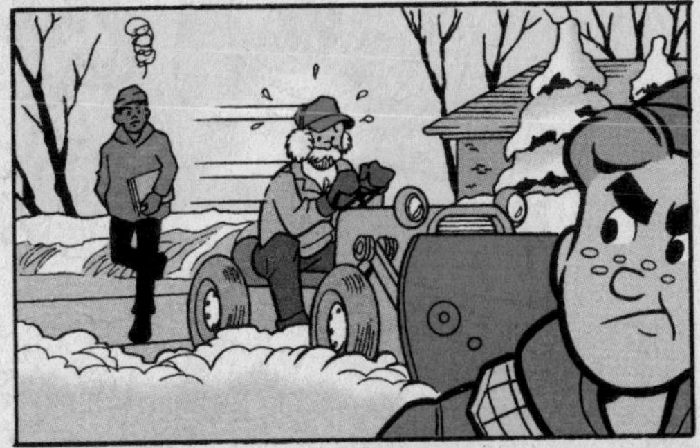

FEB.: THE BACKWARDS DANCE WAS A HUGH SUCCESS!

GIRLS ASKED BOYS TO BE THEIR DATES FOR THE BACKWARD DANCE. BOYS WERE VERY RECEPTIVE TO THIS NOVEL IDEA... WITH A FEW EXCEPTIONS!

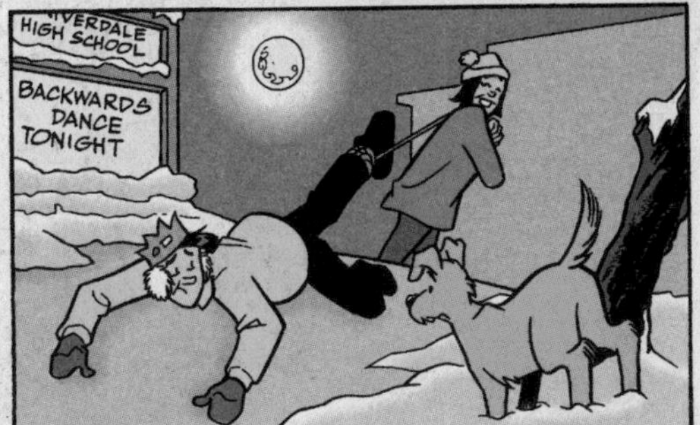
HIGH SCHOOL
BACKWARDS DANCE TONIGHT

MAY: THERE WAS A GREAT REJOICING AT THE FACULTY-STUDENT PICNIC. THE FACULTY WON THE TUG-OF-WAR TUSSEL THANKS TO PRINCIPAL WEATHERBEE'S WEIGHTY CONTRIBUTION. IN THE PIE EATING CONTEST, JUGHEAD WON FIRST PRIZE... AND SECOND PRIZE, AND THIRD PRIZE...

JUNE: WITH THE ANTICIPATION OF THE HAPPY SCHOOL YEAR COMING TO AN END, THE HEARTS OF STUDENTS AND FACULTY WERE HEAVY WITH SADNESS.

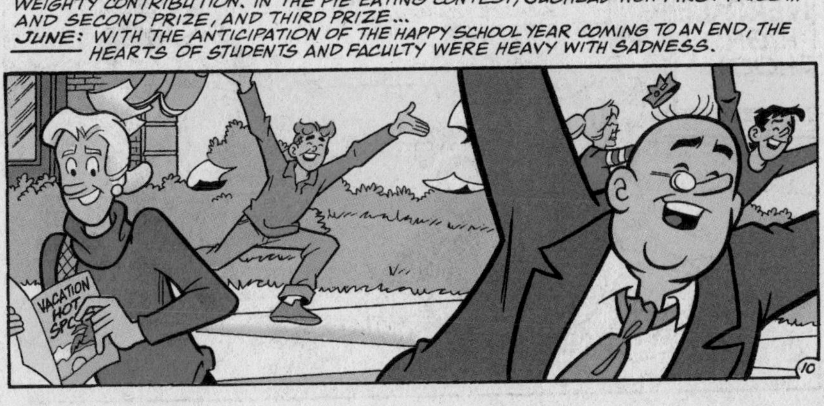
VACATION
HOT

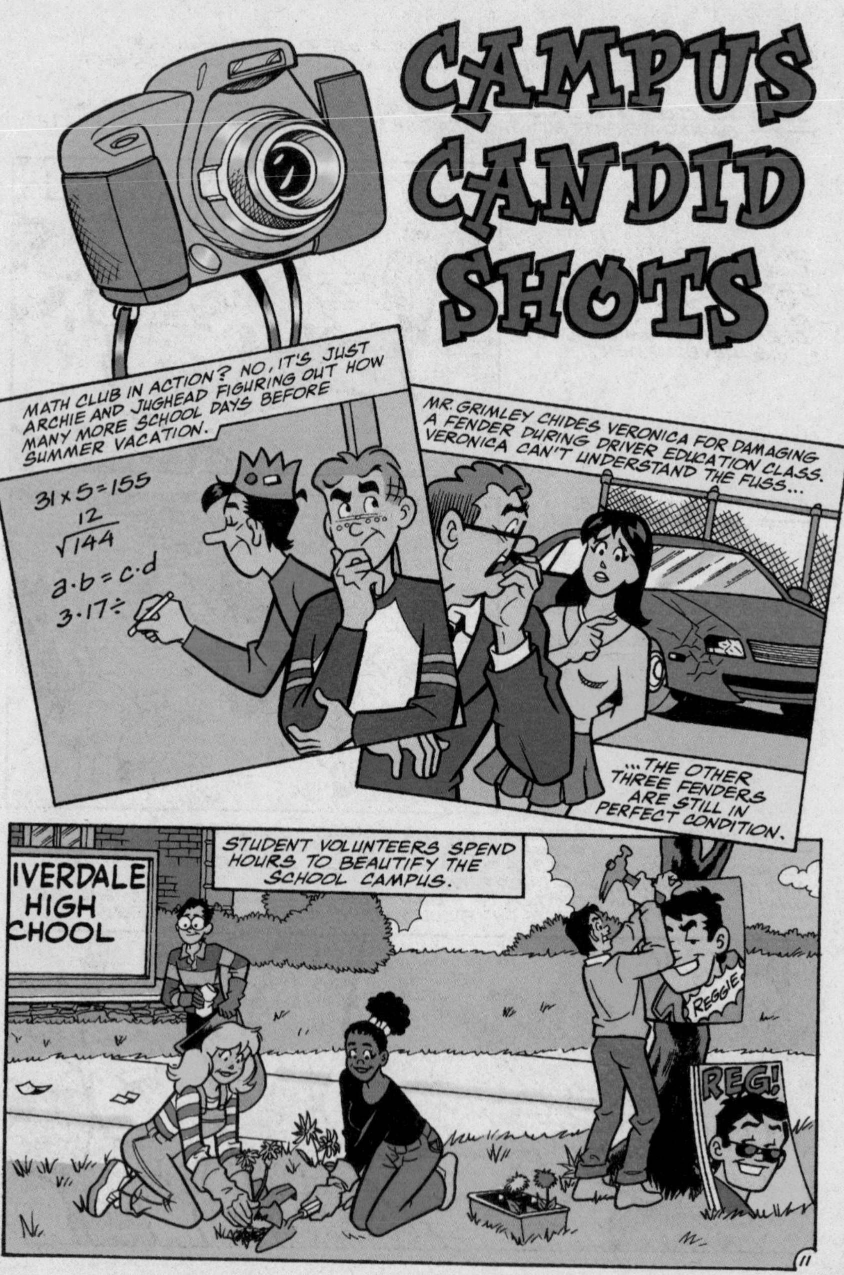
CAMPUS CANDID SHOTS
MATH CLUB IN ACTION? NO, IT'S JUST ARCHIE AND JUGHEAD FIGURING OUT HOW MANY MORE SCHOOL DAYS BEFORE SUMMER VACATION.
31 x 5 = 155
12
√144
a·b = c·d
3·17÷
MR. GRIMLEY CHIDES VERONICA FOR DAMAGING A FENDER DURING DRIVER EDUCATION CLASS. VERONICA CAN'T UNDERSTAND THE FUSS...
...THE OTHER THREE FENDERS ARE STILL IN PERFECT CONDITION.
STUDENT VOLUNTEERS SPEND HOURS TO BEAUTIFY THE SCHOOL CAMPUS.
IVERDALE HIGH CHOOL
REGGIE
REG!
11

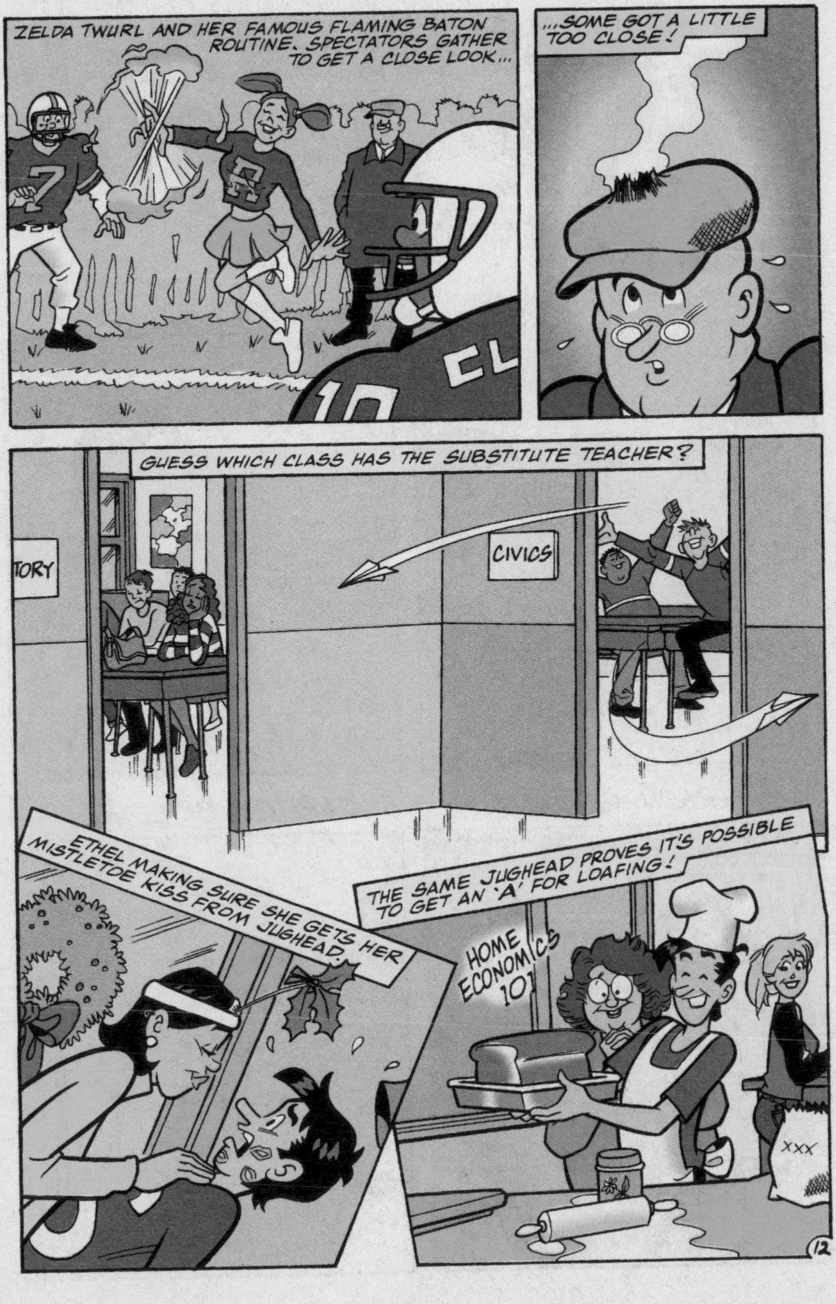
ZELDA TWURL AND HER FAMOUS FLAMING BATON ROUTINE. SPECTATORS GATHER TO GET A CLOSE LOOK...
...SOME GOT A LITTLE TOO CLOSE!
GUESS WHICH CLASS HAS THE SUBSTITUTE TEACHER?
TORY
CIVICS
ETHEL MAKING SURE SHE GETS HER MISTLETOE KISS FROM JUGHEAD.
THE SAME JUGHEAD PROVES IT'S POSSIBLE TO GET AN 'A' FOR LOAFING!
HOME ECONOMICS 101
XXX
12

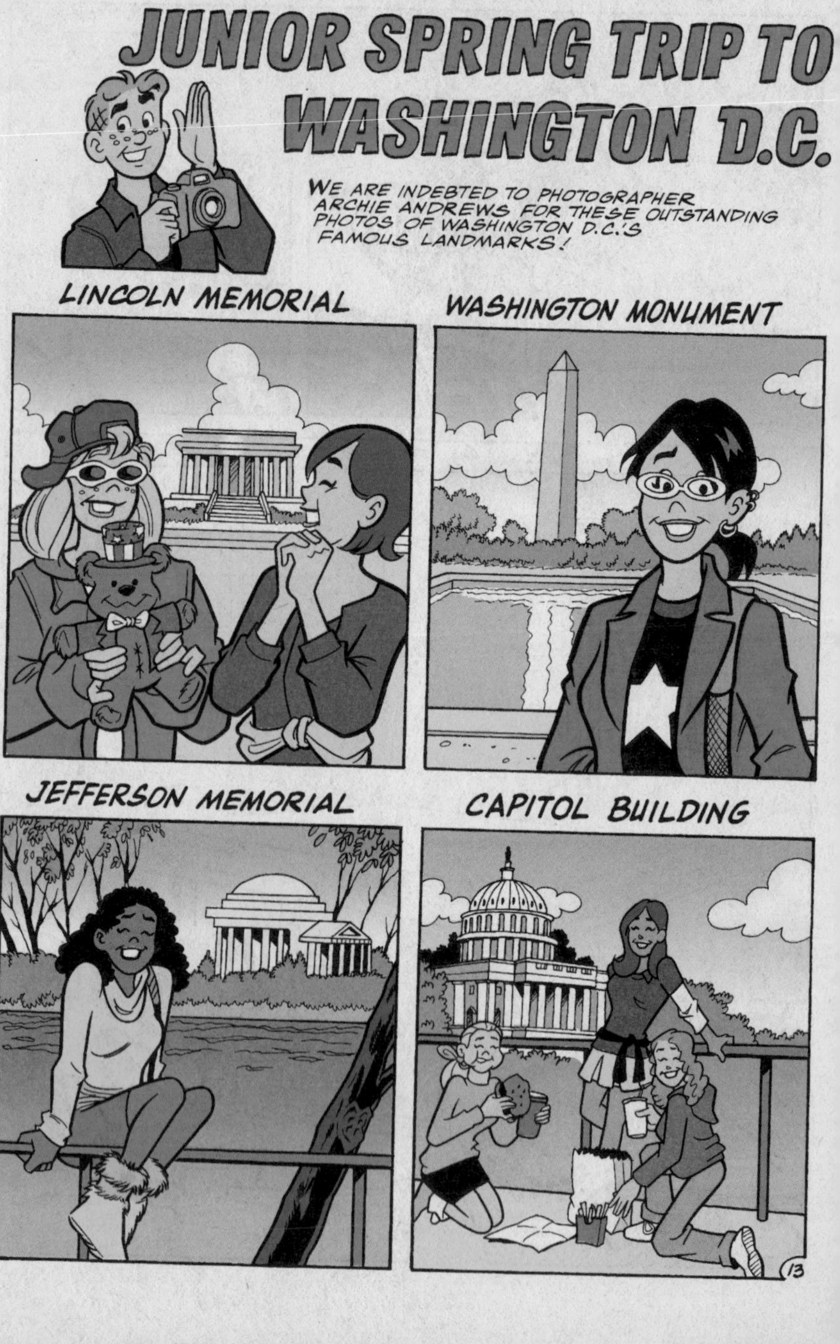
JUNIOR SPRING TRIP TO WASHINGTON D.C.
WE ARE INDEBTED TO PHOTOGRAPHER ARCHIE ANDREWS FOR THESE OUTSTANDING PHOTOS OF WASHINGTON D.C.'S FAMOUS LANDMARKS!
LINCOLN MEMORIAL
WASHINGTON MONUMENT
JEFFERSON MEMORIAL
CAPITOL BUILDING
13

A NIGHT TO REMEMBER...
THE PROM

MOOSE DISCOVERS HE ACCIDENTALLY LEFT HIS CAR KEYS IN HIS CAR ON PROM NIGHT...

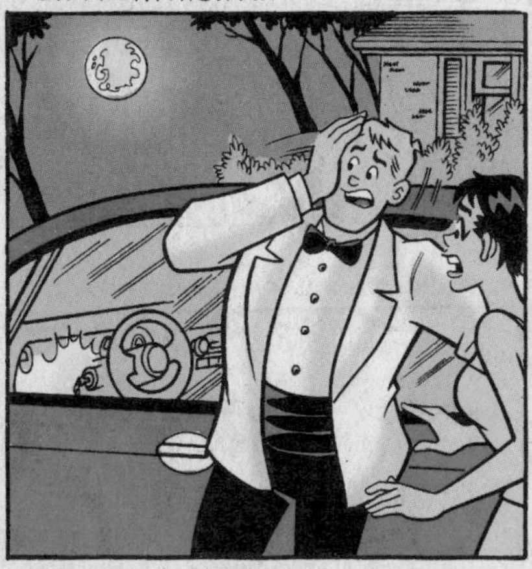

...HOWEVER, HE AND MIDGE STILL MANAGED TO GET TO THE PROM, AND ALMOST ON TIME!

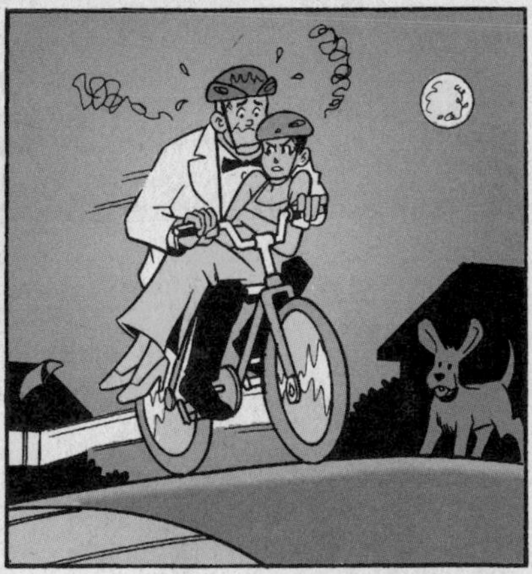

WHEN IT CAME TO PICKING HER PROM GOWN, NANCY NEEDED HER MOTHER'S HELP AND ADVICE... BUT MOSTLY HER MOTHER'S CREDIT CARD!

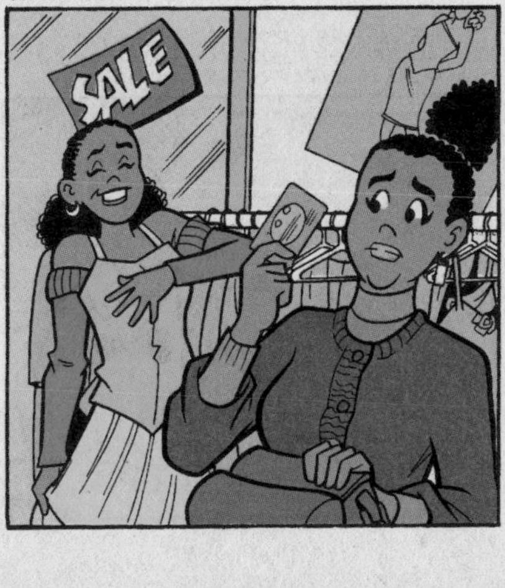
SALE

GUESS WHO GOT A SPECIAL RATE ON HIS RENTED TUX?

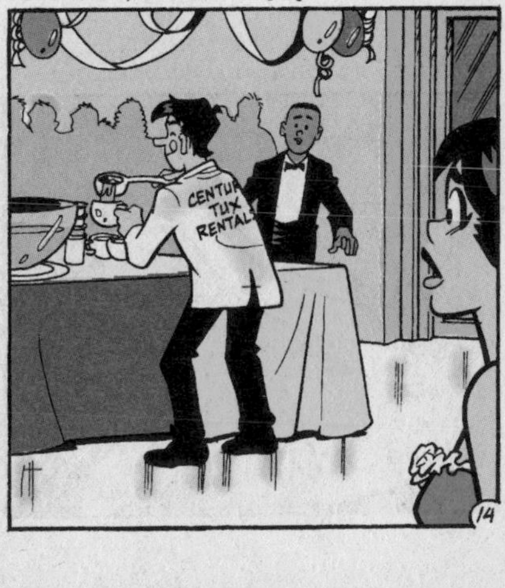
CENTU
TUX
RENTALS
14

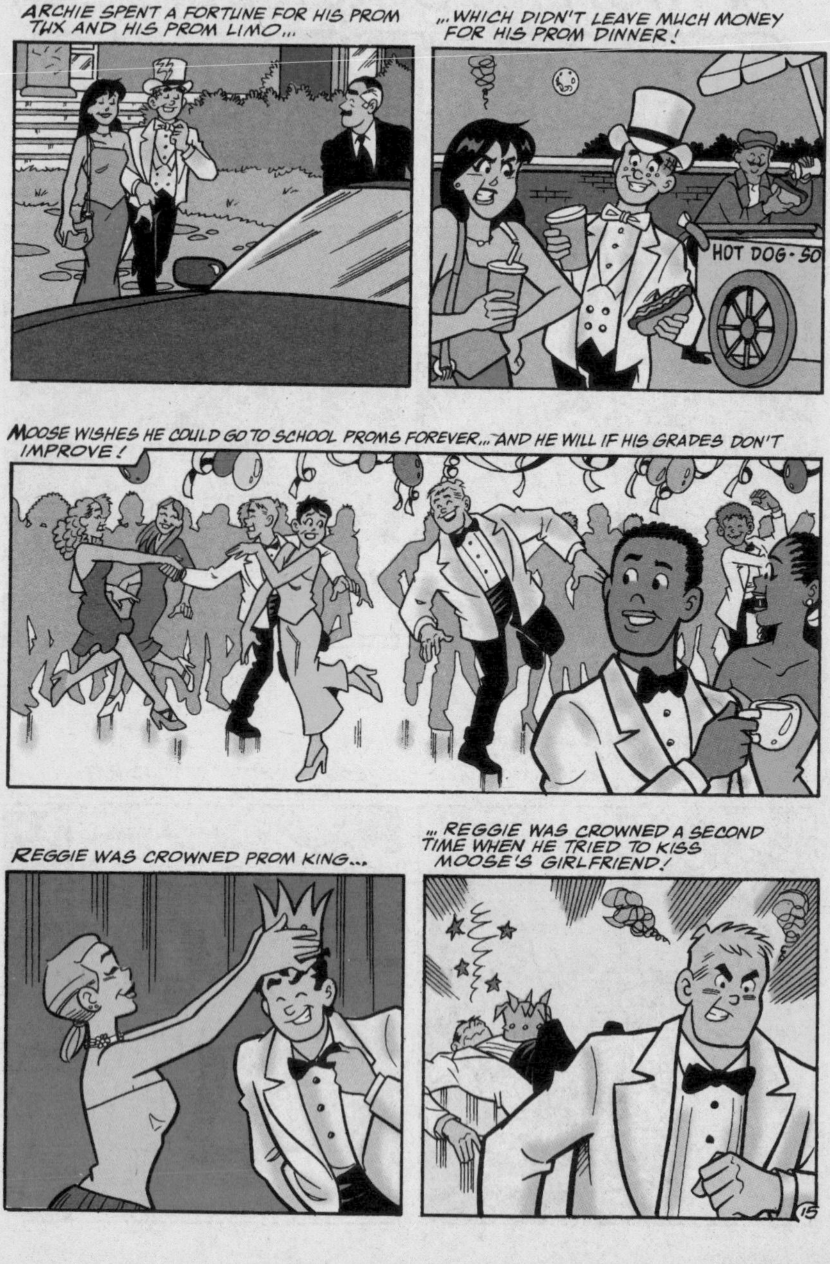
ARCHIE SPENT A FORTUNE FOR HIS PROM TUX AND HIS PROM LIMO...
...WHICH DIDN'T LEAVE MUCH MONEY FOR HIS PROM DINNER!
HOT DOG - SO
MOOSE WISHES HE COULD GO TO SCHOOL PROMS FOREVER... AND HE WILL IF HIS GRADES DON'T IMPROVE!
REGGIE WAS CROWNED PROM KING...
...REGGIE WAS CROWNED A SECOND TIME WHEN HE TRIED TO KISS MOOSE'S GIRLFRIEND!
15

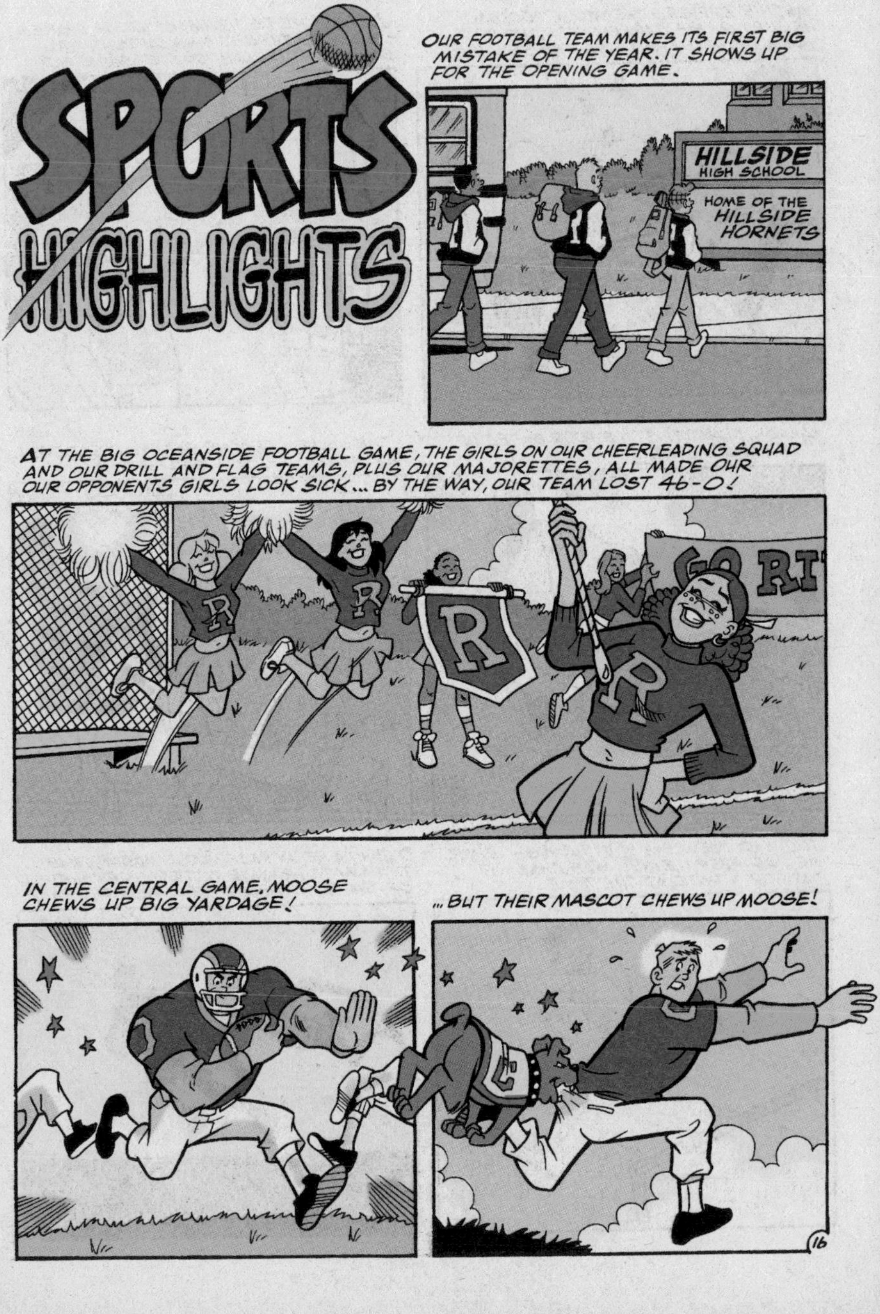
SPORTS HIGHLIGHTS
OUR FOOTBALL TEAM MAKES ITS FIRST BIG MISTAKE OF THE YEAR. IT SHOWS UP FOR THE OPENING GAME.
HILLSIDE HIGH SCHOOL
HOME OF THE HILLSIDE HORNETS
AT THE BIG OCEANSIDE FOOTBALL GAME, THE GIRLS ON OUR CHEERLEADING SQUAD AND OUR DRILL AND FLAG TEAMS, PLUS OUR MAJORETTES, ALL MADE OUR OUR OPPONENTS GIRLS LOOK SICK... BY THE WAY, OUR TEAM LOST 46-0!
IN THE CENTRAL GAME, MOOSE CHEWS UP BIG YARDAGE!
...BUT THEIR MASCOT CHEWS UP MOOSE!
16

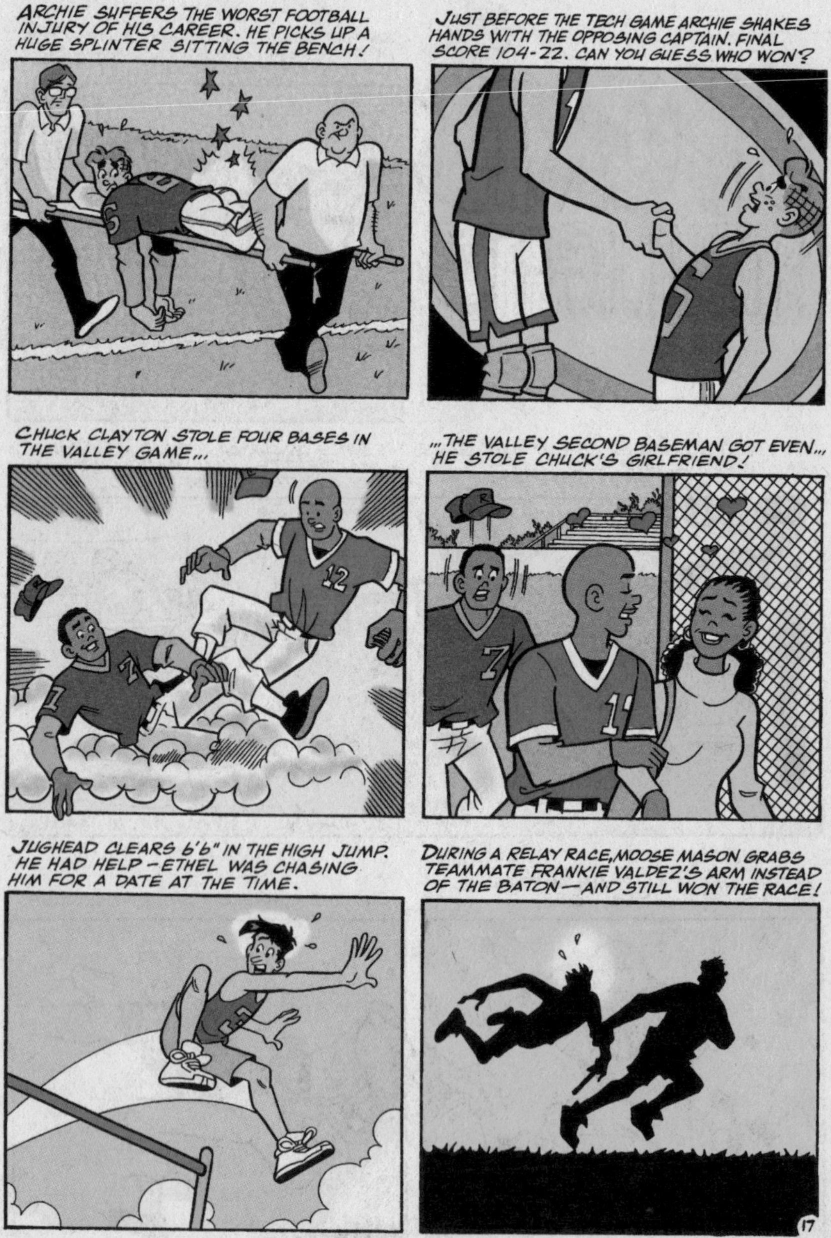
ARCHIE SUFFERS THE WORST FOOTBALL INJURY OF HIS CAREER. HE PICKS UP A HUGE SPLINTER SITTING THE BENCH!
JUST BEFORE THE TECH GAME ARCHIE SHAKES HANDS WITH THE OPPOSING CAPTAIN. FINAL SCORE 104-22. CAN YOU GUESS WHO WON?
CHUCK CLAYTON STOLE FOUR BASES IN THE VALLEY GAME...
...THE VALLEY SECOND BASEMAN GOT EVEN... HE STOLE CHUCK'S GIRLFRIEND!
JUGHEAD CLEARS 6'6" IN THE HIGH JUMP. HE HAD HELP - ETHEL WAS CHASING HIM FOR A DATE AT THE TIME.
DURING A RELAY RACE, MOOSE MASON GRABS TEAMMATE FRANKIE VALDEZ'S ARM INSTEAD OF THE BATON — AND STILL WON THE RACE!
17

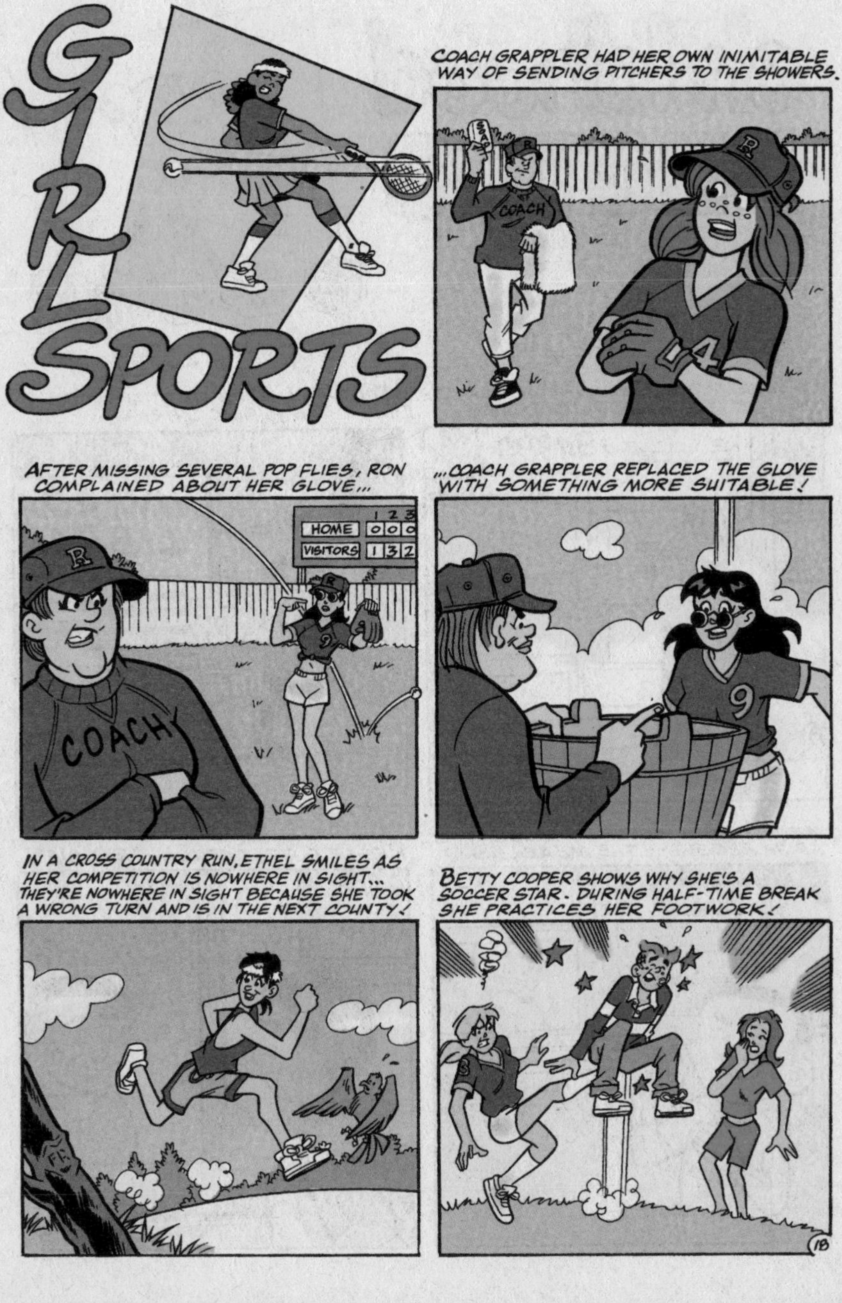
GIRL SPORTS
COACH GRAPPLER HAD HER OWN INIMITABLE WAY OF SENDING PITCHERS TO THE SHOWERS.
SOAP
COACH
4
AFTER MISSING SEVERAL POP FLIES, RON COMPLAINED ABOUT HER GLOVE...
1 2 3
HOME 0 0 0
VISITORS 1 3 2
COACH
9
...COACH GRAPPLER REPLACED THE GLOVE WITH SOMETHING MORE SUITABLE!
9
IN A CROSS COUNTRY RUN, ETHEL SMILES AS HER COMPETITION IS NOWHERE IN SIGHT... THEY'RE NOWHERE IN SIGHT BECAUSE SHE TOOK A WRONG TURN AND IS IN THE NEXT COUNTY!
BETTY COOPER SHOWS WHY SHE'S A SOCCER STAR. DURING HALF-TIME BREAK SHE PRACTICES HER FOOTWORK!
18

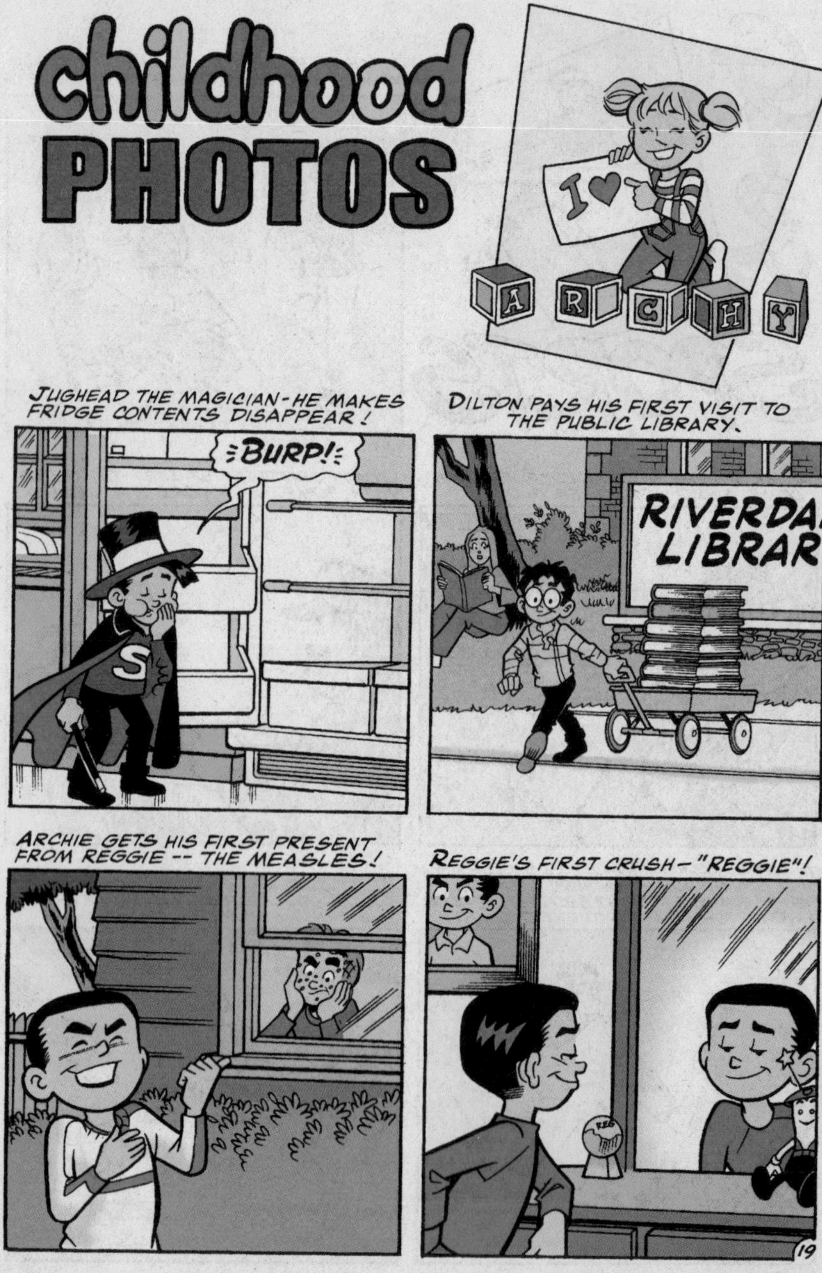
childhood PHOTOS
I ♥
A R C H Y
JUGHEAD THE MAGICIAN- HE MAKES FRIDGE CONTENTS DISAPPEAR!
BURP!
DILTON PAYS HIS FIRST VISIT TO THE PUBLIC LIBRARY.
RIVERDA
LIBRAR
ARCHIE GETS HIS FIRST PRESENT FROM REGGIE -- THE MEASLES!
REGGIE'S FIRST CRUSH- "REGGIE"!
19

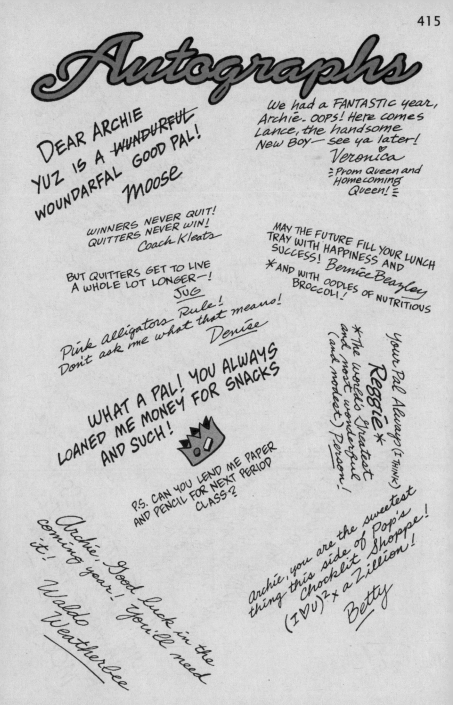

Autographs

DEAR ARCHIE
YUZ IS A ~~WUNDURFUL~~
WOUNDARFAL GOOD PAL!
Moose

We had a FANTASTIC year,
Archie- OOPS! Here comes
Lance, the handsome
New Boy— see ya later!
Veronica
≈ Prom Queen and
Homecoming
Queen! ≈

WINNERS NEVER QUIT!
QUITTERS NEVER WIN!
Coach Kleats

BUT QUITTERS GET TO LIVE
A WHOLE LOT LONGER—!
JUG

MAY THE FUTURE FILL YOUR LUNCH
TRAY WITH HAPPINESS AND
SUCCESS! Bernice Beazley
* AND WITH OODLES OF NUTRITIOUS
BROCCOLI!

Pink Alligators Rule!
Don't ask me what that means!
Denise

WHAT A PAL! YOU ALWAYS
LOANED ME MONEY FOR SNACKS
AND SUCH!

P.S. CAN YOU LEND ME PAPER
AND PENCIL FOR NEXT PERIOD
CLASS?

Your Pal Always (I THINK)
Reggie
*The world's Greatest
and most wonderful
(and modest) Person!

Archie, Good luck in the
coming year! You'll need
it!
Waldo
Weatherbee

Archie, you are the sweetest
thing this side of Pop's
Chocklit Shoppe!
(I ♥ U)² x a Zillion!
Betty

TOO BAD SCHOOL IS COMING TO AN END!
I KNOW YOU MUST FEEL DESPONDENT TOO!
MAYBE WE CAN MEET AT THE LIBRARY
DURING SUMMER VACATION AND COMMISERATE
WHILE BROWSING THROUGH SOME
ENCYCLOPEDIAS. YOUR FRIEND,
DILTON

IN THE
GOLDEN CHAIN OF
FRIENDSHIP REGARD
ME AS A LINK.
Marie

To Archie, a great pal
Our football team improved
100% this year! We won two
games, twice as many as
the year before!
Chuck

HAVE A FUNTASTIC
SUMMER OF SURFING!
Frankie Valdez

Dear Archie,
I'll never forget our movie
date! How could I, you made
me pay for both of us!
P.S.- If you have trouble
reading this it's because you
gave me this cheap
pen to write with—
Mellisa

You are an outstanding student
Archie!... That's 'cause you're always
out standing in the corridor.
Ha! Ha! I'm only half-joking!
Flutesnoot

ARCHIE, I'LL ALWAYS TREASURE
OUR FRIENDSHIP!
Midge Klump

ACHIE—STOP MESSIN'
WID MY MIDGE OR I'LL
PULVARZE PULLVAR
KLOBBER YUZ—
MOOSE

the End!